The Lady and the Minstrel

The Lady and the Minstrel

JOYCE DIPASTENA

ALSO BY JOYCE DIPASTENA

Enjoy two FREE short ebook prequel scenes to *The Lady and the Minstrel.*
Available from most online retailers.
An Epiphany Gift for Robin
The Girl by the River

Read how Gunthar and Helen fell in love in *Loyalty's Web,* Book 1 in my
Poitevin Hearts Romance series

Other titles in Poitevin Hearts:

Illuminations of the Heart (Book 2)
Loving Lucianna (Book 3)
Dangerous Favor (Book 4)

The Loves of Lyonstoke Castle
Courting Cassandry (Book 1)

Short stories
"Caroles on the Green," in Timeless Romance Anthology: Winter Edition
(2012)
A Candlelight Courting

Non-fiction
Name Your Medieval Character: Medieval Christian Names (12th-13th Centuries)

To my mother, who began this journey with me. I hope she can now see its end from the other side of the veil.

Cast of Characters

Acelet de Cary (mentioned) – a troubadour from Poitou who once served in the household of Hugh de Bury, Earl of Gunthar (appeared in *Illuminations of the Heart* and *Loving Lucianna*)

Alain de Bury – grandson of Hugh de Bury, Earl of Gunthar

Alan Hobart – steward of Ashbury Manor

Annys de Tracey – a young woman at King John's court; friend of Marguerite of Winbourne

Antony Tollerton – one of Gunthar's squires; son of Edward Tollerton

Arthur Marcel (mentioned) – father of Gilbert, Robert, and Lottie Marcel (appeared in *An Epiphany Gift for Robin*)

Brandon de Vexin – a knight of Gunthar's household; father of Ralf de Vexin (appeared in *Loyalty's Web*)

Caradoc (mentioned) – former minstrel in the household of Hugh de Bury, Earl of Gunthar

Christopher Beckford – baron of Beck Castle/Manor in Wiltshire and Halham Manor in Dorset; nicknamed "Kit"

Dickon – a villein child, brother of Emma, son of Jehane

Donnet – Helen de Bury's maid

Edward Keynes – knight served by Richard Channing as squire; brother-in-law of Christopher Beckford

Edward Tollerton – marshal of Hugh de Bury, Earl of Gunthar; father of Antony

Father Elias – village priest of Beck Manor

Father Eudes – chaplain of Ranulf de Villon

Eva – Marguerite of Winbourne's maid

Evelyn de Bury – daughter-in-law of Hugh and Helen de Bury; widow of Henry (Harry) de Bury

Felcourt – a Frenchman

Gerald Faintree – a knight whose castle neighbors Hugh de Bury's

Garoux Beckford (deceased) – father of Christopher Beckford

Gilbert Marcel – brother of Robert and Lottie Marcel

Helen de Bury, Countess of Gunthar – wife of Hugh de Bury (introduced as Heléne in *Loyalty's Web*)

Hubert – a footsoldier

Hugh de Bury, Earl of Gunthar – a counselor to King John of England; lord of Lamhurst, Norcott and Selberry Castles, and Rushall Manor (introduced in *Loyalty's Web*)

Jane Lovell – mistress of Symeon Achard, Earl of Saxton

Jehane – a villein woman, mother of Emma and Dickon

Jarrott – bailiff of Halham Manor

John Heywood (deceased) – baron of Winbourne Castle; grandfather of Marguerite of Winbourne (mentioned in *Loyalty's Web*)

John – Marguerite's groom

Leah de Villon – Marguerite's mother; daughter of John Heywood, wife of Ranulf de Villon

Lottie Marcel Hanley – sister of Robert and Gilbert Marcel

Lucy Locke – a villein; wife of William Locke

Marguerite of Winbourne (also Marguerite de Villon) – daughter of Ranulf and Leah de Villon; betrothed to Symeon Achard, Earl of Saxton

Nicholas Tybert – squire to Symeon Achard, Earl of Saxton

Odo – chaplain to John Heywood; Marguerite's tutor and guardian of her inheritance

Ralf de Vexin – one of Gunthar's squires; son of Brandon de Vexin

Ranulf de Villon – father of Marguerite of Winbourne; baron of Ashbury Castle

Richard Channing – cousin of Marguerite of Winbourne; squire of Edward Keynes

Robert Marcel – a minstrel

Stephen – baron of Romsfeld Castle; neighbor of Christopher Beckford; sought a betrothal to Marguerite of Winbourne when she was ten

Symeon Achard, Earl of Saxton – counselor to King John of England

Warin Eyvind – a knight at the court of King John

Therri de Laurant (mentioned) – a Poitevin baron; brother-in-law to Hugh de Bury, Earl of Gunthar (appeared in *Loyalty's Web* and *Dangerous Favor*)

Thomas Hastings – secretary to Hugh de Bury, Earl of Gunthar

Triston de Brielle (mentioned) – a Poitevin knight (appeared in *Loyalty's Web, Illuminations of the Heart,* and *Loving Lucianna*)

William Locke – a villein on Halham Manor

Non-fictional characters (in alphabetical order)

Arthur of Brittany (mentioned) – son of King John's deceased older brother, Geoffrey Plantagenet

Hugh de Lusignan, Count of La Marche – a vassal of King John; formerly betrothed to Isabella of Angoulême before she married King John

Isabella of Angoulême – queen of England; betrothed to Hugh de Lusignan, Count of La Marche, before she married King John

John Plantagenet – king of England

Philip II Capet (mentioned) – king of France; also known as Philip Augustus

William Marshal, Earl of Pembroke (mentioned) – one of the greatest magnates of the realm of England; known by his contemporaries as "the greatest knight who ever lived." (appeared in *Dangerous Favor*)

I

Dorset, England
December 1213

"Marguerite, what are you doing? Oh, heavens, not again."

Robert turned at the exclamation, uttered in faint tones of feminine despair by a petite blonde woman astride a graceful white mare. His hand rested on the tilting gate affixed to the raggedy fence that traced the small perimeter of the thatch and daub cottage that belonged to William and Lucy Locke. He had left the bridge-mending to fetch some cheese for his and Will's lunch while Lucy attended a sick neighbor, and had not expected to hear a lady's cultivated tones in the heart of Lyndeard Village on a day as chill as this.

A familiar resentment stirred beneath his curiosity as his gaze rested on the lady. Her hand stretched from beneath her heavy woolen cloak to reach across the neck of her mare and catch the abandoned reins of a spirited bay that danced beside her. The cuff of her glove had been turned back to expose a fur lining he suspected must feel soft as silk against her palm. A groom who looked scarce out of his teens attended her, along with a gentleman of rank judging from his equally rich and warm clothing.

"Marguerite," the lady called again, "I beg you! Oh, John, pray do something before she dirties her gown."

Robert stepped away from the gate to better view the center of the commotion taking place on the other side of the horses. He had been up at dawn with the other men, clearing the snow into two steep banks on either side of the road before they had begun repairs on the bridge. A toddler scarce tall enough to reach his knee stood cooing on one of the piles, waving tiny, delighted hands. Robert knew at once what entranced him. With the sun slid high to noonday, some of the snow had begun to melt and form puddles—lovely, glistening puddles to the eyes of a two-year-old.

Deadly, drowning puddles for a toddler who slipped and fell face in. Robert had seen the tragedy too many times. Eyes riveted on the little one's danger, Robert's swift strides had carried him half-way to the snow bank before he registered the blur that caught the child up in her arms.

A second lady, the rider of the empty-saddled bay, appeared to whisper something into the toddler's ear as the startled child began to cry. The child's disheveled brown hair hid the lady's face, but from the elegance of her skirts and cloak, Robert knew she could not be a servant. The groom, who had sprung from his saddle at the first lady's command, hesitated near the second even as Robert checked his own steps.

"Take it away from her," the lady on the white mare said sharply. "If her father sees the way it's soiled her skirts, he will have you flogged for not intercepting her. And don't think your father will spare you either, Marguerite."

Robert bristled at hearing the child referred to as though he had issued from some dog's litter. The little one's cries had tapered to a hiccoughing whimper, but these turned into panicked shrieks when the groom scooped him from the second lady's arms.

"Ho!" Robert shouted. "Put the boy down."

He surged forward again and had nearly reached the riding party when he found an unexpected hand thrust against his shoulder, shoving him back.

"Don't," a rough voice growled in his ear.

Robert glared into the warning blue eyes and tried to jerk away. He had been too focused on the child's plight to have seen the man who darted past the horses to restrain him.

"Let me go, Will."

William Locke gripped him hard by the arm. "Stay out of it, Rob. Ye'll only bring trouble on yer head an' mine, an' all for nothin'. Look."

The child's cries had brought a young, pale-haired woman running out of a nearby cottage. She paused just long enough to dip a pair of curtsies to the riding party, with a breathless, "Forgive me, milady—yer pardon, Sir Alan—if ye please, sir, I will take him now."

The woman's appearance distracted the well-dressed gentleman, who had turned his head with a frown at Robert's shout.

"Quickly, John, get rid of it," the lady on the white mare said.

William's hold tightened against Robert's twitching muscles.

The groom's well-mended homespun and well-fed look elevated his otherwise humble status above the shabby, lean-faced villeins of Lyndeard. He appeared relieved to drop the screaming tot into the woman's anxious embrace. The child flung his little arms around the woman's neck and blubbered into her trailing hair. Robert's anger still simmered, but the tension slid from his body at seeing the toddler safe in Lucy Locke's arms. William must have felt it too, for his restraining grip fell away.

"I should have known better than to let you ride into the village, even with my escort," the lady on the white mare said with some asperity. "Your father will be furious to know you've been meddling with the villagers again. If we do not get back to the castle in time to change your gown before he returns from the hunt— Marguerite, are you attending to me? Child, what in the world are you looking at?"

"Nothing, Mama," a lilting voice responded.

The tantalizingly musical note in her tones almost turned Robert's head towards the speaker, but he resisted the temptation. The lady on the white mare had twisted about in her saddle and was gazing at him and William. Robert was surprised at the softness of her pretty features. Her sharp tones had roused an equally sharp-faced vision in his mind, but he guessed now that the apprehension in her summer blue eyes lay behind her agitated rebuke of the other lady. Was this the Lady Leah de Villon, wife to the baron who owned half the fields worked by the villeins of Lyndeard Village? William's master owned the other half of the land, though in general he governed them through his steward or bailiff. William called de Villon a hard master, but what baron was not? Certainly his wife must fear him for so gentle-faced a woman to have spoken with such vehemence.

Robert felt a tug on his sleeve and mimicked William's bow. It did not matter which lord Will belonged to, defiance would only breed trouble for his friend and there was naught to challenge now. The child was safe.

"You should watch him more closely. He might have slipped into a puddle and drowned."

The same lilting voice that had answered Lady Leah carried across the winter air to tease Robert's ears again. He straightened. Lady Leah's daughter—the Lady Marguerite?—had crossed the road and stood addressing Lucy. Robert suffered a peculiar sensation as he watched her, as though the breath had suddenly been knocked from his lungs. He had met more women than he could remember in his travels about England, yet this one face had flitted through his memory again and again o'er the course of the last seven years.

No, not this face. The face of a ten-year-old girl who had been playing hide-and-seek with her grandfather in the woods on that day when Robert might have forfeited all for the sake of a book and a lute.

And yet, he thought as his lungs expanded to their normal capacity again, he could easily imagine that child growing up to look very like this graceful, diminutive daughter of a baron. In feature she strongly resembled her mother, with the wide eyes that sat beguilingly in her soft, flowerlike countenance, a small, tip-tilted nose lightly brushed with freckles, and lips that blushed a delicate shade of rose. Lovely, but not beautiful, and cast in a darker mode than her mother, her dusky hair billowing like a cloud from the confines of the fur-trimmed hood that had fallen against her shoulders. Yet her countenance held a sweetness that set her strikingly apart from the gilded haired, equally pretty Lady Leah—

"Yes, milady." Lucy interrupted Robert's thoughts as she held the child tight and bobbed another quick curtsy. "I was attendin' his mother, bathin' her face—she has the fever, ye see. Emma was supposed to be tendin' her brother, but she's only five and he must have wandered off while she was playin' with the cat. The fur is warm on her little hands when her ma' and da' have scarce enough wood for a fire—"

Lucy broke off with a panicked look, no doubt afraid her words might be taken as a complaint against the manor's lord. That she was chattering so when strangers, including Robert, usually held her tongue-tied, spoke either of guilt over the wandering child or the effect of the Lady Marguerite's smile. Robert stared. Ladies did not smile at villeins, yet this one did so almost as at a friend.

"Marguerite, that is enough," her mother said with a nip in her voice that rivaled the air that chafed against Robert's cheeks. "Step away from that creature now. You heard her, she has come from a cottage of sickness."

The Lady Marguerite turned towards her mother with a sudden flash of anger in her chestnut brown eyes. "She is not a creature. Grandfather always sent aid when the villagers were sick. And Odo taught me—"

Her mother cast a frightened look at the well-dressed man beside her. "Hush, Marguerite. You know your father has forbidden you to speak that name. Sir Alan, I pray you will not mind her. My father doted on her and let her run hoyden about his estates, but she will steady when she is wed. You need not mention any of this to Lord de Villon."

"I am not a tale bearer, my lady," Sir Alan said in a tone that suggested offense, yet Robert thought the brief glance he sent at Marguerite held a hint of fondness in it.

Lucy dropped yet another curtsy. "If ye please, miladies, may I return to the cottage? His mother will be alarmed at our dallyin'." She indicated the toddler, who now rested his head quietly against her shoulder.

"Yes, pray, away with you." Lady Leah waved a shooing hand and Lucy ducked back inside the cottage. "John, help your mistress remount. There has been enough mischief. Sir Alan, we will let you fetch more flour from the miller as we should have done in the first place, and Marguerite and I will return to the castle. And don't think I will fall for your protestations of boredom again, child. You may ride in the woods as you will as long as John accompanies you, but ride into the village again you will not."

If Lady Leah expected a meek acquiescence, her daughter instead responded with silence and a fretful chewing of her lower lip. Robert felt an unexpected flicker of dismay lest she bruise so delicate a petal, until the flicker warmed to something else as she raised her eyes and gazed straight into his.

Robert had flirted with women, both common and noble, in every county in England, but despite an admitted tendency towards impulsiveness, he had always prided himself on never losing his head over even the most dazzling beauty. He had no intention of losing his head now, either, over the merely pretty young woman studying him so frankly, not even one who spoke kindly to villeins—until her tentative smile set her brown eyes shining with an innocent vibrancy that shook him as he had never been shaken in his five-and-twenty years.

It took all his powers of self-control not to smile back.

Aye, Will, I have developed some.

He felt William watching him, undoubtedly mindful of their past together and no doubt fearful Robert might respond to the Lady Marguerite's regard with an insultingly defiant lift of his chin. Had William known all the romantic tangles his friend had dabbled in since they had last met, he might well have feared something much different pounding in Robert's chest. Except that this was different indeed, so different that Robert, who had become something of a wordsmith, could not have put a word to this emotion even if he'd tried. The only one that sprang to his mind he dismissed as too absurd even for his impetuous nature.

He nevertheless felt an almost physical pang when she broke her gaze from his.

"Thank you, John." She placed her foot into the young groom's linked hands and let him lift her into the bay mare's saddle. A moment later, she and her mother rode away as Robert's mind, mocking his own silent avowal of a moment before, swirled with schemes for how he could see her again.

William swiveled him away from the departing horses, back towards the Lockes' cottage and Robert's interrupted errand. He heard the clicking of William's tongue and braced himself for a rebuke as severe as the Lady Marguerite had suffered from her mother.

"Hold!" a voice called out from behind them. "You there. Stranger. A word with you."

Robert turned at the imperious voice. As far as he knew, he was the only stranger in the village. Sir Alan eased his horse towards Robert with the air of a man in no hurry, giving William time to drive a small punch into Robert's bicep—Robert was certain the blow would have been more hefty had it not been dealt under Sir Alan's eye—and muttered:

"What'd ye do before I got here?"

"Nothing," Robert said. "No more than you saw, anyway."

"So help me, Rob, if ye—"

William broke off as Sir Alan drew up within hearing distance. The man, with his round face and stomach, looked like one who enjoyed a good meal, but Robert had heard him barking orders to the villeins of Ashbury Manor from his stern-cast mouth and judged him a trustworthy steward in the eyes of his master the baron. At least a servant knew where he stood with a man like this, unlike the greedy, unpredictable bailiff of Halham Manor, which held power over Will.

"I presume you're the minstrel they say has wandered into town," Sir Alan said to Robert. "Can you vouch for this fellow, Locke?"

"V-vouch?"

Robert heard the stumble in William's voice.

"He does not look like a ne'er-do-well," Sir Alan said, raking Robert with an impudent glance, "though one would think if he had any talent that his tunic would be less shabby. Still, the gossip is that he has a fine voice. How long has he been with you, Locke?"

"Little more than a fortnight, Sir Alan."

"You know him from your former manor, I presume. Did he sing for Lord Christopher Beckford?"

"A-aye." Another faint stumble, though it was an honest enough reply.

"And you met him . . . how exactly? Did it amuse the baron to invite his villeins to join the entertainments at his table?"

The steward's sarcasm brought a wave of red into William's rough-stubbled cheeks. Robert forestalled his friend's response.

"A lowly minstrel accepts a meal wherever he can find it, whether from a rich, fat baron or one of his shivering but generous villeins. I have frequently been fed by both, sir." Robert barely bit off the added syllable that would have turned the term of respect into the contemptuous *sirrah*.

Sir Alan looked offended all the same, for he had not been addressing Robert. He said with a condescending glare down his bulbous nose, "I trust this shivering villein will not regret extending his generosity anew to you. Riffraff is not looked on kindly on either manor here."

"Have you heard aught to complain of me, sir?"

"Nooo." The long drawn out word sounded almost regretful. Sir Alan shot another of his stern looks at William. "Do you vouch for this fellow's honesty, Locke? That he is not some scoundrel who has pulled the wool over your eyes? Jarrott's hand will fall heavy on you if you have been careless enough to invite a thief to bed under your roof who will rob the village blind."

"He's an honest man, Sir Alan," William said stoutly.

It warmed Robert that Will's voice did not stumble now. Despite his friend's defense, he sensed William's tension and knew what he feared. But Robert had paid Jarrott, the greedy bailiff of Halham manor, a pair of silver coins to neither harass William over Robert's presence nor mention it to his absent master, Lord Christopher.

"Hmph," Sir Alan grunted. "If he's not, be assured that you'll hang alongside him."

"Is that all ye wished to ask about, sir? We need to be gettin' back to the bridge," William said.

"No, it is not all, churl. You." He jutted his plump chin at Robert. "What's your name?"

Robert's hand fisted at the epithet hurled at Will. He answered coldly, "Robert Marcel."

"Well, Robert Marcel, your reputation has reached the ears of my master. Lord de Villon said that should I see you in the village, I should command your presence at the castle tonight. He is feasting the Earl of Saxton's betrothal to his daughter. The earl is expected by sundown, so see that you arrive before Compline."

Robert's breath sucked in. Betrothal?

"Are those your only clothes, man?" the steward asked with a sniff as though at something distasteful.

The little jab in Robert's breast that followed upon his surprise almost distracted him from the disdain in the steward's voice. But a natural audacity asserted itself in his reply.

"Nay, I have a tunic of fine scarlet for when I sing before a castle hearth. Rest your mind, Sir Alan. I shall not shame your master with the garments I wear tonight."

Sir Alan grunted again. "Well for you that you don't, if you wish your services to be rewarded with silver rather than a boot to your posterior before you even pass through the gates."

He whirled his horse about bringing a curt end to their encounter and trotted away in the direction of the mill. Robert did not know which annoyed him more, the steward's condescending manner or the fact that the revelation of the Lady Marguerite's betrothal caused the memory of her smile to burn even deeper into his mind.

"Are ye sure that was wise?" William muttered.

"What?" Robert said, forcing his attention back to his friend.

"Agreein' to sing for de Villon. What if he mentions ye to Lord Christopher? Ye should not have given Sir Alan yer name."

Even with the distraction pricking at him, Robert could not resist responding with a playful obtuseness. "My dear Will, there are nearly as many Roberts inhabiting England as there are Williams."

"Aye," William said with a snap to his voice that betrayed how sorely this answer provoked him, "Robert the Harper, Robert of the Road, even Robert of Wiltshire would mean nothing to Lord Christopher's ears. But a Robert *Marcel* on his Dorset manor? He was right to name ye so, for in truth, ye are as mad as Mars!"

Robert laughed. "'Twas his grandfather who so dubbed my grandsire. I cannot help what is in my blood. But there is naught to fret over, Will. If Kit and de Villon have ever spoken, it was not on Halham Manor." He saw the way William winced at Robert's use of Lord Christopher's familiar name. "You told me yourself Kit has not visited Halham in the six years you have lived here."

"But Jarrott—"

"Your bailiff drinks so much ale it is doubtful he can remember my face, much less my name. The silver was merely to dull his curiosity when he saw you invite a wandering minstrel under your roof. But if it comforts you, I will be Robert of the Road until I leave."

"How much longer do ye plan to stay?"

Robert raised his brows. "Do you wish me to go? Even Sir Alan confessed I've caused no trouble."

"Until today, and then only because I came when I did. Don't tell me ye weren't about to tear the screamin' babe out of that groom's arms, and heaven only knows what insults ye would have hurled as ye did so. Why do ye think I left the bridge? As soon as Griff told me a party from the castle had ridden into town, I knew ye'd find a way to nettle one of 'em, or worse."

"And bring their wrath upon your head along with my own?" Despite his lifelong rebukes of Robert's hasty tongue, William had never shrunk from their friendship. Was he doing so now? There were not many men for whose opinion Robert cared, and therefore few whose rejection could hurt him. He paused to master his disappointment before he continued. "You are right. Things are not the way they were between us before. You have a wife now and must think of her safety. I will send my regrets to Sir Alan for the feast and be gone."

"To the devil with ye, Rob, that's not what I meant. That is, o' course I want no trouble for Lucy's sake, but I'm thinkin' of ye, as well. I've not forgotten what happened on Beck Manor, even if ye have."

The vision these words stirred in Robert fanned a rush of fire from his inner core that threatened to blast the wintry air around them. "'Tis not something I am like to forget, Will—ever."

Though he spoke softly, he knew from William's face that his friend understood every deathly quiet syllable.

Robert shrugged one shoulder, as though to cast the darkness behind him for now. The reckoning would come, but it would not come today. He glanced at the sun as it darted out from behind a cloud. The days were short in December. He would not reach another village before nightfall. Well, 'twould not be the first time he'd trudged along a road he could barely see in the dark.

"Just let me gather my things," he said.

"No." William caught his shoulder again, as roughly as he'd done when he'd restrained Robert from the groom and child. "Not yet. I've missed ye, Rob. I've never understood ye, but I've missed ye. There was never a moment of peace in yer company and 'tis a wonder Lord Christopher let me keep my own head for all the times I refused to shun ye. But I've never known a more loyal or honest man than ye, or a better hearted one." He shifted to place one hand on each of Robert's shoulders and gave him a little shake. "The saints forgive me, but when Lord Christopher sent me away to Halham, I missed ye more than I missed my own kin. Don't go yet." The big man's mouth curved up slowly at one corner. "There were good memories at Beck Manor too, weren't there?"

Robert grinned back. "Aye. The bonfires we lit on midsummer's eve, bobbing for apples on Saint Swithin's Day, racing the plows on Plow Monday—"

William dug a playful elbow into Robert's ribs. "Dancin' on the green with Agnes Littlemore." As soon as he said it, his friend appeared to sense his mistake.

William's broad face sobered, but Robert preempted his apology. "Never mind, Will, it is over and done. I have not thought of Agnes in years." For William's peace of mind, he knew it best not to confess to the reflections the name Agnes Littlemore pricked up now. If he could not quite remember her face, he remembered all too keenly how and why they had been parted.

The days were thankfully long past when another could choose his path for him. The Lady Marguerite's sweet countenance flowed into his mind as distinctly as Agnes's faded vaguely away. Was it possible she and the ten-year-old child were the same? If there were even a chance, how could he leave without at least an attempt to thank her? He heard again the baying of the hounds, felt again the wave of helplessness when his hands refused to abandon his two most beloved possessions on the river bank, even knowing how his former horrific punishment would pale if Kit caught him again. Had it not been for the child's quick wits and swift feet—

"Does she come to the village often?" Robert asked.

William scratched his sandy head, looking puzzled. "Who?"

"The Lady Marguerite." Robert nodded in the direction of Sir Alan riding back through the village with a large sack of flour tied behind his saddle, grateful for the timing that made his question appear to be linked to the steward and not to his wandering thoughts.

"I ain't seen her more than a half-dozen times since she came to live with her parents. That was three years ago, after her grandfather died. They call her Lady Marguerite of Winbourne for the castle she was raised at some-place in the north, though 'tis said she sometimes visited Dorset as a child. She came into Lyndeard a few times with that young groom ye saw today, bringin' bread to villeins who were sick, but her father put a swift stop to that. She has a kind heart, Rob, so don't ye go sneerin' at her when ye're up at the castle tonight."

With his oddly thumping heart, the last thing Robert desired to do was to sneer at her, but he nevertheless felt a stir of hesitation. As much as he owed her—if she had indeed been the child—he had known even then that the excitement of adventure had prompted her to aid him in his hour of need. He had been nothing more to her than an intriguing stranger. Despite the danger of losing the escape she'd made possible, he had crouched dripping wet in the reeds on the opposite side of the river and watched her run into the embrace of her grandfather, lingering until the old man bore her safely away from the path of the baying hounds. A gentleman did not interfere with another man's hunt and risk causing him to lose his prey. She would not have learned the truth from an encounter with Kit.

The child had been well-bred enough to have thought twice had she known what Robert was. And if she had grown into a woman who brought food to villeins and smiled at them, might not her generous actions yet be tinged with condescension and pity?

There was only one way to test her, and that was to speak with her himself. He did not know how he would manage that in a castle filled with her father's knights, but he trusted his ingenuity to think of something— provided he kept his engagement to sing for her betrothal dinner tonight.

He felt a pull of displeasure at the corners of his mouth. *Betrothal.* Well, her future was not his affair, only the service she may have rendered him in the past. A discrete exchange, an expression of thanks, and he would move on. Provided—

"Are you sure you wish me to stay?" he asked William.

"The roof needs patchin' before it snows again, an' the latch on the pen broke this mornin'—Lucy had to shut all the chickens up in the house—and even the surly Griff was grateful for yer help at the bridge-mendin' today. Just continue to mind yer tongue and yer temper an' lend a hand where it's needed, an' ye'll be welcome enough in the village for another sennight."

"Then I'll leave after Christmas."

No matter how useful Robert made himself, he knew an itinerant freeman who bore no allegiance to either manor's lord would be looked upon with frowns by steward, bailiff, and villagers alike if he remained longer than that. Will had been right about his name. If Sir Alan grew curious at Robert's tarrying, if he mentioned it to Jarrott, and despite the silver coins, Jarrott passed on his presence to Kit— Not that Robert wouldn't have welcomed encountering his old adversary again. There was one moment out of the debacle of their last meeting that he actually relished and would have given much for a chance to relive, now that he no longer feared the hounds.

"Eh, Rob, what are ye thinkin'?"

Robert blinked away the pleasant vision, startled by the alarm in William's voice. "What do you mean?"

"I mean I've seen that kindlin' in yer eyes before and it always bodes trouble for someone."

Robert laughed. "Not this time, Will. Robert of the Road intends to be nothing but meek and respectful for the remainder of his visit. Beginning by mollifying your wretched bailiff for being so long absent from the bridge." He clapped a hand to William's burly shoulder and spun him towards the road. "Go ahead without me while I fetch us a bite of cheese. If Jarrott complains, tell him we were detained by Sir Alan. He can hardly blame you for lingering when de Villon's steward demanded it."

Fear of the volatile bailiff spurred William's steps swiftly towards his former task, but Robert observed the way he slowed to cast a longing glance at the cottage where his wife nursed a sick neighbor. Villeins were not supposed to know how to love. Their masters viewed them as barely above the beasts that plowed their fields or the packs that hunted game for their tables. But Robert knew love when he saw it. He had observed it every day growing up in the shared glances between his parents, heard it in the tender way they had spoken to each other even when times were hard, seen it in his father's quick, gentle touch to his mother's cheek and the way she threaded her fingers through his father's thick black hair when she thought Robert and his siblings weren't watching.

Robert had heard and seen the same between William and Lucy in the fortnight that he had dwelled under their roof. That Kit had sent William away from all he had ever known to dwell among strangers had been but one more of Robert's hard-held grudges. But Robert realized now the baron had dealt his villein an unwitting favor, for Lucy had clearly brought a light to William's life he would never have found on Beck Manor.

In all his wanderings about England o'er the last seven years, Robert had never given any thought to a future hearth and home of his own. There had been too much to see, too much to experience, and far, far too many beautiful women to flirt with. He wondered if there would be any beauties at the castle tonight. Would they cast the Lady Marguerite's pretty sweetness in the shade? Or had he mistaken that lovely shimmer in her eyes?

He let himself into William's cottage, but not before he cast an impatient look at the sun, willing it to hasten its lowering across the sky. Since the pope had laid an interdict on England the Church bells no longer rang, but after a lifetime of listening to their tolls, Robert had retained a feeling for the rhythm of the hours. The sooner the hour of Compline came, the sooner he could seek his answers.

2

Marguerite shifted in her chair to the left, and then the right, seeking to catch the light from the hearth between the shadows cast by her father's pacings. With the shutters closed against the winter's chill, 'twas all she had to guide her needle. She and her mother had not spoken of the incident in the village since their return to the castle, but she had caught her mother's worried start when Lord de Villon had returned from the hunt and joined them. Neither the steward nor the groom had betrayed Marguerite, however, for whatever her father rambled on about, none of the fateful words—Heywood, Odo, or villeins—drifted to her ears.

Marguerite tried to listen, but she had been dreaming so sweetly before her father flung back the tapestry from the entrance to her mother's solar and invaded this intimate female space with his hulking and unwanted male presence. He never came here but to rail at her about some shortcoming. Even when he paused to cast a fresh piece of applewood onto the flames, the burst of scent quickly dissolved into the reek of the stables that clung to his cloak and boots. Marguerite's nose wrinkled against her will, even though she knew the instinctive recoil would only bring upon the slightly uptilted feature her father's condemnation for its dusting of freckles.

Her mother's protest tempered her father's harsh words "Still, Ranulf, a man has overlooked worse things . . ."

Marguerite reached again for her dream. The man in the village, with hair as sleek as a raven's wing and the midnight eyes she remembered so well. The same eyes, and yet grown different, eyes that held their secrets now. He had trusted her then. Not one day had passed in the last seven years that she had not recalled their meeting, the look of wild despair in his gaze when her footfall had whirled him around on the river's bank, and then at her offer, a gratitude so fervent it had consumed the fears that had driven her to try to flee from the man she loved most in all the world.

She had been but a child, despite the adult commitment she had been asked to make. It could not possibly have occurred to the strange young man to think otherwise of her in the intervening years. There had been nothing in his impassive gaze in the village to indicate that he recognized her. But she had dreamed of him, oh! so often, inventing such delicious interludes between them. Like now. Her needle darted in and out of the linen cloth, skillfully designing a string of flowers as dainty as the ones that graced the wreath she imagined his tanned fingers weaving for her thick, dark hair.

Her father's voice rumbled disagreeably in the background. "You know, Marguerite, the Earl of Saxton will be with us by nightfall . . ."

It was spring, and they sat in her mother's pleasure garden . . .

"When he approached me on the matter, I own I was stunned . . ."

He smelled of fresh air and the green wood . . .

"I had well given up hope after . . ."

She reached out a hand and touched it boldly against the breast of his rough homespun tunic, smiling at him an invitation that would surely replace the child in his memory with the woman she had since become . . .

". . . has asked and received my permission to marry you."

Her dream smashed apart. The needle jumped through the linen and pricked her finger, flinging a crimson drop of blood into the center of a delicately embroidered yellow flower. The liquid soaked into the snowy cloth and spread its stain to turn the yellow petals orange.

"Marry? Saxton?" Her father's pronouncement bounced her to her feet. "Grandfather would never allow it."

Her father's face turned almost as red as the new droplet bubbling up from her finger. "Your grandfather is dead, and you will do as you are told. You are seventeen. Seventeen! Your mother was fourteen when we wed. You should have been married long since, had Heywood's madness not left your inheritance repugnant to all sane men."

Marguerite shook away the fresh blood with such violence that her embroidery went flying. Her father had tried to force marriage on her twice before, the first time that very day she had fled to the riverbank. She should have trusted her grandfather to listen to her fears rather than trying to run away—but if she had, she would never have met the handsome young man by the river.

Even if he left the village in the morning without them ever speaking again, she would sooner die a maid than wed a man who smelled as sour as Sir Stephan had when she was ten, or who gulped and guzzled and snorted so loudly at the dinner table as Sir Humphrey when she was thirteen, all the while eyeing her as if she, too, had been a bit of choice veal waiting to be devoured.

Or an earl more than twice her seventeen years who desired her for nothing more than her lands and an heir, while he openly lavished his passions on a widow with a reputation as sordid as his own.

"I will not marry the Earl of Saxton," she repeated. She sought first for the most practical defense she could think of. "The interdict the pope has declared forbids all marriages solemnized in the Church."

"Then you will marry at the Church door, or in my own hall, where weddings are still allowed. The king himself has countenanced this marriage, and if you think my own chaplain will refuse a command by the king, even for the pope, you do not know Father Eudes as well as I."

Her back snapped stiff with resistance. "I do not care what the king says. You cannot make me marry without my consent."

Despite her bold words and the heat of the hearth's flames, her skin prickled as if smote by a chill. Her grandfather was not here this time. She had nothing but her own courage to resist her father with now, and the glint of punishment was already in his eye.

"Fool. The Earl of Saxton is the most powerful man in the kingdom. Even the Earl of Gunthar fell before his sway. They say King John does not make a move without Saxton's counsel."

"They also say he is grasping, manipulative and cruel—" the words tumbled out even as her mother, who had retrieved her embroidery, lay a warning hand on her arm "—and that he flaunts his affair with Lady Lovell boldly under the nose of the queen herself. I will not marry such a man."

The firelight glinted off the elaborate threads of the heavy cuff of her father's surcote, drawing her attention to his clenched fist. "You will do as you are told. What do such things matter set beside an alliance with Symeon Achard, Earl of Saxton? You will turn a blind eye to such affairs."

A blaze of rebellion brought her gaze back to her father's face. Despite the vein that began an angry throb at his temple, she thrust her chin still higher. "I will not! You know you have not the power to force me. Grandfather's will—"

She staggered as the flat of her father's hand smacked her cheek—of course he would not want to mar her face with his fist, with Saxton on his way to court her.

"How dare you defy me?" Ranulf de Villon's roar set the wooden beams of the solar's ceiling trembling. "After what Heywood did, this offer is a boon from the heavens. I will dispose of my own daughter where I please and the devil take that senile old man's will."

Marguerite pressed her hand to the reverberating sting of her father's blow. "Grandfather was not senile, and you cannot make me marry the Earl of Saxton!"

"Oh, can I not?"

His left hand raised to strike her other cheek, but her mother caught his arm.

"Ranulf, please, you know you will not persuade her thus."

De Villon rounded on his wife. "You, lady! Had you schooled her better, taught her to know a daughter's duty—! Who persuaded me to give her into the hands of that haughty, over-mighty father of yours and his giddy-headed wife, to be corrupted with their madness and taught the manners of a peasant?"

"I did it for peace."

The voice, so sharp against Marguerite in the village, quivered before de Villon's anger, but Marguerite knew her mother's fear was for her daughter. To Marguerite's knowledge, her father had never struck her mother. *He never dared strike me, either, before Grandfather died.*

"My father was determined," Lady Leah continued. "Have you forgotten how he threatened to cut us both off in favor of Marguerite if we defied him? He would have done it, you know he would, just as he left her his richest manor when he let you inherit the others at his death. Odo said he did it as a reminder to you not to challenge his will—"

Her mother's fingers flew to her mouth as if to catch back the forbidden name, but de Villon did not hear, for he was already roaring over her words.

"You persuaded me for peace, yet peace is what I have not! Curse you! Curse Heywood!"

To Marguerite's relief, her father fell back to pacing, his punishing hands clasped safely, for the moment, behind his back. She rubbed her fingers gingerly against the feverish heat in her cheek. The ache would fade in a few hours. Would the redness fade, as well, before the Earl of Saxton arrived?

Lady Leah pushed Marguerite back into her chair. "You are right," she said over her shoulder to her husband, "my father allowed Marguerite to grow up impulsive and headstrong. You should not have bound me to silence in the matter of her betrothal. Had you allowed me to tell her when you first spoke to the earl . . ."

De Villon gave a harsh bark of laughter. "And give her time to find a way to send word to Northumberland? I am not a slackwit, lady, whatever your father came to think of me after that mischief-making *churchman* turned his mind against me."

Marguerite bristled at the slur in her father's voice, but her mother, urgent as always to try to reconcile her husband and daughter, pressed restraining hands onto Marguerite's shoulders.

"You know all your servants are trustworthy," her mother said, "even Sir Alan, however fondly he smiles on her. Had you let me, I could have prepared her, persuaded her to her duties towards us and towards my father's lands. She is not a child anymore, and she knows it. She speaks hastily, out of shock, is all."

"I—" Marguerite began a protest, but her mother squeezed her shoulders tighter.

"Let me talk to her now," Lady Leah pled. "She loved my father. Enough that she will not wish to see his lands forfeited to the king when she dies because she was too selfish to give him an heir."

That brought Marguerite an unexpected pang of guilt. Her grandfather's will directed his granddaughter's freedom to choose her own husband, with his chaplain Odo's "guidance and consent." When her grandfather had dictated the unconventional terms, she knew he had trusted her to choose wisely, both for herself and for the future of the vast estates he had inherited from his own father and so cunningly expanded in his lifetime.

But not Saxton. Not Saxton.

"I think solitude will serve her better," de Villon said coldly, turning about to glower at his daughter. "Go to your chamber and remain there till I summon you. And you would do well to reflect that I know where to lay bruises that Saxton will not see until your wedding night."

To Marguerite's shame, she shuddered as she rose from the chair. It galled her to show weakness before her father, for she knew he viewed himself triumphant. But was he not in truth? She did not fear the beating, but marriage! She had never met the Earl of Saxton, but she had heard enough shocking gossip to appall her. And now she was to wed such a man?

Her mind tumbled and tumbled as she fled the solar and ran up the great stone stairs to her bedchamber, but no solution came to her. Even had she been able to find a knight, a squire, even a common servant to risk her father's wrath, no plea would reach Northumberland, far less return with aid to Dorset before her father forced her to the altar and the marriage bed.

Lady Leah brought Lord de Villon's summons just as the sun lowered against the horizon, setting a weak glow to the pale winter sky. Marguerite had spent the intervening hour struggling to reconcile herself to the inevitable. Perhaps the whispers about the Earl of Saxton were untrue. Marguerite had always known she must marry one day. Before she risked the force of her father's hand again, she would judge the earl for herself.

She paused on the bottom step of the circular stone stairway that led from the gallery connecting her tower chamber to the great hall of the central stone keep of Ashbury Castle. She had expected so great a lord as the Earl of Saxton to travel with a magnificent retinue but the crush of unfamiliar men, all attired in rich velvets and dazzling jewels fit for a king's court, snatched her breath away. Her mother gave her little time to recover it, shooing her gently but firmly towards the center of the hall where she presumed her betrothed-to-be awaited her. Here and there she caught sight of a face she knew, members of her father's household, bright with excitement for the event they had been summoned to witness. Suddenly her mother pulled at her sleeve, drawing Marguerite to a halt, and whispered in her ear. Marguerite lowered her gaze as was becoming to a maid. She felt the looming presence of the man before her and after a pair of throbbing heartbeats, peeked through her lashes for her first glimpse of Symeon Achard, Earl of Saxton.

She had sensed his height and mass before she dared the glance, but she saw now that his weight was pure muscle, his broad, heavy shoulders powerful rather than portly. The brilliance of his attire almost blinded her.

Precious stones flashed from the fingers of hands that hinted of crushing strength; diamonds sparkled, sewn to his collar and cuffs; a ruby pendant hung round his neck, rising and falling against a chest as square and strong as a cathedral stone. Marguerite blinked in awe, then peeped a little higher to see into his face.

Her heart stuttered uncertainly. His features bore a harsh, arrogant cast, though they had a certain rugged handsomeness. She guessed him to be past his fortieth year for his dark hair showed signs of graying near the temples. She did not realize that she had ceased to peep and was gazing full into his eyes until the shiver shuddered down her spine. She searched in vain for some hint of warmth or kindness in the hazel depths. His voice, when he spoke, cracked a bit as if fractured by the coldness she sensed in his soul.

"My lady," he saluted her, bowing over her hand, "you do me great honor."

Her eyes darted away from his in panic at his touch and caught her father's warning gaze. She drew her fingers away, but hurriedly lowered her lashes again and sank into a curtsy.

"My lord," she whispered through a throat that threatened to squeeze itself clean shut, "it is I who am honored."

Had he felt the way her fingers fluttered in his? Had he seen the revulsion in her eyes?

She felt him shift his position slightly at a nearby rustling sound. Before her downcast view appeared a pair of dainty, slippered feet, the shoes sewn with so many tiny diamond-like stones that their owner looked as if she was borne aloft by the stars. Startled, Marguerite looked up again, this time at the tall, slender woman who had joined them. The bodice of her rich blue kirtle hugged the perfect symmetry of her figure like a glove. A string of pearls and diamonds threaded through hair of flame. Marguerite had never seen so exquisite a face: fiery brows arched with elegant grace over eyes of emerald green; the flawless nose might have been carved of ivory; while lips of vermillion formed a perfect bow.

The woman curtsied to the earl with ethereal grace and the bow curved upwards into a sultry smile.

The earl took her hand in his and raised it to his lips. His cold, hazel eyes grew warm.

Warm in a way that made Marguerite squirm as though she glimpsed something indecent. She knew who the woman was before the earl presented her to the company.

"My lords and ladies," his harsh voice uttered blandly, "allow me to make known to you my Lady Jane Lovell."

Marguerite felt every gaze round from the flame-haired beauty to herself, shock on the faces of her father's men-at-arms, amusement on those of the earl's. Her cheeks burned with humiliation, but she stood quite still. No one, not even her father, seemed to know how to respond to the earl's effrontery.

Saxton himself at last broke the silence. His gaze, again grown chill, settled disdainfully on Lord de Villon. "Shall we proceed with the betrothal, my lord? My time is short."

His words threw the company into confusion. Marguerite hardly knew what followed in the immediate aftermath, for a sudden buzzing in her brain drown out all rational thought. She vaguely felt herself urged into position at the earl's side while Father Eudes' pasty, equine face swam before her vision. Her father's chaplain spoke and the earl coolly repeated his words. Then it was Marguerite's turn. She heard her voice stumbling over the first few words of Latin before her tongue froze. The buzzing abruptly ceased. She felt herself shaking and when she spoke again, the words burst from her lips in a blaze of white heat.

"I will not!"

The earl frowned a warning more menacing than she had ever seen on her father's face. "I beg your pardon?"

The chaplain suggested nervously, "Perhaps my lady did not perfectly understand the phrase—"

"Nonsense," her father said, "she speaks Latin like her native tongue. Are you mad, girl?"

Marguerite felt the drain of blood from her cheeks, but she was too angry to care. "I will not marry this man." She broke from her place at the earl's side and swept before Lady Jane. "I will not be so insulted, so dishonored in my own home! To be thus humiliated by a low, common harlot—"

Her father followed her and dealt her a slap that brought the blood rushing painfully back to her cheek. "How dare you?" he hissed in her face. "Get to your room."

The press of men in the hall parted to allow her a path to the stairs.

Marguerite fled without a backward glance at the earl, but she stumbled to a stop on the third step when she heard the chaplain say:

"My lord, does Master Odo know—? That is, I presume you have obtained his consent for—?"

She pressed a hand to the cold stones of the wall to steady herself. Her father drowned out the rest of the faltering query with a thundering curse, but her heart pounded at the chaplain's doubt. Her protest had made him hesitate. *Odo.* Perhaps he was not so far away after all.

She stood trembling. Her cheek throbbed, but she knew this was no time for cowardice. If she threw herself at the chaplain's feet, begged him to send word to Northumberland—

A hand closed on her arm with a strength that made her wince.

"Come with me," her father's voice snarled into her ear.

Her father must have seen her pause on the steps, must have guessed what was in her mind. And he surely felt her shudder as he dragged her up the stairs.

The pulsating ache in her back had not ebbed when Marguerite sat down gingerly on the edge of the ornately carved chair next to the Earl of Saxton. The couple took precedence on the dais even over her parents, claiming the place of honor at the center of the white clothed dining table. Her mother sat on the earl's left with her father beside her, far enough away for Marguerite to avoid his scowls. The welts left by her father's belt still stung, but in the end he had only wrung a half-triumph over her. She had returned to the hall and offered a stiff-lipped apology to Lady Jane, but she clung fast to her refusal of the marriage.

Her father had decided, therefore, to delay the betrothal ceremony until he found a way to make her more compliant and moved up the grand feast he had ordered on the earl's behalf. Now Marguerite sat beside Saxton as he gazed with an air of infinite boredom over the knights and ladies who swarmed the trestle tables set up below the dais. The unfamiliar faces of the earl's company overawed Marguerite, sprinkled too thinly with faces that she knew.

Then she caught the blue eyes of a sunny-haired young man who sat at a table to her left, and felt her first pang of comfort. Someone had invited her cousin, Richard Channing. Richard had been her father's page during those rare visits her grandfather had allowed her to her parents as a child. Richard's lively mischief had proved a happier distraction for Marguerite from her dismayingly ill-tempered father than had the pretty, soft-faced mother who coddled her one moment and the next left her with strange servants to run off to attend her husband's every whim.

Marguerite had not seen Richard in the last six years since he had gone off to serve as squire to Sir Edward Keynes. Her heart flooded with gratitude for his presence now. Would he remember all the larks they had shared? Would he understand the shadow that now lay over her heart?

"Beware, my lady."

Marguerite jumped at the earl's harsh voice. Had he seen her gazing at Richard and misunderstood its meaning? Before she could explain their kinship, Saxton bent his head and spoke softly in her ear.

"Lady Jane is more forgiving than I. I do not forget a slight. And my ambition will not be thwarted by a stubborn, spoiled child."

So, it was her cut of his brazen mistress that rankled him. If he expected another apology, she had no intention of giving it. He must have seen the defiance in her eyes, for his own gleamed a challenge in return. In a move surprisingly swift for a man of his bulk, he rose suddenly to his feet. The rumbling conversation in the hall fell silent as he lifted his goblet high.

"My lords and ladies, to my betrothed!"

Marguerite gasped at his pronouncement. He bowed to her, then turned back to the company and launched into a flourishing speech praising her loveliness, vaunting her undoubted virtue, and declaring his good fortune at winning the fair hand of the Lady Marguerite of Winbourne. When he finished, the company cheered. Marguerite gripped the edge of the table, barely resisting the impulse to leap to her feet and scream: *But I have not repeated the vows!* The outburst would only win her another beating. She saw her father's smile and the earl's smirk as he resumed his seat at her side.

Saxton was the king's closest counselor, the most powerful man in England. If he chose to pretend that the vows had been spoken, what man, even knowing otherwise, would dare contradict him? Marguerite felt herself trembling and drew in a deep breath, then a second and a third, trying to calm her alarm. The earl and her father thought her neatly backed into a corner. She must bide her time. She had seen Father Eudes waver in doubt. In the few years she had known him, she had not sensed a strong willed man, but perhaps he held more of a conscience than she knew. Perhaps even now he had a message flying to Odo.

The hope steadied her so that her fingers did not shake when a servant appeared beside her bearing a silver laver filled with lavender-scented water. She shook back her wide, draping sleeves to avoid inadvertently dampening them as she rinsed her hands. Her father had decked her out in a gown worthy of a future countess. Gold and silver threads wove a sumptuous pattern of leaves and vines in the rich gold cloth of her kirtle. Amethysts stiffened her collar and cuffs. Her servant Eva had brushed Marguerite's hair until it shone before binding it with a golden fret beneath barbette and fillet.

The unaccustomed splendor threatened to suffocate her.

She slid a sideways glance at the earl as the servant moved to his side with the laver. So much gold embroidery bedecked his tunic that she could not tell the color of the cloth beneath it. A heavy gold medallion with the imprint of his crest, the roaring bear, rose and fell against his wide chest, while a scarlet round cap sat a little rakishly upon his head. Marguerite saw him smile at someone seated at one of the side tables and knew who had captured his attention without following his gaze. The same naked hunger leapt into his eyes that had humiliated her when Lady Jane had made her first appearance in the hall.

Marguerite locked her teeth on her angrily quivering tongue and looked away.

The strains of the musicians hired by her father had floated down from the gallery while her father's squires paraded in the first course of the meal. But now as the company fell at last to dining, a short hush in the music was followed by a single, striking chord so near that it caused her to glance again at the floor beneath the dais. The crust of sweet white bread she had just dipped in some pepper sauce dropped from her startled fingers.

A minstrel stood in the open space between the diners where the jugglers, whom her father preferred, sometimes performed. Her breath suspended at the sight of him—the man she had seen in the village—the man from seven years ago. Had she fallen into dreaming?

"I pray you, good lords, lend me your counsel," he sang in a voice so rich and warm it swept around her like a velvet cloud. His fingers played lightly over the strings of a lute that ill-hid the scuffs and scratches on its sides beneath its veneer of polish.

> *"You who are experienced at love.*
> *I love a lady who is beauteous beyond measure,*
> *Yet I am less than a shadow in her eyes."*

Oh, if only he sang of her! She thought of that achingly beautiful moment in the village when his gaze, audacious yet oddly veiled, had snared hers before her mother had called her attention away. She had expected that he would travel on again ere she could convince her mother to allow her to return to the village and contrive a way to seek him out. Now here he stood, inexplicably . . . miraculously . . . so near that a few quick steps and she could have laid her hand in his square, brown palm.

"I sigh, I weep, I die of grief,
My heart is wounded beyond all bearing.
Yet all this pain I would joyfully endure
Might the wind carry but the whisper of my name to her ears!"

Marguerite recognized the verse he sang. 'Twas a love song popular among the minstrels who had visited her grandfather's hall, but never had the music sent through her such a delightsome shiver. The minstrel had changed his common homespun for a short tunic of scarlet. The bright, merry color accentuated the raven sheen of his close-cropped hair and complemented his even, sensitive features. Though he stood almost negligently as he plucked an interlude on the lute strings, energy rolled off his well-knit figure in waves that enveloped her as strongly as his melodic baritone voice.

"And yet, contrary heart—"

That organ somersaulted in her breast.

"Could I then be content?
A glance I would pray for next,
A smile, and then sweet kisses.
Ah! For these three boons I would . . ."

Marguerite did not hear the words that came next, for on the word "smile" she did just that and found herself nearly blinded by the responsive grin that set his face alight.

Almost instantly his face sobered again and his eyes darted away. His quick fingers did not drop so much a beat on the strings as he sang on as though nothing had passed between them.

Despite the minstrel's swift attempt to mask his lapse, Marguerite heard the ripple of murmurs through the hall and felt the shocked gazes of the company upon her. A hand beneath the tablecloth closed cruelly over her wrist, extinguishing the ecstatic glow that had engulfed her at the minstrel's smile.

"You appear to have made a conquest," Saxton murmured. "Who is he?"

Heat rose up in her cheeks, but she struck a careless tone. "A minstrel. It is nothing. Such fellows are inclined to be rather romantic."

"So long as he romances you from afar. I will have my wife above reproach in the world's eyes and mine."

Her gaze flashed down to the sideboard where the flame-haired Lady Jane sat. "I suppose it is too much to hope for the same in my husband?"

"Ah, the lady has a temper." His hand clenched her slender fingers with a slow, deliberate strength until she winced at the pain. "I will brook no defiance from you, my child. A spirited woman does very well outside of marriage, but I will have harmony within my home. You will not concern yourself with my affairs. Do you understand me?"

The veiled threat in his voice chilled her to the bone. "Yes," she whispered.

Apparently satisfied, he released her hand, but her fingers throbbed as though he still grasped them. Diverted by the minstrel, she had nearly forgotten the welts on her back, but they began to pulse again, too. Her father meant to pass her from his own harsh control to the brutal possession of this man beside her.

A stirring occurred across the hall near the arched entryway. Marguerite saw diners turning their heads towards the disruption. She followed their gazes—she dared not glance at the minstrel again—and felt her last hope crumble away. One of her father's knights stood with a mailed hand clamped on the arm of Father Eudes, who looked as nigh to fainting with terror as she had ever seen a man. The knight smiled, a firm, reassuring smile in the direction of her father on the dais. If the priest had tried to send word north, he had clearly been intercepted.

Marguerite felt the trap shut tight around her. She might be bound tomorrow, but tonight she could not bear another moment of the earl's oppressive company.

Saxton raised a dangerous brow as she stood up quickly and moved beyond his reach. "Forgive me," she murmured, "I am feeling unwell."

She dropped a curtsy to her father and a lower one to the earl, and swept from the hall before either of them could stop her.

His betrothed. Saxton's lips quirked. He had made it quite clear to everyone who mattered that he viewed Marguerite as exactly that, vows or no vows. He expected no more defiance. When the insufferable banquet finally ended, he considered himself free to indulge his desire as brashly as he did in the king's court. He rose from his chair and waited, hand extended, for Jane Lovell to sweep her way to the dais and place her fingers in his. As she did so, Lord de Villon cleared his throat awkwardly. Saxton glanced at him, his gaze sweeping past Lady Leah's troubled face.

"Yes, my lord?" Saxton asked the baron coolly.

"I—"

Saxton watched with satisfaction as de Villon's protest withered beneath his gaze.

"—er—" de Villon stammered "—um—I hope the banquet was to your liking, my lord?"

"Well, one cannot expect to find court pleasures in the countryside, but I appreciate your efforts. Goodnight, my lord, my lady."

Saxton bowed to his host and hostess, then would have led Lady Jane to their chambers but she resisted his attempt to draw her to the stairs. Ah, so she was angry. He should have told her before they left London, but she would have refused to come with him and that would have made his time in Dorset more tedious than he could bear. Now he would have to cool her temper before she would grant him the heat of her passion.

Lady Leah had described her pleasure garden in excruciating detail to the earl while they had dined. Saxton expected to find the rose bushes crumbling and bare at this season, but he judged the brisk night air would serve his purpose. And the gardens would be private. Anyone careless enough to stumble across him entwined with his mistress there should know to back hurriedly out again.

He tugged Lady Jane quite firmly out to the bailey towards the little wooden gate that opened into the garden. They passed a knot of men on the way, common castle servants, the sort that Saxton would not have spared a second glance at had one of them not been the scarlet-garbed minstrel. The fellow met Saxton's eyes boldly in the light of the torch held by one of his companions, his face as unreadable as it had been in the hall, save for that one ill-judged grin he had cast at the Lady Marguerite. Saxton walked past him, annoyed by the man's daring, but dismissive of it, as well. Saxton's little wife-to-be would not challenge him again.

Inside the garden, the nipping winter's breeze riffled his hair above the fur-lined collar of his heavy cloak, but the heat of his lust kept the cold at bay. He attempted to embrace his flame-haired lover, but she evaded him with a dagger's glare.

"Betrothed!" she exclaimed. "And you never said a word to me until we stood in the hall with Lord de Villon and his daughter. When you told me you had business to conduct with the baron, I never *dreamed*—" She flung out her hands. "Why, Symeon? How have I disappointed you?"

"You have not disappointed me, Jane." He clasped her sumptuous body in his arms before she could slip away again and possessed her lips with an almost violent force.

From their first meeting when she had arrived in the king's court a dashing young widow with a past already steeped in scandal, he had known he would not rest until she was his. Saxton was past forty, well beyond the age of falling in love. He had seduced and abandoned more women than he could number, but after more than two years, this lady still held him enthralled.

He repeated, his voice husky from their kiss, "You have not disappointed me. Nothing has changed. But the king has granted me rich honors and estates. It would be irresponsible of me not to see that they are provided with an heir. Surely you can understand that?"

They had never discussed marriage between themselves. Five years as wife to Lord Lovell followed by a string of prior lovers, had proven her as barren as she was wanton. She must have always known this day must come.

"Yesss," she admitted slowly, at last. "But why this child?"

"Marguerite of Winbourne is heiress, not only to her father's lands, but to her grandfather's vast estates. John Heywood had eccentric views, and out of reluctance to ally themselves with his heir, the barons of this realm would allow some of the richest manors in England to slip through their fingers." Saxton snorted his disdain of his weak-minded peers. "I do not care to be so foolish. What matter to me whether the churls that plow the fields be bond or free, so long as they do their work and pay their fees? With Heywood's estates added to my own, I will hold such power that King John will not dare to cast me off."

Her luscious mouth mocked. "As he did the Earl of Gunthar? All of Gunthar's lands and wealth did not save him."

"Gunthar did not understand how times have changed. He was a relic from old King Henry's days. But you have watched me with King John for years. Do you doubt that I know how to handle our liege's capricious fits and tempers? He was delighted when I told him of my scheme. I left him quite gleeful with the assurance that I will be happy to 'lend' him whatever sum he requires to refill his perennially empty coffers, once Heywood's inheritance is mine."

"And where do I stand in this scheme?" Lady Jane asked. "You heard the Lady Marguerite's outburst in the hall. She has no intention of meekly tolerating her husband's mistress. And she is so lovely and young—"

No one could whine as beguilingly as Lady Jane.

"Bah!" Saxton said. "She is pretty enough, I suppose, if one cared for dark women, but beautiful? Nay. And such wide-eyed innocence I find tiresome. Why think you I chose to seduce you rather than any of the virtuous maids at court whose charms the king would gleefully have delivered into my hands had I chosen to ask them of him?"

That won him a sultry laugh. They ever jested over which of them had first seduced the other.

"Come." Saxton caught her hand and pressed a hot kiss upon it. "I will prove my devotion to you with a ruby the size of this delicate fist on my wedding day, compliments of Lord Heywood's fat coffers. The first of many gifts from my bride's inheritance."

Lady Jane slid back into his arms with a shiver that thrilled him. A wild, wanton kiss as only she could bestow, then with their arms entwined about each other's waists, they left the garden and crossed the now empty bailey to return to the warmth of the keep.

4

Lying in her bed in the darkness, her back still pulsing from her father's punishment, her fingers still aching from Saxton's crushing grasp, Marguerite did not feel nearly as brave as she had in the bracing light of the hall. A small fire crackled and sputtered in the stone fireplace her grandfather had insisted her father build in her chamber when she was a child. Heywood had lost all his babes born on his cold northern manor save his daughter Leah. He would not, he had said, risk losing his only grandchild to the winter's harsh whims, as well.

"Oh, Grandfather," Marguerite whispered, "if you were only here now."

The firelight glowed too dimly through the heavy curtains that surrounded her bed, allowing the shadows to press in about her like some great smothering mantle. She dragged one of the blankets over her white woolen nightdress and left the bed, padding across the cold floor to kneel in the small ring of light cast by the guttering flames.

"Oh, Grandfather," she whispered again, the flames blurring through the tears that welled into her eyes, "why did you have to die? And Grandmama. I know she was silly, but oh, she was kind!" Marguerite sniffled and rubbed at her nose. "Father blames everything on you," she continued as if her grandfather sat right before her, her head resting on his knee, his rough hand stroking her hair as it had when she had been a child. "First he hates it that I am a girl, though of course, that is the one fault he cannot lay on you. But he curses you for all the rest. For filling my head with Latin and arithmetic and 'a jumble of other knowledge' he says is useless for a woman to know. He especially hates it that you made Odo teach me to read. He says it is why I am so romantic. Just because Grandmama liked to borrow those stories by Chrétien from the monastery and have me read them to her."

Well, Marguerite admitted silently, perhaps that criticism was true. Chrétien de Troyes had told the most marvelous tales of adventure and love, but Marguerite would not confess how they had influenced her heart, even to her grandfather.

She sighed. "But mostly, of course, he hates you because of what you did to Winbourne Manor while you lived, and to all your other manors after you died. He challenged your will in the courts, you know. He said that you were senile!" Her fist clutched angrily on the folds of the blanket. "But the royal courts upheld your will in the end. Father said it was because you lent the king so much money to fight his wars with King Philip that he commanded them to overlook your 'dangerous reforms.' Only of course, Father never uses the word 'reform.'" She almost giggled, until she remembered how miserable she was.

Those 'reforms' had served as her protection against all the unwanted suitors her father had tried to scrabble up for her hand after her grandfather died. Despite the papal interdict that had lain over the land for five years, her father was right. Marriage had not disappeared from the kingdom merely because the vows could no longer be declared in a church. But no matter how tempting Heywood's wide and prosperous lands, no man had wanted to ally himself with a perilous experiment that the courts had left no means of rescinding if it failed—and still worse, if it succeeded.

Until the Earl of Saxton had chosen to covet what other men feared. Even with the flames heating her cheeks, Marguerite shivered. Her father called her romantic, but she knew that real life was not like the stories that Chrétien told. Odo, Heywood's chaplain and Marguerite's tutor, had explained the expectations of duty to her after the debacle of Lord Stephen. Though Heywood would never force her into a marriage that repulsed her, Odo said, the day would come when her grandfather would expect her, as his only heir, to marry a good and honorable man as befitted her name and station.

A good and honorable man—that did not describe the Earl of Saxton! Marguerite had been fond of her grandmother, while her tutor, Odo of Wedmore, had commanded her respect, but only her grandfather had ever held her whole-hearted love and trust. One word from him would have rescued her—but he was gone, and tonight she felt achingly alone.

A soft *tap-tap-tapping* made her turn her head from the flames. A wind must have come up, stirring the old oak tree outside her window to rap against the wooden shutters. She scrubbed away the tears that tickled her cheeks and stood up. The air near the fire suddenly stifled her. The drum of the branches lured her to the window. She drew back the shutters, welcoming the rush of cold air against her face even as she tugged the blanket closer. As she'd suspected, the oak tree's barren limbs shook in the wind.

At first, she thought the low whistle no different than any other night the wind shrilled through the branches. But after a moment, she registered the subtle difference in tone. A soft, pure trill. Of all the unique colors of sound she had lay listening to in the night o'er the past three years, none of them had ever rung so true.

She reached out a hand to still the limb nearest to the window and leaned forward to gaze into the darkness. The clouds skittered across the sky, playing hide and seek with the moon, until suddenly the moon leapt out in all its white brilliance and she saw him, standing directly below her at the base of the oak. Dark hair shone silver in the moonlight and bathed the face she had dreamed of for years in all its haunting charm. The minstrel who had smiled at her so boldly in the hall.

He raised a hand. "Please, my lady, do not cry out."

"What do you want?" she called softly. "Ought you not to be with the other musicians in the gallery? What are you doing there?"

"Come down and I will tell you."

"Come down?" Was he mad? "My father would have my head!"

"What, are you afraid? Then I must come to you."

She watched with fascinated shock as he wrapped his hands around a low hanging branch and swung himself up into the tree. He climbed the branches, lithe and quick as a cat. She barely stumbled back in time to allow him room for the final bouncing step that brought him through her window.

Oh, heavens, he could not be here! Really and truly here, in her very bedchamber—!

Her bedchamber. She shot a panicked look over her shoulder at the door. "If my father finds you—" She bit off the warning on her tongue, the urgent reminder of the hounds that had chased him seven years ago, how she would not be able to save him this time if her father came in upon them. Something inside her bade her wait, yearning for him to speak first, to say that he recalled their encounter as keenly as she did.

"Shall you call your father's guards, milady? I swear on my life that I mean you no harm."

This reassurance, spoken in soft, earnest tones, stung her conscience like a rebuke. It had not entered her mind to fear him. Why did she not back away, shout for help? 'Twas no insubstantial romantic dream that stood before her, but a very solid man who had scaled a tree with such swiftness that he could surely overpower her in an instant if he wished to. Was it wise to trust from a single chance meeting that he would take no advantage of her now?

Especially when nothing in his voice betrayed a memory of her. The shadows of the chamber closed in around them, shading the features she had committed to heart, but a flicker from the sputtering fire flashed against his scarlet tunic and dully lit the rough, threadbare cloak that he had tossed over it.

"Ah," he murmured, "I thought you lovely in the village, and dazzling in the hall all dressed in gold, but to see you clad in white like an angel . . ."

His hand jerked up, stretching half-way across the space between them before she saw his fist clench and drop quickly back to his side. He had almost touched her. She could not have stopped him. His restraint encouraged her. She realized that she had allowed the blanket to grow slack, revealing more of her white nightgown than was proper. Proper! An ironic little laugh rose up in her throat. There was nothing proper about being alone with a minstrel in her bedchamber! She should command him to leave and scream if he refused. Had it been anyone, *anyone* else— But it was *him*, and instead of screaming, she found herself fighting a temptation to inch closer and comforting herself that at least he remembered gazing at her across a dusty village road.

The ironic laughter quenched on a lump of frustration. It was not enough. She did not care that she had only been a child, that it was unreasonable to expect him to see in a seventeen-year-old woman the ten-year-old girl who had helped him all those years ago.

She tugged the blanket back into its modest place and masked her hurt by demanding coldly, "What, pray tell, is your name, sir?"

"'Tis Robert Marcel. I brought my lute should you crave a song."

She refused to let his playful tone disarm her resentment. "I have heard that verse you sang tonight dozens of times."

"And yet it made you smile such a smile as to send a man's head spinning. Still, if you like it not, I know many another tune."

In truth, she could not have recited a single word of the verse, for his own flashing grin had sent everything out of her mind except him. She shifted her position to force him to turn so that the firelight fell across his fiercely handsome face, a face worthy of a man reckless enough to climb an oak tree to invade a lady's chamber. The same jolt of attraction that had pounded through her in the village and again a few hours ago in the hall, blazed through her again. She tried to distract herself with the instrument slung over his shoulder, shrouded in the same supple cloth covering that would never have protected it from the warping surge of a river. Almost she felt its weight in her hands again. And the other. What had become of the other bundle she had carried?

Her heart tripped afresh when he launched softly into verse.

> *"How merry the summer while it lasts,*
> *With bird song and the mirthful stream,*
> *And lover's heart that's true.*
> *The memory warms in winter's age,*
> *When song is gone and streams are still,*
> *And love has passed away."*

This little poem she knew, too. She had heard it sung merry, melancholy, sardonic, even bitter, but never in such fluid tones as his, or to a melody so plaintive that it hung shivering in the air, a poignant reminiscence for moments after his voice had ceased.

"Does that please you better, my lady?"

Did he banter again? She could not tell what he thought from his impassive expression or the low spoken words.

"Why are you here? What do you want?" She wished to chill him again with her dignity, but the questions instead came out barely more than a whisper.

"To see you. To talk with you. To—" His voice snagged as the truth swept the impassive mask from his face. "Oh, heaven forgive me, to kiss you!"

His hand reached out again, then hesitated, hovering just below her chin. Instead of rebuffing him, she felt herself sway towards him ever so slightly. His fingertips, calloused from his lute's strings, brushed against her cheekbone. Then her cheek cradled gently in his palm and the midnight eyes, no longer veiled, gazed into hers with a longing that took away her breath.

"I have thought of nothing but you since you gazed at me in the village today." His voice shook slightly as the words spilled out in a rush. "Then when you smiled at me in the hall, I knew I was lost. I cannot hope to court you. I am only a poor minstrel, and you are betrothed to the Earl of Saxton. But one kiss—just one!—I would cherish to the end of my days. Just one, if you will grant it—and then I will be gone."

Gone? Let him go now, when she had only just found him? Heaven could not be so cruel as to ask her to send him away so soon! If it took a kiss to bind him—

He must have taken her silence as assent, for he pulled her against his chest. He held her firmly, yet so gently that the embrace brought no pain to her back. Marguerite had never been in a man's arms before. Her heart raced so hard a pleasurable little buzz of dizziness hummed through her mind and body. He did not look like a man who often hesitated to take what he wanted and yet when he bent his head towards hers, he checked himself just short of her lips. It was that instant of uncertainty in him, briefer than a heartbeat, that nudged her leap of faith in his honor and lifted her willing mouth and drifted shut her eyes.

And then she felt his mouth on hers, gentle, warm, strong, yet somehow cautious, as if weighing something in her, as if waiting . . . for what? Outrage on her part? Resistance? Oh, heavens! If Marguerite had felt dizzy before, her senses now swam in earnest, and she wound her arms around his neck and let her body melt against him and kissed him back as if all her future hung on this one moment.

He pulled away with a little gasp, then despite his vow, found her lips again, this time with greater force. She tightened her hold, for her knees felt strangely untrustworthy. He did not smell of fresh air and green wood as she had dreamed, but of the smoke of her father's hall and a faint, fresh hint of mint. Ah! This was better than any daydream, this flurry of snatching kisses he suddenly pressed against her mouth, this quivering little flame inside her.

"Marguerite? Child, are you asleep?"

Marguerite pulled away with a gasp. "My mother," she whispered. "Oh, you must go. Quickly." She tried to push him toward the window but he did not move. "Go!"

"My lady—" She heard the husky fervor in his voice, but her mother rapped on the door, calling over his words.

"Marguerite?"

"Oh, go!" She shoved at his stubborn, solid chest. "*Go*, before she finds us together and summons help. I did not save you from the hounds just to watch my father cut you down before my eyes!" She vaguely heard his sharp breath as her mother's call grew more insistent. "Yes, yes, Mama, just a moment."

He caught her hands and held them against his breast. She could feel his heart beating strongly beneath his tunic. "I shall return," he said.

"Not here. Not like this."

"But I must see you again."

Her lips parted to protest and he bent forward to kiss them. Her head whirled. Again came the rapping and her mother's voice.

She pulled her lips away. "Please!"

"When shall I see you?"

"I don't know. I—tomorrow. Tomorrow morning, late. There is a place outside the village called the North Glade. Anyone can give you directions. I will meet you there. Now please, go."

He raised her hands to his lips, swung himself over the windowsill, and vanished into the night.

Marguerite closed the shutters, then ran across the room to admit her mother. Lady Leah still wore her gown from the banquet, her white linen veil edged with embroidery still floating o'er her pale gold hair. "Child, why did it take you so long to answer?"

"Forgive me, Mama. As I told the earl at the banquet, I felt unwell. I had Eva fix me a draught to help me sleep, then had difficulty rousing myself enough to let you in." Did she sound as breathless as she felt? She feigned a yawn and rubbed her eyes in a pretense of lingering drowsiness.

Lady Leah looked troubled and laid a hand to her daughter's brow. "Your father was displeased with your departure from the hall, but if you are indeed ill—"

"I am feeling better now," Marguerite said, then worried that she'd spoken too quickly. She yawned again. "Only I am veeery sleepy. I am sure I will be fine in the morning."

"I hope so. Your father wants you to join him and the earl in a hunt tomorrow." Lady Leah paused but did not move away from the door. "Marguerite, I realize you are unhappy with your betrothal to the earl—"

"Please, Mama, I don't think I can discuss it sensibly just now. I'm afraid Eva's potion has not entirely worn off." She heaved what she hoped sounded like a drugged sigh. "Can we talk about it tomorrow?"

"Well—if you are sure you are all right—"

"Quite sure." She kissed her mother dutifully on the cheek, then wondered with a wave of panic if Lady Leah could feel the betraying heat the minstrel had left on her lips.

Lady Leah gave her daughter a quick, surprising hug, then left the room, drawing the door shut behind her.

Marguerite raised the back of her hand where his kiss still lingered like a firebrand, and nestled it against her cheek.

5

Robert did not see the egg hidden in the straw until he felt the oval object beneath the instep of his soft-soled shoe and heard the brittle crack as his foot smashed it against the hard-beaten earth floor. A nearby hen flapped up in squawking protest, threatening to drive Robert back into the bedroom he had sought to exit. He flung up a protective arm before his face, but Lucy Locke had already dashed across the room, shooing the hen with her apron.

"Away with ye, ye wicked thing! Away! Oh, dear. Oh Rob, I'm sorry."

He leaned against the timber doorframe and crooked up his dripping foot, half-laughing until checked by the anxiety in the pretty blue eyes that surveyed the white and yellow puddle in the straw.

"The apologies should be mine, Lucy," he said. "I know every egg must be precious to you and Will this time of year."

"'Tis naught, 'tis naught. How could ye know she would choose to lay an egg just there?" Lucy gave Robert a timid smile.

An air of dangerous fragility hung about her thin eighteen-year-old figure. Robert chewed his lip to control a frown. It had taken him the better part of the last fortnight to coax her out of her shyness of him and he did not wish her to misinterpret his emotions now.

"He is so—*forceful*," he had overheard her confiding to her husband his first night in their cottage when she had thought him asleep. "I mean, he is very kind, and his smile will have all the women in the village fair swoonin', and I do like the way his eyes dance when he laughs, but—but I can almost feel somethin' simmerin' beneath it all. Somethin' hot an' dangerous—Oh, I know 'tis silly. Ye'd not have welcomed him with that big, broad grin o' yers if he was not perfectly safe."

"Safe enough for ye, sweet thing," William Locke had murmured from the darkness of their straw pallet across the tiny bedroom.

"Ye knew him on yer old manor? An' how? He's an air of the castle about him, I think, and ye but a villein."

"Nay, not the castle," William had said.

"But Will," Lucy whispered, her voice piercing in its awe, "he's got *books*. And a sword."

"For which we will be in sore trouble if Jarrott learns we've a weapon any larger than a kitchen knife in our house."

Then he had hushed her, for Robert had been quite certain that William knew him still awake and counted him receptive of the rebuke.

Now Lucy handed Robert a rag that reeked of sour milk to wipe his shoe. He bit his lip harder at the sight of her red, cracked fingers that looked brittle enough to snap off if she stepped out into the cold. He knew the appearance deceptive, but it angered him all the same. *Hot and dangerous*— Nay, the last thing he wished was to frighten her. So he offered her his most cajoling smile as he took the rag and extended the dun homespun tunic he carried in his hand in exchange.

"I wonder if you might mend that for me, Lucy?" he asked as he mopped away the yoke from his sole. "I've attempted it myself, but I think I've only made it worse."

A pale pink wave rose up in her wan cheeks and he thought she looked pleased. She brushed a strand of listless flaxen hair from her eyes to examine the tear in the tunic's shoulder more closely. "I'd be happy to do it for ye, Rob. 'Twill only take a minute."

"Come sit, Rob," William's voice rumbled from the lopsided trestle table. His friend set down two mugs of ale next to a plate of dry cheese. "How'd it go at the castle last night? Ye must have come in after Lucy and me fell asleep."

"Aye, it was late," Robert said.

He tossed the egg-stained cloth in a corner with some other rags where Clea the cat sat kneading a bed for a morning nap. Robert drew up a three-legged stool to the table across from William. Cut of hardier stock than his wife, everything about William looked sturdy and square—his shoulders, his chin, even his forehead topped by a thatch of thick, sandy brown hair. Still, Robert knew this meager plate of cheese provided little enough sustenance for the needs of so big a man. And so he sipped his flat ale and ate sparingly. He'd received some castoffs of food with the other servants after the tables had been cleared from the castle hall last night. He expected he'd be rewarded with more of the same tonight, for Sir Alan had invited him to sing again as he'd counted Robert out a pair of bright coins.

Lucy held his torn tunic against her face and breathed deeply. "Mmm. Mint. I would never have thought of pressin' mint into my clothes. I grow it in the summer for cookin', of course, but I never dare use more than a pinch, for 'tis said to make men fierce."

William chuckled. "'Ware then, 'ware, for Rob's temper is fierce enough as it is!"

Robert laughed too. He brushed away a dusting of the dried herb that clung to the sleeve of the well-worn smock he wore. "Nay, it helps keep the fleas away, is all."

He saw the humor fade from William's face, replaced by a crease of disapproval. "Still at that, are ye? An' bathin' in every river ye see, as well, I suppose? Saints! Ye're more fastidious than a lord. Ye're too much like your da, ye are, an' not for the good. I've told ye that again and again."

Robert felt a flash of resentment as familiar as William's rebuke. "Aye, you've told me a great many things through the years. Had I thought any of them worth heeding, I'd have done so by now."

He regretted the snap in his voice as soon as he said it for he saw the alarmed widening of Lucy's eyes. William should have known better than to chide him about his father, but for Lucy's sake, he sought to make quick peace with her husband.

"'Tis too chill a day to quarrel with you, Will," he said in an easier tone, pleased to see Lucy sit down near her distaff and begin threading her bone needle. "I know I said I'd help you fix the door of your coop to keep these lovelies penned, but I've someplace I must be this morning."

He scooped up a black speckled hen that had fluttered up to the table and dropped it lightly back onto the floor. Thank goodness he'd left his scarlet tunic hanging on a peg in the bedroom with his cloak draped over it to protect it from his host's errant poultry. The sturdy English broadcloth had cost him dear for the precious bright dye and must serve him well for years to come.

William must have observed his wife's distress as well, for he took a deep draught of ale before replying in equally even tones, "Someplace very important, I take it? 'Tis not like ye to beg off from a chore for a whim."

"It is just for the morning," Robert said. "I should be back by None."

William pursed his lips, not unlike the way he had at Robert after their encounter with Sir Alan yesterday. "I gather ye mean to tell me nothin' about it, then. Yer not in some sort of trouble, are ye?"

Lucy had set her needle to flying, but the needle stilled, waiting, Robert knew, for his answer. He replied with no thought in his head but to put her back at ease.

"Only if you consider falling in love to be trouble."

That won from her the delighted smile he had hoped for.

"Oh, Rob, who is she?" Lucy cried. "Is she very pretty? Is she kind? Where'd ye meet her? Why have ye said nothin' o' this before?"

Robert threw up his hand with a teasing grin. "One question at a time, Lucy, I beg of you." He felt William's steady gaze on him. He knew his friend suspicious, but William could not possibly guess the truth.

"Tell us about her, Rob," Lucy insisted.

Robert succumbed to the inviting glow on Lucy's face to reminisce on his lady's graces. "Her cheeks are fairer than the foam on fresh cream. The faintest freckles dust her nose, as though some fairy creature spilled her enchantment there. Her dark hair billows about her sweet face like a tumultuous cloud of summer, while her chestnut eyes . . ." his heart pounded in memory ". . . her eyes are full of such trusting dreams as to make a man quake in awe." He recalled his one pang of conscience at the sight of the innocence nestled in her eyes just before she had lifted her lips to his and he had tumbled headlong into their first kiss.

"Never ask a minstrel to describe a woman he's smitten with," William muttered. "What folderol ye've learned to recite, Rob."

"I wish ye'd say such pretty things about me," Lucy said to her husband with a sigh.

William gave her a crooked grin of such affection that it raised a happy, forgiving blush in her cheeks before he turned back to ask his friend, "An' where'd ye meet this beauty? Ye've teased enough girls in the village with that roguish smile of yers, but I'd have known ere now if any of them had amused ye for more than an hour. An' I know ye well enough to know ye'd not have flirted with a one of them if ye'd already given yer heart to someone."

"But he sang at Ashbury Castle last night," Lucy reminded him. "Is that where ye met her? Is she a servin' girl up at the castle?"

Robert hesitated. "No, she's not a serving girl."

"Then who is she? Tell us, Rob, for I'm dyin' o' curiosity!"

He glanced at William, who was watching him with narrowed eyes over the rim of the ale mug he'd raised back to his lips. Robert was not sure what devilry prompted him to confess, "'Tis true that I met her at the castle. Her name is Marguerite."

Lucy looked puzzled. "'Tis a pretty name, but I do not know any Marguerites in Lyndeard except for—" She broke off as William spewed a mouthful of ale across the table and burst into a coughing fit. "Oh, Will!"

She shot up from the stool and ran to her husband's side. Robert stood too and thumped him on the back.

William gasped out words between attempts to draw breath. "Ye don't mean— Ye can't—possibly— Blast it—Rob!" He struck Robert's hand away, drew a rasping chestful of air, and exploded, "Have ye lost your mind?"

"William, what is it?" Lucy cried, hovering worriedly around her husband.

He mastered his breathing and stood up slowly. "He's talkin' of the Lady Marguerite. Aren't ye?"

Robert lifted his chin in challenge. "And if I am?"

"Oh!" Lucy clapped her hands together, though the half-mended tunic she still held muffled the sound. "Oh, I knew he belonged to the castle folk! William, ye should have told me! Lettin' a young lord sleep in our hovel, as though he was a nobody like us."

"He's not a lord," William said sharply. "He's—" He hesitated, his eyes still locked with Robert's. "He's just a minstrel. A common, *lowly* minstrel who's as mad as a hare in March."

Robert laughed.

William glared at him. "Ye think it's amusin', do ye?"

"Only that I still have the power to shock you," Robert said. "You've cursed my arrogance and presumption enough times that I should have thought you'd greet this latest impudence with no more than an exasperated shrug."

He rested his foot against the lower rung of the stool he'd just been sitting on and watched the consternation spread across William's features as the implication of his words sank in.

"Please tell me ye weren't fool enough to actually approach Lord de Villon's daughter last night?" William begged.

"Approach?" Robert's blood rushed as he recalled the feel of her in his arms, the taste of her kiss . . . "Aye, I approached her."

Robert let his impassive mask slide over his face as he said it. Though 'twas a defense he'd mastered after he'd left Beck Manor, William clearly sensed mischief in the expression that suddenly shut him out.

William brought down his fist on the table so hard that the ale mugs jumped along with his wife. "Enough! Didn't ye hear Sir Alan yesterday? She's betrothed to the Earl of Saxton. Do ye think the man who stands next to the king will let ye trifle with his wife?"

"I've no intention of trifling with her." However emotionless Robert kept his face, he heard his voice come out cold.

"Then what are ye about?"

Robert searched inside himself for an answer and found himself oddly at a loss. "I don't know, Will. I realize how far beneath her I am, that it is hopeless for me to love her. But I have never felt for any woman what I felt for her last night when we—spoke."

He clung tight to his mask as he said it. He had never lied to William before. He had never concealed even his brashest actions from this man whom he counted more brother than friend. But to confess that he'd scaled a castle wall, swept the Lady Marguerite in his arms and kissed her not once, not twice, but again and again— He was not a scoundrel, however much he enjoyed a good game of flirtation. He had always trod carefully the line of playful dalliance, no matter how some of his more experienced feminine encounters had tempted him to cross it. That he should have showered kisses on an innocent maiden who had lured him with no more than a smile had been so contrary to his nature that he could not explain it to himself, much less to William.

"Ye're right when ye speak o' bein' beneath her." William's voice broke in brutally across Robert's conscience. "The noblest blood runs in her veins, and what are ye? The son of a man who was hanged for treason. A wanderer, with no place to call yer own. An' ye dared to even raise yer eyes to her face?" William gave a hard laugh, as though mocking his own question. "But o' course ye did. I tell ye, Rob, one day yer arrogance is goin' to land yer neck in a noose like yer da."

Heat flamed up in Robert's cheeks during this speech, but Lucy's little stammer checked his retort.

"His da? Is—is that true?" she asked William.

Robert forgave the way she drew back from him. 'Twas a dangerous thing to harbor a traitor's kin.

"Aye," William said roughly. "Arthur Marcel—"

"Did not betray the king!" Robert glared at his friend through a white haze of anger.

"Rob—the French silver they found—"

Robert shoved the stool so hard with his foot that it slammed against the wall. "That was Lord Garoux's black lie. My father was innocent, and so help me Will, if you still count yourself my friend—"

William's mouth set hard as Robert broke off, but he said nothing more. Robert did not trust himself to speak further, either. He snatched his tunic out of Lucy's hands and jerked it over his head. Then he stalked into the bedroom to find his belt with the tyger-hilted dagger he'd bought six months before in York. He fastened both on with a series of angry tugs, pulled his cloak from the peg and tossed it around his shoulders. That left his scarlet tunic exposed. After the briefest hesitation, he took it down too, rolled the tunic up, and slipped it into the soft, padded case that held his lute. *Just in case he did not return to the cottage before Compline.*

"Where are ye goin'?" William demanded as Robert strode through the front room again, his lute over his shoulder, and pulled open the door.

Robert paused to meet his gaze. "You are right, Will. I am as mad as a hare in March. So mad that I'm off to meet the Lady Marguerite and I will take great care to explain to her all you have reminded me of."

William looked panicked. He reached out and grabbed Robert's arm. "Rob, the earl— She's his betrothed! Ye can't—"

Robert shook him off. "Don't tell me what I can and cannot do, Will. Wise or foolish, I make my own choices now."

"Ye always made yer own choices, Rob, and remember what it cost ye."

That memory only goaded Robert across the threshold. He slammed the door behind him, his earlier words of humility dissolving in the bang. Why should he not court her? She could not love the earl, or she could not have kissed Robert with the fervor she had last night. She was a woman, he a man, and in his determined world, that was all they required to stand as equals. If she had grown from a compassionate child into a generous-spirited woman who wished to give him her heart, why should he not take it?

The first villein Robert met in a village lane pointed him to the clearing in the woods called the North Glade. Robert had hoped to find her waiting for him, but perhaps it was just as well she was not. With his blood still simmering from his exchange with William, there was no telling what folly he might have committed.

But in truth, the folly had already been done. He admitted it as the brisk morning breeze slowly cooled his temper. He paced across the frosty bracken and back again, his thoughts racing over the events of the night before.

His hopes to draw the Lady Marguerite unobtrusively aside at some point after the feast and learn if she was the child he remembered had been frustrated by her early departure from the hall. Robert guessed himself the cause, that unguarded grin he had cast her in the middle of his song. But how could he have reacted otherwise? If her hesitant smile in the village had set an unfamiliar tripping in his heart, her glowing, spontaneous one in the hall had swept his mind nigh witless. Only his musician's training had kept his fingers plucking the tune on the strings and the memorized words flowing unchecked from his tongue.

What imp had prompted him seek out the window to her chamber he could not have said. The thought merely slipped into his mind while he stood conversing with a group of castle servants in the bailey, waiting for his pay. It had taken no more than a pair of casual, offhand questions to learn which tower was hers. He did not know what he'd intended once he found it. It certainly had not occurred to him to scale the tree until the Lady Marguerite had unexpectedly thrown back the shutters and gazed out on the moon . . . and at him.

Robert's tendency to act on reckless impulse had bedeviled him all his life. He had not even realized he was scurrying through the branches until he had come even with her window. By then it was too late. As soon as they stood face to face, he'd realized he had wanted to kiss her from the moment she had smiled at him in the village. Had she shown fear, he would have returned at once to the winter's night. Had she spoken even one haughty, condescending word, he'd have left her just as quickly. But instead, she had bantered with him, unable to conceal the sweet innocence that lay beneath her attempt to chill him with her dignity.

And then she had kissed him so sweetly and what had followed had flowed as naturally from his being as the music his mother had breathed into his blood from the hour of his birth. The one kiss he had meant in all sincerity to be content with had turned into two, and then he hardly remembered anything but his swimming pleasure. He had thought that she felt it too, that mystifying yet almost tangible sense of completeness in the union of their lips.

Robert had trusted that memory to bring her to the glade today, but he had trod back and forth across the bracken so many times that his booted feet had melted a path in the frost. The former night's wind had blown out the clouds, letting thin, hazy rays fall from a pale blue sky through the barren branches of hawthorn and ash. He drew his threadbare cloak closer to shut out the breeze that nipped at him in spite of his pacings. He hoped the gesture would hide, as well, the tear in the shoulder of his tunic that he had not given Lucy time to finish mending. Lucy's shocked face when William had told her of Robert's father hovered again in his mind. Would the Lady Marguerite shrink from him if she knew, as well?

How could she not?

The fear merely quickened Robert strides. He would risk it to see her again. He tossed another impatient glance at the sky. Where was she? She had said late, but by the position of the sun, it must be approaching None.

Then the quiet air broke at last with a *clop-clop-clopping* of hooves and he turned to see her riding between the trees. Green cendal skirts peeped from beneath her cloak's hem and one soft, dusky curl escaped her fur-trimmed hood to stray over her shoulder. The crisp breeze had ruddied her cheeks so they bloomed like radiant spring roses.

She caught a sharp breath at the sight of him. "Oh! I was afraid I would no longer find you here!" Her eyes sparkled as she drew up her bay mare. An apologetic smile curved her lips. "I am sorry to have kept you waiting, but *such* a time I had escaping unseen from my father's hunting party."

Robert grasped the mare's bridle and stroked its forehead. It whinnied softly beneath his reply. "I do not wish to cause you trouble, my lady. If your father misses you—"

"Oh, he will not be surprised to find me gone. He knows that I hate to hunt. I slip away whenever I can before the party closes for the kill. It is only that if he had seen me leaving, he would have insisted that my groom accompany me and—" she paused with a blush, before finishing shyly "—and I did not wish to bring my groom along."

Robert was not immune to the sweet trust inherent in her words. It was frighteningly naïve of her to entrust herself to a stranger. *But she does not view me as a stranger.* Last night as she'd thrust him towards the window to escape her mother's discovery, she had spoken of the hounds that had tracked him as relentlessly as her father's pack surely chased their prey today. Her fervent warning had confirmed her as the child by the river.

He released her mare's bridle and stepped around to her side. "Your father is wise to insist upon such precautions. But I promise you are safe with me."

She leaned down from her saddle and set her small gloved hands on his shoulders. His palms brushed briefly against the fur lining of her cloak as he found her silk clad waist and lifted her to the ground. He stood for a moment gazing into her lovely, hood-framed countenance. If his mother had poured music into his soul, his father had branded his bold heresy upon it. One quick move of Robert's head and he could taste those heady lips of hers again. There was nothing to stop him, not even herself while she stood so very still in his grasp, as if waiting . . . as if willing . . .

But he felt his cold hands warming beneath the cloak's fur, saw the fine, soft weave of the woolen fabric it was sewn to. Her sleek, cendal gown was the final mockery to the coarse homespun of his tunic with its frayed seam at the shoulder and the shabby cloak that concealed it. Luxuries that usually fired his resentment now unexpectedly disconcerted him as he gazed again into her artless eyes. The convictions that had driven him for five-and-twenty years wavered in a rush of uncertainty.

He dropped to one knee and caught her gloved hand to his lips. "My lady."

"Oh, no, no, please!" She sounded appalled and tried to pull her hand away. "I am not a queen that you should kneel to me."

He clung to her fingers. "You may as well be a queen," he said, suddenly fierce with the realization of how unattainable he must hold her. He had been mad last night. To take further advantage of her innocence would be the act of a knave. "I should never have asked you to meet me."

"But I wanted to come. I have dream—thought of you so often. I-I do not think you remember me, though." The quivering of her lower lip betrayed her disappointment.

"Forget my little savior?" He kissed her hand again before he released it and rose. "Even if such ingratitude were in me, this would remind me of my debt every time I sang." He moved to touch the case he had left beside the log.

Her eyes brightened again. "It is your lute, is it not?" She followed him and reached her fingers to where she guessed the neck of his instrument must be. "No wonder you dared not cross the river with it. The water would have ruined it beyond repair. It was your livelihood even then."

She spoke her conclusion in firm, sure tones. So, in all these years, even with the hounds fairly baying at his heels, she had not guessed the truth. Nor did he intend to let his face reveal it when she stole a smiling glance at him.

"May I see it?" she asked.

He hesitated. He should thank her and send her on her way. But instead, he joined her when she sat on the log. He removed the lute from its case and set it in her lap.

"Oh!" she exclaimed. "The design of the rose is lovely."

Robert felt a surge of pride at her pleasure in the intricate grillwork over the sound hole. "My father carved it," he said. "He fashioned the entire instrument for my mother and gave it to her on Epiphany when I was seven years old. I helped him gather the wood late at night while old Lord Garoux slept. A minstrel who was passing through the village told us which wood was best: ash for the soundboard, boxwood for the neck, strips of maple for the ribs on the back."

She had pushed back her hood as he spoke and listened with her gaze flitting alternately between the instrument and his face, but she tilted the lute now to examine its deep, rounded body. He admired the graceful turn of her cheek, the whimsical freckles dusted across her small nose as he continued.

"The minstrel showed my father the thickness to cut the wood and showed him how to bend the ribs to form the belly so that the sound would be the sweetest. Father let me slide the pegs in their places after he carved their notches before he attached the strings. In truth, my contributions were small, but at the time, I felt for all the world as though I had labored over the gift quite as much as he."

"'Twas your mother, then, who taught you to play?" she asked when he paused for breath.

"Most of my training came later, but my mother taught me a little. She sang and played the flute, but she had to learn her way with these strings by trial and error." He touched an affectionate finger to the instrument. "I think she was born with music in her. My father did not sing, but he was clever with his hands, and brave. When the king went to war with France, my father fought too, as loyal as any baron or earl."

So determined was he to state aloud his faith in his father that it took her swift, wide-eyed glance to jar him into realizing how carelessly he had worded it. His back stiffened slightly. Well, and why should it surprise her that he spoke thus of barons and earls? Surely she had not thought him of noble birth? The weave of his clothing had been as rough seven years ago as it was now.

She smiled—some secret little smile that he could not interpret before she returned her study to the lute. "'Tis a pity it is marred," she said, rubbing a hand gently along the scuffs in the side. "Did it happen while you were running away?"

He hesitated. He had told William he would tell her everything, and with the blaze of anger still in him Robert might have done so. He had been braced then for her to shrink. But now, in this cooler moment, he wished to linger beside her, to try to pierce the mystery of what had drawn him to her. It could not be the enchantment of her smile alone. There had been too many women more beautiful than she who had stirred his passion, but never his heart.

He sensed some subtle difference in her, some unique view of the world that had prompted her as a child to help a desperate young man in a frayed, shabby tunic worthy of a serf and as a woman to comfort a frightened villein boy. But it made no sense in either a child or woman of her birth. *Kit and I played together as boys, but he never for an instant forgot the distance between us.*

Robert answered her query in a roundabout way, shaking his head as he touched one of the scratches in the maple wood. "This one happened when a neighbor boy teased my little sister by taking her doll away. In Lottie's tussle to retrieve it, they knocked against the table where our mother had left the lute so that it toppled off and hit the floor. It took our mother days to retune it, but happily no worse damage was done. This one"—he turned the instrument in her hands to point out a scrape on the other side—"happened years later at an inn. After I sang for the company they bought me a fine dinner, but I carelessly left the lute on the floor beside my chair while I ate. A servant bringing in food for another customer did not see it and accidentally dealt it a kick as he passed by." Robert's mouth curved ruefully. "However hungry, I never again failed to bestow it safely in its case before I partook of a meal."

"And this one?"

He followed her finger as it touched the third blemish in the wood, the largest and deepest of them all. He had dodged the truth as long as he could. "That is where my mother herself dropped it on the day she learned that my father had fallen afoul of Lord Garoux." Robert met the query in her gaze. "And aye, my lady, that is why I ran away."

At least, the seeds had been sown that day for the events that had come to fruition seven years later. Robert watched her face and waited. How much more he told her about his father depended on her next question.

She brushed her fingertips against one of her rose-tinged cheekbones, then shook her head so briskly that it freed her hair from her fallen hood to float like a cloud over her shoulders. "If Lord Garoux was anything like my father, I do not blame you for running away. I would run away too, if I could. In fact—" she kept her gaze fixed on the lute as she finished "—I was trying to do so the day I met you by the river."

Robert stared at her averted profile. "You? Running away? From what?" He asked her the question she had forbore to ask him. An image he had long forgotten suddenly arose in his mind. When he had swam across the river and she had met him on the other side after carrying his bundles across the bridge, her lips, rosy even then, had parted on the beginning of a plea. It had been cut short by the old man who had broken from the trees, urgently calling her name. She had turned and dashed back to the bridge, the words left unspoken . . . until now.

"You were going to ask me something that day," Robert prompted.

A blush mounted beneath the natural bloom of her cheek. "If I could go with you," she confessed after a moment. "I had not thought very clearly when I left the castle, and only realized when I reached the river that I had no idea where I was going. And then I saw you and heard the hounds, and I knew from how desperate you looked that you were running away, too. I wanted to ask you to take me with you. But then I heard my grandfather calling and knew how dangerous it would be for you if he saw you. He might have told whoever was chasing you where you had swam the river. So I ran back across the bridge to distract him."

In all the years Robert had remembered her with warmth and gratitude, it had never crossed his mind that she may have paid a price for the service she had rendered him. "But I saw you rush straight into the old man's arms," he said. "He scooped you up with such relief and love in his face, it cannot have been from him you fled."

Her chestnut eyes widened on Robert's face. "You stayed to watch me?"

"You were only ten. However desperate I was, I could not leave until I knew you were safe. I hid in the reeds and watched until I knew whether the old man meant you good or ill."

"And—and if he had meant me ill?" she asked, a slight breathlessness now in her voice. "What would you have done?"

Robert heard a soft whinny and looked up to see that her mare had wandered across the glade and stretched its neck towards the branch of a yew tree. He left the log to catch its reins again and tether it a safe distance from the lethal leaves before he turned back to answer her question.

"I do not quite know," he said. "I could have done nothing if Kit had caught me, but I suspect I would have swam back across the river to try to help you anyway. I rarely thought through the consequences of my actions before I hurled myself into trouble in those days." Robert felt another rueful tug at his mouth. If William knew how Robert had scaled her tower wall last night, he would say that his friend had changed but little since boyhood.

He felt her searching his face but he knew she would read nothing there. After a moment, she pulled off her gloves and began to gently pluck at the lute's strings.

"Who is Kit?" she asked.

"Lord Christopher, Lord Garoux's son." Robert barely heard his own answer as he resumed his place beside her, for her revelation troubled him. Had he inadvertently rewarded her kindness with harm? "From what or whom did you flee, my lady? Had someone threatened or frightened you?"

"Oh, no, not exactly. Well—well, frightened me, I suppose, but I know now that he never meant to." Her fingers picked out an aimless pattern of notes. "I mean my grandfather, the old man you saw by the river. 'Tis merely that he and my father wished me to marry a smelly old knight. I was too young to wed, but old enough to be betrothed. They brought me all the way from Winbourne in Northumberland to Romsfeld Castle to meet Lord Stephen and speak the betrothal vows."

"Lord Stephen of Romsfeld? They wished you to marry him?"

She glanced at Robert, her pretty brow creasing. "You know him?"

Robert shook his head. "Nay, we never met, but I saw him from time to time. His fields lay near to ours. I had to cross Lord Stephen's lands to reach the bridge. I'd originally meant to cross there, only Kit set the hounds on me sooner than I expected and there was no time to reach it. I know I should have swam the river on our side, it would have lost my scent and I would have made my escape before Kit even knew I was gone—only I could not bear to leave my mother's lute behind, so I made for the bridge instead."

"But once the hounds were on your trail, you knew they would follow your scent right over it." Understanding gleamed in her eyes. "That is why you looked so haunted. The only way to lose them was to swim, and that would have ruined this lovely thing." She caressed the lute as reverently as though she held a polished, shining masterpiece.

Robert sighed. "It was foolish of me. The lute was already marred, the wood grown dull, when I stood at the river that day."

"You said your father carved it for your mother in love. That makes it beautiful."

She returned to plucking the strings. He sat watching her, savoring her graceful movements and wishing he dared kiss her again.

"I am glad I found you," she said amid a series of glistening notes that still attested to the skill of his father's construction. "Glad I could run this across the bridge for you so that you could swim. What happened to the other bundle you gave me?"

His books. "It is safe with a friend. But you, lady—" his alarm flared up again "—what happened with your grandfather? With Lord Stephen?" Robert could not bear it if she had been made to suffer for his sake.

"Oh." She gave an embarrassed little laugh, the blush returning to her cheeks. "My fears were all for naught. I should have listened to Odo when he promised me all would be well."

"Odo?"

"My grandfather's chaplain and my tutor when I was small. I told him I did not wish to marry Lord Stephen and he said he would speak to my grandfather, but I did not believe it would make a difference. I knew the match pleased Grandfather, else he would not have listened when my father suggested it nor brought me to Romsfeld Castle. I did not wish to disappoint him, but when I saw Lord Stephen and smelled him and tried to imagine living always and always with him—"

Her fingers stumbled a little on the strings before resuming their steady pattern. "I was afraid Grandfather would brush aside my fear, assure me that he knew best—the way he always did with my grandmother and sometimes did with me. I could not think what else to do, so I ran off in a panic. But when I went back, Grandfather was ever so sorry and held me close and promised that he would never, never ask to me to marry anyone that I disliked. And he never did, even when I knew how badly he would like to have added Sir Humphrey's lands to his, just as he had wanted Lord Stephen's."

So, that explained why so much loveliness remained unwed. Robert was glad no serious threat had awaited her return from the river. But the thought that fell like a shadow across his mind dismayed him almost as much as the alarm her story had just subdued. She had rejected Lord Stephen and Sir Humphrey, but Robert had sung at her betrothal dinner to the Earl of Saxton less than four-and-twenty hours ago. Then she had found something in the earl that pleased her enough to accept him where she had spurned the others?

Men spoke of the Earl of Saxton all over England. Arrogant. Ruthless. Power-hungry. Licentious. And the king's right arm. Robert knew only the latter to be true. The rest were mere rumors, muttered in villages or towns that Robert passed through, or at hearth fires where he sang. Men feared the earl, hated his power and coveted his favor. Robert had given none of it much heed. After eighteen years trapped between the borders of Beck Manor, he had had a world to explore. The excitement of plying his newly chosen occupation at fairs, entertaining at tournaments, singing for merchants and barons in every county in England had consumed his curious mind and his body's restless energy. If the intrigues of the royal court had affected his minstrel's life, it had done so in so tangential a way that Robert could not have cited an instance.

He had never seen the famed earl before last night. An almost instant antipathy had recoiled through Robert, even before he had caught the hungry glances between Saxton and the flame-haired beauty in the snug-fitting gown and witnessed the way some low-spoken word had sent the Lady Marguerite white-faced from the hall. And yet the Lady Marguerite had agreed to wed him, for had she not just said that by her grandfather's word she should never be forced to the altar?

Had she agreed for wealth? For power? She was no longer a ten-year-old child to shun such advantages out of youthful impulse, especially when such a marriage would thrust her into the very center of royal prestige. And yet the same instincts that warned Robert about the earl also convinced him that the kisses in her chamber had not been a lie. She was still young, he thought, watching the lithesome sweep of her wrist as she strummed a chord on the strings. Young enough to suffer the pull of conflict between pleasing at last the grandfather she so clearly loved and indulging her still girlish heart.

Well, whatever they had shared in her chamber, her future was not his affair. She had made a woman's choice and must learn to abide a woman's consequences. In the heat of defiance he might have dared to woo a baron's daughter, but seducing another man's betrothed went beyond the bounds of honor he had sworn as much his right to claim as those who looked down their proud noses at his birth.

Gradually through the stream of his thoughts he became aware that the aimless notes she plucked had evolved into a familiar tune. Her fingers moved nimbly now, reproducing an air he had sung in many a castle and town and village square.

"You know how to play the lute," he said in surprise.

She smiled. "Not as well as you, but a little. My grandfather raised me in Northumberland but he sent me to spend the summers with my mother. When I was little, I sometimes stole away from the castle to Millie Todd's cottage. She taught me to sing and play. But one day my father caught me and forbade me to ever visit her again."

After the scene between mother and daughter in the village, Robert could guess why. "Because Millie was a villein?"

She nodded. "A poor widow. Millie's son, Simon, is paying court to my serving girl, Eva. My father would not approve if he knew. Eva is a freeman's daughter, but I begged Sir Alan not to tell when he saw Simon dancing with her on the village green. May I trust you to be discreet as well, sir?"

Robert answered, "The dalliances of your father's villeins are of no matter to me, my lady. I assure you, your maidservant's secrets are safe."

His answer seemed to please her. This time when she looked at him, her dusky eyes had taken on a soft glow. "Then since you are so trustworthy, I will show you something."

She handed him the lute, then crossed to the side of her mare. She removed something from a leather bag that hung from the saddle. When she turned back round, the glow in her eyes had become an eager sparkle.

"Millie's eldest son, Ned, carved this for me when I was eight, but then my father found out about Millie so I never learned to play it. Please, would you teach me?"

Robert leaned the lute against the log once more and stood to take the wooden flute she held out to him. He surveyed it closely, then played a flutter of notes. "'Tis a fine instrument," he said. "This Ned of yours has skill." He gave it back to her. "But I think it is not my place to go against your father's wishes."

The sparkle died so quickly that it caused a pang in his heart, but she persisted, "Oh, please? He need never know and I would so like to learn to play it." A thought seemed to occur to her. "You are not leaving Dorset soon, are you?"

He remembered his promise to William. "After Christmas. I can stay no longer I'm afraid." He pushed the words as naturally as he could past the lump that rose in his throat as he spoke them. These hours had flown by too fast. He had only just found her and did not want to leave her yet. But he had promised . . .

Her face, a charming mirror to her emotions, unlike the discipline he had mastered with his own, fell with disappointment. Then it brightened again with a determined cheerfulness.

"That is seven days from now," she said. "You can teach me for seven days. Or six, or five, or . . ." She faltered at his silence. Her shoulders slumped a little. "Oh, I am sorry. Of course you must have more important things to do than to waste your time instructing me to play the flute."

Her lips drooped so sadly at what she clearly interpreted as a rejection that Robert held out his hand for the flute before he could stop himself. Seven days. Where could be the harm? "On the contrary, my lady, I can think of no more pleasant way to waste my time than in such a task. Let me have it again."

The sparkle returned to her eyes and together they sat back down on the log. He played her a simple tune, then grinned when she rewarded him with a laugh as happy and warm as a shining summer's day. And so her first lesson began.

The sun had begun to slip low behind the trees when Robert finally called a halt. Marguerite protested, but he said firmly, "Your parents will be worried about you."

"Oh, no," she replied. "My mother will think I am still with the hunt, and my father will think I've gone home."

Robert laughed at this devious response, but said, "Nevertheless you must go. If through some mischance your father *should* discover what you have been about, you will never learn to play that flute. Remember Millie Todd."

Marguerite sighed. "You are right. But I will meet you here again tomorrow. My father likes to hunt every day, and he insists that I join them because of Lord Saxton. My Lord Saxton could not care less about my presence, he rides with that horrible Lady Jane." Her eyes grew brooding, but then she smiled. "I know I can steal away again, though. And I will try to be here earlier. You will wait for me?"

Robert hesitated at her mention of the earl. He ought not to encourage her to think she could marry a man like Saxton and still indulge whatever romantic notion had brought her to meet Robert in the glade. The earl did not have the look of a man to disregard the slights of an errant wife, however lustfully he gazed at other women.

But she is not his wife yet, and I will be gone long before she is. And however much I want to kiss her again, I swear I shall behave with such propriety that we shall part as no more than friends.

She placed her hand on his arm, pressing her entreaty with anxious fingers at his silence. Her touch, even through his sleeve, made something leap in his chest. He knew he should take the reaction as a warning, but he met her earnest eyes and answered simply, "I will be here tomorrow."

He caught the relief in her sigh. "And tonight? I know that my father bade Sir Alan invite you to sing at the castle again."

"I will be there too, my lady."

He saw the little satisfied lift at the corners of her mouth. Did she think he would assail her chamber wall again? Robert vowed to be on guard against her smiles, no matter how beguiling, as he led her to her mare and lifted her into the saddle.

7

Marguerite urged her mare up the steeply inclining road that wound around the earthen motte where the great stone keep of Ashbury Castle stood. Matters had not ended quite as she had intended when she'd slipped away from her father's hunt. In between the blissful reliving of the minstrel's kisses that had warmed her through the night, a plan had gradually evolved in her mind. Surely a minstrel, with no bond of loyalty to her father, free to come and go as he pleased without suspicion, and one moreover who might believe that he owed her a debt . . . oh, surely he would carry word to Northumberland for her? All she had to do was find a way to stall until he returned with Odo and the protection of her grandfather's will.

Her cheeks heated as she recalled the longing that had sprang in her when the minstrel had lifted her down from her mare in the glade. She could not think of anything she had experienced in her life that had been more exhilarating, more utterly delicious than his embrace in her chamber. Surely he could not kiss her like that, and then refuse to help her?

Only she had never asked him. She had grown distracted, first by the tumultuous throbbing of her heart when he sat so near her on the log, then when he had told her the story of his lute. Had he realized how his mask slipped when he spoke of his father and the lute's creation? That frustratingly unreadable expression he had mastered since their first encounter, the one he had met her with in the village, that had made his sudden, flashing grin in her father's hall all the more flustering, the one that had maddened her in her chamber until it had dissolved just before he kissed her . . . it had melted away again in the glade, vanishing in the happy memories that danced like lightning across his darkly handsome face.

She longed to know more of him, more of the man he was, beyond the power of his kisses. She wanted to see that happy light in his eyes again, the beautiful, vibrant way it transformed him. If she sent him to Northumberland, Odo might fly to her rescue, but what if the minstrel—dared she call him Robert?—did not return with him?

Ashbury Castle loomed up before her, as if to impart a warning. To risk an unwanted future with Saxton for what might be no more than a caprice of her inexperienced heart was foolishness. She knew it. Now. But there, in the glade, all she had known was the inexplicable aura of hope and safety that had enveloped her while they had sat together, talking, sharing, and finally in a second unguarded moment that had lit Robert's face and eyes afresh, laughing together over her first inexpert attempts to play the flute. Saxton and her father had felt so far away. There had been only a sweet contentment that she had wished might last forever. So instead of begging Robert to go to Northumberland and Odo, she had begged him to stay another day with her.

Marguerite trotted her mare across the drawbridge. She should dread what awaited her return to the castle—her father, the earl—but instead as she rode beneath the spiked iron teeth of the raised portcullis, her heart still sang with the final melody that Robert had piped for her before they parted. She spoke merrily to the guards who manned the gatehouse and when she emerged into the bailey, welcomed with a smile the sunny-haired young man who strode across the yard to meet her.

"Richard! What, have you returned from the hunt?"

"Your father sent me to find you." Her cousin lifted her down, his brow creased with concern, and called to a groom to stable her mare before continuing in the rattling way she remembered from their childhood. "Your father said you had likely ridden home, so I came here first, but your mother hadn't seen you. She said you had probably gone to the village, even though she says you're forbidden to do so, so I rode into Lyndeard and searched high and low for you, but no one there had seen you. So I came back here and told your mother, and this time she was alarmed because it had been so long since you left the hunt. She was about to send some guards with me to comb the woods, but then I looked out the window—we were in her solar—

and saw you riding into the bailey— Where were you, Marguerite? You have been gone for hours."

Marguerite told the only lie she could think of. "Riding in the woods, trying to my cool temper. I was angry at Lord Saxton and Lady Jane."

Even though the lingering strands of music and mirth, rather than anger, still buoyed her, she knew she had chosen the right pretense when Richard grunted.

"Well, I can't blame you for that," he muttered. "You should have heard the foul names your father called you when he turned round in his saddle and found you gone. Well, no, it's better you didn't hear them, although the rest of us did, including the earl. Not that the earl appeared to care. I don't know which infuriated me more, the way Saxton kept whispering in his redhead wench's ear, the brazen looks she kept throwing back at him, or the indifferent shrug he gave when, for all any of us knew, you had fallen into some sort of danger."

Richard's worry touched Marguerite. He could not know how often she abandoned her father's hunts. Her father had likely guessed her perfectly safe and had only been angry to be embarrassed in front of the Earl of Saxton.

She tucked her hand into the crook of Richard's elbow, but answered his speech with a playful rebuke. "You ought not to call Lady Jane a wench. Lord Saxton does not take kindly to insults of his mistress."

The memory of Saxton's displeasure yesterday bounced off the glow that still enfolded her from the glade.

"Well do I know it," Richard said with a frown. "I have been with Sir Edward in King John's court and no one dares speak a word against her there for fear of Saxton."

She tugged Richard towards the wooden stairs that led to the keep's entrance on the second story. "I did not know you came from court. It has been years since we have spoken! You have grown ever so tall."

His frown relaxed. "And you are nearly as small as ever."

"It is so unfair. I had hoped to grow at least an inch or two taller than Mama, but we are exactly the same height. Is Sir Edward good to you? Are you happy serving as his squire?"

"He is a generous master, and Lady Sarah, his wife, is the kindest creature on earth. If the king succeeds in rallying enough of his barons to go to war with France again, Sir Edward says that I may go, too, and perhaps earn my spurs."

Marguerite felt a stir of dismay. "War? Father has said nothing of another war."

All her life the kings of England and France had been in conflict. When she was eight, her grandfather had sailed across the British Sea, that channel of water that separated the two kingdoms, accompanying King John on a failed campaign to prevent the king's duchy of Normandy from falling into the hands of the French. Two years later, shortly after Marguerite's aborted betrothal to Lord Stephen, her grandfather had again followed the king on an equally fruitless attempt to win the duchy back. Though her grandfather had returned from both expeditions unscathed, some of his men-at-arms whom Marguerite had known all her life, had not. Seeking to comfort her for those who had died, her grandfather had explained to her the courage and duty required of men when summoned by their king. Marguerite had pretended to understand, for she had seen that it pleased her grandfather that she should. But even as a child, she sensed that more than duty and courage drove him to battle. Too martial a glint lit his eyes when he recounted the swing of his sword and the charge of his lance.

That gleam now shone in Richard's eye. "Likely your father hoped nothing would come of it," he said. "The king has sworn to reclaim Normandy and humiliate King Philip when he does it, but this time the barons of England are dragging their feet. Most of the barons have come to hate the king, and one can hardly blame them after what he did to William de Briouze and his family. Nay." Richard shook his head at Marguerite's questioning glance. "'Tis an ugly tale and I'll not soil your ears with it. It was a vicious and dishonorable thing the king did, but he is still our king. It is a shame to our Norman forebears to leave their ancestral lands in the hands of the scheming French."

Marguerite guessed that Richard was more eager to try his hand in battle and win his knighthood than he was to reclaim lands that had long ago been diluted by inheritance from their family. She clung a little tighter to his arm, hating for him to risk himself against King Philip's army, yet at the same time hopefully imagining the Earl of Saxton sailing away with King John, delaying his marriage to Marguerite and giving her time to—

To what? What if *he* went, too? Her heart gave a tiny wrench at the thought. But why should Robert go? Minstrels did not fight wars. *Unless he is more than a minstrel.*

She slowed her pace, not enough for Richard to notice as he followed suit, but enough to delay their arrival at the stairs until she asked the questions she had carried home with her from the glade.

"Richard, do you remember when Grandfather wished me to marry Lord Stephen of Romsfeld Castle? How you almost came to my betrothal then, too?"

"Aye, I remember. Lady Sarah, Sir Edward's wife, wished to see her sister, who was a neighbor of Lord Stephen's, and offered to spare one day of her visit to accompany me to witness your vows. Apparently I had rattled on about my 'pestering little cousin' to her whenever she asked me about my family. I was thirteen, Marguerite, and I missed you, and Lady Sarah saw it. I think she arranged the trip especially to coincide with your betrothal, just to be kind to me."

"Pestering?" Marguerite said, assuming an indignant air.

"I could hardly shake you from my heels when you visited your parents. Every time I turned around, there you were, begging me to let you fetch the arrows for my archery practice—"

"Because you were always late and I did not wish Sir Roland to scold you."

Richard went on as though she had not spoken. "And my wooden sword from—"

"From wherever you left it. You never could remember."

"—and run along beside me on my errands for your father."

"I was bored," Marguerite said honestly. "All Mama wished me to do was sit at my embroidery all day. And you loved every minute of my fetching and carrying for you. It puffed you up so much, some days I thought you might burst."

Richard threw back his head and laughed, and Marguerite joined him. How glad she was to be with him again. But their bantering exchange had not distracted her from the information she hoped more than ever now to glean.

"Lady Sarah's sister was a neighbor of Lord Stephen?" Marguerite said when their laughter had steadied. "I did not remember that. Which neighbor?"

She tried to sound idly curious, even as her heartbeat quickened. She hoped Richard would not wonder why she asked so many years after a failed betrothal.

"Lord Christopher Beckford. He and Lady Hersent, Lady Sarah's sister, had been married less than a year when your grandfather brought you to Wiltshire."

Less than a year. Had there been a long betrothal? Might Lady Sarah's sister have spent time before her marriage in her future husband's home, as was common? If so, had she known the men of her husband's household, and might she have talked about them with her sister?

She and Richard had reached the stairs. If they went inside to her mother, Marguerite might lose her only chance for answers. She sat down on the steps and rolled her eyes in what she hoped was a wry expression towards the entrance door above her. Richard responded with an answering grin, confirming that he was in no more hurry than she to listen to her mother's rebukes for leaving the hunt. If Lady Leah had seen Marguerite's return from the solar window, she knew her daughter was safe.

Marguerite sought and failed to think of some casual way to frame the thoughts in her mind. She resorted to the direct, wrapped in a fabrication. "Did Lady Sarah ever mention a man who served her brother-in-law with the surname Marcel? I remember Lord Stephen speaking of him to my grandfather."

Richard pulled at one of the blond locks behind his left ear. Marguerite remembered the gesture from their childhood, whenever her cousin grew thoughtful.

"Marcel?" He repeated the name slowly. "I don't think so. Why?"

"There was some scandal about him. I had forgotten all about it until we fell to talking of Lord Stephen and my visit to Romsfeld Castle."

"What sort of scandal?"

"I do not remember the details, only that he did something that angered Lord Garoux Beckford, something so dreadful that it made his son run away from the castle. The father may have been one of Lord Garoux's vassals . . ." She hesitated. Robert had said their fields lay next to Lord Stephen's, but Richard said the "neighbor" had been Beckford. She corrected herself to reflect Robert's obvious meaning. "Or more likely, he was one of Lord Garoux's knights or men-at-arms. He fought in France as one of Lord Garoux's soldiers. I—I do not recall much more, only that Lord Stephen was so shocked over whatever—I think he called the man Marcel—had done that he told Grandfather about it one day at dinner." She chided herself for stumbling in her attempt to make up an excuse for the non-existent conversation she had "overheard." She pressed on, hoping to cover the misstep up. "I thought perhaps Lady Hersent had written to Lady Sarah about it. You know how Mama loves to gossip with your mother, and they are only sisters-by-marriage."

"If it happened when Lord Garoux was alive, Lady Hersent would not have known anything about it," Richard said. "Lord Garoux had been dead for four years when she married his son, Christopher."

"But that—" *isn't possible*. Marguerite bit the sentence off. Had Robert not said he had run away because of his father's disgrace? She tried to remember his exact words in the glade. No, he had not said the one event had followed directly upon the other. That had been her own conclusion. But she had as good as told Richard they had happened as one. To try to probe further now could only raise awkward questions from Richard. Already he was staring down at her with a puzzled expression. Oh! She longed to stamp her foot with frustration, but dared do no more than wiggle her toes hard in her slippers. Lady Hersent had been married to Lord Christopher at the time Marguerite and Robert had met, so Lady Hersent must have known Robert and what had driven him away—and Marguerite could not ask!

She tried to dismiss it all with a laugh before Richard could inquire why she was so curious about people she had never met. "I told you I did not recall many details. Some little thing must have dredged up the scandal in Lord Stephen's mind and I heard him telling Grandfather and misunderstood that it had all happened years before. I do not even know for sure that Marcel was the name."

That was true. 'Twas an uncommon surname. Robert might have taken it himself, perhaps to conceal his association with a father who had fallen into disgrace with his lord. It would have been quite lawful for Lord Garoux to visit the sins of a parent on the heads of the children.

"Forget it," she said. "I do not even know why the old story popped into my head." She held out her hands to him. "Come, help me up and we'd best go inside. Father and the earl will be returning soon and I must change my gown for another wretched banquet. I think Father has invited half the countryside to tonight's feast."

"It is no small thing in the eyes of the world to become the Countess of Saxton." Richard pulled her to her feet, but instead of releasing her hands, he held them tight. "I am sorry for it, though. I should have wished any man on earth your husband before him."

Richard's usually cheerful face turned unnaturally grim on the words. Marguerite felt her chest constrict. Her lingering radiance from the glade began to ebb as she felt the hour of another feast with the earl draw closer.

"Did you know him at court?" she asked.

Richard moved one of his booted feet to rest on the step beside her. "I have only been there a few weeks with Sir Edward—the king is gathering his barons and knights for his new campaign against France—but I've heard of the earl, of his grasping arrogance and sordid reputation, for years. Once at Westminster, I learned quickly enough to stay out of his way. His tongue is cutting as a whip, except, of course, with the king. There he is all flattery and honey, and the king soaks it up like fresh baked bread. Saxton might have his pick of all the brides in England. Why his eye chose to alight on you—"

She drew her hands away and started up the steps, grateful to turn her face from his troubled gaze. "It is because of Grandfather's lands. He was one of the wealthiest barons in England and I am his heir."

"Aye." Richard's footsteps echoed dully on the wooden steps behind her. "They talk of you at court. They all of them covet your lands, those men who are looking for wives, and yet to govern them in your name under the terms of your grandfather's will—"

Marguerite felt her chin lift in defense of her grandfather, even though she knew her cousin could not see it. She said nothing, merely switched the hem of her gown out of the path of her climbing slippers as Richard rattled on.

"You might have had a fair husband rather than a brute like Saxton had your grandfather given more forethought to how his will would affect your ability to marry. At court they call Heywood's actions radical and dangerous, and murmur against the king for sanctioning it just to finance his wars. Even Sir Edward says—"

She whirled around so sharply that Richard had to retreat a quick step back to avoid from colliding with her. "I don't give a fig for what Sir Edward says! You sound just like Father. 'Radical. Dangerous.' How, pray tell? How is Grandfather's will a threat to anyone?"

Richard's ruddy complexion ruddied even deeper. "Don't rip up at me. If I sound like your father, then you must know exactly why. To rule your grandfather's estates might lead to dissatisfaction on your husband's lands.

Dissatisfaction might turn to resentment, and then to defiance. And what if active protests follow? What if the protests spread? They won't risk it, Marguerite, not a one of them."

"That is absurd. If anything, the barons of this realm should embrace Grandfather's example. His lands have done nothing but prosper!"

"Which, in their eyes, only makes it worse. Embrace his example indeed." Richard snorted. "Your father is right about one thing. Heywood filled your head with a great deal of nonsense. And you have your grandfather to thank for finding yourself bound to a man shameless enough to bring his mistress to his own betrothal, for no other man is so conceited in his power and cunning as to think he can rule Heywood's manors and stamp out the danger from spreading to his own."

Marguerite gave Richard a long, hard glare before she turned and resumed her climb up the steps. But a dismaying thought slipped into her mind as she went. If Robert learned of her inheritance, would he shrink from her, too?

She heard Richard's quickened footsteps, then felt his hand on her shoulder. She resisted for an instant before she allowed him to turn her around.

Though he stood below her, his tall frame brought them nearly eye to eye. "Marguerite, I'm sorry. I know how you feel about your grandfather, but it just makes me so blazingly angry that he's brought you to this. You aren't witless and you aren't blind. I saw the look on your face at the table last night when Saxton kept leering at Lady Jane. Sir Roland told me what happened at the betrothal ceremony, too."

Marguerite flushed. Her father's marshal, like his steward, had always treated her with fondness. Sir Roland had no doubt confided in Richard out of concern for her, but it only deepened the cut of her humiliation. Were all the tongues of her father's house wagging about that incident?

"It sickens me that you are to be Saxton's wife," Richard said, a savage note now in his voice. "If I knew some way to stop it—"

Her breath caught. She pulled his hand from her shoulder and held it as hard as he had held hers a moment before. "You could. Oh, Richard, you could! If you went for me to Northumberland, if you told Odo—"

A bitter glumness fell over his face. "Do you think I haven't thought of it? But your father is watching me like a hawk. I'll wager I would have found the roads out of Dorset blocked by his men if I'd tried to ride north from the hunt, instead of coming back here."

Her father had had years to observe Marguerite's affection for Richard and his for her. He would surely have anticipated that she might try to enlist her cousin's aid. *Robert. I will have to send Robert . . . if he will go.* She would ask him tomorrow, she would beg him . . . if she could find the words and the will to send him away from her.

"Milady."

Marguerite looked over her shoulder and saw her serving girl Eva standing in the open doorway at the top of the steps.

The young girl bobbed a curtsy. "Forgive me for interruptin', milady, but your lady mother is askin' for ye."

"I am coming." Marguerite set her foot to the next step, then suddenly whirled back and flung her arms around Richard's neck. "I am so glad you are here," she whispered.

He could do nothing to save her from Saxton, yet for a handful of heart-beats she drank in the comfort of his embrace. When she pulled free she felt the wetness of tears on her cheeks and ran the rest of the way up the steps before he could see them.

The aroma of course after course of mouth-watering food drifted up to the gallery where two musicians with viols, a third with a flute and the fourth with a trumpet accompanied the diners of Ashbury Castle. The little ensemble pointedly ignored Robert as he stood by with his lute, waiting to be called like the night before to the main floor of the hall for his own performance. He assumed the musicians were in the baron's permanent employment. With no ties to a noble household himself, Robert knew they viewed him as a vagrant, a light and useless fellow. He had heard it all a hundred times muttered behind his back by the privileged instrumentalists of lordly households. He made a face from his unobtrusive corner, mocking their puffed up airs as they played their slow, stately cadences, then despite the glares they slid at him, moved to the railing that ran alongside the gallery and leaned over to watch the diners. He dared not speak to the Lady Marguerite, of course, in the presence of her father and the earl, but he could nonetheless fill his gaze with her loveliness for a few hours again.

Regrettably, all he could see from this vantage point was the top of her head. A gilt circlet wound around her dusky curls which had otherwise been left unbound. The Earl of Saxton, seated beside her, wore a lavishly embroidered round cap. Robert heard the musicians' sharp whispers between their numbers, seeking to chide him for moving out of his corner. He ignored them, contentedly rapt in each graceful turn of the Lady Marguerite's wrist as she raised various morsels of the dishes set before her to lips he could not see but remembered the taste of with a pang of delight.

When the servants brought out the second course, the ensemble behind him ceased their music as tumblers appeared before the dais. Following their acrobatics, a jester in a parti-colored tunic and hose took their place and challenged the company to solve his impudent riddles. The jester was new. Robert guessed the baron was trying hard to improve upon last night's entertainments for the earl.

Robert's summons did not come until the third course. The Lady Marguerite was a vision tonight in green and gold! He caught the eager welcome in her eyes, but he dared not encourage it. The Earl of Saxton frowned heavily at her side, no doubt remembering Robert's bold smile at his betrothed the night before. Robert smothered his yearning and directed his songs to the earl and her father.

It gave Robert a chance to study the earl afresh, now that he knew the Lady Marguerite had willingly chosen him to become her husband. Her choice baffled Robert more than ever. Each look the earl tossed at his betrothed he shot through icy, narrowed eyes. His mouth softened only when he smiled at a flame-haired beauty seated at one of the lower side-boards, but even then, while his gaze held a stark hunger, no warmth gleamed in the hazel depths. Robert's hot nature recoiled from so much coldness.

He stole a glance at the Lady Marguerite from beneath his lashes, the first he had ventured in the course of the three songs he had sung. Whereas she had shifted forward in her chair when he first stepped onto the floor, she now sat well back, a slight droop about her shoulders. The light was gone from her eyes and a poignant unhappiness had blossomed in its place. Robert maintained the dulcet tenor of his voice, even as he determinedly steeled his heart against her sorrow. She had said the choice was hers. She had chosen wealth and ambition over a husband's affection and fidelity. Robert had neither lands nor gold nor status to tempt her with. It was not his place to try to ease a heart she had willingly given Saxton to break.

I will be friendly when we meet tomorrow, but nothing more. The vow ran round and round in his mind through the end of his performance. He knew he ought not to meet her at all but that, he found, was a vow he could not bring himself to make.

When Lord de Villon at last dismissed him, Robert went out to the bailey to receive his payment as he had the night before. Sir Alan was already doling out coins to the tumblers and jester, while a servant held a torch at his shoulder that snapped in the winter air. Robert had nearly reached their small circle when a woman's scream froze him in mid-step. The terror in the cry swiveled him on his heel and drove him back towards a storage shed. Robert shoved the half-open door so hard that it banged against the wall inside. He heard a thud followed by a man's groan and what sounded like a woman's now muffled sob, but he could see nothing in the blackness until a scrunching of feet joined him and the light of Sir Alan's torch threw its glow on the struggle inside.

A young man with a tangle of dark hair in his eyes had a hand clamped over the mouth of a woman who writhed against the arm he had clamped around her waist. Another man whose hair shone red in the torchlight slumped moaning at their feet. The man with the woman drove a foot into the ribs of the crumpled form on the ground and snarled at the intruders, "Get out. Take this churl with you, and get out."

Robert knelt beside the man on the ground. He was young, perhaps twenty, Robert judged. His hair was not red as it had first appeared in the torchlight, but a dusty blond. One eye was swollen nearly shut. The young man struggled to catch his breath. Robert laid a bracing hand against the coarse homespun cloth of his sleeve, but kept his gaze steady on the man with the tangled locks.

"And the woman," Robert said with a deadly calm. "Give us the woman, and we will gladly go."

The man tossed back his head with a scornful laugh. As the dark hair flipped back from his forehead, Robert realized he was more youth than man, seventeen, perhaps eighteen. Sir Alan muttered something and his servant's torch shifted to catch a glint of gilded threads embroidered in a braided border around the badge sewn to the shoulder of youth's tunic.

A roaring bear. Robert had seen the image blazoned on the breast of the Earl of Saxton's surcote tonight. The youth must be one of his squires.

Robert heard Sir Alan gasp. "Your pardon, Master Tybert, we did not realize it was you. Pick that fellow up, minstrel, and bring him along."

Robert lifted the wheezing young man into a sitting position, but repeated, "The girl?"

"The girl is none of your concern."

Robert felt a chill tick down his spine at Sir Alan's words. With the recast light, he saw now that she was of an age with the squire who held her, or younger. Terror shone in her eyes above the hand that still covered her mouth.

"My lady will not be pleased," Sir Alan muttered, as if to himself, "but—well, the matter must be between her and the earl." He said more loudly to Robert, who had made no move to obey his command, "Help the lad to his feet. There will be an extra shilling for you if you get him back to the village without further incident. He's ideas above himself to be courting a free born lass."

Robert's chill flamed away on a wave of heat that loosed an angry jibe from his lips. "You'd rather a free man debauched her."

Sir Alan stiffened at the barb. "Impertinent rogue!" but he broke off as the young man suddenly rolled out of Robert's hold and tried to make a lunge for the squire.

The squire met his attempted attack with another hard kick, this one cracking against the young man's jaw and hurling him onto his back. Robert moved swiftly to cradle the young man's head, relieved when he saw his eyes dazed but still conscious. The blow must have glanced off in the blur of his movement.

"I beg your pardon, Master Tybert," Sir Alan said. "Don't heed the minstrel's words. Get out of the way, Marcel. You, jester, get the churl up and—"

Robert did not hear any more, for a drubbing rage pounded between his ears. His hand flashed to his boot where he always concealed his dagger when summoned to a baronial hall where weapons were banned. His fist clenched around the tyger hilt, then immediately released it. Only the squire's youth stopped Robert from whipping it free. Instead, he sprang out of his coiled crouch, dodged another lash of the squire's foot, and silenced the squire's curse with a jab of an elbow to the ribcage that cut off the squire's air.

Robert pulled the girl free from the squire's slackened grasp and shoved her towards the door. "Run," he said.

The girl stumbled a few steps forward, but hesitated beside the young man on the ground.

"Run!" Robert shouted now. "I will see him safe back to the village."

The tumblers and jester who had followed Sir Alan milled uncertainly, as though expecting an order to stop her, but Sir Alan unexpectedly grabbed her arm and pushed her towards the threshold. "Haste to your mistress," he said.

She tossed an irresolute look at Robert, but something in his expression seemed to reassure her, and she disappeared into the night.

"You—" the squire gasped, struggling to straighten from his doubled-over posture "—will pay—for—that—minstrel—"

Seeing the squire's wobbly stance, Robert seized upon the memory of the kicks to the young villager to place a deliberate foot against the squire's stomach and shoved him the rest of the way off balance. The push carried enough force to send the squire stumbling back into a stack of supplies that toppled over with a crash and rained their contents over him—objects that must have smarted by the sounds of the thuds against his body.

"Touch the girl again," Robert said, "and your master the earl is not the only one who will hear how a common minstrel thrashed you."

Robert knew the pride of the knightly class. It would not matter if Robert were older and heavier than the squire or that he had merely knocked the wind from him, then knocked him down. The squire would be shamed, and the earl more so, that a man both considered beneath their notice, a mere musician, had defeated a man of warrior blood. Robert knew he had judged the squire's vanity aright when the youth lay spluttering among the supplies but did not call out to Sir Alan to stop Robert from heaving the young villager to his feet and leaving the shed together without hindrance from the steward.

The young man leaned his tall, loose-limbed body heavily against Robert as they crossed the bailey, seemingly too stunned to do more than open and close his mouth a dozen times, as though to convince himself that the squire had not broken his jaw. He seemed at last to come to himself just short of the gatehouse, whirling about so suddenly that he dizzied himself into a stagger.

"Easy," Robert said, catching him before he could fall.

"Eva." Robert heard the young man's panic. "That knave will—"

"Your lass is safe. By now she is in the castle, helping her mistress prepare for bed."

"The fiend let her go?"

Robert realized the young man must have been too dazed to have comprehended what happened after the blow to his jaw. Robert told him briefly.

"Eva's the Lady Marguerite's maid," the young man said when Robert expressed puzzlement over Sir Alan's abrupt change of heart for her safety. "Likely Sir Alan hoped to retain milady's favor once he saw a way to let Eva escape without openly crossin' the earl's squire. Did ye really knock the knave down?"

Robert felt the watchful eyes of the castle guards upon them. "Aye," he said softly. "Now hold your tongue for a bit."

The young man obediently fell silent until they were safely beyond the gatehouse and starting down the pathway towards the village. He seemed to steady as they went and finally pulled his arm free of Robert's support, muttering that he could walk by himself. Robert stayed near enough to catch him if he stumbled, but he'd seen no blood in the shed and had felt no lumps on the young man's skull while Robert had held his head. His companion's easy breathing suggested no ribs had been broken by the squire's kick, though he was undoubtedly sorely bruised.

"Are you Simon Todd?" Robert asked, and felt the young man's glance of surprise in the dark. "Rumor is a 'Simon Todd' is courting the Lady Marguerite's serving girl."

"Did Will Locke tell ye that?"

Robert could not confess that he had learned it from the Lady Marguerite herself, but he shied away from a lie. He parried the question with, "You know Will?"

"Oh, aye. He works the fields of Halham, while I'm with Ashbury. Ye're the minstrel who's been stayin' with him, ain't ye? Are ye from his old manor? Don't tell me ye're a runaway?"

From the excitement in Simon's voice, Robert sensed the young man hoped Robert would tell him exactly that. Robert kept his own voice light. "I'm a freeman, sir. Minstrelsy is my trade."

He felt Simon's broad shoulders shrug beside him. "Don't matter to me either way. I'd run away myself an' I had the courage. A rottin', miserable life this is. How do ye know Will, then?"

Again, Robert dodged a direct answer. "A minstrel meets many men in the course of his wanderings. You've guessed right enough that I met Will in Wiltshire. How did he end up in Dorset? Villeins don't just up and walk away to another manor." Aye, that question should throw Simon off the scent.

Simon repeated the story that Robert had learned from his brother when he had secretly revisited Beck Manor two years ago. Will had formerly been bound to Lord Christopher Beckford's manor in Wiltshire, Simon said, working the baron's fields with his six brothers. But six years past, plague had ravaged the village of Lyndeard and left a dearth of strong laborers for both Halham and Ashbury. Lord Christopher had transferred a number of villeins from his other manors to make up the loss, and Will had been among them.

"Imagine being forced from the only home ye've ever known." Bitterness hummed in Simon's voice. "They view us no differently than dogs, these lords. Will's father had too big a litter of sons, so the baron picks Will up by the scruff of his neck and drops him here in Lyndeard without so much as a 'by yer leave.' Oh, Will's a stoic one, no one's ever heard him complain, but there was misery enough to see in his eyes if one cared to look before he met and married Lucy Wilde."

So, things had been as bad for William as Robert had imagined they must be. William had no more heart for adventure when Robert had known him on Beck Manor than Robert's own brother had. Will's initial loneliness must have been nearly unbearable. 'Twas yet another grudge Robert had no intention of forgiving, no matter what contentment his friend had since found with Lucy.

He and Simon had reached the edge of the village now. Although Simon had walked the last stretch without a noticeable wobble, Robert asked, "Can I see you home?"

Simon stopped and shook his head. "Nay, my brother Ned's bound to have waited up for me. He don't like it that I want to marry Eva. Says she's 'above me,' like Sir Alan does, but her grandda' was a villein like us before he bought his freedom from Lord de Villon's grandfather, an' her da still works the fields like the rest o' us, just without so many fees and services. Still, Ned says I'm too bold and that I'll come to grief one day sneakin' up to the castle to see her."

"Like the grief you came to tonight?"

Simon responded defensively to the irony in Robert's voice. "The black-guard snuck up on us in the dark. We were just talkin', I swear! But I'd left the door open a bit for some light, an' one minute we were talkin' and holdin' hands and the next I was on the ground and my head was swimmin' an' Eva was screamin' an' that devil was laughin', an' if I'd had a knife on me I would have sliced out his guts."

"And the baron would have hanged you for it, if the earl didn't avenge his squire first by disemboweling you in return."

"Are you sayin' I should have let that devil rape her?"

Robert felt the sting of Simon's horror. He remembered his own nearly overwhelming temptation to draw his dagger on the squire. Had the boy been a few years older, he would have done so. But Robert also knew from experience the retaliatory power of knights and barons and was glad it had not had to fall on the young man at his side.

"Of course not," Robert said. "I only meant—" He paused. Who was he to offer practical counsel he knew he would never have followed himself? "I only meant one should be prepared to face the consequences of one's choices. That boy dealt you a nasty beating for defending her tonight, didn't he? But you were right to try."

Simon rubbed his bruised chin. "Tried an' failed." Robert heard the shame in his mumbled words. "If ye hadn't come along—"

Robert set his hand on the young man's shoulder and squeezed it. "Sometimes they win, Simon. I hate it as much as you, but sometimes no matter how hard we try to stop them, they still win." Robert had known the raw despair of defeat. Even the revenge he had sworn one day to accomplish would not wipe away his greatest failure. He released Simon, then dealt him a comforting buffet with the flat of his hand against Simon's brawny bicep. "But the squire did not win tonight. So go show Brother Ned your black eye and let him deal you a lecture and put you to bed and remember that your lass is safe as long as I am in Lyndeard."

Simon grinned. "I wish I could have seen the knave's face when ye thrashed him."

"'Twas hardly a thrashing. I merely caught him off guard and knocked him down to give Eva a chance to escape."

"Still, he'll not want that humiliatin' tale to reach the village. It'd make great sport that a minstrel confounded a great lord's squire."

"You must keep your tongue still about that, for I told him—

"Oh, aye, aye, I won't say a word so long as he keeps his filthy paws off Eva." Simon's voice sobered then. "She an' I both owe ye a debt, an' I don't even know yer name."

Robert remembered the promise he had given to William, the one he had broken in the Lady Marguerite's chamber when she, too, had asked his name. Then some staunchly loyal part of him had refused to deny the surname his father had bequeathed him. But the vague byname he sometimes assumed came easily now with Simon.

"They call me Robert of the Road, but my friends call me Rob."

Simon held out his hand. "Then I hope I may call ye Rob, too?" He grinned again as Robert met his clasp.

A few moments later they parted. Robert went on to William's cottage, hoping to find his friend long abed by now. Their quarrel of the morning felt as if it had occurred weeks ago, so much had occurred since Robert had stormed off to the glade that morning. But when he rounded the corner of one of the twisting village lanes, he saw a flicker of candlelight shining through the window of the Lockes' cottage. He sighed. By the time he let himself quietly into the small house, he had braced himself to see William sitting at the lopsided table, still dressed and judging from the alertness on his stolid face, still ominously awake.

"Good evening to you, Will." Robert closed the door behind him. "You're not waiting up for me, I hope?"

The single candle on the table perhaps made William's lowered brows appear more brooding in the shadows than they were. *Perhaps.*

"Matter o' fact, I am. Where've ye been, Rob?"

The question surprised Robert. "At Ashbury Castle, of course. I thought you knew I was engaged there again tonight."

"How should I? Ye said nothin' of it this mornin' and I've not seen ye since."

Robert realized William was right. He had left the cottage in a blaze of anger without mentioning that he had been invited to sing again. "Forgive me, I did not mean for you to worry. As you can see, I've come to no harm."

"So ye say."

Robert heard the terse clip in his friend's voice. 'Twas no trick of the shadows. Will had definitely been brooding.

"Where've ye been all day?"

Robert moved to the small fire glowing on a stone hearth in the center of the floor and stretched out his hands to their heat. "Here and there. Is Lucy in bed? You should not have sat up for me, Will, there was no need."

"I'd hoped we could talk a bit." William failed miserably to inject a friendly interest in his tones, and apparently realizing it, fell back on the directness nature had bestowed on him. "Where'd ye go when ye left us this mornin'?"

The tenacious probing did not surprise Robert, but he felt his mouth tighten as he turned to meet William's dogged gaze. "I went to meet Lady Marguerite of Winbourne. I told you I would."

"Ye spent the day with her?"

"The afternoon. She came late."

"What'd ye do?"

Robert's eyes narrowed. "What do you think?"

He saw the flush that washed up beneath the stubble on William's cheeks, but his friend stood his ground. "I'm askin' ye, Rob."

"And what do you expect me to say? That I tried to seduce her? That I failed? That she put me firmly in my place?"

"Robert—!"

Goading Will had ever been too easy. "Oh come, do you really think that's what happened? I had not believed you thought so little of me." Robert strolled over to the table and sat down across from his friend.

William looked flustered. "Now, Rob, o' course I don't think— Not but what I haven't seen ye for seven years, an' that hot blood of yers—But I know ye'd never—" Then he grew angry as Robert laughed at his confusion. "I'll have the truth from ye, Rob."

"What business is it of yours, Will?"

"I'll tell ye what business it is o' mine. Ye don't belong on either manor, an' while ye're my guest I'm responsible for ye. An' if ye can't conduct yerself properly, then—"

Robert's laughter fled. Hurt flared up in spite of William biting off the sentence. "Then perhaps I'd best leave." He knew he had finished his friend's thought when William flinched at his sudden coldness. "So we are at that again." Robert stood up and took a step towards the bedchamber.

William rose, too, and caught his arm. "Now, Rob, that's not what I meant."

"What *did* you mean?"

"Only that ye behave a bit more—more cautiously." William flung up his hands. "But I suppose that's too much to hope for from ye!"

The hurt faded on a wave of wry sympathy for William's exasperation. Given Robert's stormy past, he could hardly blame his friend. "If it alleviates your worry any, all the Lady Marguerite and I did was talk. It was perfectly harmless. I did not try to court her, if that's what you fear."

"But ye wanted to." William stared him straight in the eye.

"Perhaps. But I did not."

"But ye wanted to," William repeated roughly, "and once ye take a notion into yer head, it's hell to pay with ye, Rob. Can ye swear to me ye won't go beyond the bounds with her?"

That depended on what William considered *the bounds*. "I'd do nothing against her honor."

William waved a hand, impatiently this time. "That's not what I asked ye."

Robert felt the fire of temptation in his blood again, but he fought it back as he had ever since he had learned the truth about her betrothal. He waited a pair of heartbeats until he could inject a light note into his voice. "It is my intention to do no more than teach her to play the flute and then move on after Christmas, as I told you I would."

William groaned and dropped back in his chair. "Seven days. More than enough time for ye to fall headlong into trouble. Ye never *intend* to, but ye always do."

"'Tis a little late to chide my rashness now," Robert said. "You knew what I was when you accepted me into your house.

"Oh, aye, but I'd hoped ye'd changed."

"Apparently I have not. I am older, but no more wise."

"Aye," William said with such blunt agreement that it made Robert smile. He waited until Robert sat down again, too, then gave him a long, keen look across the candle's tiny, flickering glow. "Are ye happy, Rob?" he asked suddenly. "Are ye more content now than ye were in Wiltshire?"

Robert shrugged. "I am no less content. And I would never go back."

"Would ye not?"

"I *could* not. You know that, Will."

William sighed. "Aye."

Again Robert felt his friend's study in the dimness of the candle.

"Don't ye ever miss them, though?" William asked after a silent moment. "Gil and Lottie?"

"Of course I miss them," Robert said, surprised. "As I've missed you. Why do you think I came to Lyndeard?"

"And I'm grateful to see ye again. I never thought I would, any of ye. When Lord Christopher forced me from the manor . . ." William's gaze shifted away, as though something shamed him. ". . . I thought I'd die, I was so lonely."

Though he'd guessed it, the gruff confession startled Robert. Will had never been one to speak his emotions easily. Life was to be stoically endured, not lived and breathed with either joy or despair. That he spoke openly now of his suffering to Robert meant something serious gnawed beneath the embarrassment of laying open his heart.

"If things were different," William said, "if Lord Christopher weren't there—wouldn't ye go back?"

"Kit Beckford *is* still there. But even if he weren't, no," Robert repeated, "I would never go back." Not the way William meant. A short, furtive visit to his brother and sister was one thing, but to tie himself to the land again—? William had never understood him—none of them had—but Robert felt the gulf between them widen further than ever at his answer.

William shook his head. "If it'd been me, if I'd had a choice, nothin' could have driven me from the manor, not even to escape the fees and services ye always hated so. Nobody likes 'em, but they aren't unbearable. To give up family and friends to live yer life free but alone—" He drew a deep breath, slow and ragged. "If I hadn't met Lucy here, I don't know how I'd have borne it." He lifted his gaze back to Robert. "How do ye do it, Rob? I know ye were always restless, but Agnes was pretty and gentle and would've made ye a good wife. Why could ye not be content to marry her and plow her father's fields?"

"It was not my fault Agnes married another." Robert could have bitten his tongue off when he realized he'd responded to the old resentment that surged up in him rather than William's question. It deflected William from his baffled pain, but prompted a too familiar challenge.

"Oh, wasn't it? Ye've no one but yerself to blame, and ye know it. Ye had to go an' open yer mouth, not once, not twice, but so many times no one could keep count anymore. Why could ye not just have kept yer tongue still?"

Memory bubbled caustic in Robert's throat. The bitterness of those years pulsed afresh, like a raw wound. "No one listened to me," he said. "No one dared. I never posed any real threat to anyone and they knew it. It was not my words, but Lord Garoux's conscience—"

"Rob—yer father—"

"Was not a traitor! You shall not say it again!"

Robert did not realize how hard he'd pushed himself to his feet until his chair hit the beaten earth floor.

"Hush! Ye'll wake Lucy."

Robert leaned forward, his hands flat against the tabletop. He tried to force down his flash of anger, but it still seethed beneath his quieted voice. "My father was innocent, Will. I will prove it if it takes me a lifetime. Kit and his father have done their best to destroy my family, and if you think I will not make Kit pay—"

William rose to right Robert's chair and conveniently, Robert thought, avoid his eyes. "Lord Christopher and his da had no hand in yer mother's death."

Robert rejected the defense. "She died of sorrow, grieving for her husband. And what of Lottie? She was barely fifteen when—"

William caught Robert's shoulders and shook him. "Let it go, Rob. Ye can't change nothin' of the past an' ye'll not win a battle with a baron. Ye've made a new life for yerself, the life ye always wanted. Don't ruin it in a useless quest for revenge."

Robert might have argued further, but a great weariness suddenly settled over him. It had been over four-and-twenty hours since he had slept, so exhilarated he had been the night before from the Lady Marguerite's kisses and so restive in his anticipation of meeting her this morning in the glade. Tomorrow he would see her again. Somehow thoughts of her eased his anger. Tonight he knew he would sleep, but he hoped he would dream of her.

William let him go and made a grumbling sound in his throat. "Ye haven't heard a word I said, have ye?"

Robert pulled his attention back from a sudden eagerness for his pallet. "I always hear you, Will. It is not your fault if I never choose to heed you. But it has been a very long day. Let us resume this quarrel in the morning, shall we?"

He moved on to the bedchamber before William could object. Lucy must have gone to bed a long while ago, for the few embers still glowing in the brazier had nearly smoldered out. Judging by the size of the woodpile Robert had seen beside the kitchen hearth that morning, Will's quota of wood from the forest must have run out early. Had they not quarreled before he had thought of it, Robert would have lent his friend a wood-penny for permission to gather more. He would rectify that in the morning, before he left again for the glade.

Robert stripped down to his smock and fell onto his pallet. Even his memories of the hours he had spent with Marguerite could not quite hold at bay the near frigid cold of the tiny, draughty room. He tugged the thin, patched blanket around him and clenched his teeth together to prevent them from chattering. Will would soon be warming Lucy in his arms. Robert closed his eyes and sought to drive back the cold with a vision of holding Marguerite snug and safe against him. Come daylight, he would know the vision for the absurdity that it was, but what could it hurt tonight to dream?

9

arguerite slipped away from the early morning hunt and rode for the glade, sick with fear that she should find it empty. She had not expected Robert to dare another smile at her in her father's hall, but he had not even glanced at her. Had she misunderstood what passed between them yesterday in the clearing and the night before in her chamber? Even after he had avoided her so painfully at last night's feast, she had lain awake in the dark for hours, hoping desperately that she would hear his whistle beneath her window or him tapping at her shutters . . . But she had fallen asleep to silence, with her pillow wet and the looming threat of the Earl of Saxton hovering all around her.

Without Robert there was no hope of escape, no hope for . . . for . . . She pulled up her mare and stripped off her glove so that she could lay her bare fingers against her lips. *No hope to ever taste his kiss again.*

The latter thought almost frightened her more than the first. Two days ago he had been a romantic dream. Yesterday he had become a fascinating reality. But last night . . . last night, after the feast had ended, while she had waited for Eva to come and help her dress for bed, he had all unbeknownst to himself become her hero. She did not think she could bear it if she had inadvertently done something to drive him away.

She nudged her mare forward again, pushing through her fear, until she heard the soft strum of his lute. Tears of relief stung her eyes, but she tamped down her leap of hope. He had promised to meet her and was too honorable to go back on his word, but it did not mean that he would be glad to see her.

She glimpsed him first through the barren branches, sitting on the log with his dark head bent and his brown, nimble fingers fluttering over his instrument's strings. He looked up swiftly when he heard the clip of her mare's hooves, then set his lute aside and sprang up.

"I did not expect you so early this morning, my lady."

"Yet you are here." Did he hear the small quaver in her voice?

He smiled faintly. "Aye, just in case."

As he had yesterday, he crossed to her side and reached up to help her dismount. She set her hands to his shoulders, square and strong beneath her touch, and let him lift her to the ground. Like before, his grasp lingered for a moment on her hips. He was not as tall as the Earl of Saxton, but she still had to tilt back her head to look up at him. She could not read his expression, but she thought she caught a flicker in his eyes of something hot and ardent.

Then he frowned. "What's wrong?"

"Wrong?"

"Something has distressed you. Will you tell me?"

Was her face so easy to read? Her cheeks grew warm. She could hardly ask him why he had ignored her at the feast. He would think her childish, and what if she did not like his answer? She longed to stay just where she was, still caught in his light clasp, but feared his scorn if he guessed the truth. So she stepped away to place a more proper distance between them and seized upon the excuse of her very real gratitude.

"My distress is not for me," she only half-lied. "I was thinking of my serving girl, Eva, and her narrow escape from the earl's squire last night."

Robert's dark brows rose in surprise. "She told you of that?"

"She did not want to, but I saw her red eyes when she came to help me dress for bed. At first she refused to say why she had been weeping, but I insisted until she broke down in tears and sobbed out what had happened in the shed. She told me how you forced Nicholas Tybert to let her go. She said Master Tybert had beaten Simon and she was terrified of what more he might do, but she said you promised her—"

"Assure her that Simon is fine," Robert said. "I do not think the squire will try to harm her again, but you should keep her out of his way all the same."

"I shall do so. It was kind and brave of you to defend her." Marguerite did not know a single man of her birth who would have stooped to help a serving girl. Why had he?

She would have searched his impassive face for an answer, but he turned to loop her mare's reins around a low hanging branch. She had a thousand questions for him. She did not doubt for one moment that his birth equaled that of the noble squire he had chastised last night. The way Robert spoke in the same refined accents as she, the easy assurance in his stride, the proud way he tilted his chin when he sang before her father's hall—surely these all betrayed his noble blood? What shame had befallen his father that it had forced his son to masquerade as a minstrel?

Would the answer matter? She did not love him for his birth, but for what had taken place in the shed last night, his defense of a helpless serving girl and her villein suitor, when even Sir Alan, Eva had told her, would have turned his back.

Marguerite's breath caught suddenly, sharply enough to turn Robert about as her hand flew to her mouth.

"My lady?" He stepped towards her, his normally enigmatic expression quickening with alarm.

She thrust her hand back down to her side. "It—it is nothing. Just a silly thought that I startled myself with." She laughed, trying to sound merry, when in truth her lagging recognition of her bold thought stunned her. *She did not love him for his birth . . .* She barely knew him. How could she think of love?

To her relief, he laughed too, as if something in her had charmed him.

"The mind can be most capricious," he said, "but it requires discipline if you wish to master the flute. Did you bring the instrument along? Let us sit, then, and see if you can tame your wayward thoughts with the tune I taught you yesterday."

She retrieved the flute from her saddlebag and sat beside him on the log. For the most part she succeeded in reproducing yesterday's melody, but once or twice she fumbled in the notes. Each time he reached over and repositioned her fingers over the holes. She battled a temptation to deliberately misplay the tune just to enjoy his touch, but a little stir of pride did not wish him to think her too simple to learn.

His hands fascinated her. Deeply tanned, the square palms showed strength but no particular grace aside from the skill she had witnessed on his lute's strings. Those strings had left calluses on the pads of his fingers, but she did not find them unpleasant as they brushed against hers. Sturdy hands. Practical hands that scorned the clusters of jewels worn by her father and the earl. His life could not have been easy since he had been driven from his manor, for his hands had grown a little rough compared with the polished smoothness of the earl's. But honest hands, she sensed, for they guided hers with a firm but careful courtesy when her quickened heartbeat knew that he could have stolen so much more than kisses if he'd wished to, here alone in the clearing.

The morning slid by while he taught her one lively tune after another. Gradually his fingers lingered longer and longer over hers. She did nothing to discourage this small intimacy, but rather savored it. Each time she looked into his face, she found him smiling. Like yesterday, the music appeared to relax him, diverting him from whatever caution had formerly restrained his manner towards her. Her doubts of the night dissolved. Had he not shifted unconsciously closer to her on the log until their shoulders brushed together and the heat of his nearness made her head swim? *Could I not bask for the rest of my life in his smiles? Oh, aye! If only . . . if only . . .*

"You grow weary, I think, my lady."

He drew the flute down to her lap. In spite of her determined attempts to will it otherwise, air had begun to leak out of the corners of her mouth until notes that she had finally learned to produce with aplomb gradually began to wobble. She glanced at him in embarrassment, but found only encouragement in his eyes.

"'Tis naught to be ashamed of," he said. "Your lips will build up endurance with practice. They are merely unskilled as yet—"

He broke off with a faint flush and looked a little too quickly away from the lips he thus critiqued. But not before a swift, warm glance at them had sent a shiver through her. *Unskilled, but not untried, and eager for more lessons than the music you would teach me.* Oh, such wild, delicious thoughts flowed through her. It did not matter that the impassive mask slid back over his face as he stood. She had glimpsed his desire and knew he longed to kiss her again as much as she longed to be kissed by him.

He took her fingers lightly and drew her to her feet. "That is enough for one day. Perhaps you can rejoin your father's hunt before you are missed."

He could not have formed a better suggestion to spoil so promising a morning. Her mouth pulled together in a pout. "So that he might scold and nag at me some more?"

"Is that what happened yesterday? Then truly you must go. I would not be the cause of discord between you and your father."

"Oh, he has no need of you as an excuse to be angry with me. I need only live and breathe for that. While as for my Lord Saxton—he has no use for me at all."

Robert released her hand, bringing her a little pang of loss. Had her bitterness displeased him?

"You have chosen the earl for your husband, my lady. Perhaps he is cold today, but surely in time he will learn to love you."

She stared at him, aghast. "I—chose the earl for my husband? How can you think I would ever choose to wed such a—such a—" *monster* was the word that sprang into her mind, but she feared lest Robert judge her over-dramatic and merely naïve about men.

He frowned again, but not with the concern he had greeted her with on her arrival. His stare held almost an accusation. "You said your grandfather's will allowed you to choose."

Again her bitterness spilled out. "My grandfather is dead. I am at my father's mercy now and he has none. I am a woman and so I must do his bidding."

She saw her mother's face, sad but stern the morning after Robert had kissed her. Marguerite thought she had barely registered a word of her mother's lecture, lost as she had been in her memories of the night, but she found it imprinted starkly now in her memory.

"It is a daughter's duty to wed as her father commands her," she parroted the Lady Leah. "Once she is wed, it is her duty to love her husband, to give him heirs, no matter that he cares not for her. If he finds pleasure in another woman's company, why, a wife must close her eyes to it, must pretend not to know that behind her back all the world is laughing and pitying her. And once he has his heirs? Then he is done with her. She is of no more worth than any other piece of property which has served its purpose, then lost its usefulness." Her mother had not said that last to her, but Marguerite knew it would be true. Her grandfather had held an exceptional view of the world, but it was her father's view that would prevail. Tears of frustration burned and drove her to lash out beneath Robert's softened gaze. "That is all a woman is. A slave, a bit of property. But you are a man, you would not understand."

His chin jutted slightly up, as though she had dealt him some blow. He watched her for a moment, his chest as steady as she felt hers heaving in resentment against him and the entire male race. Then suddenly he grinned that grin that transformed his dark face with light and quieted her breast by stealing away her breath.

"I am a man, it is true, but I am very much your servant. You have but to command me to see me obey."

She did not quite know how, but she found herself seated again on the log and Robert on one knee before her in the frosty bracken, waiting as though for his king . . . or queen . . . to charge him with some great quest.

She laughed before she could stop herself. "No one obeys me, sir. But if you are in earnest, then . . . then . . ."

He cocked an inquisitive brow as she trailed off. This was her chance, but the words did not want to come. To send him away so soon felt more than she could bear. When she gnawed on her lip in silence, he shifted himself to sit at her feet and link his hands around his knees. His gaze rested keen upon her face.

"Why are you not wed? Truly, lady. Your grandfather, I am told, has lain dead these past three years. Why has your father waited so long to command you? Or has there been an understanding between him and the earl all this long while?"

She shook her head.

"Then why? For were I a knight, I would have sought your hand long since."

Her heart leapt at his admission, spoken a little gruffly. And she would have given him her hand in an instant! Oh, why did he play thus with her? He had trusted her seven years ago on the riverbank. Why would he not trust her now with the truth of his birth? But a wave of shame caught her lip between her teeth again, for she had not trusted him, either. Would he still look at her thus, with that simmering heat behind his steady gaze when she told him? Or would her explanation douse his passion? If he should rebuff her after she had woven so many hopes around him—

But he would find out eventually. In fact— "I am surprised you do not already know," she said with a feigned carelessness. If he should reject her for what followed, she would not let him see how it hurt her. "All the world knows what my grandfather did."

"Not all the world, my lady. I am only a wandering musician."

"Have you never wandered to Northumberland, then, or heard the name of Heywood?"

"Northumberland, aye, three, perhaps four years ago. I do not recall that I cared much for it. It seemed a wild, untamed land. I do not think I have ever been as cold as I was when I was there, and I have frequently been cold. As for Heywood, nay, I do not recall the name. Is there a reason why I should?"

"It is anathema among the lords of this realm. No man will touch me because of what he did in his will."

Oh, she could not bear to sit here and watch horror grow in Robert's eyes. She stood and crossed the glade to fiddle with the needles of a yew tree, one of the few splashes of green among its winter-barren neighbors.

"And what was that, my lady?"

Suddenly she wanted it all over and done. The consequences must fall where they may.

"A year before I was born, he emancipated all the serfs on Winbourne Manor, his largest fief in Northumberland. Grandfather took me there when I was scarcely more than a babe. I grew up at Winbourne, thinking all manors were managed thus, not knowing that what he had done was— unusual."

She glanced over her shoulder and saw that Robert had stood up, too. What was he thinking? Nervousness made her babble on.

"My father says the barons might have overlooked Winbourne as an aberration, except that my grandfather left charters at his death freeing the villeins on all his other manors, as well. My father challenged the will, but the royal courts upheld it, and *that's* when men stopped seeking my hand in marriage. Grandfather deeded Winbourne Manor directly to me at his death and left my father ruling the other emancipated manors in my mother's name. And they will all go to me eventually as well, because my father has no other heir."

"Ah." Robert had not moved through her speech, but she knew from this soft spoken word that he understood. "Those barons who would otherwise eagerly court both you and your lands stand askance at the prospect of risking even the appearance of countenancing a notion so dangerous as emancipated manors."

She turned, bristling as though he had thrown a challenge at her. "It is absurd! Why should a manor that is farmed by freemen be any more dangerous than one that is farmed by villeins?"

"It is the idea that is dangerous," Robert said. "Once freed, a man may choose his own fate, and what if it is not the fate his lord would have him choose? Suppose he is no longer content to farm his lord's fields before his own, or willing to remain on the manor at all? Your world would starve, my lady, were it not sustained on the backs of villeins."

A sharpened edge slipped into his voice, goading her further in defense of her grandfather. "But we did not starve! Odo told Grandfather that the men would stay if he treated them fairly and most of them did. Winbourne is today one of the richest manors in Northumberland."

She thumped her hands onto her hips and readied herself to argue his reply, but he only asked, "Who is Odo?"

"Odo of Wedmore. He is a priest who became my grandfather's chaplain before I was born. Odo was born a villein himself, though he never told us on what manor his parents served. They bought his freedom when he was a boy so that he could enter the Church. Father called him a dangerous agitator because Odo said that all men should be free and treated with equal respect. I suppose you think that idea is outrageous, too?"

Robert merely raised his brows. "Such a man as that became your grandfather's chaplain? Your grandfather must have been exceptionally broadminded."

"He—" Marguerite hesitated. She wanted to vehemently agree, but honest memory held her silent. Despite the indulgence and love her grandfather had shown her, he had been a man easily stirred to impatience; hardheaded, stubborn, and very, very ambitious to expand his estates. She remembered how his sternness had sometimes intimidated her as a child, as it had when he had wished her to marry Lord Stephen before Odo had intervened. But in the end, her grandfather had always placed her needs before his plotting and maneuvers to obtain more land.

She could not pretend, no matter how much her protective instincts wanted to, so she told the truth. "I do not know why my grandfather did what he did. What does it matter now? He freed his villeins and now no man will marry me except Lord Saxton. If my grandfather's actions offend you, sir—"

"I?" Robert said. "Offended? What has any of this to do with me? The concerns of barons and villeins alike are of no matter to a landless minstrel."

Oh! How could he speak so lightly of what she had just revealed? She could not even read his eyes now, he guarded his thoughts so closely. She must find a way to test him, then.

"You said that I might command you and that you would obey."

If her sudden change in their topic of discussion surprised him, he gave no sign. In fact, he answered with a small, softened smile. "Lady, and so I shall."

"Then if I asked you to—"

"Aye?" he prompted as she broke off.

Go to Northumberland and tell Odo that he must haste to rescue me from Lord Saxton, and you must promise, promise, *that you will return with Odo when he comes!* She could not. Now that he knew the truth, she could not risk him fulfilling the first part of her plea, while politely denying her the second.

"Lady," he said with a reassuring firmness, "anything you ask me, I will do."

A wild, wicked temptation flashed into her mind to ask him to kiss her again. She struggled to fight back a fresh wave of heat in her cheeks and merely held out her hand. Her knees went weak with relief when he took it quickly in his own. "Then will you meet me here again tomorrow?"

She held her breath through his pause.

"If you wish me to, my lady."

Her fingers flexed more tightly around his. "Will you give me your word?"

He stared for a moment at their locked hands, and then his smile went crooked. "Did I not promise to teach you the flute? I will be here."

"And—and tonight?"

"Your father has requested my music again in his hall." Mention of Lord de Villon appeared to spur him to seek the position of the sun behind the heavy winter clouds. It was impossible, of course, but she knew as well as he that too many hours had slid by since she had left the hunt. "Now truly, my lady, you must go. Your father is sure to have missed you by now, but perhaps if you—"

"I will ride home and he will think I have been there all this while."

Robert laughed, as he had yesterday when she had given the same reply. Her hand still clasped in his, he led her to her mare. "You are very sly. The earl will have his hands full with you, I think."

His words panicked her into whirling towards him. "I do not want to marry the earl."

She felt him searching her eyes and cursed him for keeping his own so successfully veiled. "He is the king's right arm," Robert said. "You will want for nothing as his wife. He will keep you warm and safe from a world more harsh and bitter than you can comprehend."

"My *life* will be bitter and harsh if I marry him. I want—" She stopped as she sensed something shift in him, though she did not know why. He had not moved or altered his breathing or even blinked.

"What do you want, my lady?"

Oh, how could he be so blind? "I want a man who will love me more than he fears my inheritance. He need not be wealthy, only generous and brave. A man of honor willing to govern my grandfather's lands at my side."

It took her a moment to feel the increased pressure of his fingers around hers, so hard was she now clinging to his. Before she could say more, he lifted her hand and bent his head to kiss it. His mouth pressed fierce against her skin, startling her with his sudden passion.

"I pray you find him," he murmured, then tossed her into her saddle and slapped her mare on the rump, sending it trotting from the glade. She twisted about to view him, and saw him standing at the edge of the trees, watching, until distance at last separated him from her gaze.

Tomorrow, she thought, her hands clenched white-knuckled on the reins. Tomorrow she would know if her inheritance had frightened him away.

IO

Robert sent the Lady Marguerite away none too soon, for he could not have contained his roiling energy for one more moment. As soon as she was gone from his sight, he locked his hands behind his back—hands that still felt the lingering thrill of her delicate fingers—and traced the inner perimeter of the glade with such long, swift strides that he nearly dizzied himself. He did not know how he had stood so still through the revelations of her grandfather. One half of him had wanted to lash out in skeptical mockery of Heywood's motivations; the other half had wanted to catch Marguerite in his arms and smother her with kisses. What did it matter why her grandfather had done what he'd done? His actions had molded Marguerite of Winbourne into a warm, compassionate woman, one who cared not only for the safety of her maid, but for that maid's tears as well. Such a lady might not look as askance on Robert's suit as he had feared. Or so the daring hope had leapt in him before she had dashed it with the very reasonable desire she should have anticipated.

"I want a man willing to govern my grandfather's lands at my side."

Who knew how many manors the land hungry Heywood had deeded to his granddaughter, each almost certainly ruled over by a castle fortress. Robert challenged many things about the order of his world, but he had enough common sense to know that particular ambition was rather beyond his reach. Manage a castle with a garrison full of knights? Even he was not that mad!

Nay, he could not live in her world. For a brief moment when he had learned her betrothal to Saxton was not by her choice and she had recited the chaplain Odo's words "—all men should be free and treated with equal respect—" Robert had dared to consider asking her to live in his, but he had quickly come back to earth again. He'd wager she had never tasted the frigid bite of a Northumberland winter the way he had. She had surely spent her childhood near the flames of her grandfather's hearths and slept at night wrapped in a profusion of the thickest blankets.

Robert did not like the Earl of Saxton. Merely thinking of the man still raised his hackles. But as he had told Marguerite, the earl would protect her in ways Robert never could. And surely, surely one day Saxton would come to love her? How could any man, even one with a heart of ice, fail to thaw at last before so merry a laugh as hers, such sparkling eyes, such grace and loveliness, her charms all the more powerful because her very essence was so pure.

Six more days till Christmas. He would indulge himself with her company that much longer, and then as he had promised William, Robert would swallow Marguerite's loss as he had the other blows of his life, and move on.

The blast of snow arrived in a violent storm, trapping Marguerite inside Ashbury Castle. For two days she flitted from her chamber to her mother's solar to the hall and back to her chamber before beginning her restless route again. Panic would not let her sit still above a handful of minutes in each place. She had passed three more days in the glade with Robert before the storm struck, learning the merry tunes he taught her on her flute. Gradually they had added duets with his lute and when her mouth grew tired of blowing, she laid her flute in her lap and they sang together instead. They had not spoken again of her grandfather and she had not asked him to ride to Northumberland.

Saxton barely glanced at her each night at the table, his gaze fixed as always on Lady Jane with whom he promptly retired at dinner's end. Perhaps it was his neglect that made the threatened betrothal seem too intangible to be real. Or perhaps Marguerite feared losing these precious days with Robert more than the possibility that her father and the earl might yet find a way to force her hand.

But with the daily hunting expeditions suspended by the snowstorm and all the men confined to the castle, her father had begun to seek more determined ways to throw Marguerite and the earl together. Marguerite managed to deflect most of these attempts, assisted by her cousin Richard and the earl's obvious boredom with her, but in the back of her mind she sensed that things would change after Christmas. Once the celebrations had come and gone, the king would surely summon the earl back to court. King John, she knew from Richard, was anxious to strike out for France and Saxton must surely go with him. Would he try again to force the betrothal vows before then, or would he insist on their marriage?

Why did I not speak? Why did I not send Robert to Odo? The inexplicable aura of safety that she felt when she sat by Robert's side had shattered at their enforced separation. She paced the galleries that led from room to room, chiding herself over and over. Even if she found him waiting for her in the glade once the storm ended, it was surely too late to send him now.

The nightly feasts had continued from the castle's stores, but with the bitter, howling winds and snow banking high around the walls, there was no way for an outside jester or tumblers or a minstrel to join them. Marguerite could barely eat or sleep for wondering where Robert was and what he was thinking and whether this time apart would cool the simmering heat in his eyes and replace it with a cold, sober assessment that the dangers of her inheritance outweighed the desire she knew he felt for her.

Her first and only thought when the storm finally blew itself out on Christmas Eve morn was that she must see him if she could. What she would do if Robert failed to be waiting for her in the glade, she could not allow herself to think. She wrapped herself in her warmest cloak, drew on her fur-lined gloves, hid her flute beneath her cloak, and hurried out to the bailey. But she stopped halfway to the stables when she recognized the Earl of Saxton and his flame-haired lady. Saxton held the reins of Lady Jane's sleek mare, while Lady Jane's maidservant and a knight whom Marguerite had never seen before waited with their mounts a discreet distance away. Marguerite had not paused soon enough to avoid overhearing Saxton's deep voice.

"Must you go, Jane? It will be unbearable here without you."

Lady Jane smiled her dazzling smile. "The king has sent his request for my return" —she nodded in the direction of the knight— "and with John, to request is to command. Do you wish me to brave his fury by remaining longer?"

"Yes," Saxton said at once.

The luscious redhead laughed. "I cannot, even for you." She raised a hand sparkling with jewels to his face. "Be assured I shall find no pleasure at Westminster without you. How long must you tarry here?"

"Not long, I trust. De Villon has agreed to my plan, but we must wait until after Christmas. Just a few more days. I will join you at Westminster before Epiphany."

"I shall await you with impatience."

Marguerite watched as Saxton, in full view of the maidservant and the king's knight, as well as Ella the laundress, Clara the goose girl, and Sir Alan Hobart who happened to be crossing the bailey at that moment, bent his head and kissed Lady Jane full on the mouth. They hung together so long, with such blatant mutual hunger, that the mounting heat in Marguerite's cheeks threatened to explode into flames. At last Saxton released the beauty and lifted her into the saddle. He watched as she and her company cantered out of the courtyard, then turned and saw Marguerite.

He looked only vaguely startled. "You are up early this morning, my lady."

"As are you, my lord." Marguerite forced herself to keep her voice very even. "Lady Jane is leaving us?"

"As you see."

Oh, aye, I have seen too much. She thought he smirked a little as his gaze roamed over her hot face. How dare he insult her so within her own home?

She refused to flinch from his repressing stare and said boldly, "Perhaps you should have accompanied her. There is nothing to keep you here."

The smirk turned into a thin smile. "There is you, my dear."

"You are mistaken, my lord. I shall never marry you. I will not repeat the vows."

His smile vanished, perhaps displeased lest Ella, Clara, and Sir Alan heard her reply as clearly as they had seen him kiss Lady Jane. Saxton crossed the short distance that separated him from Marguerite, stopping so near her that she could have touched his massive chest without straightening her arm. His height blocked the weakly straining sun and cast an ominous shadow over her. She nearly flinched, but was certain that was what he hoped, to intimidate her with his hulking size. She clenched her teeth and forced herself to remain rooted where she stood.

Saxton's eyes were chill as the snow that lay in the yard. "You will do as you are told, my girl. If you would but cooperate, we might deal very well together."

"And when I am your wife, will I be expected to make room for Lady Jane within our home?"

"If I so desire. You will obey me."

Marguerite's temper flashed at his arrogance. "I will not!"

"You will obey me," he repeated, his voice hardening, "without question. Do you understand?"

She pressed her lips together angrily. His hand came under her chin and forced her face up to his. His eyes glinted dangerously into hers.

"Do you understand me?"

"I understand that I shall be your chattel!"

His fingers tightened about her chin until she winced. "You will do well to cease these antics, my lady. You might find life considerably more difficult with me than you ever have with your father. Do not force me to show you what I mean."

Marguerite shuddered at the menace in his gaze, but he let her strike his hand away—she knew she could not have wrenched free of his grip against his will. She ran for the stables. Her mother had agreed to let Marguerite wear off her fidgets with a good, brisk ride, as long as she took a groom with her and promised not to go to the village. *Oh please, please let Robert be waiting for me,* she prayed.

"Marguerite. Where are you going, girl?"

Marguerite stopped just short of the stable door and turned reluctantly at her father's voice. She realized she was shaking from her encounter with the earl. Saxton, having apparently dismissed her already from his mind, had crossed halfway back to the keep where her father had met him. She hoped her father could not see the trembling that still held her.

"Mama said that I might go riding—"

"What, now?" Her father cut her off. "Nonsense. I sent some servants out at dawn to gather holly for the hall. I thought the earl might help them place it, as he is so tall. Your mother is supervising the Christmas preparations in the kitchens, so you must direct the draping of the greenery. And I have had the chess board brought out so the two of you might play beside the Yule fire when you are done."

Marguerite began a protest that she was certain Saxton would second, but to her surprise, he held out his arm and said, "It would be my pleasure to assist you, my lady."

Marguerite recovered herself swiftly at this unexpected response. "Yes, Father. Let me take a quick ride to clear the cobwebs from my head"— just long enough to reassure Robert, lest he be even now in the glade and wait in vain for her—"and then the earl and I will—"

Her father glowered. "Now, Marguerite. Or"—his glower lightened—"perhaps the earl would like to ride with you."

"No!" Marguerite moved so quickly away from the stables that she nearly tripped into a run. If Saxton should ever, *ever* suspect that she and Robert— "No, sir, of course we will do the holly if you wish it."

From the glance her father directed at her chin, she guessed that Saxton's fingers had left their mark there. Her father shrugged, then fell into step beside the earl as they returned to the keep, rubbing his hands together and cheerfully regaling the earl with his plans for the Christmas Eve feast. Along with the rich dishes he had ordered for the table, he had hired a troop of mummers to perform an allegorical play. De Villon had feared the storm would prevent the mummers from joining them, but with the skies clearing he had sent a servant to fetch them, along with a fresh summons for the tumblers and jester and the minstrel, if he still lingered in the village.

Marguerite felt her agitation ease just a little. She would see Robert tonight, then. He would only have to look into her eyes to know that she had been prevented against her will from joining him. Assuming he waited for her there. *Assuming he even looks at me tonight.* Save for that first evening, he never, ever glanced her way when he sang, and if his gaze inadvertently passed over her from time to time, it did so so briefly and blankly that he did not even appear to register that she sat in the hall. His distant behavior still unnerved her, however welcoming he always proved when he lifted her down from her mare the next morning. A fretting fear that she misread his attentions when they were together haunted her to bed every night, worrying her sleep until she found herself sitting, merry and safe, at his side again on the morrow.

Somehow Marguerite endured the morning with Saxton. Despite the fact that only a short time before he had flagrantly embraced another woman, he feigned such interest in and consideration for his "betrothed" that the servants, who had not been in the courtyard to witness Lady Jane's departure, whispered behind their hands and cast indulgent smiles at him and Marguerite. Saxton even let her win twice at chess after they had finished with the holly. He praised her cleverness, again conspicuously before the servants, when he forced her to take advantage of careless moves she knew a man shrewd enough to rise in power next to the king could only have made deliberately. Marguerite silently cursed his duplicity, for she knew it made her frowns appear temperamental and childish.

Her disgust at his behavior broke on relief when her mother finally summoned her to change her gown for the feast.

Weary of all the grandeur her father had forced upon her during the earl's stay, Marguerite tried to choose a subdued surcote of dark gray wool, but Lady Leah told Eva to bring out the crimson kirtle instead.

"Tonight is Christmas Eve," her mother said. "Your father wishes you to look your best before his vassals. This—" she took the gown from Eva and shook out the graceful folds "—has always looked most becoming on you, my dear."

Though not as lavish as the stiff golds and greens her father had decked her in the previous nights, Marguerite nevertheless hesitated. Her father had never approved of this particular gown. The soft, intricately woven cloth of the bodice had a tendency to cling boldly to her curves, while the neck scooped more revealingly than any other gown she owned.

"But Mama, Father has always said this gown makes me look a wanton."

Lady Leah answered with a nervous laugh. "Nonsense, my dear. He was in a temper when he said that. It brings out the blush in your cheeks more prettily than any of your other gowns. He was quite right to suggest that you wear it for tonight's festivities."

Marguerite understood instantly. With Lady Jane gone, her father wanted Marguerite to play the temptress. Marguerite vowed silently to play no such game. As Eva laced the back of the gown up tightly and Lady Leah tied on a golden girdle with pearls to emphasize her daughter's small waist, Marguerite swore she would behave so dully that Saxton would spend the entire evening gazing longingly at Lady Jane's empty chair.

Her suspicions of her father's hopes were confirmed when she joined the earl at the high table. Her dashing gown drew a glint into Saxton's hard eyes that she had only observed before in his gazes at Lady Jane. He had never looked at Marguerite thus before, not even while he had taunted her with his solicitous attentions that morning. She squirmed with revulsion when his gaze followed the line of her necklace, a gold chain with rubies and pearls sprinkled between the links, knotted so that it formed a loop that dangled just above her kirtle's dipping neckline.

For the first time at any of their meals, Saxton attempted to engage her in conversation, but she deliberately returned the most repressing, monosyllabic answers she could. Her aloofness did not appear to discourage him, even when she barely brushed her lips to the rim of the wassail cup he passed to her. Sharing a cup with Saxton repulsed her as much on Christmas Eve as it had every other night, though this time she felt compelled to at least make a pretense of observing the traditional Yuletide ritual before handing the cup back to him and asking his squire, Nicholas Tybert, to bring her a goblet of her own. Saxton drained off the wassail cup, then had the squire refill it, twice, thrice, a fourth time and a fifth. Saxton always drank heavily at their meals, but at her father's command, the wassail flowed faster and freer than the usual wine, and Saxton's consumption accelerated accordingly. As did her father's. Lord de Villon, grown boisterous, at length left the dais with a rather unsteady gait and a fat pheasant leg in his hand, to mingle among his guests. The hall grew so raucous it almost deafened Marguerite, until the now familiar figure of the minstrel stepped onto the floor. Three bold strums of his lute strings, and the din abruptly fell to a dull hum.

> *"Personet hodie*
> *voces puerulae,*
> *Laudantes iucunde . . ."*

Marguerite could not prevent herself from leaning forward to gaze at Robert as he launched into the Latin verses of a Christmas hymn. His pronunciation of the syllables was flawless. Someone had taken great care with his education. Oh, if only he would look at her! But as always, his bright, midnight eyes swept every face in the hall except hers.

A hand closed on her arm beneath the tablecloth. She looked up quickly into Saxton's face. A high flush had spread across his cheeks. His eyes gleamed down into hers and a slow smile curved his lips. "My lady, you are in great beauty tonight."

His voice did not slur, but she recoiled, the aromatic mix of cloves, cinnamon and apples of the wassail soured with the wine on his breath.

"I thank your lordship," she murmured, and tried to draw her arm away.

His hand slid down her sleeve to find and lightly grip her wrist. "We have not had a moment alone since I arrived. Come, let us step out onto the battlement."

"Leave the festivities? That would be most improper, my lord." Marguerite attempted to pull her wrist free, but his grip tightened with the strength she had come to know and dread.

His smile grew harder. "Come, my lady, there is no harm in it. The company's attention is all engaged with the minstrel. No one will observe our absence."

Only then did Marguerite realize the trap. Her father's movement away from the dais had been a deliberate maneuver to draw the company's eyes to him and away from her and Saxton. Her mother sat stiffly, staring fixedly at her husband. Marguerite knew she would not turn her head, even if Marguerite cried out to her. She threw a desperate glance at Robert, but he, too, had shifted towards Lord de Villon.

"Come, my lady," Saxton repeated, and drew her out of her chair.

Marguerite leaned lightly on the earl's arm as he guided her out to the deserted battlement. Saxton dismissed her father's guards and sent Nicholas Tybert to fetch her mantle, then set it courteously about her shoulders before sending the youth away, too. For some moments they stood in silence, looking through one of the gaps in the crenelated wall over the village of Lyndeard. It spread like a dark shadow below them in the moonlight, with one central sphere of light where Marguerite knew a bonfire burned. The villagers of Lyndeard danced caroles around the flames on Christmas Eve, as the villagers had on Winbourne Manor.

"You are very quiet tonight, Marguerite."

Saxton's height loomed even more oppressive in the dark than it did in the daylight. She struggled not to let dismay show in her voice. "I thought you did not like talkative women."

"That is true. There are certainly better ways for a man and woman to occupy their time." He moved his hand along the wall until his large palm swallowed hers.

Marguerite felt a wave of revulsion at his touch. "We should not have left the hall."

To her surprise he let her draw her hand free, but when she turned away from the wall he moved to block her retreat with surprising swiftness for so large a man.

He reached out to toy with the dangling chain about her neck. "Very pretty. Where had you this?"

"It is my mother's, lent to me for the evening—"

She broke off with a startled gasp as his long fingers encircled her throat above the knot in the chain. She tried to pull away, but his arm wrapped around her waist and jerked her hard against his body.

"Ah no, my lady, you must not try to escape from me. Hold still!"

Despite his sharp command, she shoved again against his chest. Again in vain. She might as well have sought to dislodge a stone from the castle's walls. The same lewd hunger she had often seen in his eyes when they rested on Lady Jane he now bent down on her. He must have felt her shudder, clamped against him as he held her. Saxton fondled her throat with just enough meaningful pressure to impress her with his ability to cut off a scream before it could pass the little hollow into which he pressed his thumb. Shouting would have been futile anyway. She knew this was exactly what her father had hoped would happen with Lady Jane gone.

Looking satisfied that she understood his power over her, Saxton's caress gradually slid downward, past the dangling loop of her chain to trace the scoop of her bodice. Marguerite's lips trembled, but she forced herself to still them. She would not beg for mercy from this man. She shut her eyes very tight, praying for a rescue that she knew would not come. His hand rested briefly against her thudding heart, then came abruptly under her chin. He tossed back her head and kissed her.

His mouth ground against hers, coarse and greedy. Fear and disgust slammed through her, but past them both raced anger. How dare he desecrate the sacred glow of Robert's kiss that she still cherished on her lips? Saxton's cold, rough mouth fouled the memory until in a blaze of unthinking fury, her foot flashed up, then drove down with all its strength atop Saxton's own soft-slippered foot.

Saxton freed her mouth with a quick breath of surprise. Marguerite twisted out of his slackened hold, flung back her arm, and brought her hand hard across his face. She imagined she could do little enough harm to so large a man, but her action startled him into falling back a step.

His surprise lasted less than an instant before his glare went vicious and his voice lashed out like a whip. "You will regret that, my lady."

"Stay away from me. I am not your wife yet."

He made a movement that she began to dodge, but a sudden pounding of footsteps made him whisk his hand back.

"Marguerite? There you are." Her cousin, Richard Channing, came hurrying along the wall-walk. "I've been looking all over for you. Your father is angry that you left the hall."

Marguerite caught Richard's arm as he reached her. He must have felt the way relief set her trembling, for he drew her hand securely into the crook of his elbow.

"Did he see us leave, Richard?" She could not comprehend why her father would have sent anyone to find her. Unless— She shuddered again. Had he hoped that she and Saxton might be discovered so compromised that she would feel compelled to surrender to the marriage?

"Nay, no one saw you go out," Richard said. "It was not until the minstrel spoke of dedicating a song to you in honor of your betrothal that your absence was noticed."

Robert? He had never attempted to directly salute her "betrothal" before. Had it been a lucky chance? Or had he been aware of her, watching over her all along, and seized on the ruse to send her aid?

"When it was discovered that the earl was missing too," Richard continued, "the company began to stir in a manner my uncle did not care for. He ordered me to retrieve you at once. He is very angry, though I doubt—" she caught the hostile glance Richard threw at Saxton "—that it was your fault." Richard turned to face the earl, dragging her about with him on his arm. "I'll thank you to remember, my lord, that my cousin is a lady and is to be treated as one."

"Your cousin is a shrew," Saxton snarled. "I look forward to the day when I am free to school her."

"That day is not yet, and until you are wed she will not go unprotected."

Marguerite clung to Richard, but it was Robert's faithful face she saw. Chance—perhaps. But she could not believe it, not when he had so studiously avoided even glancing at her night after night after night. He had to have known she had left with Saxton, had to have deliberately drawn attention to her absence, knowing it would compel her father to act in defense of her honor regardless of his own wishes. The calming sense of safety she had felt with Robert in the glade had become a promise fulfilled.

She did not care that Saxton followed her and Richard along the wall-walk and down the series of circular stairs that carried them back to the hall. Despite Robert's caution, surely he would dare one glance at her now, just long enough for him to see in her eyes that she had understood, that thanks to him she was safe, that he could not have won her trust more completely than he had by his actions this night.

She gazed eagerly about her as they reentered the hall. Her father frowned from his chair beside her mother. The company shifted uncomfortably around them. Her gaze swept the floor in front of the dais, the side tables, the far corners, even upwards to the gallery, then back again to the floor.

Robert was gone.

II

Robert uttered a soft curse when he nearly collided with William coming through the cottage door just as he was about to exit.

"I thought you were still at the bridge," Robert said. It had been damaged again in the snowstorm. He had hoped to avoid an encounter like this while Will labored with other villagers on renewed repairs.

"I was," William replied, "but I was worried about Lucy. She sniffled somethin' fierce durin' the night. I made an excuse to come an' check on her. How is she?"

"I tried to get her to make a tea from some of my dried mint leaves, for I've found it helpful in clearing a stuffy head, but she was afraid it might make her quarrelsome. So she's gone to a neighbor to see if she has any feverfew." Robert stepped outside and pointed at a cottage with a half-patched roof along the lane.

William glanced at the cottage and nodded. Then his gaze returned to Robert, as though belatedly taking in the cloak tossed over his shoulders. "Ye're leavin'? Without sayin' goodbye?" His gaze sank to Robert's empty hands, then returned to Robert's face. "Ye're *not* leavin'. Not without yer lute an' the rest of yer things. Then where are ye goin'?"

Robert deflected the question. "I thought we agreed that I would stay one more day."

'Twas the day after Christmas. Robert had spent yesterday's holy morn with the other villagers listening to a sermon by the village priest in the churchyard, since the interdict denied them the administration of the mass even upon this day. Afterwards, he stole off to the glade where he had hoped, though not truly expected, that he might find Marguerite. He had known it unlikely that she would be allowed to slip away unnoticed on Christmas Day, and had indeed found the glade empty. To prevent another interrogation from William, whose suspicions had steadily grown as Robert's absences each day had lengthened, Robert snared a hare and brought it back to the cottage. William had been too grateful for the bracing nourishment it had offered for Lucy's cold to remind his friend of the dangers of poaching. After they had roasted the hare and dined, Robert built up the fire with some wood he had taken from the forest along with the hare. That had stretched the limits of William's tolerance. Though Robert understood William's fear, it made him impatient all the same. Why waste a wood-penny, he said to William's chiding, when God could not possibly want some men to freeze only because other men laid greedy claim to what Nature surely intended a benefit to all?

Appreciative, despite his ingrained fears, of the gifts that had blessed his wife, and perhaps reluctant for a parting that might be their last, William had agreed this morning to Robert's request to linger another day in Lyndeard. "I daren't any more, though," William had said. "Jarrott is already eyein' ye more closely than I like."

"I know," Robert had replied. "I won't ask more than today."

He had lain awake the last two nights, staring into the darkness as Lucy's coughs and snuffles repeatedly brought William out of his snores to mutter his worries for her. Robert had lain as still as he could, not wanting to disturb them. By both mornings his muscles had ached from his body's taut discipline, for he had longed again and again to spring to his feet and accompany his warring thoughts with some sort of vigorous action. Had there been something to plow or harvest, he would have spent the night in William's fields, as Robert's father had often labored beneath the light of the moon, but nothing could grow this time of year with the fields hard frozen.

The decision had finally settled across Robert's mind in the early hours of this morning's dawn. The restlessness stilled, replaced with a resolve that anchored itself immovable in his spirit and heart. One way or another, this day would decide his future.

"Where are ye off to?" William asked again now.

Robert waved a vague hand. "I've something to attend to."

"Here in the village?"

Robert hesitated.

William groaned and ran his fingers through his sandy hair. "I knew it. Ye're in trouble, aren't ye?"

"Will—"

William's fingers left his hair to jab Robert hard in the chest. "Don't think that I can't see it. That glint in yer eye, that mulish set to yer lips— I've known ye too long not to recognize the signs that ye're about to do somethin' insanely foolish."

"Well, then, it's better that you don't ask me, is it not?" Robert retaliated for his friend's assault by dealing William a friendly but forceful buffet to the shoulder, then tried to step around him.

William caught him by the arm and spun Robert round to face him. "Don't. Whatever ye're plannin', just don't."

"I have to, Will. Let me go."

"Rob—"

"Don't worry for me. Don't I always land on my feet?"

"More like scrabbling back up like a stubborn puppy who refuses to come to heel, no matter how many times his master beats him for it. Rob, she isn't worth it." Robert stiffened, but William pressed on. "Ye know I haven't asked ye again, but do ye think I haven't guessed where ye've been stealin' off to every day? Ye've been with the Lady Marguerite, haven't ye?"

Robert pulled his arm away. He knew from William's expression that he did not need to answer.

"I've nothin' against her," William said, his voice roughening beneath the challenge in Robert's gaze. "I meant no insult to her. She's a lovely, kind-hearted lass, but nothin' can come of it, ye know it can't, and Saxton—Lord Christopher's punishments will pale next to what Saxton can do to ye if he learns o' this."

"He won't learn of it," Robert said. "Not before it's too late, anyway."

"Rob," William called when Robert turned and started down the lane, "it isn't fair to her! Ye gave me yer word ye wouldn't take advantage of her!"

Robert paused and turned halfway about. "I won't. Whatever she decides, she will do it with her eyes wide open. My word on it, William. Again."

For William's sake, Robert rehearsed to himself one more time all the practical reasons why he should stay away from the glade, even as his feet carried him there on a swift tide of hope. He knew he was mad. He did not need William to tell him that. A lady and a minstrel? Insanely foolish, indeed. But everything had changed on Christmas Eve. It had taken every ounce of self-discipline Robert possessed not to stand all night staring in rapt admiration at the Lady Marguerite in that enticing crimson gown. With the greatest effort of will he had maintained his usual nightly detachment, careful never to appear to look directly at her. William would be worse than alarmed if he knew how frowningly Saxton had watched Robert at dinner ever since Robert had knocked down his squire. Robert had not spoken of the incident, and he knew Simon Todd had not either, but there had been other witnesses to the squire's humiliation, the tumblers and the jester who likely had not been so discreet. The earl did not need his temper further strained by intercepting Robert returning the longing looks Marguerite was too young to resist casting at him from the dais.

But never for an instant had Robert failed to be wholly aware of her, every turn of her head, every gesture of her graceful hands, every emotion that flickered across her sweet face—including her disgust at Saxton's lustful glances and her fear when he had drawn her to her feet and led her out of the hall. Robert had wanted nothing more than to lunge after them, but he had been trapped by the gazes of her father's guests, fixed on him and his song. He had done the only thing he could—drawn attention to her empty chair and thus embarrass her father into sending that sunny-haired young man in search of her. He suspected Lord de Villon had dismissed Robert from his hall out of pique that Robert had interfered with a disgraceful plot to maneuver his daughter into a reluctant marriage.

Robert's hopes that he had misread the earl, that Saxton would learn, in time, to love Marguerite, had broken on the ugly reality the wassail wine had flushed into Saxton's face. So lewd a hunger as Saxton directed at Marguerite could never turn to love. That was the moment Robert had known that he could not walk away from her as he had planned. For two nights he had fought the obdurate resolve that had solidified in him that night, using every sensible argument he could conjure, and he had conjured a boundless number. But he could not leave her to Saxton's mercy, and it was clear her father intended to force the marriage along before any man of her own station could appear to challenge Saxton. Robert had little enough to offer Marguerite aside from his devotion. He did not know if it would be enough. But offer it he had sworn to do and let the choice be hers.

Robert swept aside the branches of a hawthorn tree and stepped into the glade, then froze. She had never arrived before him, yet there she sat on the log where they had wiled away so many days in music. She did not see him for her head was in her hands. Her fingers twisted through her thick, dusky hair, her distress rippling in the air between them.

"Marguerite?" Her name escaped his lips before he realized he had not prefaced it with her title. "Oh, my heart, what is it?"

She bounded up at the sound of his voice, tears glistening on her pale cheeks, then hurled herself across the glade and landed in his arms. He could not stop them from closing tight around her.

"You came." Her face pressed into his tunic's breast, muffling her sob.

Robert's blood pitched colder than the air around them as her arms wrapped convulsively around his waist. He had sent Simon Todd up to the castle twice yesterday to speak to Eva and be sure the earl had not tried to accost Marguerite again. Both times Simon had returned with the assurance that her cousin—the sunny-haired young man?—was guarding her closely, despite Lord Saxton's glares. But a long night had stretched between then and now, and her father, Robert knew, was not to be trusted, however sympathetic towards her that tall, broad-shouldered cousin might be.

He felt her body trembling against him. He could not draw her any closer without smothering her.

"What has happened?" he asked again. Somehow he kept his voice gentle when a swelling rage within him wanted to pull his dagger free and hunt Saxton down.

"I was afraid you would not come," she whispered without raising her face. "I was afraid— Oh, I have been so afraid!"

"Of what?" He barely bit off *sweetheart*. If Saxton had laid so much as a hand on her—

"That you would think I had cast you off because I did not meet you on Christmas Eve." Her voice was thick with the tears he could still feel shaking her shoulders. "And you would not look at me at dinner so that I might try to signal you, and then when you tried to salute me with a song you must have seen that I had left the hall with Lord Saxton. I'd hoped that you did it to protect me, but my father would not let me come yesterday either, he insisted that I spend all day in Lord Saxton's company, and I began to worry what you must be thinking, that you might believe I did not come because I had changed my mind about Lord Saxton and went with him willingly that night, and I was afraid you would think I did not really love you after all and that you would go away and I would never see you again!"

He let her rattle out all her frantic emotions against his chest, his heart giving an exultant jolt when the words *love you* tumbled off her tongue. Still, the ferocious question burned in his mind. He cupped her cheeks in his hands and lifted up her face so that he might catch a lie in her eyes.

"You must tell me truthfully," he said. "Did Saxton do you harm that night, or—or since?

Robert stifled his groan of relief when her head moved in a small, negating shake between his palms.

"He acts as though that night never happened, but I can see in the way he looks at me when we sit at chess or walk through the garden with Richard that he has not forgiven me." Her eyes flashed. "I do not care, I am glad I slapped him. I wish I had done so sooner, before he left a horrid, foul tasting kiss on my lips." Robert felt her shudder. No lie lurked in her eyes, but something very akin to panic replaced the burst of defiance. Her tears flowed hot against his fingers. "I have tried and tried to forget it, but the memory follows me everywhere and chokes me with disgust. Oh, please, I know it is wicked of me to ask you—a lady ought never—but I have rubbed my mouth raw and still—Oh, please, will you kiss me again, as you did in my chamber? Please make his memory go away." Another shudder, another sob—

Oh, saints, Robert had not expected a request such as this. His heart hammered with the desire he had battled ever since that wild, reckless night he had swung himself through her window. He had guarded his passion so rigorously since then, determined not to stain her honor in some careless, impulsive moment. He had meant today to lay his own truth before her, and then—only then, if she answered as he hoped, would he seal his promise to her with another kiss.

But the plea in her eyes undid all his noble resolves and his mouth drifted towards her lips like a bee drawn to a seductively blushing rose. He checked a bare inch away, struggling to master his pounding blood.

"Marguerite—if I kiss you now, I might never be able to stop."

"Then don't." Her arms left his waist and entwined about his neck. "Don't stop."

Her breath, half-whisper, half-sob, mingled with his exhale of surrender. His mouth settled over hers and met an eager welcome. She nestled, small but vibrant in his embrace, her lips quivering swiftly to a clinging fierceness.

His blood coursed and his kiss deepened. He plunged into an eddy of pleasure, but deep beneath his urgent thirst for her, something quieted deep in his core. He had felt the promise of it before, whispering along his soul in those moments when his restlessness calmed as they'd blended their music and laughter. Now his anger, his grief, his pain, all the roiling turmoil of his past grew still, swallowed up in her healing balm.

How long he drank her in like a man parched, he did not know. Their lips parted only long enough for each to catch breath before tangling together again. And again. Slow, savoring, seductive. He wanted her to taste his gratitude, but feared she could only taste his desire. If she did, it did not seem to daunt her, for she clung to him more tightly.

And that nearly proved his undoing. He had known that night in her chamber when he had set his lips to hers that she had never been kissed before. She could not understand the effect of her heated return of his kisses. He made one desperate, belated grab for caution—and felt it sift through his fingers like sand. All thought flowed away with it as passion surged. The feverish tide blotted out everything except his need for her and her answering fire.

He did not realize that in their fervor, they had begun to shift across the glade until her heel caught on the hem of her cloak and she stumbled. They fell to their knees together beside the log, the impact jarring Robert back to some sense of awareness. Her hands caught his face when he tried to draw away and held his mouth locked to hers. He nearly slid back into the intoxicating vortex, but something else swirled in, something tender and protective. She was too young to understand the danger of embraces like these, but he knew how perilously close they were to crossing a boundary he could never bring her back from.

He felt her resistance when he grasped her wrists and pulled them down a little roughly. Trying desperately to fan the ember of warning stirring up his conscience, he tore his lips from hers. "Marguerite—"

She cut off his husky qualm with another kiss.

Oh, saints. One more moment and he would lose his last restraint. He pushed her away a little too hard, for he heard her startled *huff* as her back knocked up against the log and slightly winded her. It drove the haze from her eyes, but he stood up quickly as he saw it misting back.

She gazed up at him, confusion replacing passion, then dissolving into horror as he retreated across the glade. She covered her mouth with shaking hands, then looked away with so much shame in her eyes that it nearly drove him back to her side. But he was not ready to trust himself to touch her again.

"I am so sorry." He heard the anguished break in her voice behind her muffling palms. "I should not have asked you to—You must think me as wicked as Lady Jane!"

"I think you," Robert said gruffly, "the most delightsome, adorable woman I have ever known. If I was so clumsy that you could not feel my love in those kisses, then I am as contemptible a scoundrel as the Earl of Saxton."

That brought her gaze back to his with a glow of hope that was almost painful. Her hands drifted tentatively from her lips. He was grateful for a gusting winter breeze that blew against his cheeks and cooled just a little the blood that still scalded in his veins.

She searched his face. "Do you?" she asked, in softly trembling tones. "Love me?"

He did not think he had assumed his impassive mask, but perhaps the habit had become so second nature that he no longer noticed when he donned it. "You spoke the words first," he reminded her. "Or did I misunderstand—?"

"No. Oh, no!" She scrambled to her feet.

Another flurry of air glided over him just in time to tamp his blood down another notch before she rushed back into his arms. He pressed her head gently against his shoulder to keep at bay a little longer the temptation to kiss her again.

"You were not clumsy at all." She sounded suddenly anxious, as though she had left the question hanging unsatisfactorily between them. "I wanted to believe I felt love in your kiss. Could you feel my love in mine?"

"Aye." *And your trust.* Robert prayed he might never come so near betraying it again. He leaned his cheek against her soft hair. "So then, our love for each other is settled. But there is still much we must talk of, my lady."

She gave a protesting little squirm. "Do not call me that. I liked it when you called me Marguerite. And I—I must call you Robert."

"Rob," he said absently. "And I think you are too small for so lengthy a name as Marguerite. Mae would suit you better."

Her squirming ceased and her arms slid around his waist again. He heard contentment in her sigh. "I should like that."

He tried not to think how perfectly she fit in his embrace.

She moved her head to rest her ear closer to his heart. "I wish we could stay like this forever. Just like this. But—" She stirred again, then quieted, still nestled where she was. "What is the time, do you think?"

He reluctantly parted his cheek from her hair to gaze at the sky through the trees. "The sun is still behind the clouds, but I suspect it was near the hour of Prime when I left the village. You came very early to arrive here before me. I know I lost track of our kisses, but I do not think it can be Terce yet." His gaze lowered back to the trees, then swept the inner perimeter of the glade. His hold on her slackened. "Where is your mare?"

"I left her with John."

"John?" He caught her by the elbows and pushed her gently away.

"Don't worry." Her fingers brushed the place between his eyebrows where he realized they had plunged together in a frown. "He is my groom and is completely to be trusted. Even if he knew about us, he would not betray us."

Robert cursed himself for becoming so distracted by her that he had not observed the absence of her horse. So she had not slipped away this time from hunting with her father and the earl. Robert shot another look around the trees, this time half in fear of meeting a pair of intruding eyes. "Where did you leave this groom?"

"To the west of the glade. I did not want you meeting him on your way. I was afraid he would frighten you away if you saw him, and—and I was already so afraid that you would not come at all."

"Mae, this groom of yours, however trustworthy, must surely be wondering where you are."

"Oh, he knows where I am. He just does not know about you." She smiled up at him.

In spite of himself, Robert laughed. "You had better tell me what devious story you told him, then."

She blushed a little at that. "Only that I wished to be alone to think. John would never question me. Three summers ago when I was visiting my parents, he fell into some foolish prank—he is only just my own age—and my father flogged him for it. I slipped away to the stables afterwards to clean his wounds. Father was furious when he learned of it, but Odo always said it did not matter how one was born, if I saw another suffering, God would expect me to use what gifts He had given me to help. And

Mama had taught me the herbs of healing, so I—" She stopped. "Do you disapprove?"

Robert realized he had stiffened when she mentioned the boy's punishment. He tried to relax his body but could not. "Your own age—three years ago, he would have been fourteen." The quietness she had cast over him splintered.

Her gaze faltered beneath his. "It is my father's way of discipline. I do not approve, but I had no power to stop him."

Robert barely heard her defensive response. For an instant, he had flashed back to his own fourteenth year, heard again the hiss and the snap, felt the first bite of the lash in his flesh—

"Did he learn his lesson?" Robert's question drew her gaze back to his face. "Your groom. Did he play anymore pranks after that?"

She shook her head. Something in Robert must have dismayed her, for she stared at him wide-eyed in silence. He did not know how he managed to smile—in irony, perhaps—but was glad he had when he saw her anxiety slide away.

"Good. It is never wise to challenge the whip." He managed to suppress an edge to the words. He had many things to tell her, but some things felt too harsh for today. He could not court her if his heart was full of bitterness.

The emotion was not easy to subdue, not when he had nourished it so doggedly for so long. The reckoning with Kit would come, but it must wait for another time and place. Robert would not let his adversary win by stealing the hopes of this day. He took Marguerite's hand and drew her down to sit beside him on the log.

"John has been devoted to me ever since," she said, "so I knew he would escort me here without question and wait where I told him to. Father knows him loyal enough to trust my safety to him, even though he is young."

"Then your groom, or your father, or both are fools. You could be sitting here at this very moment at the mercy of a wolf."

She smiled and squeezed his hand. "I know I am safe with you. I have always known it. I am not as naïve as you think me."

Robert forbore to offend her with a contradiction. "What happened to the daily hunting parties?"

"I dared not wait for that today. You know how late it is before I can sometimes slip away. I had already failed to meet you two days in a row. If you thought I had failed again, that I had changed my mind about Lord Saxton—"

She pressed Robert's hand still tighter. "I could not risk you misunderstand-ing, so I left as soon as I could after breaking my fast, before my father could force me to join the hunt or otherwise spend another day trapped in Lord Saxton's company." Her eyes sparkled her happiness at Robert.

"Mae." He could not let her walk blindly into a future with him. "We must think carefully of what we are about to do."

"I have thought about it. Father never returns from the hunt before Sext, and sometimes as late as None. If we leave now, we can be miles along the north road before he realizes I am missing from the castle." She sprang to her feet and tugged at Robert's hands for him to follow.

Robert stared at her, startled, but stayed where he was on the log. He had every intention of eloping with her, if she was willing after he told her about Beck Manor, but—"Miles along the north road—today?"

She looked surprised. "Of course. If we ride swiftly and are very careful not to get caught along the way, we can reach Northumberland before my father. Once Odo marries us, there will be nothing he or Lord Saxton can do. You—you do not care about my inheritance, do you?"

Robert heard the apprehension in her voice over the legacy that had driven all her suitors away except the Earl of Saxton.

"Not one whit," Robert said truthfully. "But Mae—"

Her cheeks shone. "Oh, I am so glad! You are very hard to read some-times, you know, and I could not quite tell what you were thinking when I told you about my grandfather and Odo or even today about John. But you kept meeting me even after I told you, and the way you kissed me today made me hope— I am so very glad I was right about you!"

A heaviness settled in his chest at her glow. It felt like ages ago that he had heard her speak of her desire for a husband to inherit her grandfather's lands with her. But she had kept meeting Robert, too. Whatever else he had hidden from her, she had always known him to be a mere minstrel.

"Mae—Marguerite, sit back down."

"But Rob, I don't think we should wait." She glanced at the sky and met with the same cryptic grey clouds as he had. "The longer we tarry, the more likely it will be that my father and Lord Saxton will—"

"We can't go today. Come, I told you we must talk."

She stared at him blankly. "Not go today?"

"Sit down, sweetheart."

"But, Rob—"

He pulled on her hands still laced with his. "Marguerite, please—"

"But we *must* go today! Whatever it is, you can tell me on the way. I brought a change of dress, just in case—in case you were here and—and agreed to m-mar—h-help me—" He was quite sure she had been about to say *marry* before changing the word with so vivid a blush. "You can ride John's horse. Or no, I suppose I cannot send him back to Ashbury Castle without me, my father would thrash him senseless. He will have to come with us. I will ride up behind you on his horse and he can take my mare and—"

"Marguerite, we are not going anywhere until you sit down and listen to me."

Robert could not tell which shocked her more, the sudden snap in his voice or the abrupt way he released her hands. He bit his lip at his flash of impatience. It sprang from a stab of self-doubt so rare that it took him a moment to identify it. He saw all too glaringly now how their hopes in one another had been at cross-purposes all this while. He had thought—at least, had prayed—that she might be ready to accept a modest life with his devotion over the duty she believed she owed her grandfather. But she—for some unfathomable reason, she appeared to believe she could ride through the gates of her grandfather's castle demanding to be wed to a minstrel who could then take up life at her side, ruling her inheritance. He nearly laughed out loud at the absurdity she did not seem to grasp.

He took her hands again and pressed her fingers gently. "Forgive me, sweetheart, I did not mean to sound so bearish. But truly, there is something I must tell you, and no, it cannot wait."

Still, she remained frozen where she was. Her dark eyes grew luminous in her swiftly paling face. "But Rob, there is no time. Lord Saxton is taking me to Westminster."

That drove Robert to his feet. "To the king's palace? When?"

"On Monday."

Robert relaxed a little. "That's four days from now."

"But my father is pressing and pressing him. He says it does not matter that I have refused to speak the betrothal vows, once I am in the king's court I will be accepted by all as Lord Saxton's affianced bride and the king will allow Lord Saxton to push through our marriage no matter how I protest. If my father had his way, Lord Saxton would bear me off tomorrow! What if he decides not to wait?"

Robert had studied the earl for many a night now and had observed Saxton's disdain of Lord de Villon. "Saxton will wait because he wants your father to know who is in command of you. The more your father presses, the more Saxton will dig in his heels to resist." *That is what I would do*, Robert acknowledged to himself. He hated to admit he shared a common trait with the Earl of Saxton, but Robert recognized stubbornness when he saw it, for the fault had plagued him all his life.

He passed a reassuring arm around her shoulders. "Come, Mae, sit. I intend to have you well away from here before Monday—that is, if you do not change your mind after I tell you why I was running away that day we met on the riverbank." He tried to offset these foreboding words with a playful grin, but wondered if it looked as uncertain as he felt.

Fear held her stiff for another moment. Then curiosity won the struggle in her face and she finally sank back down with him on the log.

"You said it was because your father fell out of favor with his lord. Whatever your father did, you must not think that it will matter to me. It will not change my mind about loving you."

Her vehemence touched him, but Robert shook his head slightly. "Loving and marrying are two very different things. I should have told you, before things came to—this."

He kissed her, defiant and swift, then pulled his mouth away before the wave of passion could ensnare him again. Then he drew a ragged breath and fixed his gaze on the trees across from them. 'Twould be easier to tell her if he was not looking into her eyes. But he must begin in the right place.

"A year after King John succeeded his brother Richard, he went to tour his lands across the British Sea. My father told me the names of some of the places they saw—Maine, Touraine, Anjou, then on to the lands the king inherited from his mother, Aquitaine and Poitou." Robert paused. The French names still felt odd but exciting on his tongue as he remembered the flush of excitement on his father's face when he'd shared his stories of a foreign shore with his family. "The king took an army with him to make clear his power in the minds of his new vassals, for my father said there had been some question as to John's right to the throne. He had a nephew by a brother who stood between him and King Richard whom some thought should have been the rightful new king."

"Arthur of Brittany," Marguerite said. "I remember my grandfather rebuking some of his men-at-arms when he heard them repeating a rumor that King John had ordered his nephew murdered."

Rumors had run fast and far for years after the boy's death and Robert had heard them all in his wanderings. "Some say the king did it by his own hand while in a fit of drunken rage. I suppose we'll never know the truth. But that was years after the king first toured what my father called his Angevin domains. The baron of our manor, Lord Garoux Beckford, rode in the king's ranks on that journey and among the men Lord Garoux took with him was my father. My father went for the promise of silver. Good *English* silver, for our family's sake."

Robert still remembered sitting around their smoking hearth, enrapt in his father's tales. "For the most part the king paraded peaceably through his new domains, taking hostages of vassals he did not entirely trust, though my father said there were a few minor skirmishes, particularly among the unruly barons of Aquitaine and Poitou. In particular, the friends of the Count of La Marche protested when King John married the count's betrothed behind his back."

Marguerite had begun to play with Robert's fingers, perhaps hoping to draw his attention back to her. "Our Queen Isabella. Grandfather said it was because of that marriage that the king lost the duchy of Normandy to France. But I was only four when the king married. I know only what my grandfather told me of that scandal."

Robert laid his free hand over hers to quiet it, but kept his gaze on a hawthorn tree. "I was twelve. My father said the king left immediately after the wedding for the safety of one of his own castles, but his army was attacked in the rearguard by an ambush. The king had made sure the count himself was far absent at the time so he could not interfere with the marriage, but the count had friends who learned of it, they said, through one of King John's own men. These friends hoped to intercept the king and perhaps kidnap the new queen to restore her to her rightful husband-to-be. The king and queen escaped the attack unscathed, but some of the king's men, including one of his favorite archers, were killed."

A long recital, Robert knew. He could not blame Marguerite for her impatient shiftings. But the story was important for her to understand what followed.

"Some months later, my father returned safely to England with Lord

Garoux, along with the king and his new queen. Who the king wed and the uproar it caused among barons on both sides of the British Sea meant nothing to us. We cared only for the silver my father brought back and how it would free my family at last from Lord Garoux's oppression."

Her hand, which had been attempting to turn so that her palm lay against his, suddenly stilled. "Was Lord Garoux as brutal as my father?"

Robert shrugged. "I suppose he was no more harsh than any other lord. From things that Will's da sometimes let slip, I think things were worse between Lord Garoux and my father before my parents married, although I recall twice when my father so angered Lord Garoux that he—"

Robert stopped. He had been so caught up in his memories that he almost didn't registered Marguerite's shudder beside him. He saw how quickly she averted her face when he turned his head to look at her.

A horrifying question suddenly stole into his mind. "Mae—when you said your father's 'way of discipline' was the whip, did you mean that he thus disciplines *you?*"

"N-no."

Robert's blood ran cold at her stammer. He caught her by the chin and forced her gaze to meet his. "Marguerite."

"Not the whip. H-he mostly uses the force of his hand with me, although sometimes when he is especially angry, he takes his belt, the one with the brass studs, and lays it to my back."

Fury seared away the cold and raced churning through Robert's veins. To his surprise, he felt Marguerite try to shrink from his grasp.

"Oh! I should not have said that, should I? I do not mean to criticize my father. A man may chastise the women of his household however he pleases."

Robert stared into her frightened face, appalled. "Is that what you think I am thinking?"

"I-I have never seen your eyes blaze like that before. I-I did not mean—"

Robert groaned and dragged her into his arms. He knew from her stiffness that she feared his anger directed at her when he wanted nothing more at that moment than to deal her father a taste of his own "discipline." He held her taut body against him and stroked her back, trying not to think of bronze studs bruising her tender skin.

"Mae." He heard his voice thick with his struggle to ward off the horrific vision so that his anger might not dismay her again. "You must not be afraid of me. You must never be afraid of me. I would strike off my own hand before I would ever lay it to your hurt."

She slowly melted in his arms. "I know. Oh, Rob, I know."

No, he thought, *you do not. But I will spend the rest of my life proving that you can trust me.* Assuming, that was, that she still wanted him after— "I have not finished my story, love."

He eased her away from his chest, relieved to see some of the color returned to her cheeks. She gave him a determined smile, as if anxious to assure him of her confidence.

"You were telling me of the silver your father brought back. I remember one of my grandfather's men-at-arms, poor but of noble birth, who scrimped and saved for years and years until he had enough silver to buy his own armor and destrier. At his request my grandfather knighted him, then he went off to further make his fortune and we never saw him again. My grandfather was not a cruel lord, but if Lord Garoux was and used your father and your family badly, then I can understand how your father would wish you all to be free of him."

She did not understand. How could she? "Your grandfather's man-at-arms bought status, not freedom," Robert said. "Rich or poor, he could have left your grandfather's service at any time. No law could have stopped him. That was not the way with my family."

He watched a puzzled crease form between her brows. It was past time she knew why those hounds had been baying at his heels seven years ago.

"Less than a month after my father's return," Robert resumed, "I was at the village church, copying out the Life of Saint Edward the Confessor for Father Elias when Will came running in and blurted out that Lord Garoux was at our cottage with four of his knights. Lord Garoux had never sent anyone but his bailiff to us before, and certainly had never come himself. I ran off in the middle of the story where the Pope commuted King Edward's pilgrimage in return for rebuilding Saint Peter's Church at Westminster. The smear I left on the page is still there." The words of that preempted story still burned in his memory.

Marguerite's face smudged like the ink as Robert fell into that day again.

"I pelted home just in time to see my father throw a fistful of coins in Lord Garoux's face" —*One coin bounced off Lord Garoux's cheekbone and rolled along the hard beaten earth to disappear behind his mother's mending basket*— "and Lord Garoux's knights spring upon my father" —*His father's fist hit one on the jaw, his foot drove off another—* "and my mother drop her lute." *The instrument struck the ground hard on its left side, bounced slightly, then rolled strings downward into the dirt next to his brother's feet.* "Then Lord Garoux shouted, 'Traitor!' and 'Take him!'" *The sword blade laid across his father's throat had not silenced his father's cursings.*

"My mother tried to run after them as they dragged my father out, but the knights shoved her back" *—The flat of a gloved hand to her stomach hurled her against their rickety table, knocking it over nearly on top of his shrieking nine-year-old sister—* "and when I threw myself in front of them, they knocked me down, too. I banged my head on the doorframe" *—A crack of fire against his skull, a moment of blackness, then a sickening swirl of the cottage walls—* "and when my vision stopped swimming, my mother had fainted in Gilbert's arms and Lottie was sobbing and my father was gone. And two days later, Lord Garoux hanged my father on the gallows he built in the village square, for betraying the king to the Count of La Marche."

The sharp sound of a gasp jerked Robert back. Only then did he feel his drumming heartbeat and his clothes dampened against his body with sweat in the cold and his tongue dry from his swift spilling words. He rose to his feet on a wave of pain as fresh and deep as if it had all happened yesterday. He paced the glade, unable to sit any longer amidst the vivid flashes that leapt burning through his mind.

"The day of the hanging, my mother told me to stay with Father Elias, but I tried to slip away. I wanted to be with my father, to shout to him and all the village that I did not believe Lord Garoux's lies. But the old priest caught me as I was cutting across the fields. He was a small man and gentle, but he was a lion in his strength that day. He let me scream and flail at him— I even landed a bruise on his eye—but he would not let me get past him, until I knew by the sun that it was too late. I collapsed then in exhaustion and tears. Father Elias sat with me, there in the fields, with my head in his lap, stroking my hair while I wept as if I had been a babe and not an angry, heartbroken twelve-year-old boy."

Almost, for a moment, Robert thought he felt again the cloth of the priest's coarse habit against his cheek and the touch of his fingers against his hair, but 'twas only an eddy of air swirling past him. The nip of the breeze steadied him a little, but it could not sweep away his reluctance. He did not want to stop his pacings, he did not want to turn and look at Marguerite.

He rambled now, desperate to avoid her. "My mother died a year later.

Lottie and Gilbert and I—my sister and brother—came under the care of Will Locke's father, as much as he was able to help us with nine children of his own. As a traitor's family, Lord Garoux could have confiscated our fields, he could have thrown us off his manor to starve—it would have been his right, for all his own lord, the Earl of Gunthar, chastised him and the royal courts ultimately fined him for the 'irregularity' of the execution."

As if a fine, however large, could bring his father back. He heard a faint rustling, the breeze stirring in the barren trees. He pivoted on his heel and strode back across the bracken.

"We were reminded again and again of Lord Garoux's magnanimity in letting us keep our fields and our house. Our neighbors called him merciful. But I say still he did it out of shame."

So bitterly had Lord Garoux's hated face soared up in Robert's vision that he did not see Marguerite until her hands slapped against his chest. He gazed down into eyes so stormy that he knew she thought herself deceived by his former silence. Even marriage to the Earl of Saxton must seem more honorable to her than the love of a traitor's son.

12

Marguerite felt Robert's chest heaving beneath her hands and saw the pain in his eyes before he shut her out. His mask slid firmly in place, wiping away the emotions she had watched seesawing across his face: his pride and love when he spoke of his father following the king; his misery, so stark when he relived his father's crime and punishment that she had wept with the twelve-year-old boy while the man had paced across the glade, unseeing. But Marguerite's frustration had washed out everything else in the end, for she had called his name again and again, needing him to slow down, to pause, to explain all the contradictions that left her head whirling. But on and on he had talked, never hearing her—perhaps not wanting to?

In all her aching grief for him, too much still baffled her. He *would* listen, he *would* untangle all the puzzling threads—and he would *not* stare down at her as though she had become a stranger to him.

His chest dragged up again on a ragged-sounding breath, then he shifted his gaze over her head to the trees behind her. When he spoke, his tones were as aloof as his features. "I will find a way to escort you to the protection of your grandfather's chaplain. It will not be easy—we are a very long way from Northumberland—but I'll not send you back to your father, save for this one last night. Stay clear of his temper, meet me in the morning with your maid, if you can bring her—"

Marguerite stamped her foot, crunching the frozen bracken, and closed a fist on his threadbare cloak. "Look at me. No, *look at me.*" She did not need to be able to read his face to know what he was thinking. "You doubt me, don't you? How dare you, after I have given you my heart this day? Why should I care what your father did? You are not he. You could not have dealt so honorably all these days with me if you had one drop of dishonesty in your blood. If your father succumbed to the temptation of silver, whether for love of his family or simple greed, his choice does not reflect on the man his son became."

Robert's eyes flashed with the same fire that had dismayed her when she had told him of her father's studded belt. She released his cloak, thrust back a step by the force of his anger.

"My father did not betray the king for silver! That was Lord Garoux's lie! Lord Garoux had no right to die at peace in his bed after he murdered my father to cover his own crime."

Marguerite wrestled down her fear. Robert's hands were clenched tight at his sides, but they remained at his sides. Could she truly trust a man as enflamed as he not to strike? She drew her own somewhat shuddering breath but forced herself not to back further away. "Then you have not told me everything—have you?" He started to swing away from her, into his restless pacing again, but she caught his arm. "You owe me the rest."

His face remained turbulent, the mask torn away, but he stood still, only his muscles flexing beneath her hand.

"What does it matter?" he said. "No one believed me then and no one will believe me now. Lord Garoux carried off the proof years ago."

"What proof?"

"The coins. The ones my father threw at Lord Garoux were not the same ones my father showed us when he came home. The head on the coins was different and the name—I remember spelling it out for my father, showing off the Latin I had learned from Father Elias. *Iohannes Rex*. King John."

Marguerite studied Robert in confusion. He knew Latin and spoke in the refined accents of her class; he knew how to write, for he had been transcribing the Life of Saint Edward the Confessor for the priest; his father rode in the king's army, yet had been arrested in a simple cottage. *Our cottage*, Robert had called it, one that Lord Garoux never came to.

But Robert was still speaking of the silver. "When my father threw the coins, one of them fell behind my mother's mending basket. I found it afterwards. The face stamped on one side had changed, and the cross on the back was different, too. I knew then that someone had switched the silver, but I could not think who at first. My parents hid all their money in our bedroom under a clothing chest that only my father was strong enough to move. They did not think anyone knew of the hiding place, not even my brother and sister and I. And we had not, until . . ."

He trailed off, his gaze drifting over her head again.

"Until?" she prompted, when he stared overlong at the trees.

He paused before continuing. "It took me a few days to remember the morning I ran off early to play wooden swords with Kit before my studies began with Father Elias—"

This time she cut him off. "Who is Kit?" He had spoken the name before.

Her question returned his attention to her face. His eyes were still hot, but he seemed calmer now in his anger. "Lord Garoux's son, Christopher. He was my brother's age, but Gil was too wary to befriend anyone from the castle. I was not afraid of Kit, though. My father said it is man's law that makes men serfs, not God's, that in the beginning we were all born free and one day we would all be so again, so that I need not bow down to another if I did not wish to."

His chin lifted slightly. Did he expect her to challenge him? Odo had often said much the same, only without that reckless advice at the end. Her broadminded grandfather would not tolerate impertinence from his emancipated villeins, while any villein who dared to cross her father would have felt the crack of the whip across his back. Marguerite said nothing, waiting for Robert to confide more, sensing that the answers she sought lay very close now.

When she stood silent, he continued. "My mother chided my father for his words and said that I must show respect to Lord Garoux's household, but I did not wish to bow down to Kit, so I never did. I think that is what drew him to me. He would taunt my birth in one breath, then cajole me to play with him in the next. The day after my father returned to the manor, Lottie came by to watch Kit and me with the swords, chattering the way little sisters do. She said she had woken up in the night and seen Da moving the chest and she'd heard a jingling and thought he had been hiding bells for some toy he meant to carve for her. I said there were easier places to hide bells from her than underneath that heavy old chest and after we all stood guessing for awhile what else it might be, I remembered the silver and I said it. And Kit heard. He must have told his father, and that's how Lord Garoux knew where to find my father's silver and where to plant the French coins in its place."

Marguerite felt her breath catch as the threads finally began to untangle. With convictions such as Robert's father held, was it any surprise that his father would allow himself to fall in love with a villein girl? It explained everything. It spoke to his father's honor that he would wish Robert to be educated, and to the likelihood of Lord Garoux's pride that he must seek such education at the hands of the village priest. However Lord Garoux might disregard the two boys playing together, he must have objected to the son of one of his villein women being raised in the castle alongside Lord Christopher.

"By the time I recalled all of that, it was too late. My father was dead."

Robert's words, thick with self-reproach, jerked Marguerite out of her excitement in her discovery. Her hand, still on his arm, pressed the hard muscles beneath his sleeve.

"I ran up to the castle," Robert said, "and found Lord Garoux in the bailey, about to mount his horse for a hunt, just as though he had not murdered my father four-and-twenty hours before. I was furious. I accused him right there before a circle of his men-at-arms of switching the silver, and worse, that he had done it to conceal his own guilt. I knew it was true when his face went so red, but he slapped me and called me a hysterical boy. He said if I ever spoke such slander again I would regret it, despite my youth. My mother had followed me and pulled me away with the most grov-eling apologies to Lord Garoux. I cursed her for it all the way back to the cottage."

He shoved a sudden hand through his hair and closed his eyes. "I was only a boy. I did not understand how she feared for me until we reached home. Then she held me so tightly I could barely breathe and she wept and said that my father would not wish me to throw away all he had sacrificed for me and I must promise never to speak such suspicions again. I knew then that she knew it was true, too, but I promised her to make her stop crying. And I kept my word until she died."

Marguerite stroked his arm, wishing her touch might console him as his had comforted her when she had confessed her father's beatings.

"And then?" she asked. For she sensed there was more.

His eyes snapped open and he stepped around her, two paces towards the ash and hawthorn trees before stopping with his back to her. Her heart wrenched at his rejection. Did he still doubt her?

"Then I accused Lord Garoux again. Not to his face, but to everyone in the village. I knew word of it would reach him, and it did. But too much time had passed, no one believed me by then. I did not care, I kept saying it, even after Lord Garoux's patience broke and he tried twice to make me stop." Robert whirled on her suddenly. "Do *you* believe me? Or do you think, like everyone in my village, as even Father Elias did, that I blinded myself to the truth because I loved my father?"

She moved towards him and tentatively took his hand. Would he shake her off again? "I have believed every word you have ever told me. Why would I not believe you now?"

She thought relief flickered in his gaze, but so did uncertainty. "And is that enough?" he asked.

She remembered his earlier words. *Loving and marrying are two very different things.* They were not for her. She nodded her head vigorously. "Yes. And if you will kiss me again, I will prove it."

His fingers gripped hers and he pulled her a step closer, but he made no feint towards her lips.

"Mae, you must think ever so carefully. The world will be unforgiving enough if you choose to marry a son of villein parents. If it learns that you also married a traitor's son—"

"Parents?" She must have misheard him. She thought he had used the plural, but surely he only meant his mother? "You said your father rode with the king's army. He could not have done that if he were—"

"I never said he rode," Robert interrupted, looking surprised. "He served as a footsoldier, though 'tis true that Lord Garoux had given him a sword."

"A sword? But it is unlawful to arm villeins." Oh, none of this made sense again!

"Lord Garoux gave it to my father in spite of the law. Lord Garoux said a knight can be turned for silver or ambition, but he knew my father coveted freedom for his family above everything else and promised him enough silver to achieve it for my mother and brother and sister and himself if my father returned him safe to England."

Marguerite could not but notice the member of the family he left out. "What about you?"

"My father had already bought the promise of freedom for me years earlier so that I could enter the Church, though until my fourteenth year I was only to be allowed to study half-days with Father Elias and must work the other half in Lord Garoux's fields."

"But Rob, you are not a priest. If both your mother *and* father were villeins, then that means that *you*—" Marguerite did not realize she had drawn her hand away so that she could press her fingers to her temples in an attempt to control her bewildered thoughts until she saw Robert stiffen.

"No. I am a freeman. Do you think I would have dared to court you if I were not? That I would ask you to enter that cruel world with me? Even I am not as base as that."

"I do not think you base." She caught his hand quickly again. "It is only that I do not understand. Simply running away from his manor does not make a villein free." For that had surely been what Robert had been doing that day she met him on the riverbank between Lord Garoux's lands and Lord Stephen's. If she had not been so young and he so exciting and handsome, she must have realized that truth from the first.

"It does if he escapes capture by his lord for a year and day," Robert said. "Father Elias told me it is the law. I know he did not think I would try it, and I do not think I would have if Kit had not become such a devil after Lord Garoux died. I knew Kit would punish me for the things I'd said about his father, but—"

Robert's head snapped towards the trees. He let her go, pivoted abruptly on his heel and strode across the glade.

"What are you doing?" she said as he shoved back some hawthorn branches.

"Shhh. Stay here and be quiet." He hissed the warning, then disappeared.

Marguerite stared at the bouncing branches left behind by his swift exit. Where had he gone? Why had he left? She started to follow him, then froze. Footsteps crunched against twigs and dry leaves to the left of the glade, rounded behind her, circled back to her right. It was only Robert. It had to be Robert! Still, she would have exclaimed her relief aloud when he parted the hawthorn branches and returned, but for the finger he laid to his lips.

She waited until he was beside her once more, then whispered, "Was someone there?"

He shook his head, but she did not like the look of his frown. He spoke equally softly. "I thought I heard a sound, but perhaps it was only my imagination. I hope I was wrong. The woods out there are thick and easily hidden in, and the ground too hard frozen to leave tracks." An uneasy air still lay about him. "What about your groom? Are you sure you can trust him? Perhaps he followed you and bolted back to the castle to tell your father when he saw you with me."

"John would never disobey me. You would find him right where I left him if you went to look."

Oh, she should not have said that, for Robert promptly disappeared again, soundless as a cat this time. She sat down on the log and pulled anxiously at her knuckles while she waited for him to return. She tried to join in his worry about having been seen or overheard, but all she could think of were the revelations he had shared.

Had she been a fool to have woven such high dreams around him? How could it be true? A villein! But how could she have guessed? There was nothing villein-like about him, except perhaps, she confessed now, his coarse, thread-worn clothes. The rest—his refined manner of speech, an education even most men of her own station did not possess, the way he carried himself—

Oh! It came to her in a great flash. That was what had tricked her! Odo had raised her to know the men and women who worked her grandfather's lands. Most had been humble and grateful to her grandfather for his charter, a few had remained ill-tempered or surly, but Marguerite remembered all their faces: stolid, incurious, diffident even before her. Liberated they might have become in the eyes of the law, but a charter, however magnanimous, could not transform their core. Robert's fire, his vitality, his brash self-assurance—these traits never found spark in the breasts of men born to the servitude of the fields. These were the gifts to men born free. Or a man whose father had breathed freedom into him, even when the world told him he was bound.

Now what was she to do? She did not care how Robert was born. She loved him. But—

"Mae?" She did not know he was back until he lifted up her chin. He had returned as silently as he left. She knew from the relaxed set of his shoulders that he had found John just as she had said. She also knew Robert saw too much in her face. "Marguerite, if you are having second thoughts—"

"How can you ask me that?" She felt her mouth tremble. "How could you kiss me and not know I would go to the ends of the earth with you?"

He dropped to his knees and kissed her now, perhaps to test her words. She poured into it all the truth her heart could summon.

She looped her arms loosely about his neck as he rolled his forehead against hers.

"Then what's wrong?" he murmured.

"If I asked you to come to Winbourne Manor with me—what would you say?"

Silence while she held her eyes closed.

"What would your Odo say?" he asked.

She felt a leap of hope. "He would welcome you. He was born a villein, like you. He talks just like your father, so—"

"So he would embrace me with open arms, marry us, and turn all your grandfather's castles and lands into my keeping as your husband? Marguerite, even if he did not view me as a scheming fortune hunter and drub me off your lands—"

"He would not!"

"What do I know of managing manors and guarding fortresses? For that you need a husband like the Earl of Saxton."

Her arms tightened around him in panic. "I do not want Lord Saxton!"

Robert's hand stroked her hair. "And I will not give you to him. If you wish it, I will take you to your chaplain. He will find you a husband who can care for your grandfather's inheritance."

"I do not want another husband. I want you."

She pressed her face against his neck. She knew she should look at him, but she was afraid she had already brought hurt to his eyes again. If he read how it broke a little corner of her heart to fail her grandfather's trust— She feared he was right about Odo, and without Odo's consent to their marriage, her grandfather's lands would one day be forfeited to the crown. If Robert read her face now, she would lose him. He would drag her to Northumberland, turn her future over to Odo, and disappear from her life as quietly and completely as though they had never met.

"Then I must provide for you in my own way," he said, confirming the choice she knew lay before her. "It will not be the life you were reared to, but I will do my best to see you never lack for any necessary comfort. It is all I can offer you. If it is not enough—"

"I told you I will go with you." Her voice came gruff past the lump in her throat.

He brushed back her hair, tucking it caressingly behind her ear. "Think carefully, Mae. I will never be more than a minstrel. I will give up my wandering, but it may take time to find a steady position. I cannot hide you in some knight's or baron's household where you might be recognized by some passing guest who babbles it to your father. But some merchants hire musicians, too. I have been offered such a position a time or two, but I was not ready to tie myself down. I'd not have found you, if I had."

He pressed a kiss to the top of her head. It poured courage into her. Some merciful hand of fate had brought them back together when that meeting on the riverbank should have been their first and last encounter. Gratitude flooded into the little crack in her heart, and a sweet glow of certainty.

When he pushed her gently away to force her gaze to meet his, she no longer feared what he might see.

His midnight eyes bore into hers with an implacable honesty. "Marguerite, if you marry me, there will be no going back."

She thought of her grandfather and a cold, empty future fulfilling his hopes for her and his lands. To please a dead man, however loved—She spread her hand against Robert's cheek, warm and alive with promise.

"I will go to the ends of the earth with you," she repeated. "Or to a merchant's house or to a villein's hut."

He grinned that grin that flopped her heart over in her breast. "*Not* a villein's hut. I told you, I am a—"

"—freeman." She leaned forward and whispered against his mouth, "No going back," before she kissed him.

13

Robert did not like sending Marguerite back to Ashbury Castle, but he could see no other way. It was too late to elope with her today. Her father would be too fast to follow their tracks at this hour. Robert had plans to throw Lord de Villon and Saxton off their trail before it began, but for that he must return to the village for one more night.

He was torn between relief and regret that neither William nor Lucy were at the cottage when he reached the village. He did not wish to leave William with another quarrel, but he should like to have said goodbye. It had felt like a lark two years ago when he had snuck onto Beck Manor under cover of darkness to visit his brother and sister, lingering with them for a full five days right under Kit Beckford's nose and Kit never knowing. But risking his own discovery was one thing. Returning to Lyndeard Village with Marguerite as his wife and chancing her father to learn of it was a risk Robert could never take, even to see Will again.

Robert slung his lute on his back and his empty traveling bag over his shoulder, then sought out Simon Todd to take a very loud and public leave of him.

"Thank Will for his hospitality," Robert bade the young man, striking a merry air before a gaggle of giggling villein girls who were whispering and nudging one another as they stared at him and Simon. "'Twas a jolly Christmas—I do think the lasses of this village have the lightest feet I have met for dancing—but I have stayed overlong and the road calls to me again."

Simon returned Robert's clasp of his arm. "We'll miss ye an' yer music. And they'll miss yer dancin'." Simon nodded at the girls, who blushed and giggled the harder. "Are ye sure ye won't stay to thank Will yerself?"

"I'll not reach the next town before dark, if I do." Robert released Simon's arm, tossed a kiss from his fingertips to the girls, which made them fall into shrieks of "Don't go! Please stay!" and left them all with a grin and a wave. When Marguerite of Winbourne disappeared, suspicions would not easily fall on the minstrel who had so carefully avoided looking at her in her father's hall and who had left the village the day before she vanished.

Robert stole back to Lyndeard well after midnight, bringing with him a sack full of food, two plain woolen gowns he'd bought from a candlemaker's daughter, and a warm woolen cloak, also purchased in the town. That Lord de Villon's own coins, paid to Robert for his nightly music at the castle, would pay for his daughter's "abduction" did not escape Robert's irony, but he felt not the least twinge of guilt. The baron was an indefensible brute to beat his daughter, and then sell her to a fiend like Saxton. He deserved to be humiliated. *He deserves to be flogged.* Regrettably, Robert could not linger to witness the one or deal out the other.

Lucy's deep, steady breaths attested to the success of the feverfew, for nothing more than the faintest occasional sniffle appeared to disturb her sleep when Robert let himself into the bedroom. Robert knew just as surely from her husband's shallow breathing that William still lay awake. His friend said nothing, though, as Robert stripped down to his smock and stretched himself out on his own hard pallet with the thin blanket, reaching for a few hours of rest through his thrumming excitement. How soon would he dare to pause in their flight to seek out a priest and wed Marguerite? Tomorrow night, if they made good time. The next, if his instincts prodded him to place a longer, safer distance between them and a possible pursuit first. Then he would at last have leave to kiss her to his heart's content, and, he thought with a mischievous grin he was glad William could not see, he suspected it would take a great many kisses to content him.

Robert rolled over on his stomach and folded his arms beneath his head. He wished he could have afforded a better bridal gift for her than the spring green ribbon embroidered down the center with a garland of red roses that he had wheedled from the candlemaker's daughter for a penny and a song. The food, gowns and cloak had sorely depleted his assortment of coins.

They would need every penny left to tide them over until he found a music-loving merchant to take them in. Then he would exchange the rough woolen gowns he'd bought tonight for something finer, though never, he knew with a sigh that dulled his excitement just a little, anything as fine as the whisper-soft cendal she wore when she met him in the glade.

"Rob?" William's voice rumbled low against the darkness.

Robert considered feigning sleep, but after a moment he murmured back, "Aye?"

"Did ye do it?"

"Aye."

"And she—?"

Robert paused, his mind flashing through all the revelations and emotions of this day. "She comes with me with her eyes wide open."

Robert could almost see his friend's mouth tighten in the dark, but William said nothing more and neither did he. He stared into the night, planning . . . dreaming . . . until his lids at last grew heavy with the first gray haze of dawn.

A pale sunlight had replaced it when the stirring sounds woke him from his doze. Still sprawled on his stomach, he did not move while he listened to the sounds of William and Lucy dressing. William's deep murmurs brushed against Lucy's feminine tones, but Robert did not try to catch their words. Only when some sense told him that Lucy had left the room did he at last roll onto his back to catch the bleak eyes of the man who loomed above him. Robert sat up slowly. They stared at one another for what felt like an age.

"Be careful," William said at last, "and don't let Saxton catch ye. I pray, for yer sake, I never see Marguerite of Winbourne again."

William left the room before Robert could reply, and a few minutes later Robert heard him leave the cottage with Lucy.

Robert made one last check of the items in his traveling bag. The two gowns inside left no room for his scarlet tunic. He would roll that up and stuff it, as he had once before, inside his lute's case. As for the woolen cloak . . . that, too, he had bought for Marguerite, to replace her own. A minstrel's wife might own a mantle trimmed about the hood with common red squirrel fur, but never one lined from hem to hood with the blue and white variety called vair. They would sell her rich cloak along the way, but not, he vowed, before he had sold every last possession of his own, saving his lute and his sword, to sustain them if he needed to.

From the bottom of his bag he pulled out a book, one of three he had been carrying in a smaller bag when he had first met Marguerite. Father Elias had had the book bound for him after Robert finished transcribing it. Robert flipped to the page where his startled pen had smeared the ink right in the middle of a word when Will had run into the church with the news that Lord Garoux was at Robert's cottage. Father Elias had made him cross the letters out and write them again, resuming the sentence and the transcription a few days after his father's death. For a full two pages the words in the sentences slanted as though they would topple over, the pen strikes spidery-thin with Robert's distracted grief. He knew Father Elias had meant the labor for Robert's good and indeed, in time the words became firm again. Lines that rose and dipped through tears straightened once more as grief gradually steadied into a resolve he had never shared with the gentle priest.

All these years Robert had kept it as a reminder of that day and the hard days that had followed, but he set the book aside now, along with two more that completed his small collection. The bestiary with modest sketches in it that Father Elias had given him and a medley of tales about a sly fox named Reynard that he had bought for himself years after he had run away, with the wages from a particularly prosperous Christmas season. During less profitable times of the year, Robert had consoled himself through many a hungry night with the pleasure he found amidst these books' worn pages. Even with their scuffed bindings, the fading ink of the latter two, and the smudge in the middle of the first, he knew he could have bartered a high price for each of them. Nothing, not even the lure of a thick cloak or a good, hot meal on the bitterest of winter nights had ever tempted him to part with them before.

But now . . . He swallowed the lump that rose aching in his throat. He would sell these last of all, but if it took too long to find a permanent position he would give up these old friends, too, to keep Marguerite safe and warm.

He tucked the volumes back inside his bag, then stuffed the woolen cloak in after it. His coins were not gone yet, he reminded himself as he secured the strap. His spirits sprang afresh. Yesterday's minstrel had struck out for the north, which would surely be the first direction Lord de Villon would look for his daughter. Today's minstrel would take Marguerite west, aiming for Somerset. Perhaps they would even strike deep into Devonshire for a time. Eventually he hoped to place greater distance between them and her ancestral homeland, but fate would play its hand in their future, for a generous, music-loving merchant of any shire but this one Robert must find as soon as possible.

He packed his scarlet tunic and secured his lute case. Then for the first time since he'd arrived in Lyndeard he strapped his father's sword to his side, though he arranged his cloak to conceal it. One final glance around the Lockes' small bedroom satisfied him that he had forgotten nothing. With his lute again across his back and his traveling bag on his shoulder, he let himself out of the cottage.

Marguerite should be in the glade by now. The thought lent an eager bounce to his step. He could not risk anyone knowing he had returned during the night, so he made for a back lane that would allow him to leave the village unseen. He was just short of the southward bend in the road that led away from William's cottage when a frantic voice called out his name.

"Rob? Oh, Rob, I prayed ye had not yet left!"

Robert swiveled on his heel, dismayed to hear Lucy's voice. She sped down the rutted road so fast he feared she might take a tumble over the uneven ground. He reached out to catch her hands as she reached him.

"What is it, Lucy?" Alarm pitched hard in his chest. "Has something happened to Will?"

To his relief, she shook her head. "Will's helpin' to repair the bridge. He'd clout me if he knew I'd come for ye."

Robert smiled at the absurd thought of William laying any hand but a loving one to his wife.

"Rob, I know ye're leavin' today, but if someone don't come—They're makin' sport of her at the well. Jehane, Emma's and Dickon's mum—"

The little boy Marguerite had rescued from the melted snow puddle the day she had ridden into the village and back into Robert's life. He gave a curt nod that he recognized the name, then asked sharply, "Who's making sport of her, Lucy?"

He prayed she did not mean what he knew she did. But she would not be so desperate over some mocking but harmless words by another villager.

Lucy pulled her hands away so that she could wring them. "Lord de Villon an' his huntin' party. Oh, Rob, I know I shouldn't ask ye. I-I don't know what ye can do. But no one else will do anythin' at all, not even Will if he was here. He'd stand like all the rest, grim and hatin' them but not darin' to act or even speak." She twisted her fingers so hard Robert expected to hear them crack. "They—they might not mean harm. Sometimes Lord de Villon and his men only tease the women and ride on. It is usually Jarrott who rides down from Halham drunk and bored who—"

She broke off with a shudder that gave Robert too clear an understanding of what Jarrott did with the female villeins on the manor. Robert's mouth soured with anger. They were all alike these barons, every last brutish one.

When Lucy continued, it was with a catch of tears in her voice. "Only one time last spring Lord de Villon had a guest who took a fancy to Gillot and they carried her back with them to Ashbury Castle an'—an' no one dared try an' stop them. There are men in the square again today, villagers, but they are all too afraid of Lord de Villon's whip to help. An' Lord de Villon's companion—he has the same look in his eye as the man who took Gillot and shamed her." Tears ran freely down Lucy's face now. "Rob, I've never known anyone like ye, fearless enough to stare a lord in the eye. Will told me ye're leavin' today for good and I mustn't tell anyone that ye were here last night, only—only—"

Robert did not need to hear any more. He gave her a little push towards her cottage. "Go inside and stay there. I don't care what your duties are today, don't come out until Will comes home."

"What are ye goin' to do?"

"I don't know. Just do as I tell you."

Lucy ran to the cottage, only pausing to cast a frightened look over her shoulder at Robert before she slammed the door shut behind her.

He paused a moment to try to tamp down his temper. *Marguerite is waiting even now in the glade.* But Robert could not turn his back and let Jehane be ravished. He would find a way to extricate her, then meet Marguerite, albeit a little later than they'd agreed. Being seen still in the village might raise questions and complicate their escape, but he must deal with that potential obstacle later.

When Robert reached the square, he saw Lord de Villon still astride his horse, along with Sir Alan Hobart and the sullen, swarthy squire Robert had knocked down in Lord de Villon's shed. They all carried bows and spears as if they had, indeed, been on their way to an early morning hunt when they had detoured to the village. They must have sent the rest of their party on into the forest with the hounds while they pursued their business here.

Nay, their mischief. Lucy had been right about that, for there was no mistaking the unholy leer on the baron's face. Robert saw a fourth horse without a rider on the other side of the baron and turned towards the well. Blazes. He should have anticipated the blackguard Lucy spoke of. A little knot of women blocked his view of all but the Earl of Saxton's shoulders and head where he stood near the well's wall, his dark hair topped by an angled round cap with a curling feather.

The women turned at the scrunch of Robert's footstep. "Master Marcel," one of them murmured in surprise. "We thought ye'd gone."

Saxton's large body blocked sight of his prey, but Robert heard Jehane's frightened whimpers. He shot an angry glance around the square. A few old men lingered among the women, leaning on gnarled canes, but there were three sturdy younger men as well, one villein from Ashbury Manor, two who belonged to Halham. They watched Saxton just as Lucy had described, grim and hating, but subdued.

"Cowards," Robert muttered.

"Ye mustn't say so, sir," the woman who had greeted him said defensively. Was one of the men hers? "There's nothin' they can do. Interferin' would only land them in the stocks, or worse."

Worse, indeed, Robert thought with a searing throb of memory. He had fought and lost his own battles. A villein could never win against his lord. But a free man had advantages a villein never would. Robert slipped his bag from his shoulder, leaned his lute case against it, then stepped firmly through the women.

He could see clearly now as Saxton struck the well-cup from Jehane's trembling hands.

"Bah. That is not the draught I would slake my thirst on." Jehane tried to shrink back against the rim of the well, but Saxton's arms lashed around her, dragging her against his chest so that her slender body nearly vanished in the folds of his voluminous cloak.

"Let her go!" Robert's shout rang through the suffocating blanket of fear that held the women and men alike as helpless spectators to Saxton's intent.

Saxton turned, but one arm remained defiantly clamped around Jehane's waist. Robert saw the tears on her ashen cheeks, her terror-darkened eyes.

"Well, well," Saxton drawled, "if it isn't our charming minstrel. Where's your lute, boy?"

"I've exchanged it for this." Robert pushed back his cloak, exposing the hilt of his sword with his hand resting on it.

Saxton gave a crack of laughter. "The minstrel would have us think he knows how to handle so fine a weapon," he tossed at the men still on horseback. "Shall I test him, do you think?"

The surly squire snapped out, "Go back to your music, rascal, before my master deals you a lesson for your insolence."

Robert displayed his scorn for the squire by not so much as flicking him a glance. *Marguerite is waiting*, he reminded himself. Bad enough that half the village had seen him again. He had not time to engage in an altercation with these men if he could find another way.

He eased his hand from his sword hilt, hoping to diminish the tension. "I have asked you to let the girl go, sir," he said to Saxton with rigid politeness. "Be good enough to do so and there need be no trouble."

Lord de Villon gave a crack of mirth. "What, Saxton, shall you obey this fellow? Minstrels are said to be formidable opponents, after all."

Saxton laughed along with the baron, Sir Alan and the squire, but it was the sight of Saxton's hand boldly fingering the lock of brown hair that lay along Jehane's throat that made the scene blur slightly before Robert's vision. *You think you are immune to chastisement because you deal with villeins and they are, after all, mere property to be used as their masters see fit. Well, my Lord Saxton, let us see.*

Robert pulled his sword free. "Your last warning, my lord. Let her go."

The laughter abruptly ceased. Saxton appeared to study Robert's blade for a moment, the early morning sun glinting off its well-honed edges. Saxton gave a shrug and his arm dropped from around Jehane.

Slightly surprised to have won his point so easily, Robert acknowledged Saxton's gesture with a curt nod. "My thanks." He re-sheathed his sword, glancing down at his scabbard as he did so.

"Rob, look out!"

Startled by Lucy's cry—had she followed him?—Robert glanced up to see a blur of velvet and fur and steel flying at him. He jerked his sword free again and sprang back, barely gaining space enough to block Saxton's blow. The force of it drove Robert down on one knee. If he had ever wondered whether wine-softened flesh or muscle lay behind Saxton's girth, he felt the answer now in the way his blade shuddered beneath Saxton's bullish force.

Robert saw the triumphant flash in Saxton's hazel eyes before Saxton bent forward and murmured in his ear, "Nick was right, you are quite the gallant. He said the wench might draw you out. As though I would ever soil myself with a filthy villein."

The slur of Jehane was enough to make Robert's vision sear with rage again. Saxton's sudden shove, intended to knock Robert on his back, only grazed along the edge of his sword as Robert whipped his blade and body about in a semi-circle. He disengaged with an agility that appeared to take Saxton by surprise. Saxton's sword jabbed through empty air as Robert found his feet and sprang out of reach.

Saxton recovered and whirled after his prey. Robert met him prepared this time. His sword shrieked against Saxton's in a flurry of thrusts and counter-thrusts. Anger beat hard through Robert's veins as he fought, but he strained through it for his father's voice. The lessons his father had taught him in their fields beneath the light of the moon guided Robert as surely now as they had through every game of wooden swords he had played with Kit and every skirmish with steel blades he had fought and won since leaving Beck Manor.

This is the way you parry, Robin. And this is the way you thrust—

Robert held at bay the swift defeat that Saxton's glower suggested he had expected to win. But Robert had no better success in overwhelming Saxton. Back and forth they drove one another across the square. Once, in a space through their movements, Robert caught sight of Lucy, her eyes wide with horror and guilt as she comforted a still frightened Jehane.

Robert made a savage thrust of retaliation for the villein girl's terror, then felt the reverberating shock up his arm as Saxton deflected a jab that struck very near his throat. From Saxton's violent curse and the ferocious anger that flared in his eyes, Robert guessed he had come as close as anyone ever had to spearing away Saxton's life. Their swords clashed together again, sparks exploding from their rasping metal. A vicious stab sought to slip beneath Robert's guard, but Robert knocked the lethal point aside and again leapt nimbly out of reach.

The reprieve lasted less than a moment before Saxton closed with him again. The ringing of their blades grew so deafening that Robert almost did not hear Saxton's hiss.

"Did you really think I would let you besmirch my wife-to-be with your brutish lust? You would not even know how to enjoy a woman of her birth."

It took Robert's mind an instant to shift from the battle to yesterday's rustling at the glade. Both blades stilled for a pair of breaths. *Marguerite . . .*

"You followed her?" Robert said.

Saxton's eyes gleamed as deadly as his steel. "No. My squire followed you."

Robert glanced at the youth over Saxton's shoulder, his sullen face smug with revenge.

The distraction nearly proved Robert's undoing. He heard the whiz of Saxton's blade one heartbeat before he ducked beneath its slicing edge so narrowly a lock of Robert's raven hair landed in the dirt beside his right boot.

It was not the escape that made his blood pound afresh. *Saxton knew. And if Robert did not make it to the glade before he did—*

Robert barreled his body into Saxton's while the earl was still half-turned with the strike that had sailed over Robert's head. Their shoulders collided and staggered Saxton backwards, knocking off his cap with the curling feather. Robert had hoped to throw him completely off balance, but Saxton steadied himself with a dexterous shuffling of his feet. It did not matter. Robert needed only that moment of confusion to seize the advantage. He did not give Saxton time to fully regain his equilibrium, but rained down blows on the earl's blade. Each impact drove Saxton back another step. If Robert could knock Saxton down, wound him or even better, knock him out, anything to gain time to reach Marguerite first—

Robert saw sweat sheen on Saxton's frustrated face, saw his broad chest heave as he at last began to grow winded, heard Saxton's staccato curses against the ringing of steel on steel. Then Saxton caught and held the edge of Robert's blade with his. The swords vibrated, suspended in the air between them. Saxton shifted his feet until they planted against the ground like two immovable oaks. Robert saw murder in his eyes and tried to disengage, but Saxton moved with a startling speed. He forced Robert's sword down, then up in an arc that drove Robert's sword point above his head. Saxton whipped his blade free and sliced it towards Robert's stomach.

Robert avoided being gutted with a lightning spring backward. He fended off a second strike, bounced back another step, parried, and leapt again. He landed on a spike of pain. Fire shot through his ankle. He pitched sideways, hurled off balance by the pothole his foot had slipped into in the storm-rutted square. He hit the ground hard. A loosened stone caught his wrist on a jagged edge, jarring his hand open so that his sword spun free. Teeth gritted, he tried to scramble back up, but Saxton stood over him, nostrils flaring as he shortened his blade for a thrust straight through Robert's heart.

Robert hurled himself into a desperate roll in the dirt, but the blade still found a home. Steel, chill and fiery all at once, slid into Robert's shoulder with ridiculous ease. A groan burst from his lips. He heard women screaming and braced himself through the pain for a second, lethal strike.

A shriek, this one not caused by steel, tore the air. Lucy threw herself across Robert's chest. "No!" she pled. "Please no!"

Saxton checked the blow that came near to impaling them both. Killing an impudent minstrel was one thing, Robert thought sardonically through the spreading flame in his shoulder. Destroying another man's property without permission—for that's surely how he viewed the weeping Lucy—apparently was another matter.

"Well done, my lord," Lord de Villon's voice rang out his approval of the battle's ending. "If the fellow doesn't bleed to death, he'll wear that scar for life. I'll warrant he'll not be so quick to challenge his betters again."

Saxton rebalanced his weight, then stood calmly wiping Robert's blood from his sword. Lord de Villon appeared at Saxton's shoulder, dragging a sobbing, shrinking Jehane.

Saxton's reply droned through the buzzing hum rising up in Robert's ears. "I appreciate your attempt to divert my boredom, my lord, and this little scuffle was amusing, but as for that —" Robert's blurring vision caught the jerk of Saxton's head towards Jehane "—I prefer my wenches less reeking. Tomorrow I return to Westminster. Have your daughter ready."

"No—" The word croaked in Robert's throat. Marguerite . . . waiting for him in the glade—He had to reach her . . . had to protect her . . .

Lucy eased herself away as Saxton resheathed his sword. The reddish haze of Robert's vision was fast going gray, but he struggled to shove himself up.

"No, Rob, ye mustn't," Lucy's frantic voice sounded in his ear.

He felt Lucy's hands on his shoulders, trying to hold him still as he sought to make his leaden limbs defy her. "Let me go, Lucy," he panted.

"Rob, please."

He heard the sob in her voice just before her hand slipped against him and pressed into his wound. Fire exploded through his shoulder, then blackness collapsed all around him.

14

He watched her watching the child. The high-pitched giggles rose from the floor of the hall to the gallery where she stood looking down, as slender as the day they had wed. Almost forty years later, an air of gentle regality had replaced the awkward self-doubt that had once reigned in her heart. He liked to think he'd had some hand in shaping the self-confident woman she had become. He knew he was a better man for having loved her. Even today, most would not call her beautiful. Her chin remained too sharp, her little nose too imperious, her mouth a touch too wide, but she had never ceased being lovely to him. The soft shimmer of her pale hair bore a few silver threads now. He had lost the last dappling of brown in his grey hair years ago. Now he ached at night deep in his bones, and sometimes a weariness dogged him that he would never confess to her. They had shared more joys than sorrows, but the heartaches they had passed through had been the sort that never fully healed, and this last one still struck deep.

As always, she wore the loss less stoically than he. He saw her smile at the boyish shriek and the mother's teasing laughter, but when he moved to stand beside her and she glanced up at him, he recognized the sadness he had seen too many times in his life lurking at the back of her silvery gaze.

"Did you give him your answer?" she asked.

"Not yet," he said. "I did not wish him intruding on them"—he nodded to the mother and son tossing a painted ball between them—"so I took Sir Ingram to my library and left him there to daunt him with a roomful of books he has no ability to read." Her chuckle pleased him. She knew, as he did, how men who ordinarily scorned learning as the labor of clerks found themselves unexpectedly intimidated when thrust into the presence of her husband's obsessive collection of leather bound tomes. He added, "I would not give him my decision without counseling first with you."

A touch of mischief stole into her smile. "Which means you do not wish to go. You never need my counsel to know your own mind, only when you wish to excuse yourself from some unpleasantry."

"And on my oath, I can think of nothing more unpleasant than returning to King John's court. I do not think you nearly well enough for a trip to Westminster."

"You could go without me."

"As frail as you've grown? What sort of unfeeling brute do you think you married?"

She *hrumphed* through her little nose. "I am perfectly hale, as I was the day you blamed your need to retire from his council on my 'fragility.' *You* were the one who collapsed three days after we returned home with your hand clutching your heart. You know Nigel Physician said you must hereafter lead a quiet life. Tell *that* to the king's messenger and send him back to the devil's court."

Her face, only lightly touched with the lines of age, paled during her own bantering retort. He saw the fear that stole in beside the sadness in her eyes.

"Nigel Physician, as I have told you before, is a fool," he said. "'Twas little more than an irksome twinge."

"That laid you out in your bed."

"For a day. Very well, two. Was I not back on my feet in time to see Peter off on his crusade? Our son did not seem to think me at death's door when he saw me."

"Because he was a heedless, fourteen-year-old boy and his head was filled with dreams of glory rather than the father he had not seen in more than a year."

"Tosh. I am as strong today as I was the day we met." He took her hand and kissed it. "Never fret, my dear. That little lording below needs a father, and I am all he has now. I have every intention of raising him to become a fine young knight, and husbanding *you* for a good long while yet."

He squeezed her hand to reassure her of his strength, even as he prayed his words might be true. He had outlived most of his contemporaries by over twenty years.

He distracted her by pointing to the boy below them as he ran, chasing the ball through a shaft of sunshine slanting through a window. "See how his hair shimmers in the light? Pale gold, just like Harry's." He brushed the back of his fingers against the silvering hair at her brow. "Just like yours."

'Twas not a new observation, and she laughed, as she always did at the absurdity the compliment was now.

"His mother's hair is golden, too," she reminded him, nodding at the young woman who caught up the boy and his ball and swung them around in her arms.

He watched the boy wiggle free of his mother's embrace and run off again with trill of high-pitched giggles. "I think he has his father's mischief, though. He may need a firmer hand than mine to tame it."

He spoke the hint gently. He had been a sometimes stern parent to the two sons Heaven had spared out the miscarriages and stillbirths, determined to rear them to be as independent and disciplined as his own father had reared him to be. But Peter and Harry were both gone now, one cut off in his youth in a distant land, the other in young manhood too close to home. Harry, at least, had left him an heir. He did not truly doubt his ability to raise the little scamp below into a man he could be proud of . . . provided it pleased Heaven to grant him another score of years. Nay, that asked too much of Heaven's forbearance. He knew it, and she did, too.

"Gerald Faintree has asked to see her," she confessed.

"Ah. Faintree is a good man. I would not object to—"

"But she will not see him."

"Ah," he said again. Their daughter-in-law grieved too much for her young husband. Two years. It was time she opened her heart anew. But they could neither of them bear to press her.

She let go of his hand and turned away from the scene below. She swept along the gallery with the quiet grace she had always possessed yet never discerned in herself.

"John does not like to be kept waiting," she reminded him. "What shall you tell his messenger?"

He fell into step beside her. "Unless you can provide me with an imperative reason to stay by, say, developing a sudden weakness of the lungs—"

She drew a long, deep breath and exhaled just as efficiently.

"—or a few delirious shakes—"

She extended a thin but very steady hand.

"—or a sudden, undoubtedly dangerous chill that requires me, as your devoted husband, to remain by your side in a state of sleepless agitation for your safety—"

That won a laugh as she paused to lay his palm against her cool cheek.

He sighed. "Then I have no choice but to go. I swore King Henry an oath."

She sobered. "Even though John betrayed his own father? Even though he squandered all that Henry left him out of lust for that strumpet, Isabella?"

"My dear! She is our queen." His lips twitched, amused by her spirit despite his rebuke.

She resumed her sweep towards the staircase. "You said you knew her before her marriage. You told me she loved the Count of La Marche, yet she forsook him for fat John's crown."

"John was not fat fourteen years ago," he murmured over a smothered breath of laughter.

"I have eyes of my own," she said. "I was waiting for you at Westminster Palace when you returned with the king and his new bride. I saw how she looked at him then, calculating, scheming, smug with ambition, but never with love. I hear it is still so between them. Yes, my dear, I still have my own friends at court. Why must you return to that sordid den of treachery and wantonness?"

"I have told you why."

This time the sigh was hers. "Then as your devoted wife, I shall, of course, go with you."

He drew her hand into the crook of his arm. "You needn't. I had a letter from William Marshal after Christmas. He says the king has been seething since last summer when the barons humiliated him by refusing to obey his summons to follow him to Poitou. John, Marshal writes, is like a vengeful dog, determined to tear his former lands out of the grasping hand of the King of France like a hound all a-growl to recover a stolen bone. Now that John has finally brought his barons to heel—or at least persuaded most of them to send some of their knights—I'll warrant we'll be setting sail within a fortnight. You may as well stay here and spare yourself the weariness of a ride up to Westminster and back."

"You'll not try to counsel the king to change his mind?"

He heard the anxiety in her voice. He answered truthfully. "Aye, I'll try, but rest you easy. I'll not be so blunt as to risk banishment again."

"As though I cared for that! I'd be content if neither of us ever set foot in Westminster Palace again. It is your head I worry for."

"And I mean to take good care of it. I have a grandson to raise and a wife to comfort still. I'll not let myself be provoked by Saxton again."

They had reached the great stone stairway that wound down from the gallery to the hall. She paused and turned towards him, saying a little wistfully, "I wish I might come with you to Poitou. I have not seen my brother since Peter was born."

"We are going to war, my dear. This is no time for a family gathering. If things end as the king hopes, I will take you to visit your brother in the summer. If the campaign fails—well, let us hope it does not fail." For if France won Poitou and Aquitaine, as it had won Normandy, England would be cut off from the last of its Angevin Empire, and she from the family of her birth.

She nodded her understanding of the political situation. "Well, I shall come with you to Westminster, at least, to be sure the Earl of Saxton does not humiliate you again."

Her silvery eyes flashed as she said it. A pity she could not stand in the king's council, for he was quite sure she would face down the devious Earl of Saxton more stoutly than the proud barons who groveled and fawned to win his favor. Only William Marshal, the Earl of Pembroke, held nearly equal power in the kingdom with Saxton. *And he only maintains it by employing a more diplomatic tongue than I did.*

"Very well, if you insist upon it," he said, "though I will likely have little time to spend with you once we arrive at the palace. I anticipate John will be as greedy of my attention as he always is. Tell Caradoc to make himself ready to accompany us. His companionship will cheer you, while I am—"

"Caradoc left us early this morning, before the king's messenger arrived."

He frowned. "Left us? To visit the town, I trust, to buy more trinkets to send back to his sister in Wales?"

He spoke it as though saying it would make it so, but he knew the true answer from her face before she replied.

"No, to marry the girl with the copper curls he has been praising to us for weeks. She is a cordwainer's daughter, which you would know if you had lent his prattle half an ear instead of glaring him into silence every time he sighed her name. He has been terrified of your displeasure, but I gave him my blessing and told him he must do as his heart bids him. So off he went this morning—"

"And back he will come tonight," he broke in curtly. "Caradoc may bring his new wife with him. I will send someone to see to it. A cordwainer's daughter! She will be elated for a chance to see London and the king's court at your side."

"Well," she said with a little smile, "she might if they were not most probably on their way to Wales by now. Caradoc wishes her to meet his parents, of course. Don't frown so. You know how lonely Caradoc has been since he left his home, or you would if you ever listened to a word he said. It was kind of William Marshal to send him to us after Harry died, but Caradoc was never fully happy to be in England until he met Adelin—yes, that is her name. So I gave him enough silver to pay his way back to Wales with his bride and told him to make haste, for I knew how you would be when I told you."

He muttered a curse upon the Welsh minstrel's head. A woman. It was always a woman who lured them away, from the first ramshackle troubadour he had engaged to assuage his wife's grief after their first stillborn child through the half-dozen minstrels who had replaced him, and now the dreamy-eyed, golden-voiced Caradoc. Other men kept their minstrels for decades, many raised families and died in service to their lords. What curst stroke of fortune had found it amusing to strike each of his with a love malady that inevitably prompted them, instead of growing more settled, to run off pell-mell for this reason or that with his new wife in tow, compelling him to fill the position at Lamhurst Castle all over again?

Music had proved the balm that raised his own wife from her despondency after each miscarriage and the two stillbirths. Harry had sustained her through Peter's loss, and their daughter-in-law and grandson through Harry's. But always he had seen how the music had borne her up beneath it all, bringing light again to her eyes, refreshing her perspective . . . To bear her off now to "the devil's court", as she had called it, without Caradoc's sustaining tunes—

"Perhaps you should stay here with Evelyn and Alain," he said. "That boy is handful enough for one woman. Evelyn would be grateful, I know, for your wisdom and support."

He knew she read his mind. She stretched on her toes and set a kiss to his cheek. "I will be more at peace with you. Besides, there is sure to be a profusion of minstrels in so great a town as London. I will choose one for myself to return with me to Lamhurst when you have sailed away with the king."

He could not deny his selfish reluctance to be parted from her a moment sooner than his duty to the king required. She was right. They would have their pick of minstrels in London and this time, he would be very sure to select one not only with a silver voice, but with a silver head of hair, preferably already well tethered to an equally silver-haired wife, both of whom would be happy to live out the remainder of their lives in service to the Earl and Countess of Gunthar.

<h1 style="text-align:center">15</h1>

Westminster Palace
Westminster, England
January 1214

obert must think she had betrayed him.

But what else could I have done?

"That riddler told the drollest puzzles at dinner yesterday, do you not think?"

Lady Annys de Tracey's chatter sounded like a voice speaking through a mouthful of wool, so muffled did it hum beneath the thoughts that pounded in Marguerite's head. Marguerite tried and failed to focus on her new friend's words. She knew how curiously the queen's ladies-in-waiting watched her as the newest member of their circle. She tried to force herself to set a stitch in the embroidery cloth that had fallen limp in her lap, but her fingers felt as weak as milk.

I waited for you all day—

"'Water become bone,'" Annys rattled on. She tossed a cinnamon-brown curl over her shoulder before resuming her own stitching. "That one was easy. Even I guessed he meant 'ice.'"

—until twilight filtered through the trees and I dared not stay any longer. I knew you were only delayed, as I was over Christmas, and that you would expect me to come again to the glade on the morrow, just as I had found you waiting for me—

"But it was absurd for us all to cry 'bell' for the last one. As soon as the riddler said, 'They ring me, they ring me,' we should have known it was a trap."

But when I got back to the castle, Father said the earl had changed his mind and was taking me to Westminster in the morning. I said I would not go.

In truth, Marguerite had shouted it, and had won for her defiance a blow that had hurled her against one of the tapestried walls. But Robert need not know that. The bruise that lingered beneath her eye would be faded by the time she saw him again. She wished she could speak all her worries aloud, as she sometimes talked to her grandfather beside the hearth in her chamber at home, but with Annys chattering away at her side, Marguerite dared not even move her lips. She flung her thoughts at Robert, nonetheless, as though he might somehow hear her across the space that separated them.

You will come after me, won't you? They gave me no choice. Mama stayed all night with me, readying my wardrobe. She and Father did not leave me alone for so much as a moment until I rode through the gates the next morning at the earl's side. Father would have bound me to the saddle had I tried to resist. You were my only escape . . . But I know you will come!

"'I awake and clang loudly when my master gives me a shake. I chime in the morning when his hand takes me up and tinkle a sweet night song ere he blows out the candle.' Sir Warin was so very keen-witted to guess that he meant a key on a ring!"

Marguerite dragged up a smile for the young girl who chirped away beside her, even as she reluctantly confessed to herself that her confidence in Robert had begun to wobble just a bit. She had been at Westminster for a fortnight and no word from Robert had yet come. Of course, he could not scale the royal walls as he had once scaled the walls to her bedchamber. But he knew how to write. He could bribe a servant to smuggle her a message, or someone to unobtrusively approach her when she rode into the City of London with Annys. But the servants she passed in the galleries walked by her in silence and when Annys bore her off to help her select some new ribbons or slippers or gloves for her wardrobe, no one ever pushed himself through the crowds that thronged London to slip a scribbled piece of parchment into Marguerite's hand.

There was still time. He might have tried a dozen ways to contact her and have merely met thus far with failure. He would try again. She knew he would try again! Unless . . .

Unless you felt betrayed that I left for Westminster without a word. Perhaps—perhaps I should have sent Eva to leave you a note in the glade.

But no, Mama had kept Eva occupied with a dozen tasks to ready Marguerite for the journey. The servant had no more chance to slip away from the castle than Marguerite had. What must Robert have thought when he came to an empty glade? Would he remember more than Marguerite's assertions of love at their last meeting?

Oh, why did I ever tell you about Odo and my inheritance? I know it made you doubt me. I know you feared that I might love my grandfather more than I loved you. If you waited for me all day as I waited for you, only to learn that I had gone off with Saxton after all—! Is that why you have not come? Is that—is that why you will not come?

"Marguerite." Annys's prattling voice hissed a sudden warning. "They are staring at you again. Dry your eyes."

Marguerite realized a teardrop had splashed onto her embroidery. She blinked rapidly, trying to squeeze away the moisture in her eyes, but a surge of panic that she had guessed the true reason for Robert's absence threatened to choke her.

"Has Lord Saxton done something to upset you again?" Annys murmured. "He is a beast! But do not give these cats the satisfaction of seeing you cry."

Marguerite nodded. Queen Isabella's sophisticated circle found too much amusement in the Earl of Saxton's inexperienced betrothed. Only Annys, two years younger than Marguerite, had made any real effort to befriend her, and although Marguerite was grateful, she had also caught a longing exchange of glances between Annys and Marguerite's cousin, Richard, and guessed Annys's motivations were not entirely unselfish.

As soon as Lord Saxton had introduced her to the king and queen as his affianced bride, Marguerite realized he had finally found a way to force her hand. Welcomed by the king himself, with the queen and the entire royal court looking on, Marguerite had not had the courage to protest Saxton's lie and declare that she had never spoken the betrothal vows. Saxton must have known that she would not, for she had seen his smile of triumph as she had curtsied low before King John and Queen Isabella.

Saxton had paid little enough attention to Marguerite since, for Lady Jane was also at court, but on the few occasions he spoke to her Marguerite acknowledged him with coldness. That, too, the entire court must have seen, for Marguerite had become aware that the women spoke slyly behind their hands when she walked past and the men watched her with sardonic grins.

Annys, like all the others, must have seen Marguerite's red-rimmed eyes, for she had wept for Robert every night since she had come to Westminster. She sensed that Annys hoped to win Marguerite's confidence with her sympathy, perhaps so as to confide her own hopeless feelings for Richard. Marguerite had overheard Lady de Tracey, Annys's mother, reciting the names of prospective husbands for her daughter to another matron, and Richard's name had been woefully wanting from her list, for Richard was only a younger son with little hope of advancement beyond what favor he might gain from Sir Edward Keynes, the knight he served as squire.

But though Marguerite longed to pour her heart out to someone, she did not know Annys nearly well enough to trust her yet. So she murmured to the girl's concern, "It is merely that I am still a bit overwhelmed. I have never sat in a royal court before."

"My parents brought me here last fall," Annys said softly. "They wish me to wed a rich husband, because I have four sisters who will need help with dowries. Mama says I am pretty enough to catch such a man's eye, and well enough dowered as the eldest born daughter. But . . ." She trailed off with a sigh, waited, hopefully, Marguerite thought, for Marguerite to make a comment, and when she did not, Annys set another stitch in her embroidery cloth.

Last fall. That must have been when Annys had met Richard. Marguerite wished she knew of a way to help them be together, but she did not. She smothered a sigh of her own and returned to her needlework.

Marguerite had finished outlining one flower and started on another when the bubble of gossiping feminine voices all around them suddenly stilled. Marguerite knew the reason before she even looked up. This fortnight had taught her how all the ladies fell silent when the queen rose restless from her gilded, cushioned chair and swept abruptly across the solar to stare broodingly out a window.

Marguerite had thought Jane Lovell the most beautiful woman she had ever seen until she laid eyes on Isabella of Angoulême. At six-and-twenty, the queen eclipsed every other lady of the court, even the exquisite redhead who today, as always, sat at her right hand. The queen dazzled Marguerite like an exotic jewel. Her almond-shaped eyes glistened more brilliantly than the sapphires and diamonds woven into the glossy golden braid that wound around her head. Her brows slanted over the striking eyes, flying away at the corners like one might expect to find on some strange fairy creature. Her high-boned cheeks shone finer than ivory, dusted with a faint glow of pink in their hollows.

"I once overheard Papa say that it was pure lust that drove the king to steal her," Annys whispered, as the murmurs of the other women slowly resumed around them.

With that passionate pout of the queen's full lower lip and the delicious curves of her crimson clad body, Marguerite could well believe it. She had seen the way the king gazed at his wife—with the same raw hunger that Lord Saxton gazed at Lady Lovell.

"Some say she bewitched the king." Marguerite repeated the cruel innuendos that flew behind the queen's back.

"Papa said a man like John needs no enchantment when a woman like Isabella is dangled before him," Annys murmured. Her color rose as they discussed a subject young girls their age were supposed to be ignorant of, even as Annys's eyes gleamed at sharing the wicked knowledge. "Papa was with the king in Angoulême when King John stole her away from the Count of La Marche. There have been all sorts of trouble since, and the king has lost nearly all of his father's ancestral homelands to France, merely because he could not control his passions. And now he goes to fight yet another war."

Richard's master, Sir Edward Keynes, and Annys's father, Lord Brian de Tracey, had already answered the royal summons. As soon as he arranged for the security of his castles in his absence, Marguerite's father would come, too.

Queen Isabella stood with one petite white hand resting on the window's sill, but her alluring face revealed nothing of her thoughts. What must it be like, Marguerite wondered, to have an entire kingdom rocked for one's sake? In the fortnight since she had been at court, other malignant gossip had come to her ears, as well, for the queen's circle of ladies was never happy save when slyly shredding another woman's reputation, even the queen's herself.

Isabella thought her beauty had ensnared the king's heart, but John is not a man to love. That he still burns for her all these years later, is clear. But if she thought either love or lust would bind him to her alone, she was sadly mistaken. John openly shames her with his mistresses. She has no choice but hold herself proudly, and pretend that she does not see.

Some of these spiteful words had been loudly whispered with pointed glances in Marguerite's direction, making it impossible to ignore the comparison they clearly laid between Marguerite's betrothal and the king's marriage.

As if he'd discerned Marguerite's very thoughts, a page boy entered the chamber wearing the royal colors. The boy dropped to one knee in the rushes before the queen and reverently kissed the hand Isabella extended to him.

"Your grace, the Earl of Saxton requests the company of Lady Jane. If you could spare her . . . ?"

"But of course," Isabella responded in her prettily accented voice.

Marguerite wished she could sink clear through the floor when the queen slanted her a look of pity as the redhead rose with a catlike smile and followed the boy out. At least Lady Jane spared Marguerite the humiliation of looking at her before she swept through the doorway. The other women were less tactful. They mirrored the queen's mortifying "sympathy," each staring at Marguerite before they bent their heads close to one another's and twittered behind their hands.

"Do not let them see your chagrin," Annys whispered. "Lord Saxton is callous and cold, but I know someone who would console you, if you would only smile at him."

Marguerite looked at her, startled. Annys flicked a glance at the ladies-in-waiting who were still watching for Marguerite's reaction to the page boy, then tapped a finger to Marguerite's cloth and said brightly, "However do you make such tiny stitches? Show me your trick again."

Marguerite took the hint and resumed her embroidery. Only when Annys must have deemed it safe did the girl lean over and whisper in Marguerite's ear, "Sir Warin Eyvind, silly. He is head over ears in love with you."

Annys pointed at the blue bird that Marguerite had stitched hovering over a cluster of flowers two days ago, still feigning a discussion of their stitchery.

Marguerite racked her memory for the knight of whom Annys spoke. The tall one with the nut-brown curls? It must be. Annys had said he'd answered the riddle about the key last night. She supposed he was handsome, but in love with her?

"That is absurd," Marguerite murmured. "I have not spoken two words to him."

Annys shifted her finger to the yellow bloom Marguerite had fashioned yesterday. "But he has been trying to speak to you. I know you fear Lord Saxton—who would not? It is dreadful that your parents have betrothed you to him! But methinks Sir Warin would run away with you if you would give him the least encouragement."

Marguerite released a soft huff at such nonsense. "Annys, you know my situation. The queen's ladies mock me as much for my grandfather's inheritance as they do for my dismay of the court's morals. No man will marry me save for Lord Saxton." *And the minstrel who thought himself betrayed.*

Her eyes had begun to sting again so that the green stem of the yellow bloom blurred when Annys pointed at it. "Sir Warin is a younger son with no inheritance of his own. They say he must either find a rich sponsor to serve or marry a rich wife. The gossips say he cannot be choosey in the latter. He would surely overlook your grandfather's nonsensical will, and you cannot tell me that marrying him would not be a hundred times nicer than marrying the Earl of Saxton?"

A shadow fell across them. Marguerite looked up with dismay to see that Queen Isabella had left the window to join her and Annys.

"Look, my lady," Annys said boldly. "Does not the Lady Marguerite execute the tiniest stitches? I am sure I have heard you admire them yourself."

Marguerite said quickly, "Oh, Annys, you are quite mistaken. Her grace's embroidery quite puts mine to shame."

Isabella smiled. Marguerite had learned her as vain about her needlework as she was about her beauty.

"I have indeed praised your work," the queen said. "It reminds me of how skillfully I stitched at your age, though of course, the years have only increased my needle's dexterity. It will be the same for you one day, my dear, as long as you continue to practice. It is an art men like to boast of in their women."

The queen lifted the linen Marguerite had been embroidering from her hands and studied it consideringly for a moment. Then the full, pouting mouth formed a sudden O as though a thought had struck her.

"I shall arrange for you to embroider a shirt for the earl. Something that he can wear close to his heart while he is with my husband in Poitou. The king never rides off to battle without just such a token from me. It will warm Lord Saxton to you, my child." She wagged a coy finger at Marguerite. "That, and a few more welcoming smiles from your lips. Men are fickle, as you will learn. Their flesh is not as loyal as one would wish, but their spirits and hearts can be won so long as a wife is willing to accommodate their little indiscretions. Begin with smiles tomorrow at dinner, then surprise him with the gift of a shirt. Do not be so meek as to deny him a kiss or two, if he asks it, and you will soon have his affections ensnared, though his body may sometimes wander."

It took everything inside of Marguerite not to physically shrink at the queen's words. Let Lord Saxton kiss her again? She repressed a shudder with an urgent force of will, for she dared not offend the queen by openly recoiling from her advice. Was this how the queen rationalized herself to the king's flagrant affairs? The very thought of submitting to such a marriage with the Earl of Saxton turned Marguerite's stomach sour.

She swept her lashes against her cheeks to veil the revulsion she feared she could not conceal in her eyes and prayed that Isabella would interpret it as a sign of flustered awe that Marguerite had won so great a condescension as counsel from the queen.

"You are most kind, your grace," she somehow found voice to say. "Thank you."

Isabella laughed, a rich, sultry sound. "You think me bold, child, but we are wives to bold men, or you shall be soon. I don't doubt your mother has counseled you to meekness—mothers always do—but that will never serve men such as ours. Lord Saxton will drive those blushes from your cheeks soon enough and you must return his passion just as fiercely." Isabella's dainty fingers came under Marguerite's chin, forcing her to look into the queen's eyes. Isabella's brilliant gaze glittered hard as diamonds lit with flames. "Be a tigress with him, my dear. A tigress, and though he stray, he will always come back to you."

Satisfied with this wifely wisdom, Isabella smiled, set Marguerite's embroidery back in her hands, and moved around the circle to bestow her attentions on another one of her ladies.

The queen had made no attempt to impart her advice in confidential tones. Every one of those catty women who sat in the solar must have heard every word and seen Marguerite's dismay. They would mock her even worse, now. Marguerite, face aflame with humiliation, somehow forced herself to resume her stitchery.

Rob. Oh, Rob, where are you?

But she knew the heartbreaking answer. He had abandoned her to what he believed to be her own choice—marriage to the Earl of Saxton!

16

arguerite blamed Annys for putting the idea into her head. Until her friend had spoken, Marguerite had avoided allowing her gaze to linger on anyone during dinner. At first she had been too awed by the great hall of Westminster Palace, a room of such elaborate size that it could have swallowed even her grandfather's sprawling hall as though the latter had been no more than a modest bedchamber. A row of arching Norman windows built deep into the thick stone rimmed the grand heights of the walls, their light setting agleam the trumpets in the railed gallery above the diners' heads where they announced each course with a flourish of graceful notes. Squires dressed in flamboyant colors marched in bearing rich and often exotic dishes, while others appeared at her shoulder to keep her jewel-studded drinking goblet filled with wine. The throngs of unfamiliar faces at the tables set below the dais remained for the most part, with a few exceptions, a confusing sea of strangers.

Lady Jane, no longer relegated to a lower table, joined Marguerite and her betrothed, along with the king and queen, on the dais albeit seated to the left of the queen. From the various shades of pity and amusement cast at Marguerite from those who ate at the tables set below them, she had quickly guessed that prior to her arrival, Lady Jane had dined in Marguerite's chair next to Saxton.

Marguerite had learned to keep her gaze fixed steadfastly on her silver plate, unable to bear the galling sight of Saxton and his mistress leaning forward in their chairs so that they might, while they ate, cast torrid glances at each other around the royal couple between them. Saxton never addressed Marguerite directly, though he charged the squires in what dishes to serve her. He never once asked after Marguerite's tastes, and uncertain as to proper protocol before the king, she did not challenge him even though Saxton's choices more often curled her tongue than pleased her palate.

But now, less than four-and-twenty hours after the queen's appalling marital counsel, Marguerite peeped upwards through her lashes to see if Annys's revelations were true. Sir Warin Eyvind. She judged him of an age with Robert. His curling brown hair fell over his forehead in an undeniably romantic way. He appeared happily engaged in conversation with a comely widow whose silk and jewels suggested at the very least a comfortable wealth, but after a few moments he glanced up towards the dais. His brown eyes were earnest and steady, but his gaze was quickly eclipsed by the memory of a pair of midnight eyes that danced and challenged and sometimes saw too deeply into Marguerite's soul.

She returned her attention quickly to her cawdel of salmon, but the fish tasted like ashes in her mouth. Nevertheless, she forced down several bites before she peeped at Sir Warin again. He was still gazing at her, so ardently now that she actually glanced over her shoulder to see if some beauty had stepped onto the dais behind her. No one had. Was it only her inheritance he desired? She knew herself no more than what most men called pretty. Even Robert had never praised her as beautiful when she had been—she corrected herself—had thought herself most secure in his love.

She fought back a sudden flood of vivid little moments where Robert had nonetheless made her feel as if she were the center of his existence. He had become hers. He would always be hers now. But she could not just sit helpless in her misery until marriage to Lord Saxton made the queen's horrible words a reality. She had thought, in a moment of panic, of attempting to flee the palace, of walking the two miles to London—for as Saxton's betrothed, she would never be allowed to ride out without an escort—and attempting to lose herself in the great city of London until she discovered a way to send word to Odo or escape along the roads of England to Odo's protection at Winbourne Castle. But she quickly realized that to be a vain scheme. She had but to miss no more than a meal for Saxton to wonder where she was. And once he wondered, once he sent his squire to seek her out and discovered her missing without a word, he would guess at her intent and, with the strength of the king's guards behind him, every escape from London, every road to Northumberland, would be swiftly blocked, while London itself would be combed by the guards until she was discovered and dragged back to the palace.

No, as with her father in Dorset, only someone Saxton would not suspect could carry word for her to Odo. A man like Sir Warin. Prodded into a new awareness by Annys, Marguerite felt a little stir of hope in the way he watched her as she dined. Was it possible Sir Warin might agree to do for her what she had never asked of Robert—ride to Northumberland to fetch Odo and the terms of her grandfather's will that could deliver her yet from Lord Saxton?

But he will expect a reward, Marguerite. He will expect you to marry him instead. She did not know if she was ready to let another man love her.

She was grateful for the distraction when the king fell to his daily boastings. King John always talked long and loud at dinner of how he and his army would soon trounce the French and humble the proud King Philip. At intervals he would launch himself to his feet, shouting to his barons and knights, "Shall we not, my lords?" to which they all rallied while thumping their mugs and goblets against the tables, "Huzzah! Huzzah! We will humble the king of France!"

Marguerite's response to this bombast was always to utter a fervent, if silent, prayer that Saxton would not insist on a wedding before the army's departure date, now set for early February.

The king drank as hard and fast as he boasted. Marguerite had learned that when the king's wine-slickened voice garbled his bursts of bravado into "Shalleena, mlors?", that the meal had reached its end, for the king soon thereafter stumbled out of the hall with his arm around a buxom wench, unless he dropped back into his chair and his head pitched snoring on the tabletop first.

Today though, while the king staggered a bit, slopping his wine over the rim of his cup as he shouted, Marguerite saw King John clamp the stubby, jewel-encrusted fingers of his free hand on Saxton's wide shoulder to steady himself while he waited for his knights' responsive chant to fade. The gold coronet he always wore to dinner had slipped sideways on his oiled hair. His round face, framed with greasy dark tendrils that fell to his shoulders and ruddied with drink beneath his dark beard, shone an unexpected challenge to his knights and barons.

"Trounce the French usurper we shall!" King John repeated. "But shall I do it with untested troops? Shall I?"

He appeared to have steadied his tongue along with his body, for though still slightly blurred, Marguerite nonetheless picked out his words with only a modicum of effort.

A brief pause through the hall, as though confused by the king's question, quickly filled with the response the king's future army supposed was expected of them. "Nay! Nay!" the men shouted.

"Then a tournament, my lords!" King John said with a drunken smirk. "A tournament we shall have on the morrow so that I may judge your mettle for myself. Not with blunted weapons, but with swords razor-sharp to spill your bowels and lances keen to pierce your hearts. I will take none but the strongest with me to battle, the rest of you may go to the grave and the devil in defeat and shame."

Marguerite stared at the king. Was he mad? Could he truly intend his knights to duel to the death on the very eve of an invasion of France?

Into a second lull of startled silence broke an unfamiliar sound. From his chair at her side, the Earl of Saxton laughed.

"'Tis a cunning jest, your grace," Saxton said. "Look how you've disconcerted even the bravest of them. Forsooth, they think you serious! As though you would be reckless enough to go to war with only half your knights."

The king shot Saxton a glare from bloodshot eyes. "A jest? Think you I could not crush Philip with a mere tenth of the good English knights of this realm if I wished to? Think you I am too craven to try?"

Saxton, apparently sensing a misstep, tried to speak a quick disclaimer, but the king bellowed over him.

"Philip won my lands by deceit and luck, not because his knights were more skillful than mine. If you are too fainthearted to follow me, Achard, you may go to the devil, too."

Something flickered in Saxton's cool eyes when the king addressed him by his surname rather than his title, but Saxton only sprawled back in his chair, took a leisurely drink from his goblet, then replied in unruffled tones.

"Was I faint of heart, sire, when I stood at your shoulder as you flouted the Count of La Marche and married our beauteous queen? Was I faint of heart when I rode at your side to deliver your queen mother from threat of capture by La Marche in retaliation at Mirebeau? Was it I who rebuked you for shackling the count and his ally, your rebellious nephew, and for parading them back to Normandy as a warning to their followers and King Philip that you were not a man to be thwarted?" Saxton took another long sip from his cup, then murmured as the king drew breath to reply, "Ah, nay. As I recall, that man who called your actions dishonorable was not me, but the Earl of Gunthar."

Marguerite felt the tension of the hall tick up the back of her neck as she, with the others, watched to see how the king would respond to this obvious effort to deflect his anger onto an unknown earl. She could not tell if the flush in the king's face lingered there from anger or the wine. He scowled at Saxton another moment, then tossed back his head so suddenly on a roaring laugh that his coronet slid further askew. Marguerite had become accustomed to the king's volatile shifts from high spirits to black humor and back again, so it surprised her when Saxton shifted uncomfortably at the chuckles and chortles. Or no, the torchlight in the hall must have merely tricked her eyes, for Saxton's massive shoulders shook as he joined in his liege's laughter.

The king turned a little too quickly to address the crowd in the hall again. The movement set him swaying slightly. This time he leaned forward and planted his fists on the table, so inebriated that he barely missed plunging one set of knuckles into the remains of his dinner.

"The tournament will go forth as I have commanded," he insisted. "Whether you fight to the death will depend on how badly my head pounds in the morning." He giggled, found his goblet and sloshed some more wine into his mouth. He turned taunting again to his knights. "Now ready yourselves this night how you will, in prayer if ye be cowards. As for me—"

The king banged down his goblet, then abruptly pulled the queen from her chair and into his arms. He dealt her a deep, thorough—and from the way he teetered to and fro a bit as he did it—drunken kiss. Isabella's cheeks flamed when he finished, but her eyes glowed, not with embarrassment, but with the same wanton passion Marguerite had seen too often in Lady Jane's eyes.

"As for me," the king slurred, "I shall have dancing before my lady and I move on to other pleasures. Who shall join me and my queen?"

Saxton stood with that swiftness for his size that always startled Marguerite and, to her consternation, held out his hand to Lady Jane. She walked shamelessly behind the royal couple to take Saxton's clasp.

"My lady and I will join you, your grace." Saxton raised Lady Jane's hand into the air in a flagrant gesture that shut Marguerite out as completely as though she had vanished from the dais.

Marguerite wished she could dissolve into invisibility. Too many stares had found her again on Lord Saxton's words, even as men and women surged to their feet in imitation of the king and his counselor.

At the king's command, the tables and the remains of the meal were quickly cleared away and the court musicians traded the stately airs to which the king's court had dined with a lively dancing tune. Marguerite was pushing her way through the crowd with as much dignity as she could muster to try to reach Annys's side when a man stepped into her path.

"Lady Marguerite, might you honor me with your hand for the estampie?"

Sir Warin. Smiling down at her with courtesy, not mockery, and his eyes lit with the same admiration that had baffled her earlier. She hesitated, about to make an excuse, when she caught sight of Saxton and Lady Jane holding hands in the line that was forming for the dance. Before Marguerite scarcely knew what she was doing, she gave Sir Warin a bright smile and laid her fingers in his.

He held them lightly as they danced and to Marguerite's surprise, little memories of kindness by Sir Warin o'er the past fortnight began flitting through her mind. When the comb had slipped from her hair and fallen into the rushes one night, it had been Sir Warin who had retrieved it for her before melting back into the crowd. When she had lamented to Annys of Saxton's indifference to her tastes at the dining table, Sir Warin had shortly appeared with a little bowl of rice pudding with honey and almonds leftover from the kitchens. And when she had stolen away to a corner in the constantly bustling hall in an attempt to hide her sadness as she plied her embroidery, and her needle had broken? Yes, Sir Warin had appeared at her side with a replacement borrowed from Lady Felice before Marguerite could take three steps from her chair to make the request herself.

"It is warm in the hall," Sir Warin said as the dance ended and he led her from the floor. "Perhaps a turn on the ramparts would cool us both. Will you join me, my lady?"

Marguerite hesitated. She tossed a look at Saxton and saw him leading Lady Jane from the floor, his arm about her waist, his head bent close to her ear. Marguerite's chin lifted in a flash of defiance and she laid her hand on Sir Warin's arm.

"Thank you, sir. I should indeed welcome some fresh air."

Marguerite strolled with Sir Warin along the rampart's wall-walk, glad for the brisk breeze that flowed over her heated cheeks. The winter days were still short and stars had begun to glisten in the cloudless night sky. Neither of them spoke for several minutes, but her mind rolled with memories of the myriad small courtesies dealt her by this knight since her arrival at court. She vaguely recalled thanking him for each, but absently, barely seeing him then.

On an impulse, she stopped now and pressed his hand. "I shall miss you when you are gone to France."

The darkness shadowed his face, but his free hand came up to hold hers warmly between his palms. "You honor me, my lady."

"Nay." A prick of guilt that she had not been kinder to him made her suddenly shy. "I have very much needed a friend of late. You have been endlessly patient and good. You must have thought me quite tiresome—"

"Tiresome? Never!" He caught himself up, then uttered with a burst of passion that startled her, "I shall make a name for myself in France. Your memory shall be my inspiration."

Her heart tripped a little at his fervor. If she asked him to serve her by flying a different direction, what would he say? *Speak*, a voice whispered in her mind, but a vying flutter in her breast murmured, *Not yet, not yet*.

"I think you will need no such inspiration as my poor name," she answered. "Still, I hope you go safely."

"My lady—"

Her hand still lay in his. She felt the gentle pull of his fingers as he began to draw her to him. This was what she had hoped for when she had danced with him, and yet she disengaged herself from his clasp and took a few steps away.

"What a bright night it is," she said. "Why, one can see as clearly as though a thousand candles were lit."

He moved again to her side. "Aye. Do you know the constellations?" The unaccustomed fervor in his voice was gone, replaced with the easy, relaxed tones he always used when he rendered her a service.

Marguerite lost track of the passage of time as Sir Warin pointed out one star cluster after another. So absorbed had she become with the night sky's beauties that she was surprised when she suddenly realized she was shivering. Sir Warin seemed to notice at almost the same moment, for he muttered, "Fool that I am, why did I not think to bring your cloak? You will catch a chill—"

"No, no, I am fine, truly—"

He placed his arm around her shoulders in what she knew was an instinctive attempt to warm her, but the gesture instantly turned into something more. His embrace about her tightened.

"Sir Warin, please!" She thrust her hands against his chest as he turned her towards him.

He made a sound almost like a groan, but did not release her. "I have tried not to look on you, have tried not to want you—I know you are betrothed to another, but—" He drew a painful sounding breath, then uttered roughly, "You do not love him. I know you do not love the Earl of Saxton!"

"I—"

"You cannot lie to me, Marguerite," Sir Warin said almost savagely. "You could not love such a man. I have seen the way he humiliates you, the anger and sadness in your eyes. If you will only let me, I will do all in my power to turn your misery to joy. Can you doubt my love? Have I not spent every possible moment at your side? Have I dreamt of any other woman since I laid eyes on you?"

Now, sang out the voice in her head. *He is ready for you to ask him now.*

And yet she squirmed again in his hold.

He caught her shoulders and held her slightly away from him, as though he sought to quell a misunderstanding. "I offer you no dishonor, just a loyal and honest heart. Come away with me! We will flee this wretched court. The king will not let Saxton leave his side in the midst of his preparations for war, and by the time they return from France, you will be my wife."

His wife? The word nearly knocked the wind from her. She had not expected to be confronted with the word so soon, but surely it answered her dilemma even better than her own scheme? Instead of bringing Odo to her, Sir Warin would take her to Odo and the protection of the will that even Saxton would not be able to break.

All you need do is say 'yes.'

Sir Warin appeared to find hope in her sudden stillness. He drew her into his arms and set a kiss to her forehead. Then he slowly tilted up her face. One kiss would commit her to him. A tall, handsome knight, kind, gentle—but the moonlight glanced off the brown of his eyes, caught the curl in the locks that fell over his brow, and the murmur in her breast that warred with her mind became a screaming wrench of protest.

He was all around her, his dark minstrel face lit with his lightning smiles, his laughter, his music—oh, saints! His kisses!

It was madness to cast away her future for a memory, yet cast it away she did.

She twisted her head aside before Sir Warin found her lips. Her eyes filled with tears. "I cannot," she choked. "Oh, pray let me go."

"Marguerite—"

"Sir Warin, I beg you—"

He hung onto her stubbornly. "You do not love Saxton!"

She muffled the sob in her throat. "No—"

"Then—"

"—but I do not love you, either."

She felt him flinch at the blow. A moment of aching silence pulsed between them.

"Not Saxton," he uttered hoarsely. "Then who?"

She shook her head.

"There is someone else, Marguerite. Do you think I could not hear it in your voice? I would know the name of the man who deprived me of my joy." Sir Warin's voice rang deep with bitterness.

"His name would mean nothing to you." *And it will pain me too much to speak it.*

"Still, I would know."

She realized he would not release her until she gave him an answer. She whispered past the tears that burned in her throat, "Robert Marcel. Now let me go."

Sir Warin repeated the name blankly. His embrace slackened but he did not fully obey. "Aye, I know not the man. If he cares so much for you, why has he not carried you off?"

The tears flooded up scorching in her eyes. "Perhaps he does not care so much." Her voice broke.

Sir Warin wiped the hot wetness from her cheeks. "Marguerite—"

"My, my, what a very romantic tableau."

The soft words, smooth as silk, doused over Marguerite's grief like a blast of cold water. Sir Warin's arms at last fell from around her as they both turned toward the Earl of Saxton, silhouetted in the open tower doorway.

How much had he heard? He clearly had seen too much! Marguerite stammered, "M-my lord—"

"This is not what it appears, Saxton," Sir Warin spoke over her words.

Saxton barely glanced at them as he joined them on the wall-walk, his attention fixed on some infinitesimal speck he flicked from his velvet sleeve. "Is it not?" he murmured. "Were you not, then, embracing my affianced bride?"

"You do not care to embrace her yourself," Sir Warin flashed back.

"What I choose to do with my betrothed is no concern of yours." Saxton's hazel eyes lifted now to rest on Marguerite. "I have not found her particularly anxious for my embraces, but I can assure you I will devote the proper attention to such matters when we are wed. I doubt she will find them quite as pleasant as your own."

Marguerite shuddered. How was she to live with the choice she had made if it bound her to a man like this?

Sir Warin stepped in front of her, as if to shield her from Saxton's gaze. "Direct your anger at me, my lord. It was I who acted wrongly. My lady made it plain to me my advances were unwelcome."

"Indeed?" Saxton said. "Then perhaps you should return to the hall. I will care for my lady."

Sir Warin hesitated, but Marguerite whispered behind him, "Please go." She could not take advantage of his chivalry after rejecting his heart so cruelly.

"One moment, Eyvind," Saxton said as Sir Warin moved with open reluctance towards the tower door. "You are planning to be in the tournament tomorrow?"

Sir Warin stiffened slightly. "Aye, my name will be in the lists."

"Good. I shall look forward to meeting you."

Sir Warin bowed, accepting the challenge, and then was gone.

Marguerite swept forward to catch Saxton's arm as he turned to follow the knight. "You will not hurt him!"

Saxton glanced down at her with the same glint in his eyes that had chilled her the night Robert had first smiled at her in her father's hall. "What I have claimed as my own, I do not share. I have claimed you, Marguerite."

She shivered, but not from the winter's air this time. "Am I merely so much property, then?"

"You are a woman."

She bridled at his dismissive tones. "Aye, and so I am. If you think the less of me for that, you make a grave mistake."

"It is you who have mistaken matters. Did I not once warn you that my wife's name must be free of all reproach? I do not give warnings lightly, my child, as you shall soon learn."

Her stomach was a gnarl of knots, but she refused to show her fear of him. She hoped he could see her disdain in the rigid set of her back as she swept before him down the tower stairs and across the galleries that returned them both to the hall.

17

Westminster Palace
Westminster, England
January 1214

The day of the tournament dawned clear and fair. Marguerite took her place on the canopied stand that had been erected, honored as betrothed to the Earl of Saxton to sit next to the queen. Queen Isabella, aware of Marguerite's friendship with Annys de Tracey and in a generous mood due to the king's decision to forego participating in the tourney himself and watch the entertainment with his wife, had invited Annys to join them. Annys chattered happily away at Marguerite's side, even as her eyes followed every move of Richard Channing's where he stood across the field, assisting Sir Edward Keynes to ready himself for the joust.

The king's pallor and frequent grimaces attested to his overindulgence of wine the night before. But though he still insisted his knights be armed with sharpened weapons—he stubbornly maintained that blunted swords and lances were the weapons of cowards—he had abandoned his drunken scheme of encouraging his knights to fight to the death. Marguerite knew Saxton must have played a part in the king's altered decision from the way the king glared at Saxton and muttered profanities over his name as Saxton paraded about the tournament field.

Saxton wore a forest green tunic over his mail, emblazoned with his crest, the roaring bear. Marguerite had seen the emblem many times on his jewelry or clothing, but perhaps in a bid to intimidate his competitors, he had enlarged the figure for today and added several embroidered crimson drops of blood dripping from the creature's bared and vicious-looking teeth. The same beast graced the top of the helmet he carried under his arm, but in this case, the blood had been painted on the teeth themselves. It stared menacingly at Marguerite from its unblinking eyes as Saxton stopped before the stand to salute the king and queen with his upraised lance.

Marguerite had earlier watched Lady Jane draw a yellow ribbon from her hair and tie it to Saxton's lance as a favor. It fluttered its unabashed contempt of Marguerite's pride for too many chagrining moments as the king uttered his royal blessing—"Fight this day with courage and honor. May God be with you."—in a humdrum voice that revealed his continued displeasure with his "favorite." He waved Saxton on so that he might bless the next knight and the next. Marguerite wondered if the king still smarted from Saxton's laughter last night in the hall, or if their quarrel sprang from an encounter this morning—or both.

When Sir Warin rode up to the stand for the king's invocation, Marguerite lowered her gaze in lingering guilt for the way they had parted.

"A favor, Milady Marguerite." His salutation startled her into glancing up again. To her surprise, he wore a jaunty grin. "Pray do not refuse. I shall win great glory to your name."

Marguerite looked quickly at the king, fearful that Sir Warin had offended him by addressing her before his liege, but King John sent a spiteful glance at the Earl of Saxton where he conversed with his squire, Nicholas Tybert, then nodded his royal encouragement at Marguerite. An encouragement she was not so naïve as not to realize was a command. Despite Sir Warin's playful tones, his eyes were determined. Had he lain awake all night remembering that the man she loved had forsaken her and plotting to change her mind about his proposal?

She rose reluctantly, compelled to answer as she knew the king expected. She had left her hair unbound, but Annys had merrily tied a cluster of snow-drops to Marguerite's left wrist before they had come down to the field. Marguerite untied them now and held them out to her "champion." She smiled to please the king, and bade Sir Warin, "Do not disappoint me, sir."

Sir Warin, his eyes on hers, accepted the flowers and deliberately raised them to his lips before tucking them snuggly into the side of the helmet he carried under his arm.

King John clapped his hands and cried, "Ah, my lady, sly, sly!" before he leapt to his feet and intoned with the most vigor he had shown so far that morn, "Fight this day with courage and honor, Sir Warin. May God be with you."

It did not ease Marguerite's conscience that the queen smiled archly, and Annys mischievously, as Sir Warin rode away and Marguerite resumed her seat.

In spite of her misgivings about the knight, Marguerite felt a stir of excitement when the heralds' trumpets blared and the first two contestants took their places at opposite ends of the field for the series of paired competitions the king had decreed should precede the mêlée. Marguerite had never attended a tournament before. Now that the king's bloodlust had sobered with the morning, an air of good-natured sportsmanship seemed to mark the games. One or two very young and very ambitious knights fought recklessly, but their more experienced competitors easily disarmed them. Marguerite found herself repeatedly carried to her feet with the rest of the crowd, cheering for the winners. Sir Edward Keynes unhorsed two knights before taking a tumble himself and leaving the field.

Marguerite had turned her head to listen to a remark from Annys when the herald announced, "My lord the Earl of Saxton and Sir Warin Eyvind!"

Marguerite jerked about in her seat, all her enjoyment vanishing. She watched Sir Warin and Saxton, their helmets already donned, take up their positions, then turn to face each other, lances couched for the moment loosely beneath their arms. Their horses, caparisoned in the colors of their families' houses—Saxton's in fresh, bright cloth, Sir Warin's faded and worn, reflecting his light purse—stamped the ground impatiently. The herald rode midway between them, his gloved hand held high above his head. Marguerite tried to brace herself as the lances snapped up smartly. Then the herald's hand dropped and the horses vaulted into motion with a thundering of hooves.

She winced involuntarily as the two men clashed together. Both lances splintered on the other man's shield, but only Sir Warin swayed in his seat and nearly fell. He regained his balance, exchanged his broken lance, and turned to try again. Once more he and Saxton came together with no harm done. Still, an unaccountable dread hovered over Marguerite. She tried to tell herself that Sir Warin, like Sir Edward, would be none the worse for taking a tumble, but a malicious voice persisted in whispering in her ear, *I do not give warnings lightly my child, as you shall soon learn.*

Again the ground shook with the pounding of hooves, the great warhorses bearing their riders inexorably toward one another. Marguerite heard one of the guards who attended the king mutter, "Your shield, lad, lower your shield," but it was too late. Saxton's lance slipped beneath Sir Warin's improperly held buckler, the force of the galloping horses causing it to pierce and rip Sir Warin's armor as easily as a knife might rip a piece of silk.

Marguerite screamed. She launched to her feet as Sir Warin rolled from his steed and hit the ground on the other side of his mount where the horse's body hid the seriousness of his wound from her view. But she saw the gleam of blood on Saxton's lance. The world reeled before her eyes, a sudden roar louder than the destriers' hooves filled her ears, and she sank to her knees.

Someone caught her and lowered her back into her seat. As if from a very great distance, she heard a voice calling her name.

"Marguerite, Marguerite, please answer me!"

She did not realize her eyes had closed until she opened them to see Annys's frightened face. Her friend chafed Marguerite's hands as Marguerite realized it was the king's guard who propped her up. She looked past her friend to the field where a crowd had gathered around the fallen knight. She still could not see him, but there arose the vision in her mind of Sir Warin lying white and bloodstained in the dust. She shuddered.

"Perhaps we should return her to the castle," Annys said anxiously.

A pause. Had the guard glanced at the king for guidance?

"Aye," the guard said gruffly, then asked Marguerite, "Can you walk, my lady? Then take my arm and come."

Two excruciating days passed before it was announced that Sir Warin would live. The report brought Marguerite relief for his life, but not from her guilt. His injury was severe, Annys said, and it was not known to what extent he would recover. The thought haunted Marguerite waking and sleeping. In day dreams as well as in shades of the night, she envisioned him standing before her, sometimes accusing, sometimes forgiving, but always his body and future broken because he had tried to love her.

Marguerite did not know how she managed to sit so quietly each day beside Lord Saxton at dinner. Thankfully, he never spoke to her for if he had, she was quite sure it would have shattered her restraint and set her flailing at him like a madwoman. His hard eyes gleamed with too great a satisfaction for her to doubt the "accident" the king and his court bemoaned had been anything but a deliberate attempt to kill a man Saxton had viewed as a rival. Horror of this new aspect to Saxton's character sickened Marguerite. Sickened and defeated her, for how could she ever put another man at risk by even daring to smile at him? Perhaps it was as well that Robert had abandoned her. Wherever he was, at least he was safe of Saxton's malice.

18

he Earl and Countess of Gunthar."

Marguerite looked up from her embroidery, ears pricking at the servant's announcement. Gunthar? Where had she heard the name before? There was nothing familiar about the gentleman and lady who entered the queen's solar. Their clothes bespoke wealth but not extravagance, although the man wore a pendent bearing an elaborately filigreed silver horse studded with winking sapphires. Despite his advanced age, the Earl of Gunthar carried himself as erect as a man half his years. He stood as tall as Saxton and though not as massively built, something about his broad shoulders and lean frame nevertheless emanated an intimidating power. Or perhaps, Marguerite thought, it was the hawkish cast of his features, or the stern curve of his mouth that suggested little patience with fools, or his heavily browed grey eyes that carried a light so keen she feared they might pierce clear through her if he turned his head her way.

Thankfully, the aging earl spared not a glance for any of the queen's ladies, but walked straight to the queen. Only the stiffness with which he knelt to kiss her hand suggested that the years sat more deeply in his bones than otherwise appeared.

"Your grace."

"Hugh," the queen greeted him. "I had not thought to see you again at court." Was there a bit of an edge in Isabella's sultry voice? "And Heléne. How well you are looking."

Marguerite had barely noticed the earl's wife, for the force of her husband's presence eclipsed the quiet elegance Marguerite recognized in her now. She was younger than the earl, though silver grazed the strands of pale gold hair that escaped her snowy veil. Tall and slender, she curtsied to the queen with an almost youthful grace.

"Thank you, my lady, I am much recovered," the countess said.

Marguerite caught a faint hint of an accent in her soft, pleasing voice, similar to the one the queen spoke with.

"Did you only just arrive?" Isabella inquired. "How delightful! Pray sit and take some refreshment."

"You are very kind, your grace," the earl said, "but I cannot stay. I only wished to pay my respects to you before meeting with the king." Unlike his wife, he sounded English enough to Marguerite.

"Of course." The queen's polite smile was cold. She made no attempt to encourage him to linger. "But Heléne must stay and entertain me."

"I should be honored, your grace," the countess said. "Thank you."

The queen exchanged a few more stiffly polite words with the earl, then dismissed him to go to the king.

Marguerite caught the queen's sideways glance at the flame-haired woman who sat at her side. Prior to the earl and countess's arrival, Lady Jane had been regaling Isabella with a slightly scandalous tale about one of the queen's ladies who had the misfortune to be absent and thus unable to defend herself.

"A hawking party rode out early this morning," the queen said to the countess, "but a few of my ladies kindly consented to remain behind and keep me company. Of course, you will remember Lady Jane Lovell and Lady Felice Lennar from your previous stays at court. Let me acquaint you with the Lady Marguerite de Villon, Lord Saxton's betrothed, and Lady Annys de Tracey. They are newcomers to our circle, but I am sure you will remember Lady Annys's parents."

"And Lady Marguerite's," the countess said, to Marguerite's surprise. The countess smiled, her silvery eyes as warm as her husband's had been penetrating. "At least, I knew your grandfather, Lord Heywood. He held my husband's greatest respect. We were sorry to hear of his passing. How does your mother?"

The countess knew her grandfather? Marguerite felt a little churn of excitement. She had been alone with her memories of him for so long! "My mother is very well, thank you, my lady."

"Leah was such a pretty child. You are very like her, but for your coloring."

The countess appeared about to say more, but the queen grew impatient for her guest's attention.

"Dear Heléne, do come and sit beside me for awhile. I am sure Jane will not mind relinquishing her place to you."

Lady Jane looked so startled, the queen might have slapped her. The redhead rose very slowly, clearly reluctant to "relinquish" anything. Marguerite, glancing from the simple beauty of the countess's gown to the jewel-heavy opulence of Lady Jane, realized for the first time that the resplendence that had so often made her blink in awe was actually little more than garish.

"I hope I may ask you to wait upon me later," the countess murmured to Marguerite. "I should enjoy speaking to you of your grandparents."

"Yes, my lady, I should like that, too," Marguerite said, trying not to show an unbecoming eagerness.

Lady Jane hovered possessively in front of the chair she had vacated. The countess's kind smile faded. She betrayed no indignation, but met the flame-haired beauty's sparkling eyes with a level, waiting look Marguerite sensed a man as daunting as her husband would approve of. The queen cleared her throat meaningfully. Lady Jane might be mistress of the king's most powerful counselor, but she was not that counselor's wife and countess and she stood in the presence of a woman who could claim both titles. Lady Jane stepped aside, but not without a rare flash of malice in her brilliant green eyes as the Countess of Gunthar took her place at the queen's side.

"And Papa says that Lord Saxton is furious." Annys spoke in hushed tones, even though she and Marguerite were quite alone.

As betrothed to the king's chief counselor, Marguerite had been granted a magnificent bedchamber. Thick carpets warmed the floor, while nimble forest creatures capered among the profusion of flowers woven into the tapestries against the walls. This chamber, like her one at home, had a great hearth built into one wall, but unlike the simple linen curtains that enclosed her bed there, the curtains in this chamber were made of rich velvet embroidered in gold. A servant tied them back in the daytime with tasseled ropes. A new gown the Earl of Saxton had ordered for Marguerite lay spread out on the bed. However Saxton chose to neglect her in public, he seemed determined to keep her exquisitely attired as became his future wife.

The Earl and Countess of Gunthar had arrived at court two days ago, and Annys was fairly bursting to share with Marguerite the conversations she had overheard between her parents.

Marguerite could not deny her own curiosity. "Why should Lord Saxton be furious that the Earl of Gunthar has come to court?"

"Papa says Lord Gunthar was once as close to the king as Lord Saxton is now, but Lord Gunthar did not approve of the king stealing Queen Isabella away from the Count of La Marche." Annys lifted the new gown from the bed and held it up to Marguerite's chin. "Lord Gunthar quarreled with the king about it, although Papa said the full break did not come until two years later when King John returned to Normandy to stop a rebellion by the count and the king's nephew, Arthur of Brittany. Oh, my, Marguerite! Lord Saxton may be a beast, but he has delicious taste in gowns!"

Marguerite glanced indifferently at the butter-soft yellow silk adorned with a profusion of embroidered flowers. Annys's story explained the queen's coldness towards the old earl. Marguerite suddenly remembered where she had heard Gunthar's name before. Saxton had spoken it at dinner the night before that dreadful tournament, nigh three weeks ago now, where he had come so nigh to killing Sir Warin. She clamped down the guilt that tried to surge back up inside her so that Annys would not see it. Her friend felt almost as remorseful for suggesting that Marguerite encourage the knight as Marguerite still felt for having done so.

"Lord Saxton hinted that the Earl of Gunthar did not approve of the king capturing his nephew and the Count of La Marche," Marguerite said.

"Nay, it was not the capture itself. Have you a ribbon to match this silk? Papa says what angered Lord Gunthar was the king's treatment of his prisoners. The count was of noble blood, and Arthur's blood was royal, yet King John shackled them and paraded them through Normandy as though they were common criminals."

Marguerite joined her friend in searching through the little carved casket where Marguerite kept her ribbons.

"*That* was what Lord Gunthar rebuked the king for." Annys held a blue ribbon against the silk and then tossed it back into the casket, rejecting the frippery's shade. "Papa says King John fell into such a rage there were many who feared for Lord Gunthar's head, but the Earl of Pembroke, who was a friend of Lord Gunthar's, intervened. The king remembered the grudge, however, and when they returned to England, he banished Lord Gunthar from court—" she tried a strand of red, but dropped it back in the casket as well "—although pressured by Lord Pembroke to display some small respect for the long and loyal service Lord Gunthar had given his father Henry and brother Richard when they had been king, King John allowed the story to spread that Lord Gunthar retired because his wife was in poor health."

"White goes with everything." Marguerite lifted such a ribbon out with one finger. "If Lord Gunthar was dismissed in disgrace, why has he come back to court now?"

"Nay, it must be something more cunning than white," Annys protested. She returned the white ribbon to its sisters. "Papa says the king must be growing uneasy with Lord Saxton's arrogant assumption of power. First he said Lord Saxton dared to suggest in a counsel that the king's strategy for the new war might be flawed. Then we all saw how he laughed at the king at dinner and how it displeased the king. Oh, if only the king had listened to his advice about the tournament, that poor, poor Sir Warin might never have been injured so dreadfully!"

Marguerite suspected Lord Saxton would not have been above having his squire "accidentally" hand him a sharpened lance, had the king agreed to blunted weapons.

"Papa told Mama that likely the king fears Lord Saxton has become too powerful and has called Lord Gunthar back as a rebuke and a reminder that Lord Saxton can fall from his grace as quickly as his former rival did. For they competed for influence over the king, you know. Papa says Lord Saxton played no small part in Lord Gunthar's downfall, that 'twas Lord Saxton who advised the king to humiliate his nephew and the Count of La Marche, knowing that Lord Gunthar would object and thus offend the king."

Marguerite returned her gown to the bed. She remembered the resentment in Lady Jane's eyes and thought again of Sir Warin. Perhaps someone should warn the old earl.

Annys carried over a green ribbon and laid it against the silk. She had found one just the shade of the green winding tendrils of the flowers.

"Do you think they will be gone long?" Annys said.

"Who?" Marguerite queried.

"The men who ride with the king to France. Richard said Sir Edward is taking him with him. If they fight, if there is a battle, Richard might return a knight."

If he did, he would be a no more eligible husband for Annys than he was as squire, for his future would always be dependent on serving a man of greater wealth, like Sir Edward. Annys must know that, yet her eyes shone with hope. Marguerite still carried too much despair in her own heart to dash the glow in Annys's, so she sought to distract her instead.

"Would you like to try on the gown and ribbon? There is time before dinner."

Annys nodded vigorously, and they left off talking of kings and earls and the war that lay ahead.

The Countess of Gunthar soon kept her promise and invited Marguerite to spend an afternoon with her. She and her husband had been granted a suite of at least three chambers, judging from the two doors that stood in the far wall of the antechamber Marguerite entered. The fore-chamber itself appeared to have been turned into a sitting chamber for the countess, with several elegant cushioned chairs, one near the window to catch the light while the countess plied her embroidery, though today the shutters were closed against the rain. To Marguerite's surprise, she saw in the light of the multitude of candles that lit the chamber, a book lying open-faced atop a basket spilling over with cloths and threads, with a skein of yellow yarn atop the pages, perhaps to mark its place.

The Lady Helen—for that was what everyone but the queen called her— must have followed the direction of Marguerite's gaze. The countess reached down to the basket near her feet and picked up the book with an engaging chuckle.

"We had barely been at Westminster a day before my husband visited the bookstalls in London. Hugh says he bought this to entertain me, but he was still reading it long after I fell asleep last night. I must snatch what hours of enjoyment I can from this while he is with the king. It is useless to ask my husband to read it with me, for he has no patience for revisiting ground he covered late in the night before he has reached the end."

Marguerite held out a curious hand. "May I see it, my lady?" Lady Helen gave her the leather-bound volume. "*Quatre Fils Aymon*. The four sons of Aymon. I do not know this story."

"You know how to read, child?"

"Indeed, my lady. My grandfather taught me. Does that surprise you?" Marguerite did not know why it should. Lady Helen had just confessed to knowing how to read herself.

"Yes, a little," Lady Helen said. "Your grandfather did not teach your mother to read, as I recall. I believe he raised her very strictly and married her quite young to your father." She motioned to a stool with a velvet cushion. "Come, child, sit."

Marguerite thanked her. She tried not to show her eagerness as she sank down on the stool. "You said you knew my grandfather."

"Why, my dear, I almost married him."

Marguerite nearly dropped the book. "Almost married Grandfather? But he never mentioned you to me."

Lady Helen smiled. "There is no reason why he should." She wove a needle with a red thread through her cloth. "We were all friends after I married Hugh and your grandfather married Edwina Saville, but we did not meet again after my husband retired from court. That was twelve years ago, when it was no longer considered wise to be a friend of the Earl of Gunthar."

"Grandfather would have cared nothing for that," Marguerite scoffed. "He was not so fainthearted."

"No, he was not." Lady Helen set another stitch. "I thought Lord Heywood must be the most horrid man when my mother told me I must wed him, for I was quite in love with Hugh—Lord Gunthar—and he with me. There were reasons Hugh and I could not marry in the beginning, but once Hugh made up his mind to do it, he swept away every objection with his usual efficiency." She gave a tiny sigh. "How long ago that seems. Hugh and I have been quite happily wed for nearly forty years now."

"I am glad, my lady," Marguerite said courteously, but she could not resist adding, "but my grandfather was not horrid."

The countess looked up quickly, as though realizing she had offended. "No, of course he was not. I had not met him then, you see. I was born in

Poitou and your grandfather only sent emissaries to arrange our marriage. I learned what a good man he was after my husband brought me to England. Is reading all your grandfather taught you?"

"Nooo," Marguerite confessed. "He had Odo—my tutor—teach me arithmetic and geography and—and—well, a few more subjects my father said were only fit for clerks." She felt the curiosity in Lady Helen's gaze. "It was because I was Grandfather's only heir. He wished me to understand how to manage the lands he would one day leave me."

"Your mother was his only heir before you were born, yet he did not see fit to teach her how to rub two letters together. Oh, there, I have offended you again. Forgive me, child. I have learned to be too outspoken from my husband."

"My mother says I speak too impulsively as well," Marguerite confessed, warming to the countess.

"Then we are certain to become fast friends, you and I."

Marguerite could not resist the twinkle in the countess's eye. Lady Helen was not beautiful, but Marguerite realized she possessed something the exotic queen and the ravishing Lady Jane did not: a disarming charm.

"I should like that very much, my lady."

Over the next three days, their afternoon visits became regular. Sometimes the countess tried to speak to Marguerite of her betrothal to the Earl of Saxton, but when Marguerite grew reserved, she quickly turned the subject to other matters. Marguerite liked it best when the countess shared amiable or amusing anecdotes of Lord Heywood and listened as Marguerite did the same. Sometimes they talked of books they had both read. And occasionally, the countess surprised Marguerite by speaking of politics.

Marguerite was most intrigued when the countess spoke of the young Duke of Brittany. The king's nephew may have allowed himself to become a puppet of France in an attempt to overthrow John's claim to the throne, Lady Helen said, but he had only been a boy of fifteen, and son of John's own deceased brother, Geoffrey. It had been shameful for John to put him in shackles and humiliate him before the barons of England and Normandy. And then the boy had simply vanished. Of course—the countess set a stitch so tiny to her embroidery cloth that it made Marguerite's efforts feel quite clumsy—there was no proof that he had been murdered at King John's command, or that he was even dead.

Yet 'twas as though some dark retribution had raised its hand against

King John. He had lost all the lands his father had left him—Normandy, Anjou, Touraine and Brittany to France. Only his mother's lands of Aquitaine and Poitou remained to him across the British Sea. It was from there, the countess said, that King John would base his forces to strike against his old enemy of France. But it would not be easy. Between the rumors over his nephew's disappearance and outrage at the king's high-handed mistreatment of his barons, Lady Helen believed the barons were only one more mismanaged war away from breaking out in open rebellion against the king.

Marguerite's breath caught on a gasp. "Would Lord Gunthar support such a thing?"

The countess only smiled and turned the question aside, saying she had trespassed upon Marguerite's time enough for one day.

"Pray take *Quatre Fils Aymon* with you if you like," Lady Helen said as Marguerite rose from the stool. "I finished reading it last night."

Marguerite knew herself dismissed. Her mind swirled with questions as she left the countess. Rebellion? Here in England? But all the men at court behaved so deferentially to the king. Or was their conduct merely a ruse until they discovered how matters fell out with the upcoming war? And what of those men, like her father, who rarely came to court at all?

"Marguerite?"

She froze halfway down the passageway outside the countess's chambers. The voice stole away her breath, as it did in her dreams. But she was not sleeping . . . was she? Had she imagined this entire afternoon with the countess? She shook herself. Nay, she was not alone in her bed wrapped in her painful loneliness in the middle of the night. The weight of the book in her hand attested to her wakefulness.

"Mae."

The second name, the name only *he* knew, spun her about on a confused stammer. "R-Rob?"

He moved so swiftly he was little more than a blur until his arms were around her, lifting her off her feet and whirling her around in the air. She could not see him—she had buried her face too hard against his neck—but the familiar scent of mint and wood smoke filled her senses. No vision, no shadow sprung from her longing, but solid. So wonderfully solid and strong! It was he! Her heart drubbed in her ears, drowning out his murmuring words, but she knew his beloved tones. She had dreamt them every night, even when dozing the endless hours after the tournament while she waited to hear if Sir Warin would live.

Sir Warin. Oh, she should not want Robert here! If Saxton knew—! She tried to think of silken threats and lances that ripped through mail like a knife slicing parchment, but all she could do was cling to Robert the harder and pray he might never let her go.

19

It jarred Marguerite when he put her down. She barely glimpsed Robert's profile before he turned his back to her, but he held her hand fast in his and dragged her along behind him. That was when she heard the footsteps. She could not tell whether they came from Lady Helen's chambers or climbed the stairs in front of them. Either way she and Robert would surely have been seen had Robert not pulled her abruptly into a room that opened off the passageway and shoved the back of a chair under the door latch to prevent anyone from entering behind them.

"It is likely Lady Helen's maid," he muttered, "returning from some errand for her mistress. All the men are usually safe about other duties this time of day. But it is best to be cautious." He gave the chair a confident thump with the flat of his hand. "It's not the first time the rains have stuck this old door shut."

He turned toward her then. She gazed at last into his dear, dark face and found it fiery with a passion that weakened her knees, until it smeared with her tears.

"Marguerite, what is it?" He drew her down beside him on a bench near the shuttered window. His thumbs swiped gently across the moisture on her cheeks.

"Oh, Rob, I thought you had forgotten me, or—or perhaps didn't care."

The fear felt so absurd after the fierce embrace he had just dealt her. She leaned into his arms again, pressing her face to his shoulder, then jerked upright as she felt him wince and catch his breath. Her lips parted with alarm, but before she could speak Robert leaned forward and kissed her. In an instant the world fell away and they were back in the glade on that wild, glorious day they had first spoken of their love. How could she have doubted him when she tasted his devotion and faithfulness in the union of their lips?

Yet she *had* doubted him, and the shame of it made her pull away.

"Rob—"

"Mae, if you thought I did not care, then I did not kiss you soundly enough in the woods." Oh, how she had missed his dancing, midnight eyes! "I came as soon as I could, sweetheart."

"But where were you? I waited and waited that day in the glade!"

"I could not help it, Mae. I was—detained." He kissed her quickly again. To ward off her questions? "If only you had not left Dorset. I had no time to send you word."

"Oh!" It was just as she had feared. "What must you have thought? To leave without giving you a chance to explain. You must have believed I'd deserted you, that I wasn't serious when I said I'd go with you. But oh, Rob, I could not help it, either!"

"Of course you could not, sweetheart. Did you think I would not understand? What else could you do when a summons came from court? 'Twas my own fault for—for—" The hated mask that shut her out slid over his face. "Nay, I'll not make excuses. I should not have failed you."

"But why didn't you come?" She laid her hand softly against his shoulder. "Does it have something to do with this?"

He hesitated. "Aye."

"An accident?"

"Aye."

"Tell me," she coaxed.

"Love, the 'why' is not important, other than it was stupid and careless of me. What matters is that I am here now."

Why would he not confide in her? Oh, but he was right. All that mattered was that he had come for her at last. Saxton would soon be off to war, and then there would be nothing to stop her from flying away with Robert.

Marguerite glanced at last around the room where they sat. It looked like a quarter for servants, men, judging from the stray items of clothing tossed helter-skelter about the various traveling bags, a scattering of cast off bones, one a half-eaten chicken leg that appeared to have been abruptly abandoned, and a smell of flat ale that hung in the air. Was this where Lord Gunthar's male servants housed? How had Robert known the room was here? Now that the first shock of his arrival had passed, how had he known where to find her?

She had not realized she still clutched Lady Helen's book in one hand until she reached for Robert's clasp. She set the book in her lap so that she could slide both her hands into his and hold onto them tightly, lest he slip away from her again.

"How long have you been here?" she asked him. "And where are you staying?"

"Here," he said.

"Well, of course I know you are staying in London, but where—"

"Here, Mae, at court."

She must have stared at him as though she were addled—his answer certainly confounded her—for he laughed.

"Don't look so shocked, sweetheart. It is perfectly safe, I assure you. I am Lady Helen's new minstrel."

"Lady Helen's—*minstrel?*"

"Aye. I met her and the earl on their way to Westminster. It seems Lady Helen's former minstrel ran off with a cordwainer's daughter and she was desirous to replace him. I sang for them at an inn where they had stopped for some refreshment and Lady Helen invited me to join their household. Her husband frowned when she did so. He asked me if I had a wife and when I said no, he said I was too young and they must look elsewhere, but Lady Helen exclaimed that my song enchanted her—it was a fairy song my mother taught me—and she said I must not heed her stuffy husband and that she would not allow me to say her nay. I knew they were coming to court, so it seemed the perfect way to find you."

Marguerite counted the days since the Earl and Countess of Gunthar had arrived at court. "I have spent nearly every afternoon with Lady Helen," she said. "Did you not know it until today?"

"Of course I knew it. She calls for my music every morning and evening. She talks of you to the earl while they sit together at night and I play my lute in the corner. A time or two when we were alone, she even talked of you to me."

"Did she?" Marguerite blushed. "What did she say?"

"To her husband, that she finds you clever and bright and wishes she had a daughter like you and what a shame it is that so much sweetness must be wasted on a man like the Earl of Saxton."

Marguerite's lashes fluttered shyly against her cheeks. "And to you?"

"Much the same. She has grown fond of you very quickly. But as much as she bemoans your future marriage and as compassionate as I have found her to be, I think it would stretch her tolerance beyond breaking if she knew her minstrel intends to abscond with a lady, even if it saves you from Saxton."

Marguerite lifted his hands and kissed them. "How soon?" *Oh, pray say tomorrow!*

When Robert did not answer at once, she looked up and saw he frowned a little.

"We must be careful, Mae," he said after a moment. "'Tis why I dared not surprise you in Lady Helen's chambers. She nor anyone must not suspect that we have met before. I could not approach you before I knew what hour would be most safe to speak alone with you here." He indicated the room where they sat with a curt nod of his head. "And I dare not wander too far from this area of the palace because if Saxton sees me—"

She understood at once. "He will recognize you from my father's hall and wonder how you come to be in the royal palace."

Robert's mouth crooked up. "Oh, he will know why I am here . . . because he knows about us."

Marguerite stared at him. "Knows . . . about . . ." she bounced to her feet in horror ". . . *us?*"

"Mae—"

Lady Helen's book thumped against the floor. Marguerite let go of Robert to scoop it up, but she knew her face was white when she straightened for her cheeks had gone cold. "Rob, what do you mean? How *can* he know?"

"His squire followed us to the glade and told him. Saxton tracked me down in the village. We had an—argument—and before I could stop him, he whisked you away to London."

An argument? And Robert winced when she leaned against his shoulder. Oh! She shuddered as she realized what sort of "argument" must have kept him from meeting her in the glade. But she would not ask him again. Even with his mask, she sensed that he concealed the details of that encounter out of pride. She had learned from her grandmother how fragile and dear a man's pride was. Saxton had somehow offended

Robert's, and no amount of coaxing and pleading would persuade him to tell her how.

But she could not pretend that his revelation did not panic her. She saw again Sir Warin flung out of his saddle, the blood gleaming on the tip of Saxton's lance—

"Oh, Rob, you should not have followed me. You should not have come!"

"I could not *not* come, Mae. Do you think me so shallow that I would be deterred by some vexing quarrel and leave you to the mercies of that brute?"

"You do not understand. If Lord Saxton discovers you are here—" She broke off with a shiver.

Robert stiffened. "Do you think I cannot protect you?"

She sank back down on the bench and flung her arms around his neck, Lady Helen's book clutched tight in her hand. "It is *you* I fear for. I could not bear it if he should harm you."

"I am not afraid of Saxton." Robert's breath was warm against her ear. "In fact, I look forward to meeting him again. I've a certain score that needs paying off." He stroked her hair. "Make that several scores. Has he made things difficult for you since coming to London?"

She thought of the tournament and shivered again.

"What's he done? You can't hide it from me, Mae," he said when she shook her head, "you are clearly upset. What's he done to you?"

Robert lifted her face and searched it. His dark eyes had grown hard. Did he fear he'd missed a lingering bruise?

"He's not touched me," she said quickly. "But he—he injured a friend of mine. He is wicked and ruthless and if he sees you, if he thinks you have come for me—Rob, it isn't safe for you! Go away, at least until Lord Saxton has gone with the king to the war. Then there will be nothing to stop us from being together. Just a few more days, perhaps a week—"

Robert frowned, but he said nothing for a moment. Then he stood and drew her up with him. "We will speak of this later. Lady Helen will be calling for me soon and the other men will be returning to wait on her husband."

"But Rob—"

He silenced her with a kiss, hard and swift.

"Later," he said firmly. "I will send for you soon. Wait to hear from me." He laid a finger to her lips when she tried to protest again. "Come, I will see you to the stairs."

She should have fought harder against his determination to stay, but the heat of the kiss that lingered on her lips stole all her resolve. Selfishness won the battle in her heart. She wanted him here. She wanted to know he was near her, not somewhere lost in throngs of the great city of London.

She knew from how tightly he clasped her hand that he was savoring her touch as much as she savored his as they walked down the passageway together. Neither of them spoke until they reached the stairs. A few more days and Saxton would be gone, the danger to them both passed. As long as Robert was careful—

She checked as they reached the head of the stairs. Two men stood at the foot, turned to address each other so that neither appeared to see Marguerite and Robert gaze down on them. One she recognized immediately as Sir Edward Keynes. That was not unusual. She knew he had to pass this stairway to reach the hall from the area of the palace where he was housed. She had met him before when leaving Lady Helen's sitting chamber. The other, a tall, loose-knit man with a handsome, neatly bearded profile and a soft wave in his thick brown hair, was new to Marguerite and, she suspected, to the court. It did not surprise her when Robert's clasp tightened on her hand and pulled her away from the stairs.

"Marguerite, I must go," he said softly. "I will explain everything soon."

She nodded. It would be dangerous to be seen together, yet her fingers still clung to his. Robert kissed her one more time, as though he could not get enough of her.

"I love you, Mae," he whispered. "Never doubt that."

She watched him, drinking in the bold, almost defiant strides that carried him away from her until he disappeared behind the door of the servants' quarters.

The two men were still conversing at the foot of the stairs. Marguerite drew a deep breath, then slowly began her descent, praying they would not be able to hear the strong beating of her heart.

"Lady Marguerite," Sir Edward greeted her as she joined them. "Have you just come from the countess again?"

Marguerite nodded and held up the countess's book. "She has kindly lent me this to read."

Sir Edward smiled, then motioned at his companion. "Lady Marguerite, allow me to make known to you my brother-in-law, Lord Christopher

Beckford. Kit, the Lady Marguerite of Winbourne, Lord de Villon's daughter."

Lord Christopher took her hand and bowed, missing Marguerite's shock and horror to find herself unexpectedly thrust into the company of the man who had brought so much misery to Robert and his family. Had Robert recognized him? Oh, surely he had!

She struggled for Robert's sake to smooth out her expression before Lord Christopher straightened. She expected to meet the eyes of a monster, cold and malicious, like Saxton's, but the dark grey eyes that gazed into hers looked almost warm.

"Lord Heywood's granddaughter," Lord Christopher said with a smile. "I recall how you nearly married my neighbor, Lord Stephen, when I was twenty. You remember, Ned," he said to Sir Edward, "that summer when Sarah came to visit Hersent. Our wives," he explained for Marguerite. "My felicitations, my lady. I understand my neighbor's loss is the gain of the Earl of Saxton. You shall be wife to him, I am told, when he returns from the king's campaign."

Marguerite answered as she knew he and Sir Edward expected. "That is to be my honor."

Thank heavens her prayers had been answered for the wedding to be held back until the king's army returned from France. Annys said, once more quoting her father, the delay had been at the king's suggestion, another stratagem, Annys's father guessed, to keep the Earl of Saxton unsettled in the royal favor. *And by the time he returns, I will be long gone and the wife of Robert Marcel.*

"I have come to join the king's cause," Lord Christopher said, "summoned by my liege lord, the Earl of Gunthar. And now I have arrived, it is best that I pay my respects to him without further delay. 'Twas a pleasure to meet you, my lady."

He gave her a courteous nod and set his foot to the bottom step.

"Lord Gunthar is with the king just now," Marguerite stayed him. "And the countess told me she wishes to rest."

That last was a white lie, but if he should walk in upon the countess while Robert was playing his lute for her— Oh, she must warn Robert to be ever and ever so careful until the king's army left for France!

"I see." Lord Christopher removed his foot from the step. "Then I shall come back later. My lady, is there someplace I can escort you, perhaps?"

"Thank you, but I—I was on my way back to my chamber to change my gown. I am certain it is out of your way. Thank you for your kindness, though."

She curtsied to Lord Christopher, and then to Sir Edward, then glided past them both with as much composure as she could muster. Her father could be congenial too, when it pleased him, yet she knew how easily men could show a different face to one they held power over, like a daughter. *Or a villein.* If she stayed another moment in Lord Christopher's company, memories of the pain he had inflicted on Robert might provoke her into saying something she—and Robert—might regret.

20

*L*ady Helen looked straight into Robert's eyes with a gaze as direct and searching as any he had withstood from her husband.

"You give me your word, as a man of honor?" she asked him.

Robert held his face still, concealing his surprise. Men did not often link minstrels with honor, no matter how sacred Robert himself counted his word when he gave it. He might have lashed out with a barbed pride to someone else, but in this instance he replied with simple honesty. "I would have done it without you asking, my lady."

She had won his loyalty almost from the first, not only for the generosity she had shown him since taking him into her household, but for those moments she cast twinkling glances at him in her sitting chamber, sharing her amusement over some haughty, arrogant comment Lord Gunthar made to her when stating his opinion on a variety of subjects. The only thing that had spared the old earl Robert's usual contempt for men of his rank had been the wry grins with which Gunthar received his wife's chidings. Robert found it hard to hate a man who so clearly loved and respected his wife, even if nine times out of ten when Robert sang for the Earl and Countess of Gunthar, the earl behaved as if Robert wasn't even there. Robert had discovered little beyond Gunthar's unexpected warmth for Lady Helen to mitigate the otherwise lofty lift of the earl's hawkish nose, but Robert would serve him for her sake. *Though I do not promise to always mind my tongue.*

"His men are loyal," Lady Helen said. "There is not a one of our household, knight, squire or page, whom I do not completely trust. But you are clever and quick and daring. Nay, do not feign modesty to please me. There is something about you—" She tilted her head, weighing him with an unnerving perception. "You do not fear the way other men do. I do not know how I know it, but I do. I will not ask for your word again. I will simply trust you."

This lady, nearly as tall as he, so slender even in her fifties that Robert had thought her fragile until he had seen how vigorously she moved, with a gaze as piercing as her husband's on those rare occasions the earl ceased staring past Robert and looked straight at him . . . this lady who so often twinkled at Robert in this very room with a baffling but irresistible camaraderie of spirit . . . this lady Robert would not fail.

Lady Helen smiled at him. "Go now, but bring your lute and come to us this evening. I will see to it my husband is in a receptive mood."

Usually when Robert bowed, he did it with a flourish as a punctuation to one of his performances, or with a mental shrug in a sham of deference for men who thought themselves his superior, having learned it was best to pick his battles in asserting his equality. Rarely did he bow to another out of genuine respect, but he went easily down on one knee now and kissed the countess's hand.

"Thank you, my lady." He hoped the tone of his words imparted his double gratitude, for both her confidence and her intercession. He left her with his heart beating an alternating rhythm of hope and dread.

Dread surged to the forefront when he saw the young man awaiting him outside the servants' quarters. Voices rumbled from the other side of the partially open door from men excitedly preparing to join the earl when he and his knights rode with the rest of the king's army for the coast on Thursday. Robert housed here with the earl's lower servants, those who would accompany the troops but not fight with them in battle: Gunthar's private cook, his barber, his tailor, a few of the earl's minor clerks, and his personal physician, the latter flattered to have been included at the countess's insistence, but disappointed at having been excluded from sleeping in the sitting chamber alongside the earl's squires.

Robert took the young man by the arm and drew him farther away from the door. "Did you give her my message?" Robert asked, his voice low.

Simon Todd nodded. "Aye. Did you know her parents have come to court?"

Robert gave a short nod. "Three days ago. The countess has been mourning Lady Marguerite's companionship. Lady Leah, it appears, does not think it seemly for her daughter to squander her time with the wife of Lord Saxton's rival."

If any man might have known how to counter the Earl of Saxton's despotic power, Robert judged it would have been the Earl of Gunthar in his prime. Robert found Gunthar autocratic and overbearing, but also intelligent, honest, and shrewd. There was an air about him that clearly intimidated most men, a piercing comprehension in Gunthar's keen grey eyes that seemed to weigh a man's worth at a glance, then either approve or dismiss him. Robert knew he had sufficiently passed some silent test to be trusted to serve Gunthar's wife.

But a hint of weariness lay beneath Gunthar's formidable bearing. His grey hair attested to his long life, the creases in his face that it had not been an easy one. Robert did not know if Gunthar still possessed the energy to fight against Saxton's relative youth and cunning corruption, but from the glint in Gunthar's eyes and the hard set of his mouth, Robert sensed that something had brought him to court to try.

Only days remained before the king and his troops sailed off to France. Thanks to the arrival of Marguerite's parents the morning after Robert had revealed his presence to her, Robert had not had a chance to speak with her again. With Kit Beckford prowling about the palace, Robert had not dared stray beyond this passageway. Robert had at length recommended a new glove maker to the countess, then seized upon the apprentice sent to measure her hands to go where Robert could not.

"You had best get back to your glover," Robert said to Simon. "If he reprimands you for tarrying at the palace, tell him the truth, that a servant of the Earl of Gunthar asked you to perform an errand for him."

He clapped a hand to Simon's shoulder and turned him towards the stairs, but Simon resisted with a chagrined expression that sent Robert's brows up in question.

"Rob, Lady Marguerite—she told me to tell ye that she—"

"Told you?" Robert's brows twitched down as fast as they'd soared. "I gave you a message to hand to Eva. You were not supposed to let the Lady Marguerite see you."

"I know, but she came to the door when she heard my voice."

"Blazes, Simon, I told you to keep your head down. Her father, *your master*, is at court. What do you think he will do if he finds you here instead of on his manor?"

"Drag me back an' flog me," Simon mumbled, "an' put me in the stocks. That's what he did to old Perkin Cropper four years ago when he tried to run away, an' Perkin was over fifty. It's what de Villon does to all his villeins who displease him."

"It's what they all do," Robert said. "Now you've thrown Lady Marguerite into the middle of it all. She will try to protect you, and her father is no more gentle with his daughter than he is with his villeins." Robert could have shaken the young man.

"I'm sorry, Rob. I swear I'll be more careful. I'll make an excuse not to come back to the palace until her da is off to France and her mum has gone back to the manor. Lord de Villon won't see me, I promise."

Curiosity pricked beneath Robert's vexation. "What did my lady say when she saw you?"

"First she begged me to go back to the manor, for fear o' what her father would do if he saw me. But I told her what ye told me, that 'tis madness to sit in idle slavery when there are lawful ways to escape."

"And to that she said?" Robert realized he held his breath, waiting for the answer. A baron like her grandfather choosing to free his villeins was one thing. Robert encouraging one of her father's villeins to abscond from his manor she might view entirely differently.

"She didn't say anything at first, just bit her lip and looked thoughtful. But then she smiled an' asked me what I would do when I was free. I said I'd marry Eva if she'd let me, though I confess, a year an' a day seems a cruel long time to wait."

"It will be worth it when her father no longer stands a threat to you," Robert said, "when you have money of your own in your purse to support a wife and need answer for your choices to no man but yourself."

Simon gave a reluctant sigh. "I suppose ye're right."

Robert tried to push him again towards the stairs. "Go back to the city and stay out of sight till her father is gone. 'Twill be a good lesson for you in patience."

"Rob—" Simon resisted him again. "Lady Marguerite—she says she can't come meet ye this afternoon, but she can come in an hour. Well, less than an hour now, since we've been standin' here talkin'—"

"This morning?" Robert cast a dismayed glance at the door to the servants' chamber. "But the men won't disperse from there until they go down to the kitchens to eat after the court has dined. There is no other time or place we can speak in private. You explained that to her, did you not?"

"I tried, but she wouldn't listen. She said it had to be now, as soon as she changed her clothes, because her mum would want her company after dinner, as her mum has every day since she's come to court."

Robert had known that from Lady Helen's laments, but he had trusted Marguerite to be clever enough to slip away this once. She had tricked her parents fully a week to meet him in the glade in Dorset.

Robert swore. He dragged Simon over to the door and pulled it open, then strode inside, rattling off a list of sham errands as fast as they raced through his desperate mind.

"I have just come from the Lady Helen and she has given us each a charge, if we would please her. Yes, before dinner."

The clerks he sent to the city to buy more ink for their master's voyage, the tailor to buy more cloth for the earl's hose.

"And would you mind showing my young friend here the way back to his glover's shop?" Robert said. "He's been in London for less than a week and still loses his way six times of ten."

The baker he sent to the palace kitchens to prepare a special dish for the earl at dinner, the barber to buy a new razor— "The earl said you nicked him while shaving this morning." That was true enough. Robert had over-heard Gunthar remark upon it to his wife as Robert had passed the earl leaving her sitting chamber that morning. Thankfully the physician had already gone off on some errand of his own.

As soon as Marguerite was through the door, Robert rammed a chair beneath its latch again, grateful for a morning of drizzling rain to plausibly stick the swollen wood. Then he turned to observe his love in an absurd homespun gown, with two fat, fluffy-ended braids swinging about her shoulders.

"Before you scold me for coming," Marguerite said, "I borrowed this gown from Eva and had her dress my hair like her own. Anyone who saw me would think me just another servant."

Robert looked at her delicate white hands and watched the graceful way she moved across the room. He sighed his exasperation. "'Twould take more than that plain gown to make you look like a servant."

The scolding done, he took her small, soft hands in his and bent down to kiss her. Then he led her to the bench near the window where they had sat together before, but she released him before they reached it and swept over to the corner where he stored his gear, apparently identifying it by his lute case. He heard her short, sharp breath as she touched the hilt of the sword that leaned against his bag. He had been polishing the blade earlier that morning, before Lady Helen had agreed to see him.

"Is this yours?" she asked, with a wide-eyed glance over her shoulder.

"It was my father's," he said, joining her. "Gilbert wanted to destroy it when our father died, but—"

"Gilbert?" He could see her trying to place the name, and the instant when she succeeded. "Your brother."

It pleased Robert that she remembered. "Aye. Lord Garoux had given the sword to our father for the king's wars, but it is unlawful for villeins to be armed. When Lord Garoux did not ask for it back after he hanged our father, Gilbert feared the baron had left it with us as some sort of trap. I was only twelve but had some absurd thought that I could protect us all with it if need be, so I hid it where Gil never found it."

Robert watched her trace a finger around the pattern of a rampant tyger figured into the sword hilt's circular pommel. One raised paw had broken off, no doubt the reason Lord Garoux was willing to cast it off on Robert's father. 'Twas this image that had prompted Robert to purchase a dagger with a similar, but unflawed, emblem on its hilt when he had seen the blade in a market in York.

"Lord Garoux never asked us for it," he repeated, "and neither did Kit. I thought Kit had forgotten about it until he set the hounds on me. That's when I knew he guessed I had taken it with me when I fled. A villein with a sword would be reason enough in the eyes of the law for Kit to let his pack tear me limb from limb, especially after the things I had said."

Robert regretted his frankness when Marguerite shuddered. He passed a reassuring arm around her shoulders, reminding her that he was safe and sound beside her.

"About his father, you mean?" she asked.

"No." Robert nudged her hand aside to wrap his fingers around the sword's hilt. It fit in his grasp perfectly. "Oh, that was the true reason for his anger, of course, but it was not why he released the hounds. A baron may punish 'slander' any number of ways, including cutting out a man's tongue, but he may not kill him for it. I said something much worse in the end than accusing his own father of treason. I said that villeins should be free."

If her father had ever resorted to more vicious methods of corporal punishment upon his villeins than flogging, Marguerite must have remained ignorant of it with her more enlightened grandfather, else she would not have whirled about with so shocked an expression when Robert spoke of it.

"How can that be worse than what you said about Lord Christopher's father?" she cried. "They called my grandfather mad for freeing his villeins, and the idea dangerous, 'tis true, but no one would have dared to set hounds on him. The royal courts even upheld his will!"

"Your grandfather's actions only affected his own manors, Mae. Did he ever tell you why he did it? Did he ever raise his voice to encourage other lords to free their villeins, as he had done?"

She shook her head. She would have mentioned it that day in the glade when she told him about her inheritance if her grandfather had done either.

"A baron who sets villeins free on his own manor is merely eccentric or irksomely mad," Robert said. "But a *villein* who goes about shouting that all his fellows should be free, and then runs off with a sword—*that* man might be called a dangerous agitator who seeks to upend the very order of England, by violent force no less."

Robert whipped up the sword, swinging it in a hissing arc away from Marguerite. His shoulder had well healed of Saxton's thrust, save when direct pressure was set against it. By the time he needed to use this steel again, he judged his shoulder would be fully sound.

He turned back to Marguerite and set the blade's point against the floor. "*That*, Mae, is real treason. There is not a baron in England, including the king, who would not applaud the man who put a stop to such heresy as that by any means he chose."

Her cheeks went white. "Rob, is—is that what you wish to do?"

"Upend your world?" He closed his eyes for a moment, tasting a life of freedom for his brother and sister, for William and Lucy, for every man and woman in England too weak or too frightened to fight for it. But he shook his head. "Because I spoke a truth that Kit did not like does not mean I ever thought I had the power to bring about a revolution. That is not why I took the sword. I only brought it with me to defend myself in a world I knew nothing about. It gave Kit the perfect excuse, though, to turn his hounds loose on me, which he did not dare do before."

He gazed down into her troubled face and saw she had not caught the implication of his word "before," for her worry focused elsewhere.

"But Rob, you still have the sword and you helped Simon escape from our manor. Lord Christopher might say it proves his fears of you were justified."

"Would you have me send Simon back?"

Did she hesitate out of a reluctance to return the young man to a life of bondage or because she was fearful of disappointing Robert if she answered honestly? Her reply, when it came, did not fully satisfy his question.

"N-not forever," she stammered at last. "Just until my father sails for France. If my father sees him here at court—if Lord Christopher sees *you*—"

"I am not afraid of Kit."

"Oh, I know," she said. "You are a freeman now and can legally carry a sword." He felt his lower lip curling towards his teeth and swiftly stilled it as she hurried on breathlessly, "But Rob, did you know that Lord Christopher is a vassal of the Earl of Gunthar? That is why he was coming to see the earl that day we heard him on the stairs. I have been so afraid that he might return and see you with the countess."

"He did come once, but I was careful to stay out of his way," Robert assured her. "Kit holds two fiefs from the earl, my old manor in Wiltshire, though Gunthar never visited there in my lifetime, and Halham Manor which shares Lyndeard Village with your father's villeins." He saw her surprise. "You did not know about Halham?"

She looked appalled. "My father rarely mentioned Halham's lord, and when he did he only called him Lord Christopher. How could I have guessed he meant Christopher *Beckford*? Oh, Rob, how could you be so rash as to come to Lyndeard and fairly throw yourself under Lord Christopher's nose?"

"It was the only way I could see my old friend, Will Locke," Robert answered practically. "Will says Kit never comes to Halham. But even if he did, I would never have met you again if I hadn't been 'so rash,' so don't chide me for that, sweetheart." He laughed and dealt her a quick kiss. Then he leaned his sword against his bag again and led her over to the bench. Time was passing too swiftly and he had so much still to tell her.

"I did not actively encourage Simon to leave your manor, Mae," Robert said as he drew her down beside him, "but when he saw I was leaving Lyndeard, he begged me to let him come with me. I could not tell him to stay and be content with his lot when I refused to be content myself. Besides, how else is he to marry Eva if he does not win his freedom? The men of your world—men like your father, like Kit—would never allow a villein to wed a free woman. We cannot even marry a villein from another manor without permission. My sister Lottie tried."

Marguerite must have caught the thread of bitterness that stole into his voice, for she asked, "What happened?"

Her grandfather's manor must encircle a single village, Robert thought, rather than sharing one as her father's did. Robert explained, "Lottie wished to marry a man named Albric, but he was one of Lord Stephen's villeins. They could not marry without Kit's consent, for any children she bore to Albric would become Lord Stephen's villeins and Kit would lose their future labor. Kit agreed to let them wed if Gilbert would pay him merchet for our sister's loss. Do you know what that is, Mae?"

She shook her head. "Odo told me proudly that he need not teach me the terms that rule villeins since my grandfather had none and I would only govern free men and women when he died."

"Merchet," Robert said, "is a monetary sum a villein father pays his lord to allow his daughter to marry, a sum equal to the cost of an ox. *That* is how they view us, as mere beasts of burden to cultivate their fields so that they may rest, sated and fat, off the sweat of our bone-weary bodies."

He wanted to sit beside Marguerite relating it all in calm tones, distanced from the raw memories by so many years, but anger began a slow, steady throb in his heart. He fought hard to hold his voice even.

"Our father was dead, but Gil would have paid the merchet had Kit not set it so high, higher than his father had ever asked of any villein. Kit knew we could not raise the sum. He did it purposely, to provoke us—to provoke *me*. He knew my temper. He wanted me to hit him, I saw it in his eye. He could have run me through with his sword for the offense and suffered no more than a token fine, at worst, and likely not even that, for who would blame him for putting down a dog that'd grown vicious?"

Robert felt Marguerite shift her weight, heard her begin to speak, then check herself. Without glancing at her, he plunged on in her pause.

"It was the first time Kit had presided over a manor court in the stead of his steward. I might have done just what he wanted—I had my hand in a fist

—but Gil stepped directly in front of me and asked for time to consider Kit's terms. Kit agreed and dismissed us. Gil dragged me away. He and I quarreled over what to do for days, while Lottie wept in despair. Then a week later, we came home from the fields to find Lottie hysterical. She said Kit had summoned her to up to the castle and told her that she was to marry Walter Hanley, a man who tended Kit's stables, and who was a brute and bully about the manor."

The restlessness that had driven Robert as long as he could remember overtook his resolve for control and thrust him to his feet. He fell to pacing, weaving his steps around the barber's bag of razors, the tailor's mending kit, and the pens the clerks had left lined up on the floor.

"Gilbert said we could never win against a baron, so why try and suffer? He told Lottie she would find safety in quietness and meekness, and told her to go to bed. But I could not bear to hear her weeping in the dark. So after Gil fell asleep, I bade her dress and carried her away to Albric."

Robert saw that Marguerite had risen with him, and returned to press her gently back down on the bench.

"What happened?" she asked, her eyes wide with worry.

He rubbed her shoulders lightly, more to try to distract himself from his own emotions than to soothe her concern. "I was only seventeen, Mae, and I was impulsive and headstrong. I remembered the law Father Elias had told me of. And I remembered how my father had said it was the right of all men to be free. So I convinced Albric that if he wanted Lottie, they had no choice but to flee our manors and evade capture for a year and a day. Once they were legally free, I assured them Kit would pose no further threat to their happiness." Robert felt his mouth crook up in rueful irony. "And of course I went with them, because it was my idea and I thought they should not know how to do it without me. And I wanted to be free, too."

He recalled the wild exhilaration that had flowed through him as the three of them had run together through the woods, guided only by a silvery half-moon that dappled the forest floor through the canopy of branches. Albric muttering doubts all the way, Lottie telling her beloved again and again to "trust Robin," Robert's own triumphant laughter at the thought of Kit's chagrin when he found himself outwitted, but most of all Robert's joy that he was on the verge of achieving his father's greatest dream for at least two members of their family—

And then the sound of baying hounds.

"Seventeen," Marguerite said as he felt again the shock that had rushed up his spine at the clamoring dogs. "But I met you when you were eighteen, and you were running away alone."

"That's because we were caught." At least Kit had kept the hounds leashed that time. Barons did not kill runaway villeins and lose their labor, and that was all Robert and the others had been that night. He had not yet begun his "treasonous" assertions of freedom. Robert recalled how even with the dogs howling and Lottie screaming and Albric shouting, he had not known fear. Only a naïve surprise that Kit had followed them so soon.

He saw distress in Marguerite's face as she anticipated what followed. His hands clamped tighter around her shoulders. No, he had not feared Kit then or afterwards. There had been only hatred, and a terrible guilt that still lay aching in his stomach.

"I was young, Mae," he repeated, "and so wretchedly foolish. I led them away on the spur of the moment with no notion of where to go or what to do. It was inevitable that Kit should catch us. I should have known that. If I'd listened just once in my life to Gilbert or Will when they told me to stop and *think*— But I never did, and the night ended in disaster. Kit dragged us back and gave Albric to Lord Stephen to deal with, then locked me up in a filthy cell in his castle till morning."

"Lord Christopher punished you, didn't he?" Marguerite whispered. "With the whip?"

There was no use attempting to soften the truth for her. At least Kit had spared Robert the stocks.

"Aye, Kit had me flogged." No need to tell her it had not been the first time, or the last. "He was angry. Furious that I had tried to defy him. His bailiff whipped me until I fell unconscious. I awoke with a fever and by the time it passed, Lottie had been forced to marry Walter Hanley."

That had been the darkest day of Robert's life after his father's death. In some ways it had been worse for he could not have saved his father, but if he had been more careful, more cautious—if he had thought before he acted— he might have saved Lottie.

Marguerite stood and slid her arms around his neck. "Never again," she said fiercely. "You are a freeman now and no one shall ever flog you again."

He held her tight against him and buried his face in her sweet-smelling hair. He had felt a promise of healing once in her kiss. Now her comfort swept all around him. If the guilt and anger did not fully fade, the emotions ebbed back into that bearable corner where he had learned to tamp them down and live his life with energy and optimism, though too often impulsiveness still tripped him into trouble.

"How did you ever find the courage to try to flee again?" she asked.

"The first few months were difficult," he confessed, at last sitting down with her once more on the bench. "I could barely speak to Lottie for the shame I felt. I knew that Hanley abused her, but Gilbert said I would only make things worse for her if I interfered, so I kept my distance. But I was still angry at Kit. That was when I started repeating my father's belief that villeins should be free and the more I saw it provoked Kit, the louder I said it. Kit called me a radical and an agitator. All the villagers, my neighbors, my former friends, all of them save Will Locke and Gilbert, began to shun me for fear of Kit's displeasure."

Gilbert had struggled till the end to play the protective older brother, trying, with a rare flash of their father's stubbornness, to guide Robert into wiser paths. And stolid, loyal Will, with no blood-ties to bind them, who cursed and rebuked Robert's reckless words and actions, had nevertheless refused to abandon their lifelong friendship no matter how Kit glared and Will's parents and siblings begged him to cease his association with "the troublemaker."

He felt Marguerite waiting for more. "Things changed when Hervé of Cressy came to the village. Hervé was a minstrel."

Robert heard her soft gasp. He leaned forward, his forearms resting on his thighs, and rubbed his hands together between his knees. She thought she had guessed the rest of the story, but she had not.

"I showed Hervé my mother's lute," Robert said, "and he offered to teach me something of his trade. Our duets became so popular that Kit at last invited us to the castle to entertain his household and his new wife, Lady Hersent. For awhile I'd forgotten to bait him for my excitement in the music. After we sang for him a few times, Kit became almost friendly to me. We had played together as boys. I thought he must have spent his anger on me with the flogging—" Robert barely caught himself in time to turn the word singular "—and perhaps regretted all the conflicts that had risen between us after my father's death. After Hervé moved on, Kit continued to invite me to the castle to sing alone. I believed we had at last reached a sort of truce. So when Kit began preparing to join the king's campaign to regain Normandy, I asked to go with him."

"I thought—"

Robert glanced at Marguerite and caught her puzzled look.

"You were not trying to flee with Hervé the minstrel then?"

Robert shook his head.

"Why did you wish to go to Normandy?"

"To follow in my father's footsteps. Perhaps to find evidence of his inno-cence in the lands where he was said to have betrayed the king. But Kit laughed in my face when I asked." Robert's lips tightened as the sound of Kit's scorn burned his ears again. "He said he would be mad to trust me when my father had proven himself a traitor. Like father, like son, he said. Well, I did something even my father never dared do to Kit's sire. Gilbert was not there to stop me this time, so I hit Kit full in the mouth."

Marguerite gasped, loudly now. "Oh, Rob! You said yourself Lord Christopher might have run you through for striking him!"

"He might if I had not knocked him down," Robert said. "It all came rushing over me, every wrong he and his father had dealt my family, and I lost my temper as badly as I ever had in my life. I shouted my father was no traitor and flung fresh accusations about his own. Kit clambered to his feet, infuriated, but he wasn't wearing his sword. He swung his fist at me, but I dodged and hit him again."

The satisfying *crack* of Robert's knuckles against Kit's chin trounced out Kit's mocking laughter now as it had then.

"This time when Kit fell he hit his head on the edge of the dais, for we were quarreling beneath it in the castle hall. The blow stunned him, long enough for me to leave the castle. I knew what would happen when he regained consciousness. I knew I had finally given him what he wanted, a reason to kill me if he caught me. But this time I did not run off all pell-mell. I'd inadvertently bought myself time when Kit hit his head. Not much, but enough to run to our cottage and pack a few belongings, including my father's sword and my mother's lute."

Robert saw Marguerite glance at the unsheathed blade propped up against his instrument. He had learned a few things since the aborted attempt with Lottie. This time he'd taken a weapon to defend himself with, and the lute to earn himself a living in his new world.

"I thought I could make it across the bridge before Kit recovered enough to come after me, only I had not left him as dazed as I thought. I still had enough of a head start that I could have swam the river, but I hesitated . . . and you know the rest."

He straightened and kissed her hand in renewed gratitude for the part she had played in frustrating Kit's pursuit. Her fingers brushed whisper-soft against his cheek. He turned his head to kiss them too and was rewarded with her smile.

"What was in the other bundle you asked me to carry for you that day?" she asked.

He realized he had never told her. "My books. Here, let me show you."

He led her over to his bag. They knelt beside it together, where he dug out the three volumes.

"The saint's life Father Elias gave me after I finished copying it for him."

She took the book and opened it. "This is your writing?"

He nodded and watched her study the pages, proud to know their legibility had passed the priest's strict judgment, though Father Elias teased him that his letters possessed too bold a flair for the meek-tempered priest he was striving to train Robert to be.

"This one," Robert said, exchanging the book in her hands, "is a bestiary Father Elias gave me for the moral lessons each sketch taught. It has drawings, not paintings, as you see, with allegories written by another hand than mine. These are the two you carried for me. I bought this one—" he gave her the third "—for myself with some of the first wages I earned in my new life as a minstrel."

"*Reynard the Fox*," she exclaimed. "Odo read this to me when I was ever so little." She raised her eyes, aglow with delight, to his face. "Oh, Rob, let us read it together!"

The dread he had staved off by telling her the rest of his story became an aching hitch in his chest. He reached out and lovingly twitched the fluffy end of one of her braids. "We will, sweetheart . . . when I get back."

"Back?" She stared at him. "Back from where?"

He drew a deep breath before he answered. "Back from Poitou. It is where Gunthar says the king will station his forces."

"From Poi—" Understanding dawned in her face with painful swiftness. "You are going with the king?" She scrambled to her feet. "But Rob, Saxton is going, and my father is going, and even Lord Christopher. There will be nothing left to stop us from being together—unless you go too!"

Robert rose and reached for her, but she danced away, *Reynard* clutched tight to her breast. He saw the quick swell of tears in her eyes. "Mae—Marguerite—"

"Rob, how can you even think of it? We have only just found one another again, and now you are leaving? *Why?*"

He spread his hands wide in a plea for her to understand. "For the same reason that I asked Kit to let me go with him seven years ago. To seek proof of my father's innocence."

"Your father has been dead for thirteen years. How do you expect to find evidence after so much time, even in Poitou? Do you even speak French?"

He hesitated, then shook his head.

Anger flashed behind her tears. "You go for pride." Her voice stung with accusation. "To prove yourself the equal of knights and barons and earls, the very men who view you no differently than a beast of burden, who flog you, who trample you and your family beneath their feet. But you will not go as their equal. If you think you will—"

"Of course I do not think it. They are not the only ones who fight. There are archers too, and footsoldiers, all men of humble birth. That is where I will march, among the Earl of Gunthar's men. Lady Helen promised to intercede with the earl to let me join his company."

"Rob—"

"Marguerite, I have to go. Perhaps I will learn nothing. Perhaps the trail has grown too cold, as you say. But I have to try."

The book against her breast rose and fell with her aggravated breaths. "Lord Christopher is one of Lord Gunthar's vassals. If you march with the earl's men, he is sure to see you!"

"He will not be looking for me. If I know Kit, he will not bother to look at the footsoldiers at all. I will be safer there than if I rode into battle as a knight."

Robert saw her reaching for another argument. "What if you lose your temper again? What if you confront him?"

"I will watch him only. Perhaps his father confessed to Kit before he died. He may do something, say something, that leads me to the truth. If he did and I was not there to see it . . . Marguerite, I do not know how to make you understand . . . but I have to go."

This time it was she who paced, her rough, homespun gown carelessly scattering the clerks' neat line of pens across the floor. When she spoke again, he heard the misery in her voice. "I do understand. But—" One of the pens cracked beneath her slipper as she whirled towards him, saying all in a rush, "Oh, Rob, let us be married now, tonight, before you leave me!"

Temptation scorched through him, but he shook his head.

Again anger blazed in her eyes like lightning. "The king is going to war! There will be battles, men will die—*you* might die. How am I to bear this?"

The only answer he had was to open his arms. She ran into them, dropping the book so she could fling her own about his neck. He heard her soft sob against his breast.

"Sweetheart, if it should indeed happen that I should not return—I would not make of you a widow, so young as you are."

"Do you think I shall mourn you the less for not being your wife?" she demanded, hurt turning her anger fierce.

"Nay." He laid his cheek against her hair. "But you will not lose your position or be cast alone upon the world, the wife of a minstrel who never came back from a war. That *I* could not bear."

He rocked her gently as she wept. He had not thought of following the king until he had seen Kit striding past the half-open door to the servants' quarters on his way to pay his respects to Gunthar. Lady Helen had confirmed to Robert that Kit had come at Gunthar's summons to fight for the king in Poitou. Until then, Robert had had every intention of running off with Marguerite as soon as the king and his army marched off to Portsmouth. But Robert had seen his old enemy, sniffed an old trail of lies, and everything had changed.

He let Marguerite weep softly against him for a few more moments, then dried her cheeks. "There, sweetheart, I vow I will return for you, or move heaven and earth trying."

He led her back over to his bag. He knelt, holding her hand in one of his while he rifled through his belongings with the other. There. It lay just beneath the gowns he still carried for her to wear when they eloped. He pulled out the ribbon. He had meant it for a wedding gift, but just in case his brave words about returning did not come true—

"Wear this for me, sweetheart, and think of me when you do."

He moved behind her and drew back her braids, then bound them together with the spring green ribbon with a garland of merry roses embroidered down the center.

A thump sounded against the door, followed by a curse, another thump, and a shuffling of feet as whoever stood on the other side went off to find some tool to wedge open the "swollen" door.

"Marguerite, you must go." Before he lost his will, before he forgot his duty to his father.

She turned to face him, her eyes shining with despair. "Will I see you again before you leave?"

He did not know, and he would not make her a promise he could not keep. "I'll send you word by Simon's hand."

It was the most he could offer. He pulled open the door and pushed her across the threshold, darted a glance up and down the empty passageway, then leaned forward to kiss her one more time, a kiss to bide them both through the long, lonely months to come.

21

Poitou
March 1214

The rain had ceased at noon, but the weak sun that broke from the clouds had not been enough to dry the muddied earth or warm the air by nightfall. Mist rose swirling white against the dark over the plain where the English camp had settled for the night. Robert arranged himself more comfortably cross-legged on his pallet, and continued listening to the voices nearest him while he plucked a dulcet tune on his strings. Gunthar's knights frequently talked freely to the backdrop of his music, just as Gunthar had done in his sitting chamber with his wife, so accustomed to the sounds of the minstrel's lute they seemed to forget that Robert was there.

"Saints!" Thomas Hastings exclaimed. "You should have seen his face. The Earl of Saxton gone livid! Lord Cold-as-a-Fish, sneering down his nose at us these twelve years, making us grovel for his favor, crushing anyone whose glance offended him, Lord Lick-My-Boots-or-I'll-Kick-Your-Ribs was finally disconcerted. I thought he might murder the king!"

"He's more likely to murder Gunthar, if it's true," his companion said, holding out his hands towards the fire.

"If? Who's in command of this camp, I ask you?"

Most of the men had retired to their pallets by this hour, the knights bedding closest to the fire with their squires nearby. The archers and foot-soldiers rimmed around behind them. All were wearied by their march from the king's base at La Rochelle, but the late arrival of the Earl of Gunthar's brother-in-law, Lord Laurant, who had brought his own knights to support the king, kept a few men awake exchanging news. Only Gunthar and Laurant and their personal squires had been offered hospitality by the Baron Malefay inside his castle's walls. The rest of the company sought comfort as best they could on the wide plain that stretched between the fortress and the forest on this chill March night.

Robert had been as surprised as the rest of the company to learn that Gunthar would be leading the expedition to woo the Poitevin barons of the north, with Saxton attending him, rather than vice versa. And Saxton, to his vociferous protests earlier in the day, had not been invited by Gunthar to join his discussions with the baron.

"I saw it myself," Hastings said. The flames cast a glow around his and his companion's otherwise shadow-dark figures. "The king's command took Saxton so unawares that he actually suggested the king must have misspoken. John disabused him with a smirk that drove Saxton's face white with mortification."

Robert presumed it was Hastings' position as Gunthar's secretary that had won him a place at Gunthar's side to witness the king's orders to the two earls.

"Well, now, that would have brought my master some satisfaction," the second man replied with an accent slightly heavier than the one the Lady Helen spoke with. "He was sorely insulted for his sister's sake when the king banished Gunthar from his court. He ranted for weeks when he learned of it and threatened to throw his allegiance to France. I think it was only the letter from Lady Heléne that stayed his anger and kept him loyal to the fealty he'd sworn to John."

From the man's words and accent, Robert guessed him a knight belonging to Lord Laurant, Lady Helen's brother. Robert had glimpsed the Poitevin baron briefly before he had ridden off earlier in the day at Gunthar's side. Laurant's golden beauty could not have contrasted more starkly with Lady Helen's mild prettiness. Even in his fifties, with gray brushing along his temples, Robert knew the baron's face would still enchant women young and old

"My master was astonished when word came that Gunthar was in Poitou once more, apparently restored to the king's good graces," the knight with the accent said. "Gunthar dared not come after his dismissal, Lady Heléne wrote, for fear the king would accuse him of selling the king's secrets to

France in revenge. Gunthar, consort with France! The thought would be laughable to anyone but John, who sees a traitor or spy in every shadow."

Hastings' silhouette shifted against the flames, as though some disquiet had come upon him. Robert realized he had let his hand grow still on the lute strings. Men who failed to consciously register his music often sensed the change when it ceased. Robert resumed his plucking and saw the silhouette immediately relax again.

"What is behind this caprice of the king's to restore Gunthar to his former honors?" the Poitevin knight asked.

"I know only the rumors men were whispering when I returned to court with the earl," Hastings said. "A friend who has spent more recent time in the king's court than I thinks the king has begun to fear that Saxton has grown too comfortable in his power. He told me Saxton even dared try to command the king about some silly tournament, but he thought that was only the final ember to a fire of suspicion already lit in the king's heart. You know King John. Nay, you have been spared the worst of him here in Poitou."

A movement turned Robert's head toward a shade that traveled around the perimeter of the campfire.

"It has been the king's delight from the first days of his reign," Hastings continued, "to promote one favorite so as to humiliate another, but Saxton has grown expert at knowing how to satisfy the king's passions, whether for wine, women, or perceived enemies to demoralize and debase. My friend said the king seems unready to entirely dispense with Saxton yet, but appears to wish to rebuke him for his growing arrogance, and has chosen Gunthar to frighten him with."

"Gunthar should be warned to tread lightly, then."

Robert could not alert the two knights of the man who approached them without giving away his own eavesdropping, but the newcomer's voice revealed what the darkness hid—that he was a friend.

"Gossiping about Saxton and Gunthar, are you?" Sir Brandon de Vexin spoke in the same accent as the Poitevin knight, though Robert knew him as one of the men Gunthar had brought with him from England. "My lord will cut off your ears if he hears you. He's no tolerance for rumormongers, as Hastings here knows." Sir Brandon's affable tones suggested the threat was a jest, though a true thread of rebuke ran beneath it. "The earl will want us fresh for our ride with him to the Baron de Courcelle tomorrow, so get to bed, both of you."

Hastings rose and stretched. "Are you just back from the watch? How do you think your son fares with Gunthar? Some of these Poitevin lords have been mighty foul tempered when reminded of their oaths to the king."

Hastings' Poitevin companion stood and jabbed Hastings with his elbow, which made the secretary laugh.

"And so would you feel peeved," the Poitevin said, "to be called upon to fight for a hopeless cause. If King John fails, *you* will both go safely home to England, while *we* will be left at the mercy of King Philip's retribution for choosing the wrong side in this war."

"Bed, gentlemen," Sir Brandon repeated more firmly, "or my lord will be demanding your tongues, as well, for suggesting the king might not be successful in this quest."

Robert remembered, as Sir Brandon must have, that not every man in the camp was loyal to the Earl of Gunthar. Saxton was here, and had brought along some of his men. For the most part they congregated in another part of the camp, but Saxton had made a point of ambling casually among Gunthar's men while they had eaten their evening meal. That was when Saxton had caught Robert's eyes across the campfire in the early light of dusk. Robert had kept his head down earlier when Kit Beckford walked past him, but some devilish daring in him had held Saxton's gaze steady.

It had brought Robert no little satisfaction to see the usually unflappable Saxton stand stunned on discovering that the minstrel he thought he had left disabled or dead, sat hale and defiant in the midst of his rival's footsoldiers. Annoyance had flashed swiftly behind the surprise in Saxton's eyes, followed by a gleam of malignance before he had pivoted on his heel and stalked off into the woods.

Hours had since gone by and Saxton had not returned to the camp. Robert could only guess the thoughts that must be running through Saxton's mind. Humiliated by the king, left behind by Gunthar despite his protests that he should be included in negotiations at the castle, and then, where he least expected it, rudely reminded how his betrothed had spurned him for a common minstrel. Saxton had seen Robert clearly tonight, sitting among Gunthar's men. He must realize that Robert had come to Westminster Palace with his rival. Had he guessed that Marguerite had known and that she and Robert had trysted once again right under his nose?

Aye, Robert thought with a touch of unholy amusement, it might take the entire night for Saxton to work off his multiple frustrations in the woods.

Robert slid his lute into its padded case and carefully laced it up as Hastings, Sir Brandon, and their Poitevin companion each retired to their pallets around the fire. Robert's bed was more distanced from the flames, but a little of the warmth reached him across the brisk night. He wrapped his worn cloak about him and stretched out on a pallet so thin that he may as well have lain on the mist-dampened earth for all the buffer it provided against misshapen rocks and protruding twigs. *At least 'tis not as cold as Northumberland.* He had taken to reminding himself of his brief, unpleasant exploration of the northernmost county in England whenever the cold chilled his bones and threatened to set his teeth a-rattle.

He reached for thoughts of Marguerite, memories he'd held close through all the long, muscle-sore marches behind Gunthar's mounted troops and all the cold, lonely nights when his ever-restless mind struggled against his exhausted body to let him sleep. He had been parted from her before, when he'd lain abed for weeks with a fever in William's cottage, fighting the inflammation in his shoulder from Saxton's sword wound. That had been torture enough, knowing Saxton had borne Marguerite away from Robert's protection and worrying through those weak, wretched days and nights how he would find her again and if it would be too late.

At least this time he knew her safe from Saxton, for now. And this time she knew Robert had not abandoned her, and waited faithfully for his return. But with a great sea of water between them, surrounded daily with as many foreign voices as familiar English ones, Robert felt a world away from her as he had not in England.

He had just begun to drift a little into a pleasurable reminiscence of his love when a tumult of shouts brought him upright on his pallet. Men around him sat up too, befuddled from slumber. Not having been fully asleep, Robert found his feet before they did and reached the commotion at the edge of the camp before more than a handful of knights roused themselves to follow.

Two camp guards stood over a man who had fallen to his knees. One had his sword laid across the intruder's throat.

"Hold! I tell you, I'm a friend!" Panic sounded in the intruder's voice.

The light of a torch set up on a bracket near the sentry point sent a ripple of fire down the threatening blade and lapped across the muddied face of a dazed and frightened man who looked to Robert barely past his youth.

"Friend?" the guard with the sword at his throat scoffed. "What proof have you that you are not a spy?"

"I'm English—"

"Bah. The French can buy English spies as easily as King John buys French ones. You come here wearing no badge to identify your house or the house you serve. Why should we believe a word you say?"

The sword stayed the young man from moving his head, but Robert saw him feel frantically at the cloth at his shoulder. If there had been a badge like the embroidered emblem of the Earl of Gunthar that the two guards wore on their tunics, it had been ripped roughly away from the young man's clothing. Only tattered edges of a once-sewn piece of yellow cloth remained.

"I swear!" the young man said, urgent but breathless. "I am squire to Sir Edward Keynes. We were attacked—Sir Edward was taken. My badge had a loose edge when I dressed this morning. It must have gotten torn off in the struggle."

Robert's ears pricked at the name. Keynes? Kit's wife's sister had married a man named Keynes. Robert drew closer, more in curiosity than anything else, and felt a jolt of surprise when he recognized the features beneath the mud.

"You must take me for a fool to fall for that story," the guard jeered, plunging his hand into the young man's hair and snapping back his head to bare it for the sword's edge.

"Hold!" Robert shouted. "I know him."

The guard looked towards Robert, frowning when he saw it was the minstrel who spoke. "You know Sir Edward and can vouch that this is his squire?"

Robert shook his head. "Nay, but I know him to be Lord Ranulf de Villon's nephew. I sang in de Villon's hall at his daughter's betrothal dinner. This young man is her cousin. You can ask the Earl of Saxton if you do not believe me."

The guard glanced across the field at Saxton's tent before Robert remembered Saxton had not yet returned from the woods. Or had he? The guards would not have challenged Saxton if he had returned after Robert closed his eyes.

"What if he's right?" the second guard muttered, jerking his head in

Robert's direction. "Do you really want Saxton to know how near you came to skewering his betrothed's kin?"

The first guard gave a growl, but released the young man. "What's your business here?" he demanded, still surly as he slammed his sword into its scabbard.

The squire staggered to his feet. "The king has returned to La Rochelle and sent my master, Sir Edward, to command the Earl of Gunthar to rejoin him. But along the way, we were set upon by Poitevin knights led by Sir Aymer d'Avries, the traitor!"

Robert saw the young man's blue eyes flash in the torchlight.

"Sir Aymer bade us tell the king that Poitou will not support his campaign against the King of France. Sir Aymer is a sworn vassal of King John's, so Sir Edward justifiably lost his temper. They shouted insults back and forth, until Sir Edward ended by calling Sir Aymer a coward. That enraged Sir Aymer so, he struck Sir Edward and the next thing I knew swords were drawn by both sides and we were fighting for our lives."

The squire wobbled a little, but steadied himself even as Robert took a step forward to help him. A quick flush beneath the mud and a sharp gesture from the young man's hand warned such assistance would offend. Robert stopped. He recognized pride when he saw it stamped across a face. The squire looked of an age to win his spurs, perhaps even for acquitting himself bravely of this assignment. Robert guessed he felt shamed by the panic he had shown to the guards and no doubt shrank from betraying any further weakness. Robert's step had brought him close enough to see a cut beneath the mud on the squire's cheek and a gash on his right temple.

"We were outnumbered by Sir Aymer's men," the young man resumed, "so Sir Edward shouted at me to escape and find the Earl of Gunthar. They took my horse, so I ran and ran—" He broke off, then drew himself up with as much dignity as his mud and injuries allowed. "Please, take me to the earl and I will tell the rest to him."

"Gunthar isn't here," the guard said. "He went to confer with Lord Malefay in yonder castle." He nodded toward the hulking fortress on its perch atop a steep-sided promontory. "I can take you to the Earl of Saxton if you wish. But he's not like to do anything for Sir Edward tonight, and Gunthar will be back in the morning."

The squire appeared to debate with himself for a moment. Saxton was betrothed to his cousin, but Robert remembered how angry the squire had looked when Robert had drawn attention to Saxton's surreptitious disappearance with Marguerite from her father's hall one night.

"My orders were for Gunthar," the squire said, "so I will wait for him."

The guard nodded. Robert thought he looked relieved. Saxton had not been hesitant about loosing his cutting tongue on Gunthar's men in their master's absence.

"We'll find you a bed for the night, then," the guard grumbled, "though I don't know where." His gaze swept over the knights who had followed Robert, but none of them volunteered to give up his pallet for the squire.

"He can have mine," Robert said. "'Tis scarce worthy of a squire—I am just one of Gunthar's footsoldiers," he said to the young man, "but it will keep any further mud from your clothes, if not the jut of rocks from your ribs."

Robert said the last with a grin. The young man looked startled, began to speak, then paused. "Thank you, sir," he said. Robert sensed the words had shifted on his tongue. "I would welcome a pallet, however humble. But where will you sleep?"

The question surprised Robert. Since when did a man of the squire's birth care how a footsoldier slumbered?

"I'll sleep with my cloak. It will keep me warm enough." The squire's unexpected concern prompted Robert to respond with a generous lie.

"Go then," the guard said. "I'll send word in the morning when Gunthar is ready to see you."

Robert did not insult the squire by taking his arm when his footsteps zigzagged a little, but once the young man was seated on Robert's pallet, Robert dug out his ration of wine from his satchel and put the flask in the squire's hand.

"Drink. It will steady your head. I'll warrant it must be spinning, given that gash on your temple. Let me bandage it for you."

Robert left him drinking the wine while he went to fetch some water from the stream and some strips of cloth and a healing salve from the snoring barber's supplies. By the time he returned, the wine had restored some color to the squire's pallid face.

"I know you," the squire said as Robert set about cleaning the mud from the scratch on his cheek. "I was not sure at first when you told the guard you had been in my uncle's hall, but when you grinned I remembered. You are the minstrel who made my cousin blush when you smiled at her."

"I smile at all the lasses," Robert said carelessly. "It pleases them, and a happy lass is likely to persuade her father to invite me to sing again. The more I sing, the fatter grows my purse."

The squire nodded, as though Robert's answer made perfect sense. He winced beneath Robert's hand, then stiffened into a stoic endurance. "I owe you a debt for tonight," he said. "That guard would have cut my throat had you not stayed him."

"He was on edge because of men like d'Avries who are breathing resistance to the king, but I think his companion would have stopped his blade had I not spoken."

"You did not feel how close it pressed upon my throat. I repeat that I am in your debt. Will you tell me your name? I regret to say that I do not recall it."

Robert hesitated before he answered. "I am Rob Marcel."

He knew he should not cling to the surname, not with Kit Beckford in Gunthar's camp, but if he was going to fight and possibly die for the king, he would do it as his father's son, not some nameless minstrel.

"I'm Richard Channing."

Robert had washed a ring of clean flesh around the scratch and began applying the salve. Richard sat in silence while he did so. He did not speak again until Robert turned his attentions to the gash on his forehead.

"What do you think d'Avries will do to Sir Edward?"

Robert realized the tightening of the muscles beneath his fingers was not merely a reaction to pain.

"I doubt he will harm him," Robert said, hoping his confidence would allay the young man's fears. "Sir Edward is a rich man, he will fetch a good ransom. D'Avries will likely treat him as an honored guest once his temper cools."

Richard turned his head to stare at Robert, forcing Robert to pause in his cleaning. "How do you know Sir Edward is rich?"

Robert weighed his answer. He had revealed his name. 'Twould be foolish now to confess he had known Sir Edward's sister-in-law, even under the pretense of having entertained the Beckfords as a minstrel. Come morning, Richard was likely to learn that Kit was in the camp, and learning it, would surely seek out his master's kin-by-marriage. Robert should not have told him his surname. One mention that a man named Marcel had bandaged his head—

Robert fell back on what he hoped was a plausible assumption. "Sir Edward has wealth enough to merit Lord Ranulf de Villon's nephew for his squire. I presume he therefore has silver enough to buy his freedom from d'Avries's tower."

To his relief, Richard nodded his agreement. Robert almost heard the squire gritting his teeth as Robert rubbed salve into his gash and wrapped a strip of clean cloth about his temples. Hopefully between the pain and exhaustion from all the commotions he'd lived through this day, Richard would not remember the carelessly dropped name of a wandering musician.

"There." Robert tied off the bandage. "That should hold you till morning. Now try to get some sleep. There's nothing you can do until Lord Gunthar returns in the morning."

Richard drew his muddied cloak around him and stretched out on the pallet with a sigh. Judging from his breathing, he was asleep before the rocks and twigs dug through the thin barrier to vex him.

Robert spread his own cloak on the ground, trying not to envy the thick woolen folds of Richard's mantle. Filthy it might be, but Robert had touched it in the course of cleaning Richard's wounds and felt it heavy and warm. Likely it had been fresh woven for this journey. Sometimes when Robert wrapped himself in his, he fancied he could still smell Beck Manor in the threadbare cloth, though rationally he knew the scent had faded years ago.

If Richard had behaved more haughtily, he and his fine cloak would have roused Robert's resentment, but instead he had found the squire's manners surprisingly easy. Richard had even slipped once and called Robert "sir." He had been undoubtedly muddled by the stress of d'Avries's attack, his injuries, and the guard's rough greeting, but 'twas in such moments of strain, Robert had learned, that men revealed their best or worst natures. Richard might fall among those very few nobles who were not entirely self-centered and detestable.

But Robert confessed he had not offered up his pallet solely out of compassion for the bedraggled squire. If he struck up a friendship . . . what friendship there could be between a squire and a minstrel . . . perhaps he could obtain news of Marguerite. Robert dared not write to her himself, and he had warned her strictly not to attempt writing to him. But she might send word to her cousin, asking how he fared so far from home. Perhaps if Robert led the conversation just so in the morning before Gunthar sent for Richard and subsequently released him to join his own squires, Robert could glean just a drop or two of information for how Marguerite fared, too.

The moisture-softened earth masked the sound of footsteps, but Robert caught the shadows at the edge of the camp, licked to life by the still burning campfire, just as the flames had warned him earlier of Sir Brandon de Vexin's approach. Robert did not know what instinct made him lower himself quickly to the ground to feign sleep along with the rest of the camp. It might merely be one of the guards making rounds, and 'twould not have been the first time a guard had found Robert still awake, restfully plucking his lute strings. All the same, Robert lay still and tried to match the deep, even, slumbering breaths of the squire.

There was no reason for the shadows to glance his way as they drew near to the area of the camp where he lay, but he kept his eyes slitted as nearly shut as he could all the same without completely obscuring his vision. Two men. He could not mistake Saxton's tall, massive build for one of them. Though Gunthar matched his height, no man that Robert had seen in the king's entire army bore a chest so thick or shoulders so wide as Saxton's. The man with him lacked a few of Saxton's inches and was more slenderly built . . . or perhaps he only appeared so next to Saxton's silhouette. Though too far away to make out words, Robert heard the rumble of Saxton's lowered voice, then his companion's murmured reply.

Robert's eyes started wide and his heart drubbed quick and hard, like the beat of the drums that had driven their march from Westminster to the docks of Portsmouth. That murmur might have sounded on the other side of the world, and he would have known it. Kit Beckford. With Saxton?

The two men moved on, into the deeper shades of the camp, but Robert was sure he saw them strike hands before Saxton's hulking shadow diverted in the direction of his tent. Robert lifted his head slowly to follow the shadow he knew belonged to Christopher Beckford. It moved among the footsoldiers, near enough for Robert to shut his eyes again. Kit's tent, Robert knew, lay to the east of Gunthar's, but he, like Gunthar's other vassals, had brought archers and footsoldiers of his own along to swell the ranks of Gunthar's fighting force. The king hoped an army would intimidate his rebellious Poitevin subjects where a modest embassy of knights would not. The vassals' soldiers slept according to the prestige of their lord progressively further away from the fire, behind Gunthar's more privileged troops.

When Robert reopened his eyes he saw that Kit had paused among his own sleeping men. He bent to rouse one of the soldiers. Robert strained to catch a murmured word, but he only saw a gesture. He could not see in the darkness whether it was an archer or a footsoldier who rose. The two of them chose a different path through the camp, both avoiding the betraying flames of the fire so that Robert could make no guesses by mannerism or build or a glimpse of a profile who slipped into Kit's tent a few minutes behind his old enemy.

oon arrived and Gunthar still had not returned to the camp. One of his squires, Sir Brandon de Vexin's son, rode down from the castle to say the earl and the baron were still negotiating and that likely the camp would not move on this day. He refused to let Richard ride back with him to the fortress. Robert heard Richard shouting at the boy and though Richard bellowed the king's summons as an excuse, he had done nothing but fret his worry all morning to Robert over Sir Edward's safety. Robert guessed him more hopeful that Gunthar might rescue his master than concerned they might return a day or two late to La Rochelle in contradiction of the king's command. Gunthar's squire, a curly-headed youth with quick brown eyes whom Robert had twice glimpsed with a book when Gunthar had flung some order his way, stood firm in his instructions that no one was to interrupt affairs at the castle for any reason. He left Richard fuming as he remounted his horse and rode off to rejoin the earl.

Robert had earlier taken Richard down to the river to bathe away the mud that had caked to hardness overnight. Richard complained loudly at the briskness of the water but Robert had bathed in colder, although he'd found the river, like the days in these southern climes, less nipping than he'd been accustomed to for a March in England. Saxton's squire, Nicholas Tybert, intercepted them on their return to the camp. The youth spared only a single surly glance for Robert, then bore Richard away saying his master wished to speak with him. Robert had expected Richard to return to

Saxton's tent after his encounter with Gunthar's squire, but instead Richard came striding across the field to vent his frustration to Robert.

"Sir Edward could be dead for aught Gunthar cares," Richard growled, "murdered by a Poitevin vassal of the king's. You'd think Gunthar would want to burn d'Avries's castle to the ground, but instead he sits up there groveling for Lord Malefay's support."

"I have not been in Gunthar's service long," Robert said as he dropped to one knee beside his bag, "but from what I have seen of the old earl, I cannot imagine him groveling to anyone." Robert drew out a leather pouch. "Besides, Gunthar doesn't know what happened with d'Avries. All you shouted at his squire was the king's demand that we ride back to La Rochelle."

Richard answered with a snort. The cut stood out red on his freshly washed face and his hair, still damp from the river, was frizzing up in yellow waves over a clean bandage wrapped around his head. Robert's own locks lay moist against the back of his neck. He had not been as muddy as Richard, but even on the manor he had bathed once a week or more in the river. His father had taught him the invigorating trick as a boy. When one grew weary, when the muscles screamed they could not plow one more foot of sod, a brisk self-dunking in the water set the blood a-rush again, lending hours more of energy, along with a curiously pleasant sensation of skin washed free of the dirt they tilled.

Robert poured some dried leaves from the pouch into his hand, crushed them into dust, and rubbed them on the under-tunic he wore.

"What's that?" Richard asked.

"Mint. It keeps the fleas away." Robert held out the pouch. "Here, try some."

Richard took the pouch, but hesitated. "Mint plays havoc with one's temper, and I am already cross enough."

Robert laughed. "Then you will fight more fiercely for the king. But until we come to battle, it will keep the fleas away."

Richard sprinkled a little over the clean set of clothes he'd donned in Saxton's tent, but so sparsely that Robert guessed he did it merely to not offend. He returned the pouch to Robert. "Did you bring it with you from England?"

"Some, but not enough to last two months. I bartered songs for more in the villages we passed through." Robert rubbed some of the dusted leaves on the back of his neck and up his arms beneath his tunic's loose sleeves, then returned the pouch to his bag, pulled his homespun surcote over his head, and belted on his dagger.

"That's an unusual hilt," Richard said.

Robert smiled. Steel clearly held more interest for Richard than herbs. He set his weapon in Richard's hand and watched him test the balance.

"'Tis as fine as my own. Perhaps finer. No one would look twice at this dull blade I carry."

Robert presumed Richard referred to his dagger's hilt and not its cutting edge. That hilt protruding from Richard's sheath was indeed quite simple, a shaft wrapped in leather with a metal crossbar at the base and a simple metal disk for the pommel.

Richard ran an admiring finger over the design on Robert's hilt. "Look how cunningly someone has carved a tyger into the horn overlay. They've polished it down so smoothly the edges do not even catch on the hand, even though the creature stands rampant."

The most difficult pose for carving into a hilt. With one hind foot on the ground and the other three in the air, plus the upright tail, there certainly could have been many an uncomfortable snag on the tyger to bruise the bearer's hand when thrusting. But as Richard said, the maker had sanded the figure almost flat, then stained the outline to preserve the intricate claws and tufts of fur along the creature's body.

"Where did you find it?" Richard asked as he handed it back to Robert.

"At a fair in York." Robert slid the blade back into his sheath. It startled him when Richard sat down on Robert's pallet and linked his hands around his knees. "Would you not be more comfortable closer to the fire?" *Beside the knights and other squires.* Some of them were roasting a brace of rabbits one had trapped in the nearby woods. Robert's stomach grumbled at the mouth-watering aroma, but he resigned himself to his footsoldier's ration of hard bread and cheese.

"Oh, they're a stuffy lot," Richard said, catching the meaning of Robert's glance at the men mingling near the flames. "They've been polite, but not friendly. I don't serve Lord Gunthar or any of the other men here, and I think some of them are still suspicious of the way the guards found me last night, filthy and frantic with my badge torn off. Saxton has acknowledged that he knows me, but Gunthar's men are suspicious of him, too, for which I can't blame them. I had a wretched interview with him while his squire lent me these clothes. He's laid his humiliation by the king at Gunthar's feet, of course, rather than admit he may have gone too far in his own conceit. He invited me to rest in his tent until Gunthar returns, but—well—if you don't mind, I'd rather sit here with you."

"I've little enough to entertain you with," Robert warned, "unless you'd like a song."

Richard responded with a boyish grin. "Your voice is as fine as that dagger you wear and it'll while away the time more pleasantly than answering Saxton's despicable questions about my cousin."

Robert's fingers froze on the laces of his lute case. "What questions about your cousin?"

He asked it before he realized how impertinent such curiosity sounded. He sought for a way to soften his impulsive query, but his presumption appeared to fly over Richard's head as his smile faded into a scowl.

"The sort that make me wish I dared plow my fist into his face. 'Did you know where she went every day when she left her father's hunt in Dorset?'" Richard's voice dripped with too much hostility to make his attempt at mimicry sound remotely like Saxton. "Home, I told him roundly. I found her there myself. As though she would ride anywhere else when he humiliated her by fawning all over his mistress while they rode in the woods."

Robert gathered from Richard's sarcasm that he had not said those last words to Saxton.

"'What about Sir Warin?' he asked me then. 'How long had she sought to ensnare him before the tournament? Had their disporting gone further than flirtation?' Disporting! Flirtation! The insinuating way he said it, he may as well have called her a harlot. Saints, how I wanted to hit him!"

Robert's hand fisted with the same desire. He had been hungry to hear of her, but such slurs as this? His blood churned, even as he wondered who Sir Warin was.

"'And does she really expect me to believe she spent all those afternoons sitting innocently with Lady Helen? The countess will pay along with her husband for thinking she could spite me by playing accomplice to Marguerite's fickle perfidy.' If his squire hadn't come in just then to tell me Gunthar's squire had returned to the camp, I'd have knocked him down then and there." Richard leaned his chin on his knees, looking glum. "Well, I would have tried. He's built like a boulder and probably would have pummeled me into a bloody heap if I'd attacked his exalted person." The sarcasm returned on "exalted."

"He is not invincible," Robert said, remembering Saxton winded and sweating and murderous with frustration as Robert had dodged his sword again and again in the village square, before that curst pothole had proved Robert's undoing.

"He's mad, of course," Richard said, as though Robert had not spoken. "No matter how miserable she is, Marguerite would never disgrace her name by betraying her betrothal vows. Only a self-centered ox like Saxton would feel threatened by another man merely smiling at her. You did so yourself that first night you saw her and you saw how it made him frown. Well, perhaps you weren't watching, but—"

Oh, aye, Richard Channing, I was watching.

"—he scowled at her like a jealous lover, as if he hadn't been throwing lustful glances at that red-headed strumpet of his all night. *He* may be as licentious as he pleases, but *Marguerite* must not ride out of his sight or keep an old woman company or allow a man to bow to her without Saxton suspecting her of cuckolding him behind his back. I don't care how big he is, I vow, if she were not bound to marry him, I'd—"

"What if she does not?" Robert said. Richard turned a blank gaze on him. Robert drew out his lute and began to tune the strings. "What if she chooses not to marry him? I do not suggest her guilty of Saxton's mistrust. She is too clearly a lady to indulge in sordid affairs." Let Richard think he spoke flattery, rather than from his own sweet knowledge of her. "But if she chose rather to wed a man she loves, would you think it a dishonor to her?"

"Aye, to her name, to her house. I hate it—" Robert heard the emotion vibrate in Richard's voice "— but my uncle says she spoke the vows, and betrothal is as binding as marriage."

"Nearly, perhaps, in your world. But the Church would not hold it so if some other man were to capture her heart and she chose of her own volition to give that man her hand." Robert tightened a peg and plucked one of the strings again to see if it hummed more true.

"You do not understand." For the first time, the smallest hint of condescension stole into Richard's voice. "We cannot merely marry on a whim wherever our fancy alights. There are matters of land and bloodlines and dowries and honor. Things are different among tradesmen, like cobblers and furriers and smiths, or servants like milkmaids or laundresses." Robert noticed he did not mention villeins. That would be like acknowledging the milkmaid's cow. "Or even," Richard added, "wandering musicians."

Robert wondered if Richard spoke the last with a smile intended in jest but which Robert knew he would interpret as patronizing. He chose not to look lest it spoil the tentative friendship between them, and strummed out a chord instead.

"Sometimes I wish I were a cobbler's son instead of knight's, and Annys a laundress's daughter," Richard said with a sigh. "Then no one would care if we married. But her parents will not hear of it, and neither will mine."

Robert glanced at him now. Richard's eyes gazed far into the distance. Though Robert had learned to guard his own expressions, he knew a besotted young lover when he saw one.

"Is Annys's bloodline not worthy?" Robert asked.

That snapped Richard's attention back with an indignant flash. "Of course she is worthy. Her father is a baron. What, do you think I would really marry a laundress's daughter?"

Robert refocused on tuning his lute. He knew himself better at guarding his face than his tongue and paused a breath's span to be sure he could answer evenly. "Of course not. What's the problem, then?"

"I am only a younger son. Unless Sir Edward chooses to favor me in some way someday, I will likely never be more than one of his household knights." Richard leaned his chin on his knees again, this time with a dejected air. "Even if Annys was willing to marry me anyway, I'd never be able to support a wife on those wages. I could never ask her to make a sacrifice like that."

Robert fought off a small nettle of guilt, and fanned instead the familiar stir of rebellion that rose in him. Richard might call Marguerite's marriage to Robert a sacrifice, but insisting that she marry the Earl of Saxton for bloodlines and advancement and some distorted concept of honor was far more reprehensible, in Robert's eyes. Still, the guilt continued to chafe. It had not troubled him to court Marguerite behind the backs of her family when they had all appeared to him arrogant ladies and lords and selfish persecutors of his love. But now he had come to know Richard, Robert found it less comfortable to deceive him, especially when the young squire had for the most part treated Robert quite decently, and clearly held a genuine affection for his cousin.

But continue his deceit, he must. Robert would not risk losing

Marguerite to Richard's overzealous pride and protection, simply because Robert's conscience pricked him.

Robert stood. "Forgive me, but I've a future of my own to make, and I won't do it talking here with you. Gunthar's men toss me coins if I sing verses to their liking when they're bored, and they're looking mightily bored while they await the earl's return today."

He felt Richard follow him as he moved nearer to the fire and struck a few chords on his lute. Knights, archers, and footsoldiers alike, immediately began to mill in Robert's direction.

"What will you sing for us, Master Marcel?" Thomas Hastings called out, his usually sober clerk's face brightening at the prospect of some entertainment.

"Why, sir, I would seek counsel from all those here who are experienced in love." That puffed them all up, setting his listeners grinning and jabbing one another in their ribs. "A fair lass has struck me with despair and I know not what to do. Let me tell you of her." Robert set loose a flutter of sweetly tuned notes, and then sang forth his verse. "*I love a lady who is beauteous beyond measure, yet I am less than a shadow in her eyes.*"

Because he could not speak of Marguerite did not mean he could not sing to her. Perhaps somehow she would sense him on this faraway shore, dreaming of her as he fell into the strains that won the first smile that had enchanted him in her father's hall.

Gunthar returned to the camp shortly before dusk, just as Robert was finishing off his evening rations of dried herring and raisins. From the plunge of the old earl's heavy grey brows, Robert guessed matters had not ended well between him and Lord Malefay. Gunthar sent a request for the Earl of Saxton to join him and vanished with his two squires, his marshal Sir Edward Tollerton, Sir Brandon de Vexin, and his secretary Thomas Hastings into the wide canvas tent identified as his by the pennant that flapped above it in the breeze, a prancing silver stallion on a field just shy a royal blue. Sir Brandon had held up a staying hand to Richard Channing, who sat eating next to Robert and who had started to rise to follow Gunthar, but before Richard grumbled a dozen words, Saxton crooked a finger his way as he and his own squire walked past. Richard followed him with quick, eager strides.

Robert was draining his last drops of ale and exchanging tales of a visit to Lincoln with a fellow footsoldier who hailed from there when Richard and Saxton came back out sometime later. Richard shook his head to something Saxton said. Robert could not make out their expressions in the dimming light, but Saxton stood watching through the rising mist as Richard rejoined the minstrel. Perhaps it was Robert's imagination, but he thought he could feel the force of Saxton's malignance rippling across the space between them before Saxton and his squire finally turned and walked on to their own tent.

"He offered to let me bed in his tent for the night," Richard said, sitting down beside Robert again. "As if he'd never said all those hateful things to my face about my cousin just this morning. I'd sooner sleep on a dung heap. But I'll settle for the ground next to you, if you don't object. I'll not ask for your pallet again."

"Nay, it is yours without the asking," Robert replied. "I've slept on the ground more times than I can count and have never been the worse for it. Did Gunthar say if we march for La Rochelle in the morning?"

The man from Lincoln turned his attention to the man drinking on his other side, though Robert guessed he still listened with half-an-ear. The oddity of a noble young squire eating among the footsoldiers had won Richard and Robert many a curious look.

"First he confessed to Saxton that Lord Malefay is proving stubborn in his refusal to throw his support behind the king," Richard said, "which made Saxton smug as a cat who just stole the cream. He clearly hopes Gunthar's failure to persuade the Poitevin barons to uphold their oaths of fealty will return the king's wrath upon the old earl's head."

Richard pushed a piece of dry bread through a plate of rabbit stew that one of Gunthar's knights had handed him, just before Saxton had signaled him to Gunthar's tent. The broth had cooled and congealed in his absence.

"When Gunthar finally let me speak, I told him about the king's command and what happened with Sir Edward and Sir Aymer d'Avries. But he would not commit to an action, saying only that he must 'consider matters for the night,' and then dismissed us." Richard half-raised the grease-clumped morsel to his mouth, then wrinkled his nose and dropped it back onto his plate. "Do you really think Sir Edward is safe?"

"I can think of no reason for d'Avries to harm him," Robert said.

Richard nodded. "The ransom." But he looked unconvinced and pushed away the unappetizing remains of his supper.

Despite his anxiety over Sir Edward, Richard appeared to fall asleep almost as soon as he stretched out on Robert's pallet. Robert, reclining again on his cloak, linked his hands behind his head and listened to the squire's deep, steady breathing. He could not remember the last time he had slept as soundly as Richard, even on those occasions when he lay warm in the rushes of a baron's great hall. Or when every muscle and bone in his body ached from laboring long summer days in the fields and should have left him too exhausted to do anything but fall immediately into slumber. And yet he rarely had, his mind as restless as a boy as it was this night.

The chill of the deepening night tautened those muscles now, but Robert had long since learned how to grit his teeth to bear the cold. There were no stars to gaze at, for a heavy canopy of clouds had blotted them out, so he closed his eyes and reached, as he had every night since he had left Westminster, for the one comfort that calmed his mind and eased the annoyance of the stones and twigs that nudged against his back: memories of Marguerite.

Brilliant as a golden queen the first night he had sung for her, in her shimmering kirtle woven with gilded leaves, jewels winking from the gilt netting that bound up her dusky hair. Innocent and trusting as an angel, her dark hair unbound and flowing over her white nightdress as he'd taken her in his arms in her chamber and lost his heart to her in their first kiss. Her merry laughter while he'd taught her to play the flute. The worried crease in her forehead when she had told him of her grandfather's inheritance. Their heated kisses in the glade, their sweet confessions of love, the moment when she had placed her life, as well as her heart, into his hands.

"I will go to the ends of the earth with you."

Should he have stood less firmly against her plea for them to marry before he followed the king to war? His memories might be yet the warmer tonight. Perhaps she would not feel quite so far away.

His musings snapped off and his eyes flew open, though he did not know why. He rose slowly onto one elbow and searched the darkness, but all he saw were the shapes of sleeping men. In the distance flickered the torchlights of the knights on guard. Nothing untoward could slip past them. Richard's arrival had proven that last night. Closer burned a brace of torches outside Gunthar's tent, but a guard sat on duty there, as well.

Robert lay back down, but the spell had been broken. Renewed thoughts of Marguerite eluded him, swirling away like the mist when he sought to embrace them again. He tried to subdue the strange tension that had crept over him. Richard had barely shifted, he slept so deeply. Robert tried to relax by matching the squire's breathing, slow and steady and deep. He let the whisper of the grass they slept in flow soothing into his ears.

The whisper . . . Robert bolted full upright. In his swift survey of the darkness, he had seen the pennant above Gunthar's tent hanging heavy from its pole, robbed of the breeze that had earlier fluttered it proudly. He felt no movement of air against his cheeks. He held his hand over the grass beside him, but the blades felt perfectly still.

Robert eased slowly to his feet and stared about him, but he could see nothing amiss. Except that the guard outside Gunthar's tent appeared to have fallen asleep. It was hardly Robert's place to rebuke a knight grown lax in his duties, but he nevertheless picked his way carefully through the field of sleeping soldiers until he reached the tent and set a hand on the guard's shoulder to shake him awake.

Somehow Robert knew the moment he touched the man, even though the knight's flesh was still warm. The guard rolled off his stool as Robert's hand coiled away, the torchlight catching the whites of the dead man's eyes and the black stain of blood soaking up through the back of his tunic.

Robert flung open the flap of the tent and shouted a warning before his eyes adjusted enough see within. He did not need sight, only the hairs prickling up the back of his neck. Light from the torch filtered in, gleaming silver on a dagger's blade held by a form that started and turned at the sound of Robert's voice. The figure had been bent over Gunthar's cot. For an instant Robert's stomach clenched, thinking himself too late. But the blade shone clean, untipped with blood. Robert hurled himself forward, for the form stood close enough still to whirl back and strike his target before the sleeping squire on the ground at the foot of the cot could spring up to block him.

The tent flap fell closed behind Robert, shutting out the meager light from the torch. Robert slammed into what had been little more than shadow before the darkness enclosed them and met the resistance of a hard, muscled body. His momentum threw them both stumbling against what felt like a wooden desk. Inkhorns clattered together. Parchment scattered beneath Robert's hand as he struggled to steady himself, while his other hand splayed across a broad, square chest. He sought to slide his arm across it to pin his opponent against the desk's top, but felt a swinging motion, remembered the dagger, and sprang back to avoid the dead guard's fate.

The darkness concealed the blade now, but the swish of wind just short of his nose told Robert how narrow his escape had been. He had seen the dagger in the man's right hand. A strike as forceful as the one his opponent had sought to deal him would throw his opponent off balance, if only for a moment. Robert prayed he judged the situation aright, lunged forward, found what he hoped were the man's shoulders, and shoved them down across the desk.

A loud grunt burst from the man, followed by a crack that might have been his head banging against wood. The man squirmed, shifting beneath Robert's grasp. Voices were shouting around them now, growing louder as Robert struggled in the dark to find and lock down both of his opponent's hands. A shaft of light flowed back in. The flap had been tossed open again. More shouts joined the ones in the tent, footsteps scuffled, then someone lit a candle. Whoever held it stood near enough to cast its light clearly across the face of the man Robert grappled with.

Robert froze and so did the man sprawled across the desk. Savage yellow eyes gazed into his from beneath a low, coarse brow overhung with slithery dun tendrils. The nose, flat and lumpy, looked as if it had encountered a few more fists since Robert had seen it last. The heavy lips sneered with the same brutal malice that had haunted Robert for the past seven years.

The moment of recognition broke on a wave of shattering hatred. *"Hanley."*

Robert spat the foul name out of his mouth. His opponent still clutched the dagger, glaring defiance at him. Robert knew the man's strength. He would not easily pry the blade loose with his fingers. He bent his arm and snapped his elbow down square in the center of Hanley's wrist. Hanley screamed. A satisfying sound Robert wished he'd wrenched from the beast seven years ago. The blow dislodged the dagger. Robert locked his hands around Hanley's throat and crushed his howl into silence.

unthar awoke to the sound of a shout. A dark shape hovered over him, too broad to be his squire, the only one with permission to rouse him before daylight. Almost as soon as he glimpsed the figure the tent went dark again, followed by a thump, then a mingled thud and clatter of objects he could not discern by mere hearing. Footsteps scuffled, muted by the carpet his son had sent him from the East. Gunthar cursed his old bones. He had not needed a squire to wake him twelve years ago when he had followed the king to Normandy. Then a mere shift in the shadows had been enough to wake him. The devil take old age!

"Antony!" he called.

"Here, my lord," his squire's voice replied from the area at the foot of his cot where the boy slept every night.

"What the devil is happening?"

"My lord, I don't know. I can't see—"

"Well, feel out a tinderbox and light a candle." Gunthar barely bit off adding *fool*. The boy was not usually such a dullard.

The sounds of some sort of brawl continued. Gunthar thought he heard a grunt, but Antony was shouting over it—"Hie hie hie! To Gunthar! To the earl!"—as he rattled about for a light source on the table next to the cot.

And when they come, I'll not be found sitting in bed like an old woman. Aching joints or not, Gunthar's heightened heartbeat would have vaulted him from the cot as lithely as his own squire days, had he not feared landing in the middle of the altercation he still could not see. His hearing told him the scuffle was taking place somewhere near the desk he had brought along for Hastings to more comfortably attend his secretary's duties. Nevertheless, Gunthar slid from the cot with some caution, lest his ears had at last decided to betray him along with his bones.

The tent flap flung open and men surged inside the tent, shouting their alarm and confusion. In the next breath, the squire finally succeeded in lighting a candle.

Gunthar saw two men struggling against his desk. The upper body of one appeared to have been forced down across the top by the other. They wrestled for something clutched in one of their hands. A dagger. Gunthar saw the weapon in the same candle glow that fell across the men's profiles before the man on top made a sudden, flashing movement with his arm that made the second man scream. The hands of the first whipped around his opponent's throat and cut the sound off. The snarl that burst from first man's lips and the vibrating force of his fingers left no doubt of his intent to throttle the man across the desk.

Gunthar recognized the profile of the raven-haired aggressor. "Let him go, Marcel!" he shouted at the minstrel. The minstrel ignored him. Even in the muted candlelight, Gunthar could see the other man's eyes bulging while his face blotched a dangerous purple. "Someone—De Vexin, Channing— break them up, *now.*"

Gunthar flung the command at the two men who stood at the forefront of those who had rushed inside the tent. Sir Brandon and Richard Channing leapt forward and each grabbed one of the minstrel's arms. Robert resisted, hanging doggedly on to the man's throat until two more of Gunthar's knights sprang to help pry him loose.

Robert struggled wildly against the hands that restrained him. "Traitor! Assassin!"

"Keep—'im—away—from—me," the other man croaked between loud, ragged breaths for air. He pushed himself off the desk, but leaned against it to prop himself up while he fingered his maltreated throat.

"I'll send you to hell!" Robert shouted at the man. "Blazes, Richard, let me go!"

Gunthar did not know how he did it, but the minstrel somehow wrestled himself free. From the way one of his knights lurched sideways and another stumbled back with his chin in the air, Gunthar presumed a push and possibly a punch were involved, but Robert moved too fast to be sure. Gunthar guessed his target, though, and stepped between Robert and the desk. From the rage in Robert's face, he did not know if Robert would check himself or try to throw him aside. Gunthar was not as young as he once had been, but he planted his feet strongly apart and braced himself to withstand an attack.

Robert stopped, almost breast to breast with him. Gunthar saw the flame in the dark eyes.

"Are you mad?" Gunthar hissed. "Get hold of yourself."

A seething breath blew out between the minstrel's clenched teeth. Though anger rolled off of him in palpable waves, he stepped back a pace. Richard Channing came forward to lay a hand on his shoulder. Robert brushed it off but made no further attempt to reach the man behind Gunthar.

Gunthar turned to view that man. He did not know the low brow and broken nose, the heavy mouth and the limp dun hair. The fellow was dressed like a footsoldier, though he wore no badge to identify which lord, if any, he served. Sometimes apprentices ran away from their masters or younger sons from their merchant fathers to follow some idealized perception of war. Though this man looked too old and hardened to be the victim of such naivety.

"Who are you," Gunthar asked, "and what are you doing in my tent?"

"His name is Walter Hanley." Robert answered. Gunthar glanced over his shoulder and saw the tempestuous storm still flashing in Robert's eyes. "I caught him in an attempt to murder your lordship. The guard outside is dead, undoubtedly by his hand as well."

Gunthar shot a look at Sir Brandon. "Is that true? Is the guard dead?"

"Aye, my lord."

"By *his* hand, not mine." Hanley's voice rasped through his bruised throat but he spoke stoutly. "'Twas *Marcel* tried to murder ye, my lord. I caught *him* bendin' over ye, that dagger in his hand."

Gunthar followed Hanley's gaze to the dagger on the desk and made a swift mental note: the blade was clean.

"Liar!" Robert shouted. "You rogue, don't think to see me hang in your place. I've sworn you would pay, you and your master, for all you've done to my family. Now you add murder and treason to your crimes and think I'll walk tamely to the gallows for you? Let me get my hands around your throat again and—"

"May I assume," Gunthar broke in quietly, "that you two know each other?"

"Aye," Hanley said with a savagery Gunthar could hardly blame him for, "he hates me, as ye've seen for yerself. He would murder ye and for an old grudge throw his guilt on me."

"That's a lie."

Gunthar turned towards the minstrel and found his normally impassive face as passionate as the eyes that locked with his.

"My lord, I swore on my life to protect you."

"Swore?" Gunthar repeated, surprised. "To whom?"

"To your lady wife. There is no reason for you to trust me, you have not paid two snaps of attention to me since I entered your household, but the countess asked my aid and I would not betray her. She pled with me to guard you if I could and I gave her my word I would do so."

"On your life?" Why would a minstrel who owed Gunthar no particular loyalty swear such an oath for him?

The minstrel's gaze did not so much as flicker from his. "On my life."

Helen was no fool. If she trusted this man—

"Don't heed him, sir." Hanley's rasping tones sharpened. "He plays upon yer feelin's. He was ever a clever, smooth-tongued rascal."

Robert began a heated retort but broke off as one of Gunthar's men-at-arms pushed through the tent flap, dragging a thin, wiry footsoldier with a narrow face and watery eyes that darted to Hanley before dropping to his boots. Like Hanley, his tunic bore no badge.

"My lord, we found this fellow trying to sneak out of camp."

"Indeed," Gunthar said. "Bring him here."

His man-at-arms pushed the footsoldier forward none too gently. Gunthar motioned to his squire to reposition the candle so that he might see the soldier more clearly. Then he reached down and pulled free the dagger from the sheath that lolled against the man's hip. The sheath had smeared the blood but not wiped the blade clean.

"You should have left it in my guard's back," Gunthar said dryly. "Cantwell, take Hanely and—whoever this rat is—away and see them safely bestowed for the night. I will question them in the morning. Marcel—"

Robert, he saw, was looking elsewhere. Gunthar followed the minstrel's gaze and discovered that someone else had entered the tent behind his man-at-arms. The Earl of Saxton stood just inside the entrance, his gaze locked with a studied coolness on a dancing defiance in Robert's eyes.

The silence of Gunthar's study jarred Saxton's gaze free first. He turned his attention to Gunthar. "I heard there was trouble in your tent, my lord," he said smoothly, "and I passed the dead guard outside. Allow me to be of assistance. You are undoubtedly wearied by this uproar following your grueling negotiations with the baron. Return to your rest and I will deal with these prisoners. Come with me, Marcel—"

"You are very good, my lord," Gunthar cut Saxton off, "but I am not the least wearied and I will do my own questioning. And Marcel is not a prisoner. Now if you and everyone else will leave us? You too, Antony."

The squire bowed, set the candle on the table next to the cot, and followed the knights out of the tent. Saxton hesitated, a faint crease in his brow, but he merely murmured, "As you wish," and went out, too.

Gunthar moved across the carpet, its weave warm and soft against his bare feet. The intriguing geometric designs were muted in the candle's small glow. He was not a sentimental man, but had surrendered to a whim to bring the carpet with him to Poitou. The ridiculous luxury made him feel close to the son he had lost in faraway Constantinople. It passed briefly through his mind that Peter would have been near an age with the minstrel, had his son survived that curst Crusade. It was small comfort that his son had lived long enough to send this gift to him, but one took comfort where one could.

Gunthar lit a second candle to increase the light in the tent, reached absently for his cloak and tossed it for warmth over the smock he had worn to bed, then turned to face the minstrel.

"Well, now," he said. "Tell me, if you please, your version of tonight's events."

Robert did not immediately meet Gunthar's eyes. The minstrel's gaze seemed focused on Gunthar's cloak. Gunthar glanced down at it, but he could see nothing amiss with the heavy wool or fur lining.

"It is just as I said," Robert answered after a moment. His formerly hot voice had cooled to nearly match the tent's chill. "I saw your guard outside in a slump and thought him sleeping through his duty. I came to rouse him and found him dead. Why would any man kill him save to reach you with some nefarious intent? I threw open the tent flap, saw a man bending over you with a dagger, and jumped him. We fell against the desk, we struggled, your squire lit a candle and gave me light enough to strike the blade from the villain's hand. The rest you saw." Only then did his gaze lift to Gunthar's. "My lord, you told Lord Saxton I was not a prisoner. Is it so?"

"And you told me that you were charged by my wife to guard my safety. Is it so?"

"Aye, my lord."

The words perplexed Gunthar, as they had before. "Why? I have my barons and knights to guard me, bound to me by oath. She knows that. Why would she seek an oath from a minstrel?"

"That you will have to ask her," Robert said. "All I can tell you is that I gave her my word, though I would have guarded you for her sake without her asking."

If the minstrel thought by this admission to win Gunthar's favor, he spoiled the effect by making no discernable effort to subdue a gleam of hostility in his dark eyes. What exactly Gunthar had done to enrage the fellow he found himself at a loss to guess. But where Helen was concerned, Gunthar would not tread carelessly. He had watched the minstrel with his wife far more closely than Robert had known. He thought he had taken the minstrel's measure, else he would never have agreed to let him join his foot-soldiers. The same shrewdness that had guided Gunthar's judgment of men for fifty years told him something was missing to the minstrel's story.

"Why?" he asked again, more strongly this time. "What is my wife to you that you would serve me 'for her sake?' Or is this some contrivance to win my trust, a fabrication concocted by 'a clever, smooth-tongued rascal?'"

Robert flushed at Gunthar's use of Hanley's words. "No! I am loyal to her. I am loyal to you. I'd not betray you after you took me into your household, made it possible for me to—"

"To what?" Gunthar demanded as Robert broke off. Robert pulled his gaze away and paced across the carpet. Gunthar let him cross the width of the tent and back before repeating, "To what, Marcel?"

"'Tis naught," Robert said without pausing in his strides. "Suffice it to say that you did me a service when you brought me to Westminster. You housed me, fed me, paid me fairly for my music—"

"Yet you glare at me as though I were some enemy."

"No. That is—Did I glare?" The minstrel stopped, biting his lip. "Your pardon. You must have mistaken some flicker from the candlelight."

Saints! Did the man think Gunthar would not catch the mockery in his voice, however subtly masked? For the first time that night, Gunthar's temper slipped. "Insolent fellow, how dare you patronize me? Because I am old, you need not think me stupid or blind."

The withering note Gunthar struck usually sent men into swift apologies. The minstrel faced him down with a defiant lift of his chin.

"But you may think me a deceitful rascal," Robert retorted. "Why should you believe a word I say? What could I, a common minstrel, know of swearing oaths, much less honoring them? What could *I* know of simple loyalty?" The hostility burned bright in the dark eyes again. "Why am I even here, my lord? If you doubt my honesty, why did you not let Cantwell drag me off with Hanley and that rat-faced accomplice of his?"

"Because your dagger is still in its sheath, while Hanley's sheath was empty." Gunthar watched Robert's hand drop reflexively to that distinctive tyger hilt of his. "Had *both* your sheaths held daggers, the one that lies on my desk might have been brought to cover the guilt of either of you. But only Hanley's sheath was empty. I presume he meant to pull the blade out of my heart and take it with him once I was dead."

A cloud fell over Robert's brow. He muttered, "Devil."

Gunthar hoped he meant the epithet for Hanley. "I owe you my life tonight," Gunthar said to the minstrel. "I do not know what you are concealing from me, and I will not tolerate any further impertinence from you, but that this still beats—" he thumped a fist to his heart "—I will not forget." He dropped his hand back to his side. "So you see, I am not your enemy."

Robert said nothing. His gaze lowered to the pattern in the carpet, as though considering Gunthar's words. When at last he moved, he walked over to the desk and gazed down at the dagger Hanley had left behind.

"Do you know it?" Gunthar asked.

Robert shook his head.

"But you know Hanley."

Robert turned, his eyes guarded now. This was the man Gunthar had known at Westminster, his face an unreadable mask. It was useless for him to pretend, though. He had told Gunthar Hanley's name.

Robert must have realized the futility of vacillating, too. He gave a curt nod.

"Sit down," Gunthar said, "and tell me how you are acquainted." He twitched his cloak more closely around him, then sat on the edge of his cot, thereby granting permission for Robert to obey his command.

Robert glanced at the secretary's chair with its carved wooden armrests, but chose to sink down on a stool at the foot of the cot near the pallet where Gunthar's squire slept. Gunthar sensed the reluctance in him to reply, but after a few moments of silence, Robert's shoulders lifted in a faint shrug.

"Walter Hanley is my brother-in-law."

"What?" Gunthar had not expected that.

"My sister wed him at the age of fifteen. She was not given a choice. Villeins aren't, you know. We may try to pay for permission to wed as we please, but when the baron says, 'It is my will that you marry my brutish knave of a groom,' the woman must meekly submit, even if the beast beats her every day, merely because it gives him pleasure to lord his mastery over her."

Robert's expression had gone as impassive as a stone, but Gunthar caught the way his breath quickened as he spoke. The wound was either fresh or had festered for a very long time. Gunthar held his peace and waited.

"It is little better for the kin who tries to protect her," Robert continued in that same dispassionate voice. "If he protests the brutish groom's behavior, the baron binds her kin to the whipping post and rebukes him with a flogging. The baron's will must not be challenged. The kin must be brought to heel and broken, as the baron would break the spirit of a rebellious hound."

There was only one possible interpretation of this story. Gunthar said quietly, "I think whoever this baron was, he did not succeed in breaking you."

Robert met Gunthar's eyes now, but they remained as carefully veiled as they had earlier bespoke his heart's passion. "His name was Christopher Beckford."

Gunthar's brows shot up. "Beckford?"

"I believe you know him, my lord?"

A subtle irony threaded the minstrel's voice again. This time Gunthar refused to rise to it.

"He is my own vassal," Gunthar said. "If what you tell me is true, that he flogged you and forced your sister into so abhorrent a marriage, then you must hate him for it."

Robert began to speak, then pressed his lips together hard.

"And Hanley," Gunthar added after a moment's silence. "You clearly hate him, too. So that is why you tried to throttle him tonight."

Again, that harshened breathing. The minstrel's expression did not alter, but this time his voice throbbed low against the darkness. "She fled to my brother and me again and again, bruised and weeping, pleading for our protection. Each time Lord Christopher returned her to Hanley for his— chastisement. Do you think I will forget it? Do you think he will not pay?"

Gunthar remembered the minstrel's vibrating hands around Hanley's throat, but he did not make the mistake of thinking these words applied to Hanley alone. Was this the secret he had sensed, that Robert had been born a villein? No. Robert confessed it too easily, when he might have worded his story such as to conceal that truth. But Gunthar could not ignore what Robert had just confessed.

"You are aware that Christopher Beckford is in this camp?" Gunthar said. "It is clear you ran away from his manor. As his liege lord, it is my duty to return you to his possession."

A flash of the night's earlier hostility lit across Robert's dark eyes before he masked it again. But the defiant chin came up. "I am a freeman. It has been over seven years since I left the manor."

"Ah." Comprehension dawned, mingled with curiosity. "Who told you of that law, Robert?"

"A priest with whom I studied when I was a boy."

"I see. And you have been a wandering minstrel from that time forth? I am afraid your priest neglected to explain one very important aspect of that law. For a villein to gain his freedom, he must not only evade capture for a year and a day, but he must reside in a privileged town, pay taxes, and be received into the guild." Robert said nothing, but Gunthar caught the rueful twitch of his lips. "Then you did know?"

"Aye. Oh, not when I ran away, but when you brought me to Westminster and I visited London I learned of it." Robert stood and began to pace the tent again, as though he had contained some pent up energy for as long as he could. "I do not care what the law says, seven years is more than enough time to have earned the freedom that should belong to all men at birth. Do you think it was an easy decision to run away from the only life I had ever known? I had never set foot off Beck Manor, I knew nothing of what lay beyond its borders. As miserable a life as it is, as a villein I had the assurance of a roof over my head, a bed, of sorts, food to eat, however meager. I was surrounded by people I knew, some whom I loved."

He pivoted on a flowery-centered diamond shape near one edge of the carpet and paced back the other way.

"What life awaited me as a minstrel? Would men pay me for my music or would I starve to death? At seventeen, I confess I was too impulsive to consider these questions. At eighteen—well, I was still impulsive, but I will not deny that at eighteen some doubt had worked its way into my mind."

"Then why did you leave?"

Robert tossed a glance over his shoulder at Gunthar, but whatever emotion the question stirred now remained hidden in his eyes. "That, my lord, is something you could never understand. After all, you have been free all your life. 'Tis something you take for granted as easily as you wear that fine cloak. I could never explain to you what it is to know your life is not your own."

'Twas the little shake of his head that Robert gave at the end of these words that unexpectedly stung Gunthar. Like the discipline in Robert's eyes, his tone this time betrayed no mockery or scorn. Yet Gunthar felt somehow accused, judged, then simply dismissed, as though saying anything more would be a waste of the minstrel's breath. Gunthar did not generally think much about his own villeins, though he did not tolerate random abuse of them by his bailiffs. For the most part they remained faceless laborers to him. But this man—this villein—had vibrant form and a quick wit and a courageous heart—aye, and it appeared tonight, a loyal one. He had pride, as well. Whether hot with passion or coolly impassive, that trait was stamped clearly across his features.

Gunthar had seen it even at Westminster. He had enjoyed the minstrel's skillful tunes, unobtrusively performed beneath Gunthar's conversations with his wife in the evenings. He had watched Robert frequently from beneath his lashes, determined to weigh the stranger he had taken into his household at his wife's insistence. Robert, she'd said when Gunthar queried her in private, was ever polite and considerate and willing to perform any service she asked of him. A time or two Gunthar was certain he had even caught her exchange a mischievous glance with the minstrel over something that Gunthar said. Only the joy of seeing her happy had prevented Gunthar from rebuking the minstrel from treading too near the line of presumption.

But beneath the virtues his wife praised, Gunthar had sensed a simmering restlessness and impatience in Robert. Courteous and smiling he might be to Helen, but when Gunthar addressed him, the smile faded and Robert's dispassionate replies bordered on the brusque. All his life, Gunthar had found men intimidated by his power or wealth or simply by his waspish tongue. He had learned to use his ability to daunt men to his advantage. It had permitted him few close friendships, but he had been content enough for the most part with the affection of his wife and sons. He confessed that it nettled him a bit to discover what he suspected at Westminster to be true—that Robert did not fear him. Yet there was something attractive, as well, in a man who spoke his thoughts bluntly, rather than shrinking from Gunthar's displeasure or fawning for his favor.

He watched Robert pace the carpet a few more times, lost in thoughts the minstrel's face would no longer betray, before Gunthar spoke again.

"Do you think, then, it is Beckford who desires my death?"

Robert stopped and turned, as if startled by the question. "My lord?"

"You said Hanley was Beckford's groom. It would be logical to assume that he was sent by Beckford to kill me."

Gunthar expected a swift agreement and was surprised when Robert hesitated.

"I've no cause to love Beckford, it is true," Robert said. "I believe him capable of any treachery. But I have not seen him or Hanley for over seven years. Hanley wore no badge on his tunic tonight. I do not even know that he is still in Beckford's service. I imagine the vicious cur could be easily bribed to murder a man. But Beckford—he is your vassal. What would he have to gain by your murder?"

So, Gunthar thought, *even in your hatred you can be fair.* He would remember that.

The cloak had slid from one shoulder and he hefted it back into place before he stood and said briskly, "Very well. I shall have to wait and question the prisoners. Now it is late. Get yourself some rest. Tomorrow we ride to rejoin the king."

Robert remained rooted to the eight-pointed star woven into the carpet beneath his foot. "Beckford—?"

"Ah, yes. If you are wise, you will stay out of his way."

"Then—you will not tell him I am in the camp?"

Gunthar felt a faint smile soften his mouth. "You saved my life this night, Robert Marcel. No, I will not betray you to Beckford, but neither will I protect you if you are caught. Now leave me—and take care."

Robert stared at him, his eyes as unfathomable as a midnight sky. Then he turned and left the tent.

24

The Earl of Gunthar's camp broke shortly after dawn. Robert did not know whether Gunthar had spoken with the prisoners before they set out for La Rochelle. He saw Hanley and his rat-faced companion bound hand and foot in a space cleared for them in one of the supply wagons, surrounded by mounted knights who wore the blue and silver of Gunthar's house. Robert marched with the other footsoldiers at the rear of the camp. Some of the men had grown friendly with him o'er the month and a half they had been in Poitou, drawn by the music he sang in the evenings that appeared to stir pleasant memories in them of home. A cheerful man named Hubert prattled beside him as they walked, barely pausing long enough in his ramblings to take a breath until a mounted horseman rode through the ranks and drew up alongside Robert. Hubert's jaw dropped, then he mumbled out some words of respect and quickly faded into the crowd of soldiers around them.

"Do you mind if I join you?" Richard Channing asked, swinging himself to the ground without giving Robert a chance to answer.

"Would you not be more comfortable riding?" Robert suggested.

"Bah. I am not too lofty to walk." Richard flicked a glance at where the squires rode in the company. "Besides, they are all bores. Most of them ride with their noses in the air, although that peculiar squire of Gunthar's, Ralf, I think they called him, rides with a book propped up on his saddle. *A book.* Have you ever seen anything so absurd? And when they mock him for it, he just looks up and grins, then buries his nose again. How he manages to avoid riding into a tree is anyone's guess."

Richard must be referring to the squire with the curly brown hair, Robert thought, for the one in the tent last night had been blond and he had heard Gunthar call him Antony.

"He is Sir Brandon de Vexin's youngest son," Robert said. "The reader you saw. The gossip is that the earl found the boy in his library picking out words from a book called *Metamorphoses* when he was scarcely five-years-old."

"Meta-what?"

Robert laughed. "*Metamorphoses*." He had no idea what it meant, but he had always liked the feel of odd words on his tongue. "They say Sir Brandon was embarrassed and said he should give the boy to the Church. Gunthar asked the boy if he wished to be a monk so that he could read books, but the boy answered firmly, 'I will be a *knight* that reads books,' which so amused Gunthar that he took him to be his page, and now he is one of Gunthar's squires."

"Hmph." Richard snorted. He seemed impervious to the stares he received as he walked along beside the minstrel, leading his horse behind them.

"Do you not read?" Robert asked.

"Just enough to make out the scrawl of my cousin's letters. I only learned so I would not miss her so much when her grandfather took her back to Northumberland at the end of each summer, and then when I went to serve Sir Edward."

Robert's heart tripped. He feigned a mild interest. "The Lady Marguerite of Winbourne? Does she write to you often?"

"She's sent me a half-dozen letters since we've been in Poitou. I like to read them, but answering them is a chore. My fingers feel like they turn into sausages whenever I pick up a pen. Now if Annys would write me, I'd find a way to reply, even if I had to ask that peculiar squire of Gunthar's to help me."

Robert heard Richard's heavy sigh. He suspected Richard would have liked a sympathetic ear for his impossible love for Annys, but Robert asked instead, "And is your cousin well?" Hopefully Richard would accept the query as one of simple courtesy from the minstrel who had sung at her betrothal dinner.

"Well enough," Richard said. "She writes that the Countess of Gunthar invited her to visit their estates in Kent until spring. Her mother, she says, did not like it but granted permission because Marguerite reminded her that Lord Gunthar was in the king's favor again and that they should not antagonize his wife by refusing. But Marguerite said I must not tell her father, for he would not approve. I can trust you to be discreet, can I not?"

Richard said the latter with only the slightest hint of condescension in his voice, just enough for Robert to know Richard had not entirely forgotten the difference between their stations. Robert chose to overlook it because he found he genuinely enjoyed the young man's company, and more selfishly, because of Richard's connection to Marguerite.

"Most certainly," Robert replied. Marguerite with the Countess of Gunthar? He felt a comfort in the thought. She would be cared for kindly by the countess, rather than constantly harped at by her soft-faced, sharp-tongued mother eager to see her married to Saxton.

"Marguerite said the countess invited Annys, as well. Something about cheering up her widowed daughter-in-law with 'young company.' Marguerite fills her letters with mentions of Annys. I know she does it for me, because she knows that I love her. Only sometimes I think it would be less painful if Marguerite never wrote Annys's name at all."

"You would not truly wish to be ignorant of her for who knows how many months this campaign of the king's drags on?" Robert knew how long and lonely the days and nights had been for him with no knowledge of his love. Just hearing Richard speak Marguerite's name had fallen upon Robert's famished soul as sweet, honeyed morsels.

"I suppose not," Richard agreed with another sigh, then turned the subject. "What did Gunthar want with you last night? I fell asleep before you came back to our pallets. How long did he keep you?"

"Long enough for you to fall asleep," Robert said. He knew from Richard's quick grin that he had likely not lain awake for ten minutes after the altercation in Gunthar's tent. Robert smiled, too. "He only wished to know what I had heard and seen."

Richard grew serious again. "Who do you suppose that fellow was? Was he the one who murdered the guard? Was he trying to steal something from Gunthar?"

Neither of them could see Hanley or his companion any more for the number of knights who rode behind the wagon.

"I do not know," Robert said. "And if I did, it would not be my place to say. Perhaps the earl confided in Saxton. You might ask him. Or . . ." Robert hesitated, then hazarded ". . . or perhaps he told one of his vassals, like Lord Beckford. Did you speak to the baron about Sir Edward? I have heard they are kin."

"Only by marriage," Richard replied. "Their wives are sisters. Aye, I told him of Sir Edward. He said he would help to pay any ransom that might be demanded, but that Gunthar would have more influence over winning Sir Edward's freedom than he. I've not spoken to him today, though. He was not in Gunthar's tent last night, so I do not know why he would know what it was all about. I do not think he and Gunthar are close."

Robert had seen Kit earlier, mounting his horse to ride out with the rest of Gunthar's camp. Robert had kept his head down as always as he had walked past his old master to take his own place in the ranks.

For the second time that morn, Robert heard the clip of hooves trotting among the footsoldiers and glanced up to see Saxton's squire, Nicholas Tybert, riding up to him and Richard.

"Ho, Channing," Tybert said with a smirk. "You seem to find the minstrel's company mighty interesting. Aren't we good enough for you?"

Richard flushed a little, but answered bluntly, "I would find any company preferable to yours, Tybert."

Tybert glowered, his glare taking in Robert as well as Richard, but it was to Richard he continued to address his words.

"My master wants to see you."

"Saxton?" Richard said. "What does he want now?"

"Is it my place to ask questions? I do as I am told, and I was told to fetch you."

"Very well, I'm coming."

Richard threw a grimace at Robert, then mounted his horse and rode away to join the Earl of Saxton.

Evening arrived without reaching the king's camp. Gunthar sought shelter with Lord Triston de Brielle, a Poitevin baron yet loyal to the king. Lord Triston welcomed Gunthar and Saxton, with their vassals and knights, into his keep. The archers and footsoldiers quartered within the bailey. Gunthar sent word by Sir Brandon that he should set footsoldiers to guard the outer perimeter of the castle. To Robert's surprise, he found himself assigned as one of the two soldiers to stand watch outside a postern gate at the rear of the castle wall, with Hubert, the gabbler he had marched with that morning before Richard had joined him.

"Does the earl not trust Lord Triston's knights?" Robert asked as Hubert secured a torch in the iron bracket Robert had driven into the ground.

"I marched with the earl twelve years ago, when he fought in Normandy with the king," Hubert said. "Aye, he trusts Lord Triston, but he trusts his own judgment more. He's a cautious one, is the earl. He always backs his host's guards with some of his own."

"With footsoldiers?"

"With those of us he trusts," Hubert said, a note of pride in his voice. "He says his knights may wield finer blades, but our eyes and noses are keener because we walk closer to the ground than those who ride on horseback."

Like hounds, Robert thought. *Gunthar sets us to guard the castle gate the same way he would set a dog to guard the door of his hen house.* Except that as much as Robert wanted to condemn Gunthar as a haughty, overbearing, self-centered lord who could not tell the difference between one of his dogs and one of his serfs, last night's experience with this particular lord checked Robert's resentments, almost against his will.

It was true that Gunthar had wrapped himself in that rich, fur-lined cloak of his with the casualness of a man who took such luxuries for granted, one who's mind never crossed with the thought that others less fortunate than he ever shivered in the cold. That mindless ease in his privilege had set Gunthar in Robert's mind, at first, among the detestable ranks of men like Kit and Saxton. It had not helped Robert's temper when Gunthar had repeated Hanley's slur on his honor. Robert knew he had reacted impudently. He also knew his impertinence had angered Gunthar. The earl might have responded by locking Robert up with Hanley and the rat-faced man to sort the truth of their conflicting accusations out later. *He could have sent me off with Saxton.* But instead, Gunthar had done what Robert had not expected—he had believed Robert. And he had thanked him.

And when I told him I was a villein, he did not then dismiss me as some dimwitted creature incapable of understanding what had just occurred, but he asked me, man to man, for my opinion of Kit. And then he let me go without revealing me to Kit. And now he has set me here, to guard him and his knights—not as a hound, but as one man who trusts another.

Robert's hand clenched on the hilt of his father's sword as he stood in the cold by the postern gate. He did not know what to make of the Earl of Gunthar. But Robert would not fail this charge tonight, no matter how the chilling breeze snapped about his ears and his eyes burned with weariness while Gunthar slept snug in one of Lord Triston's chambers on a bed stuffed with fleece, if not feathers, swathed in thick, padded quilts like the one Robert had seen rumpled on the cot in Gunthar's tent.

Hubert maintained his own guard's watch with surprising discipline and silence, standing alert and serious as the hours dragged on, his own hand resting on the hilt of the short sword at his waist. He and Robert exchanged words no more than a handful of times through the night. The breeze had dispersed the day's clouds so that Robert could watch the progression of the moon across stars so thick they seemed to form a white smear across the sky.

Robert presumed the moon's courses in Poitou mirrored those he had observed for five-and-twenty years in England. He guessed it, therefore, an hour or two after midnight when the postern gate gave a jarring screech of swollen wood on rusting hinges. Robert whirled towards the gate with Hubert, but Hubert challenged the shadow first.

"Halt there. Name yourself and state your—"

"Fool," a biting voice cut him off. "You were set here to keep trouble out, not to keep the earl's men trapped within. Stand back and let me by."

Robert took two soft steps away from the light of the torch and bowed his head. What was Kit doing leaving the castle at this time of night?"

"My lord," Hubert said stubbornly, "I can't let you pass unless you've got permission."

"I need no permission to dally with a wench." Kit's voice dripped thick with the contempt he always directed at men he thought beneath him. "Lord Triston's castle is woefully lacking in such diversions, but a lass in the village gave me a lovely, wanton smile as we rode past today. Keep your mouth shut and there'll be a silver coin for you when I return."

Robert saw Hubert's posture stiffen. "I can't be bribed, my lord."

Beckford shrugged. "Fine. Let us discuss this, then, with Saxton."

Hubert's stout shoulders shuddered slightly in the moonlight. "Nay, my lord, if you've got Saxton's permission—I'm sorry my lord. I did not know."

Robert could not entirely blame Hubert's sudden surrender. Saxton had taken out his bad temper at the king placing Gunthar in command by loosing his cutting, frigid tongue on Gunthar's troops when his rival was not there. Robert had seen more than one man pale beneath Saxton's abuse. Hubert must have been one of his victims, anxious now to avoid a repeat of his spite.

Robert's tongue quivered to protest, but he confessed his own cowardice in biting back the impulse. If Kit saw and recognized him before he was ready to be recognized, Gunthar would let Kit drag Robert back to the manor. Or try. Robert stood silent, his head still down as Kit's boots moved away from the castle walls. But he had no intention of letting Kit ravish one of Lord Triston's villein girls as he had whenever the fancy had struck him back on Beck Manor.

"What could I do?" Hubert muttered when Robert looked at his fellow guard. "You heard him. He said he had Saxton's leave to go to the village."

"Lord Gunthar is in command here, not Lord Saxton," Robert said. "I'm going after him."

"Who? Gunthar?"

"Beckford. Cover for me, will you?"

Before Hubert could object, Robert strode off in the direction of the village. He did not yet know what he planned to do when he got there. He did not dare confront Kit directly. But he would find some way to cause a disruption to give the girl a chance to escape if, as he suspected, she was not as willing as Kit had said.

It was not difficult to keep Kit within sight, but Robert had to move cautiously, at a distance to prevent Kit hearing his footsteps and turning around. Until at the edge of the village Kit stopped. There was a cottage on the outskirts, more of a hovel where some unfortunate—most likely, Robert guessed, some demented old woman the villagers feared—had been exiled to the farthest reaches of village society. Robert dodged into the shadow it cast just in time to avoid the angle of Kit's vision as Kit looked over his shoulder at the castle. They were too far away for Hubert to see them now, even with the moon bathing the ground with its glow of white light.

But it let Robert see Kit's profile clearly. The wave in the brown hair beneath the round cap he wore, the fine cast of his features that women called handsome. He sported a trim beard that he had not worn seven years ago, but he was still lean and muscular, and his stance was as smug as ever. Just so had he stood on that sweltering day of Robert's seventeenth summer, his grey eyes holding Robert's, smiling while his bailiff had bound Robert's hands to the post and readied the whip.

Every bitter memory had screamed at Robert to throw Kit into the fire of Gunthar's suspicion last night. Robert had seen Kit with Saxton, had watched him pick his way through the sleeping footsoldiers to where Hanley might have lain. The conclusion seemed logical. And revenge had been so tempting. But Robert had not seen the face of the footsoldier Kit had roused, had not heard what Kit might have murmured to him. Their conversation might have had nothing to do with Gunthar. Even with hatred raging in Robert's heart, he found he could not do to another what had been done to his father—accuse and condemn without proof. Not even Kit.

But Kit moved now, away from the village towards the woods to the north. Kit had a village full of villein girls to ravish if lust had been on his mind. Why head for the forest instead?

Robert followed as before. The trees made it harder to keep Kit in his line of vision. Robert had to stay close enough to hear the crunch of Kit's boots in the bracken while trying to walk quietly enough not to give his own footsteps away. Kit, apparently not expecting that someone might trail him, made no similar effort at furtiveness. Moonlight dappled the ground in erratic patches through the canopy of leaves above their heads. Robert had shadows now to conceal him, tree trunks to dart behind whenever a twig snapped beneath his boot and Kit's footfalls ceased for a moment in reaction.

Deeper and deeper into the trees Kit strode. The carpet of fallen leaves grew denser in this part of the forest, muffling Kit's steps and forcing Robert to pursue him more closely. They wove around poplars and hazel and oak, until a thick stand of bushes the height of a man threatened to block their way. Kit swept an opening through them with a swing of his arm and vanished to the other side. Robert waited as long as he dared, until fear of losing Kit drove him forward to push the branches aside as well.

He dropped them again, backing away as quickly as he could. The bushes shielded an unexpected clearing where Kit had stopped beside a tree stump bathed so luminously in the unhampered moonlight that Robert had glimpsed the thick moss grown over it before his retreat.

"Who's there?"

Robert silently cursed himself. How could he have been so careless? Kit's back had been turned to him, but Kit would have to have been deaf not to hear the rustling of the branches behind him. Robert touched his sword hilt, then eased loose his dagger instead. It made a softer sound slipping out its sheath.

"*Seigneur, seigneur, pardon, je suis en retard!*"

"To the devil with you, Felcourt. You make enough racket to raise the dead." Kit's voice sounded savage.

Robert held his breath. Had Kit confused the swishing sound of Robert's bushes with the crackling of limbs by the man who broke through the greenery from another direction to join him in the clearing? These were not the woods outside Beck Manor. Robert prayed Kit found the unfamiliar forest as disorienting as he did.

"*Pardon, monseigneur, j'ai cru voir quelqu'un dans les bois, mais c'était seulement . . .*"

"Someone else in the woods?" Kit said sharply.

"*Oui, seigneur, mais c'était seulement un chevreuil.*"

"Blazes, man, speak English. I have already warned you. I'd rather not risk my neck to some spying Poitevin who might choose to go tattling to Gunthar. Precious few of them, I have found, speak my own tongue, so unless you wish me to take this and go back to Lord Triston's castle—"

"*Non, seigneur* . . . I mean, no, milord. *Par*—forgive me, milord."

Robert moved cautiously forward, rolling silently from heel to toe until he was near enough again to part a slit through the bushes and try to see what "this" referred to. Kit held something in his hand, but he lowered it to his side, away from Robert's sight.

"Are you sure it was only a deer you saw?" Kit cast a suspicious glance in Robert's direction. Robert dared not release the branch he held lest it bounce in the moonlight. He could do naught but trust the thick branches over his own head would conceal him in shadow.

"Aye, milord. I held back from joining you until I was certain. "

Robert exhaled slowly. The short, stout stranger with Kit must have approached the clearing from an entirely different direction than Kit and Robert had, a supposition strengthened by the way Kit's body was angled away from Robert's position.

The man called Felcourt drew closer to Kit. "You have spoken to La Marche?" he asked. "Has he decided?"

"He has," Kit said. "Do you have the money?"

"*Oui*, milord, all of it. But first, what does *le comte* say? When will he—"

"Do you take me for a fool," Kit broke in, "to trust a Frenchman to keep his word? First let me see the silver."

Robert nudged the branches ever so slightly wider to better see Kit's companion. The man's balding round face frowned in the moonlight, but he untied a pouch from his belt and handed it to Kit. Kit balanced the pouch on some flattened object he held in his other hand and loosened the drawstrings. Robert heard the jingle of coins. He guessed Kit must be counting them in the silence that followed.

"It is all there, milord," Felcourt said at last with a touch of impatience, "with a receipt promising more if La Marche succeeds. Now you must give me the plans."

Kit glanced around the clearing one more time, his gaze sliding right past Robert before it returned to Felcourt. He retied the pouch, stuffed it into the breast of his tunic, then gave Felcourt the object in his hand. With the moonlight slanting down on the Frenchman, Robert thought it looked like some sort of packet, the sort made of leather he'd once seen a merchant he'd sung for bind a letter in and give to a servant to be delivered in the rain.

"It is all there," Kit said softly, echoing the Frenchman's words, "sealed, to be opened only by your king. At the proper moment, La Marche will deliver the prize into King Philip's hands."

Felcourt slid the packet into his tunic's breast.

"King Philip will hold by our bargain?" Kit asked.

Felcourt gave a derisive snort. "*Oui, seigneur,* you need not doubt *our* king's honor. He is French."

Kit swore at him. Felcourt chuckled and patted his breast where the packet hid, then shoved his way through the bushes across the clearing. Robert set the branch he'd been holding back in its place as carefully as he could before Kit turned around, then moved behind the wide trunk of an oak tree and waited for Kit to emerge.

Kit came out slowly. The shades cast by the trees hid his expression now, but he'd tossed his cloak back to free one of his arms and from the placement of his hand, Robert guessed it rested on a dagger or sword. Had he seen Robert through the branches? Or was he merely being cautious, lest Felcourt's "deer" prove to be something more dangerous?

Robert would have waited until Kit moved safely out of sight, but he was not sure he could find his way back to Lord Triston's castle on his own. In daylight he might have found his way, but he dared not wait till morning. He had abandoned his post to trail Kit and could only imagine Gunthar's disgust if dawn arrived to reveal the escaped villein in whom he had placed his trust had apparently run away like a coward. Everything in Robert's nature shrank at the thought and pressed him on in Kit's footsteps.

Kit's increasingly quickened pace suggested he knew his way precisely. Either he had been to the clearing before or someone had marked a path to guide him, but if the latter were true Robert could not see it. Gradually Robert felt the carpet of softened leaves that had muted their steps begin to thin again. The debris on the forest floor grew drier and coarser, more difficult to navigate without a betraying crunch. He reluctantly dropped further behind to place more distance between his boots and Kit's.

Then Robert sensed that something had changed. Twice Kit took a turn so sharp that Robert almost lost him. This could not have been the way they had come before. Robert would have remembered such nearly pivoting bends. He kept his dagger in his hand just in case Kit were laying some sort of trap, but Kit strode on in seeming confidence. Perhaps it was only a shortcut. Perhaps for reasons of his own—reasons Robert had witnessed in the clearing—Kit wished to return to the castle quickly before Gunthar discovered he, too, had been gone.

Kit swerved around another bend so abruptly that his cloak gave a snap in the air. Robert's heartbeat accelerated as it had the two prior times. As before, he slowed his own pace to follow Kit's movement warily, but this time when Robert pursued the swing in the new direction no shadow moved ahead of him.

Blazes! Where had Kit gone? Robert took a step forward, then paused to gaze around him. All he saw were black spectral bushes and the soaring jet trunks of trees. Kit could be behind any of them.

Another step. Another pause.

The blow came from out of nowhere, slamming into Robert's side. His left shoulder hit the ground hard, then a great force shoved him onto his back. A man straddled him—Kit, growling low in his throat. Robert's dagger was still in his hand. He swung it wildly, not caring where it landed, but Kit must have felt the motion for Robert's wrist met with a swift, strong palm. Kit tried to wrench the weapon away. Robert clung to it doggedly. Did Kit think he struggled with some unknown opponent, or had he recognized Robert? Kit cursed him twice in their struggle, but he did not speak Robert's name. Robert fought hard to hold his own tongue silent, lest Kit know his voice.

Feeling stole back into Robert's benumbed shoulder, allowing him to grapple more fiercely with his foe. They rolled and groped and scrabbled together on the forest floor, in and out of mottling splashes of moonlight. Either Kit had not drawn his own weapon or Robert had somehow knocked it free, because Kit was using two hands now to try to pry loose Robert's dagger. Whether Kit recognized him or not, Robert knew he was dead if Kit got the blade. Robert pushed and hit and shoved until he finally flung Kit on his back.

Robert scrambled atop him and pressed his forearm across Kit's throat. *Who is master now?* he thought savagely. He ran his thumb along the vein pulsing warm at the side of Kit's neck, then touched the cold edge of his dagger against it. Kit went still. *What does it feel like to be helpless, my lord? To know your life hangs on another man's whim?*

There was nothing to stop him from taking revenge. Revenge for his father's murder, for Lottie's bruises and tears, for William's aching loneliness . . . Vengeance flooded Robert's mouth, scalding and corrosive. His hand clenched tighter on his hilt. Nothing to stop him . . .

Except the dusky-haired woman with the freckle-dusted nose who waited for him in England. If he killed a man—even this miserable excuse for one—they would call Robert murderer. He could never see Marguerite again. Could he leave her to suffer alone at Saxton's hand, if it meant ending this bitter, throbbing hatred that had driven him from the day his father died?

Revenge. He would have it, but not like this. He took his arm from Kit's throat and slammed his hand against Kit's breast. The pouch of silver bulged through the fabric. Did the coins bear a French inscription, like the ones that had trapped Robert's father? If so, it was all Robert need present to Gunthar to prove that—

Robert felt the swing of Kit's arm too late to stop it. Pain exploded on a white wave through his head, then consciousness blinked out.

25

Robert did not know how long he sat on the forest floor, clutching his head against the pain that threatened to split it wide open. It had been daylight when he opened his eyes, but the trees above him swirled so sickeningly that he quickly squeezed them shut again. Memory had come back sluggishly through the merciless throbbing: Kit, the Frenchman, the attack in the woods— Eventually Robert dragged himself to sit up, urgent to get back to the castle, but waves of nausea had stayed him sitting here until his stomach ceased heaving. His skull still pounded but he finally managed to squint open his eyes. Two blurry, bloody rocks lay near him. He reached out a shaking hand. Nay, one rock only. Pain hazed and doubled his vision. He touched the side of his head and winced. A lump swelled there beneath his blood-clotted hair.

The devil take Kit. Had he lingered long enough to gaze into Robert's face after he'd struck him, or had he been in too great a hurry to flee from the scene?

Robert shifted himself over to the nearest tree and used it to pull himself to his feet. The effort sent his surroundings into another spin, but after a few moments the woods steadied again. The shrill whinny of a horse penetrated the fading buzz between his ears, and then he heard the shouts of men. Surely they came from Gunthar's camp? Kit must have led him nearer to the forest's edge than Robert had realized in the dark. He stumbled towards the sounds, using the voices to guide him as he lurched from tree to tree to support his stubbornly weak legs. Even with his blurred vision, he could see the trees thinning, and then they parted altogether to allow him a foggy image of men and horses milling about beneath the walls of Lord Triston's castle.

The distance did not appear too far, the woods having broken closer to the castle in this spot than the stretch he'd walked last night to the village. He hoped his determination would propel him successfully to join the men, but without the support of the trees, halfway there he felt his knees trying to buckle. He staggered obstinately forward another few feet. One voice shouted above the general hubbub at the castle wall. Feet came thudding his direction, the sound stopping abruptly just as Robert felt himself pitch forward.

Strong hands caught him by the shoulders and lowered him to sit on the ground.

"Rob! Saints, man, where have you been?"

Robert dropped his face into his hands. His head pounded sickeningly again and he felt disgustingly faint.

"Rob?"

Even through the thudding in his head, he recognized Richard's voice. "I'm all right," Robert muttered thickly. "Or I will be in a moment."

"But what happened? Your head—"

Robert flinched away with a groan as Richard touched the swelling left by Kit's rock. He fought the pain through several moments of silence before Richard spoke again.

"Gunthar has been asking for you."

Robert groaned inwardly this time. Of course Gunthar had. Robert found his voice, still somewhat husky. "Did Gunthar think I'd run away?"

"He does not share his thoughts with me." Richard's voice sounded tart. "I'd better take you to him. But first let me see to your head. Looks like you've taken a nasty blow there."

He helped Robert to his feet and supported him to the castle gate. Robert saw blurred wagons among the men and remembered the order that Richard had brought. Gunthar's men must be readying to continue their journey to rejoin the king. From the way the hum of conversations broke off as he and Richard passed by them, he knew men had stopped to stare their way. Richard guided Robert through the gate and into the bailey where more men and horses milled. Richard found a corner and lowered Robert back to the ground, then left for a few minutes, returning with a basin of water and some bandages.

"My turn to return the favor," Richard said as he set about washing the blood from the side of Robert's head. "Though the scratch you cleaned on my temple was nothing to this. It looks like someone tried to bash your head in with a rock. Do you want to tell me what happened yet?"

Robert shook his head and Richard fell silent again. Robert gritted his teeth through Richard's nursing, determined not to cry out or wince again. The young man had apparently obtained a salve as well as water and bandages from the camp's barber. The ointment eased some of the throbbing in Robert's skull and his vision at last began to steady. By the time Gunthar's fair haired squire, Antony, joined them, Robert could see the squire's frown clearly.

"I am to escort you to the earl," the squire said to Robert.

Richard ignored him and handed Robert a flask of wine. Robert gulped the liquid down, welcoming the bracing flow of it into his veins, before signaling to Richard that he was ready to rise.

"You should have a bandage," Richard said.

Robert gingerly brushed his hair down over the swelling, grateful that Richard had cleaned away the blood. Perhaps it was pride, but this was one part of the night's story he did not wish to confess to Gunthar.

"Nay, I will be fine now, though I should welcome the support of your arm to Gunthar's door."

Richard lent it willingly, keeping a firm hand on Robert's elbow as they followed Gunthar's squire into the great stone keep. The squire led them through the castle's hall, up some stairs, and across a gallery that took them to a chamber door in one of the castle's towers.

"I will be fine now," Robert murmured. "Thank you again."

Richard drew his hand away. Robert shifted his feet to steady himself a moment, then nodded at the squire who watched him with an eyebrow cocked with curiosity. The squire flung open the door and announced, "Robert Marcel, my lord."

Robert stepped into the chamber, where Gunthar sat scribbling away at a furious pace on a sheet of parchment atop the same desk that had been in Gunthar's tent the night Robert had struggled with Hanley. Gunthar looked up, then set down his quill pen, his gaze on Robert's face.

"So I see," he said quietly. "Thank you, Antony. You may leave us."

The squire bowed and went out, closing the door behind him.

Robert waited as Gunthar's gaze lingered on his cheeks, cold enough he knew they must be white. He hoped Gunthar would not glance at his fists, clenched tight against the faintness that still hovered at the edge of his temples' pulsing.

"What's the matter with you?" Gunthar asked abruptly. "Are you ill?"

"My lord, I am fine." Robert was pleased to hear his voice come out almost normal.

"You don't look fine. Sit down."

Robert accepted the curt invitation with relief and sank down on the nearest chair. If Gunthar felt any concern for his footsoldier's pallor, Robert saw it dissolve in the gleam of anger that stole into Gunthar's grey eyes.

"Would you care to tell me why you abandoned your post last night?"

Even though Robert had expected the question, the dry tones carried a sarcasm that stung.

"I did not abandon it," Robert said, rebelling at the word. "I asked Hubert to watch for me while I . . ." He trailed off. What could he say? He had no proof for what he had heard in the woods. He could scarcely sort out his thoughts through his head's drubbing.

"While you . . . ?" Gunthar prodded.

Robert heard the thin sneer beneath Gunthar's words and knew he had already been judged. Unable to assemble his befogged mind into a defense, he slipped into his old, familiar resentments.

"Would anything I say make a difference? There is only one reason a man of my birth would 'abandon his post,' and that is cowardice."

To Robert's surprise, the grey eyes suddenly blazed. "Coward, indeed. Two nights ago I gave you your freedom, last night I gave you my trust, and how was I repaid? You deserted your post while you were on duty—aye, I repeat it, deserted!—and this morning three men are dead. I want answers, and I want them now." Gunthar slammed his hands on the top of the desk and pushed himself to his feet with a furious glare.

Robert stared at Gunthar's wrathful face. Three men dead? Had the world turned upside-down overnight? "My lord, I don't understand—"

He broke off as Gunthar strode around the desk and pulled something out of his belt.

"Does this look familiar to you?"

Robert looked down at the object in Gunthar's hand. A dagger lay in the strong, long-fingered palm, the weapon's hilt blazoned with the image of a rampant tyger, the blade Robert had polished but yestermorn now crusted with blood.

"My dagger." His hand dropped reflexively to the empty sheath at his side. "But how do you come to have it? It was in my possession just last night."

Disdain spread over Gunthar's mouth. "Is this ruse of befuddlement intended to throw me off? If you think I have summoned you here to deal with a fool, you have dangerously misjudged me, sirrah."

Robert pressed the heels of his palms to his temples. If his head were not drumming so, he would think himself adrift in some nightmare, still on the forest floor.

"My lord, I do not understand how you come to have my dagger or why it should be covered with blood—"

Gunthar cut him off with a hard, short laugh. "Fine. If you wish to play games, I will oblige you. You deserted your post last night and this morning three men are dead. Hubert, the man who stood guard with you, dead of a dagger in the back. Cantwell, who stood guard on our two prisoners, dead of a dagger in the back. Dorn, one of those prisoners, dead of a dagger in the back. This dagger, Robert Marcel, *your dagger.*"

Robert shrank back, revolted. "*No,* sir!"

"You said it was yours?"

"Aye, but—"

"And you admitted it was in your possession. Who else could it be?"

Robert stared at Gunthar in horror as the truth pierced his pain-hazed brain. Kit. He *had* recognized Robert in the woods and had devised a sweeter revenge than silencing what his former villein had witnessed by simply killing Robert as he lay unconscious. Three men dead by Robert's dagger. Who would believe Robert now if he accused his old master of treason?

Robert did not know whether it was pain or fury that made him shake as he rose to his feet. He had only his honesty to fight back the lie. He knew it would not be enough, but he spoke it nonetheless, staring straight into the challenge in Gunthar's eyes.

"My lord, I tell you forthrightly that I have killed no one. You may believe me or not as you please, but I am not a murderer. Those men were not killed by my hand."

Gunthar held Robert's gaze for a long, probing moment, his face hard, his mouth set tight. Then he leaned slowly back against the desk and folded his arms across his chest. The grey eyes went hooded and his voice went soft. "Persuade me, Robert."

The almost gentle invitation took Robert aback. "Sir?"

"Where were you last night?" When Robert hesitated, Gunthar added simply, "Tell me."

Robert gazed at him suspiciously. 'Twas Gunthar who played a game with *him* now, but Robert could not guess his intent, for he could no longer read Gunthar's eyes. "I have no proof. You will not believe me."

"Try me anyway."

Robert swung away from Gunthar to pace across the tower floor. A frustrated energy drove him through the throbbing discomfort that made his strides still slightly unsteady. Without looking at Gunthar, Robert told him of what had passed last night: how he had followed Kit into the woods, of the scene he had overheard between Kit and the Frenchman, the silver and the packet that had been exchanged, and finally, reluctantly, of Robert's scuffle with Kit in the woods, ending with the blow to his head that had laid him unconscious in the woods all night. It stung him to confess the last. He felt a fool for not anticipating so obvious a defense on Kit's part.

He felt Gunthar watching him through it all. When Robert finished, he stopped and turned to face the old earl again.

Gunthar's heavy lids continued to veil his eyes. He said nothing for a long moment. Then he murmured, "I knew there was no love lost between you and Beckford, but to accuse him of this—! I see you will be satisfied with nothing less than his ruination and death."

Robert had thought himself braced for the doubt, but the words cut deep. He had let Gunthar disarm his caution, lull him with a pretense of giving Robert a fair hearing. Fair? From a nobleman?

"I warned you I could not prove it," Robert said. "You have but my word for what happened, and I see you are unprepared to accept that." He added, with a derisive curl of his lip, "I have learned from long experience that in contest between lord and villein, the lord invariably has his way."

Gunthar's heavy brows plunged down. "You grow insolent, sir."

Robert gave a scornful little laugh.

Gunthar pushed himself away from the desk, his eyes hard as agates. "Are you guilty of this crime, Robert Marcel?"

"No, sir, I am not."

For a moment longer they faced each other, Robert's snap hanging between them in the air. Then Gunthar strode past him to the door. Robert expected him to hail the guards, but while Gunthar reached out to grasp the latch, he did not lift it. He stood very still for several heightened heartbeats in Robert's breast. Then his hand fell away and he turned around.

"I am sorry, Robert," he said abruptly. "I want to believe you. My every instinct urges me to do so. You're a dashed hard man to read, until your eyes flash like that. And this—" he stepped close enough to touch the swelling on Robert's head with surprising gentleness "— is no lie." Gunthar's hand fell back to his side. "But it is not enough. I cannot explain this away." He motioned to the dagger, now clasped in his left hand. "You might accuse Beckford of stealing it, but there is no proof he was even in the woods."

And Hubert, the other guard who had seen Kit leaving the castle, is dead. Robert might have a lump on his head, but who was to say he had not received it in a struggle with Hubert or Cantwell or Dorn? That he had staggered into the woods, then staggered out again, disoriented by his wound, until Richard had found him and brought him back to the castle?

Robert knew Gunthar had already weighed the same conclusions when he said, "It would be your word against Beckford's, and whatever I think, you have taken the king's measure right enough. He would not accept a minstrel's testimony over that of one of his own barons. I could have Beckford searched for this silver you speak of, but do you think I will find it?"

Robert shook his head. Kit was not a fool. He would not have kept the silver where it could be easily discovered.

Gunthar sighed. "You have fallen into quite the tangle, Robert Marcel, and I do not know if I have it longer in my power to extricate you, far less unsnarl the mess the king has made of affairs in England." He slid Robert's dagger back into his belt.

Robert did not know what to make of Gunthar's words. Did he speak honestly to Robert, or did he seek to lull his suspicions to trick a confession? Nothing discernable changed in Gunthar's proud, commanding posture, yet Robert felt a sense of sudden weariness about the strong shoulders.

"I am too old for this," Gunthar said. "Sometimes I wish I had ignored John's summons and remained in Kent. We were happy there, Helen and I."

If Gunthar baffled him in other things, of one thing Robert had been sure from their first meeting: this man loved his wife. Robert remembered those evenings he had sung for them in London, the affectionate glances he had watched them exchange, the tender way Gunthar still held his wife's hand after what must have been decades of marriage, a shared camaraderie of spirit Robert had rarely witnessed between a man and woman. He knew it was absurd to take an earl as a pattern for his own life, yet often when Robert drifted into sleep, it was in a warm glow of hope that one day he and Marguerite would sit, grey-haired, like Gunthar and his countess, as much in love at the end as they were today.

Curiosity nudged aside Robert's doubts for a moment. "Why did you come to court, sir?" He had overheard enough of Gunthar's conversations with his wife to know the earl had not done it for ambition or vanity.

Gunthar raised his brows. "Who am I to defy the king's command?"

Before he could catch himself, Robert grinned. "Your pardon, my lord, but I cannot quite picture you quailing in the presence of King John."

Gunthar smiled too, his eyes lighting at Robert's shrewdness. "No, you are right. I am not afraid of John. There is more."

Robert realized in the pause that followed that his question had been impertinent. He said as Gunthar stood seemingly lost in some reflection, "Forgive me, my lord, you need not explain yourself to me. It is not my place to ask—"

Gunthar's gaze flicked back to Robert's face. "Don't apologize, Robert. It is out of character."

A rush of heat flooded out the cold that had lingered in Robert's cheeks. "My lord, indeed, I never intended to give you such an impression of me as that! If I have said anything out of place—" *If?* His flush deepened. He knew full well Gunthar had not called him "insolent" without reason. "Indeed, I know that I have! I earnestly—"

"Apologize?"

Robert caught the quizzical gleam in Gunthar's eyes. Robert bit his lip, but something had shifted the tension between them, and he felt his mouth curving upward again. "Truly, sir, I am not always so impudent a fellow as you think me."

"What I think is that you are wasted as a mere minstrel. You ought to have been a duke's son."

Gunthar did not sound mocking. Did he jest? "My lord?"

"You've the manner of one, at times. But never mind that. You asked me a question and I see no harm in answering it." He motioned towards the chair that Robert had occupied earlier. "Sit down again. I once suffered a similar blow to the side of my head and fancy I have a fair idea of the way your skull must be throbbing just now."

Robert hesitated, but when Gunthar repeated, "Sit!" with a little impatience, he returned rather gratefully to the chair.

Gunthar walked over to the desk and picked up the quill. "You are too young, of course, to remember the late king."

"Richard?" Robert asked.

Gunthar made a face of distaste. "No, I speak of Henry the Angevin. Richard . . . well, let it go." He lowered himself with just a hint of stiffness into the sprawling chair behind the desk. "I was with Henry, fought with him, during those last wars against his son, Richard, and the King of France. And I was there at Chinon when Henry fell ill, saw his face when word came to him that John, too, had betrayed him. Richard had long been a thorn in his side, but John he had loved, John's rights he had fought relentlessly to defend against Richard's grasping demands. To learn that in the end, John had thrown his lot in with Richard—It killed him, that final, cruel betrayal."

That had been twenty-five years ago. The lines in Gunthar's face seemed to Robert to deepen as he slid into those long ago memories.

"Men thought that Henry died hating Richard." Gunthar threaded the feather of the quill through his long, still graceful fingers. "Henry had the ungovernable temper of a Plantagenet, but at his heart's core, he was always a loving father and remained so, even in his most bitter defeat. Even as he cursed Richard, he begged me to stand beside his son when Richard became king, to give Richard what support and advice lay in my power. He said Richard would need what help he could get." A brief, reminiscent smile flitted over Gunthar's tired features. "Richard cared not for my advice when I warned him to stay in England. Instead he plundered the kingdom for the glory of his Crusade. But when he died, I found myself more successful with John—until his marriage to Isabella, and then that affair with the young Duke of Brittany."

"Sir," Robert ventured when Gunthar paused, "is it true what is said? That the king murdered his own nephew?"

Gunthar frowned now, his gaze resting again on Robert's face. After a moment, he set the quill down and continued as if the question had never been asked. "I warned John that the Lusignans would not accept meekly the insult of him stealing Isabella from the Count of La Marche. I warned him it would mean trouble on both sides of the British Sea. But he chose not to listen to me. He preferred Saxton's counsel and dismissed me from court. To own the truth, I found it a relief at long last to be out of court affairs."

"Then why did you return?"

"Because of my oath to John's father. I know John summoned me back to frighten Saxton. And I know he has little intention of heeding my counsel now any more than he did twelve years ago. But for the love I bore his father, I could not refuse to try."

Robert understood the call of loyalty and love, and nodded his head.

"But all of this is nothing to the point." Gunthar swept a hand sideways, as though brushing away the tale he had just told, leaving only the dilemma that now faced them. Kit's trap.

Robert jerked his shoulders square, ignoring the unpleasant dryness that stole into his mouth. "What now, sir?"

"I shall have to place you under arrest," Gunthar said. "It would be best if you surrender quietly—"

"Surrender?" The word shot Robert back to his feet. "If you think I am going to 'quietly' stick my head in Kit Beckford's noose to please you and the king—"

Gunthar's bark of laughter cut him off. "Aye, I thought your humble attitude could not last. I assure you, your head in a noose should not please me at all. And it is in the hope of keeping your head out of one that I ask you to go with my guards for now and make no attempt to escape. Will you give me your word?"

"No, sir."

Gunthar smiled. "I thought not. Is there no honor in you, Robert?"

"My lord, if I gave my word, be assured I should keep it."

Gunthar nodded. "Nevertheless, you will agree not to escape until we have reached the king's camp, at least."

"It may be too late by then." Robert knew he could not evade the guards that undoubtedly waited outside the tower door to seize him, but if an opportunity came to break away along the road—

"Will you not trust me, Robert? I wish to help you, but I cannot without your cooperation."

Trust? An earl? With his freedom and life? Did Gunthar think he was mad, or merely a witless oaf from the fields?

"Why should you wish to help me?" he challenged.

Gunthar leaned back in his chair and studied Robert with an almost puzzled expression in his steady grey eyes. "That is a good question. One to which I don't have an answer, aside from the fact that I like you, Robert Marcel. And that I cannot explain either, for a more insolent, disrespectful fellow I've never met!" He laughed, not mockingly, but with a sort of baffled humor Robert somehow sensed Gunthar directed at himself. Then Gunthar straightened and stood. He walked around the desk to lay his hands on Robert's shoulders, his face suddenly very grave. "Trust me in this, I implore you. Give me a chance to prove your innocence."

Robert felt himself unnerved by Gunthar's touch. He gripped Robert, not shrinkingly, as a noble repelled by a churl, but hard and bracing, the way William might have sought to fortify Robert, or Robert, William. The world had indeed turned upside-down.

Robert stared into Gunthar's eyes, searching for deceit, but saw only a quiet, almost urgent plea. The barrier between them blurred further. He asked one last question, simple and direct. "How?"

Gunthar's strong mouth tightened, then went slightly awry. "I do not know. But whatever course I decide upon, it will take time. You must give me that time."

No prevarication, no smooth guarantees. It was that—an honest answer that promised nothing while promising everything—that urged Robert across the gulf of doubt and won the slow nod of his head.

"Your word, then, that you will stay with my guards?" Gunthar said. "Give me that, and I will see to it that you are not bound."

And that—an exchange of faith for faith—pushed Robert the rest of the way into a wild gamble on Gunthar's integrity. He spread his hands, knowing he might be walking off a precipice he could never return from, but he heard himself consent anyway.

"Very well, my lord. You have my word."

26

Lamhurst Castle
Kent, England

Marguerite sailed over the ice, the wind whipping her hair into tangles she knew she would spend half the night combing out again, but the ecstasy was worth it. It was like flying to skate across the shallow frozen pond, impossibly supported only by a pair of shaved bones strapped to her feet. It had taken her weeks to steady her ankles enough to stand and take her first wobbly steps on the ice. She and Annys had clung to each other and repeatedly toppled over together in a heap of bruises and giggles on the hard surface, while Evelyn de Bury had glided around them graceful as a bird circling in the air, laughing and encouraging them to try again.

"I did not think I should ever learn," Evelyn had said, "but Harry held my hand fast and guided me ever so patiently, until now I can do this—" she spun around in a tight little circle "—and this."

She'd flown backwards so fast that Marguerite and Annys had both screeched in alarm, but Evelyn reversed herself with some clever maneuver Marguerite still had not learned, just avoiding colliding with the tapered bank at the ice's edge. They skated on an artificial pond on the Earl of Gunthar's wide manor, one that, according to Evelyn, her late husband had cajoled his father into digging sufficiently shallow to allow the ice to linger hard enough on the surface so that Lord Harry could share this entertainment with his new wife through the early weeks of March.

Marguerite could skate wide circles now and occasionally attempted a precarious spin, but she still preferred to keep her gaze straight ahead.

Annys had glided ahead of her today, trying to catch Evelyn's four-year-old son, who could still skate faster than either of his mother's new friends and loved to prove it with his gleeful little squeal. The child, handsome as a golden cherub and impish as an elf, had made what might have been days of dreary waiting whirl by instead in merriment.

"He will break hearts when he grows up, Evelyn," Marguerite said as his golden-haired mother coasted up alongside Marguerite.

Evelyn smiled, but Marguerite heard her sigh as she watched her son skate teasingly just out of Annys's reach. "In general he is very good, though very willful at times. 'Twas a trait of his father's, and 'tis a father's stern hand he needs."

"But surely Lord Gunthar—"

"Lord Gunthar is a grandparent and, like Lady Helen, is prone to be over-tolerant."

Marguerite caught the fond glance Evelyn cast at her mother-in-law who sat on an elegant little chair on the bank, looking up from her needlework now and then to observe the young women and the child with a smile. It had been Marguerite who had begged the countess to join them today. Lady Helen had seemed unusually reserved, almost melancholy when they had broken their fast together that morning. Marguerite had offered to stay behind and keep her company while the others went down to the still-frozen pond. When the countess had refused to allow it, Marguerite had resorted to shameless wheedling until Lady Helen had agreed with a laugh to come and watch them skate.

"Harry would not have put up with all his tricks," Evelyn said of her late husband. "But there, I'm afraid I am no more proof against his naughty coaxings than his grandparents. My lady would have me marry again, but—" She broke off with a little shake of her head, then excused herself and sailed off to scold her son for skating so many rings around Annys that Annys had grown dizzy, slipped, and skidded giggling across the ice on her backside.

Marguerite saw the worry in Lady Helen's face and glided over to reassure her.

"Annys would not laugh so if she were hurt," Marguerite said. She stepped awkwardly into the frosted grass, then sat down to remove her bone skates, her heavy skirts and mantle protecting her from the moisture. There could not be too many more days cold enough to freeze the pond, she fancied. Spring would surely begin seeping in soon.

"Did Evelyn say anything about Sir Gerald?" the countess asked. "I gave him leave to write to her from the king's camp in Poitou."

"She confessed to me that she has received a few letters from him, but she has refused to open them and says she cannot answer." Marguerite reached up to lay her hand across Lady Helen's thin fingers and said gently, "She still mourns for your son, my lady."

"So do we all," Lady Helen said. "It was so kind of you and Annys to accept my invitation to come to Lamhurst. You have lifted Evelyn's spirits. And mine." She disengaged her hand from Marguerite's and reached out to thread her fingers through Marguerite's hair. "Such thick tresses," she mused, working free a windblown knot. "My hair was once this heavy, but never had such wayward curls as these."

Despite the silvering threads among the pale gold, Lady Helen's hair, which she always wore unbound beneath a veil of white, still maintained a lustrous sheen. The countess withdrew her fingers from Marguerite's curls, though they lingered briefly on the green silk ribbon with the roses down the center that dangled from Marguerite's hair over her shoulder.

"Did you bring my embroidery, too?" Marguerite asked as the countess returned her attention to her stitchery. She loved to sit with the older woman in her sunlit solar and listen to her stories of her life with the earl while they plied their threads together. Marguerite had found the Earl of Gunthar even more intimidating than her father and Saxton. Something about him daunted Marguerite's tongue whenever she stood in his presence, but Lady Helen had apparently had no fear of tweaking him boldly when she was scarcely older than Marguerite. Perhaps the earl had been less formidable forty years ago? One day Marguerite hoped to sit with a daughter of hers and recount such warm tales of her and Robert's long and happy marriage.

"Nay, child," Lady Helen said, "this is not a day to be bound to silks and needles. Go back to the ice. Your mother will be demanding that you return to her come spring."

Oh, then Marguerite hoped that spring might never come! She had loved these days tucked away with Lady Helen and Annys and Evelyn in Kent. But she knew the time must pass for Robert to return to her. She had prayed he might do so before her mother's summons came, but the letters from her father and Richard, and Gunthar's to Lady Helen gave no hint that the king was near accomplishing the goals that had driven him and his army across the British Sea.

"I am tired of skating," Marguerite lied. "I would rather sit here with you. I think—" she hesitated lest she touch upon some tender spot Lady Helen preferred to keep private, but then she ventured "—I think you are sad today, my lady. You are missing your husband, perhaps, or—or Lord Henry?"

Evelyn's husband had died two years ago, three months after their son had been born, struck by a mis-shot arrow during a tragic hunting expedition.

Lady Helen set another stitch to the design for a pillow covering that was fast coming to resemble a flowery mead. Marguerite, whose embroidery even her mother praised, did not think she had ever seen such tiny, elegant stitches.

"My husband writes that he is well," the countess said. "And yes, I miss Harry's laughter and mischief every day. He always kept Lamhurst so lively. Alain is much like him when he was that age, but dear as the boy is . . ."

". . . he is not your son," Marguerite finished when the countess trailed off.

Lady Helen smiled at her. "No, he is Evelyn's. And whether she thinks it or not, one day she will fall in love again and she and Alain will leave us."

"But he is your husband's heir. Surely your husband will raise him here at Lamhurst?"

"When he is older perhaps. That is a decision for days to come. Still, for now Alain somehow keeps Harry close to me. It was Peter I have been thinking of today."

"Peter?"

"My other son. Our eldest."

Marguerite rocked back a little in surprise. "I did not know you had another son. Evelyn never told me."

"She never met him, though she knows of him, of course. But by the time she met Harry, he was our only surviving child." Lady Helen finished embroidering a pert tail on a hare that frolicked through the flowers on her linen square, then knotted the thread and bit it off. "My two daughters were both stillborn, the others all miscarriages. Then Peter came, and Harry. Strong, sturdy boys who withstood all the ailments of childhood and brought joy and comfort to my husband and me. My husband set Peter as squire to a friend of his, Lord Harding, Harry to one of his vassals. When Lord Harding responded to the call of Pope Innocent III and took the Cross, he asked to take Peter along as his squire. My husband was reluctant, as was I, but we eventually agreed the experience would do our son good. Would you hand me that scarlet thread?"

Marguerite searched in the countess's basket until she found the requested skein.

"We know Peter arrived safely in Venice, and then in Constantinople," Lady Helen continued as she rethreaded her needle. "He sent us a carpet from the latter with cunning designs that he wrote were popular in the East. Then everything went silent. We sent messenger after messenger to Constantinople, but none of them returned with word of him." She set about stitching what looked like a cluster of cherries on a green-leafed tree in her garden design. "Eventually muddled accounts began to find their way to us. Shocked pilgrims who said the Crusaders had not gone on to the Holy Land, but had sacked and plundered Constantinople, a Christian city. Deserting knights of the Cross who claimed their fellow 'holy' companions had become little more than paid, brutal mercenaries between feuding Eastern dynasties.

"Then finally, after two years—" Lady Helen's needle hung in the air for a moment before plunging back into the cloth "—one of Lord Harding's knights returned with word that his master had been killed in an ambush within the walls of the city by vengeful citizens whose homes had been burned by the Crusaders. He did not know how many of Lord Harding's men had escaped, but he himself had chosen to wash the dust of what he called 'the curst city' from his feet and flee back home to England."

She began a second cluster of fruit. Marguerite could not see the countess's eyes as they were fixed on her embroidery, but the kind, generous mouth quivered slightly at the corners.

"Twelve years ago Peter left us." The needle dove through the linen and out again. "Eleven years ago he sent us that beautiful carpet." Into the cloth and out. "Ten years ago this day Lord Harding's knight rode up to our gate to tell us that his master was dead. And ten years since of silence."

Ten years ago this day. Marguerite drew up her knees and wrapped her arms around them. "I am eighteen today."

She did not know what prompted her to say it. It seemed selfish and uncaring of what the countess had just shared, but the words tumbled out anyway.

Lady Helen looked up, as if startled. Then a sweet, droll twinkle lit her silvery blue eyes. "Are you?"

"It is why I begged my mother to let me stay until spring," Marguerite confessed. "I wanted to spend this day with you, because—" *Because I have grown to love you so.* She could not say that. It would sound as if she did not love her mother, too. Marguerite could not be so disloyal. She *did* love Lady Leah, but the acceptance she felt from the countess, the respect for both her heart and her mind, the contentment, the peace—All that she had lost when her grandfather died she had found anew with Lady Helen at Lahmurst Castle.

"I am honored," Lady Helen said when Marguerite paused. "Nay, more than that." Her thin fingers brushed Marguerite's cheek. "I have come to care deeply for you, Marguerite. Your bright company takes the sting from what has been a doleful day for me for ten years. How shall we celebrate, child?"

"I did not tell you that because I wished to make merry." Celebrate one's birth day? How absurd the countess must think her. "If anything, my mother would raise a lament. You must tell me honestly, my lady. Do I look older today?"

"Older?" Lady Helen repeated. "Than yesterday?"

Marguerite blushed. It sounded foolish when Lady Helen said it like that, but Marguerite's worry was real. "Of course I do not think I have changed overnight, but now that you know, perhaps you have observed lines on my brow or creases at the corner of my eyes, or—or—" Oh, she prayed no strand of white peeped amidst her curls. It would be ever so noticeable in her dark hair.

"Child, you are only eighteen. You are little more than a babe."

"My mother wed when she was fourteen. She was ashamed when I turned seventeen without a husband. I do not wish . . ." Marguerite hesitated. She dared not speak Robert's name. "I do not wish my betrothed to be disappointed when next he sees me." Her betrothed. She and Robert had spoken no formal vows, but she had pledged them to him in her heart.

Lady Helen threw back her head and laughed until tears streamed down her cheeks. "Oh, Marguerite, I am ever so glad you came to Lamhurst. Ridiculous, adorable child." She wiped the tears away. "My dear, you are as lovely and fresh as the roses that bloom in my garden, a comparison even more apt with that ruddy blush now burning in your cheeks. Nay, child, truly I do not mock you. I understand more than you know. I was eighteen when I married the earl. Until then, my mother was absolutely cruel in her indictments of my plainness and the fact that no man before Hugh had asked for my hand."

"Plain?" Marguerite scrambled onto her knees in indignation. "How could anyone call you that? You are the most elegant woman I know! Even Lady Jane Lovell looks garish and hollow when she stands next to you."

"Ah, child, that is kind, but it is not true. Hugh calls me pretty, because he sees me through the eyes of love. But I would take that a thousand times over a glorious face and figure. It will be the same for you one day, Marguerite. I did not know how young I was at eighteen. Believe me, when your betrothed returns, he will see naught but a glowing young woman—"

Lady Helen broke off, sobering as quickly as she had dissolved into mirth. Marguerite knew why. To the countess, Marguerite's "betrothed" was the Earl of Saxton, the man who had shamed Lady Helen's husband and driven him from court. She could have no illusions about Saxton's character or the likelihood that he should ever see Marguerite as anything more than a pawn. Did she think Marguerite did not know, too? They had carefully avoided discussing Saxton, both at Westminster and here at Lamhurst.

"That is a charming ribbon you wear," Lady Helen said. Marguerite thought the cheerful note in her voice sounded forced. "It is clearly precious to you. You wear it every day and I have seen how you caress it when you sit in reflection. Was it a parting gift from Lord Saxton?"

Marguerite hesitated. She could not lie to the countess, but she could not tell the truth, either. "No. But it was given to me by someone I care for, someone I do not wish to forget."

"Your cousin?"

Marguerite rubbed the soft silk boldly between her fingers. It would draw more suspicion if she shied from touching it, now that she knew the countess had been watching. "I pray Richard is safe," she said. "I pray they are all." Would the countess notice that she had not directly answered her question?

Lady Helen smiled again. "As do I, child. There, Evelyn is calling you. Go have one more skate, then we will all go back to the castle and dine."

Marguerite tied her skates back on and stood up, but before she joined

Evelyn, she leaned impulsively forward and kissed the countess on the cheek. "I am sorry about Peter," she whispered.

To her surprise, the countess put her arms around her, embracing Marguerite as she had never been embraced by her mother.

"And I am glad you are here today," Lady Helen returned softly into Marguerite's ear.

I wish I could tell you of Robert. Marguerite had never wanted to share her secret with anyone until Lady Helen held her so. She had hoped that by now, the countess might have mentioned her minstrel once or twice. Marguerite had even prayed some oblique reference to him might appear in one of Lord Gunthar's letters. Sometimes Lady Helen shared bits of her husband's news from Poitou with her guests in the evenings. But of course Robert was not a minstrel in Poitou, he was only one of hundreds of footsoldiers. Neither the countess nor apparently her husband ever spoke Robert's name.

Marguerite fought back the temptation that nearly overwhelmed her now, to share the burden of her love and fears with this woman she had come to care for so deeply. She envisioned Robert frowning at the very thought. One impulsive word, one miscalculation, instead of helping could ruin everything. Marguerite loved the countess, but she did not know her well enough to be certain that Lady Helen would not think herself duty-bound to squash so radical an idea as a lady of Marguerite's birth marrying a common musician, still less, if she knew, a former villein. What if instead of seeking reassurance of Robert's safety from her husband, the countess wrote to warn the earl that perhaps it would be best if the minstrel found some other noble household to serve—in Poitou!

Marguerite could not risk it. So she kissed the countess again and returned to the ice, where little Alain took her by the hand with so much mischief in his blue eyes that Marguerite braced herself for a hard encounter with the frozen pond as he pronounced firmly that it was her turn to learn how to spin.

27

Twice on the march to La Rochelle Robert had seen an opportunity to hazard a break for the woods, but he held to the word he had given Gunthar and made no attempt to escape from his guards. And now? Now he sat locked up in a tower prison in King John's fortress of Vauclair Castle, Robert's pallet so thin the cold of the floor seeped through it while the wind from the single barred window blew brisk against the back of his neck. The only piece of furniture the small chamber held was a stool with the burly man who sat in front of the door, glaring at Robert with a drawn sword across his knees. Two more armed men stood watch on the other side. Robert had glimpsed them each time the guard changed inside.

Robert tried to tell himself it could have been worse. He could have spent the past fortnight in some dank cell, like the one Kit had thrown him in when he was seventeen. He supposed he should be grateful that Gunthar had locked him up in a tower instead, where fresh air with the first whiffs of spring wafted. He'd been given a blanket, though not a thick one, and the food had been tolerable. But he was not free. And given the fact that he had not seen or spoken to Gunthar since that day Robert had made the rash decision to trust him, Robert stood convinced the old earl had never intended anything but deceit.

"Give me a chance to prove your innocence."

Robert had cursed himself a thousand times for believing Gunthar, and cursed Gunthar as many times twice over for being what he was—a lying nobleman to whom the word "honor" held only between men of his own privileged birth. Gunthar's objective had clearly been to trick Robert to surrender, deliver him securely to prison, and then wash his hands of him. And Robert had stepped headlong into the trap because he thought he had sensed something different in Gunthar, something honest beneath the haughty, peremptory air the old earl wore as naturally as the fur-lined mantle that swung around his broad shoulders. Robert should have known better. If nothing else, Kit Beckford should have taught him that a villein could never trust a lord.

He shifted on the pallet and saw the guard across from him tense. Robert's muscles ached from the long hours of sitting. He longed to rise and pace the little space there was, but he'd learned from a sword twice pointed at his breast that the guard preferred he stay where he was. Apparently being set to guard a criminal accused of not one, but three brutal murders, made even a brave man jittery.

Three murders. Robert's head sank into his hands. Even if he found a way past the guard blocking the door and the two men outside, even if he could manage to slip out of the castle unseen or by some miracle fight his way out, how could he ever face Marguerite again? A fugitive, an accused murderer? Nay, it had not been Gunthar's cunning alone that had seduced Robert into this wretched tower. Robert had known that day he had thrown a lifetime's caution to the winds that Gunthar's pledge to help him out of this tangle was the only way he would ever be able to return to England free of guilt in the eyes of the law and marry Marguerite. He had gambled every-thing on the Earl of Gunthar and he had lost.

He thumped his fist against the floor in frustration. He saw how his motion made the guard jump and reflexively lift his sword. A caustic laugh rose up in Robert's throat, but he bit it back. He closed his eyes to shut out the distraction of the guard's reaction. As meaningless as Robert's life would be without Marguerite, he still intended to claw and scratch to keep it. Or at least scheme. There had to be a way to escape. Somehow, at some point, surely some opportunity would arise, however narrow. If he only stayed alert for the chance—

He heard the familiar click of the door latch lifting. Was it time to change the guard already? He opened his eyes just as the guard sprang up and snapped into a stiff stance of attention.

"Sir! I was not expecting you—"

The guard broke off with a flush at the slightly disdainful lift of the Earl of Gunthar's heavy brows. "I did not think myself required to ask your permission to visit this tower."

The guard's color deepened at Gunthar's soft, ironic tones. "No, sir, of course not. That is—"

Gunthar stood framed in the doorway, but the stool blocked him from entering. The guard followed Gunthar's pointed glance at the object and hurriedly pulled it out of the way with a swift word of pardon.

"Thank you," Gunthar said, and stepped into the chamber.

Robert watched him but he made no effort to stand. Gunthar frowned, then the corner of his mouth gave a quirk. Had Robert's disrespect angered him? Gunthar could take his haughty self-importance and go to blazes.

Gunthar flicked a dismissive glance at the guard. "I'd like a few words alone with Marcel."

The guard cleared his throat awkwardly. "Your pardon, my lord, but Lord Saxton forbade me let the prisoner out of my sight."

Gunthar's gaze turned as chill as a December breeze. "Lord Saxton is not in command here."

"With all due respect, sir," the guard muttered, "neither are you."

Robert's ears pricked at the guard's reply. Something must have changed since their return to La Rochelle if Saxton's word once more carried more weight than the Earl of Gunthar's.

"You are right," Gunthar said after a moment. "The king commands now. Very well, then, remain while I speak with the prisoner." The chill gaze grew cutting. "I presume Saxton has not given orders to bar me from the tower?"

The guard flinched at the bite of Gunthar's sarcasm and hastily assured him that no such command had been given. The guard stood rigidly beside the door as Gunthar took the stool and set it down beside Robert's pallet.

Robert had propped an elbow on his knee and his chin on his fist, observing the exchange with a reluctant appreciation. Much as he loathed Gunthar's arrogance, the guard had done little but curse and mock Robert. Robert could not deny a certain pleasure in his discomfiture.

Gunthar gazed down at Robert, but his eyes now had grown unreadable. Robert held them with a gaze he knew was equally enigmatic.

Gunthar said at last, "Since it's plain you have no intention of rising, have you any objection to my sitting down?"

Robert's refusal to acknowledge Gunthar's preeminence must infuriate him as much as the guard's defiance had, yet his voice betrayed nothing now but a faint trace of some emotion Robert could not discern.

Robert waved a hand towards the stool. "Be my guest." He waited until Gunthar seated himself to ask, "Have you come to inform me of my sentence?"

He thought Gunthar paused for the merest breath before he answered in a level voice, "You have not yet been condemned."

"Have I not? But in that case, surely I am free to leave?"

The guard started forward. "My lord, the whole camp knows he's a murderer. The sooner he hangs, the better."

Gunthar quelled the guard with another crushing glance. "I do not recall inquiring after your opinion. If you insist on staying, pray hold your tongue while I conduct my business."

The guard retreated, muttering.

Robert said, sweetly polite, "Do not let me detain you, sir. I do not know what event may have served to recall me to your memory, but if you are not here to sentence me I can think of no other reason for this visit."

Gunthar studied him in silence for a moment. "I had not forgotten you, Robert."

"Had you not?" Robert's façade of indifference slipped. "I have been locked up for a fortnight with no one to talk to save oafs like that"—he jutted his chin at the glaring guard—"and I can tell you, they have not been amiable company. I ask for my lute and it's forbidden me. I ask for my books"—Gunthar's brows twitched up—"and the guards laugh in my face. I ask to see *you* and I am told you have more important things to do. Well, then, I am done with you. You have me where you want me, one step away from the noose you vowed to save me from. Go, then, and let me hang."

Robert shot to his feet in defiance of the guard and walked over to the window. He wound his hand around one of the cold iron bars, his heart pounding with resentful fury.

Silence stretched, harsh and grim. Robert imagined he could feel Gunthar's glower burning through the back of his tunic.

"Look at me, Robert."

Robert would not be tricked by the softness of the command. Robert's anger sometimes masked itself in a dangerous quiet, too. He clenched his hand tighter around the window bar.

"Look at me," Gunthar repeated.

Robert resisted for another moment, but some note of authority in the compelling voice finally turned him around against his will.

Gunthar's eyes, impenetrable as slate, held Robert's with an implacable force. "Two weeks ago I promised you my aid, and I am not a man who goes back on his word. If you would, for once, exercise some patience and give me a chance to explain, you might find yourself the better for it."

Robert did not know what game Gunthar played with him now, but he had no intention of being hoaxed by false promises again. He wrenched his gaze free of Gunthar's and turned back to the window.

The stool rasped against the floor, signaling the snapping of Gunthar's temper. Gunthar's boots echoed across the floorboards. The door clicked open. A pulse of silence. The door slammed. Robert breathed out a slow, shuddering breath.

"You'd let me do it!"

Robert whirled. Gunthar still stood inside the room, his eyes afire as Robert had never seen them before.

"You'd as soon let me walk out and see you hang as swallow your pride, wouldn't you?"

"Why not?" Robert flashed back. "What have you, Lord of Gunthar, to do with me, a penniless, runaway villein? Ha! No doubt I could hang for that alone. Go to blazes!"

Gunthar strode back, his hawkish features harsh and stern. "This defiance will get you nowhere. Try holding that insolent tongue of yours and listen to me. I have been doing what I can for you this past fortnight, but it has not been easy. The king is displeased with my lack of success with the Poitevin barons and has rebuked me by promoting Saxton again. He has placed you in Saxton's custody, and Saxton seems quite determined to see you hang. Now, I ask myself, why should the Earl of Saxton care what becomes of 'a penniless, runaway villein?' Perhaps you can enlighten me?"

Robert felt the probing power of Gunthar's gaze and let the protective shade fall back over his face. He said, his voice flat, "Perhaps he does not care to see a murderer let loose."

"His manner suggests something more personal. What have you done, Robert, to make Saxton hate you so?"

"Wounded his pride." If Gunthar expected more, Robert had no intention of giving it. "What lies between Saxton and me concerns no one but ourselves."

Though Gunthar's face remained as controlled as Robert's, his hand gave a clear twitch of annoyance. "Very well, then, tell me this. That night you and Hanley wrestled in my tent, you made your animosity towards him plain. Now then, hating him as you do, why would you be so careless as to let him escape after having killed, I presume, three men to reach him?"

The words knocked the air momentarily out of Robert's lungs. "Hanley—escaped?" he repeated when he recovered his breath. "But you said—I assumed—"

"That he was dead?"

Robert struggled to remember Gunthar's exact words when he had thrown the murders in Robert's face. His throbbing head that day had clearly muddled them in his mind.

"Are you sorry that he's not?" Gunthar asked.

Robert clamped his mouth shut. He would not have murdered Hanley in cold blood, but if the brute had died in the heat of Robert defending his sister, or Gunthar that night in the tent, Robert would not have shed a tear. But he was not fool enough to say so before Gunthar and the guard.

"And Beckford," Gunthar said. "You want revenge on him too for your sister's misery."

Robert cursed himself for having ever confided so much to Gunthar, but again he said nothing.

Gunthar sat down on the stool again. Before any other man Robert would have remained standing in defiance, but something in Gunthar's bearing compelled him to lower himself once more on the pallet.

Still, Robert replied with some heat. "I suppose you expect me to meekly accept what Kit did, to brush it all aside as merely the way of our world? After all, villeins are little more than slaves, mere property to be disposed of as you please." He felt his temper fraying afresh.

"I did not say that," Gunthar said with a maddening calm. "Is that the reason you left Beckford's manor?"

Robert ground out, "Partly."

"What more? You had better tell me. It may save your neck."

"It won't. Kit will not rest until he sees me hang like my father for a crime I didn't commit." Robert met Gunthar's gaze and held it with a bold challenge.

Gunthar leaned forward, his arms across his knees, and said softly, "Tell me."

Robert felt something in him quiver at the invitation's unexpected gentleness. He told himself it was the guard's presence and not a baffling confusion that lowered his own voice another notch.

"My father was a footsoldier in the camp of Kit's sire when old Lord Garoux accompanied the king to Aquitaine and Poitou twelve years ago." He watched to see if Gunthar would rebuke him for using Kit's familiar name rather than calling his lord's son Lord Christopher, but when Gunthar said nothing, he went on. "When they returned to England, Lord Garoux accused my father of betraying the king to the Lusignans and ordered his execution. Sir, he wasn't even allowed a trial and he was innocent!"

Gunthar straightened. "Your father was the villein that Lord Garoux hanged? I remember that incident. I did not learn of it until after—until it was too late. The act was illegal and I rebuked Lord Garoux for it. He paid a heavy fine to the crown for the offense." Something flickered in the grey eyes now. Sympathy? "It is natural that you should wish to defend your father. But someone did, in truth, betray the king. Three of the king's men died in the ambush that was set for him and the new queen. The traitor was never found."

Gunthar hesitated. Robert braced himself for the words he sensed Gunthar prepared to speak next.

"The Lusignans are one of the most powerful families in Poitou. They would pay well to defend their count's rights. Is it not possible that your father—"

"No! I tell you, my father was innocent. I asked for Kit's favor and he refused it. Like father, like son, he said. Well, perhaps there is some truth to that for with my own eyes did I see Kit sell information to the French."

"You have said this before. Have you proof?"

"You know I haven't."

"Then you would do well to guard your tongue."

Robert began a hot protest, then caught Gunthar's warning glance at the guard and fell silent.

After a moment, Gunthar remarked, "Whatever happened twelve years ago, the Count of La Marche is loyal to the king now. By the king's command, I am to ride out to meet him tomorrow and escort him to join the king's forces." Gunthar raised a hand and rubbed his chin. "I do not quite know what to do with you while I'm gone—"

Robert rose to his knees, his heartbeat quickening. "Let me come with you."

Gunthar dropped his hand with a snapping frown. "Impossible."

"But my lord—" Robert paused, then lowered his voice so that even if he strained, the guard should not hear. "La Marche is the man for whom Kit was negotiating with the Frenchman."

Gunthar looked taken aback. He asked equally softly, "La Marche? Are you sure? If you say this merely to gain your freedom—"

"My lord, I swear it is true. The Frenchman asked Kit if he had spoken to La Marche. Kit said aye. The Frenchman gave Kit the silver, then Kit gave some sort of packet to the Frenchman and said, 'At the proper moment, La Marche will deliver the prize into King Philip's hands.' I do not know what he meant, but meeting a Frenchman furtively in the woods in the middle of the night and promising some 'prize' to the King of France cannot be the action of a loyal Englishman."

Gunthar's eyes narrowed. "You did not speak La Marche's name when you told me this before."

"Did I not?" Again Robert tried to remember the details of his previous conversation with Gunthar. "I cannot recall exactly what I told you. My head was pounding fiercely that morning."

Gunthar had felt the lump on Robert's head. He would know that much was not a lie.

"I suppose," Gunthar said slowly, "it is possible La Marche is not as reconciled to the king's marriage to his former betrothed as he would pretend. But he will never admit his guilt merely to save the life of a minstrel."

"Then what shall we do?" Robert asked, scarcely realizing he spoke in the plural.

Gunthar looked thoughtful and stroked his chin again. "I am not sure. I must talk with La Marche before he reaches this camp."

"And you shall let me come with you," Robert said.

Gunthar shook his head.

"Then you will leave me here with Kit? His own henchman was caught trying to assassinate you. Who else but Kit had reason to kill three men to set Hanley free before you could interrogate him? Kit must know that you are sent to La Marche. Do you think he will not guess that I have told you of his treason? What odds will you place on my being alive when you return?"

Gunthar looked grim. "I already suspect Lord Christopher of the crime that freed Hanley," he said, taking up Kit's Christian name to differentiate him from his sire, Lord Garoux. "I have been keeping him under my eye. He is my vassal. I will take him with me to La Marche. Perhaps he will give something away when we meet the count. No harm will threaten you while I am gone."

"What of Saxton?" Robert said. "You've no power to command him to join you. He wants me dead, too. You said it yourself."

That seemed to check Gunthar. He sat a long moment gazing at Robert before he replied. "And you, alas, are no more important than your father. Saxton could strangle you in this chamber, and the king would not blink so long as he could wring an extravagant fine from Saxton to fill his coffers." Gunthar stood so abruptly that Robert rocked back on his heels. "Come with me."

Robert scrambled to his feet. The action startled the guard, who stepped forward, his sword in his hand. Gunthar made a sharp gesture. The guard reluctantly sheathed the weapon and returned to his position in front of the door.

"Let us pass," Gunthar said.

"My lord—"

"Let. Us. Pass."

Robert stood behind Gunthar and could not see the look in the old earl's eyes, but the guard blanched. And stepped aside.

28

The attack came completely unexpected. The swarm of armed knights spilled out of the woods on both sides of the road, rending the air with their battle cries. The king had ordered Gunthar to take with him all the men Gunthar had brought to Poitou, hoping a parade of force on the way to meet the Count of La Marche would intimidate those Poitevin barons who still stood aloof of the king's cause. But someone had clearly anticipated them. Gunthar saw almost at once that his men were outnumbered. He watched with horror as the ambush swept his footsoldiers down like flies. He had returned Robert's sword and dagger and set the minstrel among them. Had he—?

Gunthar had no time to search for the minstrel's dark face. He danced and whirled his horse with the expertise of a lifetime's training and beat back the hail of steel blades that swooped at him, left and right. Though Gunthar had armed himself and his knights in mail beneath their surcotes, his head, like those of his men, was bare. Their assailants wore helmets, Gunthar guessed to conceal their faces. He glimpsed no insignia on their tunics, they carried no banner with them. Gunthar saw his own standard bearer weaving in and out of the chaos, doggedly holding the earl's banner, the prancing stallion, aloft so that Gunthar's men should not lose their courage.

Gunthar blocked and parried and knocked three men from their saddles, two of them with sword thrusts that broke through iron links to sink deep into flesh. An arrow sang past Gunthar's right ear. The bolt *thwanged* home in the thigh of a squire with sunny yellow hair battling bravely only a few feet from Gunthar. Gunthar saw the young man's reflexive jerk, his startled glance at the shaft in his leg, and the spear in the hand of an enemy aimed at the distracted young man's back.

Gunthar shouted and spurred his horse. His sword caught the spear tip and thrust it away from its murderous aim. He maneuvered his mount alongside the spearman, shifted the hilt of his sword, then drove his pommel into the flap of mail that protected his opponent's windpipe. The blow would not kill, but it shut off the man's air. Gunthar heard the man's scraping gasp for breath as he reached over and pulled off the man's helmet. Gunthar did not know the man's face. But he would if he saw it again, for it would bear the flattened nose of his fist from the blow Gunthar drove into it.

Gunthar did not wait to watch the man hit the ground. He whirled his horse to the squire's side. Sir Edward Keynes' squire. He had given the young man permission to join Gunthar's company, hopeful the Count of La Marche might have news of Keynes' safety.

"Tollerton! De Vexin!" Gunthar shouted. "Get this boy off the road."

The fathers of Gunthar's own principle squires spurred forward.

"Sir, Hastings is down," Tollerton said. "And Fitzalan and Warci."

Gunthar cursed. There was no time for more, for another wave of men in helmets drove at them. His knights were shut off from his view as he found himself surrounded once more. It was clear he was the target of this ambush. It had not taken long for him to observe how his attackers had again and again woven and veered around his knights to ride straight for him. Thus far his strength and skill had held up as well as when he had fought for the king twelve years earlier. But as the battle stretched on, he felt his breath begin to shorten and his arm begin to ache.

Still he beat all his assailants back, until one devil thrust his sword not at Gunthar, but at his horse. The beast beneath him screamed and stumbled. Gunthar felt the pitch that would trap him against the ground beneath an inescapable weight if he let it. He loosed his feet from the stirrups and jumped as the horse staggered over. Twelve years ago Gunthar could have landed in a roll from which he could have sprung up nimbly. But now when he hit the ground on his shoulder, a pain jarred him so severely that for several seconds he could not even see through the agony.

Shouts dinned around him, hooves stomped and scudded, stinging dirt into his face.

"He's down!" someone bellowed. "Gunthar is down!"

Gunthar scrubbed at his watering eyes with the hand that had not gone benumbed and saw it was not his fall alone that panicked his men. His banner lay in the dirt beside his bloodied standard bearer. Men who could not see either the earl or his standard would reach but one conclusion: Gunthar had been killed.

The tide turned in an instant. His knights, desperate to escape what must now appear to them a hopeless struggle, reeled their mounts in retreat. Gunthar wanted to roar at them that he still lived, but the torment in his shoulder smothered the strength of his lungs. Then someone knelt beside him. Through the blur of tears in his eyes, he recognized the badge of the prancing stallion on the shoulder of the rough woven tunic. One of his foot-soldiers still lived.

"Give me your hand," Gunthar gasped. "Help me to my feet."

Rough, calloused fingers grasped his and pulled him into a sitting position. Something cold pressed against his throat.

"The mighty Earl of Gunthar," a voice growled into his ear, "skewered by a common stableman. Not the glorious ending a man like ye hoped for, I'll warrant."

Gunthar registered the sharp edge of steel pressed to his flesh. "Who are you?" He struggled to focus on the face that hovered inches from his. His vision slowly cleared. The low brow, the broken nose, the heavy, sullen mouth and limp dun hair. "Hanley?"

"Aye." Fetid breath blasted Gunthar's nostrils, spewed from between yellowed teeth with two black gaps. "He promised my master yer own York-shire manor if he kills ye, an' my master said he'd make me bailiff there if I did the deed. *Bailiff.*" Hanley's heavy mouth spread with smug glee. "That's nearly good as bein' a lord among my kind. They'll have to obey me as if I was the baron himself. Maybe that shrewish wife o' mine will appreciate me then, when I put a fine gown on that back that only bends to me when I beat it." His fingers plunged into Gunthar's hair and yanked back his head. "An' all I have to do is slit yer fine throat and leave ye here in the road. Let them wrangle for the privilege of claiming your death"—Hanley jerked his head at the horsemen who thundered about, trying to cut off Gunthar's knights "so long as I get my reward when we get back home."

Gunthar resisted the impulse to make a grab for Hanley's hand. The blade would slice across his throat before he could reach it. Gunthar's shoulder pulsed with a sickening pain, but he sought to play for time, even though from the chaotic speed of his knights' retreat, he knew there was little point. "You are Beckford's man?"

"Marcel told ye that, didn't he?" Hanley's glee turned to a glare. "I told Beckford he should have killed that upstart in the woods when he had the chance, before he could go prattling to ye of what he knew or guessed. But like all arrogant lords, Beckford thought he knew best. Said it would be a grand irony to see Marcel swing from a rope like his da."

"Beckford killed my two guards to set you free? And your accomplice, the one who killed the guard outside my tent. What was his name—?"

"Dorn. I muffled the guard while Dorn slid his dagger into his back. Dorn was supposed to do the same with ye, hold ye silent so as not to wake yer squire while I plunged this into your heart." The blade bit closer against Gunthar's throat. "But he panicked when he heard Marcel's footsteps and scurried away like a rat. Beckford gave me his dagger and let me finish the coward off myself after he cut the ropes from my wrists."

"And this ambush? Was this Beckford's idea? I did not think him wealthy enough to bribe this many men to mask my murder."

Hanley's eyes glinted an ugly taunt. "It won't matter to ye how he did it where I'm about to send ye."

Gunthar had stared death in the face too many times before to fear what lay beyond the dagger's slash that Hanley readied to make. He closed his eyes, but only so that he might see her face. *Helen. Forgive me for not coming home this time.*

The blade against his throat jerked, but it did not cut into his flesh. Gunthar opened his eyes as Hanley grunted. A look of shock grazed the hellish intent on his features, then Hanley lurched sideways and slumped facedown in the dirt.

Gunthar was still staring at him and the dagger protruding from his back, when someone broke from his retreating men and ran to his side.

"My lord! Saints! Are you all right? When I saw him bending over you with that blade—"

Gunthar tore his gaze from the image stamped into the hilt—a rampant tyger—and looked into Robert's white face as Robert fell to his knees beside him.

"I knew I could not reach you in time," Robert said, "so I took a chance and threw my dagger. Your men think you are dead."

"I thought you were dead, too." Pain made Gunthar's voice come out more harshly than he intended. He glanced about at his fleeing knights. "Why are you here?"

"Where else should I be? Here, give me your hand."

Gunthar did not move. "In all this confusion, you could have escaped."

His words seemed to surprise Robert. Then abruptly the minstrel grinned that flashing grin that Gunthar had observed always set Robert's face so engagingly alight. "Run from a fight? That would require more sense than I've ever possessed. Besides, I had a promise to keep to Lady Helen."

He reached for Gunthar's hand again.

"Wait," Gunthar said. "You had better look." He nodded towards the body that lay nearby.

Robert hesitated, then drew his dagger from the dead man's back and rolled the body over. Gunthar knew Robert recognized Hanley when he heard the minstrel swear. Robert glanced at Gunthar, but quickly bit off the question that tumbled half-way off his tongue. He glanced at Gunthar's hand clamped against his arm as if he would block the pain radiating down from his shoulder. Robert caught Gunthar's eyes. They exchanged a silent message. Gunthar gave a curt nod and braced himself. Robert slid his arm around Gunthar's waist and heaved him to his feet.

For the first time in his life, Gunthar almost fainted. The pain undeniably bespoke a broken shoulder. Unconsciousness would have been welcome, but also humiliating. He stood leaning against Robert, fighting back the weakness, grateful for Robert's young strength. Grateful for the minstrel's promise to Helen. Grateful for his keen eye, quick wits and honest heart.

Grateful for the day he had met Robert Marcel.

Robert had been surprised on their return to Vauclair Castle to find himself freed from the tower, though he knew himself closely watched. Gunthar and what remained of his men had returned to La Rochelle to discover the Count of La Marche arrived before them. The count had rushed out to meet them, full of apologies for misunderstanding the location of their rendezvous and appalled at the misfortune that had befallen Gunthar and his troops. Robert thought there was a sly look about the count's hard, handsome face, but the king himself had joined them and thrown an arm of friendship around the count's neck. Even through the pain etched into Gunthar's drawn face from the jostling ride to rejoin the king, Robert caught the old earl's long, measuring look at the count before Edward Tollerton and Bandon de Vexin, the only two of Gunthar's men who had been searching for their master's body amidst the turmoil of the ambush, bore Gunthar off to see his shoulder tended to.

La Marche also brought the black news of Sir Edward Keynes' death. Sir Edward had made a rash attempt to escape from his captors and been killed by an arrow from an overzealous guard. The revelation, together with the wound in Richard's thigh that rendered him inactive, sunk Richard into a glum depression which Robert spent his time seeking to lift for wont of any other useful occupation allotted to him in the king's camp. Thus matters stood for a week before Gunthar's squire, young Antony Tollerton, summoned Robert to Gunthar's presence.

The great lords of the king's council housed within the comfort of the castle, while the rest of the army dwelt without in the open or in tents. Robert followed the squire into a tower chamber quite different from the small cell he had been shut up in for a fortnight. This chamber was spacious, with tapestries on the walls and shutters that could be closed on the barless window that let in a golden stream of light. The carpet with the curious patterns Robert had seen in Gunthar's tent the night he had fought with Hanley spread over the floor again. Gunthar sat behind the same wide desk that had stood in that tent, too. His face looked grayer than it had before the ambush, and lines of lingering pain dug deep. His left arm hung in a sling while his right hand sifted through a pile of parchment sheets, many of them important judging from the broken red wax seals that Robert glimpsed.

"Robert Marcel, my lord," the squire announced.

Gunthar looked up. It may have been a trick of the light, but Robert thought the lines in his face eased a little.

"Thank you, Antony. You may leave us." When the youth was gone, Gunthar motioned Robert towards a stool. "Please, sit down. I had meant to talk with you before this, but I have been—occupied." He indicated the stack of documents.

"So I see," Robert said. "I am at your service, sir."

Gunthar smiled. "You have proven that. I am well aware that you have saved my life twice now. You needn't think I shall forget it."

The quizzing light in Gunthar's eyes made Robert flush a little. Was

Gunthar chiding him over their clash in the tower cell, when Robert had made his lack of faith in the earl all too plain?

Robert shifted at an unexpected jab of guilt. "I do not think it, sir. Indeed, I do not doubt that I myself live at this moment due to your intercession. But I do not understand why."

"Why you are free, you mean? Ah. Well. I hinted to the king that certain evidence had come to light pointing towards your innocence. Fortunately he chose to believe me and release you, for the time being, into my custody."

"But there is no such evidence. You said yourself—" Had Gunthar lied for him? Then he saw the expression on Gunthar's face. "What is it? What have you found?"

Gunthar looked down at the pile of documents and smoothed his free hand over them. He said, sounding almost wistful, "I wish you would trust me, Robert."

"My lord, you know that I do."

"Do I?" Gunthar glanced up, his grey eyes twinkling. "Lad, I believe I am well enough acquainted with you by now to know that you trust no one but yourself. And perhaps that is not such a bad policy to follow. Still, I believe I will keep what I know to myself for the present."

That spurred Robert to his feet. "Keep it—? My lord, you cannot! You've no right—"

"How shall you wrest it from me, Robert?"

A surge of frustration drove Robert across the floor. He stopped just short of the edge of the desk and fisted hard the hands that longed to shoot out and shake the earl.

"Very wise," Gunthar murmured, his gaze still alight with that provoking amusement. "It would do you no good to assault me."

Gunthar's silent laughter, gentle as it was, infuriated Robert. "If this is your idea of gratitude, you might as well have locked me back up in that wretched tower. Withhold your evidence of my innocence and Kit and Saxton will see me hang."

Gunthar's face sobered. "You know they are allied?"

That took Robert aback. "Saxton and Kit?"

"You know they are."

"I know nothing of the kind." Robert suspected, but he would not make the mistake of throwing about accusations he could not prove again.

Gunthar looked down at the pile of documents. He ran his thumb along the edge of the stack. After a moment, he said, "Before you killed Hanley, as he held his blade at my throat, he confessed that Beckford had freed him and killed his accomplice and my guard with your dagger. He said Beckford had promised to make him bailiff if Hanley assassinated me."

"Hanley? Bailiff of Beck Manor? The man cannot even read!"

Gunthar shook his head. "Not the Wiltshire manor you fled from. Norcott Manor in York. *My* manor."

"Yours?" Robert understood none of this.

"Perhaps Beckford meant his bribe to Hanley as a joke. As you say, the thought of raising an illiterate stableman to bailiff is absurd. Likely Beckford knew Hanley would be too dangerous to keep alive if he succeeded in killing me, especially since Hanley knew that Beckford himself had been bribed with the promise of one of my estates. If Hanley were apprehended for my murder, his link to Beckford would be too obvious. If Hanley escaped, his potential ability to blackmail Beckford is not something that would have let Beckford sleep long at peace in his bed at night."

Gunthar tried to rearrange his sling and grimaced. Robert rounded the desk, saw how the cloth had become askew, and repositioned it to a more comfortable angle.

"Thank you."

From the tightness now of Gunthar's smile, Robert guessed the shifting about had hurt his shoulder, but it would have more ease now Robert had settled it thus.

"There is only one man in the kingdom I know," Gunthar continued, "so filled with conceit that he might think he has the power to usurp a portion of my inheritance after my death and give it to someone other than my heir."

"Saxton," Robert said. "Perhaps he was duping Beckford as much as Beckford was duping Hanley."

"Perhaps, though the king has proven he has little enough respect for his barons' rights. It is not beyond possibility that he should agree to slight me thus after my death to intimidate the other lords. In any event, Beckford clearly believes Saxton's promise, else he'd not risk his neck by agreeing to the plot. The problem is—" Gunthar hesitated before his mouth twisted up in grim irony. "Hanley is dead and his confession died with him. This time it is I who have no evidence. I told the king I could prove your innocence. Prove it I will." Gunthar said the words strongly. "But you will have to give me more time."

Robert paced away from the desk. "Hanley was a fool, but Kit is not. He would never be so careless as to gloat of the scheme. And why should he fear you, when he has Saxton's support? If you challenge him he will deny everything, Saxton will side with him, and the king will believe Saxton. It is your word against theirs, and you are out of favor with the king."

"For now. But Saxton would not have bribed Beckford to kill me if he did not fear me. John is fickle. I can play on that. He granted me your freedom, did he not? I cannot change the king's cruel, grasping nature, but if I accomplish nothing else, I will find a way to stop Saxton from ravaging the kingdom with him."

Robert might have doubted Gunthar's ability to achieve that vow once, but no longer. Not after the man who had guarded Robert in the tower had yielded his fear of Saxton to whatever he had seen in Gunthar's eye. That made Robert's decision easier. If Saxton fell, Marguerite would no longer need Robert to protect her.

He paced across the carpet, his toe swiveling on the diamond pattern in the corner before returning to face Gunthar again across the desk. He blamed Gunthar for putting the idea into his head. Robert would never have run from a battle where men he fought with back to back might depend on his sword to defend them. But this—this was different. Gunthar would stop Saxton, aye, but Hanley was dead and Kit would never concede his guilt if he thought it would save Robert. The guard who crumpled before Gunthar did not have Kit's incentive for silence: keeping his head attached to his shoulders.

Robert could see no other way for himself through Kit's trap.

He leaned forward, his palms flat against the desk's nicked wood. "Let me go, sir. You say the king has placed me in your custody. Let me escape."

Gunthar frowned. "Impossible."

"Why? What matter to you whether I live a deserter or die a murderer? I swear I'll never cross to England." How could he go back now? Every man in the camp save Gunthar still believed he had killed three men. He could never marry Marguerite with this stain on his name.

"Nonsense. You shall be neither deserter nor murderer." Gunthar rose and came around the desk to grip Robert's shoulder lightly. "There is a knighthood waiting for you in England after all this is over."

Robert blinked. Surely he had misunderstood. "What?"

Gunthar smiled, but his gaze was keen and searching. "Sir Brandon de

Vexin told me he saw you during the battle. The attack cut down two-thirds of my footsoldiers, but Sir Brandon said you survived because you wielded your sword as skillfully as any knight he knew. Young Richard Channing fought bravely, too, and there is no question that he will be knighted. And you saved my life when my own vassals and men-at-arms were scattering about me like the wind."

"They thought you dead, sir. They were seized with panic."

"You weren't."

Robert waved an impatient hand. The offer was ridiculous. "Sir, you are very gracious, but you magnify my deeds out of proportion."

"But the offer stands. Will you refuse it?"

Robert stared into Gunthar's eyes. Saints! He was serious! For an instant, Robert wavered. He cared nothing for a knighthood himself, but for Marguerite—to have something to offer her beyond a life of hopeful benevolence by some music-loving merchant—a hope Robert knew he could not truly guarantee should come to fulfillment. If he failed her, if necessity required him to drag her from town to town, performing for pennies and sometimes no more than a crust of bread—how long would her love for him last then?

A knighthood. One he had earned for himself, not the fortune hunting position she had offered him through marriage. If things were different, if he did not stand so blackly accused— But he did stand so.

"Thank you, sir, but I cannot." He wanted to turn away, but Gunthar's gaze still held him.

"Are you thinking you would not be accepted by the others? It is probably true. They would never forget your origins. It might mean little for yourself, but in time your house would come to be accepted. While it might be of little use to you, it could mean much to your sons."

"I shall have no sons."

Gunthar's brows shot up. "Why, what is this? Have you some notion of entering the Church?"

Gunthar's surprise broke his compelling gaze and allowed Robert to swing away from him to pace the carpet again.

"No. My lord, I cannot—" Robert locked his hands behind his back, clenching them with determination "—*will* not go home marked a traitor and a murderer. I could not face—"

He bit off the words, but Gunthar asked, "Could not face who?"

"My family."

Did Gunthar see the way his fingers twitched at the lie?

"Not your family, Robert. Who?"

Robert bit his lip. Even though Gunthar could not see it, his silence did no good.

"There is a woman. Of course! How could I have been so blind?"

Curse the old man's shrewdness.

"You will not face her, an accused murderer, but you will allow her to think you a traitor and deserter."

"She will never know. When I do not return, she will think me dead."

"Someone will tell her."

"No!" Robert whirled about. "She must never know. Oh, would I'd never met her."

He thrust a distracted hand through his hair and resumed his pacing. No, he could not truly wish for that. But it would have been best for her if she had never met *him*. His heart ached with such brutal force, that he'd have torn the throbbing organ from his chest if he'd had the power.

He felt Gunthar watching him. Robert knew his passionate reaction was likely to raise questions in the old earl's mind that Robert did not want to answer. He struggled to master himself, to don his familiar mask, but the pain was so great he did not know if he'd succeeded when he turned back to Gunthar.

"Forgive me, sir." At least his voice came out steady now. "My affairs are no concern of yours. Why do you trouble yourself with me?"

"I wish I knew." Robert saw too much curiosity in Gunthar's eyes. "Is she a London girl? This woman you're afraid to face?"

"I'm not afraid to face her. I'm—"

"Ashamed?"

Robert felt the tension in his cheeks and knew his mask had failed. "Would you not be?"

"You think she will doubt your innocence then?"

"Nay—aye—Why should she not? What does she know of me save for what I have told her, and how is she to know I spoke the truth? Oh, aye, she will believe me, but only because she is so innocent of the world." He ran a hand through his hair again. "She is worthy of a far better man than I."

"You underrate yourself, Robert. You are a man well worth any woman."

Robert stared at Gunthar, startled by the forthright note in his voice.

Then in spite of Robert's frustration, he laughed. "This from the man who called me insolent and disrespectful."

A wry gleam in Gunthar's eyes acknowledged the hit.

Robert gave a small shake of his head. "Forgive me, sir, but I fear even your forbearance would be tried if you knew the lady of whom we speak. She is no villein's daughter."

"So I'd guessed. I thought, perhaps, a merchant's daughter, or a soldier's."

"No, sir." Robert sought to change the subject. "Sir, what do you mean to do with me, since you won't allow me to escape and I am in your custody?"

Gunthar gazed at him a moment longer, then walked around the desk and sat down once more. Robert watched him shift awkwardly through the pile of documents with his free hand.

"You remember my secretary, Sir Thomas Hastings? He was killed during the battle."

"I am sorry for it," Robert said. "He seemed a good man."

"Aye, he served me well." Gunthar selected a document and slid it across the table. From the middle of the stack he pulled out a blank sheet of parchment and pushed that across as well, together with a quill and the inkhorn. "Copy the first few lines of that for me, if you please."

Robert expected an elaboration of the request, but when Gunthar merely sat waiting Robert gave a faint shrug, took up the quill, and sketched out the words.

"That will do," Gunthar said after Robert had written out several lines. "Now read it back to me."

Robert obeyed, trailing off as he reached the end. Gunthar reached out his hand to retrieve the materials, laid the two parchment sheets side by side, and appeared to compare them.

After several minutes, Gunthar looked up. "I thought as much," he said softly. "Who taught you to read and write?"

"A priest."

"The same priest who told you of the law of a year and a day?"

"Aye."

Gunthar leaned back in his chair, a puzzled line between his brows. "Why should such pains be taken to teach a villein boy to read and write? Are you sure you are not the son of some nobleman—?"

"Some baron's byblow, you mean?" Robert cut him off. He would have flared up in offense if any other man had asked him that. He would have flared at Gunthar if the earl had asked it a week ago. He felt the change between them that allowed him to answer calmly instead. "No, sir, I am quite sure of parentage. I am a villein's son, but villeins dream, too. My father dreamed of being free." He saw again his father's dark face and heard his beloved voice speaking the familiar, rebellious couplet. He repeated it now to Gunthar. "'When Adam and Eve first walked the earth, who then was lord and who was serf?' Whether those words were his own or he learned them from another, I do not know. I only know that he spoke them all my life."

Robert refused to flinch from Gunthar's frown. Did he think Robert's father's words as heretical as Garoux Beckford had? How could a man of Gunthar's birth think anything else?

Robert continued when Gunthar sat silent, "My father could not afford to buy freedom for all of us, so he paid Kit Beckford's father to let me enter the Church when I turned twelve. The village priest began my training, but my father died before I took the vows, and . . ."

Whatever Gunthar thought of Robert's father, he finished Robert's trailed off thought with piercing insight. "You found you wanted more than a life in the Church." The frown smoothed out. "Well, that is not such an unreasonable desire. And have you found what you were looking for instead?"

Robert hesitated before he murmured, "I thought I had."

That unwelcome curiosity lit Gunthar's eyes again. "What's her name? The woman you left behind."

Robert paused again, but he knew that evading the question would only arouse Gunthar's suspicion. Neither could Robert admit the truth. However tolerant Gunthar might be feeling since Robert had rescued him from the ambush, the earl would surely balk at a villein's marriage to a lady.

Robert compromised. "Her name is Mae."

"Mae? Is there nothing more?"

"It would mean nothing to you." Or too much.

To Robert's relief, Gunthar nodded. "Very well." He shuffled the pile of parchment in front of him. "Do you know, Robert, I've half a mind to employ you as my secretary."

Once again, Robert thought he heard Gunthar misspeak. "My lord?"

"I've fallen behind since Hastings' death. Even if I did not have other duties to attend to, my shoulder would make it impossible for me to catch up with all this." Gunthar waved a hand at the documents piled before him. "This all needs to be set in order as soon as possible. You have a fair hand and have demonstrated that you can read. Will you help me?"

"My lord, I hardly think I am qualified—"

"You may leave that to my judgment. Your wage will be the same as Hastings'. And perhaps—perhaps after you think about it, you will change your mind about the knighthood."

Robert shook his head. Gunthar's fall had surely addled his brain.

Gunthar's eyes gleamed shrewdly. "'Twould make a fine wedding gift for your bride. Methinks she could only be proud of you."

Robert supposed the earl meant to be helpful, but his harping on Marguerite only kept the hurt raw. "My lord, this offer of yours changes nothing. I still stand accused of murder. I cannot face her thus. I have nothing to give her."

"You will be cleared. And I offer you something to take her. Why do you smile?"

Robert lowered his eyes. The vision of him serving in Gunthar's household with the Lady Marguerite as his wife seemed suddenly quite absurd. He feared Gunthar would not appreciate the jest. "Thank you, sir, but I cannot."

Gunthar sighed. "You are a stubborn man, Robert Marcel. Very well, we are come to this. As your guardian, I am appropriating your services as my secretary."

Robert's amusement vanished. "You are what?"

"Appropriating your services. It will do you no good to argue. You are in my custody, remember? I am responsible for you, and I can think of no better way to keep an eye on you than this."

Before Robert could reply, the door opened and the gilt haired squire stuck his head into the room. "My lord, the king has asked you to attend him."

"Thank you, Antony," Gunthar said. "Tell him I am on my way." He rose from his chair, adding briskly to Robert as the squire left, "You may report to me tomorrow for directions in your duties. Now I must go meet the king." He strode to the door and pulled it open.

Robert realized himself dismissed. What could he say, in any case? It was true that he was in Gunthar's custody, and in his debt as well. What harm could it do to serve as his secretary, at least for now? Robert moved towards the door, but Gunthar's voice arrested him again.

"One more thing. It may be some time before I have the sums necessary with which to pay you, so in lieu of that and in token of my—appreciation—for your past services in my behalf, I would like you to accept this."

Gunthar drew a ring from his left hand, disturbing the arm in the sling enough to make him wince slightly. He held the ring out to Robert. Robert took it and studied the jewel in the palm of his hand. A gold-worked braid nested a blood-red garnet in its center. Robert glanced up and saw a disquieting twinkle in the old earl's eye.

"I believe one of my archers, a fellow by the name of Wat Mortimer, is a rather accomplished silversmith. If you do not care for the ring yourself, you might speak to him about cutting it down to fit a smaller finger."

Robert felt his face warm, but Gunthar was already striding past him. He had no choice but to voice his thanks and follow Gunthar out of the room.

29

Ashbury Castle, Dorset
April 1214

My lady Marguerite,

I send to relieve you of any concern you might have for my safety. The king's campaign goes well. I would not have you believe me indifferent to your comfort while I am away, hence I send you my squire, Nicholas Tybert, to wait upon you until my return. Prepare yourself against my coming and for that Happy Event which we both so anxiously anticipate, from whence I may at last call you My Own.

Ever yours,

Saxton

Marguerite stared at the letter in her hand, then raised her gaze to the squire's sullen, smirking face. *Sent to wait upon me, indeed. To spy upon me, more like. Or—*She suppressed a shudder, mindful that her mother stood near. This was the squire who had spied upon her and Robert in the glade, who had told Saxton of their rendezvous and thus prevented Robert from meeting her that fateful day that had sent her off instead with the Earl of Saxton to Westminster Palace. Had Robert and Saxton met again in Poitou? Had Saxton done something wicked—something irrevocable to prevent Robert from returning to her? Was the squire's presence intended as a message Saxton preferred not to commit to ink and parchment?

Her skin pricked cold even though the days had finally warmed with the coming of spring.

Her mother swept across the floor of the hall in a rustle of silken skirts.

"Why, it is delightful to see you again, Master Tybert! Welcome!" Lady Leah gave the youth her hand and let him bow over it.

Marguerite acknowledged the squire with a shallow curtsy, but she could not bring herself to smile. "I am glad that Lord Saxton is well," she said, motioning to the letter she held. "And is Lord Gunthar the same and the men of his camp? His wife, Lady Helen, has become a dear friend of mine. It should grieve me to hear ill news of her husband."

"My lord Gunthar suffered an injury to his shoulder some weeks ago," the squire said, "but he is healing fair, as is your cousin from a small wound he received in a skirmish. Your father is also well, my lady."

If Lady Helen had received word of her husband's injury, it must have come after Marguerite left her, for *that* the countess would surely have shared. Marguerite saw the rebuke in her mother's eye. She should have asked about her father and Richard before the Earl of Gunthar. But Marguerite was too frightened to care. She racked her mind for some way to inquire about Robert. Lady Gunthar believed Marguerite and Robert had never met and had never spoken to Marguerite of him, but Saxton's squire could not know that.

Desperation made Marguerite bold. "It saddened Lady Helen that her husband took her minstrel with him. I am just back from visiting her this fortnight. She talked to me often of the young man—Robert, I believe she called him—and how much she missed his music. I should like to be able to write to her and assure her that he is safe."

She saw the shade of uncertainty that passed across the squire's face. That alone gave her courage. If Robert were harmed, surely the squire would glory in speaking it in behalf of Saxton. But Marguerite's stated intention of sending his answer to Lady Helen must give him pause to lie.

After a brief hesitation, Tybert answered with a scornful sniff. "I do not know, my lady. One does not pay attention to minstrels on a battlefield."

Marguerite took comfort from his equivocation. Robert must be safe. Or at least have been so when the squire left Poitou. She wrapped herself in the assurance like a comforting blanket against a winter's chill.

Marguerite tried for several weeks after Nicholas Tybert's arrival to hold her tongue and let her mother prepare her wedding trousseau without resuming the quarrels they had engaged in before the squire's coming. The squire all too frequently asked Lady Leah if she could spare a messenger to carry letters from him to his master in Poitou.

"For I was given strict instructions by the earl to keep him apprised of your lady daughter's health and spirits," Tybert said. "He is most solicitous for her well-being until he is privileged to assume the tender care of her himself."

Saxton's feigned concern for her infuriated Marguerite. She knew it was Saxton's way of trying to manipulate her while he was gone. If she knew his squire was watching her and reporting to his master, perhaps it would intimidate her into the meek, subservient betrothed he hoped to make his wife when he returned.

But we are not betrothed. I never spoke the vows. And so she reminded her mother again when her exasperation at the squire's endless recitals of Saxton's consideration finally broke her patience.

Lady Leah spat the pins she'd been holding between her lips into her hand, for Marguerite knew her mother could not pronounce her name in rebuke without spilling the pins otherwise.

"Marguerite, pray do not begin that again. Do you *want* another beating from your father when he returns home? You know he will have his way in the end. You would save us all a great deal of pain and grief if you would only bend to his will to begin with."

"I will not." Marguerite stood on a padded footstool while Eva measured and pinned the hem of the two-dozenth gown her mother had ordered since Marguerite's return from Lamhurst Castle. She had overheard Nicholas Tybert tell her mother to spare no expense on her trousseau, for Lord Saxton would reimburse the cost of them all when he returned.

"He would have his countess's wardrobe second in beauty only to the queen's," the squire had said.

"I will not repeat the wedding vows," Marguerite declared now, "any more than I did the betrothal vows. If you will insist on decking me out in these monstrously expensive fabrics, it will only be to the earl's disadvantage, for I shall never wear them."

Marguerite did not fear the threat of another beating by her father. Robert had sworn to protect her.

Her mother handed more pins to Eva and motioned for her to continue working on the hem of the heavy velvet gown that would be given to the embroiderers when it had finished being fitted to Marguerite's figure.

"Child, you have surely been mistaken in Lord Saxton," Lady Leah said. "Would he have sent Master Tybert to attend you if he did not care for you? The earl clearly wishes very much for you to be his bride."

"Oh, yes, so that he might inherit Grandfather's estates through me."

Lady Leah frowned at her daughter's tart reply. "The land has stood too long idle under Odo of Wedmore's hand. It is time a capable man took charge of them."

"Not Lord Saxton!" He would bleed her grandfather's inheritance dry!

"Yes, Lord Saxton," her mother said firmly. "I can think of no one better suited to make the land prosper as it should." She continued over her daughter's "Hmph!", "What my father was thinking when he appointed Odo—"

Marguerite rose instantly to her former tutor's defense. "Odo is a very good man."

"That is true, my dear," Lady Leah agreed. "I have never questioned his honesty. But a villein-priest cannot be competent to know how to administer such estates as my father left behind. There has been a great deal of waste under his management."

"I have never heard of any." Marguerite crossed her arms, then uncrossed them at Eva's faint murmur that the movement disturbed the line of the hem.

Lady Leah smiled. "Of course not, my dear. Such things are for men to deal with, not women. But your father has kept a careful eye on Odo's conduct, and you may be sure that he speaks the truth."

Marguerite mumbled another *hmph*. She did not believe a word of it, but it would do no good to argue Odo's competence with her mother. Whatever Marguerite's father said was her mother's unquestioned truth.

Marguerite continued to protest the gowns, but her mother ignored her and the fittings went on.

Another six weeks passed. In spite of herself, Marguerite's spirits began to droop. The king showed little inclination of either winning his goal or returning speedily to England. Her father never wrote himself, but Saxton's letters always carried news of him and her cousin Richard. Once or twice a letter even came from Richard himself, though rarely more than a few lines. But from the man Marguerite spent every free moment dreaming of and aching for, came only silence. How should it be otherwise? It could only have been taking a dangerous chance for Robert to send her a message. But to know nothing at all of him was nearly unbearable.

Marguerite knew she would have found greater patience to wait if she had remained with Lady Helen. She missed the countess's consoling strength. She missed Evelyn's friendship and her son's mischief. Marguerite even missed Annys. Lady Leah reluctantly allowed Marguerite to correspond with the countess and from her Marguerite learned that Evelyn had accompanied Lady Helen to visit Sir Gerald Faintree when he was sent home from Poitou with a wound; that Alain had caught a fish from the pond as large as himself; and that Lord Gunthar claimed his broken shoulder had mended as good as new, though Lady Helen expressed her suspicion that he said it merely so she would not worry. But silence. Silence about her minstrel. This stifling ignorance of Robert would drive Marguerite mad!

She sat late one morning on the floor of her mother's solar, knees drawn up and chin resting on her knees, staring into the empty hearth. A fire was rarely needed in these late days of May. Her mother hummed softly as she embroidered near the light of the window, most likely unaware that the tune she had chosen was one that Robert had sung for them on a winter's eve that seemed now to Marguerite nearly a lifetime ago. Marguerite thought her heart would break with longing to hear his voice again.

The humming stopped. "I know it has been exhausting for you, love," her mother said. Had she seen the slump of Marguerite's shoulders? "But the fittings are very nearly done and you will see that it has all been worth it in the end. I do not doubt that Lord Saxton will be most satisfied with his bride."

Marguerite felt too despondent to argue again. She did not want any more quarreling. She wanted comfort. She wanted reassurance. She wanted to feel safe and secure again, as she had with her grandfather. But he and her grandmother were gone. Her mother would not let her return to Lamhurst Castle and Lady Helen. There was no one for Marguerite to turn to, no one she could confide in, no one to quiet her fears . . .

And then she saw his face hovering in vision against the darkness of the hearth. His patient smile. His calm eyes.

She scrambled up to cross the room, then fell to her knees beside her mother. "Mama, let us go to Northumberland."

"Northumberland?" Her mother looked startled, but understanding swiftly filled her eyes. "Oh, no. Your father would never—"

"I know he would not like it, but he is not here and it has been over three years since I have seen Winbourne Castle!"

"And Odo," her mother said.

"Yes—and Odo," Marguerite confessed. "What if Lord Saxton decides to banish him? What if he refuses to stay and serve the earl, even if Lord Saxton asks him? Mama, please, *please* let me see Odo one more time. I promise—" she drew a deep breath but knew it was the only way "—I promise I will not ask him to interfere with my marriage to Lord Saxton. Only let me see him and I will not quarrel with you or Father anymore."

Oh, Rob, please come back to me in time to save me from my vow!

Lady Leah gazed a long moment at her daughter, then wiped away the tear that trickled down Marguerite's cheek.

"You think I do not understand," her mother murmured. "I love your father now, but it was not easy to leave my home at fourteen to wed him. Your father and I did not meet above twice before our wedding day." She stroked away another tear. "I pray you will find such love with Lord Saxton. But if it will help to allay your fears, then you may say goodbye to Odo. Tell Eva to pack your things. We will leave in the morning."

30

It had been foolish to expect to find things the same. Marguerite acknowledged that when she saw how familiar tapestries had been re-hung on different walls in the great hall of Winbourne Castle, when she smelled sweet woodruff instead of the blue iris her grandmother loved sprinkled in the rushes on the floor, when a young hound lolling before the hearth lifted his head to gaze at her instead of old Parcival, her grandfather's faithful mastiff. But the faces were most disheartening. She did not recognize a single servant. Lady Leah reminded Marguerite that her father had set Sir Oliver Braybrooke as Winbourne's castellan after her grandfather's death. Braybrooke and his wife, Dame Gytha, greeted Marguerite and her mother with respect, but Marguerite sensed no warmth in their courtesy. They were strangers and had brought in strangers to serve the castle. Marguerite could not excuse herself quickly enough to seek the retreat of her old bedchamber.

But things were different there, too. The bedding and pillows had changed. The cushion on the chair where she sat to brush her hair as a child had been fraying when she'd left, but it still jarred her to see it recovered with a different patterned cloth. At least the tapestry over the bed remained the same: a forest scene with a family of deer, some rabbits, and a bird gracefully soaring in the air. She recalled her long hours spent weaving it, the helpful hints from her grandmother, the undeserved praise from her grandfather even when the threads around the bird had gone slightly awry, the soft-spoken encouragement of Odo—

Why had he not been in the hall to greet her? Whatever else her father had changed, he had no power to dismiss Odo of Wedmore or alter his authority over this or any other of her grandfather's manors.

When they gathered to dine after Marguerite and her mother had rested, Marguerite ventured to ask after her old tutor.

"Is he well, Sir Oliver? I expected him to join us." Nicholas Tybert hovered over Marguerite's shoulder, carving meat and setting it on her trencher.

Dame Gytha answered after she and her husband exchanged glances with Marguerite's mother. "Master Odo is a very good man, but he knows his place, which is not at the same table as his lady."

Marguerite drew her brows together. "But Grandfather always included Odo at the table."

Again Dame Gytha looked at Lady Leah before she said, with a trace of haughtiness in her smile, "Forgive me, my lady, but your grandfather was an eccentric man who saw fit to honor a villein cleric. Things are different today. Of course, my husband and Sir Miles, our steward, do nothing without consulting with Master Odo, but he does not presume to take a place within the castle."

Marguerite dropped her spoon with a splash into her bowl of almond soup. "You mean he has moved out?"

"Oh, he remains on the grounds, of course," Dame Gytha assured her. "He has built himself a dwelling a few feet within the east wall. You may see it from the upper windows."

Marguerite opened her mouth to protest, but Lady Leah caught her eye and frowned. Marguerite let it go for now and finished her dinner in silence, while her mother and Dame Gytha exchanged vapid pleasantries and Sir Oliver smiled politely through his boredom.

As soon as dinner ended, Marguerite pled a headache from the long day's travel and slipped away from the hall only long enough to stay her mother's suspicions and throw a light mantle around her shoulders. Then she left the keep through a side door and crossed the bailey to Odo's cottage. It was little more than that, though built within the protective walls of the castle rather than without in the village. Marguerite hesitated outside his door. She knew her mother would disapprove of her coming here rather than summoning Odo to the castle to wait on her. Perhaps Odo would not even be glad to see her. But he was the reason she had come.

She raised her hand and knocked briskly on the door.

It took a few moments for the door to swing open. A tall, slender man in his mid-forties stood in the frame, dressed in a dark, unobtrusive robe that reached to his ankles. His dark hair showed streaks of grey, but oh! how welcome she found his smooth, tranquil face and the familiar warmth of his grey eyes.

"Lady Marguerite! What are you doing here? You should have waited for me in the keep. I intended to come see you this evening."

"I did not wish to wait so long," she said, forcing a cheerfulness into her voice she did not feel. His formality shook her confidence. But she asked on the same bright note, "May I come in?"

"Of course, my lady, forgive me." He stepped back to allow her to enter.

Marguerite gazed around the room. Judging from the single door across from her and the size of the structure she had observed from outside, she guessed the cottage held no more than a modest bedchamber beyond the second door. She had not thought to wonder before, but did so now: had Robert grown up in a cottage like this? With a fire on a grate in the center of the floor spreading the room with a hazy smoke that failed to adequately float upwards through the hole cut into the roof? Perhaps his father had carved a rack of cooking tools for his mother, like the ones that hung on Odo's wall. Their larder would not have held venison, though. Villeins were not permitted to hunt in the forest, but her grandfather had shared his forest rights with Odo, and from the remains of a bowl of venison stew that she saw on the table, he still took leave to exercise it. Nor, for all Robert's learning from his village priest, would his parents' cottage have possessed a shelf full of books like the one that ran beneath that window to her left.

"Why did you move out?" she asked Odo abruptly. "You must find this cottage ever so small after living with us in the castle for so many years."

"It serves my needs," he said. "A man of God should be reminded of his humility. If I had stayed in the castle, I may one day have become as puffed up as Sir Oliver. It was not worth my soul to battle him for position out of pride. Wherever I live, the management of the manor remains in my hands and that is all your grandfather asked of me."

No, she thought, *he asked more of you than that.* Odo had final say over whom she should or should not marry. But she had promised her mother not to involve Odo in her quarrel with Saxton.

"You should have sent for me," Odo said. "It is not proper for you to be here."

"Not proper to visit my old tutor, my old friend?" She held out her hands to him. "I have missed you, Master Odo."

Her smile faltered when he did not take her fingers.

"My lady—"

The rebuke in his eyes, gentle as it was, set her lip to trembling. "Please." Tears pricked her eyes. She could not bear it if he rebuffed her. "P-please— do not chide me. I have been so unhappy."

To her relief, his face creased with concern and he opened his arms. She slid into them without a word. They closed about her with all the tenderness she remembered as a child.

"Little mistress, what is it? Will you not tell me?"

She nestled against him, desperate for the safety his embrace promised. But she could not answer. She had given her mother her word.

"Only say you are glad to see me," she whispered.

"Little one, of course I am." She felt the tension of his hesitation before his body relaxed and his fingers stroked her hair. "When you left, the heart went from Winbourne. You bring us light once more."

She leaned into his soft, dark robe. How many times had he lifted away her burdens and fears by holding her thus and promising that all would be well? And somehow, he had always magically made it so. Or so it had seemed to her as a child. But this time as she let the moments pulse by, the worry that lay like a weight on her heart failed to melt away.

At last she slid from his arms and sat down on stool near the bookshelf. She drew out a green bound volume and flipped through the pages without seeing the words. "You have heard of my coming marriage?" she asked.

"We have all heard," he said in his quiet way. "Winbourne will be glad of her mistress once more. Lord Audley has offered me a position in his son's household, and I—"

She looked up in alarm. "Odo, you must not leave Winbourne. Grandfather would never have wanted that."

He watched her with his hands folded, pale against the dark background of his robe. "My duties here are nearly finished, my lady. Upon your marriage, the management of your estates will pass into your husband's hands. I will need new employment."

"But did Grandfather not grant you a sufficient annuity?"

"Quite sufficient, but I do not care to be idle. Lord Saxton will doubtless desire to have his own men about him. The Audley position is a good one."

Marguerite returned her attention to the book and flipped another page. "Are you acquainted with the Earl of Saxton?"

"No, my lady."

"But you have heard of him?"

"Of course. One knows that he is counselor to the king, that he holds manors of his own in the south, that he stands second only to the king in wealth and power. Your grandfather always wished a grand match for you, but even he never conceived of attempting a marriage as illustrious as this."

"Grand," she repeated. "Illustrious. Is that all you know of Lord Saxton?"

Odo moved to pick up the bowl from the table and placed it in a washing tub. "As you know, we are somewhat isolated here in the north. I am not the court watcher that your grandfather was. Your father sent a messenger some months ago to inform us of your betrothal. I know only what that courier told us." He turned away from the tub to gaze at her. "Do you not wish to marry Saxton?"

She bit down hard on her tongue, remembering her promise to her mother. Sitting here, so near to Odo, memories began to filter back. She loved her grandfather without question, but he had been a hard man, sometimes impatient with her childish needs. When her stomach had knotted with doubts and fears, she had not run first with them to Heywood, though he had always been the one in the end who banished whatever trouble beset her.

"An illustrious marriage," she repeated. She traced a large, illuminated B with her finger on the vellum page in her lap. "Suppose I had not wished for such a match. Would Grandfather have forced me?" She lifted her eyes to Odo's. "Would you have let him?"

Their gazes held a long moment. Odo said softly, "Your grandfather loved you, Marguerite."

"Aye, because *you* taught him to."

"Nay, child—"

She rose suddenly, setting the book on the shelf top. The memories cascaded into her mind with incandescent brightness now. "Why did Grandfather change his mind about my betrothal to Lord Stephen seven years ago? He was pleased enough with the match at first. He would not listen to me when I begged him not to make me marry Lord Stephen, he said

I did not know what was best and that Lord Stephen would make a fine husband. So I ran to you and wept and wept in your arms. You stroked my hair, just as you did today, and promised all would be well, and then—then suddenly, Grandfather was no longer pleased with Lord Stephen. I remember the terrible row he had with my father about it. But why should he change so suddenly, unless *you* had said something. He always listened to you."

Odo shook his head.

She took a swift step towards him, then stopped. "Do you deny it?"

"My child, your grandfather would have loved you without any word from me."

"He did not love my mother so," Marguerite said. "He did not balk at marrying her to a man she had met but twice, or consult her desires."

"He was older and wiser with you."

"Aye, he had a wiser counselor."

More memories of her grandfather tumbled in. She did not doubt that Heywood loved her, but by nature he had been reserved and reticent. Words of affection fell awkwardly from his tongue, as though he had only recently learned to speak them. By their very rarity, she had always known them sincere. But he almost always shared them after he had spent some interlude with Odo, reassuring some fear of hers, praising some new clever learning she had mastered from her tutor, even sharing an uncharacteristically gentle joke.

"Would he not have been very different without you beside him?" she said. "Would I not have been raised as my mother was and be married even now?" Her new insight told her it was true. She took another step towards Odo. "Why did you stop him?"

Odo did not answer.

She stepped near enough to lay her hand on his arm. "Odo?"

He placed his hand over hers. "You were so very frightened, and you were only a child. It is a crime to marry children at so young an age and leads to much unhappiness."

"But why did you care? You were naught but my tutor. I had no claim on you."

He smiled. "I loved you, Marguerite. You were so bright, so merry and full of life. The one thing I have regretted in life is that I had no children. I was more rash and foolish than you knew in those days. There were times I let myself pretend that you were my daughter."

She did not slip quietly into his embrace this time, but flung her arms around him. "I wish I were."

Again he stroked her hair, but his voice was gentle. "Nay, child, do not wish that. My children would have been villeins. I have lived in both worlds, little one, and yours is infinitely more pleasant."

"Infinitely," she repeated bitterly. "Would I were a villein. Everything would have been so different."

"That it would, but not for the better."

"Yes, yes, for the better!" Had she been born a villein with Odo as her father rather than the rough Lord de Villon, who then would have cared if she married Robert? She rested her head against Odo's shoulder and sighed. "I remember you saying once that villeins were bound only because it pleased the selfish vanity of stronger men to make them so."

"Not stronger, Marguerite." A rare, hot note stole into Odo's voice. "I'd set the muscles of a man who works the fields from sunrise to sunset any time against the strength of a knight who swills wine all day and rehearses with the quintain only when his neighbor irks him or the king calls him to war. The knights are better armed, better organized, better trained than vileins. But the order between them is precarious. One day the balance will tip, and then—"

He broke off as Marguerite suddenly laughed. No wonder she had found Robert so easy to accept when she had heard words like these all her life. Odo looked down at her, surprised.

She said, "How angry you used to make Grandfather when you said to him things like that."

Odo gave a rueful smile. "Aye, I taught him much, but not all that I wished to. He never understood completely."

She stepped back so that she could see into Odo's face again. She remembered the question she had not been able to answer when she had stood in the glade with Robert and told him why no man would marry her but Saxton.

"Odo, why did Grandfather free his villeins?"

An expression slipped across Odo's tranquil face that she had never seen before. She had not time to put a name to it before he turned away and walked across the floor, slow and reflective, unlike the quick restlessness of

Robert's movements. He reached the bookshelf and paused to gaze out the window before he spoke again.

"I met your grandfather when I came to Winbourne Manor as a new young priest appointed to the village church. My superiors had banished me to this isolated corner of the realm hoping the long, chill winters here might cool the passionate heat of my heresy. Then, as now, I believed that all men should be free and railed a little too loudly against the barons who viewed their villeins as chattle and who did not wish my preachings to stir those villeins up to think they were anything else."

He turned and walked over to the wash tub, keeping his back to Marguerite. "Your mother was married and gone by the time I came." He poured a jug of water into the tub and began to clean the empty bowl of stew. "My words angered your grandfather, as they had the other barons. But instead of cursing me and threatening to thrash me off his manor, priest or no priest, if I did not stay my tongue, Heywood did something that confounded me. He made me his chaplain and took me into his household." The rag Odo held swished in the water. "He said he did it to silence me, that my words should reach no further than the walls of his keep. He dressed me in fine clothes, sat me at his own table to dine. And he listened to me. Aye, in anger, at first, arguing always that I was a fool and sparing no words in telling me why."

Marguerite gathered up the spoon and knife from the table, with a dish of bread crumbs and a crumble of cheese, and carried it to Odo so that she might stand beside him and see his face.

He took the dish and utensils from her but did not place them in the water. His gaze met Marguerite's.

"Then one day your grandfather laughed and said I would never change. And he said he respected me for it. *Respected* me."

A gleam of pleasure lit in Odo's eyes. Marguerite could only imagine how bright his surprise and delight had shone as a young man all those years ago.

"He said too many men failed to hold to their convictions when challenged by a man of power or, he added, for your grandfather had a strong streak of self-honesty, a domineering temperament. Then he clapped me on the shoulder and said that I might say what I pleased to him. And ever after, even when he frowned, even when I angered him, something between us held our friendship fast."

Odo smiled at Marguerite before submerging the objects he held in the tub.

Marguerite found a dry cloth to wipe the bowl and spoon and knife as Odo washed them. His story quickened fond memories of her grandfather's goodness, but it had not answered her question.

"But why did he free his villeins?"

Odo's hands grew still in the water. He let go of the wooden plate, so that it skimmed floating in the tub. His smile faded.

"It was just after word arrived from Dorset of your birth that a fever swept through the village. It took no lives, so we felt no fear for your grandfather when the illness struck him down. His constitution had always been strong, your grandmother and I had no reason to think he would not recover quickly. But day by day he worsened until he grew so weak we realized he would not live to see another morn."

Again, an unfamiliar shadow fell over his features. "I was his chaplain. It was my duty to shrive him of his sins. As he lay confessing through both our tears, begging for the pardon of Heaven, the thought slid into my mind that perhaps I could make something good of his death. I knew I was exploiting his fear—that was *my* sin—but I did it nonetheless. I reminded him of our old quarrel and I said—may Heaven forgive me—I said that to be absolved of the deadly sin of greed by which he had cared more for the prosperity of his lands than for the sweat of the men who made them prosper, he should grant to his villeins on Winbourne Manor what heaven had blessed him with at birth—freedom."

Odo took up the cloth that swirled in the water and scrubbed at the plate so vigorously, Marguerite feared it might splinter.

"I saw how he struggled against the idea. But when the justice of God stares one in the face, even a lifetime's unyielding beliefs can crumble."

Marguerite nudged Odo aside and took the plate to wash it herself. She kept her gaze focused on her task that he might not think he saw blame in her eyes. There was none in her heart, but she sensed he still carried remorse for what he viewed as a betrayal of her grandfather's friendship and feared what she might think.

"He was too weak to write the order himself, so he commanded me to do it, and I guided his hand as he signed his name to it. To be sure I would not stand accused of coercing him to the deed—" Marguerite heard the self-mockery in Odo's voice "—he summoned two of his knights to stand as witness. The fever had not let him rest in peace for days, but after he signed the order, he slept as quiet as a babe. I stayed at his side, wishful to be there when he slipped away. But come morning, he still breathed. By noon, the fever had abated. By nightfall, he was asking faintly for a spoonful of broth.

"The long and short of it is, your grandfather recovered and when he did, like the honest man he was, he stood by his word and freed his villeins. I think he was surprised when the yields of the fields increased and the manor prospered more than it had done before. I confess, I was a little surprised, too."

Marguerite set the plate aside to give Odo a quick hug. "Perhaps it was not a sin, then. Perhaps it was a prompting of Heaven that made you speak those words."

"Perhaps. I have prayed that it was." Odo led her to the stool and pressed her down, then drew a chair from the table to sit near her. "Your grandfather changed after that. Oh, not all at once. He was still impatient and ambitious. But he seemed to grow more thoughtful. No one was more stunned than I when he went to Dorset to see his new granddaughter and came back with you. He said your father was brutish and low-minded and he would not have his granddaughter reared by such a man. He repented the day, he said, that he had wed his daughter to de Villon." Odo waved a hand. "And you know the rest. Except, perhaps, for the end."

"Tell me of that," Marguerite begged.

His face settled back into the smooth, quiet lines that had always soothed her distress.

"That last time your grandfather fell ill, he seemed to sense that he would not receive a second reprieve. He was older then and awaited death more calmly. Only after he had said his goodbyes to you and your grandmother and sent you away—only then did he tell me of his will and the clause that would emancipate his other manors when he was dead. The revelation wrenched my heart. Difficult as it was for me to turn away the gift, I told him that he need not make that gesture again to win the grace of Heaven. He was a good man and Heaven would judge him so. But he said this time he did not do it for the sake of his soul alone, but in gratitude to me. He thanked me for showing him how to love you and your grandmother, and wept only that he had not known how to love your mother, too."

Marguerite wiped away the tears that blurred in her eyes. "Grandfather *was* good, wasn't he?"

"Yes, little one. And he *did* good when he freed his villeins and let them choose how they would live and whether they would serve him."

She remembered how she had told Robert that most of the villeins had stayed and how the manors had thrived when worked by freemen. That, she guessed, was what had given Odo his tranquility. The knowledge that however it had come about, his people were free, the land had flourished, and her grandfather had died content.

A sharp rapping fell on the door. Odo rose to open it. Dusk had gathered so that she could not make out the features of the man in the doorway, but she recognized the sullen voice.

"I am looking for the Lady Marguerite. She is missing from the keep. Her mother said she might be here."

Marguerite stood. "I am, Master Tybert. Yes, I will come with you now." She crossed to the door, but paused to take Odo's hand. "Thank you. I will come again tomorrow."

"My lady—" Odo began.

But Marguerite cut his protest off. "You may argue if you like, but I will be here. And you will dine with us at the castle for the remainder of my stay. That is not a request, Master Odo. Remember, I am your mistress now."

Odo returned her mischievous smile. She dared not embrace him again in front of Nicholas Tybert, but she pressed Odo's fingers and knew from his squeeze in response that he understood her grandfather's gratitude echoed in her heart.

31

arguerite met Odo the next morning as he was coming out his door. It was irksome that her mother had insisted Nicholas Tybert accompany her to see her old tutor, but it was better than spending no time with Odo at all. Odo begged her pardon, saying he had been asked to visit a man in the village who had suffered an injury. Marguerite immediately said that she would ride with him and sent a protesting Nicholas Tybert off to the stables to saddle her mare.

"Your mother will not like it," he warned her as he placed the reins in her hand. He added more firmly when Marguerite merely bade him boost her into the saddle, "The *earl* will not like it."

"The earl is not yet my husband," Marguerite replied. "Now pray do as I bid you, Master Tybert."

Since Tybert had been ordered by Lady Leah to attend her daughter throughout the morning, he accompanied Marguerite and Odo into the village. Marguerite talked cheerfully with Odo along the way. She found her spirits lifted further when they reached the village. Unlike Winbourne Castle, which continued to unsettle her with its mix of the familiar and altered, Winbourne Village seemed exactly as she remembered it. The lanes and cottages spread around the square green common, with the mill a little further along the way, and dominating all, the tall village church, the only structure besides the castle itself that was built of stone. This time of day most of the men and women with their children were working in the fields, but one anxious-faced woman came hurrying out of the third cottage on their left when Odo drew up his horse. Unlike the too often gaunt villeins on her father's manor, this woman's cheeks shone rosy and plump.

The woman wrung her hands as she dropped a curtsy. "Oh, Father Odo, thank ye for comin'."

It jarred Marguerite a little to hear Odo addressed by his priestly title. It had been ever so long since she had heard someone call him so. Grandfather had only ever called him "Master Odo," and when he had become her tutor, Marguerite had done the same.

"Gilles insists his ankle is no more than sprained," the woman rambled on, "but the way it's all swolled up, I'm quite certain he broke it when he fell from repairin' our roof yesterday. Ye'll know. Pray come in, an'—" She broke off with a curious look at Odo's companions.

Marguerite smiled at her. "Good-day, Mistress Joan."

The woman gasped. "Milady Marguerite?" She dropped another curtsy, this time with her hands clasped in surprise at her ample bosom.

Marguerite glanced at the squire's heavy frown. "Yes, Master Tybert," she said, "my grandfather used to let me come to the village with Father Odo"— she would have the squire know how Odo was to be respected—"and help him comfort villagers who were in distress."

Odo had only allowed her to enter cottages of villagers with injuries such as Mistress Joan's husband, for her grandfather had lost all his children to illness save Marguerite's mother. But Marguerite had learned the villagers' names and families and how to be kind and heal.

"That was very broadminded of your grandfather." The squire spoke it with a subtle slur of insult in his voice. "But the earl will not be so liberal with his wife's conduct. I really cannot allow you to enter that cottage."

"Not allow me?" Marguerite swung herself off her horse, took Mistress Joan by the arm, and marched straight towards the cottage door.

Tybert flashed off his mount and moved to block them.

"Marguerite, child." Odo spoke gently from behind them. When she turned her head she saw the quiet laughter in his eyes at her confrontation with Tybert. Nonetheless, he said, "It will do no harm to indulge Lord Saxton's squire in this. I will not be long. Wait for me here."

"Indeed, I will not," Marguerite said. "I wish to see Master Gilles for myself."

Odo moved to her side and touched her shoulder. He said softly into her ear, "You've a generous heart, little one, for which I have always been glad.

But I think in this instance you defy the earl's squire out of pride. That is a sin I will not tolerate in a former pupil of mine."

Marguerite blushed, but before she could argue or beg Odo's pardon, she caught sight of a gentleman on the other side of the lane leading a lame horse towards the blacksmith's shop up the way.

"Pray, who is that?" she asked Odo. The gentleman had passed them now so that she could only see his back, but something about him seemed familiar.

Odo followed her gaze. "That is Sir Matthew Eyvind's son, Warin. Sir Matthew is castellan of Lord Audley's Northumberland fortress a few miles west of here, where young Warin has been recuperating from a wound sustained in a tournament some months ago. Marguerite, is something wrong?"

Marguerite knew her blush had paled, for her cheeks now felt cold. "I know him," she said. "We met at Westminster. Go along with your visit, Master Odo, while I speak with Sir Warin."

She heard Tybert's quick protest and told him curtly to hold her horse, then hurried off down the lane.

"Sir Warin!" she called.

He turned around, startled. His brown curls tumbled over his forehead just as she remembered. Her pace quickened almost to a run. She did not realize she had extended her hands until she found them warmly clasped in his.

He gazed at her, amazement in his eyes. "Lady Marguerite! Is it, in sweet truth, you?"

"Yes, indeed it is. I am so happy to see you well. I feared you might die after that dreadful accident at the tournament, and all because of me!"

Guilt bubbled up in her afresh as she remembered Saxton's warning to them both, Sir Warin rolling off his horse, the blood on Saxton's lance. Accident? Nay! She clutched Sir Warin's fingers tighter and searched his handsome face. Aside from confusion, she saw no lingering pallor or lines of pain.

"But my lady," he said, "how do you come to be here? Is your home not in Dorset?"

"Oh, yes, in general, but Winbourne Castle is mine from my grandfather. I did not know your family came from Northumberland."

Sir Warin laughed. "It seems we know very little about each other, after all." He stopped as Tybert approached them, leading Marguerite's horse along with his own.

Marguerite said quickly, "Sir Warin, this is Nicholas Tybert, my—attendant."

She withdrew her hands rather abruptly from Sir Warin's. The squire was sure to write to Saxton of this encounter.

The squire bowed. "Your servant, Sir Warin."

"Master Tybert." Sir Warin inclined his head politely. He registered no recognition, but she supposed men did not always take note of other men's squires.

"Are you indeed fully recovered?" Marguerite tried to mask the eagerness in her voice, but she had to know how Sir Warin fared. "You took such a dreadful fall."

He smiled down at her. "I am very well now, I thank you. 'Twas my pride that suffered the deepest wound. It shames me that I took such a tumble while wearing your favor."

Marguerite felt her cheeks warming again. She wished Tybert had remained beside the cottage. "Do you come often to the village?" she asked the knight.

"I like to ride out daily. My horse cast a shoe a few miles back, and so you find me headed for the blacksmith's shop."

"Then I will not keep you," Marguerite said, disappointed to see him depart so soon, but sensing Tybert's impatience.

Sir Warin hesitated, appearing equally reluctant to leave her, then said, "Do you like to ride as well, my lady? I should welcome your company. I find it tediously dull riding alone."

Marguerite knew she would find the days tedious as well with her mother and Dame Gytha. She could not spend every minute with Odo. He had duties to attend to that could not always include her.

"I should love to ride with you," she said. "Tomorrow morning?"

Sir Warin agreed with the charming smile she remembered from the king's court. She felt Tybert watching her, but when Sir Warin held out his hand, she gave him her fingers once more and allowed him to kiss them. What harm could there be? Saxton was far away in Poitou and could not harm Sir Warin again.

Lord Audley was an influential man who would not look kindly on the cutting of his castellan's son, and so Lady Leah reluctantly gave her permission for Marguerite to ride with Sir Warin, so long as Nicholas Tybert accompanied them. Sir Warin treated Marguerite with the same consideration and courtesy as he had at Westminster, solicitous but respectful, so much so that she quickly lost her fear that he might overstep the bounds with her again. Marguerite soon found herself riding daily with him. He seemed content with her friendship, helping her while away the mornings after the long nights she spent wakeful in her bed missing Robert.

When Lady Leah received an invitation from Dame Eleanor Eyvind to dine with her and her son, she felt obligated to accept for the same reasons she allowed Marguerite to ride with Sir Warin. But lest the young knight should be tempted to forget to whom Marguerite was betrothed, Lady Leah dressed her daughter in one of the gowns from her wedding trousseau. When Lady Leah refused to let Marguerite wear Robert's ribbon beneath her snow-white veil, Marguerite tied it around her wrist. She had told her mother it was a gift from Lady Helen's daughter-in-law, Evelyn, and she was afraid she would lose it if she left it behind.

Dame Eleanor, a plump, cheerful matron, greeted them with an apology that dinner would be delayed, due to a small fire that had had to be put out in the kitchen, requiring both the lamb stew and pork tarts to be cooked from scratch.

"Let us sit here and coze while we wait," Dame Eleanor said to Lady Leah, leading her to the table draped in a flowing white tablecloth on the dais. "My husband left only a few men to guard the castle in his absence and I told them they need not join us until I send them word, so that you and I might have a chance to get to know one another. You do not mind if their wives join us? We have none of us been to London in years and were hopeful you could tell us of the latest fashions there. If your daughter's gown is evidence, we shall be hard pressed to find enough hours in the day to embroider such deliciously exotic designs into our cloth."

She gave an affable chuckle and motioned each of her household ladies to their chairs, but when Marguerite would have seated herself beside her mother, Dame Eleanor shook a genial finger at her.

"Nay, my lady, you will be bored by our prattle. Take her away, Warin, and show her the gardens. The larkspur are lovely this time of year. We will send this fine young squire of my lady's to call you when it is time to dine."

Nicholas Tybert protested, but Dame Eleanor insisted that he stay and tell them how fared the king's campaign in Poitou when he'd left it and whether the squire had met there Lord Audley or Sir Matthew or anyone else Dame Eleanor and her ladies might know.

Marguerite was glad to slip free of Tybert's supervision for once, as well as her mother's frown.

"I thought I should never get you alone," Sir Warin said, echoing her thoughts as he drew her into a garden thick with the scent of roses, their lush red blooms mingling with chaste white lilies. Spikes of larkspur in shades of blue, pink and purple fringed the paved walkway that wound charmingly through a lawn sprinkled thick with violets. The sun was hours yet from setting and bathed the colors of the garden in a golden glow.

Marguerite laughed a little. "Master Tybert is very earnest in his duties."

"He guards you well," Sir Warin agreed. "Did he come up with you from Dorset?"

So, he truly did not remember the squire from Westminster. Marguerite hesitated in her answer, then strove to strike a light note. "He was very generously sent by Lord Saxton to attend me. Is it not kind of my lord to so concern himself with my comfort?" She paused in their stroll and bent to inhale one of the roses.

"He would be a fool if he did not," Sir Warin murmured. "But I am glad Master Tybert is not here now." He drew Marguerite's hand through his arm, laying gentle fingers over her wrist and inadvertently trapping Robert's ribbon beneath them. They walked a few steps further down the path. "I had hoped for a moment alone with you. I did not wish to say my goodbyes with my mother and all the household looking on."

"Goodbyes?" She looked up at him, surprised.

"Aye. I am fully recovered of my injury now. It is time for me to join the king and his army."

Marguerite whirled in front of him. "No! Why must you go? The king has done well enough without you until now."

"It is my duty to go," Sir Warin said with that same condescension that had always colored her grandfather's voice when he had spoken exactly such words to her grandmother. "Lord Audley has sent for me and I cannot hold back. I could not pay the scutage even if I wished to."

And he did not wish to. Marguerite could see it in his eyes, the gleam of martial excitement at the prospect of battle. Again like her grandfather. She had even glimpsed it in Robert, though he had tried to mask his going purely under the guise of finding the truth about his father. Why must all men be so war mad? She spun away from Sir Warin so that he could not see the panic in her face. Death came with war, and it did not discriminate between knight and footsoldier on the battlefield. Indeed, how much more vulnerable must the poor footsoldier be without the protection of shield or armor? Marguerite wrapped her arms around her stomach as it pitched with the dread that never hovered far from her.

"I do not expect you to understand," Sir Warin said from behind her. "My only regret is that I must leave you thus. But I shall come safely back for you, I vow it."

That startled her into turning around again. "What?"

Sir Warin's face had hardened. "You need not guard yourself with me, Marguerite. That young squire was sent to spy upon you by the Earl of Saxton. The earl is villainy itself and I'll not leave you to his mercies. When I return—"

"Sir Warin, please," she cut him off. "Take care what you say." Her gaze darted down the path the way they had come. If Nicholas Tybert came upon them—

"Saxton is a thousand miles away and can do us no harm, though he has done his best to make me fear his spite."

Saxton would not be a thousand miles away when Sir Warin went to Poitou. How could he speak so foolishly? Impatience struggled with a fresh surge of guilt at his reference to that calamitous tournament.

"It was my fault what happened at Westminster," she said. "I ought not to have encouraged you there." She blinked rapidly and hard until the vision of that horror retreated. Let him think the sun's brilliance stung her eyes. "I will not make the same mistake again. I will not encourage you to hope where there is no hope."

Sir Warin reached out for her hand and raised it very gently to his lips. "My lady, there is always hope."

She shook her head.

"Surely you can see it," he pressed. "The chances that we should ever meet again after London were too slim to even imagine. Yet here we stand, together, in Northumberland, as if by a miracle—"

"No." She resisted when he tried to draw her to him. "Sir Warin, I had very good reasons for coming to Northumberland. 'Twas no miracle. I had no notion I should find you here."

She tried to pull her hand away, but he held onto it stubbornly. "Miracle or no, I know only that I have found you again. Marguerite, will you tell me that you have obtained happiness with Saxton since we parted?"

She tried to suppress a shiver at the thought of Saxton, but failed. Sir Warin saw it. His face glowed with triumph.

"No. I knew you could not love such a coldhearted felon as he."

Before she could anticipate his intent, Sir Warin pulled her into his arms and kissed her. His mouth was warm and sought to command a response, but it roused only anguish in her. It should have been Robert standing here, holding her, kissing her . . . Tears flooded her eyes.

She twisted her face away. "Sir Warin, pray let me go!"

"Marguerite—"

She tried to squeeze out of his arms. "I have told you I cannot love you. You will only bring pain to us both."

"How shall there be pain if you do not love me?" he demanded.

"Love, no, but I have thought you my friend and believed you thought me no more than the same."

"Friend?" He repeated the word, his voice hoarse. "How can you not have seen how I adore you? How I love you! Only give me a chance to win your heart."

"You cannot. I have told you—there is another—" She pushed against his chest. Why would he not let her go?

"Aye," he cut her off, "this Robert Marcel who cares so much for you that he abandons you to the Earl of Saxton. You are deserving of a better man than that."

"He did not abandon me." She tried prying at Sir Warin's arms.

"You said—"

"I did not know. I thought—But he *did* come."

Sir Warin's embrace abruptly slackened and she finally slipped free. But the surprise in his face quickly turned obstinate again. "Then where is he now?"

Marguerite tasted the tang of bitterness on her tongue. "In Poitou, with the king. Where else? He, too, has his duty."

She moved away to sit on a decoratively carved wooden bench a few yards down the path. The ribbon at her wrist fluttered on a sudden gust of breeze. She caught it between her fingers and rubbed the place where one of the embroidered roses had grown flattened, the dye smudged. The place where she had caressed it every night in her bed for three and a half long months, remembering Robert's touch when he had woven the gift into her hair and the promise he had made her. *I vow I will return, or move heaven and earth trying.*

She heard a footstep and felt Sir Warin stop beside the bench.

"Tell me of this man. Is he a very great knight? He must be if he would challenge the Earl of Saxton for you."

She closed her eyes and reached for her memories. As always, Robert's dark face steadied her. "He is a very good man. Honest, brave, true . . ."

"And he loves you." She heard the faint hint of wistfulness in Sir Warin's voice, as though he hoped for an answer other than the nod of her head that she gave in reply. "And you love him." These words came more heavily.

"Yes," she whispered.

His hand came beneath her chin and lifted up her face. She opened her eyes and let him gaze into her heart.

He sighed. "So I see." His thumb moved to wipe away a tear that trickled down her cheek. "Then there is nothing more for me to say." He took her hands and drew her to her feet. "Perhaps it would be as well if we returned to the hall before your squire comes to call us."

He tucked her hand in his arm again, but to her relief and gratitude, engaged only in careful, detached observations of the garden's sundry beauties as they walked. By the time she rejoined her mother, she had blinked her eyes dry once more. If she could not smile cheerfully, she smiled nonetheless, and knew by the way her mother's worried face relaxed that her demeanor reassured Lady Leah that naught but a proper courtesy had attended her daughter's stroll with their hostess's son.

32

arguerite hesitated outside of Odo's cottage. It was barely past dawn, but the faint glow beneath the planks of the door told her that Odo had risen early. She half-wished she had found the cottage dark. She would have returned to the keep and left him to his slumbers. But delay would make it no easier. This was the reason she had come to Winbourne. She had not realized it until she had lain awake all night reliving again and again her exchange with Sir Warin. Would she confess to the knight what she would not to her beloved Odo? No. She could turn her back on everything else in her world. But she could not turn her back on Odo without him knowing why.

She scratched at the door, chiding herself for cowardice for not knocking boldly. But Odo's keen ears heard, for he responded with dismaying promptness. The door swung open. He stood inside the threshold garbed in a dark, ankle-length tunic of the unobtrusive style he always wore, his unembellished silver crucifix shining white against his breast.

His grey eyes registered surprise when he saw her. "Marguerite." He glanced at the pale pink spreading in the sky behind the towers of the keep.

"It is very early, I know," she said, "but . . . may I come in?"

"Of course, child." He took her arm and guided her gently over the threshold. The brace of candles on the table threw into relief the concern on his face. "Is something wrong? Is there trouble in the keep? Or news of your father—?"

"No, no, my father and everyone in the keep are well," she said quickly.

"It is not that. It—it is just that I could not sleep, and I needed someone to talk to."

He smiled and closed the door. "Then I am glad I am here for you. Come, sit down and tell me what troubles you."

She sat with him at the table. She recognized the ledgers on the parchment sheets that spread beneath the candles.

"You are reviewing manor accounts at this hour?" She drew one of the sheets to her and scanned the columns. "You have changed the distribution of wheat to rye. But Grandfather always favored the rye in winter."

"Aye," Odo said, "the rye is easier to cultivate, but there is a great demand these days for high quality wheat. Noblemen and sadly, even many priests, are no longer content with the black rye bread their peasants eat. Your tenants work harder to grow the wheat, but they are willing for the greater return it brings us."

My tenants. All these years since her grandfather's death Odo had labored to make the manors prosper for her, and for the husband she would one day bring to govern these lands at her side.

Odo slid the ledger sheet out from under her hand. "I hope it is not misgivings of my judgment that makes you lie awake at night and draws those shadows under your eyes?"

She glanced up, startled. Did her face betray her so? She had hoped to find comfort and peace at Winbourne, but even here all she had found were sleepless nights aching for a man who felt a world, and nearly a lifetime, away from her. She felt the faint trembling of her lips before she turned her face away.

"Come, little one, whatever weight you carry in your heart, let me share it. When have we ever kept secrets from one another, you and I?"

She rubbed her hands together. Why should she be so nervous, and of Odo, of all people? At last she said, "I am leaving Winbourne tomorrow, Master Odo."

Again Odo looked surprised. "This is very sudden. Did you not tell me you had come for a month?"

"Yes, but—my mother agrees it is best we return to Dorset."

How could she stay longer and risk another encounter with Sir Warin? He had admitted during dinner that it would be another sennight before he actually left for Poitou. Lady Leah had been relieved at her daughter's announcement this morning. She had never wanted to bring Marguerite to Winbourne in the first place.

"I shall miss you, child," Odo said. "I have enjoyed spending time with you again. But I shall see you soon at Westminster. I trust your father knows that nothing he could conceive would succeed in barring me from attending your wedding to the earl."

Marguerite bit her lip. "There is something I must tell you before I go. For friendship's sake, I would have you hear it from me rather than from my parents, or—or through gossip." She met the chaplain's steady gaze. "I *can* still trust you, Master Odo?"

She thought she saw a flicker of hurt in his eyes, but it might have been a trick of the candlelight.

"Of course you may. What have I done to make you doubt me?"

"Nothing," she said quickly. "It is only—I think Grandfather would not be pleased with what I have done."

"And what is that?"

"I am afraid," she said, dragging out the words now, "that you may not be pleased with me, either." When he said nothing, she drew a deep breath, then let her declaration tumble out. "Master Odo, I am not going to marry the Earl of Saxton."

She braced herself for his shock, a frown, a rebuke. But Odo only sighed.

"I feared as much," he said.

Marguerite stared at him. "You—you are not angry?"

"Angry? When have I ever been angry with you, little one?" He spread his hands on the tabletop. "You are aware how difficult this makes things? You are already betrothed to the earl."

Marguerite was too startled by his response to contradict him. How could he know? He could not, of course. But she had confessed her unhappiness to him that first night at Winbourne. She had not spoken against Saxton, but Odo was clever enough to have guessed, and there had been time since then for him to make the inquiries about the earl's character that he had neglected to make when her father had sent him word that Saxton had asked for her hand.

"The earl is a very powerful man," Odo said. "Spurning him will cause a towering scandal."

"I know." Her throat constricted with emotion. How like him not to chide her, but to speak only words of support.

Odo shuffled the parchment sheets together until they formed a neat stack. "Perhaps the earl can be made to understand. Surely he has no desire for an unwilling bride."

Marguerite thought of Sir Warin and the tournament and shuddered a little. "You do not know Lord Saxton, Master Odo. His pride would not allow such a thing."

Odo frowned. "Pride is a very grave sin, but a very prevalent one. I am sorry to learn of it in the earl. Still, there can be no real shame in giving you up to a man of young Eyvind's standing."

Marguerite stared at the chaplain as he laid the ledger sheet on top of the pile. "Eyvind?"

"Sir Warin is a younger son with no lands of his own," Odo said, riffling through the pile with his thumb until he located a certain page that he slid from the middle, "but I have known him for years. He is an honorable young man, a brave knight, and he holds Lord Audley's favor. It is not unlikely that Audley will be generous in his wedding gift to you." Odo dislodged a second sheet and laid it beside the first. "It will not be the grand match your grandfather always wished for you, but it will be a good match, and if it contents you, it would have contented your grandfather as well."

Marguerite bounced up from the chair. "Odo, are you saying you think that Sir Warin and I—?"

He looked up at her. Whatever expression he saw on her face sent his brows soaring. "Is it not so? You said you had met him at Westminster and you have been much together of late, happily I thought."

Her fingers flew to her lips, half-muffling her, "Oh!" She dropped her hand back to her side. "Odo, I have no wish to marry Sir Warin."

She saw Odo's brows descend again, puzzled. "Not marry—? But you said—"

"Not Sir Warin! Oh, 'tis true" —she blushed— "that he has come to care for me. But I have been honest with him, telling him that he must not hope for my hand. And now—now I must be honest with you, too."

"I wish you might!"

She bristled defensively. "I did not mean to deceive you. How was I to guess you would think—"

Odo stood up, too. "Marguerite, be frank with me. Is there a man or is there not?"

She wished Odo were not so tall. It made the long, black shadow the candles cast over her unusually daunting.

"Yeesss."

"But not Sir Warin."

"No." This word she said more firmly.

Odo's face went hard in a way she had never seen before. "Then who?"

His sober stance made her hesitate. But this was Odo. If she could not trust him, she could trust no man on earth. "His name is Robert Marcel."

She sensed Odo reflecting in the moment of silence that followed.

"I am not familiar with the name," he said at last. "Does the earl know?"

Marguerite smiled without amusement. "Oh, yes, he knows. He found out—Oh, what does it matter how? He knows, so I need feel no guilt. He certainly knows I've no wish to marry him."

"You said the earl was too proud to give you up."

"Well, he shall have to. I am going to marry Rob."

The crease in Odo's brow deepened, then his face smoothed out again. He pressed her back into her chair and moved his own to sit alongside her. "Marguerite, of what like is this man? This Rob?"

His softened expression encouraged her. "Oh, Odo, you should like him. He is—he is wonderful!"

That made Odo smile. "Of course he is, child. But tell me about him. Where did you meet?"

That made her hesitate again. "In Dorset." She watched his face cautiously. "At my betrothal dinner."

"So long ago?" He frowned afresh. "He approached you at your betrothal dinner, knowing you were pledged to another man?"

"It was not like that," she faltered. "Not exactly. I think he did not mean to come between Lord Saxton and me." She remembered Robert's long reluctance to speak his heart to her in the glade and said with certainty, "Nay, I know he did not. But I was so unhappy, and he was so kind, and—and before we knew it, we fell in love."

Odo's look of displeasure deepened. "I must know more of this. Tell me of his family. Who are they? What is their position? Who does this man serve?"

"H-he serves the Earl of Gunthar." She hoped Odo did not notice the stumble in her answer.

"Gunthar?" The frown lifted. "He and your grandfather were friends. I never met him, but your grandfather admired Gunthar as he admired few men. Does your Rob hold lands from him?"

"No, he holds no lands . . ."

"Then he is one of Gunthar's men-at-arms?" Odo asked as she paused. "Or a squire, perhaps, with hopes of knighthood?"

"Nooo . . ."

Odo looked puzzled. "What, then?"

"He—he is a minstrel." There, it was out.

Odo rarely gasped. That he did so now, she knew, reflected his shock. "A what?"

Marguerite slid from her chair to kneel at Odo's side. She found his hands and held them. "He is a minstrel now, but he was once a villein, like you." She squeezed his fingers pleadingly. "Oh, Odo, how can you disapprove?"

Odo still looked stunned, but he said sharply, "Marguerite, you must not judge your young man by me."

"Why not? You are quite the best man I know."

"Marguerite." He shook his head, but she saw a smile twitch at the corners of his mouth. "I did not raise you to be such a minx as this. Flattery will not win my consent to this mad request."

"Oh!" She released his hands and flounced up. "I do not request your consent to anything. That is not why I came here."

Odo's face went more stern than she had ever seen it. "If I do not consent, by the terms of your grandfather's will you will forfeit your inheritance. You know this, Marguerite. I cannot let you marry thus. You have responsibilities."

"Responsibilities? To what, pray?"

"To your family, your inheritance." Marguerite began another protest. "To your grandfather."

That cut her off. It was the one weapon Odo possessed to wound her, and he had used it.

"Marguerite"—his voice gentled, even as it grew more throbbing—"I gave your grandfather my solemn oath that I would care for you and for the lands he loved. He was more than my patron. He was my friend and I will not fail him in this. I will not ask you to marry the Earl of Saxton if you do not wish it, but I expect you to do your duty by the love I know you bore for your grandfather and marry a man he would approve of. A man trained to guard his castles and manage with wisdom the estates he left you. If not Lord Saxton, then a man like Sir Warin."

Marguerite swept across to the bookshelf and gazed into the morning light gathering outside the window. She knew what Odo wanted from her. She knew what her grandfather would have wanted, had he lived. *But you did not live. You left me alone and I have found someone to love me and I cannot live my life for a memory, however dear.*

She twisted her hands together until they hurt. How could she say it without causing an irreparable breech between her and Odo?

"Child." She heard his footstep as he came to stand behind her.

"I am not a child." She had never rebuked him for the endearment before, and even without glancing at him, sensed his surprise. "I am a woman. And I have made my choice."

She heard his soft, indrawn breath. "Very well." At least his voice was even. "Then you are old enough to act with sense and not with passion. Your grandfather left the management of his manors in my care, but he and I both knew I had not the skill to guard his castles. It is why he allowed your father to appoint castellans after his death. Do you think a villein-born minstrel will possess more understanding of defending fortresses than a villein-born priest? No, Marguerite. For your grandfather's sake, I cannot agree to this."

"I have not asked you to," she repeated, her resentment swelling. She had known this moment must come, yet hated that it had done so. To part on such terms as this with Odo would break her heart.

"Do you imagine the Earl of Gunthar will smile on this match?" Odo's tones confirmed his implacable disfavor. "He will turn his minstrel off for such presumption. What shall this man give you then? What sort of life? Come, my lady, you are too clever not to know what you will give up if you marry him."

It stung to hear Odo resort to the formal "my lady." He did not think her eyes were clear. But nothing had ever felt more right than this. "Oh, yes, I know what I shall give up. A man who offers me wealth and position, but no warmth, for there is no warmth in him. I will not live that way, Master Odo. I have been lonely for too long. Rob may offer me few comforts, but he brings me love and happiness."

"Loneliness can be a poor reason for marriage, and especially for such a marriage. I will stop this wedding with Saxton, but Sir Warin would offer you a better match."

"No!" She turned quickly. "You must do nothing about Lord Saxton. I promised my mother that you would not interfere. I will handle the earl myself." Even knowing the gesture would displease Odo, she lifted her chin. "Rob and I will handle the earl."

Odo's mouth grew tight. "How do you know this minstrel is not merely after your wealth? Your inheritance is considerable, and you are very young and pretty. I know how the men of your own birth have shunned you and why. How they fear governing your free manors on their one hand will stir up their own villeins on the other. If one of them has found the courage to defy his peers, he should not be lightly and callously dismissed for a cunning intriguer."

Her face grew hot. "How dare you! When *you* are clever enough to know that Sir Warin would never marry me if I were dowerless. But he is a landless younger son and so has no villeins for my free manors to stir up. However sincere he might be in wanting me, *he* is the one who wants my inheritance as well, not Rob."

Odo's lip curled in a rare manifestation of scorn. "And you are so sure of that because—?"

"Because I offered it to him! I begged Rob to govern my lands at my side, and he refused." That appeared to take Odo aback. She reached out an earnest hand to his arm. "Oh, Odo, how can you judge him thus when you do not even know him?"

Her eyes burned with relief at the swift tenderness with which Odo's hand covered hers. "Marguerite, you cannot expect me to stand silent while you propose to me an intent that will alter the course of your life in ways you cannot possibly foresee. The love that I bear for you compels me to try to make you understand—"

"I do understand. I thought you would, too. You would if you could meet Rob."

"Perhaps." But Odo's mouth remained grave.

"I did not flatter when I said he was like you. He thinks, like you, that all men should be free. Have you not said the same all my life? Shall I not honor him for his beliefs?"

"Because you honor him, you need not marry him."

"Oh!" She pulled her hand away. "It was for the love I bear *you* that I came here today, rather than riding away tomorrow without telling you of my intent. But I do not ask your permission. I shall marry Rob no matter how you frown. No power that Grandfather granted you will stop me, short of locking me up in a tower."

The merest hint of a smile brushed across Odo's lips. "I would," he said, "but you would never forgive me if I did. And that I could not bear."

Though they stood a pace apart, his affection enfolded her as strongly as if he had taken her in his arms.

"Then if you cannot trust Rob," she said, "trust me. He does not marry me for my inheritance. He is too—" She bit off the word *proud*, remembering how Odo condemned that trait. "He wishes to provide for me himself, as any honest man would." Odo would like that in a man. She hoped. She hesitated, then asked the question that had nagged in the back of her mind ever since she had made her decision in the glade. "What will happen to my lands—when I marry without your consent?"

"I suspect your father will fight to claim them in his own name," Odo said, "but without another heir by your mother the crown will likely demand that they stand forfeit, if not before your father's death, then certainly after. Your grandfather's lands are too fat a prize for King John to overlook."

She did not care about the other lands, she had never lived on them. But Winbourne. Her chest hurt at the thought of this castle, her home, one day going to strangers.

Odo must have seen the emotion in her face. "If you wish me to fight to preserve them for you—"

She shook her head. She remembered Robert's strong refusal in the glade when she had asked him to govern Winbourne with her. Even had she found Odo willing to bend, she knew Robert never would. She had made her choice long before she had set foot once more on Winbourne. She had chosen Robert and nothing, not Odo, not this manor that she loved, would alter that.

"You are so sure of this man?" Odo asked quietly.

That question eased her heart. "Very sure." She gazed at Odo's dear face. The ache ebbed into regret. "I wanted so much for you to understand."

Light flowed through the window now, setting a soft glow to his features. "I do understand, little one, better than you think. Whatever else this Rob might offer you, he will not offer you a life of ease. You've no notion how difficult things are outside your own world, the struggles that take place each day to survive. You were not reared to such a life. And you are so young."

"Young enough to learn," she said. "And I am willing. And if I am not strong enough—if I should die—then I shall die as Rob's wife, and have no regrets."

Odo gazed at her, grave and worried. "I cannot dissuade you?"

"No. But you might give me your blessing." She held her breath for his response.

He laid a gentle hand on her head. "You have that always."

A lump swelled in her throat. She reached up and set a kiss to his cheek. "Thank you," she whispered in his ear. "Someday I will bring Rob to meet you, and then you will see that I chose aright."

She prayed Heaven might be kind enough to bring about such a day. But if it did not . . . She embraced Odo and let herself out of the cottage before he could see her tears.

33

La Rochelle ~ Poitou
May 1214

The stationer thumped the bundle of parchment down on his counter. "The Earl of Gunthar usually sends his squire."

"The squire had other things to do today." Robert had feared he would have to rely on the limited French he had learned as Gunthar's secretary to communicate his mission, but to his relief, the stationer spoke a heavily accented English. He must have found it to his benefit to learn the tongue of the English troops who passed through the city of La Rochelle

Robert scanned the shop shelves with their rows of quill pens, pots of vari-colored ink, pumice stones, wooden boards for book covers, and dozens of other items for bookmaking and correspondence. He pointed to a stack of parchment double the length of the sheets on the counter. "How much for those?"

"Those are for folding into quires. This is what you want." The stationer gave a confident pat to the stack. "Good parchment, precut to your master's needs."

"If I cut those down myself," Robert said, his finger aimed steadily at the larger stack, "it will save you the trouble of sizing more like this for Lord Saxton's secretary, or even the king's." His other hand tapped the bundle on the table. "And for sparing you the labor and time, I will only ask one-half off the price."

The stationer sniffed. "Gunthar's squire never quibbles with my prices but lays out whatever silver I ask."

"I am not a gullible squire, and I know inflated prices when I hear them."

349

In truth, Robert had no notion how much parchment sold for in Poitou or even the ratio of English shillings to Poitevin deniers. But he had never known a shopkeeper in England who would not squeeze a customer for as much as he could and imagined Poitevin shopkeepers could not be much different. Gunthar might be rich enough to shrug off being exploited, but it went against Robert's thrifty grain to dole out a farthing more than he deemed something was worth.

"I will give you two-thirds," Robert said, "and pay you full price for the ink." He saw the regret in the stationer's eye that he had already named the cost of the latter. "Come, I can see from your shelves that you have no more parchment sized for correspondence. You'd have to cut those down to make more anyway. 'Tis a fair offer I make to do it for you."

"Three-fourths."

"Two-thirds and not a denier more."

The stationer studied Robert, taking his measure, then sighed. "Very well, sir."

Robert glanced at the soft wool of his sleeve when the stationer called him *sir*. Gunthar had insisted Robert trade his rough homespun for something more befitting a member of his inner household. Robert had bought a new tunic with the income Gunthar paid him, but he had kept the color and cut subdued, not wishing to encourage more remarks about his opportunistic advantage of Gunthar's advancing age than Robert already overheard muttered rather loudly behind his back by men throughout the king's camp.

The stationer pulled up a footstool to help him reach the larger parchment. Robert heard him mumble "English pinchfist," under his breath, but the stationer forced a thin smile as he handed the stack to Robert. Robert counted out the agreed upon coins, slid the parchment and ink into the leather pouch he had brought for that purpose, and started back to the fortress where the king and his army were housed.

Gunthar had kept Robert in close quarters ever since their return to La Rochelle. Gunthar's shoulder was healing. He had cast off his sling, but he still spent hours a day dictating to Robert correspondence delegated to him by the king. When Robert was not inscribing semi-official letters in Latin to the Poitevin clergy and baronage, he was writing an endless stream of instructions from Gunthar to the officials he had left in charge of his manors in England. Occasionally, when the earl was rushed, Robert even wrote a reassuring report to Lady Helen that her husband was safe and well. Robert had glimpsed one of Gunthar's own handwritten notes to his wife. Such illegible handwriting from a man as educated and refined as the Earl of Gunthar had sparked Robert into laughter before he could check himself. Gunthar had merely grinned and shrugged, and after that Robert had known how sincerely his talents were needed.

Still, much as Robert loved the smell of parchment and ink, he had begun to chafe at his weeks-long confinement to the office Gunthar had set up in the castle. He had not really expected Gunthar to agree to let him take the squire Ralf's place in buying more parchment for Gunthar's never-ending correspondence, but after a hesitant pause, Gunthar had tossed Robert the pouch of coins and simply told him not to dally along the way.

Robert tried therefore not to drag his feet about returning to the fortress. But it had been so long since he had felt this free. The quickest way back to his destination was through the apothecaries street, but someone's pigs had gotten free and were foraging so noisily through the refuse in the drainage channels that a perfume maker, a spice seller, and an herbalist came charging out of their respective shops shouting obscenities and swinging their brooms.

Robert veered north and found himself in the street of smiths. The din was different here. Goldsmiths, silversmiths, and a pewtersmith shouted invitations to view their wares at a swarm of disinterested men and women who, like Robert, had chosen this detour to avoid the pigs. A few yapping dogs running free in the street ran over to the shopkeepers, some of whom tossed them scraps, while others drove them away with a flapping of hands that were thankfully empty of brooms.

Robert could not afford silver or gold, and had no need of the blacksmith's services at the end of the street. But when the pewtersmith hailed him, he wandered over to survey the items laid out on a trestle table set outside beneath the window. Poor man's silver, some called the composite metal, and surely this pitcher with the lion engraved on its side and these elaborately garlanded candlesticks were polished to so high a sheen as to rival their more expensive counterparts in the neighboring silver shop.

Gunthar had paid Robert well. He picked up a pendant of rich blue glass that cleverly mimicked a sapphire, with six pewter rosebuds studded at intervals along either side of its chain. The way the glass glistened in the sunlight could not be more enchanting than the sparkle he envisioned in

Marguerite's eyes when he imagined himself clasping it around her neck. Thanks to Gunthar, the purchase price lay within his means. Robert had more money than he had ever earned in his life. But . . .

He sighed and set the pendant back down. Gunthar would find a better secretary than a makeshift scribe drafted from the battlefield when they returned to England, and it was absurd to think Robert could continue as the earl's minstrel once he had absconded with Marguerite. He would need every shilling he had earned to support Marguerite in relative comfort until he could find a position in a less public household than Gunthar's. She would be pleased enough with Gunthar's garnet ring, he told himself. Assuming Gunthar truly found a way to absolve Robert of the murders, for Robert did not know how he could return to Marguerite at all, otherwise.

He turned away from the pewtersmith and rejoined the crowd that flowed down the street. Some paces ahead of him strolled a man with a spring green mantle and a red, curling feather stuck in the embroidered band of his black round cap. Robert's hair prickled along the back of his neck, some instinct flaring into recognition before the active thought flashed into his mind. *Kit.*

Somewhat to Robert's frustration, Gunthar had kept him too busy to pursue his suspicions of his former master. Every time Robert mentioned it, Gunthar said he would deal with the matter and commanded Robert to return to his correspondence. Even if Kit were headed someplace entirely mundane, Robert could not resist the urge to follow him now.

After all, this is why I came to Poitou. To sniff out Lord Garoux's mischief against my father, and what did I do but find you ear-deep in mischief of your own. Treason and murder . . . what else are you up to, Kit Beckford?

With so many people milling in the road it was easy to follow him without Robert drawing attention to himself. He saw Kit at length turn aside into the blacksmith's shop. Robert fingered the dagger at his hip. Gunthar thought Robert's sword might prove too great a provocation when so many knights still mistrusted him, but he allowed Robert to continue to carry the smaller blade. Robert paused just outside the smithy's door.

"You came alone?" a subdued voice said from within. It carried the same accent as the stationer, though less heavy.

"As you see." Kit's voice. Robert would not forget those smoothly smug tones to his dying breath. "The smith?"

"An old friend of mine. He went off without question and will not return until Sext."

Robert had learned that the canonical hour that fell midmorning in England in the spring, remained at midday year round in Poitou. The Church bells still chimed the hours here, where no interdict lay to smother them.

"I cannot stay long," he heard Kit say. "I am supposed to be drilling Gunthar's squires. I told them the hilt of my sword had loosened and that I must come to the blacksmith's to mend it. But Gunthar will not like it if he learns that I left."

"Then let us not waste time. Lock the door from within," the first voice said, "then come with me."

A mundane sword repair did not require locked doors. Awash with suspicion, Robert slipped around to the back of the smithy before Kit could glimpse him near the door. The window at the rear that helped relieve the smoke from the forge was shuttered, but it appeared that the latch had not caught. A crack of light escaped from inside where the wooden boards had not fastened tight. Robert maneuvered as close as he dared to the opening. As he'd hoped, the occupants had retreated to the rear of the smithy to continue their conversation.

"And so?" the voice with the Poitevin accent said. Robert wondered if Kit had insisted on English as he had with the Frenchman in the woods, the better to guard against foreign eavesdroppers less likely to have learned the English tongue than the stationer had.

"And so," Kit replied, "with the Earl of Saxton's help, it is arranged, my lord. Saxton has convinced the king to be generous in his terms with you. The marriage of John's daughter to your heir will irrevocably bind your loyalty to him, especially as John will, of course, take your son back to England as hostage for your future good behavior."

Robert's heart thudded. Gunthar had told him just this morning of the king's decision to marry his daughter, Joan, to the son of the Count of La Marche. The Poitevin scheming with Kit in the blacksmith's shop must be Hugh de Lusignan.

"You told Saxton of our plan?" the count said sharply.

"I am not a fool. Saxton would be aghast if he knew. He'd see my neck in a noose and yours on a pike. He suspects I am involved in something . . . let us say, subversive, but he's no notion what and said he'd ask no questions if

I helped him to remove 'an obstacle in his path.'" Kit responded with the coolness he always struck when he thought himself in command of a matter.

"How did you give yourself away to Saxton?"

"He stumbled upon my first encounter with Felcourt near the river by Lord Malefay's Castle. I'd seen Saxton storming about the camp earlier, lashing every man he saw with that curst icy tongue of his. He must have been out walking late at night, trying to cool his temper, when he came across us. I turned and saw him watching us, but he did not stand near enough to overhear our words. He'd seen Felcourt pass me money in the moonlight, though, and he took my pouch when Felcourt fled, and turned out the coins and saw they were French. And he guessed—subversion."

That must have been the night Robert had seen Kit and Saxton return to Gunthar's camp together. Kit had obviously changed location for his next rendezvous with the Frenchman, not knowing that Robert would follow him.

"Saxton is the king's man." The count sounded angry and wary. "He rode with John to Angoulême when John stole Isabella from me. I will never forget Saxton's gloating face alongside the king's when they bound me in shackles and dragged me to Normandy. You expect me to trust him now?"

"You may safely trust his own willful ignorance," Kit replied. "Saxton is an Englishman and says the king should be content to be one, too. He said, 'I've no interest in Normandy, Poitou, or any other foreign domains. So long as whatever it is you conspire does not touch England itself, I prefer to remain deaf and blind. If it returns us all the sooner to our homes, then I might actually thank you. And my gratitude will be the more abundant if you help me with my obstacle.'"

"His obstacle. He means Gunthar, of course." Robert heard the hard cynicism in the count's voice. "Word is all over the camp that the two of them are vying for influence over the king. A pity. 'Tis said that Gunthar spoke for me when the king bound me in chains. But if he is the price for Saxton's unwitting help, then so be it." A pause. Then, "What has Saxton offered you?" in the same sneering tones.

"One of Gunthar's manors." Kit said it as lightly as if such benefices fell into his lap every day.

"And when he learns that our 'subversion' will, indeed, touch England?"

"Ah, who is to say how deeply it will do so? That, I suppose, will depend on whether England loves King John as much as they loved his brother, Richard."

Hearty laughter rang from both men through the shutters. The jest eluded Robert. He had only been ten when the last king died, and to villeins, the passing of one sovereign and succession of another had scarcely been noticed.

"Do you suppose Saxton will view it thus when he learns what he unknowingly countenanced?" the count asked. Caution tinted the remains of humor in his voice.

"I think when that revelation strikes him, he will be astute enough to choose discretion."

"I suppose we shall have to try again with Gunthar to keep Saxton quiet, then," the count said. "I hope you do not blame me that the mercenaries I set on Gunthar seven weeks ago failed? The captain told me one of Gunthar's own footsoldiers turned on him in the middle of the battle and had his blade to Gunthar's throat . . . ?" The count trailed off, a subtle question in his voice.

To Robert's surprise, Kit did not answer immediately. Had the men drawn away to another part of the smithy? Robert drew in and held a deep breath as he nudged the shutter closest to him inward just enough to allow him to peer with one eye through the wider gap. A murky orange glow from a forge that had been allowed to cool from a yellow blaze in its master's absence, cast the only light in the otherwise darkened room. Robert could only see one man, but he recognized the profile of his former lord. Kit held a poker in his hand and was passing it in and out of the small fire that still guttered in the forge.

"Aye," Kit said slowly, the first hint of displeasure coloring his cool tones as he spoke to the man beyond Robert's vision. "The footsoldier was mine and he'd have finished off the job your mercenaries bungled had that upstart *minstrel* not interfered." He made a sudden, savage stab at the flames.

"The man Gunthar appointed as his secretary?" asked the elusive count. "He is no stranger to you, I take it."

He must have noticed, as Robert had, the malicious slur in the way Kit spoke the word "minstrel." So, Kit had indeed recognized Robert in the woods the night they had struggled. Then he had known for weeks that Robert was in Gunthar's camp.

"I knew the man some years ago. He was a troublemaker then, and he is a troublemaker now. I want him eliminated along with Saxton's obstacle. You must ask the king that the betrothal of your son to his daughter, along with all accompanying pledges of loyalty between the house of Lusignan to the house of Plantagenet, be recorded. And because of bad blood between you both in the past and to insure against any 'accidental miswording,' the recording must be done by a magnate acknowledged by you both as a man of scrupulous integrity. Even the king will agree that will eliminate Saxton."

The corner of Kit's mouth lifted in snide humor to the count's responsive chuckle.

"The obvious choice will therefore fall on Gunthar," Kit continued, "and Gunthar will bring his secretary to inscribe the actual words. The rest should be easy. That is, if you are sure your uncle's castle can repulse an assault by the king's troops."

"Mervant Castle is impregnable," the count said proudly. "By the time they realize—"

A sudden baying made Robert start away from the window. One of the hounds he'd seen earlier in the street had wandered around the back of the smithy and set up a greeting, bowing and wagging a friendly tail.

"What the blazes!" thundered the count.

Robert heard the swift tread of footsteps echo against the workshop's wooden floor. He ran, darting around the hound, but the shutters slammed back so quickly he could not be sure if the count had glimpsed him. The hound followed, barking excitedly. They rounded the smithy together, but Robert checked when he reached the street. Kit already stood in the smithy's doorway, scanning the crowd that flowed past. He must have bolted for the entrance, hoping to catch any fleeing eavesdropper when the count made for the window.

Robert's heart pounded. How was he to reach the crowd without being seen? While Kit's head was turned the opposite way, Robert picked up a stray stick, flung it at Kit's feet, then pressed back along the side of the smithy as the dog ran yapping to Kit. When Robert peered around the corner, the dog was leaping about Kit with the stick in its mouth, distracting him with its pleas to play. Robert eased himself into a cluster of men striding past the smithy, but when he knew himself even with the door, he could not resist casting a glance Kit's way. Kit must have tossed the stick, for the dog had run off, leaving Kit free to catch Robert's eye. Robert held his gaze in challenge, then calmly walked on.

Gunthar dropped down in the sprawling chair behind his desk and curved his long, tapered fingers around the lions' heads at the end of the armrests. "Well, that was an ugly scene. You'd think after nearly fifty years, I'd be accustomed to watching a Plantagenet swearing and blaspheming and frothing at the mouth while he destroyed the furniture with his bare hands and threatened to lop a man's head from his shoulders. I'd have felt sorry for John's victim if it had been anyone but Saxton."

Robert noticed that Gunthar still frowned across the desk at him. He set down the pen he had been using to translate Gunthar's scrawls into a decipherable document. "The king believed you then?"

"Nay, he did not give me a chance to tell him. The count must have panicked when he realized you'd overheard him and Beckford, for he never returned from the blacksmith's shop. According to the guards at the city gate, he fled the town yesterday before the bells of Sext." The fingers of Gunthar's right hand thrummed against the lion's head. "The king summoned his council this morning to vent his rage, and Saxton bore the brunt of it. John raved that Saxton had shown clear sympathy with the Lusignans by persuading the king to pledge his daughter to the count's heir. The count proved his perfidy, John screamed, by breaking the truce he and John had struck and fleeing like a felonious rebel to hold his uncle's castle of Mervant against him. For there can be little doubt that is where the count has gone." Gunthar's hand left the armrest to rub his left shoulder.

"The count told Beckford his uncle's fortress was impregnable," Robert said. "Perhaps you would be more comfortable with the sling again, sir."

"Nay, it's the damp. My bones would ache the same with or without a sling."

Robert rose and crossed the room to pour out a goblet of wine. He and Gunthar had worked in a curious sort of harmony over these past weeks. Robert had expected the earl to treat him with at least a subtle condescension designed to remind him of his lowly birth. But while there had been a few sharp clashes between them, those had mostly fallen in the early days, before Robert had discerned that an acerbic quip from Gunthar usually occurred when the earl grew tired or when his shoulder pained him. Robert acknowledged himself too defensive of remarks that, in retrospect, were no more barbed at him than at any of Gunthar's other men. So Robert had learned to bite his tongue at the rare flashes of ill-temper, and to watch for lines of weariness or discomfort in Gunthar's face.

Gunthar took the goblet from Robert with a faint twinkle in his eyes. Robert always poured wine to ease Gunthar's still mending shoulder when he rejected the suggestion of the sling.

"I was not going to snap at you," Gunthar murmured. "My ears are still ringing too loudly with John's oaths to leave me with the enthusiasm to summon one myself."

"I did not think it, sir," Robert said, resuming his seat on the other side of the desk. "You have not snapped at me for a fortnight." *Until yesterday.*

"And you have exercised an unnatural restraint by not retorting the way you used to." *Until yesterday*, lay the unspoken echo between them. "Aye, I say unnatural. If you were not born with a hot rejoinder on your tongue, then I have lost my last wit to judge a man."

Robert laughed. "My father had a hot temper, though he never turned it on his family. My mother always said I was too much like him."

"We all of us are, alas. Too much like our parents until someone comes along to steady us a bit. I hope your lass will do that for you, as mine did for me."

Robert picked up the pen again and resumed his transcription. 'Twas not the first time Gunthar had tried to lure him into talking of Marguerite. As always, Robert dodged. "Tell me the rest, sir. I can finish this while I listen."

He heard the soft swish of Gunthar drawing a drink before he answered.

"John cursed us all as gullible fools for believing the count's reconciliation with him genuine. Of course, John was the gullible one and he knew it, which only made him shout at all of us the louder."

"You weren't fooled." Robert glanced up. "I saw the long, measuring way you studied the count when we returned from the ambush. He has a sly, arrogant look about him. You saw it, I am certain. Did you suspect him of setting the ambush on us even then?"

Gunthar took another drink. "I have known Hugh de Lusignan for over twenty years and he has always been 'sly and arrogant,' as you put it. Aye, I suspected him. I did not think he would so easily forgive his humiliating shackling by the king. I confess, though, I thought the count had set the trap to flaunt his defiance of John and establish himself the leader of those still holding out against John in rebellion. It is not the first time an enemy of the king's has tried to send him a message by murdering me."

Robert dropped the pen, alarmed at these words. "The count has tried before?"

"Nay," Gunthar said. "Eight-and-thirty years ago, in Henry's day, by another traitor long since dead. It is a risk all take who stand on the king's high council. A strike against any of us while on an errand representing the king is a strike against the king himself. And I was on the king's errand that day, sent to escort the Count of La Marche to John's camp here in La Rochelle. I knew from what you told me you'd overheard in the woods that Beckford and the count were—let us say, less loyal than they strove to appear. And of course, I'd guessed from the attack in my tent that Saxton wanted me dead, and that he had likely enlisted Beckford's assistance. But it had not crossed my mind that Beckford would draw the count into Saxton's feud with me."

Gunthar took one last sip from the goblet, then set it down. "John must carry some doubt of the truth of his own accusations, for when he was done screaming, he ordered Saxton out of his sight, but left him at liberty. I have not been at court for twelve years, but from the look on Saxton's face I gather John had never turned on him like that before. 'Twas the first time I have seen fear in Saxton's eyes." Gunthar leaned forward, his elbows on the desk, and laced his fingers together. "'Twill make him the more dangerous. I do not fear a repeat of the attack in my tent. I have my guards about me, and they are at heightened alert since the ambush. But you—"

"I am not afraid of Saxton." Robert said.

"Then you are a fool," Gunthar replied. "You have most inconveniently saved my life twice. Saxton will not forget that. He tried to revive the charges against you to the king, but John was too maddened over the Count of La Marche to listen. While John was kicking over a bench in the hall and stomping it into firewood, he even accused Saxton of pettily setting you up to spite me, solely because I favored you. Then he shouted that he wished to hear no more of the matter and that if Saxton were the loyal man he insisted, he would have his men ready to ride with the king's at dawn tomorrow to bring down the walls of Mervant Castle."

Robert pushed himself half-way up from the chair before he caught himself. "I am no longer suspected of the crimes?"

"Not by the king. At least, not for now. But do not expect the men of the camp to dismiss their doubts of you so easily. And above all, do not underestimate Saxton's ability to land on his feet."

Robert scarcely heard him. His mind tumbled with joyful visions of his reunion with Marguerite, unstained by lies and black allegations.

Gunthar slapped his hands on the desk, reclaiming Robert's attention. He held Robert's eyes with a gaze so stern Robert had seen other men crumble at it. He recognized the annoyed flaring of Gunthar's nostrils when Robert failed to even flinch.

"He means you harm," Gunthar said of Saxton. "Why can you not get that through your skull? And it is not only because of me. If you would but tell me how you angered him, I would know the better how to protect you."

It still baffled Robert why Gunthar should wish to, but it stirred a little pool of warmth in him, as well, to hear Gunthar say it.

"Thank you, sir, but I am quite capable of protecting myself."

"What, with that impetuous head of yours that sent you chasing after Beckford yesterday? What if he and the count had caught you? Do you think they'd have let you leave that blacksmith's shop alive?"

Robert shrugged. "They did not catch me."

He had told Gunthar everything, except that he had let Kit see him. Gunthar had cursed him too roundly for taking the risk he had by listening at the window. Then Robert had lost his temper when Gunthar let it slip that he had only allowed Robert to go to the stationer's shop because Gunthar had sent Beckford out to drill his squires for the day and knew Saxton had been with the king.

"I do not need to be guarded like a child!" Robert had flashed.

To which Gunthar had replied with a glacial dryness, "A child would have obeyed me and come straight back like I told you to."

Robert had stalked out of the office, knowing any other lord would take his abrupt departure as an unforgivable insult, but knowing, as well, that Gunthar would have inexplicably forgiven him by morning. And so Gunthar had, behaving as though the quarrel had never occurred until just now.

Gunthar glared at him across the desk, then flung himself back in the chair with an exasperated sigh. "If I get you back to England in one piece, it will be a miracle. We may at least thank the heavens that Beckford has not glimpsed you yet."

Robert bit his lip. Gunthar had told him that Kit had not fled with the count. Why should he? Again Robert had no proof of what he'd heard, and yesterday Saxton was still in favor with the king.

"We ride with the king tomorrow as well," Gunthar said. "And much though I should like to leave you here, you proved yourself too good a fighter during the ambush and the king is demanding every man who knows how to wield a sword to join his assault on Mervant Castle. Saxton will be with his own troops, but Beckford is one of my men. I suppose it is useless to ask you to keep your head down?"

"I could not see the enemy with my head down, sir."

Reluctant laughter gleamed in Gunthar's eyes at Robert's reply, but he held his mouth set firm against a smile. "At least try to keep it attached to your shoulders, then. It was trouble enough to replace one secretary. If you have any pity at all for a weary old man, you will save me the necessity of replacing two."

Gunthar pushed himself to his feet, wincing only slightly before cautiously rolling his left shoulder. Robert's own humor dissolved in fretting concern. He hoped it was only age that slowed the bone's knitting and not some unseen complication. If anyone should stay behind from a battle, it should be Gunthar until both his arms were hale again. He would not, of course. Robert wished the earl would at least wear the sling until they came to the walls of Mervant. *But he will not do that, either.*

Gunthar picked up the goblet and swallowed another mouthful of wine. "Finish those documents I gave you. That should keep you out of mischief for the rest of the day, at least. Then bring your lute to my chamber this evening." He paused. "That is, I would enjoy one or two of your songs, if you would?"

Robert knew it was not easy for a man as powerful as Gunthar to request rather than command. He wondered why the earl made such an effort to do so. Gunthar worked Robert hard during daylight hours, but it was rare he did not ask for Robert's music before they retired for the night. Gunthar said the songs reminded him of Lady Helen.

"Certainly, sir," Robert said.

Gunthar set down the goblet with a tiny *thud* against the wood, then gave a curt nod of thanks and went out.

34

John had a multitude of faults, Gunthar said to Robert as they watched Hugh de Lusignan, Count of La Marche, kneel abjectly with his uncle Geoffrey before the king, but when roused to an Angevin wrath, John also had his father's military genius. That genius had devastated the rebellious Lusignans.

Mervant Castle, that "impregnable fortress," had fallen on the eve of Pentacost after less than a full day's assault by King John's army. The count in dismay had fled with his uncle to the castle of Voucant, but after a three day siege, the king's battle engines had threatened to bring those walls down, as well. Nephew and uncle gave up the fight and threw themselves on the king's mercy.

At Parthenay on Trinity Sunday, King John accepted renewed homage and fealty from the Count of La Marche and Geoffrey de Lusignan. Those Poitevin barons who had formerly held themselves aloof from the king, came quickly to heel at seeing the powerful count thus discomfited. They gathered together at John's command to witness the marriage contract between his daughter Joan and the count's heir. Robert wondered if the count would insist that the Earl of Gunthar record the contract, as the count and Kit had once plotted, but the sly, arrogant count apparently knew himself no longer in a position to challenge any demand the king chose to make, and so the king's clerks were summoned for the recording instead of Robert.

With his greatest opposition now removed in Poitou, King John at last determined himself strong enough to confront the forces of King Philip of France. His first goal was to retake the lost Angevin lands of his fathers. And so at the beginning of June, the army marched northwest towards the borders of Maine.

Robert had resumed his place with the footsoldiers. With Hanley dead, and unaware that Kit knew Robert was in the camp, Gunthar thought the anonymity of his infantry the safest place to keep Robert hidden. But on the second day of the march, everything halted. Fever struck overnight and spread swiftly through the army. Among others of Gunthar's men, it laid low his body squire, Antony.

Thrice a day, Gunthar sent his second squire, Ralf, for reports on the ill in his camp. Lest the rest of his hours remain idle, he drafted Robert to fill both their time by dictating a flood of fresh orders to the officials on his English manors. Only when Ralf came back an hour before dusk, weary and worried for Antony, did Gunthar attempt to distract the youth by ordering him to address the documents Robert had written, and excused Robert to fetch some supper.

Robert sat outside Gunthar's tent to eat his bowl of bean and herring stew. He smiled and made room on the bench when Richard Channing joined him with a bowl of his own.

"Between those two wretched earls, I thought we'd never get to talk again," Richard said with a grimace.

Robert had observed during the march how Richard rode with Saxton's troops. What Saxton had done with that surly squire of his, Nicholas Tybert, Robert could not guess, but he had not seen the youth since before Saxton had locked Robert up in that tower in La Rochelle. With the death of Richard's former master, Saxton appeared to have commanded Richard's service in Tybert's place.

"Absurd, is it not, that Gunthar has made me his secretary?" Robert swallowed a spoonful of onion-laced broth.

"That was a rare piece of luck for you. You never told me you could read and write. You'll find your purse well-lined when we get back to England."

Richard gave Robert a playful jostle with his elbow before slurping his stew rather noisily. Robert's pleasure at seeing Richard dimmed a little when he remembered how he was depending on that well-lined purse to enable him to run away with Richard's cousin.

A footstep crunched. Robert set the bowl in his lap and looked up at a tall, broad-shouldered knight who paused before them to glance from Robert's face to Richard's.

"Your pardon, gentlemen. I am looking for Richard Channing. I was told I might find him here."

"I'm Channing," Richard said.

The knight smiled and drew a folded sheet of parchment from his belt. Robert saw the red wax seal it bore.

"I bring you greetings from your cousin, the Lady Marguerite of Winbourne." The knight handed the parchment to Richard. "She hopes this finds you well and trusts your wound has healed?"

Richard rose as he took the letter. "Oh, yes, long since," he said with a guilty flush. "I suppose I ought to have written, but it is such a bore." He tossed a teasing glance at Robert. "I ought to have had you write it for me, eh, Rob?"

Robert rose, too, studying the knight's strong build and the cocky brown curls that fell over his forehead. "Gunthar leaves me no time to write for myself," he said lightly. "How then for you?"

Richard laughed and broke the seal on the letter. Robert resisted a temptation to shift near enough to catch a glimpse of his love's hand and perhaps a word or two of her welfare. He battled his impatience until he saw Richard cease scanning the parchment and begin to fold it closed again.

"Is she well? Your cousin?" Robert strove to sound no more than politely interested.

"Oh, aye," Richard said. "She is visiting her grandfather's manor. Things are 'different.' The castellan's wife has changed some of the tapestries and they are planting wheat instead of rye this year." He rolled his eyes, then looked back at the knight. "It was good of you to bring me this. Have you just arrived from England? How is it you come from my cousin?"

Just what Robert had wondered.

The light of the day was dimming, but Robert thought a faint, ruddy color stole into the knight's face. "I suffered an unfortunate mishap before the king set sail and was forced to spend time recuperating at my father's home in Northumberland. I met your cousin while out riding one day and she was kind enough to befriend me. I am quite recovered now, and so I have come to join my father in support of the king. I offered to bear any letters your cousin wished to send her father, and she asked if I would carry this one to you, as well."

"Thank you," Richard said. "Will you tell me your name?"

"Sir Warin Eyvind."

Richard looked startled. Robert saw him stare hard at the knight.

"Eyvind? But I remember you now. That 'unfortunate mishap' was the blow you took in the tournament at Westminster." Richard glanced at Robert. "Saxton dealt Sir Warin a strike with the lance that pierced his mail and came near to piercing his heart."

Sir Warin's color had deepened on Richard's mention of the tournament, though he sought to shrug his humiliation off with an easy smile. "I fought carelessly that day. That I fell while wearing your cousin's favor is my only shame."

Robert fought a downward turn at the corners of his mouth, but he must have made some movement, for Richard glanced at him again.

"Forgive my manners. Sir Warin, this is Rob Marcel. He serves as secretary to the Earl of Gunthar, but prefers to be known by his trade as a minstrel."

Robert refused to bow, but he gave the knight a curt nod of his head. "Your servant, Sir Warin."

Sir Warin inclined his head more slowly. His gaze slid over Robert's tunic and hose. Though an improvement over his much-patched homespun, Robert knew the quality of the cloth still set him beneath a man of Sir Warin's status. Robert recognized the gleam of disdain in the knight's eyes when they returned to Robert's face, as he did the challenging lift of Sir Warin's brows when Robert held his gaze boldly.

"Sir." The knight spoke the acknowledgment almost as a rebuke.

Robert felt his temper slipping, but just then the flap of Gunthar's tent pulled back and the squire Ralf looked out.

"Marcel, the earl is asking for you."

Robert excused himself to Richard and Sir Warin, and went inside the tent.

"Light the lantern before you go, Ralf," Gunthar said to the youth.

Ralf obeyed, returned Robert's smile, though rather wearily, and left him alone with the earl.

"Sit," Gunthar said. "I forgot the instructions to Rushall's bailiff, reminding him to double the winter sowing of rye this year. I already sealed the letter to my steward, so I'll have to send independently to Osborne. And I've thought of another matter or two that might need tending at Selberry and Norcott Castles. My chaplain can carry the orders for me into York-shire, he has family there whom he will be glad to see." Gunthar paused. "Do you mind? The courier is leaving in the morning and I would prefer these all go at once." He waved a hand over the stack of sealed parchments that lay before him on the desk.

"Of course I do not mind, sir." Robert sat down, sharpened the quill, and drew over a blank parchment sheet.

But even as he recorded the earl's new instructions, distraction nagged at him. Just because a man had arrived bearing letters entrusted to him by Marguerite, Robert told himself he had no cause to doubt her faith. Sir Warin had been a neighbor to her grandfather's manor. Perhaps she had known the family since childhood. It was natural that on learning Sir Warin was coming to Poitou, Marguerite should send letters to her father and cousin by his hand. No, Robert should not be concerned by a tall, handsome knight with tumbling brown curls who moved with an athletic grace Robert had observed stirred sighs of admiration in women.

But what had been that talk about Sir Warin wearing her favor in a tour-nament? And what was she doing at her grandfather's estate in Northum-berland? Robert had clung for all these long, lonely months to the sweet promises they had exchanged in the glade. But before she had whispered, "I will go to the ends of the earth with you," she had asked him to govern her grandfather's lands with her. He had tried to explain why he could not. He thought she had understood. Had this long separation given her time to reconsider? Had the sacrifice he had asked of her begun to seem too great?

"What's the matter with you, Robert?"

Robert blamed the fluctuating light from the lantern for causing a beat to pass before his vision focused on Gunthar's face. "Sir?"

"You haven't heard a word I've said."

"Yes—yes, I have."

Gunthar waited, but Robert realized he was right. How long had his hand ceased moving across the page?

Gunthar gave a crack of laughter. "You're a poor liar, boy. First you come in here looking cross as a bear, then you sit there staring into space like you're a thousand miles away. What were you thinking of so deeply?"

Robert felt his face heat. "Nothing. I was just— Nothing." He cursed himself. He had become too comfortable with Gunthar if he had allowed the earl to glimpse his vexation with Sir Warin. Robert drew his impassive mask back on. "Forgive me, sir. My time and my thoughts are yours. My mind shall not wander again."

Gunthar looked amused, but he did not pursue the matter. He resumed his dictation, reeling off three more letters before he finally dismissed Robert to seek his bed.

Robert gave Gunthar's letters to the courier in the morning. When he returned to the tent he found the squire, Ralf, sitting on the bench where Robert had supped with Richard the night before. The youth rather half-heartedly buffed Gunthar's sword. Robert pushed back the curls that had fallen into the squire's eyes and frowned when he found the ruddied forehead warm.

"It won't do any good," Ralf muttered, when Robert told him to go see Gunthar's physician. "All he did was bleed Antony and make him drink something so horrid Antony said it'd have been less wretched to die."

Robert bit back a laugh. He'd seen inept barbers bleed their patients nigh to death in an attempt to "heal" them, but Gunthar's physician seemed a judicious man. Robert had stopped by to check on Antony before coming back to the tent and had found him already more alert than yesterday.

"Go," Robert said firmly. "I will take care of the earl's sword."

Robert took up the buffing cloth and sat down to polish the blade. The sun had melted away the clouds this morning, casting a bright luster along the steel and sparkling off the sapphire that studded the silver pommel. Robert tilted the sword, admiring its beauty, but the hilt felt cold and foreign when he wrapped his hand around it. He thought of the rampant tyger with the broken paw figured into the pommel of his father's sword. For all its imperfection, that hilt seemed always to caress his palm, warm and alive, when he held it.

A shadow fell across him, prompting him to look up.

"Is there aught I can do for you, sir?" Robert asked. Had Sir Warin come looking for Richard again?

Sir Warin hesitated. "I thought you were Lord Gunthar's secretary. Ought you not to be about the earl's correspondence?"

"The courier left a good hour ago, so Lord Gunthar had no need of me today." Robert caught Sir Warin's glance at the buffing cloth and the sword.

"The earl's squire showed signs of contracting the fever. I sent him off to rest."

Sir Warin shifted from one foot to the other, betraying an awkwardness Robert guessed was not natural with him.

"I find I've little enough to do myself," Sir Warin said. "Would you mind if I sat with you?"

That took Robert aback, but he concealed his surprise and made room on the bench for the knight.

"Channing says you are a clerk who prefers to be a minstrel." The inflection in Sir Warin's voice hinted of a query, as though the statement required an explanation.

Robert resumed work on the sword. "I was a minstrel before ever I was a clerk. I only serve the earl temporarily as secretary. Why pretend to be what I am not?"

"Minstrel, clerk, and soldier," Sir Warin murmured on a musing note. "I have heard you are skilled with the sword."

"Skilled enough to protect myself and fight for the king."

"You will forgive me, but you do not look like a man who was raised to such tasks."

Robert glanced up again. Sir Warin's study once more rested on his clothes, then fell to weigh Robert's hands. The years had smoothed a bit of their roughness but could not erase their sturdy squareness or the stubborn stamp of a lifetime's hard labor. Robert could not see the expression in the lowered eyes, but his mind leapt quickly enough to recall the disdain he had seen in them yesterday.

He kept his voice even despite his annoyance. "No, you are right. I was raised to till the land."

Sir Warin nodded, as though he understood. "A free farmer."

"A villein."

Sir Warin's head jerked up. "A vil—But were you pressed into service then?"

Robert ran the buffing cloth down the blade a little more forcefully than a good shine required. "I serve Lord Gunthar by choice."

"He freed you?"

"He never owned me."

"But you said—"

"That I was raised a villein, not that I am one still."

He felt the intensity of Sir Warin's gaze, searching his profile. "Forgive me"—Robert braced himself as Sir Warin repeated the words that supercilious knights and barons often used to preface some patronizing remark—"but are you not rather young to have earned enough to buy your freedom?"

Robert kept his eyes carefully on the cold steel of Gunthar's sword. "I did not buy my freedom, Sir Warin. I took what was rightfully mine."

"I do not understand."

"I did not think you would." Robert looked up to meet the knight's gaze. "What do you want from me, sir?"

"Want from you?"

"Nay, let me guess. You have heard the gossip in the camp. Everyone here knows my roots are common, I have not tried to hide it. A rustic, the knights here think me. A yokel, a bumpkin with ambitions above my station. And so you came to see for yourself. You wonder why the earl has seen fit to elevate me thus, and like your fellows, wish someone would put me back in my place."

Sir Warin's face reddened. So Robert had guessed aright.

"I know why the earl has favored you so," Sir Warin said. "The men also tell how you saved his life."

"And have they told you," Robert asked, "how I viciously killed three men?"

"Were you guilty of that, I'm sure you'd not now be free."

These words might have tempered Robert's irritation with the knight had Sir Warin not spoken them with such a condescending sniff. Sir Warin gave no sign of realizing he had offended with his tone. He leaned his forearms on his thighs and rubbed his hands together as though they were chilled, for all that the sun was warm. Robert could not for the life of him fathom why the man lingered beside him on the bench.

Robert had buffed all he could of the sword, from its tip to its silver pommel. He set it aside and pulled over Gunthar's shield, grown dusty and smudged from their march before the fever had struck the camp. No doubt Gunthar had ordered Ralf to wipe it clean, as well.

After several moments of silence between them, Sir Warin asked rather abruptly, "Marcel, have you ever been to Westminster?"

There was no reason to avoid an honest reply. "Aye, I was there in the service of Lord Gunthar."

"And Dorset? Have you ever been there?"

Robert scrubbed at a stubborn smear that clung to the white paint of the prancing stallion. This question, coupled with the former, made him hesitate. But it was absurd that the knight should suspect anything. He hoped Sir Warin merely thought him distracted when he took a moment to answer. "Aye, I was there once."

"Is that where you met Richard Channing?"

"No, I met Richard here in Poitou."

"Yet you know his family resides there?"

"A great many people reside in Dorset," Robert said lightly. "I suppose Richard might have mentioned it."

"And his cousin, Marguerite? Has he mentioned her, as well?"

"He speaks of her often. They are very close."

"Aye, so she told me."

It took all of Robert's self-discipline not to shoot a glare at the knight. Why had Marguerite been telling Sir Warin anything? What had happened between them in Northumberland? He rubbed a little harder at the smear.

"Among all those people who reside in Dorset, did you never lay eyes on the Lady Marguerite de Villon? Or perhaps you knew her as Marguerite of Winbourne?"

Sir Warin sounded very much like a man who was fishing, but for what? There was no possible way he could know. Robert considered a lie, but as Gunthar had said, he knew he did it badly.

He hedged. "The name is vaguely familiar. I daresay I might have seen her. Of what like is she?"

"Oh, but very lovely! Fresh as a flower and innocent as a lamb. Her dusky locks float like a cloud about her cheeks of roses and cream. She has an enchanting tip-tilted nose, soft glowing eyes, and lips . . . lips as sweet as wine."

Robert's head whipped towards the knight before he could stop it. Sir Warin's lids drooped over his eyes as if in some memory, but he turned to catch Robert's gaze before Robert resumed his work on the shield.

"You remember," Sir Warin murmured.

Robert cursed himself. He tried to cover his misstep with a careless tone. "Aye, a lovely lass. Most charming. But is she not betrothed to the Earl of Saxton?"

"Aye, but it is no love match."

"Few marriages are, I fear."

"But this one—this one I cannot in good conscious allow."

Robert's breath sucked in a little too sharply. "What do you mean?"

"Ah, if you had seen her, you would know. She is a woman who was made for love. Saxton does not deserve her."

"And you do?" The veriest hint of an edge slipped into Robert's voice.

"I shall make her happier than the Earl of Saxton."

Robert waited until he knew he had successfully shuttered his eyes before he looked again at Sir Warin. "Do you think Saxton will step aside for you?"

"Lord Saxton does not worry me," Sir Warin said. "She does not even pretend to love him. But you—" A small frown brushed his mouth. "I had feared you might be more of a problem."

Robert blinked. "Me?"

"You, sir. Marguerite will not marry me while her heart is given to another." That thinly veiled disdain stole across Sir Warin's handsome features once more. "But it is plain to me now that her 'love' is no more than a girlish infatuation. I shall certainly not let it trouble me further. She will thank me for it one day."

Robert's breath slicked in again. "Will she?"

"Of course. I will certainly provide for her better than you could. She would find no joy as a minstrel's wife."

Robert bit off the retort that sprang to his tongue and willed his face to remain impassive. "I do not understand you, sir. Why should I wish to provide this woman with anything?"

Sir Warin's brows shot up as though astonished. "But are you not, then, the man whom she meant? I could have sworn yours was the name."

This pronouncement so startled Robert, he barely prevented his jaw from dropping. "She named you my name?"

"Aye. 'Robert Marcel,' she said. She would not have me because of him."

Even as this answer warmed him, Robert felt a small flash of frustration. How had Marguerite been so careless as to give Sir Warin his name?

But he would not allow surprise to trap him. He returned his attention to the shield, moistening his thumb with his tongue and combining it with a firm pressure to finally scrub away the smudge on the stallion. "You thought she meant me? I do not see how she could remember my face or name from the many musicians who have surely performed for her. No doubt you misunderstood."

"I heard aright," Sir Warin said dryly. "Yours was the name. I shall not soon forget the pain it caused me."

"'Tis some marvelous coincidence, then. Surely you are not suggesting that the Lady Marguerite is in love with me?"

"'Tis no coincidence. She told me he marched with the king. I searched half the camp after Lord Gunthar summoned you last night, and the other half this morning, but there is no knight here who matches the name, nor squire nor archer nor even footsoldier. Except for you. As for love—" Robert felt Sir Warin shrug beside him. "I can only suppose that Marguerite was so desperate to escape from Saxton that she was willing to accept any man in his place, even you. But I will relieve you both of that burden."

"Sir Warin—"

"Come, you will accept it for the best." Sir Warin set a patronizing hand on Robert's shoulder. "Allow me to offer you some advice. You will do better to serve Lord Gunthar as you are doing now than to seek advancement through such a marriage. Simply wedding Marguerite would give you no place amongst us. It is quite unlikely that you would be allowed to inherit her lands, and you cannot truly expect any man would accept you as his vassal? The thought is laughable. Marriage to Marguerite would not raise you to her level. It would only drag her down to yours."

Robert stared into Sir Warin's handsome, haughty face. "You think I would marry Marguerite to become one of you?" Revulsion shot him to his feet. "I would sooner throw myself in the river than become like you. A pompous, pretentious, arrogant, smug—"

"How dare you?" Sir Warin cut him off, his face going pale with anger.

Robert gave a harsh laugh. Sir Warin surged up from the bench, his hand flexing into a fist. Robert's muscles tensed to deflect a blow. It was how men like the knight always dealt with insolence.

But Sir Warin checked himself. "I did not come here to quarrel," he said through his teeth. "Only to confirm my reluctant suspicions. You are mad as well as scheming if you think you can seduce an innocent, gently bred lady without chastisement. I would not be worthy of my spurs if I allowed a lowborn villein to despoil her."

His slur of Robert's birth fired the resentment that seemed bred into Robert's very bones. "Because some arrogant lord once dubbed you on the shoulder with his sword, fastened a pair of gilded spurs to your heels, and proclaimed you a knight, you think yourself above me? To the devil with you! I have served men like you before. 'Nobles,' you call yourselves, yet you are more base than the humblest cottar. You and your fellow knights are nothing more than pleasure-seeking, luxury-loving, self-satisfied—"

"Why, you impertinent rogue!" Sir Warin's fist half swung up before he caught himself.

Robert's gaze flicked in scorn from the fist to Sir Warin's white cheeks. "While men like you are gorging and guzzling and wenching, your 'lowborn villeins' slave in your fields to keep your tables laden with food and your cellars swimming with wine. It is on the backs of my people that you and your kind sit warm and sated within your castle walls. Yet by what right do you sit thus warmly, while your villeins shiver and die in the cold?"

Sir Warin's brows drew together as though Robert's question puzzled him. "It is the order of the world. Some must plow, while others fight or pray. Each serves the other. Your people plow the fields for us. We protect them from wars and such disasters, and allow them to work in peace. You and your people should be grateful—"

"Grateful?" Robert felt the clenching of his own fists now. "You'd do better to give them all swords and teach them to protect themselves."

Sir Warin stared at Robert as though he conversed with a halfwit. "Who, then, would plow the fields?"

"It is not so difficult," Robert said with a contemptuous laugh. "I am sure you could learn."

A stunned gasp scraped from Sir Warin's throat. "Are you suggesting—? What, would you give villeins swords and lead them against us? Would you have them rule over us? Your words are treason!"

Robert was well aware of this. He looked away from the knight, reaching through his anger for some elusive grain of control before he talked himself into a hangman's noose, then received something of a shock. The Earl of Gunthar must have heard their quarreling voices, for he stood at his tent's entrance, watching them. Robert could not read his eyes, but something in their cool regard slammed against his heat. Robert's temper flared, then inexplicably tamped a notch. He drew several deep breaths and turned back to Sir Warin.

"You did not come here, sir, to argue over the social order of the kingdom. This woman of whom you told me—I do not know why she should speak my name to you, and can only say that she made a grave mistake. You'll gain no satisfaction from trying to pin the name to me."

"Will I not?" Sir Warin muttered. Hostility still held his face livid.

"I think not," Robert said. "Lord Gunthar is waiting for me now. Good-day to you, Sir Warin."

Robert turned away from the knight and walked the short distance to Gunthar. He did not know what he expected Gunthar to say, but the earl only met him with a mild query.

"Where's Ralf? It is not part of your duties to shine my armor."

"Ralf has the fever," Robert said. "I sent him off to rest."

"You might have called another servant."

"You said my time was my own today. I am not used to being idle." Robert wished he could tell what Gunthar was thinking. Since the earl held his face as impassive as Robert had learned to hold his, he was left to guess, and he guessed the worst. Robert drew a protective wall of distance between them. "Shall I go check on your squires, my lord?" he asked, carefully polite

"I suppose someone should." Gunthar sought to probe Robert's gaze, but Robert maintained their shield. "Very well, go look after them. And I would welcome your music this evening, if you would be so kind."

At least Gunthar meant to keep whatever rebuke he intended private. "As you will, my lord," Robert said, then bowed and left, grateful that his errand sent him the opposite direction from where Sir Warin still stood.

ou haven't changed. You will never change."

Robert whirled towards the soft, sardonic voice. He had just stepped out of the tent where the sick of Gunthar's camp had been laid to shelter them from the summer sun. Even though the words issued from the shadows at the side of the tent, he knew who spoke them. He moved into the shadow and found Kit Beckford, seated on one of the barrels of wine Gunthar had sent for his physician's use in treating those who had fallen victim to the fever. Robert could not read Kit's eyes in the obscuring shade, but he lifted his chin. It was not so dark that Kit would not see that.

"I heard you with Sir Warin." The heel of Kit's boot thumped dully against the wooden barrel as he swung his foot. "'Give them all swords. Learn to plow your own fields.' I should have known when I lost count of the floggings that there was only one way to put a stop to your sedition."

Robert closed his fingers around his dagger's hilt. He wished he could see Kit's hands, but they were lost in the folds of the mantle he wore.

"I am surprised someone has not already done it," Kit said. "Put your head in a noose. When exactly are you planning to lead this great uprising of yours to free the villeins of England?"

Robert refused to be baited. "You speak to *me* of treason?"

"Ah." Another thud of the boot. "I have wondered just how much you heard in the woods and the blacksmith's shop. Have you told Gunthar?"

Robert was not fool enough to answer that. Let Kit continue to wonder.

The swinging boot punctuated his silence.

"Gunthar was a great man, once," Kit mused. "Some said the most judicious man in the kingdom. But age is the enemy of even the great. There is no better evidence that Gunthar has grown senile than the way he dotes over you, as a man might over a curious toy or a favorite hound. If you think you are more to him than that, then you are madder than you were on Beck Manor."

"And yet Gunthar is still standing," Robert said, "while Saxton and La Marche are in disgrace. And you—you do not know what to do next."

"Oh, I know." Kit slid off the barrel. "I know exactly what to do. The only question—is when."

Robert whipped free his dagger as Kit took a step towards him. Kit flung out his hands to show them wide and empty.

"Not today, Rob. I have other plans for you, and however much you hate me, you will not strike me down unarmed."

Robert knew Kit would not have been so forbearing had their positions been reversed, but he lowered the dagger to his side. Kit took another slow step forward until they stood face to face. Robert felt the enmity rolling off his former master, as strong as the bitter rancor in his own heart.

"You have been a barb in my side from the day you were born," Kit murmured. "The only way to deal with a thorn is to pluck it out and burn it. That's what I intend to do. Gunthar will not always have the power to protect you. The reckoning between us will come." He shrugged. "But not today."

He strode out of the shadow, but not before knocking his shoulder hard against Robert's on his way past.

Gunthar leaned wearily back on his cot and rubbed his eyes. How much longer would this wretched campaign drag on? The king had spent hours shouting at his council again, as if blame for the fever that held his camp immobile lay at their feet. John, impatient after four months of trying to browbeat his Poitevin subjects into supporting him, wished to make an immediate assault on the French. Gunthar stood convinced they should first seize the seaport of Nantes. It would provide a more convenient base than La Rochelle for the king to launch an attack on French troops from the north. How to convince John was the problem. Saxton was already seeking to regain the king's favor by opposing every suggestion Gunthar made, especially when those suggestions contradicted the king's stubborn pride.

So far, Gunthar had managed to stroke the king's conceit effectively enough to countercheck his rival, but he found the effort exhausting. And he worried about his men struck low with the fever. Despite his physician's most diligent efforts, one of his knights had died tonight. Experience told him there would be more. He always grieved for the men he lost, but the squires were the hardest. He prayed most earnestly of all for their recovery. Their parents entrusted their sons to his care, and having lost two sons of his own, he knew the broken hearts behind even the most stoic-faced knight's acceptance of the news.

Gunthar closed his eyes behind the hand that lay across them and tried to force his troubled mind to focus on Robert's music. The minstrel had been playing and singing faithfully for hours. Gunthar knew he should give Robert leave to seek his own bed, but reluctance held him silent. He had sought in a multitude of ways to justify his interest in the minstrel. At first, he had merely been grateful. Gunthar owed the man his life, and though Robert brushed the act aside as no more than "duty," Gunthar was not one who left his debts unpaid. He had been drawn to Robert's boldness and straightforward manner, and intrigued to discover a man he could not intimidate, though Robert's sauciness still occasionally annoyed and provoked him.

But tonight, as he thought of the sons he had lost, the answer came to him in a keen, bright flash. Peter, his heir, murdered so far from home by a vengeful mob retaliating against King Richard's lawless crusaders. Harry struck down by that errant hunter's arrow. Gunthar loved his wife with every mote of his being, but there was an empty place in his heart that even she could not fully fill. One he had not thought could ever be filled again. Then had come Robert. The man's daring, his direct honesty, even his impulsive foolhardiness at times, were traits Gunthar recalled in both his sons. He had seen the similarities at a glance, but he was not so taken with the minstrel that he had not seen the differences, as well. His sons' tempers had been a good deal more even than Robert's would ever be, and as sons of an earl they had not the need of so sharp a tongue to teach others of their value. Robert, he guessed, would be of an age with Peter, if his son had lived.

I am growing unconscionably sentimental in my old age. Robert is not my son.

No. But since they had met, Gunthar's loneliness had eased.

He turned his head now to study Robert's darkly handsome face in the light of the low-burning lantern. Even the minstrel's vast repertoire had at last given out and Robert had ceased to sing, only sitting and strumming some restful chords in dreamy silence. Their conversations over Gunthar's correspondence by day and between Robert's songs by night had grown comfortable, at times even warm. But tonight Robert had avoided any kind of meaningful exchange by taking almost immediate refuge in his music.

Yet that was the very thing . . . the pensiveness of the evening shadows, the fluid melodies . . . that often broke down Robert's barriers.

"What are you thinking of, Robert?" Given the minstrel's earlier reticence, Gunthar did not really expect a reply, and was surprised when Robert smiled a little sleepily.

"Home, sir. I was dreaming of home."

"And of your lady?"

Robert usually avoided all talk of the woman he had left in England. But he looked tired tonight, perhaps too tired to be evasive.

"Aye, and of my lady. I dearly miss her."

"Aye," Gunthar said, "I miss my lady, too. I have never met a finer woman than my Helen. I did not deserve her, but I have thanked Heaven every day for the eight-and-thirty years that she has loved me." He smiled at Robert who still looked a little lost in the wistful chords he plucked. "Shall you bring your lady to meet me when we return to England?"

A misstep. That appeared to startle Robert back into his caution.

"I-I don't know, sir. I do not know that I shall see her again."

"Why not?" Gunthar pressed, despite the stiffening of Robert's features. "You are not still worried about the murder charges? They have been dropped."

"For now. But you said it is only because the king is annoyed with Saxton. If he regains the king's ear—"

"Oh, I think Saxton will not pursue it again. We both know who really killed those men, and from what you've told me, Saxton is too deeply ensnared with Beckford to risk being exposed in such an investigation as I would demand."

"That was not your former opinion."

Gunthar heard the tartness in Robert's reply.

"I know. But things are different now. *I* hold John's ear, and I do not intend to lose it again. You need not worry yourself, I will take care of the charges." *Even if I have to buy the king off.* "You are free to seek out your lady with a clear conscience."

"It is not that simple."

It seemed simple enough to Gunthar. "Because . . . ?" he probed gently.

"Because . . ." Robert plucked a slightly discordant chord ". . . because it may be that I am being selfish. I told you she is no villein's daughter. There are other suitors who could offer her much more than I."

The doubt in Robert's voice seemed as easy to dispense with as Saxton's false charges.

"Do I not give you sufficient means of support? If not, I—"

"No, sir," Robert said quickly, anticipating the offer Gunthar was about to make. "My pay is more than sufficient. You have been most generous."

"Then what? I do not see your difficulty." The minstrel's notions could be exasperatingly puzzling at times.

Robert's hand grew still on the strings. Gunthar watched the struggle on Robert's usually impassive face. The lateness of the hour had, indeed, relaxed the minstrel's defenses.

"But I shall not continue as your secretary when we return to England," Robert said at last with hint of desperation Gunthar had never heard from him before. "You surely have other clerks, and I shall return to my minstrelsy. And I am not sure it is fair of me to ask her to live as a minstrel's wife."

"Is that what you wish? To live out your days as a minstrel?"

"I enjoy my music," Robert said, as if the question had been a challenge. "It has been my life for seven years."

"Do you never grow weary of wandering? Would you not settle down, even to win the hand of your lady?"

Robert hesitated. "The only other trade I know is farming. I suppose I might be able to obtain some land and be accepted as a free farmer, but—"

Gunthar heard the unhappy way Robert broke off. *But you do not want to be tied to the land again.*

"There is another alternative, I believe." Gunthar said it carefully. The man could be as skittish as a colt when he thought he was being commanded or patronized. "You have served me well as secretary. I think I shall not find a better one in England."

Robert stared across at him, the lantern's light dancing against the dark reflection of his eyes. "You mean—remain as I am now?"

"Why not? I could use your continued services. You have lightened my load considerably by your efficiency. Whomever the priest that taught you, he taught you well." Gunthar saw Robert's lip curl between his teeth and knew that he was tempted. "Well?" he said when Robert hesitated in his reply.

"Perhaps. I—I don't know."

'Twas a frustratingly ambivalent answer from a man who always knew his own mind, no matter how maddeningly provoking. Hoping to clinch the matter, Gunthar said, "Your lady would be welcome in our household. I must admit, I am curious to meet her."

Gunthar had known the words were a gamble. He sighed as Robert's gaze shifted down to his lute, breaking their frank contact.

Robert plucked a series of seemingly random notes before saying, "You are very good, sir, but must I decide tonight?"

"I suppose you think you must consult your lady first? But that is not the way things are done, lad. A man chooses his own future, the woman merely gives her assent."

Even in the lantern's light, Gunthar caught the merriment in the minstrel's eyes as they glanced up again.

"Is that the way your household works, my lord?"

The scamp. Robert had spent too many evenings at Westminster listening to Helen tease and reprove her husband, while Gunthar let her tweak him to her heart's content. Gunthar chuckled. "That's the way it is supposed to work. But women do have a way of attaining their own will, in spite of us. They're a dangerous breed, lad. You'd do well to take heed."

Robert laughed. "It is too late for that, I'm afraid. I am quite lost."

This answer emboldened Gunthar to inquire, "How did she win you?"

To Gunthar's pleasure, Robert did not look away this time. The merriment turned almost mischievous.

"She smiled at me. The most bewitching smile I have ever beheld. There was no need to do more."

"Perhaps she set a spell on you."

He heard Robert laugh again before he began to pluck a more cheerful tune on his lute strings.

Gunthar smiled. He had half-feared that Robert's indignation with the strange young knight today would mar the tentative friendship Gunthar had formed with the minstrel. Robert's initial aloofness tonight had deepened Gunthar's foreboding. He did not know who the knight was or why he had been talking to Robert to begin with, but Robert's anger had clearly been roused. Gunthar was used to Robert's quick temper by now. He had discerned the knight's lofty air and heard the condescension in his voice. Robert's pride being what it was, Gunthar had not been surprised at the minstrel's sharp reaction. But beneath the pride and anger, Gunthar had caught something he had not been aware of before. Bitterness. Robert had viewed the knight as a symbol of oppression towards those born to less privilege, like himself.

How, Gunthar wondered, *does he view me?*

What had pierced Robert remoteness tonight, Gunthar did not know. He suspected that Robert did not know, either, but Gunthar was grateful for it. The minstrel had been lured into confidences he had long since given up hope of hearing. Whatever had prompted Robert to abandon his tightly-held caution, Gunthar was enjoying it and meant to encourage it as long as he could.

"Will you tell me nothing more about her?"

Another pause. *He means to parry.*

"I would surely bore you with an enumeration of her charms."

At least he parried gently. But Gunthar could be stubborn, too. "Then where does she come from? Surely you can tell me that."

"What does it matter, sir? It would tell you nothing about her."

"Which is ever your goal," Gunthar murmured. "Why are you so secretive? What is it you fear?"

The cheerful tune turned vaguely reflective. "I told you once that I am quite beneath her station. The world will not smile upon our marriage."

"Do you expect me to frown, as well?"

"Perhaps."

The word startled Gunthar into sitting up on the cot. "You believe that? After all this time, you still believe I would not stand by you?"

"If I marry her, you will see that I have been cautious with good cause. I know your intentions are honest and good, my lord, but—Well, one day you will see."

Robert let the rest go with a little shake of his head.

Gunthar listened for several moments to the subdued strains of the lute.

Absurd to feel hurt at the minstrel's reply. He heard Robert shift on the stool. It must be past midnight. He should send Robert to bed.

Instead, he said, "Then if you will not tell me about your lady, let me hear something more of yourself."

"But I have told you everything." Robert sounded surprised. "You know of my father, my sister, my quarrel with Kit, my flight from the manor—"

"Those were events," Gunthar said. "I know your views on practically nothing."

"My views?"

"Your views, your philosophy, what you think of life."

Robert raked a chord that jarred Gunthar's teeth together, then slapped his hand against the strings, throwing a silence almost as harsh about the tent.

"I think you would not care to hear my philosophy."

Gunthar thought again of the haughty young knight. But he had to know. So he said, as calm as Robert's voice had gone deadly flat, "You are wrong. I am very curious."

"Are you?" The dark eyes flashed up, and this time there was no laughter or warmth in them. "I believe you overheard me meticulously explaining my views to Sir Warin Eyvind this morning. My opinions have not changed since then."

Gunthar thought himself braced for the blunt break of companionship between them. One hand fisted in regret, but he could not condone the minstrel's reckless theories. "You mean about lords and villeins? But the order is necessary, Robert, to maintain the stability of the world."

"And is cruelty also necessary, my lord? And starvation and fear?"

"Nay, I abhor such things as much as you. That is not the question here."

"Isn't it?" The lantern light seemed to leap in the minstrel's eyes. "Do you own villeins, my lord?"

"Well, of course I do. I have told you—it is necessary. But they are well treated. I do not think they go hungry."

Robert's face darkened with what could only be a rush of angry blood to his face. "Did you hear my question? I asked if you 'owned villeins,' and you agreed without a thought. You claim to own men as you would a piece of property. You forget, my lord, that *I* have been 'owned' so." The pace of his words quickened with his passion. "You said once that I ought to have been a duke's son, but I am not. I was born to villein parents, and because of that one caprice of fate, I am to be owned and driven and beaten like an animal, like an ox or a horse. But I am none of those things. I am a man! I have the power of reason and choice. And I choose to be a man and to make my own destiny. Who shall try to stop me? You, my lord?"

"Nay." Gunthar hissed it through his teeth.

Robert shot to his feet and strode across the tent, but at the entrance he paused. Gunthar saw the lift and fall of his shoulders and heard the intake of several deep breaths.

"Forgive me." The darkness muffled Robert's voice, or perhaps it only sounded thus through the smothering tightness in Gunthar's chest. "I meant no disrespect. I told you, you should not like my views."

"Robert—" Gunthar said as the minstrel pulled back the tent flap "—what do you think of me?"

Gunthar could read no sign now in the stillness of the minstrel's back. The silence stretched so long it grew nearly intolerable.

Then Robert said so softly Gunthar had to strain to hear him, "I think you are a very good man, my lord—who does not understand."

The tent flap fell shut and left Gunthar alone.

36

*H*ad it all been a dream?

Nine months. Nine months since she had seen or heard from Robert. Had it ever been real? His kisses? His laughter? His love? Marguerite drew up her knees on the window seat of the solar she shared with her mother at Westminster Palace and stared out at the gold-leafed elms and the rusty oaks in the distance. So long since he had climbed that winter-barren oak tree outside her chamber at Ashbury Castle and caught her boldly in his arms. She had clung to his memory for nine silent, dragging months, his ribbon with the rose now rubbed to fraying her only evidence she had not imagined it all. She had counted the days, the minutes, devouring every clumsily worded letter from her father sporadically relaying news of the king and his war, for some hint of when Robert might return.

At the critical moment, her father had most recently written, when the king's armies had at last been poised to meet the French in battle, his Poitevin vassals had refused to fight. Her father wrote of John's frustrated rage as the barons of Poitou melted away in a cowardly mist. The king had been stymied, forced to sit helplessly while his ally and nephew, Emperor Otto of Brunswick, engaged the French on a sweltering day in July on the plains of Bouvines and suffered a resounding defeat. One thousand dead. Nine thousand captured. It could not have been a more thorough or humiliating debacle. Even word that the pope had finally lifted the interdict on England could not temper King John's fury. It had taken another two-and-a-half months for Cardinal Robert Curzon to negotiate a truce with the enraged and still intractable John, but at last the king had gathered his discouraged army and sailed once more for home.

Her father had sent the news on the eve of their departure and instructed his wife to bring their daughter back to Westminster to greet her betrothed upon their return. Marguerite could not fly there fast enough. It had been unbearable to hear nothing of Robert for so long. She sighed and leaned her head against the stone-ensconced window frame. Would Lady Helen come to meet her husband, or would Lord Gunthar go straight to her to their castle in Kent? If the latter, would Lord Gunthar take Robert with him to restore the minstrel to his wife? How much more of this endless, aching separation would Marguerite be required to endure?

Lady Leah came in with a tripping, eager step, her face aglow as Marguerite had not seen it for months.

"They are here! Up with you, child!" Her mother clapped her hands, whether from joy or in rebuke of her daughter, Marguerite was unsure. "How long have you been sitting all askew like this? Just look at the creases in your gown. Here, let me straighten your veil."

Lady Leah brushed a smoothing hand over Marguerite's skirts, sighed when it failed to remove the crimps in the cloth, then twitched into place the white veil that had slid aslant when Marguerite rested her head against the wall.

"Child, child," her mother moaned. "What will the earl think of you?"

Her mother stood at her back now, trying to shake out the crumpled folds and could not see how her daughter's fingers fisted on her skirts to stop their trembling, worsening the creases in front.

"Father is back with Lord Gunthar?" Marguerite could scarcely breathe, her heart hammered so hard in her chest.

Her mother's hand checked its sweeping motion. "Lord Gunthar?"

Marguerite was grateful her mother could not see her blush. Her mind had been too fixed on Robert. Of course Lady Leah meant the Earl of Saxton, not the Earl of Gunthar. Marguerite's heart sank, though she tried to rebuke it. If Saxton had returned with the king, surely Gunthar had come, as well? Soon—oh, soon, Robert would seek her out!

"I was thinking of Lady Helen," Marguerite said quickly as her mother rounded again to face her. "She will be so joyful that her husband has returned to her safely. I hope his shoulder has healed soundly."

Lady Leah had ended her daughter's correspondence with the countess when they returned from Winbourne Castle.

"Marguerite, I have warned you," Lady Leah said. "You must mind your tongue when your father comes. You will soon be Lord Saxton's wife and there must be no more talk of Lady Helen or her husband." She frowned, then twitched Robert's ribbon behind Marguerite's shoulder so that the veil would conceal it. Her mother had long since admitted a reluctant defeat at Marguerite's insistence to keep it threaded through her hair.

Marguerite turned with her mother as footsteps sounded outside the door. In strode her father with the Earl of Saxton at his shoulder, their clothes still dulled by the dust of their journey. She saw genuine pleasure light her father's eyes when they fell upon her mother.

"Lady. I could not have wished for a fairer sight to greet me."

Her mother's face shone with happiness. A man did not embrace his wife in public, but de Villon dared to cup Lady Leah's elbows and set a kiss to her blushing cheek. Lady Leah curtsied to her husband and then to Saxton, then bade her daughter forward.

"Come, Marguerite, and welcome your father home."

Marguerite stepped forward and mimicked her mother's curtsies. "Sir. My lord."

Her father brushed a faint, dry kiss to her forehead, but Saxton bowed over her hand, then held it lingeringly in his.

"I hope you will forgive us, Lady Leah."

Marguerite shivered. She had forgotten how Saxton's harsh, cracked voice set her flesh pimpling like a blast of frost.

"We should not have come to you still soiled from our travels, but I told your husband I could not bear another hour ere I laid my claim to this once more." He raised Marguerite's hand to his lips.

"Oh!" Lady Leah turned her radiant gaze on Lord Saxton and her daughter. "You have come to an accord with my husband?"

"Indeed." Saxton's fingers closed with a firm, possessive strength over Marguerite's when she tried to draw away her hand. "We settled the matter before we sailed from Poitou. A month hence I shall have the great honor of calling your daughter my wife."

Saxton gazed a glinting challenge into Marguerite's eyes. She felt her father watching her, too. Everything inside her shrank from Saxton's touch and shuddered at his words, but she held herself still. *Robert will come for me.*

He will *come for me.* She had doubted him once. She would not doubt him again.

"A month?" her mother echoed on a note of disappointment. "Why, I had hoped— Her trousseau is ready now."

"And there is nothing I should like more than to wed her this very night —" in spite of herself, Marguerite did shudder now "—but the king is, let us say, understandably in some chagrin at the unfortunate turn matters took with the French. We must give him time to restore his good temper, that he and the court may rejoice with us on that felicitous day when your daughter and I pledge our troth."

Saxton rubbed his thumb against the back of Marguerite's hand with a slow, sensual pressure, rousing such revulsion in her that she threw her mother's warning to the winds. "Has Lord Gunthar come with you and my father? If not, I shall have to write to Lady Helen. She has become my dearest friend and will not wish to miss our wedding."

Saxton abruptly released her fingers. "My lord Gunthar obtained leave of the king to linger behind on his lands in Kent while the rest of us rode up to Westminster. By the king's command, he will rejoin us soon."

He spoke curtly, and Lord de Villon scowled at Marguerite. Her father quickly drew Saxton's attention away, as if fearful that his daughter had offended with her mention of Saxton's rival.

Marguerite rubbed her hand furtively in the folds of her skirt as the two men talked, trying to rid her skin of Saxton's touch. She was disappointed that Robert was not yet at Westminster, but a measure of relief nevertheless flowed through her. Gunthar must still be in the king's favor if he had not been banished again. Then perhaps the king was still displeased with Saxton? Oh, she prayed it might be true! But Saxton had named a date—a month—quite confidently. Alarm fluttered in her stomach. Did he speak so because he had conceived a plan for disgracing the Earl of Gunthar again before a month was out? Marguerite must find a way to write to Lady Helen and warn her! Perhaps it would be best if Gunthar remained on his lands in Kent. Robert would find a way back to Marguerite on his own. She must trust in him. She *would* trust in him.

"Your husband's knights were fortunate to escape. I lost two men to the fever, but others lost many more. Gunthar, I believe, suffered the loss of three knights and an archer, along with four of his footsoldiers, which he could ill afford after so many of them had been mowed down in the French ambush."

Marguerite's attention whipped to the conversation between Saxton and her parents. Ambush? *Footsoldiers?*

She exclaimed before she could check herself, "But Father wrote that the king never directly engaged the French forces."

Saxton smoothed away a crease in his sleeve more successfully than Lady Leah had done with Marguerite's skirts. "The king never did. Alas, the Earl of Gunthar was not so fortunate. A brutal band set upon his company when they rode out to meet the Count of La Marche. Gunthar tumbled from his saddle and broke his shoulder in the fray. His knights managed to rally around him and deliver him to safety, but the slaughter of his footsoldiers was terrible. 'Tis why he asked to remain in Kent, that he might bear the news himself to the bereaved families of his fallen soldiers."

Saxton's cold eyes lifted and gazed into Marguerite's with such malicious satisfaction that she knew. Robert had been among the fallen.

She stumbled to the window seat and sank down onto the cushions before her knees gave way.

"Marguerite!" her mother cried. "Child, what is it?"

Her mother came rustling after her as Marguerite covered her face with her hands. Shudder after convulsive shudder slammed through her. *Rob. Oh, Rob, no!*

"Marguerite?"

'Twas her father's voice that rolled like dulled thunder through the roaring in her ears. Oh, saints! She must not faint in front of him. She lowered her head nearly into her lap to fight the clawing whiteness spreading over her mind.

"Perhaps this will help."

Someone pulled away her hands and forced up her chin. Cool metal pressed against her lips, then the tart flow of wine in her mouth and a bracing fire down her throat. She blinked the mist away and gazed up into Saxton's hard face as he lowered the goblet he had set to her lips.

His smirk. Oh, that hateful smirk! She had known Saxton a monster, but to stand there, so glib about another man's death, knowing how his words would drive a dagger through her heart—

Her mother's palm tested her forehead and cheeks. "She does not have a fever." Her mother took her hands. "But her fingers are like ice. Let me take her to her chamber."

"No!" Marguerite could not bear to have her mother or anyone with her. How could she explain the sobs fighting to wrench free of her chest? She heaved in several deep draughts of air, desperate to suppress her shock until she could escape her parents and Saxton.

But she could not stop the stuttering way her words came out. "I—I am—w-will be fine. It is merely—that I forgot to break my fast this morning. The faintness came on me so swiftly, but I am—w-will be fine." She kept her lashes lowered to hide the tears gathering beneath them. She knew if she looked at Saxton and saw his relish at her distress, she would lose all control and fly flailing at him.

"How could you be so foolish, girl?" her father growled.

"Forgive me, sir. I will lie down and send Eva to fetch me something to eat. Forgive me, Mama. My lord."

She dipped a quivery curtsy to her father, and with her head down, to Saxton, then swept trembling from the room before her mother could follow her.

Her hand was on the latch to her chamber when Saxton's words fought their way through the drowning waves of pain. Gunthar's footsoldiers, mowed down by the French—but at least four had lived to die later of the fever that had struck the king's camp. If four had lived, might others have escaped? She leaned into the cool stones of the wall beside the door, her tears flowing freely now, her sobs muffled behind her hand. Why would Saxton lie about something so easy to prove? If Robert still lived, he would come to her. Unless Saxton knew some other cause that would prevent Robert from coming in time to stop their marriage. It would be in Saxton's malignant character to torment her with a vicious fabrication.

Or it is true, and Robert lies buried in France.

She would not believe it, not from Saxton's lips alone. Lady Helen would know. If Robert had returned with Gunthar, he would be with them now at Lamhurst Castle.

Marguerite would write boldly to Lady Helen and ask of her minstrel. What matter what Lady Helen might think to receive such a query? She would reply in her kindness and Marguerite would know whether to weep or to wait. But who would carry the letter for her? Her parents would not allow her to send one of their servants—

Richard. Marguerite whirled from the door and ran for the stairs. Richard had written to her of Sir Edward's death, of how Saxton had taken him into his service and knighted him before they had left Poitou. Then Richard must have returned to London with Saxton. She must find him. Even if he could not ride into Kent himself, he could surely find some carrier to bear Marguerite's message to Lamhurst?

She flew down two flights of steps, the second one curved so that she did not see the man coming up them until she collided with his chest.

"Oh!" she gasped. "Pray forgive me."

"Marguerite?"

Strong hands closed about her shoulders. She looked up into the handsome, trimly-bearded face of Sir Warin Eyvind.

"I was coming to look for you," he began, then stopped. "What's wrong?"

She felt the cold in her cheeks and realized fear still held the blood from them as it battled with hope in her heart.

"Have you seen my cousin, Richard? I must find him at once!"

"Saxton has sent him on an errand into the city."

She was too frantic to more than faintly register Sir Warin's hand stroking her arm gently through her sleeve. She met his eyes and said, "Then you must go."

"Go where?"

She cast a glance at the rising stairs behind her. Saxton or her father could come upon them any minute as blindly as she had run into Sir Warin.

"Come," she said, "we cannot talk here. Let us go out to the gardens."

The fall air nipped briskly at her cheeks. She had not realized that she had tugged the cuffs of her sleeves over her palms to warm them until Sir Warin abruptly unlaced his cloak and swung it about her shoulders. Fashioned for his tall frame, the heavy folds nearly swallowed her diminutive figure.

She did not have time to argue. Her mother would eventually come to check on her in her bedchamber, and if Lady Leah found it empty— Marguerite would have to convince Sir Warin quickly to help her. She did her best to hold the cloak's heavy folds so that the hem might not drag on the ground as they walked. She led Sir Warin to the secluded arbor where o'er the past few weeks, she had sometimes taken to sitting and dreaming of Robert when she wished to escape from her mother in the solar. It panged her heart to remember those days now. How long ago had the French ambush occurred? *How long might I have been dreaming of a dead man?*

She sank down onto a prettily-carved stone bench before her knees could give way, as they had in the solar. Sir Warin knelt in the periwinkle at her feet and brushed his thumb across her tears.

"I trust you have brought me here to confide in me the cause of these?" he said.

She drew his hand away. "Sir Warin, I know that I hurt you in Northumberland, but—but I hope in spite of that, I may still count you as a friend?" He did not answer, but she interpreted the strong press of his fingers on hers as a signal of affirmation. "I need someone to carry a letter for me into Kent. My father will not spare me a servant, and—and I do not think Lord Saxton will lend me Richard . . ."

She trailed off, hoping Sir Warin would understand and offer his services.

A small frown hovered on his mouth. "Where in Kent?"

"To the Countess of Gunthar, at Lamhurst Castle." What excuse could Marguerite give? "I—I wish to inform her that my father has set the date for my wedding to Lord Saxton."

"Is that why you weep? Marguerite, you do not need the countess's aid to escape from Saxton." Sir Warin bowed his head and scattered her hand with kisses.

"Oh, what are you doing?" Marguerite cried. "Sir Warin, stop!"

She tried to pull away, but he held hard to her fingers and only kissed them more fiercely. Dismay drove her to her feet in a frantic effort to shake him off. Her movement jarred him into releasing her hand, but when she would have swept from the arbor, he blocked her retreat.

"Marguerite, you do not need him. I will save you from Saxton."

"This is unpardonable, Sir Warin. I ask you for a simple favor, and you—" She broke off as the pronoun he used registered. Her heart vaulted against her ribs. "'Him?'"

The frown plunged fully over Sir Warin's mouth. "That rascal, that upstart, that rogue of a minstrel. I knew at a glance he had pulled the wool over your eyes with his shamming ways. If he ever intended anything but to seduce you so that he could boast of it to his lowbred fellows—You can't think I would stand aside and let him ruin you, any more than I will let you marry Saxton?"

Marguerite gasped. A minstrel? One who triggered this outburst at her mention of Lamhurst Castle? "Sir Warin, did you meet Rob in Poitou?"

Sir Warin looked almost savage. "Did you think I would not hunt the length and breadth of the king's camp to take the measure of the man who stood between us? Marguerite, what were you thinking to encourage such a vagabond?"

This time when her knees surrendered, it was with relief instead of shock. "He is alive." The words burst on a sob as she sank back onto the bench.

"Did someone tell you otherwise?" Sir Warin's face blurred amidst her fresh tears so that she could not see his expression.

"Lord Saxton. He said there had been an ambush by the French, and then a fever in the camp . . . When did you see Rob last? He was well, wasn't he?"

To her horror, Sir Warin shrugged. "He served the Earl of Gunthar, and I did not. How should I know the state of Gunthar's troops at the end of the campaign? Once I saw Marcel and realized the absurdity of his courtship of you, I dismissed him from my mind."

She leapt up again. "Then you must ride to Lamhurst for me and see if he—"

Sir Warin shook his head. "Nay, Marguerite, I'll not sustain you in this farce. He never meant anything honest by you. As well ask a fish to walk on dry land as expect a man of Marcel's birth to comprehend such ideals as integrity and love. You are well rid of the scoundrel."

"How can you say that? How dare you say that?" She clamped her hands into fists, so angry and bewildered and frightened that she feared she might strike him. "Then you will not help me?"

"To escape from Saxton, aye." Sir Warin's face softened. He reached for her hand, but she whipped them both behind her back. She saw the flicker of hurt in his eyes, but he said, "Marguerite, I do not ask you to love me—yet. Only to come with me. Only let me save you from Saxton's villainy."

"Exchange one villain for another? I think not, Sir Warin." She pulled off his cloak and shoved it against his chest.

Her release of his cloak forced him to catch it. His knuckles clenched white on the cloth. "Marguerite, I know you think me cruel to deny you, but this man—if he lived—would bring you nothing but grief. If I did not care for you more than I care for my pride, I might let these stinging words send me away. But I love you—"

"Love? No, you covet my lands, just as the Earl of Saxton does. You thank the heavens that you might have a wife who is young and pretty to go with them, but if I were a milkmaid or a goose girl or, heaven help you, a villein's daughter, would you still want me then?"

Want. It was the wrong question, for she had seen his desire and knew it to be real. Just as she knew the dismay that flashed across his features now betrayed the honest answer of his heart.

"The question is ludicrous," he said. "You are not a milkmaid or a goose girl, though in truth, you betray your youth by challenging me with so absurd a fantasy."

"And if it were not a fantasy?"

He drew his lips tight. "If you insist I play this game, then you know I could no more wed such a creature than I can allow you to sully yourself with Marcel."

Sully? Her fingers itched to slap him for the slur. She locked them together still harder to resist the temptation, but she made no attempt to conceal the bitterness in her voice. "How can you think I could love you when you speak thus of a man merely because of his birth? I could never care for anyone so unchivalrous. If Robert is dead, I will marry the Earl of Saxton. I would sooner be miserable with a man I loathe than with one whom I hold in contempt."

"Marguerite!"

He called her name as she darted around him, but she ran on to the palace. Marry Saxton? But why not? If Robert were dead, nothing else in her world would ever matter again.

37

nnys de Tracey flounced away with an unhappy pout. Marguerite tried to rouse herself from her numbness to reason with her, but the effort felt too great. She had passed the last fortnight alternating between stubborn hope and black despair until today she sat in exhaustion, grateful that her mother had left her alone for a few hours in the solar until Annys had come in.

Every morning in the buoying light of day, Marguerite had risen from her bed with the conviction that Robert lived and that she had only to continue waiting as she had for so many months for him to come for her. But every night when darkness gathered, the doubts pressed in on her again, provoked anew by the pitying looks Saxton slanted at her from his narrowed eyes whenever he paused in his string of seductions long enough to look her way. Lady Jane Lovell was no longer at court. 'Twas said she had allowed her affections to drift to another man during the war, and that Saxton had rewarded her with so sore a snub when he returned that she had withdrawn to her late husband's estates humiliated and, without Saxton to pay for her extravagant tastes, in penury. Now Saxton whispered in the ear of a different beauty each night, flooding a new paramour's cheeks with blushes before they disappeared from the hall together.

Marguerite had found no way to send a letter to Lady Helen. Saxton kept Richard so occupied with his new knighthood that she never even crossed her cousin's path. Sir Warin had tried to speak with her a few times, but with so grim a look about his mouth that she knew he had not softened to help her. And so she could do naught but wait, and wait some more.

"Marguerite, please."

Marguerite at last glanced up and saw Annys's hands laced together in the plea. "I've not the courage to go alone."

Marguerite shook her head. "It is not safe, Annys. Not unless we brought a squire or groom."

"But that would spoil everything! No servant of my parents would keep my confidence, and I do not like the look of that squire who waits on you. His eyes shift about too much and that sullen mouth of his—I like him not, I tell you."

"That is because he belongs to Lord Saxton, so you may be sure he would not keep our confidence, either." Marguerite sighed. "The scheme is madness. My grandfather took me to a fair when I was a little girl. Even with my grandfather's servants about us, we were endlessly jostled by the crowd. And for two young women alone?" She shook her head more sharply than before.

"We can dress like servants ourselves so we do not draw attention, and once we are there, Richard will protect us."

"Annys—"

"Please! I cannot speak to Richard here at court with my parents watching. My father has granted Lord Ordley permission to marry me."

"Oh!" Marguerite slid off the window seat and embraced the other girl. "Annys, I am sorry."

She felt Annys's shoulders shake with tears. Marguerite understood a shattered dream. Saxton had knighted Richard for his service to the king in Poitou, but Lord Ordley was a wealthy widower who could advance not only Annys's future, but the future of her sisters. Richard might now be a knight, but he was still penniless. Annys's parents would never let them marry, and Marguerite feared that Richard's ideals of chivalry would prevent him from trying to fight for Annys's hand.

"Then help me," Annys pled into Marguerite's ear. "My parents have seen our glances. They will not let me speak with Richard, even to tell him good-bye. But I pressed a note in his hand when I passed him in the hall yesterday, saying I would be at the fair today. It will be my only chance to tell him—" she gave a little gulping sob "—how much I wish things were different—and that I will never, ever forget him."

Annys's plight struck Marguerite to the heart. "Very well, I will come with you." Perhaps it would do her good to escape for a few hours to a place where she had not spent so much time dreaming of a lost love of her own. "Do you have a plainer gown than that to wear? Then come with me, and we will both borrow something from my maid."

Marguerite had remembered little but the alarming crowds from her childhood, but as she and Annys moved from booth to booth of alluring wares, she found her dejection challenged by the lively commotion of the late autumn fair that had come to the outskirts of London. If anyone stared at the two unaccompanied young women in their rough servant gowns, they were too distracted to notice. They pored over tables with glass, pottery, and mirrors from Italy, leather and steel from Spain, and fine woolen cloth from Flanders dyed in bright colors. Merchants with connections to the Crusader lands had brought exotic textiles to vie with the Flemish wool: muslin, damask, and a delicate new fabric made from silk that the vendor called gauze. Marguerite held up a length to Annys's face and *oooh-ed* to find the cloth so sheer that she could see Annys's features, though indistinctly, through it.

"Annys! Marguerite! I thought we'd never find you in this crush."

Marguerite turned at the sound of Richard's voice, but her gaze glided past his face as he joined them to stare into the midnight eyes of his companion. She swayed towards him before she could stop herself, followed by a stumbling step—

Only Robert's swift move to meet her preempted her from crying out his name. His arms swept around her, clasping her hard to his chest even as he murmured into her ear, "Take care, you mustn't know me. Feign a swoon, if you can."

Joy and relief easily buckled her knees, but it took all the self-command she possessed not to fling her arms around him. She somehow managed instead to let them swing limply at her sides, allowing him to make his embrace appear no more than a quick-thinking move to catch her.

"Marguerite!" she heard Richard exclaim.

"Oh!" Annys cried. "She should have told me she was ill. I would never have teased her to come."

Marguerite made a pretense of reviving. She raised her hands to Robert's waist, intending to push him away, but her ear had somehow found the rhythm of his heart and refused to part from its strong, reassuring cadence.

"There, I think she is stirring." His voice set a warm vibration against her ear. "Lady?"

He cupped her chin and forced it up and away from his chest. She saw the warning behind the bright fire in his eyes, drew a deep breath, and finally eased some distance between them, though he kept a light clasp on her arm lest she succumb again to her "faint."

"I am not ill," she said, seeing the alarm on Richard's face. "Only—only—" she resorted to the same excuse she had given her parents, since neither Richard nor Annys had been present when she had used it before. "I merely neglected to eat this morning, and turned too quickly when I heard you call. A passing dizziness seized me, but I am fine now."

"You are not fine," Richard protested. "I had best get you back to the palace."

Marguerite drew away from Robert's touch to prove to her cousin that she was steady. "Indeed, you shall not. You have come to talk to Annys, and I shall not let my carelessness spoil that. Perhaps—perhaps your friend—" she flicked a glance at Robert because it would have drawn more notice from her cousin if she ignored him "—will escort me to find something to eat while we await your return."

Robert bowed. "It would be my pleasure, my lady."

Richard chewed his lip a moment as he glanced from Annys to Marguerite, then back to Annys. His beloved clearly won the battle for his conscience.

"Very well. Oh, I suppose I should introduce you first. Marguerite, this is Rob Marcel. We met in Poitou, but I thought you might remember him. He is the minstrel who sang for us at Ashbury Castle."

Marguerite affected surprise as Robert bowed again. "Is he so? Forgive me, sir, for not recalling you."

"I would not expect you to, my lady." To Richard, he said, "I will guard your cousin well for you."

Richard nodded and took Annys by the hand. "We should not be gone long," he said on a sigh, then led Annys away into the crowd.

Robert's hand closed boldly over Marguerite's when they were gone. She shut her eyes and savored the strength of his fingers. *He was alive. And he had come for her.*

She opened her eyes again as Robert pulled her into motion, drawing her away from the knot of spectators that she had not noticed before. Though Richard, like Marguerite and Annys, had assumed a humble attire for their rendezvous, Marguerite's "fainting spell" had attracted unwanted attention. She was happy to sweep along at Robert's side. She did not care how many people stared. *He was alive.*

"How long have you been back?" she asked when they had wandered far enough to escape the curious gazes.

"I returned to Westminster with Gunthar and Lady Helen last night. Gunthar engaged me as his secretary in Poitou and insisted that I stay with him in Kent until he finished his business there. I wished to send you word, but I decided it was not worth the risk. If Gunthar suspected—He is a shrewd man and could easily upset all our plans at this point. Besides, I trusted when you saw your father and Saxton return to court, you would know I'd follow them soon."

Her fingers flexed convulsively around his. "Lord Saxton told me you were dead."

That brought Robert up short in his stride. "He what?"

"He said there had been an ambush, that Lord Gunthar's footsoldiers were slaughtered."

Nothing could spoil the beauty of Robert's face to her sight, not even the black glower that fell over it. He swore under his breath. "The devil take that villain. Nay, hell would be too gentle a place to send him."

"Was it not true about the footsoldiers?"

"Aye, it was true, but *I* was not slaughtered, and he knew that full well. Mae, if I'd known, I swear I'd have moved heaven and earth to let you know I was safe."

All the fears and loneliness and tears of the past nine months fell away to hear him speak again the cherished diminutive of her name. She smiled and pulled him back into a stroll.

"All that matters is that you are here now. Only—" her smile faltered. "My father and Lord Saxton have set a date for our wedding, a fortnight from tomorrow."

Robert sent her a swift, sharp glance, but said nothing. He paused beside a booth displaying steel mirrors, ivory combs, and other trinkets to catch a woman's fancy.

"Lord Saxton has been trying very hard to win back the king's favor during Lord Gunthar's absence," Marguerite said as Robert released her hand to pick up one of the combs carved with roses that had been painted red, with winding green garlands. "Perhaps you should drop a hint to Lady Helen that he has been working mischief against her husband."

Robert nodded, but the only words he spoke were to the merchant, inquiring the cost of the comb. Apparently he found it too high, for he sighed a little and set it back down.

The idea came to her in a flash of inspiration. "Oh, Rob, why do we not leave the fair now and be married ourselves? We could be miles away from London before anyone knew we were missing!"

She followed Robert's glance at the merchant who cocked an interested eyebrow at her exclamation. Robert led her a few steps away, then saw a space between two booths where they could discourse out of the way of the crowd, and guided her there.

"Things are complicated at the moment, Mae," he said. "I am under an obligation to Gunthar and can hardly desert him without a word."

"What sort of obligation?"

"During the ambush Saxton told you of, Gunthar's secretary was killed. How Gunthar guessed that I knew how to read and write I do not know, but he engaged me to take Hastings' place. He has paid me well since that day. I have managed to save up a comfortable sum—" Robert paused, studying her with one of those impassive gazes that she had nearly forgotten so frustrated her. "Comfortable in my eyes, at any rate. I daresay it will seem small to you, but you realized when you agreed to marry me that life would be— more challenging than you are accustomed to?"

She swiveled an impatient toe into the dirt. Why was he speaking such nonsense? She waited for him to continue.

"Marguerite," he said after another short silence, "if you are still willing to take a chance with me, I believe I have saved enough to give us a fair start in the world, at least."

"Still willing? Oh, you are teasing me! Of course I am willing! And if things become difficult when the money runs low, I can sell my jewels—"

"Sell your jewels?" His jet brows snapped together. "Nay. If you think I'll not be able to support you as my wife, then you'd best think again about marrying me."

"But Rob—"

"I'll not live off your jewels, anymore than I would agree to live off your grandfather's inheritance, even if I were not 'just a minstrel.' Do you think me as shallow and idling as that pompous boor you met in Northumberland?"

Her face warmed beneath Robert's gaze. "Do—do you mean Sir Warin? He told me that he met you in Poitou. But Rob, you must also know then that I told him I would not have anyone but you!"

"Then you'll take me as I am, lady, a poor minstrel who means to sustain you with all the energy I possess and not sponge off the dregs of your wealth."

This was absurd! How could they stand here quarreling when all she wanted was to throw herself in his arms and beg him to kiss her? She reached out a hand to his arm.

"Rob, please. I—I know I was childish and romantic when you courted me in the glade, but I have grown up a little since then."

He drew in a short, sharp breath. "What's that supposed to mean?"

She felt the blush rising in her cheeks again. "I turned eighteen in March." She held her breath, waiting for his gaze to search for signs of aging in her face.

"And so? I turned six-and-twenty last month. What has this to do with anything?" His eyes narrowed as though with suspicion, but they never left her own.

"It is only—that I do not wish you to think—I have unrealistic expectations for you. I trust you to care for me, I do! But I can help. I can sew and embroider if we need more money, and the jewels mean nothing to me, truly they don't. I will have no need of diamonds or rubies as a minstrel's wife."

Robert looked away. "I don't like it when you talk that way, Mae. It reminds me how unworthy I am of you."

"Rob—"

His eyes flashed back to hers, alight with an anger that dismayed her. "Sell your jewels? You deserve a man who can shower you with diamonds and rubies, who can lavish silks and furs upon you. I dare not even buy you a comb like the one here at the fair, for fear it might cost you a future meal. Marguerite, I cannot even ensure you will have a bed to sleep in at night or a fire to keep you warm."

The anger lashed not her, but himself.

She curled her fingers into his arm and shook it slightly. "If I wanted jewels and silks and combs, I would marry Lord Saxton, or even Sir Warin. I care not where I sleep, so long as I am with you, and I need only your arms to keep me warm." *Look in my eyes now and you will see I speak truly.* If there were not so many people who might glance their way, she would convince him with a kiss.

He brushed a thumb across her cheekbone. "You are so young. I pray you will not regret your choice one day."

She shook his arm more roughly now, bringing a slow smile to his lips at the rebuke. His gaze shifted to her hair and she tensed a little. Lady Helen had assured her that her hair remained quite dark, but she was nine months older now.

He touched a spot in her hair near her ear. "You are wearing my ribbon."

His fingers slid down the band to the end that dangled over her shoulder. It had become so customary to thread it into her tresses that she had forgotten she had donned it that morning. She thought his smile grew more assured.

"We will discuss your jewels if it comes to that. It's my hope that it will not. I still hope to find a position in some well-to-do merchant's house where you may at least be comfortable." The smile dimmed again. His gaze drifted to the crowd and he murmured, as if to himself, "I do not like to desert Gunthar after all he has done for me, but it cannot be helped. He will be angry, but I think he will not be surprised."

"We will write to them both," she said. "I will wish Lady Helen to know that I am happy and safe. Only I think we should leave right here from the fair, before Lord Saxton can do us any more ill."

"Your cousin will be frantic if you disappear under his nose. We owe him rather more than that, I think."

She had forgotten about Richard. She joined Robert's scan of the crowd, wondering how soon he and Annys would return to look for them. "How did you meet Richard?" she asked.

Robert told her of Sir Edward Keynes' capture and how Richard had come stumbling into Gunthar's camp, how Robert had stayed the nervous guard's hand and bandaged her cousin's head, and the friendship that had grown up between them. "And I feel like a traitor plotting and planning to steal you away from him."

"If he had a grain of sense, he would do the same with Annys."

She did not realize her fingers still lay on Robert's arm until she felt the sudden tensing of his muscles.

"Brace yourself, love," he said softly, "we're about to be undone."

Marguerite had been looking in the crowd to the left, when she realized she should have been looking to the right with Robert. If she had, she would surely have seen the man who loomed over the heads of the men and women swarming past them. But it was too late now, for the Earl of Saxton had already recognized them and was parting a path through the masses, shoving anyone out of his way who hesitated too long to move himself or tried to protest his rudeness.

Robert swept Saxton a bow as he reached them. Though her heart was thudding unpleasantly, Marguerite emulated Robert's boldness and swept Saxton a curtsy.

"Good day to you, my lord," Robert said. "A marvelous day for a fair, is it not?"

Saxton looked briefly taken aback by Robert's audacity, but he rallied, "Indeed. The palace was abuzz with the amusement of this affair, so I came to see for myself. I confess, I did not expect to come across a diversion quite so farcical as this, though." He lifted a brow at Marguerite. "Have you been enjoying yourselves?"

"We were," Robert murmured on a thinly veiled insult before she could reply.

That brought Saxton's brows back down with so malignant a gleam in his eyes that Marguerite might have shrank had Robert not stood so impervious to it that it held her equally firm.

Saxton's features went hard and sharp as flint. "I hoped you'd be content with the unnatural advancement Gunthar's senility bestowed on you," he said to Robert. "You might have lived out your life in peace in Kent, leeching off that doddering old man. I sought to deal her a kindness, telling her you were dead." He indicated Marguerite with a curt nod. "Now she will have to grieve for you anew, for if you think I will allow this insanity to continue, you are more feeble-witted than the lord you serve."

Marguerite saw Robert's coolness slip at these slights Saxton cast at the Earl of Gunthar.

"We will see who is the feeble-wit," Robert said, "when Gunthar stands at the king's side watching you lay down your neck on the headsman's block alongside that traitor you trusted too well to try to murder a good and honorable man in Poitou."

Saxton's breath slicked in between his teeth, but the dangerous flaring of his nostrils quickly stilled.

"The French have long hated the Earl of Gunthar." His voice fell soft and light as an early snow. "He has helped the kings of England harry and obstruct French interests in Plantagenet lands for decades. If they feared to see him at John's side again and set a mark on his back, that had nothing to do with me."

"Unless the mark was not set on him by the French. Though whoever set it surely used a false-hearted Englishman who plotted other plots with the French king's agents." Robert's mouth took on a provocative tilt. "Perhaps you were ignorant of the false-hearted Englishman's treason, perhaps you were not. Do you suppose King John will be inclined to split those hairs? You know the king better than I, my lord."

Marguerite did not understand this exchange, but the swiftness of the pallor that rose in Saxton's face startled her.

"You can prove nothing," he said, "against either me or the false-hearted knight."

Robert only shrugged.

Again Saxton's nostrils flared, but this time his gaze turned savage. "And I suppose your own conscience is clear?" He whipped his head so abruptly towards Marguerite that she had not time to brace for the glare that thrust her back a step. "I will leave you for now, my lady, but think carefully before you commit yourself to this man. Ask him how his dagger found its way into the backs of three Englishmen in Poitou. Three *dead* Englishmen, Marguerite. Aye, ask him that."

A smirk snaked up the corner of Saxton's lips before he turned on his heel and strode again into the crowd.

Marguerite stared after him, aghast. "Rob, w-what did he mean?"

Robert spun her round by the shoulders, his face as white as Saxton's had been. "Marguerite, it's a lie, like his lie about the ambush. You cannot believe I would do such a thing?"

"Of course not!" she said, yet she could not stop her gaze from dropping to the tyger-hilted dagger at his hip.

Robert pulled her behind one of the booths they stood between. Marguerite knew she had nothing to fear from him, and yet she flinched. A guilty man might seek the advantage of such privacy to intimidate a sudden threat. Or try to silence it.

Robert jerked the dagger free. Marguerite recoiled, a reflexive cry surging into her throat. Then she found the dagger in her hands, Robert gently curling her fingers around the hilt before he released it in her grasp. He spread his own fingers wide very slowly, palms up and empty of anything that could harm.

Her eyes met his, then darted away in shame. But not before she had glimpsed the hurt in his gaze.

"Rob—"

"Nay, love, why should you believe me? All you've ever known of me is what I've told you, and how are you to know if I spoke the truth?"

She gazed earnestly into his eyes now. "I *do* know. All those days in the glade, you treated me with nothing but honor. When Saxton cornered me on my father's battlements—" She shivered at the memory that rose up to disgust and sicken her. "There was nothing honorable in the way he kissed and touched me that night. If you had not sent Richard to find me—Oh, Rob, *please* forgive me. You have shown me again and again that I can trust you." She held the dagger out to him.

"Listen to me first," he said. "I told you before I left why I had to go to Poitou. I found Kit Beckford in Gunthar's camp, as I hoped I would. And he was up to his father's tricks. I followed him one night into the woods and overheard him conspiring with a Frenchman to do harm to the English cause."

Marguerite had forgotten how Robert fell to pacing when he grew restless or stressed. He strode back and forth before her, lithe and beautiful as a stalking cat, as he continued.

"But Kit caught me and we struggled and he struck me on the head with a rock. When I woke up my dagger was gone and Kit had used it to kill three men in the camp. But I could not prove it was he and still cannot. The evidence—the dagger—pointed to me for the crime. They locked me up for it for a time. But Gunthar believed me when I told him I was innocent. He stood by me when there was no one else."

She was surprised to see Robert's cheeks redden faintly as he chewed briefly on his lower lip, but what troubled him about this memory she could not guess.

"Gunthar won my freedom, but the charges—they were never formally dropped. Gunthar says the king has forgotten them, but Mae, I know Saxton hopes to revive them. Had he not seen us together, he might have believed me still in Kent in Gunthar's household when you disappeared. But now he will know you have fled with me. Gunthar has overlooked many things in my conduct with him, but elopement with a lady? Nay, he will wash his hands of me for that. Bad enough that I condemn you to a future as a minstrel's wife. If Saxton resurrects the charges—Mae, I may have to flee. I will be an outlaw."

He stopped, but he did not turn to face her at once. She saw from his profile how his mouth turned down in a frown.

"If you expect this story to frighten me away from marrying you, you have misjudged me, sir. You are not rid of me so easily as that."

He shook his head. He said nothing, but the frown did not lighten.

She stepped near enough to press the dagger back into his hands. "If Lord Saxton tries to threaten us here, then we will leave England. We can go to Poitou. It is still English territory. I speak French, I can teach you."

Robert slid the dagger back into its sheath. "I know a little already. Gunthar carries on much of his correspondence in the tongue. I suppose Poitou might be the answer." He sighed. "I should have been more cautious than to stand thus in the open with you. Now Saxton has seen us, we are sure to be watched when we return to the palace." Robert set a finger to her quickly parting lips. "For all we know, he is still nearby, watching us even now, or has set a servant to do so, so do not ask me again to abscond with you from the fair. I will find a way to get us both out of the palace, but for now, we must be satisfied with this."

He bent down and kissed her. Hunger, thirst, joy, elation all flooded through her at once. She tried to throw her arms around his neck, but he caught her wrists and held them short.

"No," he murmured against her mouth. "If I let you do that, we will stand here kissing till the sun falls and the moon rises—or until your cousin finds us and plants his fist in my face." He kissed her again, swift and hard, then released her. To her surprise, mischief danced in his eyes. "Close your eyes, love, and hold out your hand."

"Why—?"

He cut her off by repeating his command more briskly. So she obeyed and extended her palm up, expecting him to place something in it. Instead, he took her hand and turned it over, then the cool, metallic feel of a ring slid over her third finger. Her eyes fluttered open before he spoke permission and she stared down at a blood-red garnet nestled in a golden braid.

"Oh!" she exclaimed.

"Do you like it?"

"It is beautiful!"

His dark eyes shone his pleasure and he dealt her another kiss that left her breathless. Again he held her arms at bay when they ached to embrace him, but when his mouth left hers with obvious reluctance, he pressed it to her hand, then kissed the ring.

"A pledge, Mae." His voice came low and ragged. "A token of my love for you."

"And mine for you!" she cried.

"Then give me a pledge in return. Swear to me, on your oath, that you will never marry Saxton."

"Of course I will not. I am going to marry you."

"Aye, but—but if something should happen—don't look like that, love, I fully intend to run off with you. But should Saxton intercept us—Mae, you know what he is. I want your pledge that you will not marry him, no matter what happens."

Her fingers wound around his, clinging at the awful vision his words raised. "Rob—"

"Marguerite, you must promise me. Even if he threatens you with my safety—or my life."

She shrank from that. "Oh, Rob, how can I?"

He caught her shoulders. "Promise me."

She tried to resist, to refuse, but he gazed so relentlessly into her eyes that her will crumbled before its force. "I p-promise."

"On your oath."

"On—" He shook her when she faltered. Tears blurred his face, but the resolute press of his fingers wrenched out the rest. "—my oath."

He dragged her then against his chest and threaded his hand into her hair, drawing her head back where it had rested before, to savor the beating of his heart. He made no attempt this time to prevent her arms from winding around his waist. She drank in his strength and love like a woman nine-months parched for water or wine, until she heard Richard calling their names.

e knows about us. How does he know about us?"

Robert went stiff at the voice that hissed from within the chamber. He had been on his way to deliver a letter he had copied for Gunthar to the courier, when he had glimpsed Kit Beckford sauntering down the passageway. Robert had veered away from the stairs to follow him, moving so softly that Kit had not heard his footfall. Why was the villain at Westminster? The war had been over for a fortnight, with no new moves by the king to bind a minor baron to the court. Kit should have returned to Wiltshire by now. Unless he was up to some new devilry. Robert had a duty to expose it before he ran off with Marguerite, if he could. 'Twould be one last service he could perform for Gunthar, while perhaps at the same time settling his own score with Kit once and for all.

And so he had felt little compunction about cracking open the door Kit had closed behind him. The voice that greeted Kit startled Robert. Even though he had known Kit and Saxton had allied against Gunthar, he had not expected to catch them meeting so boldly together right inside the king's palace.

"Marcel guesses, nothing more," Robert heard Kit say, sounding cool to the hissing warning in Saxton's voice.

Robert and Marguerite had only been back a few hours from the fair. He set his eye to the crack and saw Saxton standing directly across from the door, but he could not see Kit. From the glower on Saxton's face, Robert's dig about Saxton losing his head must have struck a rare nerve of dismay in the man.

"How can you know what he guesses and what he knows?" Saxton demanded. "I have no intention of risking my head merely because you were sloppy. If you failed to cover your tracks, if you had the *stupidity* to let him or anyone link your name and treason to me, I will crush you so fast you'll be staring the devil in the face before you even know you are dead."

From the pause that followed these words, Robert assumed they had given Kit some pause. He tried to make out something about the room where the two men stood. He thought he saw a desk, smaller and less cluttered than the one that Gunthar used, and a chair, and behind it another door leading—where? A bedchamber perhaps?

"The plan was good," Kit said, an edge now to his voice. "Gunthar should be dead, and Marcel either with him or waiting for the hangman's noose. How was I to guess that he would rescue Gunthar, and that you would be so clumsy as to lose the king's favor and with it, the murder charges I did my best to hang around Marcel's neck?"

Saxton so lost his arrogant smugness now that he hurled a string of obscenities at Kit.

A figure passed in front of the crack, startling Robert into jerking back his head and gripping his dagger's hilt. When the door did not whip open, he looked again and saw that Kit had moved from his former position out of view to sit in the chair at the desk. He sat with such an air of nonchalance, Robert knew this chamber must be his. But Robert recognized the nervous fidget in Kit's fingers as he turned a quill pen between them. Saxton's massive build and the power that projected from it had clearly intimidated him.

Kit did not let it show in his voice, though, when he said, "That blasted *minstrel* cost me a fortune from France. If I remove his threat, will you hold to your bargain to give me Gunthar's manor?"

"How can I? You bungled the matter so, Gunthar is still alive."

"I know a way to bring them down together. But I need your help, my lord. If you want Gunthar included in the bargain, that is. Otherwise, I will content myself with removing only the thorn that is Robert Marcel." Before Saxton could reply, Kit's gaze flicked over his shoulder. He frowned. "I am certain I closed that door behind me."

Robert's lips twitched in a silent curse. He sprang away and dodged through another doorway along the passageway, praying it might be a servants' quarters, like the one he lodged in near Gunthar's chambers. It was, and thankfully proved at this hour to be empty. He stood with his back to the door, listening to the sound of footsteps that halted on the other side.

"No one was there," Saxton's voice rumbled. "I placed you in this chamber because no one ever comes to this part of the palace. Now if you've a plan, let's hear it . . ."

The sentence died away as the footsteps resumed, cutting off with a stiff *click* as either Kit or Saxton shut the door firmly behind them this time. Robert sent a swift glance about the room he stood in. The floor was bare of furniture or trappings from any servants, and the half-open shutter sagged on rusty hinges. *No one ever comes to this part of the palace . . .* Then presumably no one, including the king, knew Kit was here.

Robert dared not linger and hope to listen further, so he carried Gunthar's letter on to the courier. As he went, he turned over again and again in his mind what Saxton and Kit could be plotting between them now, but could come to no answer. In any event, he planned to be well away from both Westminster and London with Marguerite before Kit could put whatever nefarious scheme he intended into action. Robert knew that Saxton would be expecting him and Marguerite to flee and had likely already set up the means to stop them. But Saxton could not prevent Robert from leaving the castle on an errand for Gunthar, though Robert knew he would likely be followed. But if Marguerite could slip out again concealed as a servant—Well, there were a few knots to be worked out, but the wedding was still a fortnight away. There was time for Robert to think of something.

Having delivered the letter, Robert turned his steps back to Gunthar's suite. *I know a way to bring them down together,* Kit had said of Robert and Gunthar. Robert would have to warn Gunthar before he eloped with Marguerite, for he did not think he could forgive himself if this man he had so grown to respect should come to harm because Robert was not here to guard him.

Gunthar had asked Robert to rejoin him when his errand was done. Robert strode through Lady Helen's sitting chamber—he knew her with the queen at this hour—and let himself into one of the two chambers beyond it which Gunthar had set up as an office. But he no sooner stepped across the threshold than he realized that Gunthar was not alone. The great chair with the lion-headed armrests had been pulled out to the side of the desk where a woman sat, nearly lost in the chair's vastness.

Robert checked his stride. "Forgive me. I did not mean to intrude."

Gunthar stood near the window, appearing to study the woman in silence, but he glanced up at Robert's entrance.

"'Tis no intrusion, lad. This woman is here to see you."

"Me?" Robert moved closer to gaze at the woman. Mouse-brown hair hung lank about her pallid cheeks and the shadows beneath her brown eyes made them seem too large for her sharp, pretty face. Robert felt a punch of recognition. "Alice?"

She sprang up from the chair. "Oh, Rob, I'm so glad ye've come at last. I'm at my wit's end to know what to do!"

Robert caught her hands and held them hard. "But Ally, what are you doing here? How did you find me?"

"Lord Christopher told us ye worked for the earl, so I just asked at the gate and they sent me here.

Robert released her and turned, flushing slightly, towards Gunthar, but Gunthar forestalled him.

"Nay, you can explain later, lad, if you feel the need. I have tied Mistress Alice's tongue with my company long enough, but it is clear she is urgent to speak with you. You'll find it more private here than in your lodgings."

Gunthar offered "Mistress Alice" a smile that ducked her head so quickly Robert knew it disconcerted her, then left her and Robert alone.

"Rob—" the woman began in a trembling voice.

Robert led her back to Gunthar's chair, then drew up his own in front of it. "Ally, what's happened?" He touched her drawn face. "You look ill."

"Not me." The words sounded choked in her throat and her eyes sheened with tears. "It's Gil. Oh, Rob, he's dyin'." She sank into his arms and sobbed.

Robert stroked her lank hair, but his mind whirled. Gilbert, his brother, dying? And Kit had sent Gil's wife all the way to London to tell Robert of it? Nay, Gilbert had scarcely been sick a day in his life. It must be some sort of trap Kit had laid.

Alice snuffled and pushed herself away to wipe her cheeks. "I'm sorry. I thought I'd braced myself for it. I knew long before we reached London that he'd not recover, but when I saw ye—"

"Are you telling me Gilbert is in London?"

She nodded. "An' Lottie, an' the children. Lord Christopher made us bring them, to hold them over Gil's head."

"Lottie?" His sister, too? What infernal mischief was Kit planning? *And what has the villain done to Gil?*

Alice was frowning, in that way she had when she blamed Robert for bringing trouble down on her husband's head. Robert tried to bide his anger until he knew the full story.

"Tell me what's happened," he said.

She scrubbed away her tears with the curt, practical gesture that was characteristic of her. "Lord Christopher wants ye back on the manor." She used the name they had all called Kit by while his father, Lord Garoux Beckford, had lived. "Though why he cares after all this time I can't tell ye. He worked hard to retrieve ye when ye first left, an' was furious when he failed. He fined Gilbert for yer misbehavior—it made for a hard winter for us."

Robert knew all this. He'd learned it two years ago when he had visited his brother's family without Kit's knowledge, but he sensed Alice's distress and let her ramble.

"I thought Lord Christopher had forgotten about ye after that. Then last week he came to our cottage, sayin' he had ye cornered and was goin' to prove yer villeinage and drag ye back for the punishment ye deserved."

"I've been gone seven—nearly eight years now," Robert said. "He's never pursued me before. The courts will ask him why." And hopefully doubt Kit's claim. Robert remembered, though, how he had confessed the truth to Gunthar. Gunthar had kept his secret close for all these long months, even from the vassal he owed the truth to. But if the courts asked Gunthar, a man so honorable that he served a king he despised out of the loyalty he felt for that king's father, would such a man lie to the law that ruled the land? For a runaway villein?

"Lord Christopher's goin' to present yer kin in court to testify against ye," Alice said.

Ah. "So that's why he's brought Gil here. But the law requires at least two male kinsfolk of mine as witnesses." Robert had made use of Gunthar's library during his time at Lamhurst Castle. "My parents both were the only children to survive in their families, and that plague that came through the year I left took the menfolk closest to us in blood. Masters hardly take the time to keep their villeins' genealogy for Kit to trace our line for certain back further, so what is he thinking?"

"He's thinkin' he'll try to use yer sister, Lottie. If the judge excludes her for bein' a woman, he's goin' to try Will Locke."

"Will?" Robert sat back in his chair in surprise.

Alice nodded. "Lord Christopher hopes he'll be accepted as a witness, since the Lockes became yer foster family after yer parents died."

"It won't be allowed. The case will be dismissed and I'll be declared legally free." Robert sprang to his feet on a wave of excitement. The mistake of his youth, his failure to bind himself to one town and a trade for a year and a day, wiped out with one miscalculation on Kit's part. Free. And Robert's children, too. He had not even thought of the threat to them before. Children of a runaway villein would be considered villeins, as well, if their lineage could ever be proved.

Except— Robert's spirits plunged a little. He would have to hire a lawyer to fight Kit's charges. He could afford it, now, with the earnings Gunthar paid him, but it would seriously deplete the nest egg he had so carefully hoarded for him and Marguerite. And if the court proceedings lingered past the time for Marguerite's wedding to Saxton—

"Gilbert made the same objections," Alice said, "but Lord Christopher brushed it aside, sayin' he had influence in court."

Of course. "Saxton," Robert muttered.

Saxton had money enough to sway the courts to Kit's side and buy allowance for Robert's sister or William to testify. Even if Gunthar overcame his scruples to counteract Saxton, how could Robert let Gunthar expend a small fortune to win Robert's freedom, only for Robert to turn around and run away with Marguerite? The thought brought a small, sickish feeling of guilt to his stomach.

"Gil would have lied for ye."

Robert did not realize he'd fallen to pacing until Alice's words brought him up short. He turned and saw something very like accusation in her eyes.

"He would have tried, to set ye free, but ye two look so much alike, I told him no one would believe him. But now—now he won't live long enough to say anythin'."

Kit would not have deliberately harmed Gilbert if it would frustrate his plan against Robert. Robert returned to his chair and took Alice's hands again. "Tell me what happened."

He felt the weariness and fear in her clasp. Her tired eyes looked larger than ever. "There's been fever in the village for the past fortnight. Gilbert, who is never ill!—he took the sickness hard. I begged Lord Christopher to wait until he was well before we set out on the journey, but Lord Christopher was unyielding. He let us travel by wagon, but we left in a terrible storm that soaked us all to the skin. By the time we reached London, even the escorts he'd assigned us agreed that Gil could go no further. They've housed us in a damp, dreadful inn to await Lord Christopher's summons. I came to find ye, because—Rob, my da and brothers all died of fever, I know the death signs and I have seen them in Gil's face. I—" for the first time her voice broke "—I do not know if he will last the night."

Robert fought his own dismay for a moment, then drew her to her feet and placed a bracing arm around her shoulders. "Take me to him," he said.

The storm Alice and her family set out in had passed London two days before, but the air of the inn where they had taken refuge still clung with a chill, autumn damp. No one had provided even a paltry brazier to warm the sick man on the cot. Robert guessed that once Kit had realized Gilbert would not live to fulfill his usefulness to him, he had decided a handful of charcoal was not worth the expense. Robert swallowed the acrid rancor that rose in his throat as a woman and two small, huddling figures beside the cot turned. The woman gave a small cry and ran into Robert's arms.

"Lottie," he whispered into her tangled red hair. He embraced her hard while she clung tight to him in return. He felt a stinging at his eyes. He had never thought he would be able to hold her thus, safe from the nightmare of her marriage. "Did Kit tell you about Hanley?"

Her head nodded against his shoulder. "That he was killed in Poitou. Robin, I swear I did not pray for his death! But—oh, was it wicked of me to feel relief when he did not come home? It has felt so strange to sleep at night without fear."

Robert felt a sudden vengeful satisfaction that it had been his dagger that had delivered her. "Did Kit tell you how Hanley died?"

This time he felt a negating shake of her head.

"Lottie—"

Alice interrupted them, leading over the two children.

"Tom, Edyth," Alice said, "I've brought yer Uncle Robin to help us. Say hello to him."

Robert released his sister and dropped down on one knee, the better to look into the faces of his nephew and niece. Even in the light of the single candle someone had set on the table, he could see the dark Marcel coloring he remembered from his visit to them two years past. Lottie had inherited her red locks from their grandfather, who had been known as Gilbert the Red before Kit's grandsire had dubbed him Marcel. The children's noses and ears were red from the cold, for their heads were uncovered and Robert had lived their life long enough to know how threadbare the cloaks they wore.

He twitched the thin mantle closer about the little girl, checked by her wide, doubtful eyes from warming her with an embrace. "Well, Mistress Edyth," he said with a determined smile, "and do you remember me?"

The little girl, scarce six-years-old, leaned into her mother's skirts, but her eight-year-old brother planted his fists on his hips. "Don't mind Edyth, sir, she's just a baby. I remember ye. Ye told us splendid stories 'bout knights on gleamin' chargers, who rode to splendid battles. Have ye become a knight, Uncle Robin? Ye told us ye would someday."

Robert sent a guilty glance at his sister-in-law. He had sung them all some of the ballads he had learned in his new minstrel's trade when he had visited them, most of which had indeed been magical tales of warrior knights pursuing glorious quests, and he had fallen to boasting a bit, just to indulge the shining awe in young Tom's eyes. Alice's mouth pinched in displeasure now, as it had then.

"This is not the time to speak of such things, Tom," Robert told his nephew. "Perhaps later I'll tell you of my adventures, but now—"

"Oh, sir," Edyth suddenly piped up, "have ye come to make Da well?"

Robert gazed into the child's wide, trustful eyes. He felt Tom watching him hopefully, as well. He could not promise what he knew they wanted, so he said nothing, but smiled at them both again. He tweaked Edyth's raven braid, ruffled her brother's hair, then got to his feet. At a nod from Alice, Lottie shepherded the children into a corner while Alice led Robert over to the cot where her husband lay.

Robert had prayed all the way to the inn that Alice's bleak conviction had merely been over-wrought nerves. But as soon as he took up the candle to allow the small light to fall over his brother's face, he knew. He, too, had seen death too many times on the manor not to recognize the dangerous hollows in his brother's cheeks, the over bright eyes, the rattle in his labored breathing and the convulsive shivers that shuddered through him, in spite of the fiery skin that met Robert's palm when he laid it across his brother's forehead.

"Oh, Gil." The groan broke from Robert's lips before he could stop it.

He was not sure at first if Gilbert heard him, though the bright eyes fixed on his face. "Robin." Gilbert's voice came pathetically weak.

Robert fell to his knees and set the candle on the floor to free his hands so he could grasp Gilbert's fingers. They, too, burned in his touch. He could not see the sickness with the little flame set below the cot. It made it easier to wrap himself in the memory of his brother in the prime of his health, two years Robert's senior, taller, a little lankier than Robert, but solid-chested and one of the strongest men on the manor. He had the same black hair and eyes as Robert, though Robert recalled that Gilbert's rarely flashed and then only when Robert had tried his steady patience to its limit.

"Gil, let me fetch a physician. The Earl of Gunthar will lend me his, I am sure. His skill pulled many a man through the fever that struck the king's camp in Poitou. He can help you—"

"Nay, Robin—" Gilbert broke off with a coughing fit.

Alice poured a mug of water from a pitcher on the table Robert had been too distracted to notice. He did not like the stale smell of the mug or its contents, but no other liquid lay at hand, so he raised his brother up to allow Alice to pour some of the drink down her husband's throat.

Gilbert gulped, coughed, drank, then pushed the mug away. "Too—late—for a—physician," he rasped. "Ally knows."

"Gilbert," Alice protested faintly as Robert laid him back down.

"Come, Ally," Gilbert said, his voice a thread of the robust tones that Robert remembered, "we're too old to play games. Still—I won't leave you unaccounted for." His hand groped to find Robert's fingers again. "You'll take care of them for me, won't you, Rob? Alice and the children?"

He spoke with the same precise accent as Robert and Lottie, the one their father had taught them. Robert cradled his brother's hand between his, trying desperately to pour some of his strength into the weakened frame. "Of course, Gil. Don't worry yourself."

Alice had picked up the candle, allowing Robert to see how Gilbert's teeth fretted his lower lip.

"I don't want—to burden you," Gilbert said after a pause, "and of course they'll return to the manor—but—if you could just keep an eye on them for me—from a distance, to keep yourself safe—see they come to no harm—"

"Yes, Gilbert, of course. It'll be no burden." It meant Robert could not flee with Marguerite to Poitou, but he would find a way to care for his brother's family while raising one of his own. He would find a way.

Gilbert lay frowning now. "I know you've made a new life for yourself—I don't want you to lose that. You know why I've come?"

"Aye, to witness against me at court."

Gilbert closed his eyes. "Aye. But he'll fail now. There'll be no blood kin to testify. Even if they let Lottie speak, it won't be enough. You'll be free—"

"Gil, don't." Robert's throat ached so, he could hardly choke out the words. "If by returning to Beck Manor, your life could be spared—"

"I know," Gilbert cut him off. A faint flicker of a smile. "But you've fought hard for your freedom. I've never begrudged you that. That's why—I asked Ally—to fetch you."

Robert waited for more, but Gilbert lapsed into silence, as if exhausted with their exchange. Robert brushed the damp locks from the feverish forehead and hoped he'd fallen asleep. The silence drew Lottie back to the cot to stand worriedly beside her brothers.

After several long moments, Gilbert's dried lips moved again. "Kit hates you, you know."

"I know," Robert said. Only some deep stress could cause Gilbert to utter Kit's familial name.

"And Saxton." Gilbert's heavy lids fluttered open. "Promise me—one more thing—"

"Anything."

"Robin—Saxton's betrothed—Kit told us— You'll ruin yourself—! Promise me—"

Gilbert's voice rose in agitation, but Robert, so startled by these words, blurted out, "Kit knows about Marguerite? How?"

Alice laid a hand to her husband's shoulder to quiet him. "I will tell him." She turned towards Robert. "Lord Christopher feared Will Locke would refuse to testify against ye, so he went to Dorset to confront Will himself, hopin' to intimidate him into obedience. Lord Christopher came back to Beck Manor all a-rant about what he called 'the new heights of your inconceivable arrogance.' He said Will's wife let it slip that ye had seduced the betrothed of the Earl of Saxton."

Robert beat back the small blaze of anger that surged up towards Lucy Locke. Who knew what threats Kit had made against her husband, for

Robert guessed that Will had proved as obdurate about participating in Kit's scheme as he had about abjuring his friendship with Robert through all those hard years on Beck Manor.

"Seduced her, no," Robert said, rising from his knees. "But I do intend to marry her."

He felt Lottie start beside him and was glad it was too dark to see her eyes.

"Rob, have sense," Gilbert pled. "You've a chance to gain your freedom from Kit. Don't throw away your life to Saxton."

"I love her, Gil. I cannot help it, any more than you can stop loving Ally."

He felt the comfort of Lottie's hand slide into his, but Gilbert suddenly pushed himself up on his elbow.

"Rob, I can't face them. Ma and Da—" Gilbert's voice was hoarse, strained, desperate. "I told Ma I'd take care of you and Lottie when she died, and I've done nothing but fail. The floggings you bore, Lottie bound to that wretch, Hanley—but at least you escaped to the better life they always wanted for you. How can I tell them I let you throw it all away for a woman I don't even know?"

"Gil—"

"Promise me, Rob. Give me your word you'll give up your mad plan and get out of London before Kit and Saxton can kill you, for I know that's what Kit intends this time. I saw it in his face when he said he means to drag you back to the manor."

"Promise him," Alice hissed into Robert's ear as Gilbert fell back to the cot, spent and coughing from the rush of words.

"Ally, I can't." Robert started to fill the mug again, but Alice knocked it from his hand and drummed frantic fists into his chest.

"He's dyin'! Promise him and let him go in peace!"

Robert caught her shoulders and held her away from him. "I can't, don't you see? If I promise I must keep my word—and I cannot."

"Ally, stop," Lottie said when Alice tried to strike him again. "If Robin loves this woman, you and Gil have no right to ask him to abandon her."

Robert's breast ached with grateful affection. Lottie had always understood his heart better than Gilbert. But he could not bear to let his brother die in such distress. He turned back towards the cot. "Gil, I promise they will understand. Da will understand."

He stopped, realizing that Gilbert had ceased coughing and truly fallen into unconsciousness this time. Robert stood with the two women beside the cot for several long, silent moments until they heard the frightened whimpering in the corner and remembered the children.

"I will take them back to the palace," he murmured to Alice, "and find someone to care for them." He could not let them stay here in this wretched place, only to watch their father die.

Alice nodded curtly, but jerked away when Robert tried to set a hand to her shoulder. He debated bringing a physician back with him, but knew it would do no good. He sought out the innkeeper before they left to pay for a brazier and charcoal, warm blankets for the sick man, and clean wine in case Gilbert woke again. But some dismal, oppressive spirit told Robert that his brother would not. He only prayed that Gil would linger long enough for Robert to be at Alice's and Lottie's side when his brother's breath grew still.

39

Gunthar watched the way Robert pushed his hand through his hair for the fifth time, accenting the crease between his brows while he copied Gunthar's scrawl into his own neat, legible writing. Legible if inaccurate, anyway. Gunthar finished scanning the transcribed letter and laid it down. This was the third one where Robert had transposed or completely misrecorded a good dozen words on the parchment. He never made such careless mistakes, it was one reason why Gunthar had retained him as his secretary.

"What's troubling you, Robert?"

Robert looked up at him, rather blindly for a moment, Gunthar thought, before the dark eyes snapped into focus.

"Are there more errors?" Robert pulled the letter back over to him, dismay in his face.

Gunthar had observed the gradual relaxing of Robert's impenetrable mask when they were alone together during the final months of the campaign in Poitou, though he could summon it back quickly enough if Gunthar tread too closely on any matter the minstrel held private. And he had certainly started their session today with the old aloofness shielding his thoughts. It was why Gunthar had refrained from asking him where he had been for the last nearly forty-eight hours. Robert had simply disappeared with the woman in the rough homespun gown and shown up with a stiff, reticent apology two days later.

None of his correspondence had been so pressing that Gunthar felt the need to make an issue of the unusual behavior. He knew the minstrel had not run off, for his gear had remained in the servants' quarters. Gunthar had long since realized the need to exert considerable leniency with Robert if he wished to keep him in his employ. At Gunthar's age, he had little patience for training a new secretary when Robert filled the role so efficiently. Today's puzzling lapses were little worse than a minor nuisance. Robert had a cunning way of scratching the errors off the parchment with his penknife and inserting the corrections so skillfully that Gunthar would have had to hold the parchment up to very bright light to see where the changes had been made.

Robert blew off the ink dust, sketched in the altered words, and slid the letter back to Gunthar. Aye, even today with distraction so clearly nagging at him, the corrections appeared completely seamless. Still, Gunthar saw how quickly Robert's attention drifted away again as he sat waiting for his next instructions.

"Is there anything I can do, lad?"

Gunthar was not sure why he asked that particular question, but he knew it struck some unguarded need when instead of responding with his usual instant deflection, Robert hesitated. Something flashed in the minstrel's eyes. Temptation. To unburden something in his heart? Gunthar held his breath. He had waited months for this.

Robert glanced away. Passed a tongue between his lips. Looked back at Gunthar and almost spoke. He stopped himself by curling his lip between his teeth so hard Gunthar was surprised there was not blood on it when he released it.

"Thank you, sir, but it is naught. I missed a night's sleep is all and there are cobwebs in my head. You have another letter, I see. I will be more careful with this one."

Robert had made the same promise three times before, but Gunthar simply slid the letter across the desk, knowing his own disciplined features revealed nothing of his disappointment.

It must have to do with the woman. There could be no other explanation. Gunthar had not forgotten Robert's revelation in Poitou that he had fallen in love with a woman above his station. For a former villein, this might have referred to anyone from a merchant's daughter to the queen herself. The truth was, though curious, Gunthar had not spent a great deal of time musing over the matter, until a wan young stranger had shown up in this very room in urgent search of his secretary two days ago.

She had not looked particularly remarkable to Gunthar at first, with her worn, patched gown and limp tendrils of nondescript brown hair. It had seemed impossible that so rough a creature could be Robert's secret love. But shy of Gunthar as she had been, he had quickly discerned a quiet dignity about her, while her shadowed eyes had held a solemn strength he judged might attract a man of Robert's mettle. Gunthar had also caught the swift charge of familiarity between them, though from Robert's surprise she had not come at his bidding. At best, she had the look of a lower servant. Likely she was some man's neglected love child, a man with status or wealth just respectable enough to have given Robert pause. What had he called her? Alice, yes, that was it. Gunthar had struggled to recall the name Robert had once let slip in Poitou. It must certainly have been Alice, and yet—

Gunthar watched Robert's hand shove through his hair again and smiled a little wryly. The boy was as maddening to him as ever. It was clear Robert was profoundly disturbed about something, but he had made it clear he would not confide whatever it was to Gunthar. And Gunthar really had no time to try to interfere with whatever it was. The king was sending him to York in the morning to mediate between two rather disruptive barons. He should like to have taken Robert with him, but his wife had been too glad-some of the minstrel's music once more for Gunthar to steal him away from her again so soon. The king had offered Gunthar one of his own clerks to fulfill his need for a secretary. He should not be gone longer than a fort-night. If Robert had not regained his powers of concentration by the time Gunthar returned, he would investigate the minstrel's two-day disappear-ance, whether Robert welcomed it or not.

"Read that over when you finish it," Gunthar said, "then bring your lute to the sitting chamber. I promised my wife you would sing her some of those new tunes you learned in Poitou before I leave tomorrow."

Robert nodded so absently, Gunthar might have wondered if the minstrel had even heard the request if he had not known Robert long enough to be confident that some corner of his mind had registered it. He studied those two deep grooves between the jet black brows another moment, then left the office to join the countess.

He found her cheerfully plying her embroidery in companionship with the Lady Marguerite. The girl's wedding to Saxton lay a little over a week and a half away and her mother, no doubt fearful of her future son-in-law's disapproval, had been reluctant to allow Marguerite to spend time with Gunthar's wife. Seeing Helen's disappointment, Gunthar had pressed Lady Leah rather firmly to reconsider her hesitance. He knew he would not be able to intimidate Saxton into such compliance once Marguerite was his wife, but her mother had dissolved nicely beneath the subtle menace he had let slip into his gaze. He had learned from his father that one need not carry out a threat, so long as another perceived that one might.

He bent to set a kiss to his wife's cheek. "What do you two discuss so earnestly?"

Helen's silvery eyes laughed up at him. "Merely gossip, my dear. You do well to interrupt us."

He moved to stand behind his wife's chair so that he could gaze across at the Lady Marguerite. Although he knew his wife enjoyed the girl's company, he knew little of her beyond the fact of her betrothal to Saxton. Gunthar had once counted her grandfather among his friends, but when the king had dismissed him from court he had for the most part severed old relationships lest they be stained by his own disgrace. Marguerite had her mother's prettiness and her father's dark coloring. Gunthar was grateful to her for keeping Helen's spirits up when, at Helen's insistence, he had taken Robert and his music with him to Poitou. Harry's death had been a hard blow to them both and not a day had passed in Poitou that he had not worried for his wife. Even after Lady Leah had summoned her daughter away from Lamhurst, Helen had written to him of their continued correspondence. From the bright tone of her words on the parchment, she had continued to be buoyed by their friendship. Perhaps there was something he could do to show his gratitude to the lass before her marriage to Saxton cut the strings of their association.

Marguerite said, her dusky head bent over her stitchery, "So Sir Gerald has finally persuaded Evelyn to put away her grief?"

"Not quite that yet," Helen replied, plunging her needle with its blue-purple thread through her own linen, "but she no longer refuses to see him when he comes to call. I have hopes for a match between them. He is a good man, and patient with her. I think he will make her happy again in time."

Gunthar had been surprised to find Sir Gerald Faintree attempting to court his daughter-in-law when he returned to Kent. Helen had not mentioned it in her letters, perhaps because she had known Gunthar's initial impulse would be to frown the young man away. But Helen had said they must not be greedy of Evelyn and their grandson merely because they still missed Harry, and he knew she was right.

Marguerite glanced up from her embroidery and smiled. It took Gunthar a moment to realize why. He was playing with a lock of Helen's pale gold hair that had spilled out from beneath her veil. It was something he often absently did when he stood or sat near his wife and fell into contemplation of one subject or another. A wistful expression misted into Marguerite's chestnut eyes, her gaze fixed upon his fondling gesture. Her embroidery drifted into her lap and he observed how her fingers moved to caress a ring she wore, a gold-worked braid with a blood-red jewel nested in its center.

Gunthar mastered his surprise in an instant. He could be mistaken. The slender fingers that rubbed the stone obscured his ability to judge it clearly.

"What do you think of this pattern, Marguerite?" Helen held out her linen on which she had begun to stitch a series of interlocked garlands of violets and snowdrops.

"It is charming, my lady," Marguerite said. "But how did you weave the petals together so cleverly just here?"

She reached across the space between them to point at the cloth, baring her bejeweled hand. If she had slapped Gunthar with it, it could not have stunned him more. With a sudden burst of clarity, he recalled every detail of that conversation in Poitou. Not Alice. Mae. The girl's name was Mae, or—Marguerite?

He waited a heartbeat before he said, "That is a very fine ring you are wearing, my lady. A garnet, is it not?"

She glanced up at him, her eyes flaring wide. *She has not your powers of self-possession, my lad.*

She hesitated before saying with betraying breathlessness, "Yes."

"May I see it?"

Again she paused. This time the smile that curved her rosy lips was clearly forced, but she must have thought the ring safe from recognition for after a moment she extended her hand to him.

He held her fingers lightly and the last of his doubts vanished. "A very fine ring," he repeated. "A gift from—your betrothed, perhaps?"

"Yes," she said again, but her gaze fell from his as she drew her hand away.

She repeated her earlier query of Helen and focused a little too intently, Gunthar thought, on his wife's explanation of her stitchery pattern.

He waited for a lull to fall in their exchange before he remarked to Helen, "As I must leave you so early tomorrow, my dear, I have invited Robert to join us when he finishes the letter I gave him. I thought you would enjoy his music."

"Oh, yes," she said, smiling up at her husband. "He told me he learned some new songs in Poitou, but you kept him so busy at Lamhurst, he had not time to sing them for me. Are you taking him with you tomorrow?"

The hand that held Marguerite's needle gave a jerk in her cloth, but she steadied it quickly.

"Nay. I have robbed you of his company long enough." The rhythm of Marguerite's stitches smoothed. "I hired him to serve you, not myself. I forget his common roots sometimes, he is so clever. I should not like to lose him, like we have our other minstrels. I think we must find him some clear-eyed bride among our household before he runs off after a pretty but totally unsuitable lass. His head is too hot and he is unlikely to consider the consequences of a pair of dreamy eyes until it is too late." He observed the tiny frown that brushed Marguerite's lips before he glanced at his wife and saw her puzzled look.

"There was nothing unsuitable about the woman that Caradoc married. Oh, are you thinking of Acelet? Heavens, Hugh, that was over thirty years ago. You only disapproved because you thought his departure would sadden me, and because Joslin— Marguerite, what are you doing?"

Marguerite had folded her embroidery and placed it in her workbasket. "If you and my lord are to be parted tomorrow, you will wish to be alone today, so I will leave you."

"Nay, child, stay," Helen protested. "Hugh and I will have the entire evening to ourselves. Do not go yet."

Marguerite stood, her basket in her hands. "You are very kind, my lady, but I—"

She broke off as the door opened and Robert entered the chamber with his lute. A soft, rosy shade stole up into her cheeks.

"My lady," Gunthar said, "I do not believe you have met my secretary, Robert Marcel. Robert, the Lady Marguerite de Villon, a friend of my wife's."

Marguerite gave Robert her hand, her smile over-bright. "How do you do? You must forgive me, I was just leaving—"

"But no, Marguerite," Helen said. "Pray stay. Once you are married, I will not see you again. You have some knowledge of music, do you not? You and Robert must perform something for us together."

"Perform? With your secretary?"

She made an admirable attempt at confusion, Gunthar thought.

"He was my minstrel before he was my husband's secretary, and a delightfully accomplished one. One song, Marguerite. Hugh, you do not mind?"

"Whatever pleases you, my dear," he said, though in truth, this did not please him at all. The boy was madder than he'd thought. No wonder Saxton wanted Robert out of the way!

"I would be honored to have you join me," Robert said to Marguerite. "A moment, my lady, my lord, while we discuss what to sing." He bowed to Helen and Gunthar, then led Marguerite to a corner of the chamber.

Gunthar watched them conversing in whispers. Marguerite's hands fluttered in a telltale sign of agitation, but no betraying emotion flickered across Robert's face. Except that the furrow still dug between his brows and he gave one small but sharp shake of his head. At least, Gunthar thought he did. Blazes! He wished he could read the man.

He took a chair beside his wife and waited. Robert did not seem inclined to linger long with his love, but guided her back to her chair, then drew up his minstrel's stool near—but not too near—Marguerite. He struck a series of sweet chords on his lute as a prelude before Marguerite began to sing a well-known *chanson*. After a few measures, Robert's rich baritone joined her simple but true soprano.

Gunthar sat back, crossing his arms and ankles. A low simmer of anger burned in him. As lenient as he had become with Robert, this—the marriage of villein and lady—was unthinkable! It was the one act of audaciousness by Robert he could not condone. And she! How a woman of Marguerite's breeding could have encouraged such foolery—!

They certainly made a handsome couple, though, seated as they were side by side. Even their voices blended in charming harmony, weaving together so instinctively Gunthar knew they must have sung thus together many times before. How long had this been going on? It was his duty to stop it, of course. Just as soon as he returned from York—

By which time it could well be too late. Saxton must view Robert as a serious threat rather than a passing infatuation of his bride-to-be's, else he'd not have tried so hard to blame Robert for those murders in Poitou. If Robert attempted to do something rash and dangerous, like trying to run off with the girl, no law in the land would object to Saxton defending his honor and that of his betrothed's by hunting and cutting down a wild, wanton minstrel.

Whatever Gunthar's stern opinions on Robert's behavior, he could not allow that. Nay, he could not wait to act. He would make Robert come with him to York and keep him there until after Marguerite was safely wed. He would drag Robert there if he had to—

He paused, struggling with the domineering temperament that was accustomed to commanding and seeing men obey. But he knew he could not command Robert. The man had been bound to obey others' commands for too many years and had set his heart hard against submitting again to another's arrogant authority. He would only dig in his heels and refuse. Gunthar would ask him, though. He would promise to return him to London in time for Saxton's wedding, saying he had been ordered by the king to attend, then once in York, arrange matters so to prevent the fulfillment of his promise.

Robert would never forgive Gunthar for the subterfuge. He believed himself very deeply in love, and he held his grudges fiercely, as he had shown with Kit Beckford. He would blame Gunthar when he lost Marguerite. Gunthar felt a rare, foreign lump in his throat. It would grieve him to lose the minstrel's friendship, but it would grieve him more to let him throw away his life on the whim of a man like Saxton.

40

Somewhere in the inklike hours of the night while the men around him in the servants' quarters lay snoring and snuffling, the numbness of his brother's death had worn off and a low, seething anger began to burn in Robert's belly. By the time he rose in the gray of dawn to transcribe one last letter for Gunthar, the seething had become a blaze. He kept his gaze carefully turned from Gunthar's shrewd eyes, knowing how anger could strip the veil from his own.

Gunthar took the letter from Robert's hand and in the small silence that followed, Robert envisioned him folding the parchment and affixing the seal. Gunthar's chair scraped against the floor. Robert rose, knowing that Gunthar had done the same.

"You are sure I cannot persuade you to change your mind?" Gunthar said.

"You've no need of my services in York. You will have the king's clerk. I have missed your lady wife and would stay and cheer her in your absence."

He caught the swirl of the hem of Gunthar's cloak. Gunthar had thrown it across the back of his chair while he dictated the letter and must be donning it for the journey. Robert waited for Gunthar to move towards the door.

"Look at me, lad."

Robert drew a long, slow, silent breath and thrust the anger down hard. Only when he was sure that he had clamped it as tight as he could did he obey Gunthar's request. Gunthar had asked him a dozen times last night to accompany him to York today, and Robert had excused himself each time. Gilbert had died scarcely four-and-twenty hours ago. Yesterday Robert had been so befogged with grief, so distracted with how to care for Lottie and Alice and the children, so frustrated to know how to escape in the midst of all these troubles with Marguerite when he knew how Saxton was watching them both, that when Gunthar had asked a gentle query, Robert had nearly poured out the whole to him.

It would have been a mistake. Nothing could have saved Gilbert. Gunthar might have helped with his brother's family, but once Robert spilled out one need, he feared in his present state he would spill out it all, and despite the friendship that had grown between them, every instinct in him still warned that Gunthar would never stand quietly by and allow Robert and Marguerite to wed. Gilbert's death had left Robert so shaken, he did not trust himself not to succumb to Gunthar's sympathy and confess a fatal admission that would lose him Marguerite once and for all. And so, he had remained silent.

He felt the probing power of Gunthar's gaze trying to pierce his thoughts. When Gunthar finally looked down to fasten the brooch at the neck of the cloak, Robert knew the veil over his eyes had held.

"I will be back before Saxton's wedding. Would it be too much to hope you can keep your head out of mischief until then?"

"Have I given you cause to think I intend to fall into mischief?"

He thought Gunthar paused before answering. "I suppose not. Beckford is in Wiltshire, and Saxton has not brought up the murder charges with the king for months."

Kit was concealing his presence at court from Gunthar?

Gunthar pulled on his gloves and stepped towards the door, then turned. His hand clapped against Robert's shoulder.

"Come with me. For the company. I will show you Norcott Castle and the apples I used to steal from my father's orchards there. They remain some of the finest fruit in England."

Norcott Castle? In York? Saxton has promised it to Kit when you are disgraced, or worse. But I intend to deal with that.

Robert had never felt less like smiling in his life, but he forced his lips to curve upwards. "Another time, sir."

He reached for something more to say, but his mind felt vaguely hazed and a dull throbbing nagged at the back of his eyes. So he left it there until Gunthar turned away.

When Gunthar pulled open the door, a thought sliced through the disorienting muddle: Robert would not see him again. One way or another, Robert would be far, far from Westminster and London with Marguerite before Gunthar returned.

"Sir."

Gunthar looked back, raising his brows when Robert hesitated.

"Thank you."

"For what?"

For believing me when no one else would. For bearing with my temper and tongue. For being a man I could choose to serve for the rest of my life if things were different. They were not different, though. Marguerite would be an unhealable break between them.

"Thank you for not asking where I vanished to for two days. I will explain when you get back." It was the first lie he had ever told Gunthar. It would also be the last.

Gunthar nodded and went out.

Robert stood a long time beside the desk when he was gone, letting the anger bubble back up. The floggings, the humiliations, Lottie's marriage and abuse, Gunthar nearly murdered twice, and now—now Gilbert dead. True, the fever could not be laid at Kit's feet, but he had drenched Gilbert and his family in the rain, housed them without warmth in one of the foulest inns Robert had seen in all his years of wandering, then refused to let Alice take her husband's body back to Beck Manor for burying. Robert had arranged for a Christian burial in a London churchyard, but what comfort would that bring to Alice and the children when they longed to visit Gilbert's grave in years to come?

Robert slammed his hand against the desk top. *The devil take you, Kit Beckford. Aye, the devil shall take you today.*

Fury throbbed in Robert's head so hard it blurred his vision for a moment. But he did not need clear eyesight to remember the way to Kit's door.

"I know you are in there, you dog!" Robert pounded against the wooden boards blocking him from the chamber where he had listened to Kit and Saxton just days before. Saxton said no one came to this part of the palace. Then no one would hear him shouting except Kit. "Let me in, you coward! Hiding behind a sick man and his children—! If you had a quarrel with me, you should have faced me like a man, not skulked behind your helpless villeins like a spineless cur!"

Silence answered him. Robert kicked the door in fury, then wrenched the latch. It thrust downward easily in his hand. The door swung open. Robert hesitated, wary lest a trap lay inside. No voice challenged him or bade him enter. Was it possible that Kit still slept? Nay, there was too much light emanating from the room, the lapping glow of a fire mingling with the smooth flood of early sunshine. Kit would not have left the shutters open all night, or a hearth fire burning in the antechamber while he slumbered beyond in his bed.

Robert stepped cautiously across the threshold, his hand on the hilt of his dagger. A blast of heat greeted him first, moistening his cheeks with perspiration. He moved to the door that stood in the wall behind the desk. He hoped Kit had heard him shouting outside and taken refuge in the chamber that lay beyond. He hoped Kit stood waiting for him with sword drawn so there would be no stain on Robert's conscience when he ended this feud in blood. Robert pulled free his dagger, thrust down this latch like the other and kicked the door wide.

He sprang into empty darkness. No shout, no slicing sword to dodge. Just silent, cheating space. Light from the antechamber flowed in behind him, showing the dim outlines of a rumpled bed with a pallet at the foot, perhaps for a squire. So Kit had slept here last night, at least, though if there were a brazier or another hearth, he had let the embers burn out.

Robert returned to the antechamber, disappointment souring his mouth. Where would Kit have gone at this hour? The brightness of this room, in contrast with the one behind him, almost made Robert's eyes ache. The thrown back shutters countered the purpose, it seemed to him, of a fire on the hearth. Together they filled the room with so much light—

Together. Why? What might one need to see so clearly at this hour of the day? Robert knew what he should wish to see. He had needed such light of his own only an hour ago. He moved to the desk where he had seen Kit sit and conspire with Saxton. It seemed too much to hope that he might find anything more telling on the desk than an unstopped inkpot or a quill tossed to the side rather than tucked neatly in the pen stand with is fellows. His heartbeat tripped when he saw the parchment. There were words. Bold and black, but ceasing half-way down the page. Kit had been interrupted.

Robert picked up the sheet. He realized his anger still flared too hot when he had to rub his eyes to clear them. Aye, there now. In the mingling of hearth light and early sunlight he could see as plainly as if he stood outside at noonday.

I, Christopher Beckford, vassal of Hugh de Bury, Earl of Gunthar, from whom I hold the barony of Beck Castle in the county of Witshire and also Halham Manor in the county of Dorset, do bear witness that of my own knowledge the man who calls himself Robert Marcel, formerly minstrel and now secretary to said Hugh de Bury, sold information to the French on King John's movements during the late campaigns to recover the king's rights in Poitou. Furthermore, that said Hugh de Bury knowingly gave comfort and protection to the traitor, Robert Marcel. Also by conspiring with the barons of Poitou whom he was sent to win to the king's cause, Hugh de Bury instead discouraged them from sending their support to the king, and thus—

The words broke off there. Except for the name inscribed in a different hand, flaring arrogance at the bottom of the parchment.

Testimony witnessed by Symeon Achard, Earl of Saxton, on . . . A blank had been left for the date, but next to the name a seal had already been stamped into red wax: the roaring bear of Saxton's crest.

So that was the trap they had set for Gunthar. Accusing Robert of Kit's own treason and Gunthar of knowing and protecting him. One part of Robert's mind raced with questions—what proof did they intend to lay, would they bribe other witnesses to support the lie, and who? But these thrummed only dimly against a renewed flood of fury that pounded through him. If the two miscreants thought Robert was going to stand idle and let them ruin the best man he had ever known—

He grabbed up the penknife on the table, then slashed it down the parchment, slicing the sheet neatly in two. Less neatly was the way Robert's fists crumpled up the divided sheets before he flung them into the hearth's flames. A rage he could scarcely control followed the parchment with the inkpot and the pens and the penholder and a pumice stone and lastly the penknife.

Robert looked for something more to throw, but through the open window floated the sweet chime of a church bell. It startled him at first, so out of place it fell against the tumult in his blood. A second chime rang calm and pure, like the eddy of autumn air that glided across the room to wash his heated cheeks. It took a third dulcet peal to draw him to the window. He could not read the sky. The foliage without was too thick, concealing the window and any occupants within. But he knew what the bells signified. The hour of Terce. The priest had said he would bury Gilbert's body after the mid-morning prayers. At least now that the interdict had passed, his brother could be buried in consecrated ground.

Robert plunged both hands into his hair, pressing his palms against his temples. He struggled to master the ragged breaths of anger that heaved his chest. Alice. He had to find Alice and Lottie and the children and take them to the churchyard. He had paid one of the palace cooks to let them huddle a few nights in the kitchen where Robert knew they would be warm. Between a funeral mass and a burial plot for Gilbert's body and lodging for his brother's family, Robert's carefully hoarded nest egg was rapidly dwindling.

But he could not think of that now. In truth, he found himself struggling to keep two thoughts in his head at all. All he wanted to do was find Kit and thrash him as Kit had thrashed Robert so many times on the manor. But Alice needed him. He leaned his palms flat against the window frame and pulled in several more chestfuls of air. Vengeance would have to wait— again.

The anger did not fade away so much as the weight of an implacable exhaustion gradually repressed it during his brother's burial. Robert fought it, for he had much to do when he returned to the palace, but he had scarcely slept for the last three nights. No matter how many times he shook himself, the vigorous motion failed to clear his head or drive energy back into his limbs. His head ached from fatigue and worry. How was he to decide what to do with Lottie and Alice and the children if he could not think straight?

He noted how the children shivered as they stood by the graveside. It was warm for an autumn day. He hoped they were not sickening. He gave Alice his cloak to wrap them in, the thick, woolen one he had bought in Poitou. Lottie's hands swept up and down her thin sleeves beneath her own patched mantle. Robert frowned and laid a hand to his sister's brow, but it felt cool enough. Lottie started to say something, then fell silent as the priest began to intone a prayer.

After the burial, they trudged back to the palace, scarcely speaking, but when they reached the palace kitchens, Robert made another grab at mental clarity through the thudding that pulsed against his temples.

"Send the children to sit by the cook fire, Ally, while you and Lottie come with me to my quarters. The men I lodge with will be about their duties elsewhere this time of day. We can talk of what we should do next."

He tugged at the neck of his tunic. He had grown too soft in Gunthar's service. During frigid winter nights on the manor, he would have welcomed a blast of heat such as the one that met them at the kitchen door.

Alice looked as drawn and weary as he felt, but she nodded, settled the children in a kitchen corner, then followed him and Lottie.

Robert checked when he opened the door to the servants' quarters and realized he had misspoken about its emptiness. Several men stood conversing within. The headache wobbled his vision again, forcing him to blink several times to clear it before he could make out the faces.

He saw William Locke first. Robert had nearly forgotten why Gilbert had been brought to London, to prove along with Lottie and Will Robert's villeinage in a court of law. Well, Gil's death would put an end to that. Without at least one male blood relative to testify, the courts would not take the word of a woman and an alleged foster brother. Two men stood near William, dressed in forest green tunics with badges sewn to their shoulders. Robert's eyes hazed briefly, blurring the image on the badges, and by the time his vision cleared his attention had fixed on a third man's face.

Richard Channing returned Robert's gaze, his eyes a-sparkle with accusation. *He knows about me and Marguerite.* Robert hated that he had deceived the young man, but there had been no other way. How had Richard learned of it? His gaze swept back to the badges affixed to the green tunics. He saw the image clearly now. A roaring bear. The emblem of the Earl of Saxton. So that explained Richard's knowledge and the presence of Saxton's surly squire who stood beside him.

Someone appeared to be kneeling behind the other men, for Robert caught movement in the small spaces between them. He saw Saxton's men lay their hands to the sword hilts as Robert stepped into the room. He reached for his dagger, bracing himself to confront Saxton as he stood. A hand clasped Richard on the shoulder and moved him out of the way. But it was not Saxton's cool gaze that Robert met. It was the dark grey eyes of Kit Beckford, gleaming with the same mocking satisfaction they had held each time he had bound Robert to the whipping post.

"Ah," Kit said. "I did not know if you would come back from the churchyard of your own accord after I found the parchment in the fire."

It did not surprise Robert that Kit knew where he had been. He had known himself watched ever since Saxton had discovered Robert and Marguerite at the fair.

"What are you doing here, Kit?" Nothing honest, not with Saxton's men at his back. Robert saw the gleam dim in those gloating eyes as it always did when Robert had the audacity to address his "master" by the familiar diminutive that should have been reserved only to Kit's family and friends.

"Insolent to the end, I see." Kit looked at Alice. "My condolences on the death of your husband. I assure you, it was not what I intended."

The anger that had come upon Robert in the middle of the night began to bubble again. "The court won't hear your case now," he said. "You as good as freed me by drenching Gilbert in the rain."

Kit scratched at the beard that trimmed his chin, a gesture of studied nonchalance. "I would like to have dragged you back," he admitted. "I should like it to have been my hand that humbled you and silenced at last your impudent tongue. Others, alas, will have the pleasure now of punishing you as befits your crimes against the crown. Instead of seeing you swing from a rope on Beck Manor, I will have to content myself with the sight of your head on London Bridge every time I ride past it."

Robert heard Lottie gasp beside him and felt a punch of shock in his stomach. "I burned your infernal lies."

"And you thought that was the end of it? What was written can be rewritten, Rob. Really, you should have tried to run when you had the chance."

Kit was right about the false testimony he had transcribed. Robert would have known that if his mind had not been so muddy.

"What are you talking about?" Richard demanded. He gazed with narrowed eyes from Robert to Kit. "I did not agree to come here to give my witness to a lie."

"You came because you are Saxton's man now," Kit snapped. "You accepted your knighthood from him and—well, I will spare you the embarrassment before these men of the rest."

Robert followed the flick of Kit's eyes to Saxton's men. Richard's face ruddied. The silent mortification of knowing his cousin loved a minstrel must be bad enough, without hearing it spoken before men who might spread it through the entire court.

"You have not been asked to do anything dishonorable," Kit said, "only testify of what your own eyes see."

There was a pause, then Richard nodded. He tossed Robert a glance of angry betrayal before Kit motioned him and the squire, Nick Tybert, to one side. Their movement lay open to view the travel-worn bag that Robert had carried with him for seven years.

"Is this yours?" Kit queried.

The bag remained fastened shut as Robert had left it that morning, with his lute leaning against it in its case, and his sword in its scabbard. Prevarication would be useless. Richard had seen the lute case and the tyger with the broken paw on the sword hilt too many times in Poitou.

"Aye, it's mine," Robert said.

"Perhaps you will consent to show us the contents?"

"Perhaps I will not. What I choose to pack in my own bag is no concern of yours."

"But it may concern the crown if Lord Gunthar's barber speaks true."

"His barber?" The round-faced man with the skillful scissors who quartered with Robert in this room was not the same who had served Gunthar before the king's campaign. That earlier servant had died of the fever in Poitou. Gunthar had hired another in La Rochelle to take his place and brought him back with him to England.

"Master Tybert here"—Kit gestured toward Saxton's squire—"shared a few drinks and several games of dice with the fellow in a tavern last night. The fellow lost, repeatedly, did he not Master Tybert?" The squire nodded. "When it was time to settle, to Master Tybert's surprise the man paid not in copper coins, but with a single silver one. Did I mention that he was very drunk? The fact that the coin bore not the imprint of our good King John, but that of King Philip of France, might not have been surprising from a man from Poitou, but he told Master Tybert—but Master Tybert can finish his own story."

Nicholas Tybert looked only too pleased to do so. "I said to the fellow, 'Does the Earl of Gunthar pay his servants in French coins now?' He answered, 'Nay, the earl pays only in English coinage. But that minstrel of his who sometimes acts as the earl's secretary, he challenged me to a game of dice three nights ago, and when he lost, he gave me this.'"

"I remember that game," Robert said. "But I paid him in English coins. Copper, not silver."

Tybert smirked. "That was not the story he told. I thought the coin suspicious. All of us remember the two murdered guards in Gunthar's camp and how your dagger was found bloodied beside the second guard's body. And that it was Gunthar who turned the king's mind from hanging you. I did not like to think that you had got the coin from Gunthar, for that should mean that you and he were in some unholy alliance together with the French. But that judgment was not mine to make. I took the coin and the barber to my master and bade him repeat his story. My Lord Saxton listened and suggested we search your belongings for the truth."

The truth. Robert snorted. The barber had not been long enough in Gunthar's service to put loyalty to the old earl over Saxton's ability to bully or bribe him into saying whatever Saxton wanted. Robert glanced at Lottie's and Alice's white, frightened faces, at William's grim, worried one, at the two men wearing Saxton's badges who had undoubtedly been sent to arrest him. He did not need to look at Kit again. The trap was springing shut and Robert had no way to stop it.

"It is easy enough to prove whether the barber spoke truly or not," Kit said. "Just show us the contents of your bag."

You mean the French silver you have planted there. The bag might appear undisturbed, but Robert knew what he would find when he opened it. He had a sharp, vivid memory of his father's fury, throwing his own switched coins into Lord Garoux Beckford's face.

"Or shall I look for myself?" Kit bent towards the bag.

"No, I will do it." Robert stepped between Kit and the bag. He had little choice but to dance to the tune Kit piped for now.

Robert knelt and slowly unlaced the strap. When had Kit done it? While Robert watched his brother's body being laid in the ground? Or earlier, while he had been flinging Kit's "testimony" into the flames? Had he done it himself, or sent someone else? Whoever it had been had been cunning. Robert did not know if he would have noticed the contents had been disturbed, they lay so near where he had left them this morning.

He lifted out his books, bound together by an embossed leather strap he had bought in La Rochelle, and set them on the floor beside him.

"Why are you here?" Robert asked softly. Only Kit stood near enough to hear him. "All of these men, even Richard, have a connection to Saxton, except for you. I thought he wished to maintain as much distance from you as possible."

"Saxton has no notion I am here. I was preparing to send Will back to Hallham, since he is of no use to me now, but he pled with me to let him see you one last time."

Though Kit spoke softly, too, Robert knew he lied. Kit wanted to be in at the kill and had used William as a ruse to "coincidentally" be waiting for Robert when Saxton sent his guards.

Robert removed a tinderbox and some candles he sometimes lit to read by when he could not sleep at night. "Yet you told me most of the barber's story as though you had heard it from his own lips." *Or invented it yourself.*

Kit shrugged. "Tybert told me while we waited for you."

Quiet as the words between them flew, Kit was playing it cautious. Out came Robert's change of hose, his soft-soled shoes, and the leather bag that held his dried mint. "And Gunthar? I read the accusations you penned. How do you intend to prove any of that?"

"Gunthar's fate is in his own hands. All he needs do is shun you when you are brought before the courts, declare himself ignorant of your perfidy, confess that you deceived him. His integrity is so famed in the kingdom that even the king will hesitate to challenge Gunthar's word if he swears it."

Kit's voice sank still lower, to barely more than a whisper as Robert pulled out his second work tunic.

"But if he attempts to stand by you, to defend you, after your treason is revealed beyond all doubt—I do not think even Gunthar's reputation can survive the firestorm of suspicion *that* will stir up. And that is when I will lay my sworn witness of his complicity before the courts. I was in his camp when he treated with the Poitevin barons, I overheard your tryst with the French agent in the woods, I may even have overheard whispered conversations between you and Gunthar. Gunthar cannot successfully deny any of it, unless he first repudiates you."

Robert had not realized how dry his lips had grown until he passed his tongue between them. "How do you know he will not?"

Kit bent down as if to peer into Robert's bag and hissed in his ear, "Because he thinks you are innocent. He is my liege lord and I know him. If he believed you guilty, he would throw you to the headsman's axe. But he will not turn his back on one of his own house whom he believes has been falsely accused. That will be his downfall."

Robert was not so sure. Gunthar had professed to believe him thus far, but serious fissures still lay between them. They had not spoken again of Robert's views on villeins, but Robert knew a man like Gunthar could never countenance a "philosophy" that Kit rightly termed sedition in the eyes of the law. And there was Marguerite. When Gunthar learned that Robert had concealed from him so presumptuous an ambition as that—

He stared down at the final article of clothing in the bag: his scarlet minstrel's tunic. He'd had no need for it in Poitou or since his return as Gunthar's secretary. That would change when he eloped with Marguerite. *If I elope with Marguerite.* Below the merry cloth lay Kit's snare. He closed his eyes and sank for one moment into the memory of how honey-sweet Marguerite's lips had tasted at the fair. He was glad he had been allowed to kiss her one last time.

He opened his eyes again with a deep drawn breath. Stalling would not delay the inevitable. He removed the scarlet tunic. All that was left was his wooden money box, also purchased in Poitou as his earnings from Gunthar had outgrown the leather pouch where he had formerly carried his coins. Robert had kept the box locked and wore the key around his neck.

It did not surprise him that Kit swooped down to scoop the box out, or that Robert glimpsed foreign markings on the box as he did so that told him this was not the same box he had bought, or that Kit drew his dagger to pry open the lock before Robert could protest that the box was not his and prove it by presenting a key that did not match the lock.

The lock jittered and popped, then Kit threw open the lid. He drew out a silver-white coin and held it out to Richard and Saxton's guards to view. Robert observed how Kit did not so much at glance at the inscription on the coin before he quoted triumphantly, "*Philipus Rex.* See, gentlemen. Not *Johannes Rex,* as read the coins of our good King John, but *Philipus Rex.* King Philip. Where, I ask you, would a mere minstrel, or even Lord Gunthar's secretary, obtain such coins as these? One or two, perhaps, he might have brought away from Poitou, but a shower such as this?"

Richard reached out with cupped hands to catch the tinkling stream of silver that Kit poured out of the box.

"And—what is this?" Kit said, as though startled. He pulled a folded sheet of parchment from the box, flipped it open and read, "In recognition of your services, in agreement set forth on the third day of March in the thirty-fourth year of our reign, we issue the promised sum and do likewise promise silver and lands as formerly agreed when the usurper John of England is delivered into our hands.'"

Kit held out the parchment, like he'd held out the coin, to Richard, to the guards, and last of all to Robert. At the bottom of the parchment stamped into red wax sat a king enthroned, encircled with the letters FRANCORVM REX PHILIPVS DI GRA. Robert knew this Latin, like he'd known the Latin on his father's coins fourteen years ago: *Philip, by the Grace of God, King of the Franks.*

41

obert had forgotten the receipt the Frenchman had handed to Kit in the woods along with the coins. Stamped with King Philip's own seal. Of course Kit would want that to force those he dealt with to hold to their word once he had delivered—

—the usurper John of England—

The words knocked the breath out of Robert. The King of France had long accused King John of stealing the throne that should have gone to John's elder brother's son, the young Duke Arthur of Brittany. Could Kit truly have been so brazen as to plot with the Count of La Marche to sell King John to the French crown? Kit would have to be mad! Discovery would mean worse than a hanging, worse even than the headsman's axe. A traitor of that magnitude would be cut down from the noose before he was dead and forced to watch his own bowels drawn out of his belly and burned before his eyes. Then his body would be quartered and gibbeted along with his head throughout the realm of England.

"What further proof of Marcel's guilt do we need than this?"

Kit's words slammed through Robert's ears like a thunderclap and sent through him a single sickening shudder. The condemning receipt had not been found among Kit's belongings. It had been found among Robert's.

He heard the scream of swords scraping free of their scabbards, but all he saw was Kit's face blurring in a red haze. Robert sprang from a coil he had not realized he had drawn his body into. His fist smashed into Kit's mouth. Robert followed him down to the floor, vaulting both their bodies into a roll. Saxton's guards would not dare strike so long as he kept close enough to Kit to risk their swords hitting the wrong man.

Robert got off another few satisfying punches before the threat from the guards forced him to allow Kit to pivot Robert onto his back. A cacophony exploded around them, women screaming, men shouting, feet scuffling. Robert and Kit punched and scrabbled against each other, Kit on top, then Robert, then Kit again.

Kit finally landed a blow that set Robert's ears ringing. The red mist before Robert's eyes thickened. He slapped his hand out wildly and felt the thrust of Kit's nose against his palm. He spread his fingers, splaying them over Kit's face, trying to blind him while Robert's own sight slowly cleared. Robert's other hand groped for his dagger. His fingers brushed the hilt, but the sheath lodged trapped between their bodies. Robert muttered a curse of frustration, then felt Kit's lips part in an audible snarl. Kit's face shifted despite the limpet-tight hold Robert sought to maintain. Robert whipped his hand away seconds before Kit's teeth could snap down on Robert's thumb.

They swore and cursed at one another while some clamor raged around them. Robert thrust his fingers into Kit's hair and jerked sideways as hard as he could, yanking, dragging until he levered his other hand against Kit's shoulder and shoved and shoved. He could not force Kit onto his back, but he managed at last to fling him onto his side. They grappled thus together for a moment until, as if in the same second of time, both realized that their positions had pinned Robert's hip and dagger against the floor while laying Kit's blade exposed to its master's hand.

Robert's hand flashed down to lock over Kit's as it clamped around his hilt. Twice the blade began to slip free. Twice Robert slammed it back into its hold. The third time, Robert let his grasp grow slack, his fingers sliding loose to Kit's wrist. The dagger slid out. Murder glittered in Kit's eyes. But in that instant of triumph, Robert fisted his hand around Kit's wrist and slammed it down between their faces against the stones of the floor.

Kit swore and snarled and cursed as Robert wrenched at his wrist, smashed his hand against the floor again, wrenched and smashed and wrenched until Robert saw the shift of the blade in Kit's benumbed fingers. Robert tore the dagger out of Kit's battered hand, scrambled to his knees, drove another blow into Kit's face, then lunged atop him.

He had the point of the dagger at Kit's throat when a man shouted, "Rob, stop!"

Robert realized that his action had bared his back, a clear, clean target for a sword thrust by one of Saxton's guards.

"Call the dogs off," Robert snapped at Kit, pressing the blade against the throbbing vein at the base of his throat, "or I'll slit your throat, I swear I will."

"Rob!" The voice behind him grew more urgent, but he could not identify it through the pounding rush of blood in his head.

Kit's eyes spat pure hatred. "Kill me and you'll hang as a murderer."

"Better that than being drawn and quartered for *your* crime. You shattered my sister's life and now my brother lies dead because of you. You and your wretched sire have destroyed everything I ever loved." Even his future with Marguerite. Robert could never marry her now. If by some miracle he escaped unscathed from this room, from the palace, from London, he would be a fugitive, an outlaw. "You owe me blood for blood. Call your dogs off," he repeated, "or I'll settle our account here and now."

Robert almost hoped Kit would defy him. One swift stroke of the dagger's blade and perhaps all the pain and bitterness would flow out of Robert's heart on the crest of vengeance finally satisfied.

"Robin, don't!"

That voice he knew. His sister knelt at Kit's head. Robert pressed the edge of the blade warningly against Kit's throat and looked up into Lottie's pale, lovely face. The cheeks that he recalled so starkly stained with the purpling imprint of her husband's bruising hands were smooth and clear beneath her pallor.

"I can't let him go," Robert said, following Lottie's terrified glance at the dagger in his hand. Kit would wreak revenge for this day on Lottie and Alice, perhaps even on the children. "Lottie, I can't let him go."

"You can't kill him. Robin, you're not a murderer!"

Robert was not so sure. Through the drubbing of his temples he saw his father's beloved face, saw again his mother's tears, Lottie's vile abuse by Hanley, Gilbert gaunt and white and still upon the cot—

"Rob," the man's voice called again, "leave him to me. We'll tie him up, then I'll smuggle you out of the palace."

Kit gave a low growl. "And hang in his place if you do, Channing."

Robert punched the edge of the blade up beneath Kit's chin to cut off the threat before he looked round. To his surprise, both of Saxton's guards sprawled unconscious on the floor. His gaze shot to the sword in Richard's hand, then to the squire who struggled to free himself from the lockhold William had clamped him in. William looked equal parts terrified and determined as he held Tybert's arms twisted tight behind his back. It was one thing to refuse to shun Robert when he defied the manor lord, it was quite another, Robert knew, for William himself to assault a man or youth of noble birth.

"Let me go, you filthy churl," Tybert swore at William. "When Saxton learns of this, he will lop off your hands before he kills you."

Richard swung around and clouted the squire so hard with his fist that Tybert slumped silent in William's hold. Robert met Richard's gaze for one instant, then flipped the dagger over in his hand and cracked the hilt into Kit's temple. Robert hoped Kit would awaken to as abominable a headache as Robert had when Kit had hit him in the woods with the rock.

"What are you doing?" Robert said as Richard sheathed his sword and held out a hand to pull Robert to his feet.

"The devil if I know," Richard replied. "I was mad as blazes when Saxton told me about you and my cousin, but lend my name to such villainy as this? I found you the morning you came stumbling out of the woods, I cleaned the wound to your head. A blow like that would have laid you out for hours, but even if you had not been unconscious when those men were killed in Gunthar's camp, why would you come back after you'd murdered them and run? None of Beckford's accusations make sense. Besides—" Richard shrugged slightly "—you stayed that guard's hand the night I arrived at the camp so muddied that he took me for spy. Now we are at quits."

Robert hesitated, then nodded and let Richard pull him up. He watched William lower Tybert to the floor as gently as a babe, as if such care might somehow mitigate his offense against the squire.

"I'm sorry, Will," Robert said. "I never meant to drag you into this."

"Ye never mean any of yer mischief," William growled. "But I'm glad I was here to help."

"We need to tie these men up," Richard said to William. "Gag them, too, to give us more time to—"

"Wait," Robert said. He stared down at Kit. His head lolled to one side and a knot already swelled where the dagger's hilt had struck him. Robert felt someone lean softly into his side. He wrapped one arm around his sister as her arms wound around his waist. "I can't let Kit take you back to the manor, any of you. You know what he will do." He looked up to meet William's eyes.

Lottie said, "He won't hurt Ally or me, no matter how angry he is. We're still too profitable to him."

You mean still young enough to bear children. More villeins to till Kit's fields, more chattle to bring profit to his coffers. Lottie was right, however bitter such "safety." No baron would squander the potential of future labor merely to spite a young woman's menfolk, any more than he would put down a broodmare because a stallion proved unbreakable.

Robert looked across again at William. "Come with me, Will. If Richard can find a way to smuggle us out, come with me."

William shook his head. "I can't leave Lucy. Besides, Beckford took me from Wiltshire because he needed me on Hallham Manor. I'm young and strong. He needs me there."

Perhaps. Robert prayed it would prove so. "He'll not let you escape unscathed for this day, though. At the very least, you'll taste the whip for it."

"Ye bore it," William said. "I'm no less a man than ye."

Despite the stout words, Robert saw a gleam of fear in William's eyes. Robert fought back a selfish wave. It would not be like before, when he'd had the whole of England to freely explore. He'd live his life alone, in hiding after this. It would have been more bearable with William at his side. But it would also be more dangerous for Will than a flogging, however savage. No, Robert would not ask that of this man he counted as a brother.

He pressed the heel of his hand to his head. It still throbbed from the raucous brawl with Kit. Lottie reached up to lay her fingers, rough but cool, against his cheek.

"Robin—"

"Can you bind them?" Richard's voice broke across Lottie's. He spoke to William. "Use their own belts, then take the squire's dagger to cut gags from their tunics. Be quick, before they wake up." Richard kicked the guards' swords so they spun far out of reach of their owners, lest the men begin to stir before William finished his task.

William hesitated.

"I will help," Robert said, but Richard stayed him.

"Nay, we must be going. Strap on your sword, then give me your cloak and your lute."

Robert obeyed the first two requests readily enough, but balked at the third. "What do you want with my lute?"

Richard pulled the cloak's hood over his fair head. "I mean to set a false trail if I can. The lute will help my disguise."

Robert's fingers locked as tight on the strap of the instrument's case as it had that day he stood frozen at the edge of the river, listening to the bay of Kit's hounds.

He felt Lottie's hand on his. "Let it go, Robin. It's not worth your life."

She could not understand, none of them could. It was a physical tie to his father, a tangible memory of his father's love for his mother that had embraced Robert, too, and held him warm and secure as a boy in a world so bitterly uncertain and cold.

Lottie pulled at his fingers. "Robin—"

She had not helped their father gather the wood, or sat at their father's side and watched his brown, calloused hands so skillfully fashion the neck and the belly. Their father had not confided in *her* the story, while he had carved the lute's rose, of the day he had stolen into Lord Garoux Beckford's gardens to steal some flowers of the same name to weave a garland for their mother's hair before they had wed. And it had not been Lottie their father praised with his flashing grin when Robert had slid the tuning pegs in so proudly.

Richard held out an impatient hand. "Hurry."

What if when Robert let it go, the memory of his father's face and voice and smile and love went with it?

William looked up from where he had pulled one of the guard's hands behind his back and was beginning to wind a belt around them.

"Ye won't forget him, Rob," William said, his voice gruff but firm. "Seven years ye were as good as dead to me. I never thought I'd see ye again, but I didn't forget ye. An' ye won't forget yer da. He's buried too deep in yer heart for that."

Robert was wrong. He saw in William's eyes that *he* understood, how, Robert could not fathom. Doubt eddied through him, but with his gaze fastened on the promise in William's eyes, Robert drew a long, slow, painful breath, then swung the lute case into Richard's hand.

"Take care of that," Robert warned, "and return it safe to me if you can."

Richard nodded, a little too carelessly for Robert's comfort, but there was nothing more Robert could do. He knelt to shuffle the contents of his bag back in and re-secure the strap, then flung the bag over his shoulder. Then he turned to Lottie.

"When Will is through, take him and Alice to the kitchens and stay there until Kit finds you. It will be best if none of you are here when he wakes up. Let him think I sent you away before I bound and gagged him." He looked at Richard. "He knows you played a part, though."

"Only that I knocked Saxton's guards down and let you escape," Richard said. "Saxton sent men to watch the exits in case you slipped away from Beckford. I'll try to draw some of them off so you can cut out without being seen."

However angry Saxton might be at Richard, Robert knew the young man carried a certain protection for now: he was cousin to the woman Saxton intended to marry.

Robert gave his sister a quick, rough hug—so much to say between them, and no time to say it. He kissed Alice, then turned to William.

The villein rose and cuffed Robert on the ear. "Take care, ye fool."

Robert laughed rather shakily, then with a husky sigh, followed Richard from the room.

But outside in the passageway, Robert caught Richard by the arm. "You have to save her from the marriage."

Richard frowned. He did not pretend not to know whom Robert meant.

"I don't like it any more than you," Richard said. "It sickens me to think of Marguerite as Saxton's wife. But what can *I* do to stop it?"

"You must think of a way. Find a way to stall. If you win him the time, Gunthar will do the rest. He is determined to bring Saxton down."

"Gunthar is an old man."

"Aye, but shrewd. If anyone can expose Saxton for the villain he is, it is Gunthar. But if Saxton marries Marguerite first, if she is his wife—if Saxton falls, Marguerite will fall with him. It will ruin her—and she will bear the brunt of Saxton's fury."

Robert saw from the blanching of Richard's face that he understood her danger.

"I'll stop it, Rob, I swear."

Robert pressed a hand to his head again. Everything was happening too fast. His head ached and his eyes burned and his limbs felt like lead. If he could only sit a moment and rest and think—

A shout from the end of the passageway near the stairs snapped him back into focus. Three men came surging toward them with swords drawn. Green tunics, badges on their shoulders—more of Saxton's guards. Instinct, training, and the burst of vitality that flooded body and soul in the heat of a battle, swept Robert's weariness to the edge of his consciousness. He flung the bag off his shoulder, whipped out his own sword and sprang down the passage to meet his attackers. He deflected a blow from the left and the right before he heard the clang of Richard's blade joining in the skirmish. Together they held the three guards at bay, though their opponents fought stoutly enough to prevent Robert and Richard from reaching the stairs. Robert suffered only one moment of panicked distraction when he saw that Richard had failed to follow his example with the bag and that Robert's lute still swung from the young man's shoulder. The strap bounced down Richard's arm, the case swaying wildly into the path of a descending sword thrust before Richard pivoted out of the way and cast the case off with a force that sent it and its precious contents banging against one of the walls.

Robert gave a shout of horror, but heeded a whistling of steel in the air to duck beneath the blade that sliced sideways towards his head. He did not lose his concentration again, not even when a door along the passageway opened and a woman's crisp voice exclaimed, "What is going on out here?"

Lady Helen. That door led to her sitting chamber. Her cry checked the guards just long enough for Robert to see his chance. He lowered his head and rammed through them. The sound of feet pounded behind him but it was not until he reached the bottom of the stairs and heard Richard calling to him and the guards still above shouting at "my lady" to get out of their way, that he stopped to catch his breath.

"They'll be after us any minute," Richard panted. "If Saxton sent more men to your quarters, then he's likely doubled watch at the exits, as well. We'll have to find somewhere to hide you for now."

"Where?" Robert said. "I don't know the palace." He had run errands for Gunthar and thus knew the way to the courtyard and from there the way to the city, but except for the day he had followed Kit, he had limited himself inside the walls to Gunthar's section of the royal fortress to avoid any unpleasant encounters with Kit or Saxton.

Richard hesitated, then seemed to make a quick decision. "I have a friend who will ask no questions." He described hurriedly the stairs and passages Robert should take. "Tell him I sent you. You'll be safe there until the hunt quiets down. I'll come for you as soon as I find a way to smuggle you out."

"Treason?" Lady Helen's voice shrilled from above them. "Why are you tarrying here? Be after him, then!"

Richard slapped Robert on the back, a blow that sent Robert once more into motion. Richard ran alongside him as long as he could so that if the guards glimpsed them, they would think the two men still fled together, but when he and Robert skidded around a corner, Robert dashed up a narrow, winding flight of stairs while Richard rushed straight on.

By the time Robert reached the door in the location that Richard had designated he did not know which might burst first, his thudding head or the hammering heart from his chest. He leaned against the timbered boards, struggling to steady his breathing. He prayed he had not mistaken the route. The pain had grown so fierce it had twice blurred his vision so severely that he had overshot two turns and had to double back both times.

He fisted a hand and thumped on the door. He should have asked Richard for a name. What if Robert had confused the path? He did not know if he could clear his muddled mind sufficiently to contrive what to do next. He thumped again. Perhaps the occupant was elsewhere in the palace this time of day. Should Robert let himself in? Richard had said his friend would ask no questions. In desperation, Robert reached for the latch, but felt it thrust downward before he could apply any pressure. The door swung open. He stared into a pair of wide chestnut eyes in the sweet, flowerlike countenance he had thought he would never gaze on again.

He had come. Finally he had come! Marguerite had passed a torturous three days waiting for Robert to find a flaw in the guard Saxton had set around them both since the fair, a chance carelessness Robert perceived or a distraction he created that would allow them to fly from the palace. It had taken all the faith she could summon not to lose hope as the days slid closer and closer to her wedding. She thought the heavens had smiled on them at last when they had unexpectedly found themselves together in Lady Helen's sitting chamber yesterday. But Robert had replied to her urgent, whispered questions with a puzzling vagueness and even a hint of impatience, cutting her off with a rather curt, "I will send for you soon."

She chided herself now for her doubts. He had come for her, just as he had promised! It was time. After all these endless months of waiting, it was finally time!

"Now?" she breathed. "Am I to come now?"

To her surprise, Robert backed away from her, a rare expression of alarm on his face.

"This is a mistake," he said. "He could not possibly have meant—" Robert broke off, flinching at something that made him press the palm of his hand to his head.

She glanced anxiously up and down the passageway. Since the fair, Nicholas Tybert's companionship had been nearly unshakeable. Except for today. Marguerite had not seen him since she had broken her fast early this morning. She had felt more worry than relief in his absence, for why would Saxton call him away unless Saxton thought he had somehow severed the threat that Robert posed?

Now Robert stood at her door, hair disheveled, face flushed and chest heaving like he had just come from a battle. Something was wrong. She reached out a hand to his arm and tried to pull him inside.

"No." He resisted her tug. "I can't stay. I must have muddled Richard's directions."

"Richard sent you here?"

"The exits were blocked. He told me he had a friend—"

"You were trying to leave the palace?" To flee? Without taking her?

"I had to! Kit found the letter among my things. I dropped it in the skirmish—"

"The letter?"

"My bag! Then Richard threw my lute— Oh, saints, if it is broken—"

She could not make heads or tails of these disjointed replies. "Rob, stop. You are not making sense."

He squeezed shut his eyes and shoved a hand through his thick, raven hair. "I can't think through the pounding. I am so tired, Mae. If I could only rest for a moment—"

On an impulse, she reached up a hand to his brow that his gesture bared. The heat in his skin was not from some battle or chase.

"Rob, you are ill!"

He shook his head and tried to pull away when she tugged at him again. "I can't come inside. It's not safe for you—"

"They won't look for you here," she said and prayed it was true.

She saw the longing glance he sent at the chamber behind her, but he set his mouth stubbornly. She felt her heart begin to thump. If someone wandered into the passageway and saw him—her mother's chamber was only steps away from Marguerite's own.

"Come inside," she pled. "Just to sit and catch your breath."

He started to shake his head again, then winced as though the movement brought him pain. This time when she pulled at his fingers, he took one shuffling step towards the threshold, then surrendered to temptation and stumbled the rest of the way into the chamber. From there she had no trouble urging him across to the bed, where he sank down with a groan and dropped his head into his hands.

"Eva," Marguerite said to the servant who turned from Marguerite's elaborately decorated wardrobe to stare, startled, at Robert, "close the door and bolt it."

Eva held a soft blue surcote with tiny gold sunbursts embroidered all over the bodice, but she flung the garment over a chair and quickly obeyed her mistress. The servant and her young suitor, Simon, had long been confidants to Marguerite's and Robert's love. When the door was locked, Eva folded her hands and lowered her gaze, as if seeking to allow Marguerite and Robert as much privacy as she could.

Marguerite nudged his hands away from his head to feel for some lump or knot that might be causing him pain. His hair ran silky fine through her fingers, thick enough that she had to plunge deep to find his skull, but she could locate no injury. She sat down beside him on the bed and laid her palm to his heated cheek.

"Can you tell me what's happened?" she asked.

He hunched forward, his arms resting on his thighs. It took him several moments to answer and when he did, his voice came almost slurring. "Coins switched— The murders in Poitou— Kit—that devil! I could have ended it between us! Why did I listen to—?" Suddenly Robert's head snapped up. "Gunthar! Kit said—but Saxton wants him disgraced, or better yet, destroyed. When Gunthar denies me—they must have a second plan!" He twisted to catch Marguerite's wrist. "Mae, someone needs to warn him. You must go to the countess and tell her—" He stopped to press his free hand to his head again.

Before his lids scrunched shut, she glimpsed the brightness of fever in his eyes. His fingers burned like bands of fire around her wrist. No wonder his head ached so!

"Never mind," she said. "You can tell me later. You need to lie down and rest."

"No time," he said on a pant. "I cannot stay here—"

"Rob, you are too ill to go anywhere. Can't you feel it? You are burning up!"

He ran his hand over his cheek and brow, but his heated palm would not register an equal heat in his face. But when he sat so still, she knew that he finally sensed the fire radiating inside him.

"I thought—I was only tired," he murmured. "But Gil—my brother—he died of the fever yestermorn just after the bells rang Matins."

"Died?" She sprang up from the bed, panic strangling in her throat.

He reached for her fingers. "Mae, I—I will be all right. But it is not safe for you for me to stay here."

"Lie down."

"Marguerite—"

"Lie down!" She shoved at his shoulders and felt as startled as he looked when he tumbled backwards into the blankets.

He tried to raise himself onto an elbow, but must have suffered another wave of pain in his head, for he fell back again and plunged both hands into his hair with a groan.

"Rob—" she struggled to keep her voice calm when all she wanted to do was scream out her fear "—let me find something to ease your headache, then sleep for just an hour or two. Then—then I will let you go wherever you please." A safe enough promise to make. If he were as sick as he seemed, he would not be going anywhere for a long while.

Robert's fingers twisted in his hair. At last he let out a long, slow breath and nodded. Marguerite called to Eva. Between them they unfastened his sword and dagger, then helped Robert shift his position so that he stretched out against the pillows. Marguerite stroked his brow gently, praying he might find her touch cool and soothing. She ran possible remedies frantically through her mind. He already smelled of mint, as he always did. Perhaps some pennyroyal oil would be strong enough to ease his head. Surely they kept some prepared in the kitchens? And she must find something for his fever, too.

"Milady." Eva spoke softly from beside her. "It is nearly time to dine. Your mother will be coming for you and you are not finished dressing."

"I cannot go. I cannot leave him—"

"Mae—" Robert's eyes remained closed, but he drew her stroking hand away. "You have to go. It would—rouse too much suspicion—to stay."

He was right, of course. The entire court was expecting her to sit on the high dais beside Saxton, as she always did. If Saxton was searching for Robert, Marguerite's absence was the surest way to draw him here. But it was almost more than Marguerite could bear. What if Robert worsened while she was gone? What if he— She fought back the horror of his muttered words: *My brother died of fever.*

"Eva—" Marguerite's voice trembled "—you must take care of him for me. Find some linen and bathe his face while I am gone."

"He should be bled, milady."

"We need a physician for that, and there is no possible way to smuggle one into my chamber. I will find some herbs." How, when, Marguerite did not know. "No one—" she turned to look at Eva "—*no one* must know he is here. Not even Simon."

The young, fugitive villein was still apprenticed with a London glover, counting down the months to a year and a day when he could claim his freedom and Eva's hand in marriage.

"Yes, milady."

Marguerite felt a soft pull on her hand. There was no time to dally, yet she sank down on the bed beside Robert. He did not open his eyes. His thumb rubbed the stone of her garnet ring.

"I do not expect you to wear it forever." The words came on a dry whisper between lips that scarcely moved. "Only—that when you look on it —you remember that I loved you."

"You are not going to die," she whispered fiercely.

He said nothing for a long moment. Then he murmured, "Warn Gunthar. And do not wait for me. Richard—will protect you now."

His hand fell away and lay quiet on the bedclothes. Did she imagine it, or had his breathing grown easier? Perhaps what he needed most was simply to rest. She slid her fingers through his hair one more time, then stood up and motioned at Eva to bring the surcote with the golden sunbursts.

Saxton handed her into her seat at the high table, then bent forward, his hands on the chair back, and murmured into her ear, "You look very charming today, my dear. I begin to look forward to our wedding night."

Marguerite said quietly when he took his place between her and the queen, "You cannot force me to wed you, my lord. You may drag me to the altar, but you cannot force the words from my lips any more than my father forced the betrothal vows from me."

"Can I not?" Saxton's eyes gleamed, but a blast from the trumpets that announced the first course preempted whatever more he had intended to say.

The queen drew Saxton's attention away as the squires began to serve.

Since their return from the war, the Earl of Gunthar and his countess had sat to the king's right when they dined, displacing the former preeminence of the Earl of Saxton. Usually Marguerite thought Saxton tried a little too hard to appear unconcerned, but while talking each day to the queen, Marguerite frequently caught him sending long, measuring glances down the table at his rival. She observed that the Earl of Gunthar was absent today, his place taken by the Lady Helen who endured with dignified composure the king's neglect while he leered at various women seated at the tables below them.

Marguerite wished Saxton would leer at one of his new lovers. Instead, whenever the queen's demand for his attention lapsed, he hovered solicitously over Marguerite, carving meat for her or directing tidbits of dishes be placed upon her plate. She did her best to ignore him and the way a cross-looking Nicholas Tybert with a bruise on his temple repeatedly filled his master's wine cup while they ate.

Marguerite was in no mood to deal with Saxton's games just now. Robert lay desperately ill in her chamber and she had to find a way to make him well again. Did the palace have an infirmary garden? Surely they must have, although Marguerite had only ever been to the queen's flower gardens. How would she justify a sudden interest in medicinal herbs when she had shown none before? She could not claim illness herself. That would bring her mother to her chamber. She could ask Eva to feign a chill, but that would not explain the oddity of a lady wishing to concoct a remedy for a servant, even her own.

"I did not flatter, my lady." Marguerite flinched away from Saxton's wine-effused breath. "Because I find pleasure with others, do not think me blind to the promise of pleasure I anticipate with you."

"You are drunk," she said.

"I am never drunk, though I will not deny that wine can add a welcome— zeal—to sport of any kind."

His hand snaked over hers beneath the tablecloth, so repelling her that she nearly started to her feet.

"Careful, my lady. Would you have the entire court see your blushes? Modesty is not a virtue here, as I should think you would have learned by now. Nick, fill my lady's cup again."

Marguerite wished she had the courage to throw the wine in Saxton's face. He was right about the king's court. Too many smirking courtiers and ladies were gazing at her heated cheeks. Even the queen sent her a sly, amused glance.

Saxton fondled her fingers. When she tried to shake him off, his hand locked over hers, his thumb clamping against the garnet on her ring. He could not know. Oh, surely he could not know that Robert had given it to her? Saxton had not spoken of their encounter at the fair or so much as mentioned Robert's name, but from the cold, menacing way he had gazed at her since that day, she knew he had not forgotten, forgiven, or intended to ignore.

"You were wise to snub young Eyvind when you came into the hall," Saxton said. "Aye, I saw the way he swarmed to you like a bee to a nectared rose. Drink, my lady. You do not need two hands for that."

She reached for a tansy cake instead, but it tasted like ashes on her tongue. How long would this interminable meal continue?

Saxton nibbled at a parsnip fritter while he resumed playing with her other, hidden hand. "Eyvind is a fool to show his desire for you so openly. If I'd known he would be such a nuisance, I would have aimed my lance more precisely at the tournament."

Marguerite had spurned Sir Warin's every attempt to speak with her since she had parted from him so angrily in the queen's garden.

"Sir Warin is no threat to you, I vow it."

Saxton's thumb slid beneath the sleeve of her cornflower blue tunic to rub a sensual circular pattern alongside the inside of her wrist. "Not at the moment. But I should not like him to indulge in the hope that he can pick up the pieces of your broken heart."

Her revulsion of Saxton's touch made it difficult to concentrate on his words. She tried again to disengage herself, but again his strength prevented a retreat.

He took a long draught from his goblet while he nudged her sleeve higher. "You know that Marcel is on the run?"

That snapped her eyes to Saxton's face, everything else fading except for her terror. He had guessed! But how could he? What if his words were a feint to trick a fatal answer from her? If he knew Robert was in her chamber, Saxton would have sent guards to seize him.

Oh, saints, what if he had already done just that?

He must have seen the panic in her eyes. It flashed into her mind that she had as equally ready a cause to blame it on as the truth.

"Rob—on the run?" She allowed the words to stumble from her lips. "From what?" she gasped, then quickly affected scorn. "Ah! It is another lie, like when you told me he was dead. You think if I believe it, I will cease my resistance to our marriage. Even if it were true, you would be no less loathsome to me, my lord."

To her disgust, Saxton looked almost amused. "Loathsome, am I? Alas, my child, your shudders will not lessen my enjoyment of your charms."

He smiled and slid her sleeve all the way to her elbow. Her stomach gave a pungent heave. *It is not as if he is touching me indecently,* she told herself with a desperate grab at self-control. *It is only my arm.* But she realized suddenly it was more than that. It was not lust alone he sought to impart with his caress. It was power. He bared her arm and stroked it boldly, almost publicly because he could. And he wanted her to know she had no way to stop him.

Saxton took another drink before murmuring, "Where is he?"

Hope leapt through her revulsion. Saxton would not ask if he knew.

As long as he touched her, Marguerite could not control the sickened trembling of her hand as she dipped her spoon into a serving of creamed leeks, but there was no tremor in her voice when she replied. "How should I know? I do not believe he has run away at all. He may have started for York with Lord Gunthar to throw you off the track, but he will be back for me. I shall never be your wife."

"Nay, I sent men to arrest him this morning, but he eluded them. He is a traitor to the crown and I have the evidence to prove it. You play a dangerous game if you think to conceal him from me. It is not only my wrath you risk, but the king's."

Marguerite dropped her spoon—she would be ill if she placed another morsel of food in her mouth—and whirled again on Saxton, her eyes flashing wide in genuine shock and swift anger. "Traitor? Oh, that is your basest lie yet!"

His fondling touch ceased, clamping now in a grip that made her wince. "I do not need a lie this time, Marguerite. Where is he?"

She saw her chance to deflect him. "You think Rob would hide behind me? Fah! It takes a coward's mind to suspect another man of skulking behind a woman." She remembered Robert's horrified face when he'd realized that he stood at her door. He would never have crossed her threshold if he had not been so ill he could barely see straight.

Saxton's eyes glinted dangerously for a moment and she realized the word "coward" had infuriated him. He shoved her sleeve halfway to her shoulder, his grasp clearly visible above the table now, then jerked her towards him until his lips brushed her ear.

Laughter burst from the diners at the tables below the dais as she tried in vain to squirm away from what they clearly interpreted as an amorous nuzzling by the Earl of Saxton of his bride-to-be. But the words hissing into her ear on an exhale of wine-soured breath were anything but passionate.

"Aye, I suppose the man is too proud for that. Well then, if you do not know where he is, there is someone who does and you are going to persuade him to tell me."

"Let me go!"

"That is a futile request, my lady. You are mine to do with as I please. Who do you think will stop me? The king?"

Saxton's hand was suddenly in her hair, twisting about her head, and then his mouth covered hers in a rough, coarse kiss.

"Heigh ho, Saxton, will you ravish the wench in front of us all?"

The king's voice rang on a gleeful note above the roar of hilarity and applause from the hall.

Saxton caught her wrist as her hand flew up to strike him. He murmured against her lips, "How fond are you of your cousin Richard? I have him locked up in a cell that only you can deliver him from."

His breath was hot, but the whispered words were icy with a menace that froze her in her chair and allowed his mouth to rove unchallenged over hers. Her stomach flopped and flopped, but he had Richard—and if she were not careful, he would find Robert, too.

Marguerite only vaguely registered the muting of raucous laughter through the thudding horror in her ears. She hated it that she betrayed her fear with a sob when she abruptly found her mouth freed. She scraped her knuckles across her lips till they hurt, not caring who mocked her, desperate to scrub away the taste of him. Her gaze flicked to the lower tables where her mother sat with bowed head and reddened cheeks. Her father stared at one of the walls of the hall, his face like a stone. In spite of Marguerite's desire to defy Saxton, another sob rasped out of her throat.

"I beg your pardon, my lord," a woman's cool voice spoke, "but I find something in the meal has disagreed with me. Might I borrow the Lady Marguerite to assist me to my chamber?"

Before Saxton could object, the Lady Helen drew Marguerite to her feet. Marguerite's teeth chattered, she shook so hard in relief. The countess's cheeks glowed with a bright, angry color rivaled only by the fire that had set her silvery eyes ablaze. Saxton rose swiftly with a restraining touch to Marguerite's arm, but when the countess failed to shrink from his looming height and merely raised her brows in a silent challenge, Saxton checked the half-spoken word he'd begun to speak in rebuke. Marguerite followed his glance at the king. John had leaned back in his chair in a grinning sprawl to observe how Saxton would respond to a remonstrance by his rival's wife. Marguerite knew that though Saxton might hesitate, his pride would not allow him to back down, least of all from a woman.

"My apologies, Lady Helen," he said, courteous but cool, "but my Lady Marguerite is urgent just now to speak with her cousin. Are you not, my dear?"

Marguerite remembered Richard. What had this monster at her side done to him? She had no choice but to whisper, "Yes."

Saxton motioned Nicholas Tybert to Lady Helen's side. "Allow me to lend you my squire's assistance in her place."

"My thanks, my lord," Lady Helen said with a briskness that belied any actual faintness on her part. "Then I shall leave behind my own squire to attend my lady and bring her to me as soon as she is finished with her cousin. With my lord husband on an errand for the king and my daughter-in-law in Kent, I find your lady's company and comfort indispensable to me."

A squire with curly brown hair joined them at her gesture. Did Lady Helen fear that Saxton might to take Marguerite away and ravish her, as the king had jested? Marguerite did not think he had any such intent—at least, not now. She swept her hand across her mouth again, then reached with gratitude for the squire's arm. She did not realize she was still crying until Lady Helen wiped away the tears on her cheeks.

"Come to me as soon as you can, child," she murmured. Then to the squire, "Have a care to her, Ralf."

The squire nodded and placed his hand protectively over Marguerite's. He was near her own age, but Saxton's glare appeared to bounce off of him. Saxton shrugged slightly and turned to the king.

"Then if you excuse us all, sire?"

John rubbed his hands together. The scene between Saxton and Lady Helen appeared to have delighted him. "Indeed, indeed," he said in dismissal, "your departure will be welcome. I cannot remember the last time the queen and I dined alone."

Perhaps inspired by Saxton's example, he leaned forward and blew through leering lips into the queen's ear, as if a hundred people were not sitting below the dais watching them. The queen's full-throated laughter floated after Marguerite like a sensual purr as Saxton led her out of the hall.

The room that held Richard was small but comfortably furnished with a chair, a table and candles, a cot near a window-slit, and a flickering brazier that drove off the autumn chill. Richard rose from the cot when he saw Marguerite. He looked pale, his clothes rumpled, his hair disheveled. Then her gaze caught a bandage on his hand.

"Oh, you are hurt!" She swept across the floor to him as Saxton told the squire to wait outside and closed the door in the youth's face.

Richard scowled. "It's little more than a scratch. I was stupid enough to let myself be disarmed by a fool of a guardsman."

Marguerite began unwrapping his hand to check on the wound's severity.

"You are here for one reason, my lady," Saxton spoke coldly from behind her. "To persuade Channing to tell me where he has hidden Robert Marcel."

"Go to blazes," Richard threw at him. "Even if I knew, I would not tell you."

She glanced up at him. Why was he protecting Robert? She heard the tread of Saxton's footstep as he joined them. She shrank closer to Richard. Her cousin was tall and broad-shouldered, but Saxton's massive build made him appear to loom over them both.

"Beckford said you helped Marcel escape. He is a traitor and will hang when we catch him."

"I don't believe a word of it," Richard said. "Anyone could have planted those coins in his bag. If that is all the proof you have—"

"I have Beckford's witness of what he saw and heard in Poitou. I watched him write out his testimony and set my own seal to it. Whom do you think King John will believe? A lowborn minstrel or a baron of the realm?"

Marguerite did not understand this exchange, but she knew the answer to Saxton's question. Whatever trap he had laid, he had drafted a man who had abused Robert, who had hunted him with hounds like a beast of prey, to help Saxton lay his plot. But that man was a baron. The royal courts would not accept the word of a former villein over any testimony sworn by Lord Christopher Beckford. Marguerite felt heartsick.

Richard's wound did not look deep. She bound his hand back up, then realized that he'd hesitated at Saxton's words.

"Where is this testimony?" Richard asked. "Why did you not show it to me before you sent me with Beckford to witness Marcel's arrest?"

"It exists," Saxton said curtly. "I can show it to you before the day is out. If that is all you needed, then I have wasted the end of a meal that I was thoroughly enjoying."

Richard said nothing. Was he wavering in his defense of Robert?

"It is a lie," she said. "Richard, whatever he has told you about Rob is a lie."

Richard looked down at her with a frown. "Is it, Marguerite? Has Marcel not been courting you behind all our backs? Are you not in love with him, then?"

She saw the anger and accusation in his eyes. But she also saw that he knew the truth. Dissembling would be useless.

"Yes," she whispered, "I am. But—"

"You and a common minstrel! Marguerite, have you lost your wits?"

She bristled at that. "Rob is a good man, and an honest one. You fought alongside him in France, you called him a friend. If birth alone determined a man's integrity and honor, you would not be locked up in this room by *that*." She sent a pointed glare at Saxton.

Saxton shrugged it off, then gazed coldly at her cousin. "The question for you, Channing, is not whether I am more honorable than a 'common minstrel,' or even if I am telling the truth. The question is simply whether you wish to hang with Marcel when we catch him."

"You would not dare," Marguerite said.

"There will be nothing I can do to stop it. Your cousin chose to help a traitor escape. He will have to bear the consequences of that misguided choice—unless, of course, he decides to tell us where Marcel is."

"All this"—she waved a hand at the narrow walls—"imprisoning my cousin, threatening to hang him, accusing Rob of murder and treason when you know he is innocent—merely out of spite because I spurned you?"

Saxton slanted his wintry stare at her. "It is not about you anymore, Marguerite. It is not even about your lands."

Richard gave a derisive snort. "I knew it! It is about Gunthar."

If Saxton's gaze had been a knife, it would have plunged through her cousin's heart. Marguerite shuddered almost as deeply as she had when Saxton had kissed her in the hall.

"I've been thinking and thinking since you locked me up here," Richard said, "and it's the only thing that makes sense. Someone tried to murder Gunthar in Poitou—twice. Who else would want him dead but you? And you must be afraid that Rob knows it."

The betraying expression vanished behind Saxton's glacial stare. "I can think of any number of enemies the old man might have, beginning with the French. Gunthar has been a thorn in their side alongside his Plantagenet masters as far back as old King Henry's days. Slander my name again and you will find your neck in a noose, with or without Marcel alongside you."

"Do you want to know why I helped him escape?" Richard said, his voice hot with contempt. "Because as much as it galls me to think of Marguerite mingling her blood with a man of his birth, it repulses me more to think of her with a cur like you."

Saxton made a sound very like a hiss. Marguerite cried out in surprise and pain when his hand clamped down on her arm.

"This visit is over," Saxton snapped. "It would have been faster with your help, but I do not need you to find Marcel. I have all the exits blocked. He is trapped in this palace somewhere, and sooner or later my guards will track him down. Bid your cousin farewell, Marguerite, for this may be the last time you see him before his trial."

She struggled as Saxton dragged her towards the door. "Let me go! Richard!"

"This is no bluff, Marguerite," Saxton warned. "The king *will* hang your cousin, I will see to that. Think on it for the night. You had better do the same, Channing," he said over his shoulder.

"I don't think you have the power to carry out that threat," Richard said, "or you'd not have needed Marguerite to 'persuade' me. Gunthar still has the king's ear, doesn't he? And for some reason I don't understand, you think you need Rob to bring him down."

"Gunthar will be in York for a fortnight and mishaps can be arranged. The minstrel is a mere irritant it will give me pleasure to snuff like a candle's flame."

Marguerite flashed out an infuriated foot and kicked him. Saxton swore, then slammed her so hard against the door that her head banged against the wood and sent the room spinning. She heard shouting and a thudding sound. When her vision cleared, Richard was on the floor and Saxton's sword point was at his throat.

Even as she screamed, Saxton stepped back and resheathed his weapon.

"You are a pair of children playing with fire," he said. "Beware, my lady. One word of anything that has passed within this room to Lady Helen, and a 'mishap' may be arranged for your cousin, too."

He pulled open the door and shoved her through with a hand to the small of her back. She stumbled, then whirled, but found her way blocked by his hulking body on the threshold. A hand touched her arm. She glanced at Lady Helen's squire.

"I am at your service, my lady," the youth said quietly.

His frank eyes shone a challenge at Saxton. The squire had served Lady Helen at the king's table and must have seen with everyone else the vile way Saxton had humiliated her there. Did he think Marguerite needed his defense? He did not even have a sword. His courage touched her, but she could not let him risk Saxton's anger for her sake.

"Thank you." She heard the tremor in her voice and tried to master it. It would give Saxton too much satisfaction to know how his threats against Richard had shaken her. She prayed that Richard was right, that Saxton's talk of hanging was mere bluster. "I—I wish to rest. Pray tell Lady Helen that I have a headache—"

"Lady Helen is skilled in herbs," the squire said. "She will know how to ease your head. My orders were to escort you to her sitting chamber when you finished speaking with your cousin."

A mulish look settled around the youth's mouth that reminded her oddly of Robert's stubbornness. Robert. She could not go to Lady Helen until she had spoken with him again. She must tell him that he was right about Saxton laying a trap for Gunthar. They must work out a scheme to extricate

Richard from his danger and find a way for all of them to slip past the guards that Saxton had set at the palace exists.

She felt Saxton watching her, waiting to see how she would reply to the squire. Surely he would understand that putting Lady Helen off would be worse than refusing and stirring questions from the countess?

"I will come to her directly, then. Only—only I must tell my parents about my cousin, first. Beg an hour's grace from my lady." She caught the squire's frowning glance at Saxton. "You may see me to the stairs near my chamber and wait for me, if you like."

The squire nodded and escorted her away to the sound of Saxton locking the door of Richard's prison.

Marguerite let herself into her chamber with the key she had hidden in a small pouch tied to her girdle. Eva started up from the chair next to the bed. "Oh, milady, thank goodness ye've returned."

Marguerite shut and bolted the door. "What is it, Eva?"

She hurried across to the bed, half-afraid that Robert had wakened and fled while she had been gone. He remained where she had left him, but the flush on his cheeks had deepened by several dangerous shades. His face sheened with sweat. When Marguerite laid a hand to his dampened forehead, he opened his eyes, but she knew from their feverish glaze that he did not see her.

"He talks," Eva said, "says things I can't understand, but he hasn't properly wakened. Milady—" she hesitated, her frightened voice wavering "—I've known some who've died of the fever."

Panic pitched afresh in the pit of Marguerite's stomach. "He is not going to die."

I won't let you. Don't you dare die! She grabbed up the cloth that Eva had left swimming in the basin on the table and began to wash Robert's fiery cheeks.

"Fetch more water," Marguerite said. "As cold as you can find it." The water in the basin had long ago turned tepid.

"Yes, milady."

Marguerite barely heard the door click shut behind the maid. Robert flinched from the cloth and tried to roll away, but he did not fight when

Marguerite caught his chin and pulled him back to her. His hand plucked restively at the sheets. She knew how they must burn against his body, how he instinctively sought for cooler bedding against which to lie. She soaked the cloth, then laid it against his brow.

"Oh, Rob," she whispered, "you are in such terrible danger."

He murmured something she could not understand and tried to jerk his head away again, but again she held his chin.

"And Lord Saxton is making horrible threats against Richard for helping you." She wiped away the perspiration that had already remoistened his cheeks. "And I think you are right that Gunthar is in danger, but Saxton said if I tell Lady Helen— Oh, Rob, I don't know what to do. Please wake up and tell me what to do!"

She knew he would not. He could not even hear her plea. She had helped nurse her grandfather in his last illness, but Odo had sent her away for the worst of her grandfather's delirium. It had begun just like this, with glassy-eyed stares, and muttered words she could not comprehend, and feverish thrashings that had required Odo's strength to hold him still while the wife of one of his men-at-arms had pulled Marguerite protesting from the room. The next time she had seen her grandfather his cheeks were white instead of red, his eyes closed peacefully, and his chest grown still.

She dropped the cloth on the bed and sank to her knees, clutching Robert's burning hand. Every other fear collapsed, swallowed by her terror of the fever. Odo and her mother had taught her how to heal, to think calmly through an illness so that she could treat it effectively, but she did not feel like a levelheaded woman when Robert tried to bounce his hand away and flung himself half-sideways on a mutter and a groan. He had become her anchor in the unsteady sea her life had become since her grandfather's death. If she lost him, her very foundation would crumble and the only thing waiting to catch her would be the soul-blasting coldness of Saxton's embrace.

"Don't die, don't die, don't die." She clung to his hand and buried her face in the bedclothes, sobbing like she had in Dame Ismena's lap while the fever had scorched away her grandfather's life.

"Mae."

She looked up, hope clawing through her terror when he spoke her name. Robert stared blindly at the ceiling. Her heart sank. It was only the delirium. Then his hand pulled free and landed gently on her cheek. His thumb brushed away a tear, once, twice—then dropped back to the bed as his lids slid shut on a sigh.

Marguerite kissed his fingers, then scrubbed away the rest of her tears herself. She could not help him if she let fear turn to hysteria. Odo was right. The sick needed discernment and composure in those who nursed them. She drew a deep breath to calm herself, then stood up to freshen the cloth and bathe his face again.

Robert continued to mutter and fret, but this time she held her alarm at bay. When he was well, they would deal with all their problems together. The most important thing now was to safely break his fever. She needed to search the herb garden, or send Eva to do so. Marguerite should have thought of that when she'd sent her servant to fetch the water.

It felt like hours before Eva returned, though Marguerite knew it was only because the days darkened so early this time of year. She lit candles and continued to apply the cloth while she chattered away with forced cheerfulness, reassuring Robert he would soon be well again, even as his tossings and turnings grew increasingly agitated. When the door finally opened, Robert gave a shout and flung himself over to lie on his stomach.

Eva pushed the door shut, her eyes glistening wide with alarm in the candlelight. "We must keep him quiet, milady. Milord Saxton's squire is quarreling at the top of the stairs with a young man who claims he is Lady Helen's squire." Eva joined Marguerite at the bedside. "Fresh water from the well. This should keep the water cool for him." She indicated the clay pitcher she held.

Marguerite carried the basin to the window and poured the old water out, then set it on the table for Eva to refill.

"What are they quarreling about?" Marguerite asked. "Come, Rob, this will feel better against your face." She dipped the cloth in the cool water. When he resisted her efforts to roll him onto his back, she sighed and set the freshened cloth to the back of his neck.

"The squire with the curly hair said he will not leave until he escorts you to Lady Helen's sitting chamber, but Master Tybert said Milord Saxton will not like it and that he should go away. From the look on both their faces, Lady Helen's squire is being very stubborn."

Marguerite dipped the cloth in the water again, then knelt on the bed so she could reach Robert's averted cheek. She should have realized Saxton would set Tybert to watch her again. He would insist on coming with her if she went to the herb garden, and wonder why and tell Saxton she was acting oddly. She might risk sending Eva—but what if Lady Helen's stubborn squire lost his patience in waiting for Marguerite and he and Tybert brought their quarrel to the door of her chamber? The wisest thing would be to draw them both off by going to sit with Lady Helen for an hour. But she could not leave Robert alone while she did so. Eva must stay and bathe his face and come for her if—

Marguerite pushed away the *if*. One hour. Surely Robert would not worsen before then. If she clung to her lie about the headache, perhaps she could wheedle some helpful herbs from Lady Helen.

Only that thought gave Marguerite the strength to leave Robert in Eva's care.

Lady Helen lifted Marguerite's chin and gazed into her eyes. Marguerite wondered how Robert had learned to veil his thoughts so completely. She struggled to mimic him. She held her face perfectly still, but Lady Helen's silvery eyes were nearly as incisive as her husband's.

"A headache, hmm?"

"Yes, my lady. I thought—perhaps you might have some feverfew? Or some yarrow or masterwort? I-I think I may be coming down with a chill."

Lady Helen gave a soft snort through her small, straight nose. "Might this 'chill's' name be the Earl of Saxton?"

She laughed when Marguerite felt herself blush, but Lady Helen's eyes went angry.

"His treatment of you at the king's table was unpardonable. I wish I'd been near enough to slap him. 'Tis no wonder you have cried yourself sick. I will have Donnet make you some primrose tea that will ease your head. Some chamomile will soothe your eyes. I keep some in my chamber. Sit while I fetch it."

Tea would do Marguerite no good. Lady Helen would expect her to drink it here. "My lady, wait."

Lady Helen turned halfway to the door of her chamber. She raised her brows when Marguerite hesitated.

"It is late and I should not impose on you," Marguerite said. "If—if I might only have some yarrow or—or masterwort if you have it, my own maid will administer it and I will retire to bed."

Lady Helen's gaze dipped to Marguerite's hands. Marguerite realized she was pulling anxiously at her fingers and quickly stilled their motion.

"You need not pretend with me, Marguerite," Lady Helen said quietly. "I will help you in any way I can. If I knew a way to stop your wedding to Lord Saxton, I would do it in a heartbeat."

Marguerite's lips began to tremble. So much inviting sympathy lay in Lady Helen's face that the tears she thought she had mastered began to well up again. "I do not know what to do," she whispered.

Lady Helen's arms were suddenly around her and Marguerite crumpled weeping against her shoulder. Lady Helen let her cry out her fears, stroking her hair with kind, gentle strokes that made Marguerite's heart ache with love for her. Her father had called such comfort "coddling" and rebuked her mother from holding her during the long, grieving days that had followed her grandfather's death.

The rhythmic touch of Lady Helen's hand gradually quieted Marguerite's sobs.

"Alas, child," the countess murmured, "I do not know what to do for you, either. The Earl of Saxton is a powerful man, not to be spurned lightly. I have puzzled and puzzled over a way to extricate you, but you are not my daughter—I wish that you were! But you are not—" her voice went a little husky "—and as Hugh would remind me, I have no say over what becomes of another man's child."

Marguerite knew it was true, but she felt safe in the countess's arms, nonetheless, and made no effort to draw away.

Lady Helen leaned her cheek against the top of Marguerite's head and sighed. "It was different when your grandfather wished to marry me. Hugh surpassed him both in wealth and influence and therefore was able to appease Lord Heywood's pride. But I think the young man you love has no such advantage over the Earl Saxton—has he?"

Marguerite cursed her body for stiffening in the countess's embrace. She feigned ignorance anyway. Lady Helen could not possibly know the truth! "I do not know what you mean, my lady. I do not need to be in love with someone else to despise the Earl of Saxton."

"Certainly not. But I am neither stupid nor blind. It was not Lord Saxton you dreamed of when you caressed the ribbon in your hair last spring, and it was not Lord Saxton who set your eyes aglow yesterday when you blended your voice so prettily with my minstrel's here in this very room."

Marguerite pushed away from her in dismay. "I did not glow. I scarcely looked at him." Oh, curse her tongue as well as her body! "It was merely the words of the song that—that set me dreaming a bit."

Lady Helen laughed again, a merrier sound this time. "Indeed, you avoided looking at Robert rather too pointedly, except for when you conversed together over your song. I own, I doubted my suspicions for a moment when Robert showed himself no more than respectfully polite to you. But you, Marguerite, your eyes give far too much away. I have a great many questions for you—where and how you met, when Robert gave you my husband's ring—but that must wait. First you must explain to me this folderol about—"

"Your husband's ring?" Marguerite glanced with surprise at the garnet on her finger.

"Ah, he did not tell you where he got it, then? Of course I recognized it yesterday, as I am sure my husband did. Hugh has worn it intermittently for years and it was on his hand the day he left me for Poitou. I thought he'd lost it, until I saw it on your finger. I hoped at first that he had given it to one of our knights who had become smitten with you—until I saw how you looked at Robert yesterday." Lady Helen paused and her brows knit slightly together. "I wish it *had* been a knight. You know you cannot wed him, Marguerite."

Marguerite abandoned evasion for defense of the man she loved. "And why can I not?"

"You are not so foolish, child. He is a minstrel, and you a lady. Such a marriage—child, it simply cannot be."

Marguerite swished away from her across the room.

"Marguerite, pray do not think me hard. If you were my own daughter, I would counsel you the same. Robert has shown himself a loyal servant to my husband and me. I believe him an honest man, and he certainly has beauty and charm enough to set any woman to swooning—don't stare, child, I told you I was not blind. But there are some barriers that cannot be breached."

Lady Helen's eyes showed sympathy, but the set of her generous mouth was firm.

"You speak of station, my lady, of birth," Marguerite said. "Is that why you married your husband? Because he was an earl? Did you marry him for wealth and the influence he wielded at court? Or because he won a pair of gold spurs when he was one-and-twenty?"

"Of course not. But this is not the same."

"So you would not have loved him if he been a yeoman instead of a lord? Or a baker, or a carpenter, or a tanner—or a minstrel?"

Lady Helen was silent for a very long time, but Marguerite knew the answer, for she had seen the countess gaze at Gunthar. Marguerite was not the only one whose eyes betrayed her heart.

"You intend to run away with him, then." Lady Helen said it as a statement, not a question. "Does that mean you know where he is?"

Marguerite crossed to stand beside the chair where she sat when she visited the countess, thus averting her expression from Lady Helen. She dared not say the truth. She did not think Lady Helen reconciled to Marguerite's decision, and even the most affectionate parent might misguidedly try to interfere "for one's good." But she needed Lady Helen's help desperately. Yarrow or masterwort—

"He is in trouble—" Marguerite began, but Lady Helen cut her off.

"That I know. I saw Robert and your cousin fighting their way past a pair of Lord Saxton's guards, and when I inquired of the guards the reason, they spoke some folderol about treason. I know little of Robert's background and their story might have given me pause but for the clear faith my husband places in him. I do not know what passed between Robert and my husband in Poitou, but the light he has brought to Hugh's eyes can only have been placed there by an exceptional man. Hugh must have guessed something was afoot, for he could talk of nothing last night but his desire to take Robert with him to York. Now I know why Robert refused to go."

For me. Marguerite pulled at her fingers again.

"Did he come to you for help?" Lady Helen asked.

This time Marguerite chose a lie. "I found him. No, I will not say where. Only—" She turned with her plea to the countess. "My lady, he is ill. He is so very ill. Please, I need something to help me break his fever."

Lady Helen looked startled. "Fever?"

"He said his brother died of it. Oh, my lady, I am so afraid."

"Oh, my dear." Lady Helen swept across the room to embrace her again. "That is what you want the yarrow for?"

Marguerite nodded fiercely in her arms.

"Marguerite, you must take me to him. I will bring medicine, and—"

Marguerite shook her head as vehemently as she had nodded. "My lady, I cannot. You mustn't ask me."

"Do you think you cannot trust me?" The countess sounded hurt.

"It is not that. Lord Saxton is watching me and if he sees you with me—It is too dangerous."

Lady Helen held her a moment longer, then seemed to make a decision. "Wait here." She vanished through the door to her bedchamber and returned a few minutes later with a jar with a wooden stopper. "Dried yarrow leaves," she said as she placed it in Marguerite's hands, "mixed with elderflower and a little pennyroyal. Make it into a tea for him to drink, very hot. You may also bathe his hands and face with it—"

"Yes, yes, my lady, I know." Now that she had the remedy, Marguerite bounced on her toes, anxious to return to Robert.

Lady Helen stayed her with a touch to her arm when Marguerite turned to leave. "Did Robert tell you what Lord Saxton has accused him of?"

"No, my lady, he was too ill. But Lord Saxton said Lord Christopher Beckford has sworn testimony that he witnessed Rob in an act of treason when they were in Poitou."

"Lord Christopher has laid testimony? Before what court?"

"No court as yet. He wrote it in Lord Saxton's presence and Lord Saxton affixed his seal to it. When my cousin Richard asked to see it, Lord Saxton said he would show him the evidence tonight."

"Tonight?" Lady Helen stared over Marguerite's head, as though suddenly lost in thought.

"Yes, my lady. May I go to Robert now? If the fever worsens—"

Lady Helen returned her gaze to Marguerite's face. "Yes, child, of course. If that does not help" —she indicated the jar— "I have other remedies that we can try. If you will not trust me with his whereabouts, at least promise you will return and let me try to help."

"Yes, my lady." Marguerite flung her arms around the older woman in a quick, grateful hug. *"Thank you!"* Marguerite had her hand on the door latch before she looked back. This was not gratitude, to let fear of Saxton bind her tongue when Lady Helen's own love was in danger. "Perhaps you should send for your husband."

"Would you take him to Robert if he returned?"

Marguerite shook her head.

"Then he can do no more for you than I have done. He is fulfilling a royal commission and would not thank me for calling him back before he concludes it."

Marguerite knew she should press the countess harder, but she needed to return to Robert. It would take days for Gunthar to reach York, time enough to persuade Lady Helen to change her mind once Robert was out of danger. Marguerite spoke another breathless word of thanks and flew from the room.

44

arguerite had never seen anything more beautiful than Robert's eyes, clear and bright once more, dancing in their old teasing way as he dragged his hand over the black stubble on his cheeks.

"I must look like a bear," he said. "You should have shaved me while I lay raving."

"You thrashed about too much. Besides," she added shyly, "I have no experience with shaving men. I might have nicked off your ear."

He gave a shout of laughter, which she hurriedly leaned forward to muffle with her hands against his mouth. The fever had finally broken three days ago, and though pale, Robert's strength was returning as rapidly as his spirits. He had fluctuated between a restlessness to be away and long spells of seeming contentment to have her sit near him and distract him from the weakness that originally kept him bound to the bed by teaching him how to play chess. But today, when she had to leave him to dine and later to sit with her mother, she returned to find him on his feet and pacing. Both times he had only returned to the bed when she had informed him that Nicholas Tybert stood watch outside her door, thus frustrating any attempt at escape that he might be considering.

Despite his laughter now, he had directed enough quiet, serious gazes at her since he'd grown strong enough to sit propped up against the bolsters for her to guess that was the thought roiling in his mind. And she knew that if she let him give voice to it, there would be no altering his decision.

Surely this would change his mind? She pulled her hands away and kissed him. He tasted slightly of garlic and pepper from the pork stew she had had Eva bring up from the kitchens when Marguerite knew Nicholas Tybert would be waiting on her in her mother's sitting chamber. She was glad Eva was not here now. Marguerite had given the girl leave to visit Simon Todd at the glovemaker's after they'd coaxed Robert back to the bed. She hoped the faithful servant was enjoying an embrace as delicious as Robert's swift, zestful return of her kiss.

His vigor reassured Marguerite as much as it delighted her. During the worst of the fever he had grown delirious, shouting out Kit Beckford's name, a few times coupled with his brother's or sister's. The anger in his voice had raged almost as hot as his body. But when he had cried out Marguerite's name, it had been on a note of despair. She had not asked him if he remembered, for he'd professed no recollection of his other rantings when she told him of them afterwards. But it troubled her. What latent fear had burrowed in his heart that her name had fallen from his lips with such distress?

She felt his hand on her cheek, nudging her gently away. She resisted letting him put too much distance between their lips. "I shall have Eva bring up some fig pudding when she gets back," she murmured before he could speak. "'Tis not that I object to garlic on a man as ravenous as you've been the last two days, but a little ginger and honey would be a pleasant variation."

He let her roll her forehead against his. "I'd rather have an apple tart," he said. "I thought the scent was wafting from your hair until you kissed me. What other treats did you enjoy from the royal kitchens today?"

"It was apple-almond pudding. We also had pears in syrup, and elder-flower cheese pie, and custard tarts, and hippocras, but I did not drink any of the latter . . ."

"Why not?" he asked when she trailed off. His hand played with one of her curls that had tumbled over her shoulder. "Honey and cinnamon and cloves and a few other spices I've forgotten, all heated in wine. I've not drunk it above twice in my life. Once a generous merchant granted me a cup to warm me before turning me out on a winter's night. The other time—"

"The other time?" She closed her eyes and let Robert's touch drive away the memory of Saxton draining goblet after goblet of the heady wine while she sat in stiff dread of another assault at the dining table. Thankfully, Lady Helen had drawn away his attention by discoursing with the king with questions that repeatedly drew Saxton and the queen into their conversation.

"The other time," Robert said, "an audacious and lovely lady in a very rich gown thought to heat my blood enough to let her seduce me. But she did not smell of apples or taste like honey and she had no beguiling freckles on her nose, so I drank the wine and thanked her, then turned *myself* out in the winter's night."

His eyes teased. He drove away her stir of jealousy with the kiss he dropped on her nose before he pulled her lips to his again in a kiss both possessive and tender. She kissed him back fiercely, pouring into their exchange every hope and dream she had ever woven around him. Into their embrace flowed all her visions of their future, the roads they would travel together, the children they would raise, the joys and tears they would share, her hair silvering like Lady Helen's while his greyed, their love burning as bright at the end as it did upon this day. She would bear anything—she would bear everything, as long as she could bear it at his side.

He broke off the kiss with a gasp. The teasing was gone, replaced with a wretchedness she had never glimpsed before in his strong, dauntless face. But it was the other expression that flickered in his midnight eyes that sank her heart like lead as he buried his face in her hair. It had not been enough. She had promised him her very being in their embrace, and still his decision stood against her like flint.

"I have to go." His muffled voice thrummed hoarsely against her neck. "Marguerite, you know I have to go."

She clung to him, even as his arms around her tightened. "You cannot. Nicholas Tybert—"

"You have to draw him away from the door. It is you he guards, not me. He went to dinner with you, didn't he? And to your mother's? I should have gone then. I told myself I should go—but I could not bear to leave you without one last kiss." His mouth pressed warm through her hair against her throat.

"Then take me with you," she pleaded.

"You know I cannot do that. I am wanted for treason."

"Then I will follow you on my own! I will not stay here and marry Saxton!"

"I would not ask that of you." He eased her away. His eyes were very bright, not with fever, but with determination.

Before, she had only been able to glimpse his emotions in laughter or passion or anger. Since the illness, his every thought had lain bare to her. The sheer force of the love that glowed from his eyes when he gazed on her shook her so hard that it had repeatedly knocked the breath from her lungs. But an obdurate resolve always flowed in swiftly behind the fervor, tinged with a pain that might have flattered her more than his ardor had the purpose she read behind it not terrified her so.

"Rob—"

"Marguerite, Richard gave me his word that he would protect you from Saxton. Once I am gone, Saxton will have no reason to keep your cousin imprisoned. I told him—but there is not time to explain it all to you. Trust in Richard and in Gunthar. They will keep you safe."

"But Gunthar has not returned. His chair was empty at the table again today." Saxton had dropped a veiled threat in her ear at dinner days ago that had frightened her away from calling on Lady Helen again.

Robert frowned at her words. She tried to divert him by setting the chessboard back on the bed between them and arranging the ivory pieces.

"Let us talk of all this later. You need to gather more strength before— Would you rather be white or red this time?"

He clasped her hand with his brown, calloused fingers. She glanced up at him and suffered the now familiar punch to her lungs.

"Mae—"

"Rob, please don't—"

"Hush, love, I need to say this." He stared for several moments at their hands where his thumb rubbed across her knuckles. "When I left the manor," he said at last, "I did not know what I wanted beyond my freedom. I thought it was wanderlust that drove me north and south and east and west along the roads of England. Restlessness has vexed me all my life. If I could only see enough, I told myself, and taste enough and touch enough, surely the dissatisfaction would eventually be sated and I might learn what it was to be quiet and content."

He paused, then cupped her hand in both of his and raised it to press a kiss into her palm. His lips burned a vow into her flesh.

"I have never felt so still as I have these three days, sitting here with you. I understand now what I never comprehended on the manor, how my father bore the discontent I felt simmering in him when I was a boy. Being with her—my mother—quieted his soul. I shall ever be grateful to you, Mae, that for these too-brief days, you have quieted mine. And I shall love you always."

She flung the chessboard out of the way so that she could throw her arms around his neck again. "Rob—you cannot ask this of me."

"Sweetheart, I have no choice. I will be an outlaw."

"I do not care! I only want to be with you. I will follow you anywhere." She felt him shake his head. "Yes, yes! You cannot stop me!"

His hand stroked her hair. "Marguerite, you are wiser than this. And I would sooner let them hang me than have you share my shame."

She shuddered against him, thinking of the danger he faced. "But it is all a lie. Even Richard says it is a lie. Saxton said he would show Richard evidence of your guilt, but he never did. Richard challenged him with it when Saxton took me to see him again. Saxton insists the evidence exists, but surely he is only bluffing, trying to shake Richard's and my faith in you!"

"He has it."

Marguerite tried to sit up, startled by Robert's words, but he held her head against his shoulder.

"I have seen it with my own eyes. Marguerite, they have everything they need to condemn me. That it is a lie will make no difference. I will not stay here longer and set you at risk, and I will not take you with me. So kiss me just once more, and then you have got to let me go."

She tasted nothing but despair in his lips this time, and her own shattered dreams, and the salt of her tears. Some sound sought to break through her pain, but the anguished thudding of her heart drown it out until Robert stiffened, wrenched his mouth from hers and cursed.

"Take him." The voice snapped like a whip from behind her.

She sprang to her feet and started to whirl about, but hands knocked her sideways. She saw a blur of green and brown that resolved into four men. Saxton's colors! She spun unimpeded now to find the door standing wide and Saxton on the threshold, watching with an icy sneer as his guards dodged Robert's fists and feet to wrestle him from the bed.

"No!" she screamed through the expletives Robert hurled at his attackers. He had no weapon. His dagger and sword lay in the corner where she had removed them during his fever.

She lunged to grab up his dagger and would have flung herself into the fray, but Saxton moved and blocked her. He held her wrists locked in his merciless grasp and forced her to watch helplessly as his men overpowered Robert and dragged him from the room.

"You monster!" she cried. "You villain! Let him go!"

Saxton mocked her with the thin curl of his lips. "Your humble words of supplication nearly overwhelm me."

He shook the dagger out of her hands with a strength she could not withstand, then shoved her onto the bed.

She rubbed at the bruises he'd left on her wrists. "What are you going to do with him?" she demanded.

Saxton shrugged. "He is a traitor. He will hang."

"No—" The word strangled off, as if the noose had jerked tight around her own neck.

Saxton walked over to her and reached one finger to trace the soft curve of her cheek. "One wonders exactly how you have been entertaining Marcel these past few days. Or may one surmise the answer from the passionate scene that met our eyes when we arrived?"

She struck away his hand. "'Twas nothing that your filthy mind might conceive. Rob is a gentleman."

"A villein gentleman? 'Tis a contradiction in terms, my dear. Ah, well." He turned away and strolled towards the door.

Marguerite leapt from the bed to catch his arm. "He is not going to hang!"

Saxton gazed down at her with narrowed eyes. "Is he not?"

Panic rolled in her stomach. "Ah, please—" Saxton's cold face bleared through her tears. "Please—"

"Come, this is better. I've endured enough of your spirit and spite. How well can you beg, my lady?"

She stared at him, uncomprehending for a moment, until the implacable glint in his eyes thrust her to her knees. Her own vow rushed back. *I will do anything for Robert, even bear this humiliation.*

"Please—spare him."

The glint pierced like steel. "I—think—not."

Her heart lurched against her ribs. "Please! I will do anything—"

"Anything? Come, my lady, be more specific."

He gazed down at her, cruel and taunting. The weight of his malignity threatened to crush her cowering to the floor. She clung desperately to one last strand of pride to keep her kneeling upright.

Her mouth felt as though it had been stuffed with wool, but somehow she managed to speak around the stifling wad. "What is it—you want?"

He stroked his chin, as if considering. "We are discussing a life, are we not? What say you, my lady? A life for a life? That seems fair."

What riddle was this? "I d-don't understand."

"Don't you? Gentleman or not, it will soon be all over the court that you've harbored a man in your chambers for close on a week. If there is to be a brat, there must at least be a plausible possibility that it might be mine."

Her face drained white. "But Rob—h-he didn't— I swear—!"

"And *I* am willing to believe you, but you cannot expect the king to be so credulous, and the court will follow his lead." The intent in Saxton's gaze was obdurate and brutal. "Your life, Marguerite, for Marcel's. Are you willing to give yourself to me here? Now?"

She followed his glance to the bed and flinched.

"I can bury him in prison or in the ground. It is all the same to me."

It would have been easier if Saxton had asked her to die. Her stomach churned, her body convulsed with shudders. But there was only one answer she could give. *Anything. Anything—*

He saw her defeat and reached down his hand. She placed her violently shaking fingers in his.

"Marguerite?"

Her head turned towards the door to discover that it still stood open. She could not see the woman distinctly through her smearing tears, but she knew Lady Helen's voice. Marguerite's sob of relief shamed her. She hated herself for her cowardice, but when Lady Helen swept across the floor and knelt beside her, Marguerite pulled free her hand and crumpled into the countess's arms.

"Child, I came as soon as I heard." Lady Helen kissed her and wiped her tears, then stood and confronted Saxton. "You have done your mischief here, my lord. There is no reason for you to linger where you have no further business to be."

Saxton returned her gaze coldly. "She is my betrothed. And she has been concealing a man who is wanted by the crown. I have a perfect right to question her."

"Then do so somewhere more appropriate than in her own chamber. You may be betrothed, but she is not yet your wife. Let us retire to my sitting chamber and you may question us both. Robert was my minstrel, after all.

Perhaps you suspect me of concealing him from you, as well?" Her silvery eyes blazed at Saxton with a depth of contempt Marguerite had never seen anyone dare to his face before.

Saxton's mouth gave a twitch of anger, but he answered the countess with a mocking bow. "I would not dream of accusing *you*, my lady. Alas, your husband is another matter. It appears that he and Marcel—"

"—were involved together in nefarious affairs in Poitou?"

Saxton looked genuinely taken aback when Lady Helen finished his sentence.

"Perhaps even treasonous affairs?" she added. "And you have evidence of this, I presume? A written statement by a witness, perhaps? If that is so, you can show it to me."

Again his lips twitched, but he replied without a beat of hesitation. "I assure you, my lady, we found all the evidence we need among Marcel's belongings. French silver and an incriminating letter—"

"Was my husband mentioned in this letter, or even alluded to?" She allowed Saxton's silence to stretch out to make her point. "I did not think so, because my husband is an honest man whom you can convict only with perjury. I have no explanation or defense for anything that Robert Marcel may have done, but this child—" she motioned at Marguerite "—was surely ignorant of it. If Robert beguiled her—" Lady Helen shook her hand for silence when Marguerite protested "—we must ascribe that to her youth and innocence. An innocence I have no intention of allowing a devil like you to despoil."

Saxton's lips curved insultingly. "I think you have no say in whether I despoil her or not, my lady. If she is not yet my wife, she is no less mine. Ask her parents." He gave one of his hateful, self-assured shrugs. "Nay, ask Marguerite herself."

Marguerite wrapped her arms around her body in a vain attempt to stop its shaking. She must not be so weak, so selfish when Robert's very life depended on her response. But she could not bear to look at the countess as she stammered through teeth that chattered as though she stood in the snow, "Th-thank you for coming, m-my lady, b-but I d-do not require your p-protection."

"Hmph," Lady Helen snorted down her straight little nose. "I have lived a good many years, my lord—" again she addressed Saxton "—and I know the conceit of men's pride. I can guess what you are thinking passed between

Marguerite and Robert, and I can guess what you think you intend to do about it. But if you hope to ravish this child you will have to do it in front of me, for I have no intention of leaving her here alone with you."

Lady Helen folded her arms and glared at Saxton, fairly glowing in her anger. The countess was a tall woman, but Saxton's hulking build made her look thin and fragile. One swipe of his massive fist would throw her off her feet, and he looked incensed enough at her defiance to deal her such a blow. Marguerite leapt up and tried to move between them, but Lady Helen's arm shot out to restrain her.

"If you were wife to any other man—" Saxton hissed. He threw a gaze full of black promise at Marguerite. "A reprieve for you, my dear, but a small one. Even my Lady Helen cannot deny me your bridal night. I shall simply move up our wedding—to Friday, I think. Aye, three days from now. The choice is yours, my dear. If I rise a satisfied husband on Saturday, Marcel may live to see the sun rise that day. If not—I will raise his head on a pike, instead."

Marguerite shivered. Lady Helen started to embrace her, but Marguerite stepped quickly away with a shake of her head.

"Fr-Friday," she said. "I-I will be ready and I—I w-will not disappoint you."

Saxton allowed himself a smirk of triumph at Lady Helen, then bowed and left the room.

Marguerite sank down on the bed when he was gone and covered her face with her hands. How could this be happening? Only moments ago, she had been loved and safe in Robert's arms, and now—

"Marguerite—"

She remembered the kisses Saxton had pressed on her before, and shuddered and shuddered. How would she bear it? A lifetime as his wife! *But Rob will live—Rob will live—*

"Child, look at me."

She could not obey the countess until she steadied herself, but when she tried to draw in a calming breath, it scraped through her throat on a gasp. She wanted only to be left alone, to curl up on her bed and weep and weep until she grew numb.

The bed dipped with the countess's weight as she sat beside Marguerite. Lady Helen stroked her hair with soothing fingers and simply waited.

"My lady, I thank you for your defense," Marguerite at last choked out, "but—I have no choice but to marry Lord Saxton."

"Come with me to my chambers," Lady Helen said, "and we will talk of it."

Marguerite shook her head. "There is naught to talk of. *Nothing* will change my mind."

Lady Helen sighed. "I cannot leave you here. What if Lord Saxton comes back?"

"I—I will lock the door."

The door. Marguerite's head abruptly bounced up. She had been so careful to keep the door locked or bolted while Robert lay ill and then recovering. How had Saxton and his guards forced their way in? How had they even known Robert was here?

Richard. Saxton must have broken Richard and made him tell! No one else knew she had concealed Robert here, not even Lady Helen. Marguerite rose and swept across the floor to view the door. There was no splintering of the wooden planks. She had left the bolt undone so that Eva might easily come and go if Marguerite was distracted with Robert, but the servant always carried a key and carefully locked the door behind her when Marguerite sent her on an errand. Marguerite tried the door latch and felt it slide smoothly downward into an unlocked position. She took a step back in horror. No. No—

Lady Helen joined her and took her hand. "Please come and sit with me. You should not be alone just now."

But alone was what Marguerite wished to be. Alone to think through this apparent betrayal. It could not be what it seemed! She saw the countess's worry and sought to allay it as best she could. "Please, I just need a little time. I will come to you in an hour. I promise."

Lady Helen looked doubtful, but nodded. "One hour, then. Do not fail or I will come and fetch you to me."

Marguerite carefully bolted the door behind the countess, then fell into sweeping strides about the room. Is this what Robert felt when he paced? This simmering energy, this low-burning rage? If what she suspected proved true, she would be as merciless as Saxton in her retribution.

45

Gunthar stared out the window, listening to the slow, hollow thudding in his chest. Anger brimmed deep beneath the turmoil of other emotions swirling through him, emotions that memory held too painful to name. He had not expected to live long enough to experience a loss like this again. *It is not the same,* he told himself for the hundredth time since the news had reached him. He welcomed the tread of the footsteps that turned him towards the door, offering at last the distraction he'd been praying for this last hour.

Helen paused on the threshold of her sitting chamber, clearly startled to see him, but he noted the swift flow of relief that flooded into her eyes.

"Hugh!" She flew to his side with the speed of a woman half her age. "Oh, thank goodness you've returned."

Gunthar took her slender hands in his and bent to kiss her before he said, "Helen, where have you been, and what in thunder has been going on in my absence? I received your courier on my way to York, telling me to make haste with my return but giving no explanation. It is not like you, my dear."

"Yes, I know, and I meant to explain, but it has all grown so complicated."

He frowned to see her pallor, the lines of worry pleating her brow. "So I've heard." Her eyes widened in question. "I have been back for nearly an hour, time enough to receive some jumbled account of treason and fugitives and the Lady Marguerite's disgrace." He paused and felt the grim tightening of his mouth. "I understand Marcel is in prison."

Helen rarely looked helpless, but it was the only word he could put to the expression in her eyes. "It is all so dreadful. Saxton claims that Robert carried a letter proving treasonous dealings in Poitou. Christopher Beckford was sent to arrest him, but Robert escaped—"

"—and hid himself in his lady's chamber?" Gunthar cut her off with a ruthless snap. "I had thought myself some judge of character, but this—! This, indeed, is behavior worthy of a—churl."

"Hugh!"

He released her hands, unmoved by her reproof. "What word would you prefer I use? Coward? To hide behind a woman and ruin her honor? I had hoped better of him than this." Anger surged over the clash of other emotions and sent Gunthar to pacing.

"I have just come from Marguerite," Helen said, "and if you could see her distress— Hugh, she loves him painfully. But you must have guessed that. She wears your ring."

Gunthar grunted. "I gave it to Robert as payment for a service he rendered me. I told him to give it to his lady love. How could I guess he would be so mad— *Blazes*!" He spun on his heel and strode back the other way.

"I do not think Robert meant to 'hide behind her,' as you say. Marguerite told me she found him in the palace, ill. She came to me for a remedy, which I gladly provided her, but she would not confide to me his whereabouts."

Gunthar swept on in his wife's pause, only half-hearing. Disappointment weighted his stomach and clogged his throat in a way he'd never known.

"I spoke with Lord Christopher," Helen continued. "He told me they found French silver among Robert's possessions, and a letter, but when I saw what he was writing, I— Hugh, are listening? Do *you* think Robert is guilty?"

"If they have evidence, what I think is irrelevant."

"Is it? And if Robert is innocent? What chance do you suppose he will have now that he is in Saxton's power?"

"None." A chair was in his path. Gunthar dealt it a shoving kick that sent it scraping across the floor, out of his way. "Devil take that boy. Why did he not come to me? Did he think I would have denied him my aid?"

A crisp laugh halted him and turned him about with a rare glower at his wife.

"That is why you are so nettled. Your pride is hurt!"

"Nonsense. I care not a rap for the scamp."

Helen laughed again. She took his hands and swung them chidingly. "Oh, my dear, you mustn't lie to me, I know you far too well." She gazed up at Gunthar with her too-discerning eyes. "Do you think I have not seen it? The way you keep him at your side, the way you jest with him as you did only with Harry and Peter?"

It is not the same, he told himself again, ignoring the resumption of that empty, drubbing throb. He started to speak lest she think he had forgotten their sons, but she set her fingers to his lips.

"No, you needn't try to explain. Marguerite has lightened my days, too." She moved into his arms and laid her head against his heart. "What are we to do?"

He leaned his cheek against the top of her silken veil, smothering down the hurt she had perceived that Robert had not trusted him when Gunthar had sensed him in trouble. "I do not know. I feared Robert might tumble into some snare, but I intended to be back in time to prevent it. It was undoubtedly Saxton who suggested to the king that he send me to York. Saxton must have feared I would interfere with his plans for Robert—" Gunthar released her to drive a fist into his palm. "Blazes! I should have taken him with me."

"He would not have gone," Helen said. "Not with Marguerite's wedding so close."

That was Gunthar's deepest regret of all. He should have found a way to sever that relationship before he'd left for York.

"The fool. Why could Robert not have fallen in love with a merchant's daughter?"

"We have little say about whom we love," Helen murmured. "I would have loved you still had you been a pauper."

"You would have had more sense," Gunthar said, though his heart warmed at the glow of sincerity in his wife's eyes. "But all this is nothing to the point. I cannot stand by and watch Robert hang."

"He will not hang, if Marguerite has her way. She has agreed to marry Saxton in exchange for Robert's life."

The first sliver of hope cracked the gloom that had enveloped Gunthar since word of Robert's arrest had greeted his return to court. "At least one of them has a grain of sense, then. As soon as she is safely bound to Saxton, I will—"

"Hugh, you cannot think I would allow such a thing? Marguerite marry Saxton? It would be obscene!"

Gunthar frowned. "Helen, you are not her mother. It is not within your power to decide whom Marguerite de Villon marries and whom she does not."

"Nor is Robert your son," she retorted, "yet you cannot tell me you have not meddled in his life as though he were, or that you are planning to continue to do so, beginning with telling *him* who he can and cannot marry."

It did not improve Gunthar's temper that his wife hit so near the mark with her accusation. It was not that he had no sympathy for the young woman Helen had grown fond of, but fear for Robert made him answer impatiently. "It is ridiculous to compare the Lady Marguerite's plight with Robert's. Being Saxton's wife will undoubtedly be unpleasant, but Robert— Helen, he has been arrested for treason. You know the king's temperament and Saxton's malevolence. Deprive Saxton of his bride and he will see Robert hanged for very spite."

"But if he is innocent, you will find a way to—"

"A man vicious enough to attempt to murder me thrice will not let Robert escape him now he has him in his power. Saxton's wedding to Marguerite will buy me time to—" Gunthar stopped as Helen's face went white.

Her hand pressed to her mouth, her eyes flaring with horror. "Saxton— tried to murder you?"

Gunthar realized his carelessness too late. "Helen—"

"Don't 'Helen' me!" He winced at the fire in her eyes "Why did you not tell me? Did you think it of such little import that I would not care?"

Gunthar knew she would not be content until she had the story. He told her briefly of the two incidents in Poitou. "There was a cutpurse in Cambridge where I stopped two days ago, as well," he added. "At least, that's what he claimed to be when his shadow caught my eye—I have been very wary since Poitou—and I whirled to block and strike the knife from his hand. Your courier's arrival interrupted my questioning, but he remains with my guards. I cannot prove he was sent by Beckford or Saxton—yet— but there was something about his face. I am almost certain I saw a man who very much resembled him among Beckford's camp in Poitou."

"You may not have proof," Helen said, "but I have." Before he could ask of what, she swept into their bedchamber and returned a moment later with a rolled up sheet of parchment in her hand. She thwacked it into his palm. "Read *that* and tell me what you think."

Gunthar pulled open the roll and read. So. Here at last was proof, indeed. Saxton's seal set to a half-written document accusing Gunthar of conspiring with Robert Marcel in treason against the crown. That Saxton had sworn his witness to an unfinished accusation suggested a malice and fabrication that even King John's suspicious mind would reject. But it did not show Saxton's hand, or even Beckford's, in the assassination attempts. And it would not deliver Robert. All this document proved was that Saxton had attempted to take advantage of Robert's "crime" to implicate and disgrace Saxton's rival. The king might be indignant enough to dismiss Saxton— perhaps even imprison him—but Robert would remain in prison, too, waiting for the gallows.

"How did you come by this?" Gunthar asked.

"It was something Marguerite said. I went to question Lord Christopher. Yes, I did not know he had come back to court, either. I asked him for the story of Robert's arrest, but he hovered rather too near to his desk while he told me, as if there were something he did not wish me to see. I gave him my hand to kiss and saw what looked like fresh ink stains on his fingers. Do you remember how, when he came to Lamhurst to swear his fealty to you after his father death, he told us he never retired to bed without drinking some saffron tea to help him sleep? I hazarded the chance that he still carried the spice with him, and asked him if he had any he might spare me to dye this gray out of my hair."

Gunthar lifted his wife's veil and slanted a stern study on her tresses, lest he find their pale gold spoiled with garish yellow streaks.

She laughed. "It was only a ruse to send him to his bedchamber to fetch the spice. In the few moments he was gone, I slipped around his desk and found that scroll, unfinished as you see it now. There is no doubt that Lord Christopher guessed I took it when he found it missing after I left him, but he could hardly challenge me over it."

"When was this?"

"Three days ago. As soon as I realized what it was—" she motioned at the parchment "—I sent the courier after you."

"That must have been when Beckford decided to send his 'cutpurse.' He would not have dared rewrite this, knowing you had a copy, but he must have feared Saxton's fury when Saxton learned how Beckford had let you spoil their plot. He surely hoped his third assassin would accomplish what the former two failed to do."

Helen gazed at him with that worry it always grieved him to see in her eyes. "What shall you do now?"

"What you brought me back to do. Confront Beckford and see if I can wring the truth from his perfidious throat."

"You won't find him in his chambers," Helen said as Gunthar started towards the door. "I set Ralf to watch him. He said that though Lord Christopher still sleeps in the palace, he spends his days in a tavern in the city, perhaps to avoid Lord Saxton as much as he can."

"Then Ralf shall ride with me," Gunthar said. "Find him and tell him to meet me in the stables."

Marguerite rubbed her cheek where the sting of her father's hand still lingered as she mounted the stairs to Lady Helen's chambers. After the countess had left her, Lord de Villon had cornered his daughter in a rage, calling her strumpet and harlot and swearing it was only Saxton's desire for an unblemished bride that spared her more than his one impulsive slap. His curses and slurs had humiliated her, for he had sworn them all in front of her mother's tears. Neither of them, she knew, would believe Robert had acted honorably with her. So she had stood silent, absorbing the lewd names her father called her, sick for the shame she saw in her mother's eyes, still terrified for Robert and despairing over her future with Saxton.

But her mother's weeping had curiously kept Marguerite's own eyes dry. They remained so as she tapped on the countess's door. Marguerite would not linger long. Just long enough to thank Lady Helen for all of her kindnesses, for as Saxton's wife, Marguerite knew she would never be allowed to see the countess again.

Footsteps sounded behind her, skittering up the stairs she had just traced. She turned at the anxious mingling of voices, just as Lady Helen's door clicked open. A young man with dusty blond hair dragged a woman with a tear-streaked face toward Marguerite. Marguerite felt herself go chill as he threw himself on his knees at her feet.

"Simon." She glanced from the runaway villein to the brown-haired lass who knelt weeping beside him. "Eva. What is this?"

She already guessed. Nay, she already knew. But she would make them tell her, nonetheless.

Simon Todd gazed up at her through a swollen eye and spoke through a cut on his lip. "Milady—" his chest rose and fell with rapid gusts of breath. "I've come to confess to ye—my base cowardice—an' my betrayal of yer confidence. I'm willin' to accept any punishment ye see fit."

Simon? It had been Simon?

"They came to my master's workshop when I was alone. I would never have told them, milady, but—"

Eva had been weeping into her hands, but at this she threw back her head and cried, "No, no! Ye must not lie for me, Simon. Milady, it was I—it was *I* who told."

A soft rustling sound brought Lady Helen through the doorway to stand beside Marguerite. Marguerite did not look at her. She merely waited, while Simon put his arm around Eva, but Eva shook herself away from his embrace and stood up.

"The men said they would kill Simon if I didn't tell. I was so afraid—" She could barely speak through her sobs. "They bound him an' put a sword to his side an' said—if I wasn't tellin' the truth—he would die. If I didn't help them—he would die. So I told them—where Rob was hidden, an'—an' I gave them the key to yer door."

It brought Marguerite no satisfaction to find her suspicions were true. She watched Eva sink back to her knees, waiting for her mistress's judgment. Marguerite tried to gaze on them with pity—would she not have done the same as Eva? But she found that compassion came hard. If the betrayal had affected Marguerite alone— But the servant had thrust Robert into the cruel, vindictive hands of the Earl of Saxton. Marguerite could no more forgive Eva than she could forgive herself, for if Marguerite had not loved Robert, his life would not be hanging by such a slender thread.

Simon put his arm around Eva again. Emotion struggled in his face, dread battling with determination.

"Is there something more?" Marguerite asked. The coldness in her voice shocked even her. She had never felt so hard. So bitter.

Simon hesitated. Eva whispered something to him, but he shook his head and muttered, "No, she has the right to know."

"Know what? Tell me, Simon!"

He winced at the bite of Marguerite's demand.

"Milady—Rob's been—"

Panic plunged through her as Simon's courage appeared to fail him. What had Saxton done? Before she could speak again, a man rounded the top of the stairs and strode towards them.

"Tell her, boy." Gunthar's bark startled Simon to his feet. The earl glared not at the villein, but past him into Marguerite's eyes.

Marguerite felt Lady Helen's hand on her arm. The countess addressed her husband with a calmness that jarred against Marguerite's turmoil.

"Well, Hugh? Did you speak with Lord Christopher?"

"No." Marguerite saw condemnation in the gaze that held hers fast and flinched without knowing why. "I was detained by events in the square. The *public* square, my lady. Tell her, boy," he repeated to Simon. "Tell her how the Earl of Saxton keeps his promises, how he bargains. Tell her what security her *sacrifice* brings to a man she says she loves."

The potent force of Gunthar's glare dismayed Marguerite in a way that Saxton's never had. She tore her gaze away to plead with Simon's less formidable presence.

"Simon, please—"

Simon drew a breath before he replied. "Milady—Rob's received a public flogging—as a punishment for his crimes."

Marguerite swayed, as if the lash had cracked down across her own soul, but she did not realize she was near to fainting until she felt arms half-leading, half-carrying her across some space her blurred vision could not clearly see. A chair appeared beneath her. She heard the curt snap of a command from Gunthar, then a cup of wine pressed into her hands. She drank at the countess's urging. The robust liquid poured a vibrant energy into her limbs, and with it came a torrent of anger greater than any Marguerite had known before.

"Oh, but he shall pay for this!" She sprang from the chair, her fists clenched tight.

"The deed is done, my lady," Gunthar said. He stood across from her in the countess's sitting chamber, still holding the bottle of wine. "There is nothing you can do now."

She swept across the room like a caged lioness. "We shall see what I can do. Oh, the liar, the villain! *How* Saxton will pay."

Lady Helen stepped into her path and caught her hands, forcing

Marguerite to stop. "Calm yourself, child. Robert is hurt, to be sure, but he is alive."

"And shall I do nothing?" Marguerite said. "Shall I not punish Saxton for this?"

Lady Helen tucked a lock of hair behind Marguerite's ear, her silvery eyes awash with worry. "Marguerite, Robert would not want you to place yourself at risk for him."

Marguerite laughed, short and bitter. She pulled away from the countess to whirl on Eva, who hovered near the doorway with Simon. "*You*. You are free to find yourself a new mistress, if you can. And *you*—" she glowered at Simon "—I should report you to my father and have you dragged back to the manor—but I will not. Go where you will, but do not come near my sight again."

"And what of you, my lady?" Gunthar's voice rapped almost savagely across the room. "Do you bear no blame in this?"

He towered over her, his broad-shouldered build less massive than Saxton's, but somehow more daunting, for where Saxton intimidated with coldness and bullying force Gunthar's terrible gaze stripped away all her defenses and pierced her to the very heart. The pain, too briefly smothered beneath her rage, cascaded over her again.

"I know the blame is mine." Her mouth trembled, her throat tightening with fresh tears. "But how could I have guessed—Rob would come to this— merely because I dared to love him?" She put out a hand to stay an impulsive move from the countess and swallowed the aching lump. "My own judgment is assured, my lord, and I will not seek to evade it. Eva"—she turned to the girl, weeping again at Simon's side—"there is one more service you may perform for me. Pray seek out my Lord Saxton and request an audience for me at his earliest convenience."

Eva curtsied, looking joyful that her mistress would trust her with any kind of task, and dashed away to obey.

"Marguerite," Lady Helen exclaimed, "what do you mean to do?"

Marguerite curtsied to the countess. To Gunthar she bowed her head, unable to bear his gaze again.

"My lady, my lord, I shall ever be grateful for your kindness to me, but I must not keep Lord Saxton waiting."

She swept from the room behind Eva before Lady Helen could attempt to stop her.

46

Marguerite had heard rumors of the Earl of Saxton's "audience chamber" where he sometimes attended to royal business on behalf of the king, but she had held so little interest in Saxton's life that it had not crossed her mind to wonder what this room might be like. Though the chamber, spacious as it was, was dwarfed by the great hall of Westminster Palace, she nevertheless stood astounded in the doorway. Tapestries rivaling those of the king's hall in their brilliant colors and designs draped the walls. Into each in some manner or other had been woven an image of a roaring bear, the one on the tapestry behind the dais daringly wearing a gilt coronet. Beneath it stood a chair of highly polished wood, lavishly trimmed in gold with rubies that winked like eyes in the carved bear heads of the armrests. Rubies, emeralds and diamonds twinkled like stars in the shield carved into the back, forming a ring around the roaring bear at its center. Saxton's emblem was even emblazoned on a gold disk attached to the bottle of wine on the silver table set beside the chair.

Did the king know that his counselor had surrounded himself with so much presumptuous glory?

It took her a few moments to summon her wits and gaze at the man standing on the other side of the chair. Or was it a throne?

"To what do I owe this pleasure, my lady?" Saxton wore a surcote of rich green velvet trimmed with sable fur, his chest spangled with chains and jewels.

She stepped tentatively further into the chamber. Her footsteps through the rushes released a mingling of so many heady fragrances that it nearly made her head spin. Curiosity briefly overcame her.

"What do you do here?" she asked.

"Listen to petitions that bore the king, deal out fair judgments—or foul, depending on how much the suppliants can pay."

She turned slowly about, taking in the tapestries. "Does Lord Gunthar have a chamber like this?" If so, did he display his emblem so boldly? Did he have a chair that rivaled the king's?

"Gunthar is not ashamed of his wealth and he knows how to flaunt it when it pleases him . . . but no, not here at court. He conducts such business in the royal hall, as does the king. Does my audience chamber shock you, my lady?"

She stopped turning to meet Saxton's eyes. "No, of course not."

She glimpsed a glint of amusement before his gaze fell from hers to roam slowly over the clinging lines of her gown. The soft, intricately woven bodice of soft crimson wool with its boldly scooping neckline had darkened his eyes in just such a manner at her father's castle the night he had attempted to assault her.

Marguerite had had her hand around the hilt of Robert's dagger, considering how to conceal it for this interview, when she had grudgingly realized that trying to punish Saxton with steel would not help Robert. Even if she killed this monster before her, Robert would remain in the dungeon where Saxton had undoubtedly flung him. No, only honey might save her love. Then honey, instead of steel, she had decided to offer.

Her heartbeat skipped at his lingering, sensual gaze, but she glided across the rushes and held out her hand. He took her fingers in his and guided her onto the dais. She had drunk a goblet of wine before she came to keep the color in her cheeks and steady herself from shrinking from his touch.

His mouth lingered hot and moist on the back of her hand. "All this"—he gestured around the opulent room—"you will share at my side. I will deck you in jewels and gowns that will make the queen herself weep with jealousy. The Countess of Saxton will be the envy of every woman in the kingdom. No small consolation, my lady, for the burden you seem to think it will be to be my wife."

Jewels and gowns—all bought with my grandfather's wealth. No, she must not let Saxton trip her temper. She must focus on why she was here, not on the past or the future.

She withdrew her hand, feigning as an excuse her desire to sweep her fingers over the green velvet cushion with the red and gold embroidery that softened the seat of the chair for its occupant. *Coward,* she chided herself. Avoidance would not win this game he forced on her. She noticed the goblet on the table stood half-empty. How many cups had he drained off before she came? No matter. The hotter his blood ran, the better.

She turned to speak, but he preempted her.

"Sit, my lady. Nay, not there—"

She was almost grateful when he checked her from sitting in his chair. Built for his massive frame, she feared it might swallow her, or at least deplete her courage if she sank into its depths.

"That is mine. You may sit here."

She had not seen the smaller, prettily carved chair that had been pushed towards the back of the dais. The smooth wood was embellished with silver and rubies. He pulled it forward and waited for her to sit on its red cushion.

"I was about to send for you when your servant told me of your desire to see me. I have news that I believe will please you." She tried not to squirm when his gaze drifted again to her bodice. "Your cousin is no longer locked up."

"You have freed Richard?"

"Aye. I have sent him off to Gloucester, to Sir Edward Keynes's widow. I thought she might appreciate the support of her late husband's squire as she mourns her husband's death." Saxton's finger came suddenly under her chin and lifted her face to his. "There must be no more foolhardy attempts to rescue you, my girl. Your cousin was very reluctant to go, but I am afraid I gave him no choice."

She mastered the panicked impulse to pull away from Saxton's touch. Richard, gone but safe. It was better thus.

"I daresay you will doubt me," she said, "but I have come to apologize. I have been very foolish to defy you, my lord."

"Have you?" She heard the dry skepticism in his voice.

Honey, she reminded herself. *Only honey will save Robert.*

"Indeed," she said, relieved when her voice did not quiver. "I have had all morning to reflect. The blame was not all mine, you know." She fluttered at Saxton what she hoped was a look of coy reproof. "You humiliated me with Lady Jane. I was angry, I will own it. And I was afraid. I had never known anyone like you. You are very intimidating, my lord. Robert was dashing and young and romantic, but—but I know now that marrying him would have been a mistake. He could never have given me a tenth of this!" She cast her wide gaze about the chamber, genuine awe of the sumptuous surroundings bubbling up again.

"Is that all you want from me, my lady? The trappings of my power?" Saxton brushed his thumb along her lower lip. "What about my passion? Will you welcome that, as well?"

She kept her mind fixed fast upon her aim. "I will be a good wife to you."

"By shuddering every time I touch you? There is a certain entrancement to such fear, it is true, but there are times a man prefers to be flattered by a woman's—desire."

She clamped down the nausea in her stomach and stood up. "I am not shuddering now," she said and stretched herself up to slide her arms around his neck.

He reeked pungent with wine this close. The fumes saturated her senses as his mouth came down on hers, rank and plundering. *Don't shrink, don't tremble—don't be sick.* She could not return his kiss, even for Robert's sake, but she managed to beat back her revulsion and let Saxton ravage her lips as he pleased. What matter if everything inside her recoiled, so long as she could make him believe she wanted him?

Her mouth pulsed from his forceful assault when he finally raised his head. His eyes were nearly black, they had grown so dark.

"That was almost convincing." His wine-soured breath spewed across her face. From the thickness in his voice, she knew him roused despite his doubts. "You have grown most cooperative for a woman who just this morning called me a villain. It is my experience, my dear, that a woman is at her most provocative when she is after something. Now, what might that be?"

This small speech gave her time to dislodge the lump of disgust in her throat. "You mistake, my lord. I—"

"Do I?" He kissed her again, long and deliberate, but less bruising. "Perhaps—" his lips moved to the curve of her cheek "—having considered the matter—" his mouth pressed down more roughly against the base of her neck "—you find our bargain insufficient?" He eased the gown away to bare her shoulder for his kiss. At last, he raised his head on a husky sigh. "What more?"

"My lord—"

"No more games, Marguerite. I have granted you Marcel's life. I suppose you want his freedom, as well?"

She knew she must not sound desperate, but the plea spilled out of her. "I will marry you without complaint. I will surrender—all you ask of me—when you ask it of me. He will be no further threat to you, I swear!"

A familiar disdain broke through the lusting haze in Saxton's eyes. "Marcel has never been a threat to me."

Hope flamed in her. "Then—"

"But I don't like the man, my dear. Besides, if I released him—I should have no guarantee of your good behavior." Saxton's hand twisted in her hair, jerking back her head before he possessed her lips again.

The flame seared from hope to outrage. She would give her all for Robert, but not for this mockery that would leave him entombed in his prison at the whim of Saxton's abuse. She raked her nails down Saxton's cheek, then spat out the taste of him when he reared up his head on a gasp.

She recognized the savage fury in his eyes and knew what was coming. She tried to flinch way, but he held her tight with one arm while his free hand fell in a bruising blow across her face.

"Shrew."

"Fiend!" she shot back. "You lied to me! You said he should come to no harm."

Saxton struck her again. "I said he would live, no more."

She could hardly see Saxton for the tears of pain in her eyes. "You had him flogged like a common criminal!" She twisted wildly in Saxton's grasp, but he held her fast. She tried lashing out with her feet.

Saxton pushed her against his chair so hard that she fell across one gold-trimmed arm and knocked the air from her lungs. She struggled to right herself, but a third blow threw her into the voluminous depths of the chair.

"He is worse than a common criminal," Saxton snarled. "He is a traitor."

"Liar! He is innocent, and you know it."

"It is time you learned your place, my lady. I'll be called a liar by no one, man or woman. You shall rue that word on your lips and these stripes on my face."

He dragged her out of the chair and this time she saw that his hand had formed a fist.

"That's enough, Saxton. Hit her again and forfeit your life."

Saxton whirled toward the doorway, dragging Marguerite with him. "This is none of your affair, Eyvind. Stay out of it."

Saxton's voice was deadly, but Sir Warin flashed back, "I make it my affair. Hit her again and I swear I'll run you through."

Marguerite's left eye was swelling shut, but she glimpsed white anger in Sir Warin's face and the blur of a drawn sword in his hand.

"Try it," Saxton snapped, "and you'll hang as an assassin." Despite these words, he flung Marguerite away with such strength that she collapsed like a rag doll at Sir Warin's feet. "Your reprieve will be short lived, my lady," Saxton's voice reverberated above her. "We've a lifetime together to avenge this."

She turned her head and saw him touch the scratches on his cheek before he strode from the room.

She covered her face, shrinking from the horror of her rashness as she had not from Saxton's abhorrent kisses. What had she done? She had enraged him, when she had meant to seduce him to her favor. What if he took his fury out on Robert? What if her folly brought more pain to the man she loved? The throbbing of her eye paled to insignificance beside her vision of the lash across Robert's back.

She felt someone beside her. Sir Warin. His arms went around her before she could raise her head, drawing her against him.

"He is gone now." Sir Warin murmured. "I will never let that blackguard touch you again. Marguerite, I've come to take you away."

She struggled to comprehend his words through the nightmare image of Robert's suffering. "Away?"

"When I heard of Marcel's capture and that Saxton had moved up your wedding, I came looking for you. Your serving wench sent me here. Saints! When I saw Saxton standing over you, your eye all ruddy and his fist raised to strike you again— I should have speared him like a squealing pig!"

The images that had tormented her into donning this gown and attempting to throw herself on Saxton's lustful mercy rushed back in on her, shutting out Sir Warin's wrath. Robert bound to the whipping post, then tossed broken and bloodied into the dark, dank bowels of the palace dungeon. No name and rank to win him an honorable prison, like Richard had enjoyed.

Her hand curled into the sleeve of the arm that held her. "You must help me."

"The horses are already saddled," Sir Warin said. "I will have you away from here before nightfall."

She threw back her head with a gasp. "No! You must take me to Robert. Please—"

"To Marcel? He is in prison."

"I must see him! If you c-care for me at all, you will help me." She hated playing with Sir Warin's affections, but she was desperate. However wretched Robert's state, she had to know for herself that nothing worse had befallen him than Saxton's flogging.

She could see nothing through her left eye now and its swelling had drawn her right one into a squint, but she knew Sir Warin's answer in the harsh silence that followed her plea. She tore herself from his arms with a sob and ran for the door.

"Marguerite, wait." Sir Warin caught her arm. "If I do this, will you come with me?"

She had forgotten how much it hurt to cry through a swollen eye. Her father had stayed his hand from her face for nearly a year—since Saxton had come to claim her. "I cannot. If I do, Saxton will k-kill him. Saxton s-said— he would let Rob live—if I will be his wife." Oh, how she prayed her clawing of his cheek had not destroyed their bargain!

She tried to pull herself from Sir Warin's hold, but he stilled her with a kiss so swift and gentle, it was over before she could protest.

His lips brushed against her ear. "If this is the test you ask of me, then so be it. But only this once, Marguerite. You must not ask me again. And I do not promise to let you sacrifice yourself for Marcel. You will forget him. In time, you will forget him."

She did not know whether Sir Warin spoke with conviction or hope, but she would not argue with him now. All that mattered was that he take her to Robert.

"Give me a few hours to make arrangements," Sir Warin said. "I will send for you when I am ready."

Marguerite pulled the hood closer around her face, grateful for its concealing folds from the curious gaze of the guards who stood outside the dungeon door. Sir Warin spoke to the men in low tones, then she heard the chime of a money bag. A moment later, the door grated open on hinges that screeched with rust. One of the guards handed Sir Warin a lantern, while a second removed a torch from its wall bracket. Marguerite saw only darkness yawning ahead, so thick the torchlight illuminated only a pair of steps at a time as they began their descent. With her free hand, she hugged tight a cloth-wrapped bundle. Her other clung tight to Sir Warin's arm. Twice she slipped on stones grown slick with age and damp. Each time Sir Warin steadied her. She wheezed on the mildewed vapor that filled her lungs and tried to cough it out. Sir Warin pressed something to her nose. A piece of linen soaked in rosewater. She would have thanked him, but the oppressive darkness smothered her voice.

After her second slip on the steps, Marguerite kept her gaze on her feet and the limited pool of light that surrounded them. She did not raise her eyes again until they reached the bottom of the steps. The torchlight danced against a wall across from her, sending red fire down a pair of demonic serpents that slithered there. She almost cried out before she recognized the truth. Chains with manacles, mercifully empty—for now.

The guard motioned towards the darkness on their left, then without speaking turned and remounted the steps. Marguerite tried to brace herself for the moment when the retreating torchlight vanished, but she gave a violent start all the same when the door clanged shut above them. The lantern's candle cast a small, muted glow from behind its horn shades, illuminating nothing but the murky presence of the man beside her.

Sir Warin slid open one of the horn panes so that more light flowed into the cell. The small flame still fought weakly against the gloom, but she could see farther now, to the man who lay face down a half-dozen paces away. Sir Warin took a step towards him, but Marguerite whispered a plea. Sir Warin hesitated, then surrendered the lantern to her. It trembled in her hand, not only from the cold. She walked slowly to where Robert lay. He sprawled stripped to the waist, his head buried in his folded arms. The stripes on his back looked black in the dim glow, she guessed with blood that had dried. He must have heard them coming, her coughs against the mildew, but he made no movement. Did he sleep or lie unconscious?

She knelt beside him, setting down the lantern and the bundle she carried. She reached out a hand towards his shoulder, then hesitated lest she hurt him and brushed her fingers against his hair instead.

"Rob?"

His whole body jerked on a gasp. "Marguerite?"

He started to push himself up, but she caught his shoulders as gently as she could and pressed him back down. "Lie still. I have brought some ointment to ease your pain."

She felt no comfort when he obeyed her. It was not his nature to surrender so easily to a command . . . unless the whip marks burned too badly to defy her.

"What are you doing here?" Robert sounded slightly dazed, his voice strained. "How did you get in?"

"Hush. We will talk later."

"Marguerite—"

"Be still." Anger for the suffering Saxton had laid on him made her voice sharp.

She thought she heard Robert sigh, but could not be sure with his face turned away from her. He did not speak again. She unwrapped the bundle. She had filled a wineskin with fresh water from the well and used it to dab clean his stripes with a soft, woolen cloth, then gingerly rubbed the salve into the angry cuts. As careful as she tried to be, she knew her touch must sting, but though Robert winced a time or two, he made no sound.

Gradually she felt his tight muscles begin to relax. Only when his tension eased enough to convince her that he found the ointment soothing did she at last wipe clean her hands and begin to stop the jar. She was certain the ointment had worked when he spoke again.

"Marguerite, we must talk *now*."

She reached out a hand towards the lantern, but when he did not lift his head from his arms, she finished sealing the jar and placed it back in the bundle.

"How did you get in?" Robert asked. "You did not come alone?"

She hesitated. Sir Warin said he had only seen Robert in Poitou, long enough to judge him unworthy of her, not that they had ever spoken. There could be naught for Robert to suspect. Robert had never met the knight who escorted her. "Sir Warin brought me."

"Sir Warin?"

"Sir Warin Eyvind. He is a friend, you may safely trust him."

She braced herself for more questions, but they did not come. Even if she had lessened Robert's pain, he must be weary from the throbbing and loss of blood. She would have to find a way to come again, for he could not apply the salve himself when the numbing wore off. She glanced at the dark shadow that was Sir Warin. He had said he would only help her this once, but surely she could persuade him—

The stirring sound warned her. Robert was finally shifting to sit up. She whisked her attention back to the lantern and swung shut the horn pane. But before she could speak the excuse she had formed for casting them into an obscuring dimness, Robert's fingers laced so tightly around her wrist that it startled out a gasp instead. His hand slid over hers until it found the latch on the pane, then he slowly eased it open once more. As the light returned, she saw his gaze fastened on her face. He drew one sharp intake of breath. His eyes flashed in the candle's light, but his voice came soft—too soft.

"Who did this to you?"

She had spent the interval waiting for Sir Warin bathing her eye in cool water until the swelling had subsided a little, but she knew the marks remained stark. "N-no one. I fell."

He gave her wrist a little twist. "Do not lie to me, Mae. Did Saxton beat you? Or your father?"

She said quickly, "No one beat me. I angered my Lord Saxton and earned a smart slap, that is all. It is nothing—"

She broke off, dismayed by a ferocity she had never seen in Robert's eyes before. He swore, then jerked her suddenly into his arms.

"Ah, Mae," he groaned, his face buried in her hair, "is this what I have brought you to? Oh, would that we had never met."

She flung her arms around his neck. "No, no, no! You cannot mean that! Oh, Rob, I love you so much!"

His breathing sounded ragged, as though he were in pain, but she had felt him ease beneath the ointment. Had she embraced him too hard? She began to pull away, but his own arms tightened around her, dragging her close again. He held her thus until his breathing steadied, then slowly nudged her gently away. She tried not to flinch when he touched her bruise, but failed. He slid his fingers away from her eye, but kept a firm hold on her chin so that she could not look away. "Why did Saxton hit you?"

His hard gaze compelled an answer. "I-I scratched him. I wanted to tear his eyes out!"

"Why?"

"Because of what he did to you! He swore you would come to no harm, and he lied!"

Robert's mouth took on a wry twist. "If a flogging is to be the worst of my punishment, I shall get off easily indeed. 'Twas not the first time I've been flogged."

She had forgotten. On the manor, when he had tried to flee with his sister. But that story was ancient, a lifetime ago for them both. This cruelty was fresh, the after effects witnessed by her own eyes. Her fury at Saxton flared higher.

"That does not excuse my Lord Saxton. He promised me your safety."

"Why should Saxton promise you anything concerning me?"

She tried to turn away her face, but his fingers tightened on her chin. "Mae?"

She could not tell Robert the truth.

She did not need to. His lips grew taut. "Marguerite, you have not been so foolish as to attempt to bargain with the Earl of Saxton?"

She struggled to keep her expression still, as she had with Lady Helen. "What would I have to bargain?"

"Yourself, perhaps—for my life?"

Despite her efforts, she knew he read this truth, too.

"What of your oath to me?"

"Oath?" Could he feel her guilty flush warming her face beneath his touch?

"At the fair. The one you swore to me. Marguerite, I hold you to your pledge."

How dare he? When he had forced her to speak those wretched words against her heart and conscience. She grabbed his fingers and pulled them from her chin. "You cannot. I have given my assent to marry Saxton on Friday."

She wondered if the rebellion in her eyes reflected the flash in Robert's. "If you think that by sacrificing yourself you are performing me a service, you are wrong. Saxton will not let me live."

"He promised—"

"Like you promised me?" Robert's voice lashed sharp as the whip she had imagined stinging over his shoulders. He flung an arm at the darkness that engulfed them. "Is this what you desire for me, to live out my days confined to this filthy pit? I would sooner die!"

She could not see through the murky shadows to judge the size of the cell, but she could feel the cold and damp seeping through her clothes, smell the rankness mingling with the mildew, hear the scurrying of creatures she had struggled to shut her ears to while she and Robert had conversed. A shudder wove through her, as deep as any she had suffered from Saxton's embraces. Her hasty temper had ruined any chance she might have had of cajoling Saxton into releasing Robert from this appalling tomb, yet the alternative was more than she could bear.

"Marguerite—" Robert spoke softly again "—you will do me no service by marrying Saxton. You will only make my imprisonment more bitter." He found her hand in the dark. "You will keep your pledge to me?"

Her eye began to ache again as tears welled back up. "Oh, Rob, how can I? I have not the strength."

"Richard—"

"Lord Saxton has sent Richard away." Not that she would have gone with him, no matter how her cousin had begged her.

She hated the silence that stretched between her and Robert. He had leaned back into the shadows so that she could no longer see his eyes or expression.

"I see," he said after what felt like a deafening eternity. "Sir Warin."

She did not register that Robert had pitched his voice as a summons until she heard Sir Warin's footsteps drawing near.

"No!" She scrambled to her feet as Robert stood. "Don't send me away. Not yet." She could not leave him like this. She *would* not.

"I do not want your sacrifice, Marguerite. You speak to me of what *you* have not the strength to bear. Well, *I* cannot bear the vision of you with Saxton. Do not be so cruel as to leave me here in this pit with that horror to haunt me. I beg you—" Robert's voice cracked "—keep your oath to me."

That rent in his strength that had never so much as wavered before benumbed her with alarm and held her in silent confusion as Robert placed her hand in Sir Warin's.

"Keep her safe," Robert said.

"Rob, *no*." The words screamed inside her head, but fell as a whisper from her lips.

"Marguerite—" Robert's hand hovered lightly on the back of hers "—if you love me, you will do this for me."

Anything. She had said she would do anything for him. She would have given her life—but he was asking her to give his. This had not been the test she had been prepared to meet.

Robert's hand withdrew. Sir Warin picked up the lantern, then exchanged a silent gaze with Robert.

Everything inside of Marguerite shrieked to throw herself back into Robert's arms, but when Sir Warin tugged her gently away, her feet stumbled along at his side. She held her tears submerged beneath the choking ball in her throat until the dungeon door clanged shut behind them. Then blind of Sir Warin and the staring guards, she collapsed to the floor and sobbed until there was nothing left in her but the dry, gasping heaves of despair.

47

In the bundle that Marguerite left behind, Robert found a tunic he guessed she had meant for him. They had taken his old one when they'd flogged him. The dungeon cell was foul, but no colder than the winters he had spent on the manor. Still, he was grateful for the thin warmth offered by the garment she brought him. Whether it had been hours or days since she left him, he could not tell. A guard had brought him food twice, or so they'd called it. Robert rejected the rotting smell of it, aided again by Marguerite's kindness. There had been some hard bread in the bundle, along with the tunic, and some chunks of dry cheese, and a wineskin with water that tasted fresh. He hoarded the latter carefully, knowing that thirst would drive him to drink from the bowl of fetid liquid the guards had left before hunger drove him to the rancid food. He'd hidden the bundle and its contents in a corner of the cell where the torches the guards carried would be least likely to cast their light.

The darkness had felt stygian at first while he had lain on the meager pallet they had given him, absorbing the pulsing burn left by the lash, and hating and hating Kit Beckford. Saxton had given the command, but Robert had no doubt that Kit had suggested the flogging. Robert had found Marguerite's jar of ointment, too. He could reach the stripes across the small of his back to rub in more when the numbing wore off, but no higher. The throbbing had long since returned across the breadth of his shoulders. He set his teeth hard, as he had at the first crack of the whip, and sought to smother the smart beneath his anger. To succumb to the pain would be to let them win.

The tormenting memories of Marguerite were harder to subdue. Her visit had distracted him from his bitter thoughts of Kit, but Robert had found little comfort in his exchange with her. Never to see her again, never to hold her— Robert hugged his knees to his chest. Had Sir Warin made off with her? Had Friday come and gone? Was Marguerite safe—or had Sir Warin failed and was she even now Saxton's wife? Robert leaned his head against his knees, groaning at the awful possibility. He told himself he must trust that Sir Warin would deliver her from Saxton. But the visions of failure were difficult to keep at bay in the dark.

The clank of the door broke the wretched images apart, as it had the other times the guards had brought him food. The visions would return soon enough, but Robert breathed a prayer of thanks for the respite. He did not lift his head at first. The guards always hurled abuse at him when they brought him the slop, no doubt hoping to provoke some response that would give them leave to deal Robert a beating. Robert had shown his contempt of his gaolers by ignoring them, but now a black thought stole into his mind. The chance was slim to impossible that he could dart past the guards, no matter how fast he moved. Would they thrash him if he tried, or would Saxton condone a more final rebuke to a show of defiance? If Marguerite had not the will to sever herself from Robert, then surely either way, it would be worth the risk?

He looked up and felt the sting of the torchlight against his eyes. It blinded him, as it had the other times they had come, but the disorienting blaze would clear before they finished reviling him. While the guards railed, he would be able to see and judge their weapons, shut off his mind from the consequences of failure, launch from the pallet—

Even before his flame-bleared sight fully cleared, he recognized his mistake and understood why the streams of invective had not yet fallen. His mind vaulted into an unexpected tumble as he rose, for the man before him should have been far away in York, safe from Saxton's trap and dusting his hands of all association with the minstrel who had betrayed his trust along with the king.

Robert flicked a glance at the fair-haired squire who held the torch. By the time he looked back at the tall, broad-shouldered man the squire accompanied, Robert's gaze had steadied on the familiar hawkish face. He met

Gunthar's eyes squarely. Robert could not read their expression, but was certain condemnation must lie behind them. He lifted his chin and waited for Gunthar to speak.

Gunthar did not do so for a long moment. Robert's heart beat so hard it began to thud in his ears.

"Well, Rob?"

The two soft words floated through the drumming. Never before had Gunthar used the shortened form of his name. It set Robert's lip oddly trembling. A flurry of emotions he could neither identify nor understand collided in his breast and spurred a rough response. "Am I to hang, sir?"

Another pause, this one measured. "There is no sentence passed as yet."

If Gunthar meant his reply as a comfort, it rang hollow in Robert's ears. "I *will* hang. You know that. Kit will not let me live."

"Lord Christopher has no say now in your fate. And Saxton, thankfully, is dawdling."

Dawdling? There could be only one reason for that. Marguerite's bargain. Robert had to stop it. If Sir Warin failed—

"You must know by now what they found among my things," Robert said. "They have evidence of my treason. Go to the king. Tell him—tell him—" *I confess*. The king would have to act then, whether Saxton liked it or not. Robert would be hanged. Marguerite would be freed from whatever promises she had made to Saxton. Gunthar, by turning his back on Robert when Saxton appeared to hesitate, would prove his superior loyalty to the king. Robert had only to speak the words. *I did it. I am guilty. I betrayed the king.* "Tell him—"

"Tell him what, Robert?"

Robert struggled again, and failed. He could not say it. To die a confessed traitor would be to betray his father's memory. *What else was to be expected? Like father, like son*, they would say. Kit would see it trumpeted from one end of England to the other. Robert's silence would not stop that. But his love and faith in his father must remain unchallenged to the end, at least by his own word.

Still—

Robert flung himself to pace the narrow confines of the cell. "They cannot let me live," he repeated.

"That has yet to be determined," Gunthar said with a maddening calm. "Traitor they think you, aye, but with whom did you consort? You were a mere footsoldier, a minstrel. No one believes you plotted alone against the king. If you will reveal the details of the conspiracy and the names of your accomplices, other heads will adorn the gates of the city, while you may suffer no more than imprisonment."

That choked Robert almost as much as the visions of Marguerite and Saxton. To remain here, a perpetual prisoner, trapped in the damp and the dark and the stench and the cold, trapped, trapped—The dread of it stifled his lungs and clogged his throat.

"No." The word croaked past the horror that sought to snag it. "I'll not remain here, caged like some animal. I'd sooner they hanged me."

"Don't be a fool." Gunthar's voice gruffened. "It is always better to live than to die."

Robert whirled on Gunthar and gestured at the cell, as he had for Marguerite. "*This* is not living. How can you think I could bear this?"

He sensed hesitance in Gunthar before he replied. "Lord Christopher has ventured another suggestion. The decision, of course, is the king's, but if it will persuade you to cooperate, he offers you freedom—of a sort."

Robert stared. "Freedom? Kit—?"

"He argues that you were merely a doltish pawn, greedy, but too clod-dishly ignorant to grasp the weight of your actions. If you will surrender your accomplices, he will take you back to Beck Manor—discipline you— and see to it that you never leave there again."

"Go back—to the manor?" Had Gunthar lost his mind?

"Would it be so bad? I will agree that a villein's lot is hard, but life as a villein would not have brought you to this." It was Gunthar's turn to sweep a hand towards the narrow walls. "You spoke to me once of security—"

Robert had thought he could not feel more miserable, but he was wrong. How could Gunthar—*Gunthar*—throw that in his face? Anger and resent-ment swelled behind the hurt with an almost savage force.

"A secure slavery!" he flashed.

Gunthar's tall frame gave a small but discernable jerk. "'Tis not slavery, Robert." His voice went sharp. Defensive?

"Oh, is it not?" Robert allowed his lip to curl.

Gunthar's strong mouth twitched downward in the torchlight. "I do not say it is pleasant, or with a bad lord, always fair. But your father owned his land and could not be separated from it, nor could your lord separate your family. You could plant what crops you wanted. You could sell the excess for profit. It is not slavery."

"Nor is it freedom," Robert said, "or Kit could not drag me back because I failed to join a guild and labor in a city for a year and a day." Every humiliation, every grudge and abuse from Robert's former life washed back over him, then burst out of his heart. "For eighteen years I submitted to the authority of men who called themselves 'my betters' because the law said I must. I have paid the tithes and the tallage, a fourth of our harvest each year for the right to live in our house—the wood-penny to keep our hearth fire burning, our best hen every year, and other fees, too many to name. I left my brother's fields at the reeve's summons to labor on the baron's demesne three, four, five days a week at the height of the harvest. What matter if his villeins' crops spoil, so long as his own stores are gathered in?"

Gunthar began to speak again, but Robert pressed on, bitterness scalding in his veins like venom. "My father died at one baron's whim, another condemned my sister to a vicious marriage. That same baron's plotting forced my brother into a storm that drenched him to the bone while he was stricken with fever, then forbade him any care that might have saved his life." That grief, still so fresh. "Of what worth, after all, is the life of a villein? We are not men and women who breathe and want and hurt. We are beasts, possessions like cattle or mules to be worked for another's profit. Worked and extorted by men like *you*, so that you and your kind might live in luxury and ease."

Robert did not realize he had pointed a finger at Gunthar's breast until he heard Gunthar splutter a protest. But the old earl's face faded in the angry haze of memories before Robert's eyes. He saw now only the fur on Gunthar's cloak and the gold threads of his tunic glistening in the torchlight and the jeweled rings on his hands. The tall, shadowed form contorted into every bone-crushing baron of England.

Robert lowered his finger but said, "Be frank with me, my lord. Have you any notion of what real hunger is? I mean true hunger. To watch your winter store grow thinner and thinner because you had not time to harvest more." He clenched his fist, remembering the fear in those wretched days. "What if spring comes late? What if the food runs out? What if the lord whose crops you saved does not see fit to save one or two mewling brats from a villein's too-large 'litter' by sharing from his own rich larder?"

Will Locke's tiny sister in Robert's eleventh year. The memory blazed

Robert on. "To feel the chill of the winter air digging at you night after night after dreary, hopeless night. To have naught but a rag for a covering and no wood left for a fire because there is no grain left to spare for a wood-penny and the manor lord has declared the timber of the forest off-limits without one. The lord, who himself sits warm and fat and at his ease behind the shelter of his castle walls, wrapped in furs, gorging on food and drunk with wine. Multiply that misery a thousand, ten thousand times among men, women and children whose only crime it was to be born a villein."

Gunthar's face came back into focus. He stared at Robert, stark and rigid.

"Why, my lord?" Robert said. "Can you tell me? Were not all men, in the beginning, made free? Is not that what we are taught?"

"You speak treason." The words hissed from between Gunthar's teeth.

"I speak truth!" Robert shouted. "Deny it if you will, but truth remains truth. If I die, I will die for that truth rather than for some twisted lie of Saxton's."

"And would you, then," Gunthar demanded, "consider yourself my equal? Would you be earl or duke? Or prince, perhaps? Holding lands, fighting wars, ruling kingdoms?"

It was not the sarcasm in Gunthar's voice that stung so, but his stubborn blindness when Robert so ached for him to understand.

Robert spread his fingers, almost in a plea. "I would be your equal in freedom. I would claim the right, as do you, my lord, to direct my life without fear. I do not want your castles and furs and jewels. I want only what I can earn fairly—freely—for myself. I ask what should be every man's privilege, to live and work as I please, so long as I do so in peace." Gunthar answered with silence. Why could the earl not see? "Is it too much?"

Gunthar gazed at him from beneath plunging brows, his mouth drawn hard and forbidding. "What you ask is impossible."

"But did you not once offer me a knighthood? What did you intend, then, if not at least a step towards equality?"

Even as he said it, Robert shook his head. 'Twas a fool's question, and he knew it. Gunthar had not offered a knighthood to Robert the villein, but to Robert the minstrel. The other barons would look askance at Gunthar's action, but such advancement of a man of lower status was not completely unprecedented. A minstrel, at least, was a free man, a very different thing from offering the same to a villein.

Gunthar had treated Robert more fairly than any man ever had, even after learning of Robert's origins. Robert had almost dared to count him as a friend. But he knew he had pushed the old earl too far in this. Gunthar was a man of vast land holdings, a man who walked with kings. To claim freedom and equality for villeins would shake his world—would shake the kingdom itself to its very roots.

"Suppose you were free," Gunthar said, the edge in his voice confirming Robert's thoughts. "Would you lead an insurgency against the baronage, against the king? Would you alter the entire order of the English realm?"

Robert responded with a fresh burst of honest anger. "You ask if I would change the order? I answer 'yes!'—if I could so without leaving behind a tide of hatred and bloodshed. But the time is not right. The land is not ready. Even if I were influential enough to lead such a rebellion, I would not do it. It could only cost villein lives and their lot is hard enough. It would certainly be harder once the rebellion was crushed."

Frustration flickered across Gunthar's face. "Then what is it you want?"

"Just what I have said. Freedom for myself and what family I might have. Freedom to live in peace." Robert glanced at the squire who held the torch and saw how the youth had lowered his eyes. To mask his reaction to Robert's exchange with his master? Robert looked back at Gunthar, still frowning, still severe. Robert's anger seeped away, leaving an aching pulse in its place. How could he hurt like this for the loss of any man's favor?

He gestured again at the walls. "But it is useless to speak of freedom while I remain condemned to this pit. I do not know why you came here, my lord, but I will not accept Kit's offer. Tell the king of my treason—my true treason. It is the last thing I ask of you." He gazed bleakly into Gunthar's eyes, then dropped the veil back down over his own. "I am grateful for all you have done for me, but I shall not hope to see you again." *Or anyone else.*

Robert turned away and moved from the torchlight into the deeper shades of his prison. He closed his eyes. It was over. Everything that mattered was over now. Marguerite, now Gunthar— Robert would not retract his words if he could, and Gunthar would never forgive him for speaking them. Yet Robert strained his ears, listening for Gunthar's departing footsteps, for the final clang of the dungeon door.

But no footstep stirred. Robert stiffened. The sound of breathing still hummed behind him. He opened his eyes and saw shadows against the wall, cast there by the continuing torchlight. *Why did Gunthar stay? What more did he want?*

"Why did you not come to me?"

The words fell soft and gruff. Robert swung about, bewildered by the note he could not place in Gunthar's voice.

"When you knew yourself in trouble, why did you not come to me?"

Robert raked his mind for Gunthar's meaning. "When they found Kit's silver among my things? You were not here, my lord."

Gunthar made an impatient gesture. "Of course I was not here. But before that—you told me nothing."

The accusation took Robert by surprise. Had Gunthar never believed him, then? He felt himself bristling in the sting of disappointment. "I told you that Kit was a traitor. I told you what I saw and heard between him and the Frenchman in the woods. If my word was not enough—"

"You did not tell me of Marguerite."

The name hit Robert like a blow to the stomach. Why should he be startled that Gunthar knew? It must be all over the palace that Robert had been found in her chambers.

"Marguerite de Villon," Gunthar repeated. "Did you think your affair with her to be of so little import as to not be worth the telling? You rate yourself very high indeed if you dare aspire to her hand. The villein who would be lord to a lady."

"Let the king hang me, then," Robert snapped. "Dead men have no use for aspirations."

"Your insolence grows tiresome, sir."

"I did not ask you to come here. If you find my views and ambitions so objectionable, then by all means, go."

"And leave you to hang? I'll not give you that satisfaction, Robert Marcel. You will yet live to humble yourself before me."

Gunthar laughed then, not caustically, but in the familiar, rueful way that caught at Robert's heart.

"Fool." Gunthar joined him in the deeper shadows and reached out to grip his shoulder. "Do you think I'd abandon you now? You may be insolent and disrespectful and have an inordinate amount of pride, but I've stood by you too long to give you up merely because we disagree. We will leave the question of villeins for another day, but a man who would so vehemently argue so dangerous a view has no reason to lie to me concerning other things. I cannot condone your courtship of the Lady Marguerite, but I do not believe you guilty of Saxton's charge and I will not let you hang."

Robert blinked. He had surely misunderstood. Gunthar was only offering to—oh, saints! *I will not let you hang.* Did he mean—? "I won't remain here in this pit!" Panic balled in his stomach at the thought.

"No," Gunthar agreed, "you must not remain here."

"And I won't go back to Kit's manor!"

"No," Gunthar said again, "not even long enough for me to buy your freedom."

The words stunned Robert. "Is that what you meant to do?"

Gunthar did not answer. He did not need to. Robert knew Gunthar would not have said it if it had not been true. The revelation shamed Robert. He had not meant to assault the decency he knew lay at Gunthar's core, but when memories of Robert's past pressed upon him, his tongue ran too swift and hot. Gunthar had not deserved the lashing Robert had loosed on him. But Gunthar had spoken roughly, too, none of his words more painful than his cutting denouncement of Robert's love for Marguerite. The one breach neither of them could span.

But now Robert let his anger go. He supposed he and Gunthar had both been shaped by their births and the lives that fate had dealt them. Yet Gunthar had lingered in this hellish pit long enough to seek to heal what he could between them. Robert would not reject the gesture again. Nor would he permit Gunthar to allow the inexplicable bond they had come to share spur him into disaster. Gunthar called Robert arrogant, but Gunthar, for all his virtues, had a dangerous overconfidence in his own haughty judgment. And if what Robert suspected were true, he was about to throw himself into the lion's den for Robert's sake, if he had not already done so.

That matter of returning Robert to his former manor. If Gunthar attempted to support Kit's suggestion to spare Robert's life, Kit and Saxton might twist his words into a suspicious sympathy for a traitor.

"Sir, you have not tried to speak to the king on my behalf, have you?" Robert did not give Gunthar time to reply. "It would do no good. They found the French silver in my bag. You must not try to defend me." A confession became more urgent than before, for it would protect both Marguerite and Gunthar. "Tell the king what I said here today, that I have fermented rebellion among his servants, the villeins of his kingdom. Have him send examiners to me. I would gladly tell them what I think—"

Gunthar cut him off with a grunt. "I've no doubt you would, just as I have no doubt that Saxton is already considering which torture methods would be most effective in loosing your tongue. It is not your views on villeins that he will wish to hear, however. Do you recall those accomplices I said were the price of letting you escape the noose?"

Oh, blazes! How had Robert not seen it from the first? "He does not want me to name the Count of La Marche. He wants me to name you."

"Helen found Lord Christopher's half-written 'confession.' I could lay it before the king and expose Saxton for the jealous schemer that he is, but there is no benefit in his fall for you. As you say, Lord Christopher planted his evidence too well. He seems to think himself secure in your guilt, for I have not been able to shake him from his story."

"Kit would never confess to save me," Robert said. "But if you know a way to drive Saxton from court—if he fell from the king's grace, surely it would stop his marriage to Marguerite?"

"Perhaps."

Gunthar could not know how that single word gave Robert hope. Then the wedding had not yet taken place.

"Sir, you must show the king that devilish lie Kit was writing. For your sake and for hers—"

"Do not tell me how to conduct my affairs, Robert."

"But—"

"I am not inclined to heed the advice of a man who held so little faith in me that I had to discover the truth of the woman he loved by seeing my own ring on her finger."

So that was how Gunthar knew. Why had Robert not thought of that risk the day they had all sat together in Lady Helen's sitting chamber? Because he had been too distracted with his brother lying ill in a damp, miserable inn.

"My lord, you said it yourself. If you had known, you would not have let me marry her."

"Perhaps not. But neither would I have cast you aside."

It came to Robert suddenly, the elusive note in Gunthar's voice. Robert had hurt him with his lack of trust. Shame swirled again into his throat, even though he knew there had been no other way. He could not have given up Marguerite, even for Gunthar.

The dungeon door jangled open and a ball of light appeared at the top of the stairs. "My Lord Gunthar," a man's voice called, "I have allowed you all the time I dare. If Lord Saxton learns I let you in—"

"I am coming," Gunthar said.

"You should not have come here," Robert murmured. He did not doubt the squire's loyalty to his lord, but a listening guard was dangerous. "It will lend credence to Saxton's charge that there is something between us. It will do no good to show the king Kit's lies if you contradict them by suspicious actions. You must wash your hands of me. You must—"

"More unsolicited and unnecessary advice. When I need guidance from an inexperienced puppy, I will tell you."

"Puppy?"

Gunthar laughed at Robert's indignation. "You are a mere lad who, you will in honesty agree, has not always displayed the most level head." Again he gripped Robert's shoulder, this time pressing hard. "I will deal with this. Do not lose hope, Robert. I will not fail you."

Robert's hand came up to clasp Gunthar's. "My lord, I pray you, be careful. If any harm falls to you because you had the folly to befriend me—" fear and affection roughened his voice "—I could not live with myself."

He could no longer see Gunthar's face in the shadows, but his fingers tightened on Robert's shoulder. "Thank you for that," Gunthar murmured. He released Robert. "Come, Antony," he said to the squire.

Robert took two strides after them as Gunthar and the youth retreated to the steps, then he stopped and let them go. He knew nothing he could say would alter Gunthar's intentions. *You hold too much confidence in your own wisdom, and it is going to land your head on the block.*

Robert could not allow that to happen. His former plan slid back into his mind. Surely it would not be long before the guard brought him more slop to eat? Perhaps surprise would be his ally, perhaps he would succeed in disarming the guard and breaking past him, lunge unimpeded up the stairs, dodge around however many men stood watch outside. If not, if he fell into battle and a sword thrust stopped him—well, at least he would die fighting for his freedom. *And you and Marguerite will be safe.*

Gunthar paused at the foot of the steps and turned back round. "Before I go, give me your word you will do nothing foolish."

Robert stiffened. "Sir?"

"I know you, Robert. I have lost all I intend to lose in this life. If you ever held any—" Gunthar paused "—respect for me, you will sit on that pallet and be still and wait—and have faith in me."

Respect. Robert wondered what word Gunthar had intended to speak instead. If he only knew the depths of Robert's loyalty. None of their painful exchanges in this cell had altered a single mite of the devotion Robert realized he had come to feel for this man. How could he sit and do nothing while Gunthar put himself in such danger? And yet he sensed from the timbre of Gunthar's voice that to refuse again to trust him would somehow wound Gunthar to the soul.

Nevertheless, alarm for Gunthar's safety pounded a refusal in Robert's breast. He clamped his teeth hard until he managed to quell the fiery words on his tongue. Even then, he found himself unable to speak the vow Gunthar asked. The best he could do was give a slow, reluctant nod.

He knew Gunthar took it as a promise. A few moments later, Gunthar and his squire had mounted the steps, the door clanged shut, and Robert was once again doused in darkness. The horror of being trapped eternally in this pit did not ease, nor his worry for Gunthar recede. But Robert returned to his pallet with a strange quiet in his heart.

48

Marguerite caressed the blood-red garnet where it still nestled against her finger, then raised a challenging gaze to Sir Warin's face. "I shall wear it to my dying day."

His handsome mouth tightened in his trim-cut beard, but he gave a curt nod.

"And this." She touched the ribbon that flowed from her dark locks over her shoulder. "I shall wear this always in my hair." *Say you will not tolerate it. Tell me again that I will forget him. Anger me into saying I will not go with you. Please!*

"If it will bring you comfort, then so be it," Sir Warin said. "But we must not tarry longer. Come." He held out his hand. "Keep whatever vow you made to him and come."

They stood in her chamber where she had gone to gather a few things for their flight. Tomorrow was her wedding day to Saxton. Two days had passed since she had visited Robert in his prison. She had dithered until this morning, unable to reconcile herself to his plea for her to elope with Sir Warin, but the nightmares had at last worn down her resistance. That hellish cell with its reeking stench, chill dankness and the skittering sounds that still made her flesh crawl. No way to ever get Robert out. *Do not be so cruel as to leave me here in this pit.*

She picked up the bag that held a single change of clothes and a handful of other small items and gave it to Sir Warin. Saxton's squire no longer hovered around her door since Robert's capture, but Marguerite knew her comings and goings from the palace were still watched. She glanced down at the servant's gown she had once more donned. It would not do to be seen with her hair billowing about her shoulders in its normal way. She should braid it again, like Eva's, if she hoped to slip away unrecognized.

She divided her thick locks into three sections and began weaving them into a plait with the ribbon. *I am not stalling. I am not.*

"Marguerite, we must be on our way."

"I am almost ready." She heard the breathlessness in her voice as her fingers worked. She had promised to marry Sir Warin in Royston this very night, for the wedding vows would prove a protection from Saxton if he caught up to them. She hoped he would not try to make of her a widow once she was another man's wife. She hoped he would not catch them at all before they reached Northumberland. Once at Winbourne Castle, Odo and her grandfather's will would finally seal her forever safe of even Saxton's blackest machinations.

Sir Warin had laid their plans carefully. Marguerite would leave the palace first, keeping her face averted to appear a common servant on an errand for some lady. She would walk into the town to avoid being known by a stable hand, then wait for Sir Warin to join her at the blacksmith's shop. He had already arranged for a second mount to be awaiting her there. He had arranged for a priest to be awaiting them in Royston, as well. Sir Warin's aim was to pause only long enough to wed Marguerite, then if the clouds did not crowd out the moon, ride on through the night to place as much distance between them and a pursuit by Saxton as possible. Marguerite prayed for clear skies. Sir Warin had made little effort to restrain the warm gazes he cast at her, and she suspected he half-hoped, despite the risks, for a night at an inn. She did not think she was ready to grant him a husband's rights yet, even if doing so might make her a less desirable prize for Saxton to attempt to reclaim.

"Marguerite, love—"

Sir Warin attempted to take her hand, but she snatched it away. "I am not your love. At least . . . you shall never be mine. You know that?" She saw the hurt in his eyes but stood firm against an impulse to soften her words. *Say it. Say that I will forget Robert in time. Make me so angry that I forget instead that hateful prison and the vow he made me swear and fling you from my sight.*

"You wound me, deliberately I think, but it will not turn me from the adoration I hold you in. Marcel entrusted you to me. He was not the man I thought him." These words startled Marguerite and Sir Warin saw it. "He could have begged you for his life, implored you to marry Saxton to save him. Instead—well—" This time she did not pull her hand away from his. "I misjudged him in Poitou and I regret to see a man of honor suffer for Saxton's spite. But I cannot save Marcel, and neither can you."

Her fingers lay stiff in his for a heartbeat, then weakened in defeat.

"But perhaps I can."

Sir Warin turned, clearing her view to the door that his tall frame had been blocking.

"Simon?" Marguerite exclaimed. Simon Todd grinned at her from where he stood on the threshold. The bruises on his face had begun to fade, but the lingering marks reminded her of the betrayal that had cost her and Robert everything. She spoke coldly to him. "If you are looking for Eva, I have dismissed her."

His grin disappeared. "I know. It was kind of ye to find her an apprenticeship with Jonet the ribbon maker." He glanced at Sir Warin, then said, "May I speak with ye a moment, milady? Alone?"

Sir Warin looked disdainfully at the villein. "Who is this?"

Marguerite was about to reject Simon's request when something in the urgency of his gaze checked her. "A glover's apprentice. He has come to measure my hands for a fresh pair of riding gloves." It was a lie, but it could not hurt to allow Simon a word or two. *I am not stalling.*

Simon gave a brief bow. "Perhaps I can measure them now, if 'tis not inconvenient, milady?"

Marguerite noticed that his eyes were very bright, as if with some excitement.

"It is not at all convenient, young man," Sir Warin said. "Go away."

"No," Marguerite stayed him. She said to Sir Warin, "It will only take a moment. In case he tells my mother that I turned him away. Wait outside and we will be through in a trice."

Sir Warin grunted and crossed his arms. "I see no reason to leave you alone with a tradesman's apprentice."

To be truthful, Marguerite saw no reason, either. She had little enough to say to the cowardly runaway, and if Simon had come to apologize again for Eva, Sir Warin's presence would keep his muttered words blissfully short.

Simon looked annoyed with the knight, but he drew out a piece of parchment and a bit of chalk from a pouch he wore around his neck. He laid the parchment out on the table beside her bed. Again he slid a glance at her, this time one that seemed to hold a warning. She arranged herself to stand with her back to Sir Warin so that she could whisper, "Well, what is it?" while Simon traced her right hand.

"Milord Gunthar wants to see you. Now."

"Now?" She glanced over her shoulder at Sir Warin, who watched them impatiently. "I cannot—"

"Milady, it is for Rob."

Her heart lurched. "What—?"

Simon silenced her with a small shake of his head, then jerked it very slightly in Sir Warin's direction. He traced her other hand while her mind raced with questions, then slid parchment and chalk back in his pouch and bowed to her again.

"Thank ye, milady. The order should be ready in a week. If I can be of any further service to ye—"

"Thank you. And yes, you may indeed be of service." She resisted the impulse to spin about towards Sir Warin and turned herself slowly, as if the idea came to her as she turned. "This young man has been courting my maid. I am leaving her behind so that they may be married, but if I were to leave the palace on his arm, any observers would guess I was she in this dress."

Sir Warin studied Simon for a moment, then to Marguerite's relief, nodded. "Aye, it will be a good feint," he said. He pulled out a coin and dropped it in Simon's red, calloused hand. "Keep your tongue still about milady's affairs and there may be a reward sent to you at the end of her journey."

Simon bowed to the knight.

"Oh," Marguerite said when Sir Warin would have followed them from the chamber, "Sir Warin, I have changed my mind about my shoes. I would rather wear my red ones for our wedding. Will you fetch them from my wardrobe, please? I left my footwear in a bit of a jumble. Simon and I will start for the blacksmith's while you search and you may bring them when you come."

If Gunthar had naught but false hope for her, she would meet Sir Warin late with a fabricated excuse for her delay. But if Gunthar had found a way to save Robert—well, she still wore Robert's ring and ribbon. Sir Warin knew where her heart lay.

Gunthar weighed the slight woman in front of him. They stood in Helen's sitting chamber, but he had told his wife nothing of his plan and sent her to spend the afternoon with the queen. He trusted no one on earth more than he trusted Helen, but he loved her even more. If something went amiss, if the escape of an accused traitor to the crown, or even an attempted escape, were ever traced back to Gunthar—No. He would never allow her and their grandson to suffer the consequences of that with him. This scheme must leave no tracks. No one must know but himself and these two young people before him.

He caught Marguerite's glance about the empty room, her surprise when she did not see his wife. An unsightly bruise still smeared around her eye, but the swelling had faded. Gunthar had been as disgusted as Helen had been horrified when Marguerite appeared at dinner with her eye nearly swollen shut two days ago. The king had teased Saxton for the scratches on his cheek, dropping loud and lurid hints as to their source that had set the entire court twittering and joining their monarch's suggestive glances from Saxton to his betrothed.

Coward. Gunthar had said it to Saxton's face at the end of the meal while the king and the court were withdrawing. That was the only word that Gunthar could summon for a man who beat a woman. Saxton had hissed at Gunthar's insult and fisted a hand where his sword would be when they were not in the presence of the king. But something had checked Saxton from challenging Gunthar. Perhaps the unfinished document that bore Saxton's seal that Gunthar had locked up in his office?

"My lord," Marguerite said when Gunthar continued to stand silently watching her, "Simon said you had something to say to me about—about Rob?"

She spoke Robert's name somewhat shyly, reminding Gunthar that this was the first time she had been in his presence since she had learned that he knew of her and Robert. The last time he had been in a less than charitable mood with her, and from her white cheeks that day, she had known it.

"You were a pair of fools to fall in love," he said abruptly. "But I was wrong to blame you as I did. Saxton is the villain in this, not you. I believe I can stop him from marrying you, if you wish it?"

She shuddered. "How can you ask me that?" Her hand moved reflexively to touch the bruise near her eye.

Gunthar felt his revulsion of Saxton stirring again in his belly. "I have certain evidence that I believe I can spin to Saxton's detriment, I hope even to his dismissal from court. I think your parents will not wish to wed you to a man who stands in the king's disgrace." He saw the leap of hope in her eyes and regrettably snuffed it. "Do not let your spirits soar too high, for the nature of the evidence I possess will in no way benefit Robert. Rack my brain as I can, I can find no way to acquit him of the treason charge."

"But he is innocent!"

"As I have no doubt. But my faith alone will not convince the king."

"My lord, Robert told me he would rather die than remain in that prison. He begged me to—to—"

"To do something rash, no doubt, that would provoke Saxton and the king to hang him," Gunthar finished for her. He was all too aware that Robert had not actually promised to remain meekly in the dungeon and wait for Gunthar to act. All the more reason for Gunthar to set his plan swiftly in motion. "He is in a black mood, and I cannot blame him. He is altogether too hasty, so we must not wait longer. Will you help me break him out?"

Marguerite gasped, then swept across the floor to stand directly in front of Gunthar. "Anything," she said. "I will do anything for him."

Gunthar wondered if she had scratched Saxton with this same fierce sparkle in her eyes. She looked so soft and sweet and small except for her radiant gaze. Gunthar guessed it was that which had drawn Robert to her, this fiery pluck that her flowerlike features belied.

"The green tunics with Saxton's badge on the shoulders that Saxton dresses his guards in," Gunthar said. "We need two of them. One for the young man here." He nodded at the glover's apprentice. "And one for Robert to wear."

To Gunthar's surprise, Marguerite glared at the apprentice. "We cannot trust him, my lord. He gave away Rob's whereabouts to Saxton's guards. If it weren't for *him*—"

"Nay, my lady, he was not the one who told," Gunthar said. "I overheard what they said to you that day. This young man, I believe, bore a sore beating rather than speak whatever he knew. It was your maid who told."

"It's true," the apprentice—Simon, was it?—said, though he looked miserable remembering that day. "I knew Rob was with ye, milady, Eva told me he was in yer chamber, but I'd have let them beat me to death before I'd have told 'em. After all Rob did for me in bringin' me to London, findin' me a position and payin' to begin my apprenticeship—for he did, milady, he paid my master to take me on, just so I could win my freedom and marry Eva when I do. I'd never have betrayed him, and neither would Eva—"

"Except that she did," Marguerite cut him off.

Simon returned her angry gaze rather helplessly. "They threatened to kill me."

Gunthar watched Marguerite's hands curl so tightly into balls that her hands shook slightly. "I know," she said, more softly after a moment, "and I should forgive her for that, but when I think of Rob in that pit, I cannot."

"Then let us get him out," Gunthar said simply. "I trust this young man, so you must do so, as well."

She returned her gaze to Gunthar, doubt struggling with hope in her face. "My lord—can we truly do so? Set Rob free?"

"Can you get us the tunics? Saxton must keep some in his chambers. I cannot search there, but as his betrothed—"

Marguerite nodded, anticipating him. "I can make an excuse to visit his chambers, but how to persuade him to give me the tunics . . ."

Gunthar thought she might touch her bruise again, perhaps in fear of confronting Saxton, but she only looked thoughtfully puzzled as she trailed off.

"I will keep Saxton away from his chambers and occupied," Gunthar said. He might not approve of a marriage, but he felt a trust to keep her safe for Robert, as well as for his wife.

Marguerite brightened. "Then it will be easy. I will say I wish to embroider one of his shirts as a wedding gift and ask his servants to let me in to choose one. I will look for the tunics while I do so . . . Oh, yes, I am certain I can find them. Then what will you do?"

"Then this young man—" he motioned to Simon "—will pretend to be one of Saxton's guards and relieve the watchman outside the dungeon door. He will let Robert out. Robert will don the second tunic so as not to be known as they leave the palace together. I will meet them at a certain location in London that I have told Simon of. From there—" Gunthar hesitated. The rest would strike away the joyful glow of anticipation that had flowed into her eyes. "I have vast resources, my lady. I have places I can hide him from all searches of the king. He will be safe—but he will still be wanted. You cannot go with him."

Marguerite gasped, and now her eyes flashed defiance. "I can. I will!"

"My lady, a simple minstrel I can conceal. But a great heiress who has sat at the royal table for nearly a year? Even I have not the power to change men's memories of your face. You would be too great a danger to Robert. I cannot allow it. And if you truly love him, you will not ask it again."

He saw the way she flinched, as if he had laid a blow upon her as mighty as Saxton's fist. Gunthar did not intend to hide Robert forever. He still hoped to somehow prove the minstrel's innocence. Perhaps Saxton would break in time, or Beckford, and confess the truth of their deeds. But Gunthar could make Marguerite no promises, for that might take years, or never come to fulfillment at all. Better to sever it now and let her find love elsewhere in time. Better for Robert, too. A marriage between them had never truly been possible.

Yet for the first time since he had uncovered the truth of their courtship, Gunthar found himself regretting that it was so. He knew his part in their separation would forever remain a rift between him and Robert. If Beckford and Saxton had not forced Robert into this cruel situation, perhaps—just perhaps, Gunthar might have convinced himself to bend rather than lose the minstrel's friendship.

Marguerite wrapped her arms around herself as though trying to contain the pain that crimped her face. Gunthar had never had a daughter and had left the comforting of his daughter-in-law to Helen when their younger son had died. He knew nothing to say or do to ease Marguerite's heart.

"Shall—shall I go to Saxton's chambers now?" The words sounded wrenched from her.

"In an hour," Gunthar said. "I have asked an audience with the king then, and requested that Saxton be present."

When Gunthar would show the king the document Beckford had been writing. It would not help Saxton's cause that one of his own guards appeared to have helped a prisoner escape while Saxton stood arguing his innocence before the king. Whether for scheming against his rival or for freeing an accused felon, Saxton should be gone from court before nightfall, if he were not clapped in the dungeon in Robert's place.

49

Once again Robert could not tell the passage of time in the hellish darkness of his prison. Sitting, waiting—trusting—none of these came easily to him. The deeper the darkness pressed in on him, the murkier his mind seemed to grow. He hugged his knees to his chest, gritting his teeth against the return of the pain in the stripes on his back. He had allowed Marguerite's ointment to wear off, for the throbbing welts were the only thing that kept him grounded in reality when he felt his will slipping into the nightmare of this cell.

Have faith. Have faith. Gunthar is no fool. Except where Robert was concerned. Why would an earl risk himself for a minstrel? *For a villein?* Yet that was exactly what Robert had let Gunthar go off to do. *And if he loses his head for it?* Robert did not think he could bear the grief and shame of knowing he had been the cause. After he had hurled so many hurtful, bitter words at the aging nobleman—*But there were warm times between us, too. Times when I forgot the cruel world he represented, when he treated me with fairness, when we bantered and jested together almost as friends.*

Robert rubbed his eyes, though he could see little enough in the gloom. *If by some miracle we both come through this, I swear*—He caught himself just in time. If a rescue by Gunthar gave Robert even the slenderest chance to find Marguerite, he would be away with her in an instant. *But I will find some way to show you my gratitude, someday, somehow.* Robert vowed it with every particle of his existence.

An existence that had begun to feel increasingly ephemeral in the fetid blackness, until the muted click of the door made his body jerk so savagely it reminded him of his solidity. Almost instantly, he knew something was wrong. No torchlight pierced the darkness. And the door had never opened with anything but a ringing *clank* before. He knew it stood wide because light flowed in faintly from the guardroom beyond. He thought he saw a shadow, but it vanished too quickly in the gloom at the bottom of the stairs.

"Who's there?" He rose slowly to his feet. Silence, but he knew he was not alone from the way the hair prickled on the back of his neck. "What do you want?" When no one answered, he shouted, "Guards!"

"They won't come." The whispered words slithered so eerily on the air that the hair soared on Robert's arms, as well.

"Who are you?" Robert asked again.

"A restless spirit," the whisper rippled. "A spirit come seeking revenge."

Robert sensed rather than saw the sudden move. He pivoted sideways and felt a rush of air pass by him.

"Revenge? For what?" He backed against the wall as he said it to prevent an attack from his rear.

"For my life, what else?"

Absurd as he knew it, Robert's mind flew back through his years on the manor and through the span since he had left. Was there someone he could have saved whom he had not? Will's sister? Robert's brother? Oh, please, not his father! He did not believe in spirits, but what else should make his flesh crawl like this?

"Ye sent me to the devil. Now it's ye're turn to stare him in the face."

A quickened footstep warned Robert this time. He dodged again, but recognized the sound that hissed past his ear. It had whirred all around him on that bloody day in Poitou, when someone had tried to murder Gunthar and cover it up by mowing down his soldiers. Spirits did not wield steel blades.

The uncanny fear slid away. He had merely been alone too long in the dark. If he could keep the voice talking, discern its position—

"You have not told me my crime," Robert said.

"Ye murdered me, Robert Marcel. The devil takes especial joy in murderers. Ye'll see his flames soon enough."

Another footfall, another dodge, another hiss of steel. Robert realized his moves had bared his back. Where had his assailant gone? Robert started to turn—or would that be a mistake? "I've murdered no one. Go back to hell and burn alone."

A snarl. A familiar one? Something niggled in the back of Robert's mind as he rotated towards the sound.

"Ye left me to bleed out my life in Poitou, yer knife in my back. If that ain't murder—"

"I did not kill those men—" Robert began, then stopped. He had not killed the two guards or Walter Hanley's accomplice, but he had flung his dagger into one man's back. *"Hanley?"*

This time a chortle, the same short, vile sound the brute had cracked each time the law had allowed him to drag Robert's sister out of Robert's protective arms. But it was impossible!

"You're dead. I saw you dead!" Robert pressed a hand to his brow, wondering if his fever had returned.

"Ye cut me down like a dog." The whisper rasped up a notch, nearing the vicious tones Robert remembered.

"You would have killed Gunthar."

"Ye cost me a fine future as well as my life."

"You—" Robert broke off. His brow was as cold as the cell in which he stood. He had no fever . . . and he was not arguing with a ghost. "You did not die."

Hanley laughed again. "Did I not?"

"My aim was bad," Robert snapped. "I should have struck more closely."

That turned the laugh to a growl. Robert's eyes had finally adjusted to the muted light filtering in from the guardroom. When Hanley lunged this time, Robert saw a shadow. He did not try to evade the assault again, but flung himself full forward and slammed the "spirit" to the floor. Robert groped for the dagger he could not see, reached a little too high, and felt the blade slice into his hand. He bit off a gasp of surprise and pain, but he knew where the weapon was now. He slid his hand down to grip Hanley's wrist. For a few moments his grasp held as they grappled, then spikes of fire shot through Robert's palm, scorching into his wrist and arm.

Robert's hold faltered. In the distraction of the pain, Hanley rolled his body with sudden force and flung Robert away so hard that Robert landed on his back. A wave of agony swept through his body, this one almost blinding, as the unhealed stripes from his flogging exploded in their collision with the floor.

Hanley was atop him before the white sheen that had burst before Robert's eyes began to fade. The chill edge of the blade bit against his throat as the darkness swirled back in around them.

"Ye should have struck more closely." The voice, no longer masked, dripped with rancor. Robert struggled to reassert his focus through the throbbing across his shoulders. "Ye're a fool, Marcel, ye always were. Thought yerself too good to labor in the fields. Thought yerself too good to marry yer sister to me. She could have been a bailiff's wife, but ye robbed me o' that when ye saved Gunthar. Well, think o' this when I send ye to the flames. Who'll have your da's land now that ye an' yer brother are gone? Yer brother's brat of a son? Nay, Beckford said he'd give me the fields to tend for yer nephew until the boy has the misfortune to tumble into the well. All I have to do is slit yer throat."

Robert pushed the pain to the rear of his mind with a massive exertion of will. Everything had changed in an instant. The dungeon door stood open and apparently unguarded. If he could only reach it—

Hanley had always delighted in goading a helpless victim. He had Robert at his mercy. It should not take much to prod him to gloat.

"Why did Kit send you?" Robert asked. "Saxton will hang me soon enough."

The blade's edge pressed a little deeper but did not pierce Robert's skin. "Saxton says it's enough to keep ye in prison, but as long as ye live there's a chance ye'll convince someone besides Gunthar that Beckford was the true traitor to the king. Without ye, Gunthar has not even the flimsy suggestion of what ye claim ye 'witnessed.' Beckford hoped ye'd come back to the manor where he could kill ye stealthily once the world forgot about ye. But Gunthar told the king ye'd refused. An' so—"

"Kit planted the silver in my bag?" Robert interrupted, trying to deflect Hanley's attention away from the dagger's purpose for another few moments. Robert inched his good hand along the floor, groping for . . . he did not know what. Something, anything to defend himself with.

"Nay, he sent me to do that while ye were buryin' yer brother."

"You switched my money box." All Robert's hand could find were tufts of stinking hay that some gaoler had spread who knew how long ago to prevent slipping on the damp-slicked stones when guards came to view their prisoners.

"It made for a quicker swap," Hanley said. "It panicked Beckford when he saw his chambers ransacked and some letter he'd been writin' in the fire. He said it was ye an' that ye'd likely sent word to Gunthar an' that he must spring his trap before Gunthar returned an' spoiled it all."

Robert crawled his fingers further through the straw. "Did Beckford tell you how he won the silver?"

"Ye think he shares his secrets with me?" Robert could practically hear Hanley's sneer. "All he said to me was, 'There's a bailiff's post for ye if ye kill Gunthar for me.' Well, that's treason enough, ain't it? Gunthar's counselor to the king. If Beckford an' Saxton wanted Gunthar in the grave, I knew better than to ask why."

"Greater safety in ignorance," Robert agreed. His fingers bumped up against something. "But you spoke Saxton's name. You knew the order came from him?" He tilted the object and felt something cold and thick and wet flow over his hand. The slop they brought him to eat.

"Saxton's been pullin' all the strings," Hanley said, "except this one. Beckford says Saxton will be enraged, but he can't bring ye back from the dead an' he can't expose Beckford without exposin' himself, so there's nothin' Saxton'll be able to do. Beckford ain't afraid of him anymore. Or he won't be once I do what he sent me to do."

Hanley did not need to shove his hand into Robert's hair and give a jerk to further bare Robert's throat to the knife, nor did he need to taunt Robert before he struck by sliding the blade in a caressive threat along the pulsing vein of Robert's neck. But the vicious nature that Robert remembered prodded Hanley to do both, and in that delay Robert grabbed up the bowl and smashed it into Hanley's head.

Or where he hoped Hanley's head might be in the dark. Robert knew as soon as the bowl struck that he had only managed a glancing blow to Hanley's skull, but it was enough to shift Hanley's balance. Hanley howled. Robert threw the bowl aside and swung his fist. He connected with something, chin or cheekbone. Whichever it was, the punch toppled Hanley off of him. Robert scrabbled to his knees as Hanley's grunt gnarled into a growling curse, then bit off as something chimed like a bell in the air.

The dagger. Robert must have knocked it flying. It would not have rung so in the straw. It must have hit one of the walls. Robert lunged towards where he thought the sound had come from, praying as he had never prayed before. Hanley followed him, close as the shadow he had first appeared to be. Robert reached the wall first, clawed in the straw, found the hilt, closed his fist around it and whirled.

The blade sank into flesh as Hanley flung himself on Robert. Hanley grunted, his arms locking around Robert in a sudden, convulsive spasm. Then the spasm relaxed and Hanley fell away.

Robert rose, the dagger still in his grip. He stood taut for several minutes, listening, wary, but no sound stirred. Gradually the sting in his palm and the ache in his back began to revive in his consciousness. He tore a strip from his tunic and bound up his cut hand as well as he could. Then he moved to the base of the steps. How had Hanley gotten in? Would Robert find dead men in the guardroom, or had Beckford bribed the guards to look the other way?

Gunthar had told Robert to sit and wait and trust, but surely he could not expect Robert to do the first two now? He mounted the steps as quietly as he could and peered cautiously around the doorjamb. He blinked against the torchlight until his vision adjusted. The guardroom stood empty, save for a pair of stools and a table with some scattered dice. *It is not a question of trust*, Robert insisted to himself. No man with a grain of sanity could fail to take advantage of an apparent unobstructed route to escape.

He stepped into the guardroom, then stiffened. A booted leg sprawled out from beneath the table that blocked his view of the rest of the body. He moved around the table for a better look. A man slumped face down, dressed in a tunic the same green shade that Saxton's guardsmen always wore.

Keep walking. This will be your only chance. If the man is dead, you cannot help him. If he is unconscious and wakes to see you, he will raise the alarm. But if Hanley had left the man wounded, Robert could not abandon him to bleed to death, even if he served Saxton. Robert knelt and rolled the man over— and gasped.

Simon Todd—in one of Saxton's uniforms? Alarm supplanted Robert's shock as he searched the young man for fatal bloodstains, then sighed with relief when he found none. Simon's chest rose and fell in reassuring breaths. Robert slipped his hand carefully to the back of Simon's head and found a knot beneath his hair. Robert rocked back on his heels. What was Simon doing here? Who could have sent him, and dressed like this? Robert could think of only one explanation.

Marguerite. Robert had used Simon to carry messages between them early in their courtship, she knew Robert trusted Simon. She must have enlisted the young man's aid in some mad scheme to break Robert out of the dungeon, but Hanley had come upon Simon first and struck him unconscious. But Marguerite would not know that. Was she waiting even now for Simon to bring Robert to her, to smuggle him out of the palace? Oh, saints, did she mean to come with him?

The temptation tore through Robert a thousand times more painful than the ache from his flogging. But it was one thing to run off with her once Gunthar cleared his name, as he presumed Gunthar was seeking to do. It was another to do so with Kit's black accusation still hanging over Robert's head. He glanced back at the door to the dungeon, but no matter how he longed to prove to Gunthar his faith, he could not make his feet move an inch back towards that loathsome cell. Gunthar, who risked his own freedom, perhaps his own life seeking to defend Robert. *Someday I will show you my gratitude.* If Robert fled, he knew his guilt would be sealed in the eyes of the king. But he could not return to the cell, and fleeing was the best way to ensure Gunthar's safety. There would be no hope of him defending Robert after this, and Gunthar would know it.

But Robert could not take Marguerite with him. Even if they succeeded in fleeing the palace together, she would be an outlaw's wife, condemned to a life on the run, always looking over their shoulders, never a moment of peace, a surety of safety. And if they failed, if Saxton caught them, caught *her*—

No. Robert stood. He would not endanger her so.

He strode determinedly across the guardroom, then stopped again at the door. How was he to escape the palace without guidance? He knew only one exit, the one he always used to conduct business for Gunthar in the city, and he had passed through it too many times not to be recognized by the guards there. Gunthar must know other ways, but Robert could not risk Gunthar being seen with him.

Escape was well-nigh impossible, then. Robert could ramble around the palace looking for a way out, only to most likely be cut down or recaptured and thrown back into that pit. Or— His gaze narrowed on the torch burning in a bracket on the wall. It was not Marguerite who had brought him to this cruel pass, or Gunthar, or even Saxton. Only one face danced in the flame. Then so be it. If events took the turn Robert supposed they inevitably must, he would take his old foe with him.

50

The panic that followed the shock in Kit's face when Robert burst in on him was the sweetest sight Robert had ever seen. Kit sat in his chamber, scribbling out some correspondence at the desk where he had written those devilish lies against Gunthar. The pen dropped from his hand with a tiny bounce. He glanced at Robert's bloodied dagger and stumbled up so fast, his chair pitched over.

"Your henchman failed in his appointed task," Robert snapped.

"Hanley is dead?" Kit's face went white.

Robert kicked the door shut behind him. "He'll never touch my sister again. And *you—*"

Kit flung out a hand. "Stay away from me. My squire will be back from his errand any moment."

"Good," Robert said. "Then let's not dally." Aye, sweet, to watch the way Kit retreated when Robert took a step towards him. "You've played the game a little too well, Kit. Let's see, just what options have you left me? I can go back to that hellhole." Robert shook his head, his gaze steady on Kit's. "The king can hang me as a traitor. Or he can hang me as a murderer." Robert shrugged. "Or both. One will bring me greater satisfaction than the other, though. Can you guess which?"

Kit checked for the merest instant, then resumed his retreat a little to his left. But Robert had seen it, too, Kit's sword leaning in the corner.

"You think you can reach that before I plunge this through your heart?" Robert said, raising the dagger.

Kit stopped. He passed his tongue between his pallid lips, but he had steadied his panic now. "I offered you another alternative, Rob. Come back to the manor."

"So you can hang me quietly, like your father hanged mine? Hanley told me why you want me back."

"Hanley is a fool. It was pathetically easy to manipulate him with the most absurd lies. Why, he actually believed me when I said I would make him bailiff of Gunthar's manor. Nothing I told him was true."

"It was true enough that you sent him to kill me. He had this at my throat."

Kit's gaze flicked to the dagger again. "You had grown too close to Gunthar. I let my fears overcome my judgment. But it is not too late. Come back, Rob."

"As your slave?"

"As my servant. I could use a man of your talents."

Robert began to circle, forcing Kit to follow and move away from the sword. "I asked to serve you once. Have you forgotten? What was it you said seven years ago when I begged you to let me accompany you to the king's wars?"

Kit's eye kindled now, for that had been the day Robert had hit him and fled from the manor. The insult still rankled. Good. Even so, Kit held his temper and his tongue.

Robert answered for him. "'Like father, like son,' you said. Well, you have proven the truth of that proverb, haven't you? Did you meet the Count of La Marche during that campaign? Did the count merely recognize a treacherous heart when he saw one, or did he seek you out because of he knew of your father's black deed?"

"It was your father, Rob—"

"Nay, that was a lie!" Robert shouted. "You know it was a lie!" He leapt at Kit, jabbing at the air just to see Kit flinch. Kit stumbled back against the wall. "Say it. Tell the truth of what your father did. He planted those coins on my father, just as you planted yours on me."

"I didn't—He didn't—"

"The truth, Kit, or so help me—"

Kit thrust out both his hands as Robert dropped into a crouch to spring again. "Wait. Rob, wait. I do not know the truth, I swear it. My father never told me. I know only that he and your father were friends, and then one day they weren't. He took guards to your cottage, he found the silver, he hanged your father—and he was never the same afterwards. His temper grew short, his hand grew swift and heavy in a way it had never been before, and never heavier than when someone spoke your father's name. That is all I know. I swear it on my mother's grave."

Robert stared blazingly at Kit. Truth, or another lie? He heard a sound behind him. The latch of the door being turned. He lunged, taking pleasure in Kit's gasp as Robert's hand closed on the front of his tunic. He swung Kit over to the door and nudged the tip of the dagger into his back.

Kit took the hint and barred his squire from entering with his arm across the doorway.

"My lord," a young voice said, sounding startled, "is something wrong?"

Kit hesitated. Robert knew himself secure from the squire's sight, half-blocked by Kit's body, half-blocked by the door.

"Tell him to call Saxton," Robert whispered. "Get him here alone." As well kill two birds with one stone. Lest Marguerite's resolve should fail her.

"I need to speak with the Earl of Saxton," Kit said. "Pray ask him to attend me here."

"My Lord Saxton is with Lord Gunthar and the king," the squire said.

The words nearly sent a shudder through Robert. Saxton was undoubtedly countering Gunthar's accusations against him to the king, arguing as eloquently as he could for Gunthar's downfall. If Gunthar, in the course of their verbal duel, spoke Robert's name with the slightest hint of sympathy, Saxton would pounce on him with all the mercy of the bloody-toothed bear he liked to sport on his tunics. Robert could only pray he was not already too late to stop it. He gave Kit a meaningful punch with the dagger.

"It is urgent," Kit said to the squire. "Tell my Lord Saxton—tell him it concerns Robert Marcel." Another warning jab. "And tell him to come alone."

"I will try, my lord." The squire sounded doubtful, but Robert heard his footsteps fade away from the door.

Robert reached around Kit to push the door shut, then shoved Kit so that he fell against the desk.

"So," Robert said, "how shall we pass the time while we wait?"

Kit righted himself to glare at Robert from beneath the waves of brown hair that had tumbled into his eyes. Robert imagined he must find it galling to be so manhandled by his own villein.

"I do not think we have discussed my brother," Robert said, "and how you dragged him through a rainstorm when he could not even stand for a fever, then housed him in a filthy, leaking hovel of an inn and let him die. Or shall we reminisce about my sister and that abomination of a marriage you forced her into?"

Kit's chest rose and fell in angry breaths. "Your sister was a very comely villein whom Hanley requested as payment for certain services he'd rendered me. I owed him a debt—and it is a lord's prerogative to dispose of his property however he sees fit."

Kit's face hazed red. Robert would show Kit how his "property" could bite. Robert flew at him again. Kit's hand moved in a blur, then suddenly Robert could see nothing but a stinging, burning blackness. He scrubbed wildly at his eyes, felt something strike his hand, and the dagger jerked free. A blow landed in his stomach, doubling him over. He swung a fist, but found only empty air. By the time he caught his breath and had teared away enough of the sting to gaze blearily across the room, Kit had gained the sword.

Robert glanced at the black stains on his fingers and then at the object Kit had dropped at Robert's feet. The inkpot from the desk. Robert wiped away as much ink as he could from his eyes and face with his bandaged hand. He did not dare take his wobbly gaze from Kit long enough to see where the dagger had spun.

The power was Kit's, now. Robert tautened his body, ready to spring away from a thrust, but Kit leaned on the sword, the point against the floor. Robert felt himself being weighed by those dark grey eyes.

"If I were to ask you one more time," Kit said, "to come back to the manor—if I offered to split the remaining silver with you, to let you buy your freedom and serve me as a freeman—if all I ask in return is that you bear witness against the Earl of Gunthar—what would say?"

"I would tell you to go to hell."

"Because you think Gunthar will raise you higher than I can?"

"Because it would be a lie."

Kit snorted his disgust. "My father was right. He said that Marcels were too honest, that they did not know where their interest lay. Scrupulous upstarts, he called you, studying with priests to learn to read, coveting freedom—Did you know your father tried to buy his freedom once? What foolery! My father put a stop to that. It was before you and I were born, but my father said that yours did not learn his lesson. He told me when he warned me against you before he died."

Robert's heart warmed through these words. His father, an honest man. Honest men did not commit treason.

"What else did your father tell you?" Robert said. "How to plant French silver on innocent men?"

Kit smirked. "You gave me that idea, Rob, fourteen years ago when you ran up to the castle to accuse my father and he slapped you before your mother dragged you away. I remember how I lay awake for nights, fearful that your words might be true, until I realized that it did not matter. Whatever my father might have done, yours should have obeyed him, like a faithful hound obeys his master's command."

Robert swore at him. "We are not hounds, though your father was a cowardly worm to conceal his guilt behind a man who fought and bled for him."

Kit's face turned wrathful. "Arthur Marcel was a rabid dog who needed to be put down. Madness ran in your family. It was my own grandfather who named yours. Marcel, he called him, son of Mars, and so you have all been with your mad tempers and heretical views. For three generations you have been the bane of my family. The idea that your people and ours could ever be equals—! Gilbert was the only one of you with sense enough to live quietly. Lottie I let Hanley tame. But you—"

"I refused to submit," Robert said. "I refused to be your lackey."

"Fool," Kit replied. "Did I care what your ideas were? But you refused to keep a still tongue in your head, you continued your subversion of others."

Robert remembered all the reproachful, cutting backs turned on him by his neighbors. "They did not listen to me. They feared you too greatly. I was no threat to you."

"Ah, but you were young. In another generation you would have appeared to have authority. You had to be stopped."

"I recall the floggings well, but they have not changed my thoughts."

"Nor tamed your arrogance. I will enjoy putting an end to your insolence once and for all. And when I am done with you, I'll see that the rest of your family joins you."

Robert took a hot step forward before he caught himself. Kit had raised the sword. "You will not harm my family."

"And how will you stop me? Those brats of your brother's would not be the first villein pups to accidentally fall down the well or into a fire. Lottie is still a comely wench and there are other churls on the manor who covet her, churls who know how to keep their wives silent and obedient. I will not allow another Marcel to rise and harass my son as you have me, and your father mine. One way or another, I will put an end to you all."

Robert knew the threats were a deliberate provocation, but fury overwhelmed all the warnings that trumpeted in his head. He barreled at Kit, but dodged as well, avoiding the vicious swipe of the sword, and lashed his arms around Kit's waist. They lurched across the room together, Kit struggling to free himself, Robert clinging to keep their bodies too close to allow room for another sword thrust, until he saw it. The dagger, lying beside the window.

A sudden shove by Kit and something rammed up against Robert's back. The desk. Kit had maneuvered him against it. Kit got one fist free and slung it into Robert's chin, knocking him into a sprawl across the top. Kit had all the room he needed now to raise his sword and arc it downward. This time, adrenaline charged through the pain of Robert's stripes, rolling him hard to his left to land on his knees on the floor. A respite only. Even as he rose and whirled, he braced himself for the thrust of steel he knew he had neither the speed nor power to evade.

To his surprise, no blow struck him. Kit lingered over the desk, swearing a string of blasphemies. The sword. Kit had struck so savagely the blade had embedded itself deep in the wood. Robert lunged again, knocking Kit away from the sword's hilt. They grappled for several minutes, Kit trying to regain his weapon, Robert struggling to reach it first, but Kit finally succeeded in throwing Robert aside long enough for his hand to lock on the hilt again. Robert dove for the dagger. And again the two men faced one another across the room.

Kit raised derisive brows. "Do you think to stop me with that?"

Robert's hand clenched on the dagger's hilt. "I'll stop you, Kit, I swear. Your threats to my family, your plot against Gunthar—I will stop it all."

Kit's eyes narrowed. "How much did you tell him?"

The barbed question surprised Robert until he remembered that Kit had asked it once before and Robert had refused to answer. Kit's invitation to return to the manor took on a new cast. He'd been feeling Robert out, trying to gage how deeply Robert had thrown in his lot with the old earl. Had he hoped that Robert would so view Gunthar as the pinnacle of the lordly presumption he hated, that he would refuse to confide to him all he had learned of Kit's actions?

There was no further reason to dissemble. "I told him everything. Gunthar knows you sent Hanley to murder him. He knows I overheard your plot with the Count of La Marche—"

Kit's sharp-drawn breath cut him off. "He knows about the king?"

"The king?" Robert's mind flashed back to the receipt they had found with the silver in his bag. Kit's own voice had read it out. . . *'we do likewise promise silver and lands as formerly agreed when the usurper John of England is delivered into our hands.'* The sheer audacity of the scheme still stunned Robert. "You and La Marche were going to sell King John to King Philip of France!"

Robert had not had time to tell Gunthar of that before Robert had been arrested, but from the enraged look on Kit's face, Kit interpreted Robert's answer as an admission.

"Have you any idea what the reward would have been? There was no limit to what I could have asked! But you—!" Kit whipped up the sword, pointing it at Robert's breast. "You ruined everything. La Marche took fright when he realized we'd been eavesdropped upon in the blacksmith's shop. He feared we'd been exposed, he abandoned all our schemes and fled. That desertion so angered King John that Saxton nearly lost his head to the king's rage, and I nearly lost mine to Saxton."

"And believe me," a cold voice dripped from the doorway, "I have repeatedly asked myself why I allowed you to keep it."

If Kit had gone white when he'd first seen Robert, he blanched the color of wax at seeing Saxton standing on his threshold. Saxton's hand rested with deceptive casualness on the sword hilt at his side. Four still-red stripes stood out against his cheek. Marguerite said she had scratched him—and earned a blackened eye for it. Robert gripped the dagger tighter. He had fought Saxton once. Saxton had greater skill than Kit. But Robert would see him pay for Marguerite's blow and every other hurt he had dealt her before any hangman's noose passed around Robert's neck.

Saxton's scathing gaze swept from Kit to Robert. "How did you escape?"

Pay, aye—but Robert was enjoying Kit's pallor too much not to succumb to the temptation to prolong his dismay. "Why, Kit's henchman was clumsy," he said. "I easily overpowered him and—"

"What henchman?" Saxton turned his glacial stare back to Kit. "What is he talking about?"

Kit looked too nonplussed to answer, so Robert did it for him. "The man he sent to kill me in the dungeon. This belonged to him." He indicated the dagger, watching as Saxton took note of the blood on the blade

"I told you I wanted him alive." Saxton's voice bit like the lash across Robert's back, but this time, Robert was not the victim.

Despite his waxen cheeks, Kit finally found his voice. "Aye, so he can convince Gunthar of my guilt and hence the king. What matter to you if I hang?"

"None, I can assure you," Saxton snapped. "First you fumble the assassination, then you prevaricate with one absurd excuse after another for why you have not completed the document we agreed upon, and now this—! You have been nothing but a bungling—"

"Document?" Robert interrupted. "You don't mean Kit's 'testimony' against Gunthar, do you?" Kit turned from waxen to a sickly green. This was as good as twisting the dagger between his ribs. "The one you signed your name and seal to before Kit even wrote it?" Robert paused for a potent beat. "The one in Gunthar's possession?"

It was Saxton who paled now. So Gunthar had not yet shown it to the King?

Saxton's fingers gave a betraying twitch of alarm on his hilt. "Is it true?" he demanded of Kit. "Does Gunthar have it?"

Kit appeared to struggle for words and failed again to find them. So Robert said, "Gunthar came to me in the dungeon this morning." It had felt like an eon between Gunthar's visit and Hanley's, but if longer, Saxton need not know it. "He told me of the document, he told me what it said—and what it did not yet say. He told me he meant to lay it before the king. The Earl of Saxton, plotting against his rival, a man who currently stands in the king's trust and good will. Will the king find that amusing or dangerous, do you think? Who might be next to fall victim to your pride and malice? Some other royal counselor who might challenge your power? The king himself?" Robert held Saxton's eyes. "Do you think Gunthar is not with the king right now making that very argument?" And Saxton was no longer there to defend himself.

Again Saxton's gaze sliced to Kit. "You called me away."

"Marcel had that dagger at my back," Kit said. "How could I know why you and Gunthar were with the king?"

Saxton stepped from the doorway, his sword sliding free of its sheath. "And the document came into Gunthar's possession—how exactly?"

"His wife—"

"Fah! You cast blame for your own deceit on a woman?"

Kit backed away as Saxton advanced. "I have not deceived you. To the devil with you, Rob. Do you think I don't know what you are trying to do?"

Saxton's gaze remained locked on Kit. "I should have dragged you back to camp when I found you with that Frenchman and told the king exactly what I heard. I should have offered to lop off your head myself. Incompetent buffoon!"

Kit swore at him. "If you had not provoked the king in the first place with your overweening conceit, Gunthar would still be tucked away in Kent, that *minstrel* would never have come to Poitou, and I'd be a wealthy man. *I* should have driven my dagger into your back and left you for the wolves in the woods."

Saxton lunged and brought down his sword with a ringing clang on Kit's blade. Robert sprang out of the way as their flurry of parries carried them too near the window, but Kit caught sight of his move and shouted when Robert came near the door, "Stop him, you fool! He's getting away!"

Saxton swung round on the instant and stepped into Robert's path to escape. Robert fell back from the open doorway. Saxton and Kit still had the superior weapons. Robert needed to play for time until he could come up with a plan to disarm one or the other.

"You said you wanted me alive, Saxton. Why?" Robert knew the answer, but Saxton did not know that.

"A poor choice of words," Saxton said, placing his broad physique squarely in front of the threshold. "It is not that I *want* you alive. It is merely that you are more useful to me thus."

"It was never my intention to be useful to you."

Saxton smiled grimly. "No. But it gives me an adequate hold over Marguerite."

The memory of her sullied eye nearly tripped Robert's temper into another angry spring of his body, but he caught the gleam in Saxton's eye and knew that was what he hoped to provoke. Robert choked the impulse back, but said, "She will never marry you now."

"No?" Saxton raised his brows in cool mockery. "Do you think I will not find a way to talk myself out of Beckford's bungling? He forged my signature and stole my seal or made a copy. He wished to implicate me because—well, I shall think of a very good reason. I assure you, I shall be most convincing and come tomorrow, the Lady Marguerite will be my bride." Saxton cast a derisive glance at the dagger when Robert cursed him. "Shall I tell you my plans for our wedding night?"

"You'll never lay a hand on her."

Saxton sneered now. "And how will you stop me?"

"I'll not return to the dungeon, Saxton. Not alive."

"No?"

"No." Robert held up the dagger. "Do you think I would not turn this on myself sooner than go back to where I was? What hold will you have over Marguerite then?"

Saxton's brows twitched down. "What sort of foolery is this? I offer you life—"

"You offer me death of the most hideous kind. I will not go back."

Saxton snapped up his sword. "So be it. Marguerite need not learn of your death, after all, until after we are wed. 'Twill make a fine wedding gift, I think."

Saxton thrust with a blurring speed, but Robert bounced back with his own quick litheness—and collided with Kit, who had apparently been rounding behind him for a nefarious strike of his own. Robert somehow managed to avoid being spit on Kit's sword, but they both hit the floor in a tangle of limbs.

Robert cursed and Kit swore while they thrashed to free themselves of their chaotic entanglement. Above them Robert saw Saxton smile. Murder gleamed in his eyes. Saxton gripped his hilt with both hands and raised the point of the blade above their struggling bodies, poising it to spear the two men together as one might impale a pair of fish. Robert flailed on top, Kit beneath him. One more kick and Robert freed himself of Kit's ensnarling leg. Robert shoved Kit hard, spinning his body after him. Saxton's sword caught and ripped the back of Robert's tunic.

Kit's fist clouted Robert on the chin again, but from the way Kit sprang up with a snarl, Robert realized it had been but a reflexive move to clear a path to Saxton. Kit dove to recover the sword he had dropped, ducking out of the way of Saxton's arc towards his head, and then the two men locked once more in battle. Their blades scraped and shuddered and showered sparks around them. Robert dragged himself out of the way of their lurching feet, then pulled himself up with the help of a chair near the wall. And then he watched, knowing the only way the scrimmage could end. Kit was skillful, but Saxton was faster and stronger. Kit jabbed. Saxton parried. Kit shifted nimbly and thrust. Saxton rebuffed his every feint and gambit. Then Saxton's steel flashed like a streak of white fire and Kit stumbled back, looking startled as the breast of his tunic stained scarlet.

Saxton's smirk of triumph as Kit crumpled just short of Robert's feet was his mistake. Robert whipped forward, snatched the sword from Kit's lax fingers, and before Saxton could check his gloating, rained down such a hail of blows on Saxton's unready blade that Robert forced him back and back again. Saxton's sword whirled and spun, but only in defense, unable to recover the advantage and execute an offensive blow of his own.

Saxton hissed, like the snake Robert had always thought coiled at the center of the villain's soul. "If you kill me, there will be worse than a hanging for you, Marcel."

"What shall they do to me?" Robert said. "Lop off my head? Carve me into quarters? I'm going to die no matter what I do. But I am not going to die alone. You asked how I would stop you from so much as touching Marguerite again. Like this—" Robert levered Saxton's blade away from his body "—and this—" he drove a kick into Saxton's stomach, fury lending it such force as to slam Saxton into the wall "—and this." He shoved the edge of Kit's blade against Saxton's throat.

"Drop it," Robert snapped when Saxton's arm flexed as though to make a move with his own weapon. Kit's blade nipped against Saxton's skin, spilling a drop of blood onto the blade. Saxton dropped his sword.

Robert held Saxton's gaze until he saw the arrogance flicker away, ebbed out by a slowly pooling doubt, then a widening of the eyelids as an expression flowed in that Robert observed with relish. This man who had inflicted so much terror on others, who had humiliated, threatened, and beaten Robert's love—at the end, when he stared death in the face, Saxton finally tasted fear. Let him go to the devil this way. One quick slice of Kit's sword, and it would be done.

51

obert," a voice spoke sharply from the doorway, "put it down."

The ringing of Robert's battle with Saxton had drown out the sound of approaching footsteps. How long had Gunthar been on the threshold?

Robert pressed the blade closer to Saxton's throat. "No, my lord. I can only do the world a service by ridding it of this vile scoundrel."

"Robert—"

"He beat Marguerite. He tried to murder you. You said yourself he has plundered the kingdom and terrorized men high and low. He does not deserve to live another day upon the earth."

Gunthar's tall frame came into view from the corner of Robert's eye. "That is not your judgment to make, lad. Put down the sword."

But Robert held the blade steady. "Who will judge him if I do not? He is already plotting how to undo the damage of Kit's document. I will not let him free to further harm Marguerite or create one more hour of havoc with your life."

"It is only your life that concerns me," Gunthar said, "and I will not see you throw it away like this. There is no need. I have come to arrest the Earl of Saxton."

That startled Saxton into daring to turn his head. Robert allowed it, along with a glance of his own to the side. Gunthar had not come alone. Several men stood behind him, dressed in the colors of the king's guards.

"How dare you presume—" Saxton began, but Robert punched off his outrage with another nudge of the blade.

"I told you," Robert said, "he is already plotting his own defense. He means to throw the blame for everything onto Kit. There will be no one to witness against him."

"*I* will witness against him."

The ragged voice startled Robert. He had thought Kit dead, but Saxton's thrust must have missed his heart. Kit had managed to drag himself onto his elbow, but from the flow of blood between the fingers that clutched his breast the wound would not be easily staunched, if it could be staunched at all.

Kit's eyes blazed at Saxton with hatred. "For this—" his fingers curled deeper into the stain on his tunic "—I will tell you everything. How I plotted with the king's enemies to sell King John into the power of the French. How Saxton overheard it all and blackmailed me. He said he would turn his head to my crime if I would murder the Earl of Gunthar for him."

Robert's gaze remained on Kit, but he felt the jerk of Saxton's chest in a sharpened breath beneath his hand.

"That is a lie!" For the first time since Robert had known him, the cool, arrogant Earl of Saxton sounded alarmed. "Sell the king? I would never have turned my head to *that*. He lies!"

Kit's own breath rattled painfully through his throat. "Who will you believe, my lord?" he asked Gunthar. "A devious fox like him or a dying man's confession?"

"And the silver in Marcel's bag?" Gunthar asked.

Kit hesitated. His face was drawn so white Robert feared he might faint before he answered. Kit spoke at last through lips that barely moved. "Mine. Planted . . . at Saxton's command." His shoulders slumped and he rolled back to the floor. Saxton cursed him. Kit's body convulsed slightly in a silent laugh before he spoke again. "Your aim was too good, my lord . . . and I do not care to die alone." He turned his head and met Robert's eyes as if realizing he had paraphrased Robert's own words to Saxton. "The game is yours, Rob. I will make full confession."

To avenge himself on Saxton for his own death, Robert thought, for Robert knew it unlikely that Kit would live the night.

Robert felt a hand on his. He tensed and whirled his head, thinking

Saxton sought to break free, but it was only Gunthar attempting to draw Kit's sword away from where it still pressed against its target. Robert finally lowered the weapon, but he kicked Saxton's sword across the room before he stepped back to allow two of the king's guards to flank Saxton on either side.

"Farrand, Milston," Gunthar said, "place my Lord Saxton under arrest and escort him to the tower. Leyland, bind up Lord Beckford's wound and you, Cuttridge, fetch some wine to brace him."

Saxton swept them all with a deadly glance, but this time Robert knew he had no power to fulfill the threat he tried to impart. Still, Saxton blustered, "If you think this is over, Gunthar—"

Gunthar lifted his brows, and surprisingly Saxton broke off. Robert had rarely seen Saxton and Gunthar eye-to-eye like this. Saxton had the more hulking build, but Gunthar stood every inch Saxton's height and something about the implacable set of Gunthar's shoulders, the haughty turn of his mouth, the uncompromising air of command his still strong form wore as easily as an old, familiar mantle, made Saxton appear inexplicably small.

"What I think is of little import, my lord," Gunthar said. "What the king thinks is all that matters now."

He nodded at the guards and they escorted Saxton out. Robert wished they might throw Saxton in the dungeon instead of a tower, however drear the latter, but even for traitors he knew one man's birth stood privileged over another's.

Robert said nothing as Gunthar found his shoulder and steered him over to a chair. He sat silent while Gunthar issued commands to the guard who sought to slow Kit's bleeding and the man who brought the wine. Bolstered by the liquid, though he sipped little enough of it, Kit began to talk.

He told how he had met and been befriended by the Count of La Marche eight years earlier when the king had sought to regain his lost duchy of Normandy from the French. Still angered by King John's multiple indignities and humiliations upon himself and his family, La Marche had enlisted Kit during King John's new campaign as a go-between with the French to plot John's downfall. John had already proposed a betrothal between his daughter and La Marche's son to try to repair the break between them. He had even agreed to seal the betrothal in the stronghold of Mervant Castle, which belonged to La Marche's uncle. Deep in the night while the castle slept, La Marche planned to lure the king with a woman to leave the safety of the walls and deliver him into the arms of the King of France. The

Frenchman with whom Kit had arranged the details insisted King John would merely be held to ransom, as his brother Richard had been on his return from the Crusade, though La Marche urged Kit to strongly hint that England would little mourn should King John fall victim to an "accident" before any ransom could be raised.

Saxton had known of the plot, Kit insisted. He feared Gunthar's return to power with the king and wanted Gunthar dead. When Hanley failed in Gunthar's tent, Kit appealed to La Marche to arrange the ambush that had come so near succeeding and killed so many of Gunthar's men. When Gunthar had escaped that, too, they had next planned to murder him, as well as Robert, when Gunthar came to witness and Robert to record the betrothal. La Marche would say they had gone with the king to guard him when John left the castle and must have been killed by the French who abducted him.

Kit's voice grew increasingly weak and halting through this recital, but Gunthar prodded him remorselessly to also tell how he had planted evidence of his guilt on Robert when they both returned to Westminster. Robert knew it vital that Kit reveal every detail in the presence of the king's guards to establish Robert's innocence beyond any remaining doubts, but after the first few words, Robert stopped listening. He'd learned everything he needed to from Hanley and now that Robert's blood had ceased to pound with the energy that had driven him through his confrontations with Hanley, Kit and Saxton, he felt exhaustion taking hold and his back begin to burn intolerably again.

"Carry Lord Beckford to his bed," he heard Gunthar bid the guards at last. "Try to keep him alive long enough to send for a clerk. It would be helpful to have his confession in writing, though you will all stand witness of what you heard should he fail to revive."

Robert glanced up and saw that Kit had fainted. Robert waited until the guards had carried Kit out before he asked Gunthar, "What will the king do to La Marche?"

"His future son-in-law and one of the most powerful men in Poitou?" Gunthar strolled over to the chair where Robert sat. "John will wish to burn his lands to the ground, of course, but after the defeat at Bouvines this summer, it is unlikely he could assemble a sufficient army to follow him across the British Sea again. La Marche's head is likely quite safe for now. Saxton's is another matter."

Robert hesitated. Nothing would give him more pleasure than to see Saxton's head on a pike. But . . . "Sir, I am not sure that Kit was telling the truth. In La Rochelle, when I overheard him with La Marche, Kit said that Saxton did not know of their plot."

"No?" Gunthar did not look disturbed. "Perhaps he learned of it later. Has that occurred to you?"

Robert supposed it was possible. Saxton was clearly guilty of so many other crimes that whatever punishment he received would surely be just.

Robert wished the guard had left the wine. He took a moment to try to master the weariness stealing through his bones and rebridle the pain. When he thought he could speak without a tremor of either, he said, "How did you know I was here?"

"It seemed the obvious guess. You'd not have made it through an exit alone and there would have been a hubbub in the palace if you had tried. When Simon Todd told me there was a dead man in your cell and that you appeared to have fled—"

"Simon? He came to you?"

"Of course. I was the one who sent him to free you."

"*You?* Sent Simon? I thought—"

"What did you think? That I would not keep my word to you? That I would leave you in that pit?"

"No." Robert said it as forcefully as his aching, exhausted body would let him. "I meant to wait as you bid me. But then Hanley came and everything changed—"

"And you charged off headlong into Beckford's and Saxton's arms, rather than coming to me." *Again* hung unspoken in the air.

Robert bit his lip, then murmured in his own defense, "Saxton said you were with the king, so I could not have come to you if I'd wanted to."

Gunthar grunted, reluctantly acknowledging Robert's point, but responded, "As if that excuses *this*." He gestured at the tumbled state of Kit's chamber. "If I had not arrived when I did, if you had slit Saxton's throat, you would have hanged, you know. You should have waited for Simon to revive. I had a perfectly good plan for your escape. But why I should expect you to do anything sensible I suppose is a question I will take to my grave." He dealt Robert a brisk cuff on the side of the head. "Young fool."

Another time Robert might have bristled, but he was so tired and relieved and grateful that he laughed instead.

Gunthar smiled, though his eyes remained serious. "While Saxton and I were with the king, Simon was going to arrange for your escape from the dungeon. We dressed him as one of Saxton's guards so the men who watched your cell would ask no questions when Saxton appeared to send one of his own men to relieve them."

Gunthar lifted Robert's bandaged hand, studied it silently for a moment, then let it go.

"You were to don a second uniform of Saxton's, then Simon would guide you through an exit in a part of the palace where your face would be less familiar than at the door you usually pass through. Saxton and the king I meant to distract, meanwhile, with Beckford's unfinished document. But Saxton got called away. His departure troubled me, but I made haste in his absence to show the king Beckford's parchment. The king grew so enraged that by the time Simon came seeking me, John was already thundering at me to take his guards and bring Saxton back to the council chamber to explain himself."

Robert shifted uncomfortably in the chair, trying to ignore the fiery welts on his back. "You said Simon found Hanley in the cell?"

"Aye. He said someone followed him and struck him from behind before he could enter the dungeon."

Robert felt Gunthar's eyes following his movements and stilled.

Gunthar continued without a pause. "Simon awoke to find the cell door open and took a torch to see what had happened. He found Hanley, dead, in Saxton's second uniform. Hanley must have donned it hoping it would assist in his escape after he murdered you. Or perhaps he thought it would help throw suspicion away from Beckford if one of Saxton's own guards had been seen fleeing from the scene of your death. In any case, he did not succeed, thank the heavens. But when Simon told me about Hanley and that you were gone from the cell, I guessed what had drawn Saxton away. I knew he had gone after you, and I knew this was where your grudges would bring you."

To Kit. It was over. The lies exposed, Robert's family safe, Robert free—He had expected vengeance to taste sweeter, like Kit's fear of him had. Instead, Robert felt slightly numb, as though it were all a dream.

He pushed his thoughts to function when they did not seem to want to. He supposed he should make his freedom legal. How much might Kit's heirs demand from him? Had he saved enough from the wages Gunthar had paid him? But he would need every coin he had hoarded for the future. He supposed he could take up a trade in another city and labor there for a year and a day. Wanderlust no longer drove him. His restlessness had found contentment long ago in—

Robert dared not let himself complete the thought. Gunthar's disapproval in the dungeon still stung too deeply and Robert was too grateful just now to start another quarrel.

"So," he asked, cautious of Gunthar's answer, "what happens now?" Would he have to stay in London to add his testimony of Kit's crime?

Gunthar startled Robert by gripping his chin and turning his head slowly from side to side. "Well, I suggest we begin with a bath. You look monstrous. How badly are you hurt?"

Robert caught Gunthar's glance at his bandaged hand. "A scratch, nothing more. A few bruises. Nothing that won't mend." Including the stripes on his back.

"Well, then," Gunthar said, "come with me. A bath and a shave and a change of clothing. It would send Marguerite into hysterics to see you like this."

Robert's breath hitched in his lungs. "Marguerite? You will let me see her?"

Gunthar's mouth curved wryly. "I doubt I could stop her." He released Robert's chin. "Do I still think this marriage is mad? Aye. But you've fought a grand fight for her. If she is still willing and you still want her, I'll not stand in your way."

Robert saw a flicker in Gunthar's normally hooded eyes. Those words had not come without cost to some deep, high-born part of him. What had caused him to speak them? Robert did not understand Gunthar's change, still less why Gunthar had ever supported him through the most improbable situations. But Robert suddenly understood the warmth that rose glowing in his own heart. It was more than respect or esteem for an honest man, more even than gratitude. He had grown to love Gunthar. And never had Robert loved him more than he did as he rose from the chair and left Kit's chamber with Gunthar's hand resting lightly on his shoulder.

Robert was not sure where he'd thought Gunthar would send him to clean up, but he'd not expected to find himself in Gunthar's own bedchamber. Gunthar's fair-haired squire, Antony Tollerton, directed the servants who carried in pails of steaming water for Robert's bath. The youth had been well trained to maintain an impassive face when heaven only knew what thoughts must be racing through his head at being sent to wait on a man whom everyone in Gunthar's household knew had once served as a common footsoldier in the earl's camp. But Antony remained unflappably polite and respectful, and at last Robert was clean, his several-day's growth of beard shaven off, the cut in his hand treated and rebandaged, and a numbing salve rubbed into the lash-marks on his back.

Robert dressed hesitantly in the clothes laid out for him. He had never worn silk before and felt guilty at the pleasure he experienced in a fabric that whispered so smooth and soft against his skin. Gunthar came in just as Robert finished putting on a pair of embroidered shoes. The earl surveyed him from his freshly cropped head to the slightly too small slippers on his feet, then whipped aside an embroidered sheet from a six-foot-tall object that stood in one corner of the room. Robert had only seen small, round mirrors at an occasional fair. Now he stared, astonished, into the highly polished surface of one tall enough to capture his entire image from head to toe.

"They're hard to come by in this size," Gunthar said, apparently seeing the stunned look on Robert's face. "I bought it for my wife shortly after our marriage. She was unsure of her looks back then. I wished her always to be able to see herself as I do, vibrant and strong and lovely."

It must have cost Gunthar a small fortune. But then, Robert had seen a glimpse of Gunthar's wealth in reviewing records as his secretary, and he knew Gunthar was worth multiple small fortunes many times over.

Robert rotated curiously before the mirror. The silk tunic, just shy a royal blue, fell in graceful folds to his knees. Silver scrollwork had been embroidered at the cuffs and around the neck, and a silver girdle with sapphire studs looped around his waist. Even his hose felt made of silk. Robert turned about the other direction. Never had he been dressed in so much finery. A duke's son, Gunthar had said to him once. But the eyes that gazed back at him from this exotic reflection were the same eyes he knew from the likeness he saw of himself when he gazed into a pool of water. All the finery in the world would not make him other than he was.

"Are you ready?" Gunthar asked.

Robert turned away from the mirror. "Does Marguerite know I'm free?"

"I sent my wife to tell her while you were at your bath. I imagine by now they are waiting for you beyond that door."

Robert's heart hammered as Gunthar pulled the door open, but when Robert stepped across the threshold, he discovered a third person had joined the two women in the sitting chamber.

"You knew this would be my choice," he heard Marguerite murmur. "I never hid my heart from you."

"I pray you will not regret this someday," the tall knight with a cocky brown curl tumbling over his forehead replied, frowning down at Marguerite. "If he fails you—"

Robert stiffened, for *if* had sounded to him very much like a *when*. He took another swift step into the room, catching Sir Warin's eye and cutting off anything further he might have said. Sir Warin's frown deepened, but he executed a series of bows.

"My ladies, my lord." One curt nod to Robert. "Marcel." Sir Warin allowed his gaze to rest long and regretfully on Marguerite before he turned and left the room.

One brief moment of uncertainty held Robert still, but then he met Marguerite's eyes and saw all he needed to waiting for him there. Two more steps and he caught he her about her waist as she flew into his arms. He whirled her around and around, his face buried in the sweet-smelling cloud of her hair, until he, at least, was dizzy. He heard her whispering his name over and over in his ear in a voice that hiccoughed with sobs. Everything fell away except for her, the scent of her, the feel of her, and the promise in her lips when he kissed her.

At last he set her down and cupped her tear-bedewed cheeks in his hands. He saw the answer in her eyes before he asked, but still he whispered, "Marguerite, will you come with me?"

Her smile nearly giddied his senses again. "To the ends of the earth," she said, "or to a merchant's house or to a villein's hut. I will go anywhere with you."

He kissed her again, lingeringly, before the world intruded with a subtle clearing of a throat. Robert's cheeks warmed at the twin twinkles in Gunthar's and Lady Helen's eyes. He held Marguerite's hand tightly as he crossed the room to where Gunthar had moved to stand beside his wife. Then Robert released Marguerite's fingers and did something he had never willingly done before any man. He fell to one knee and bowed his head to Gunthar.

"My lord, I do not have words to thank you, for my life, for my love—" he glanced at Marguerite, then again at Gunthar's embroidered shoes. "I have been unforgivably arrogant and insolent to you. Why you bore with it—with me—" his voice thickened with remorse. "You said once that I should live to humble myself before you, and you spoke truth. I live by your grace, and I would be very much your servant."

"If I thought," Gunthar said, his own voice a little gruff, "this humility of yours would last above four-and-twenty hours, I'd be worried your spell in the dungeon had irreparably addled your brain. Get up, man. There is much to discuss, but who stands the deepest in whose debt is a subject we will save for another day."

Robert rose, but before he could speak Lady Helen swept up from her chair and set a kiss on his cheek. He gazed, startled, into her silvery eyes. "My lady?"

"For keeping your promise," Lady Helen said, "to bring him home safely to me."

She cast a chiding look at her husband that hinted of some continued displeasure with him. She had not thanked Robert before. Had she learned at last of the assassination attempts in Poitou? Robert had not thought she would be pleased at being kept in the dark about her husband's danger, though if Robert had stood in Gunthar's shoes, Robert owned he would not have told his wife, either.

Lady Helen reached behind her chair, then set something in Robert's hands. He stared, disbelieving for a moment. The last time he had seen this, it had been bouncing against the wall outside Lady Helen's sitting chamber. Robert fell back to his knees, landing on both of them this time. He frantically undid the laces even as he struggled to brace himself to find naught but a splinter of wood inside the case. But when he drew the case open, there it lay, miraculously still in one piece, marred only, he discovered as he tilted the lute this way and that, by one deep, fresh scrape in the side that had joined the other scars of its life.

"My lady"—Robert blinked back a stinging moistness in his eyes—"how do you come to have this?"

"I heard the uproar outside the door when Lord Saxton's guards came to arrest you," Lady Helen said. "I went out to see what was happening and I am afraid I accidentally stepped into the guards' way and allowed you to escape." Robert saw mischief in her eyes. "When they finally ran off after you, I found that left behind." She nodded at the lute. "Is it much harmed?"

Robert sat down on the floor and pulled the lute into his lap. He ran his fingers over the strings, plucked out a discordant melody, then sighed. "I'll be tuning it for the next month, I suspect, but—" He looked up at Lady Helen, praying she could see what he knew his words so inadequately relayed. *Thank you.*

Her cheeks glowed with that pretty color that Robert had so often observed brought tenderness into Gunthar's eyes when he watched her. She said, "Marguerite, child, come sit by me again. Hugh, set a chair for Robert beside her and we will discuss the wedding."

Marguerite gasped at the countess's words. "My lady, you said that Lord Saxton had been arrested."

Robert jerked shut the case, stood, and possessively reclaimed Marguerite's hand. Had something gone awry with Saxton? Had the king already changed his mind about his duplicitous counselor?

"Absurd child," Lady Helen said, "I mean your wedding to Robert. It must be handled with some care, I think."

She motioned to the empty chair. Robert relaxed a little and walked Marguerite over to it. He sat down near her in the chair that Gunthar pulled forward so that Robert could keep his fingers entangled with Marguerite's.

"Are you thinking of her parents' objections?" Robert asked. "Once we have exchanged the vows, there will be nothing they can do. In fact—" He glanced at the window. The light promised at least another hour till dusk. "Mae, if we were to leave now, go into the city and find a priest—"

Her eyes sparkled her eagerness at his words. Robert's blood pounded. To have her as his wife this very night—

"And then what?" Gunthar's rough question broke the spell. "Do you imagine her father will not ride hell-bent after you and do his best to make his daughter a widow before dawn?"

Robert fought a wave of irritation. He supposed engaging in swordplay with her father would not be the best way to begin their marriage. "What do you suggest?" he asked Gunthar.

Frustration lent a tartness to Robert's voice that set a triumphant gleam to Gunthar's eye. So much for his humility.

"I suggest," Gunthar said, "that you exercise a bit of patience."

"I have been patient. I have been patient for nearly a year!"

"Because you were five hundred miles away from her and had no choice."

"Hugh," Lady Helen rebuked her husband, "have a little sympathy for their feelings. As I recall, someone hustled me off to my wedding night quite contrary to my father's wishes."

If Robert had not known Gunthar better, he might have thought Gunthar's cheeks tinged red. But Gunthar never blushed.

"I am merely suggesting," Gunthar said, "that it might help to still the gossip a little if the Lady Marguerite weds a knight of my household rather than my secretary."

Gunthar might as well have thrust an iron rod down Robert's spine, Robert felt himself go so stiff. "Sir, I told you in La Rochelle—"

"I remember what you said, lad," Gunthar cut him off, "but things have changed considerably since then. You will soon be absolved of all suspicions laid against you. There is no logical reason for you to refuse."

No logical reason? Robert could think of a dozen!

Marguerite's fingers twitched in his hold. "I do not understand. Rob, what is he talking about?"

"He is talking foolery," Robert said. "My lord, I do not even know if my freedom is secure from Kit's manor."

Gunthar made a hrumph-ing sound through his nose. "I will send his widow compensation for that in the morning. And before you get your hackles up on that obstinate neck of yours, you can pay me back just as swiftly as you like. I will even lend you enough to buy your sister's and sister-in-law's freedom with her children from Beckford's heirs. The wages I give to my men-at-arms is more than I pay my secretaries, however, so you'll be quit of the debt faster if you swallow your pride and trust me to know what is best."

Surprise that Gunthar knew about Lottie and Alice bit off the hot rejoinder on Robert's tongue, until he guessed that Gunthar only remembered that Robert had mentioned them to him in their conversations in Poitou. Were they still in the palace somewhere, he wondered, or had they gone back to Beck Manor?

Robert could not fail to be grateful for this offer, but he knew Gunthar would lend him the money even if Robert remained his secretary. He glanced at Marguerite's bewildered face. Would a knighthood please her? Once Gunthar had accepted Robert's determination to marry her, Robert had hoped Gunthar might wish to retain his secretarial skills. There was no man on earth Robert desired to serve more! But a knighthood, to join the very men he had so despised?

He ventured an obvious objection. "Sir, I have not been trained to be a knight. I should not know how to go about any of its obligations."

"I've seen you with a sword, Robert, and you have skill."

"I'd be of no use in battle. Your armor would stifle me. I could not fight among such men. Sir, I cannot even ride a horse!"

Gunthar gave a shout of laughter. "Can you not?"

"No," Robert said, nettled by Gunthar's humor. "Villeins are not allowed to travel far enough to need a horse, and we couldn't afford one if we were. And if you recall, I served as a *foot*soldier in Poitou, not as part of your cavalry."

"I did not mean to offend you. It is merely that with all your other un-villein-like learning, it seems rather ridiculous that you should never have mastered so simple a task as riding a horse."

"I never had the opportunity," Robert muttered.

"Well, it is not too late to remedy that," Gunthar said. "You are still young enough to learn. And if we are called to another war I will see that your scutage is paid, for once knighted you cannot resume your place amongst the footsoldiers."

"Then what use will I be?"

"I shall find a use for you, never fear. I do not let my people stand idle." Gunthar paused as if considering, though Robert had a suspicion he had already worked out the details of Robert's agreement in his mind. "I've a keep in need of a castellan," Gunthar said after a moment. "A defensive position only, and one I've no doubt you could be trained to fulfill. Oh, aye, I shall think of something suitable to your talents, never fear."

Lady Helen rose and moved to lay a hand on her husband's arm. "Let us leave Robert and Marguerite alone to discuss it. This decision will affect her, too." To Marguerite she said, "Hugh and I shall go speak to your parents. They will have surely heard of Lord Saxton's arrest by now. I will do my best to convince them that it may be a convenient time to allow you to visit me again in Kent. If your father proves reluctant, Hugh will use one of his intimidating stares to remind them which earl is still in the king's favor, won't you, my dear?"

"Indeed," Gunthar said. "Though I think Robert and I might wish to leave Westminster in the morning, before it occurs to her parents just who has been released from the dungeon."

Gunthar gave Marguerite a nod, apparently unaware of how his words unsettled her as he led his wife out of the sitting chamber.

"Leave in the morning?" Marguerite echoed, shifting about in her chair to gaze at Robert in alarm. "Does he mean just you and he? Without Lady Helen and me?"

"Who knows what whim he's taken into his head?" Robert said. "Whatever it is, be assured I mean to marry you much sooner than later." He ran a thumb lightly across her cheekbone. "And so, sweetheart? Do you wish to be a knight's lady?"

He realized her hand was still tucked in his and that he gripped her slim fingers a little too tightly. He tried to ease his grip while he awaited her reply.

She gazed at him for a very long moment before she answered. "You've donned your mask again," she said. "After your fever, you lost it for a time. I could read your heart as I never could before. That's when I knew—" her voice quavered slightly "—that you loved me—more than I'd even comprehended."

"Sweetheart." He started to pull her into his arms, but she held him away.

"I am not finished. Now I cannot tell what you are thinking again. Do you wish to be a knight? Because I will go with you just as you are. I never asked you to be other than you are."

No, she never had, even when he had sensed the longing in her for her grandfather's inheritance, not for the wealth it would have brought her, but for her love of the land and her grandfather's memory. Robert could not give her that. But with Gunthar's help, he could give her this, life as a lady at Lamhurst Castle with a woman Robert knew loved her as a daughter. If a knighthood sat ill upon him, he would never let her know.

"Gunthar said a knighthood would be a benefit to our children one day," Robert said, "and he is right. For their sake, as well as yours, I will accept his offer."

He tried to kiss Marguerite again, but again she stopped him, his mouth just short of her lips. "Rob, you must be honest with me. Is that what *you* want?"

"Just now, all I want is to kiss you."

Her hand slid over his mouth to check him. She gazed at him, uncommonly stern. "Rob."

What *did* he want? He did not need to search as deeply as she appeared to think he did to find the answer. He wanted a home, with children who felt as secure in their parents' love as he had felt on the most bitter-cold day on Beck Manor. And whether it be in a cottage or on the road or as a knight in a castle, he wanted to build that home with her.

He removed her hand and kissed her, fiercely and as thoroughly as he dared before their wedding. After a brief moment of resistance, Marguerite reciprocated his passion with an exhilarating zeal. Into their exchange cascaded the release of all their pent up fears and ardor and love. He had despaired of ever holding her again, of ever tasting her sweet, willing lips, of feeling the quickening of his pulse when her lilting voice fell upon his ears, of a future that only held light and meaning if they walked into it together.

Light was all he saw now with her, and a hope he never intended to let anyone wrest from him again.

It took them both several minutes to catch their breaths when he finally released her. Her eyes glowed as radiant as her cheeks.

"Did I satisfy your question?" he asked.

She nodded. "You promise we will wed sooner rather than later?"

He grinned. "That is one battle of wills I promise I will win."

Epilogue

Marguerite had always known herself to be short of stature, but she never felt more tiny than when she gazed at herself in the Earl of Gunthar's six-foot tall mirror. Robert had told her of it in the evenings when they walked together, hands clasped, in the gardens of the various castles they slept in at night. His single experience with the mirror had sufficiently awed him that he had repeated the tale to her many times o'er the last fortnight. None of his descriptions had prepared her to see this particular image reflected back at her, though. A pearl circlet ringed her dark hair like a shimmering halo of snowdrops. The ones sewn to the bodice of her azure silk gown cast a similar effect, mimicking swirls of frost against the bold blue background of the cloth. Pearls ran in trickling strands over her shoulders and down her sleeves to the wide hanging cuffs that exposed a white tunic beneath, with silver thread-work that set it a-glisten. The same precious, tiny round jewels sprinkled over her skirts. Even her white silk slippers were sewn with them from toe to heel.

"You are a vision, child."

Marguerite saw Lady Helen's image join her in the mirror's reflection. Were there tears on the countess's cheeks? Marguerite turned away from the glass and saw her suspicion confirmed.

Lady Helen whisked the tears away with a smile, but her eyes remained moist. "Yes, I know it is absurd of me. I am happy for you, Marguerite. I promise you these are tears of joy."

"But my lady, how is this possible? Rob and the earl were still quarreling just last night over the timing of our wedding. Lord Gunthar insisted that Rob be knighted first and that is still nearly a month away."

Marguerite could not have been more stunned when Hertha, the maid Lady Helen had given her to take Eva's place, had summoned her to Lady Helen's chamber and bade her dress in this elegant gown, for, she said, Marguerite was to be married in just a few hours.

Lady Helen dismissed Hertha with a nod of her head, then took Marguerite's hands, her silvery eyes all a-twinkle. "Robert may not yet be a knight, but he nevertheless threw down the gauntlet to my husband this morning. He says he cannot sleep anymore for thinking of how much he wants you, and without sleep he cannot concentrate on his training. And besides that he says he made you a promise and will carry you off to fulfill it tomorrow if my husband forces him to tarry without you one more day." She tucked a stray strand of hair behind Marguerite's ear. "And as I have good cause to know and have warned Hugh, Robert is a man who keeps his promises. I suspected it would be thus, so I had this gown shortened for you. You will consider it my wedding gift to you, I hope, and the pearl circlet, too."

Marguerite suddenly found that she could scarcely breathe. "So we are really, truly to be married today?"

"As soon as you are ready. I imagine Robert is already pacing the chapel waiting for you to join him."

"Oh!" Marguerite pulled off the pearl circlet, tossed it on the great, wide bed that belonged to the Earl and Countess of Gunthar, caught up an ivory comb that lay nearby on a gilt-trimmed table, and began frantically dragging it through her hair. "Oh, I cannot let Rob see me with all these tangles in my hair!"

"My dear, my dear." Lady Helen laughed and took the comb away from her, then skillfully began to work free the knots that Marguerite's hectic actions had worsened rather than loosened. "I have never seen such thick hair as this, Marguerite, but there are not as many tangles as you think. What were you doing before Hertha called you?"

"Sitting in your gardens. There is a wind today." Marguerite did not add that she had been silently cursing Lady Helen's husband for his insistence on putting the knighting before their wedding.

Lady Helen patted and fluffed Marguerite's hair, then set the circlet back atop it. "There, now. Robert is waiting for you, child, and I think he will not care a whit if you have a hair or two out of place. I thought you would be eager to join him."

"I am. Oh, I am! It is just so sudden!" She hesitated. "Are there to be many of the earl's men there?"

Robert had insisted rather too fervently on their evening walks that followed his long days with Gunthar, that she deserved a very grand wedding at the door of the tall, looming church that dominated Lamhurst Castle's sprawling village. The more passionately he had declared it, the more certain she had been that he shrank from the very thought.

"His knighting will of necessity be public," Lady Helen said, "for there must be no doubt of the Earl of Gunthar's will in that matter. But Hugh and I have agreed that a quiet, private wedding within the castle chapel will be sufficient, if you do not mind such modesty? We have asked Sir Brandon de Vexin to attend, and his son Ralf, whom Hugh has determined to assign as Robert's squire when he is knighted. Sir Edward Tollerton, his wife, and son Antony shall be there, as well. It is best to have a few additional witnesses that there may be no doubt of the validity of what takes place today."

Marguerite knew Lady Helen was thinking of Marguerite's father. Lord de Villon would like nothing better than to void his daughter's marriage to a former villein, once he learned what had happened. Nevertheless, for one small moment, she wished her mother was here. Though she had rarely succeeded, Lady Leah had tried her best to protect Marguerite from her father's bursts of temper. Marguerite had always known her mother loved her—not as well as she loved her husband, but in Lady Leah's own weak way, Marguerite had felt her mother's affection. But there was no changing what was, and the tiny ache of loss in Marguerite's heart had been filled by this strong, warm, compassionate lady who stood before her.

Marguerite took Lady Helen's arm. "Let us go now," she said. Quickly. The sooner she was bound to Robert, the sooner she would be forever free of her father's power. *And the sooner we will no longer have to part after Robert kisses me goodnight at my chamber door.*

She prayed Lady Helen could not see her vivid blush as she swept out of the room at the countess's side.

The great chapel of Lamhurst Castle could have engulfed the entire cottage Robert had been raised in. Its high, vaulted ceiling soared over Robert's head. A great three-paned stained glass window arced over the altar. The pane on the left portrayed the passing of the Keys of the Kingdom from the Lord to the Apostle Peter, the one on the right two women at the tomb with an angel sitting on the stone that had been rolled away from the entrance, and in the center stood the scene of the crucifixion. Sunlight streamed through the glass, setting all the colors ablaze and making the angel and his halo glow like holy fire. The radiant light spread over the great marble altar below the glass, with its exquisite carvings and trimmed about the top with a layer of red velvet.

The same rich cloth and color that Robert wore. He tried not to shift uncomfortably in his new clothes. The cloth felt too luxurious, the gilt embroidery too bright, and the crisp red round cap on his head felt foreign to his scalp that had always preferred its freedom or the loose confines of a hood.

Gunthar muttered for the sixth time, "This is a mistake."

He and Robert stood waiting in the chapel for Marguerite and the countess to join them. Father Matthais, the white haired chaplain, had drawn the other witnesses to another part of the chapel to converse with them so that the earl could talk with Robert alone.

"If it is, it is *my* mistake," Robert said, "and one I am determined to make."

"It would better if she married a knight."

"She will be wife to a knight in a month hence."

"It is not the same. A lady of Marguerite's birth to wed my secretary? It has already raised brows, even among my own men."

"You think they will be less shocked when you set your blade to my shoulder to dub me *Sir Robert?*" Robert smothered a quiver of dread at the thought.

"Many of them will frown within," Gunthar confessed, "but they will play the parts I expect of them and treat you with respect."

Robert gave a small shake of his head. One could not dictate respect from others. That was something that could only be earned. But Gunthar had commanded men for too long to recognize—or perhaps admit—that his haughty authority had its limits.

"I wish, just for once," Gunthar said, "you would trust me to know what is best."

This day had nothing to do with trust and everything to do with Marguerite alone. Robert returned the challenge in Gunthar's eyes with his own fierce resolve. He was surprised when something flickered in the grey depths of Gunthar's gaze and Gunthar looked away. It was unlike him to break contact so quickly.

Then slowly, as though rolling through Robert's being in a soft revelation, the answer to Gunthar's stubborn desire to delay the wedding unfolded to Robert's mind.

Gunthar had spent the last fortnight dragging Robert and, at Robert's and Lady Helen's insistence, his wife and Marguerite, on a tour of his many castles and manors. Robert's glimpses as secretary into the earl's wealth had not prepared him for so much land and power as lay at Gunthar's disposal. William would have called Robert mad as a hare in March to think he could serve so great a man as this as a knight, and many a time o're the last fourteen days Robert feared it might be true.

His doubts might have overwhelmed him, had Gunthar not spent so much time sharing with him unexpectedly personal reminiscences. The orchard at Norcott Castle where he and his friend, John Lee, had raided his father's apple trees as youths and both earned a beating for the theft from his strict-minded sire. The training field at Selberry Castle where he had learned after many an ungainly tumble to outwit the quintain. Rushall Manor, where his father had set him for a year to master the fine details of supervising bailiffs and reeves and yes, villeins, and learn what was required to make fields prosper. Claredon Castle, which still carried the poignant memory of where he had been visiting when word arrived of his father's death. And the even keener cut of the day he had stood on the battlements of Hawkham Castle, how the village below had blinked out of sight when the courier had come with the news of the ambush at Constantinople that had cut off the life of his son, Peter, and how in Gunthar's shock the words had drubbed in his head: *How will I tell Helen? How will I tell Helen?*

Each story had ended with Gunthar's hand resting on Robert's shoulder, as it had the day of Saxton's arrest, though from the faraway haze in Gunthar's eyes, Robert suspected the old earl had not realized his own gesture. Robert refused to consider what it might signify, but each time he'd found a lump swelling up in his throat.

These moments remained more vital in Robert's mind than any of their quarrels, and there had continued to be a fair number of those, most of them centered around the event about to take place this day.

"This is a mistake," Gunthar repeated for yet a seventh time. "We should wait until after the knighting. 'Tis only another month. I do not understand the need for this haste."

This time Robert did not rise to the provocation. Instead he said simply, with his new glow of perception, "You are afraid I will change my mind. That once I have wed Marguerite, I might leave like your other minstrels have." Heaven knew the knighthood meant little enough to him, but he would not tell Gunthar that. He said, with a quiet vibrancy in his voice that sprung from the depths of his heart, "I am not they. You need have no fear, sir. If you wish to bind me to your house, there is no surer way to do it than this."

Robert turned at a slight rustling sound from the doorway. He stood a moment, dazzled. Marguerite had always been lovely, but this glorious be-pearled woman hovered on the threshold like some fairy queen frosted with snow. For an instant he feared he stared at some stranger who had flown beyond his grasp. Then his eyes met hers and he saw the sweet light that shone there. The fairy queen faded away, leaving only own dear, cherished Marguerite. He smiled and held out his fingers to her. She tripped swiftly across the floor to clasp them. If her hand had been carved for him at birth, it could not have fit more perfectly in his.

To Gunthar, he added, "The man who made it possible for me to claim this as my own—" he cradled Marguerite's palm between his "—need never fear my irrevocable loyalty to him."

He felt his smile crack into a grin, so much joy abruptly burst into his breast. Everything he cared most for now stood within the walls of this chapel. Marguerite, Gunthar, Lady Helen. All that could have been added more was Lottie and Gilbert and Will. Gilbert was gone, Lottie had been safely removed with Alice to Gunthar's manor of Rushall, and William—well, Robert suspected Will would be a great deal happier hearing about Robert's good fortune than standing in the middle of an earl's grand chapel.

Marguerite's elegantly extravagant attire made him self-conscious of his own elaborate robes again. Gunthar must have suspected he would not succeed in talking Robert out of his decision, else Robert knew he would not have sent him such a rich surcote to don this morning. The clothes felt too pretentious to him, but he acknowledged he could hardly be wed in his old frayed homespun or his scarlet minstrel's tunic when Marguerite stood before him all a-glimmer in her fairy gown.

And then all thoughts of velvets and jewels vanished as he lost himself in her eyes again. It felt as though they gazed at one another for an eon, but when he finally tore his adoring stare from her to look back at Gunthar, he knew it had only been minutes. Gratitude flooded up in him, for without the old earl, this blessed day would never have come.

"I will stand your man forever," Robert swore. "And I will not refuse the knighthood. You have my word on that."

Gunthar's face at last relaxed and he nodded, accepting the honor that would hold Robert to that promise, as he had so long ago in a darkened tent in Poitou. Finally Gunthar smiled.

He clapped Robert on the shoulder and turned him towards the altar. "Go, then, and wed your lady, and may your lives be as long and happy as Helen's and mine have been."

Moments later, Robert and Marguerite stood before Gunthar's chaplain, Marguerite's hand floating to Gunthar's arm as he came to stand beside her.

"Robert, wilt thou have this woman to they wedded wife . . ."

Robert listened to the recital of vows he was expected to swear to, then stated firmly, "I will." He slid a sideways glance towards Marguerite to catch the way her rosy lips trembled.

"Marguerite," the chaplain continued, "wilt thou take this man to they wedded husband . . ."

"I will." Her voice quavered when the chaplain finished, but she smiled on the words, and Robert released a breath he had not realized he had been holding.

"Who presents this woman to be given to this man?"

Robert noted how the usual wording had been subtly altered to recognize the earl who stood in place of Marguerite's father. Gunthar had no authority either by blood or by law to usurp Lord de Villon's role in the marriage ceremony, but this part was only a traditional formality. It was the vows between Robert and Marguerite themselves that would bind them, not the desirable, but unnecessary consent of her father.

Robert met Gunthar's eyes for a moment. It did not escape either of their irony, he knew, that this man who had once stood most adamantly against their marriage was now the man who replied to the chaplain, "I give this woman," and placed Marguerite's right hand in Robert's.

"Repeat, now, after me . . ." the chaplain began.

In the same strong tones he had used before, Robert did so. "I, Robert, take thee, Marguerite, to my wedded wife, to have and to hold from this day, for better, for worse, for richer, for poorer, in sickness and in health, till death do us part, if holy church will ordain it: And thereto I plight thee my troth."

"Now, milady . . ."

Marguerite's voice came shy but staunch this time from beside him. "I, Marguerite, take thee, Robert, to my wedded husband, to have and to hold from this day forward, for better, for worse, for richer, for poorer, in sickness and in health, to be gentle and obedient, in bed and at board, till death do us part, if holy church will ordain it: And thereto I plight thee my troth."

Marguerite withdrew her hand. Ralf, the squire with the curly brown hair who had occasionally assisted Robert with the earl's correspondence and whom Gunthar had chosen as Robert's future squire, brought forth a silver ring and set it, together with a few coins of silver and gold, upon the bible that Father Matthais set on the altar. The chaplain made the sign of the cross and cast his eyes heavenward.

"Bless, O Lord, this ring, which we bless in thy holy name, that whosoever she be that shall wear it may abide in thy peace, and continue in thy will, and live, and increase, and grow old in thy love; and let the length of her days be multiplied."

He closed in the name of the Lord, then sprinkled holy water over the ring and handed it to Robert. Robert again repeated after the chaplain:

"With this ring I thee wed, and this gold and silver I thee give: and with my body I thee worship, and with all my worldly chattels I thee honor."

He placed the ring over Marguerite's thumb, then first and second fingers, invoking the Trinity, then on the word "Amen," slid it onto the third finger of her left hand where the vein that ran to her heart reflected the inward affection that would always spring fresh between them. Then, with wedded hands laced tightly together, they knelt before the altar while Father Matthais invoked the wedding prayer over their bowed heads.

Later, in Marguerite's spacious bedchamber that tonight would be theirs, after several highly charged kisses between them, Robert murmured against

Marguerite's mouth, "I warned you once that if I kissed you, I might never be able to stop."

"And now you don't have to," she said with a giggle and a blush before resuming their exchange of passion with equal eagerness.

"Except—" his hand tangled in her thick hair to pull her just a breath away from him "—that Gunthar—" he surrendered overlong to the caress she pressed back to his lips before parting for another breath "—has insisted on this curst wedding dinner for us."

For several long, zealous moments, they both allowed more kisses to supplant the call of duty. The scarlet round cap had long since tumbled from his head, and the last time he had opened his eyes long enough to check, Marguerite's circlet of pearls had gone dangerously askew. Robert much preferred this zestful fire between them to the thought of having all of Gunthar's men-at-arms stare at him and Marguerite for hours where they would be seated on the dais as the bridal couple in a hall even larger than the chapel. But while Gunthar had guessed at and respected Robert's instinctive desire for a small, quiet wedding, he'd pointed out the practicality of acknowledging it before as wide an audience as possible, the better to quell any challenges that might come from Lord de Villon when he heard of it.

There would be an even larger crowd at Robert's knighting, he warned, watching carefully for Robert's reaction. Robert had held his face impassive, but responded with a curt nod that had appeared to satisfy Gunthar's final doubts.

"The dinner, sweetheart," Robert at last repeated, and this time held her reluctantly but firmly away from him. "Comb your hair and straighten your circlet."

She giggled again. "And you had better put this back on." She ran her fingers through his hair, smoothing it down for him before handing him his cap.

When they both felt themselves presentable, he started to lead her from the room but to his surprise, she resisted.

"Rob, wait. I—I have something for you. But I do not know if it will please you."

He let her tug him back to sit on the bed, in no hurry to join the crowd in the hall, while she moved to a painted wardrobe in the corner and appeared to rummage through her gowns. She pulled something out from beneath them, then recrossed the room to set it in his lap.

She had embroidered a new case for his lute. He ran one finger over the delicate stitches that spread a myriad of tiny, golden rampant tygers all over the casing's cloth.

"So this is how you spent your time while I toured Gunthar's manors with him and worked on his correspondence."

And listened as he sought to explain to me the duties of my future knighthood. Gunthar had kept Robert close beside him during daylight hours, perhaps to try to forestall this very day, but the evenings in the gardens, those precious, too short hours of twilight, had always belonged to him and Marguerite. Robert had spent a fortnight trying in vain to retune his lute to strum sweetly again after it's collision with the wall in Westminster Palace. But that had not stopped him and Marguerite from singing together in the gathering dusk all the ballads and tender songs he had taught her in the glade where they had fallen in love.

"There is more," she said. "Open it."

He looked up, surprised to see her twisting her fingers, then unlaced the case. 'Twas not his mother's old, scuffed lute that stared up at him, but the polished face of a fresh-made instrument. Instead of ash, this soundboard was made of spruce with a flower-centered decorative knot of whirling, interlocked tendrils forming the rose. When he turned it over, he saw the ribs of the belly alternated in light and reddish hues of walnut instead of a single shade of maple. He glanced at Marguerite and saw her tensely waiting face before he bent his head again, plucked each of the strings, tuned them ever so slightly, plucked them again, then strummed out a chord of exquisite clarity and pureness.

"I could not carve it for you, as your father did for your mother," Marguerite said, sounding somewhat breathless, "but I sold one of the rings my grandfather left me—only one!—to pay a lute maker to fashion this for you. Are—are you angry with me or—or offended?"

He played out two more chords, set the lute on the bed, stood up and kissed her soundly.

"How could I be angry or offended?" he said. "I will likely never get my mother's lute back in tune, and although I wish you had not had to sell a jewel for me, I'll not scold you on our wedding day. Perhaps one day when this"—he waved at her gift—"is scuffed and worn, our son will show it to some lady with a charmingly freckled nose and she will call it beautiful because it was given in love to his father by his mother."

She flung her arms around his neck and hid her face shyly against his shoulder. "Oh, Rob, I hope I give you many sons."

He kissed the top of her head, then murmured in her ear, "And daughters, too."

He laced the lute back into its case with the golden tygers, then at last led her from the room.

She stopped on the other side of the door as he pulled it closed behind them. "No more 'goodnights' from here," she said. Her face glowed with a brilliance that rivaled the sun through the stained glass windows he had stood in awe of earlier. "After dinner—after we walk in the gardens—no more parting when we say goodnight."

"No more partings." Finally, she was his, and he was hers. Father Matthais had said, "Till death do you part," but Robert could imagine no end to his love for her. He did not know how it could come to pass, but somehow there whispered along his soul a promise of forever.

Glossary of Medieval Terms

Bailey – the courtyard of a castle

Battlement – the top of the castle wall with openings for shooting arrows through the **crenels**

British Sea – the English Channel – The term "English Channel" did not come into use until the early 18th century. Prior to that, this strait between England and France was labeled "the British Sea" on many historical maps. An example can be seen on the website for the Old Map & Clock Company http://www.oldmap.co.uk/England-and-Wales.php

Canonical hour – one of seven prayer times observed by the Catholic Church during the Middle Ages; the hours were announced by the ringing of bells which assisted people in determining the time of day

Castellan – custodian of a castle appointed by the castle's lord to govern the fortress in the lord's absence; may or may not be a hereditary position

Cendal – a variety of silk

Chemise – a woman's loose undergarment

Compline – the seventh canonical hour of the Catholic Church; in 13th century England Compline fell between 7-8 PM at the equinox, between 5-6 PM in midwinter, and around 9:20 PM in midsummer

Cordwainer – a shoemaker who makes shoes from new leather, as opposed to a cobbler who repairs worn shoes or makes shoes "cobbled" together from pieces of old leather

Crenel – the gap or notch between two merlons on the castle wall

Crenelated – a wall with gaps for firing arrows, etc.

Dais – a raised platform in the castle hall

Denier – a French coin

Demesne – the land owned by the lord of the manor

Destrier – medieval warhorse

Drawbridge – a bridge that can be raised or lowered to permit access across a ditch or moat into a castle's bailey

Fees and services – what separated the freeman (or free farmer) from the **villein**. After paying rent for his land, the freeman owed only nominal services to the manor lord, whereas the villein owed the manor lord innumerable "fees", including: tithes to the Church; a yearly tax called tallage; the **wood-penny**; fees to grind their grain at the mill; a hen or eggs for permission to keep poultry; **merchet**; heriot (the villein's best beast or chattel forfeited to the lord of the manor when the villein died); mortuary (the villein's second best beast or chattel forfeited to the Church when the villein died); and many more. A villein also owed "services" to the manor lord, including week-works (a certain number a days per week the villein was required to work on the lord's demesne) and boon-works (extra days a villein was required to work on the lord's **demesne**, usually during the height of harvest season). Villeins could also be summoned to help with repairs around the manor or at the manor house.

Fortnight – two weeks (from "fourteen nights")

Feudal contract – Feudalism was a military system in which a man of lower standing (the vassal) swore fealty (from the Latin word for fidelity) to a man of higher standing, who became his "lord." The two men thus entered into a contract in which the vassal promised to fight for his lord when called upon, in return for which the lord promised to protect the vassal from all external threats and forces.

Gallery – a balcony; also a long passageway open on one side that connects various parts of a castle

Gatehouse – the heavily fortified entrance to the castle complex

Interdict – an ecclesiastic censure by the Catholic Church that excludes individuals or groups from enjoying certain Church rites – In 1208 Pope Innocent III placed all of England under an interdict in an attempt to force King John to accept the papacy's choice for the Archbishop of Canterbury. Thanks to King John's stubbornness, this interdict lasted six years, from March 1208 - July 1214. During this time, all church services and sacraments were suspended except for baptisms in private houses, confession, and the last rites. Mass could not be performed (although later some masses were allowed to limited groups behind closed doors), marriages could not be solemnized inside a church (though they could be performed elsewhere, such as on the porch or at the door of the church) and the dead could not be buried in consecrated ground. The hope was that the king's subjects would be so outraged at being denied the blessings of the Church that they would pressure the king to bow to the pope's demands, but in actuality, the people of England overall appeared little disturbed by the interdict and found ways to simply continue on with their lives.

Kirtle – a long gown worn by women

Laver – a basin of water presented by servants for diners to rinse their hands before they dine

Manor – agricultural estate owned by a lord; sometimes attached to a castle, sometimes attached to a fortified manor house

Merchet – a fine or fee paid by a **villein** for permission for his daughter to marry, within or without the manor

Merlon – the part of the fortified castle wall that juts up between two crenels (gaps or open areas)

Motte – the raised mound or hill on which a castle was built.

Mummers – medieval entertainers whose performances often included dancing and plays

None – the fifth canonical hour of the Catholic Church; in 13th century England None fell around 12:30 PM at the equinox, 12:30 PM in midwinter, and 12:40 PM in midsummer; on the continent None fell between 2:30 PM at the equinox, 1:40 PM in midwinter, and 3:00 PM in midsummer; in the 14th century, None shifted on the continent to match 13th century England

Parchment – material made from animal skin used for pages of books or other writing

Poitevin – a resident of Poitou

Poitou – a region of west-central France ruled by King John of England during the Middle Ages

Portcullis – a grated gate usually ending in spikes that dropped vertically to seal off the entrance through the castle's gatehouse

Prime – the second canonical hour of the Catholic Church; in 13th century England Prime fell around 6:00 AM at the equinox, 8:00 AM in midwinter, and 3:40 AM in midsummer

Quintain – a device for squires and knights to practice fighting on horseback. A quintain consisted of a revolving post with an object (like a shield) on one end and a sandbag on the other. The squire or knight would attempt to ride at the object and strike it with their sword or lance and then get out of the way before the sandbag could whirl around and hit them.

Quires – in medieval bookmaking, a quire consisted of four sheets of parchment folded, creating eight leaves with sixteen sides

Rampant – in medieval heraldry, a creature in a rearing stance with one rear foot on the ground

Russet – a coarse homespun cloth, usually a reddish-brown hue

Scutage – a tax paid by a knight in lieu of military service to the crown; abuse of this tax by King John was one of the contributing factors leading up to Magna Carta

Sennight –one week (from "seven nights")

Sext – the fourth canonical hour of the Catholic Church; in 13th century England Sext fell around 10:30 AM at the equinox, 11:00 AM in midwinter, and 9:40 AM in midsummer; on the continent Sext fell around 12:30 PM at the equinox, 12:20 PM in midwinter, and 12:20 PM in midsummer

Shilling – an English coin equal to twelve pence (pennies)

Smock – a loose, blouselike garment

Solar – a small, well-lit room, usually the domain of the lady of the castle

Spurs (to earn one's spurs) – when a squire became a knight (around the age of 21) he received a pair of golden spurs, hence the phrase "to earn one's spurs" meant to earn a knighthood

Surcote – also known as the surcoat or super-tunic; a secondary tunic worn over an under tunic, usually more elaborately decorated

Tallage – one of the fees owed by **villeins** to their lords; basically a land tax, sometimes a fixed amount, sometimes determined "at will" by the lord of the manor

Terce – the third canonical hour of the Catholic Church; in 13th century England Terce fell around 8:00 AM at the equinox, 9:20 AM in midwinter, and 6:30 AM in midsummer; on the continent Sext fell around 8:30 AM at the equinox, 9:40 AM in midwinter, and 7:00 AM in midsummer

The hall or great hall – the central living space of the castle inside the keep; the ceremonial and legal center

The keep – the central tower and main residence area of the castle

Trenchers – large slices of stale bread, cut either round or square, and used as "plates" for medieval dining

Tunic – a sleeved, loose-fitting outer garment worn by both men and women; could be worn alone or under a surcote; for a man, could be knee or ankle length

Tyger – in medieval heraldry, a fanciful creature with the ears of a wolf, a tufted mane, and a pointed snout

Vair – grey and white squirrel fur worn by the upper classes

Vassal – see **feudal contract**

Vielle – a bowed, stringed instrument of the Middle Ages; forerunner of the violin

Villein – This term is often used today as interchangeable with "serf", but in fact a "villein" was an unfree peasant on the higher social end among the serfs, while a "cottar" was at the bottom of the social scale among the serfs, the scale being determined by the amount of land one possessed and the number of fees and services owed to the manor lord. Whether villein or cottar, both were "unfree" peasants. At the same time, they were not slaves. Serfs at any level could not be sold, although the land they worked on could be sold and thereby bring the serf under the authority of another manor lord. Each serf held some land of his own on which he could raise crops to support himself and if he managed to grow any excess, he could sell that excess for profit. Serfs had some rights and privileges that the manor lord was (in theory) required to respect. It was technically illegal for a manor lord to separate a serf from his lands and send him to work on a different manor, although one manor lord in *The Lady and the Minstrel* does exactly that with one of the characters. It was also illegal for a serf to leave his land and go live somewhere else, with the exception of the Law of a Year and a Day as described in this story. Although Robert's mother was a cottar and his father a villein, I use the term "villein" throughout *The Lady and the Minstrel* to simplify the class of unfree peasants for the reader.

Wall-walk – the walking space behind the fortifications (**merlons** and **crenels**) on the battlements; also known as the allure

Wattle and daub – building material for medieval cottages; a "wattle" (latticework of wooden strips) was dabbed or "daubed" over with a sticky composite of clay, sand, and straw to form the walls

William de Briouze – an English baron, once a favorite of King John, who for obscure reasons (possibly over the death of Arthur of Brittany), lost the king's favor in 1208; when William fled to France to escape King John's persecution, his wife and eldest son were captured, imprisoned and, according to reports, were starved to death; William died in exile in 1211

Wood-penny – a penny required of **villeins** before they could gather dead wood from the forest

Thank you for reading

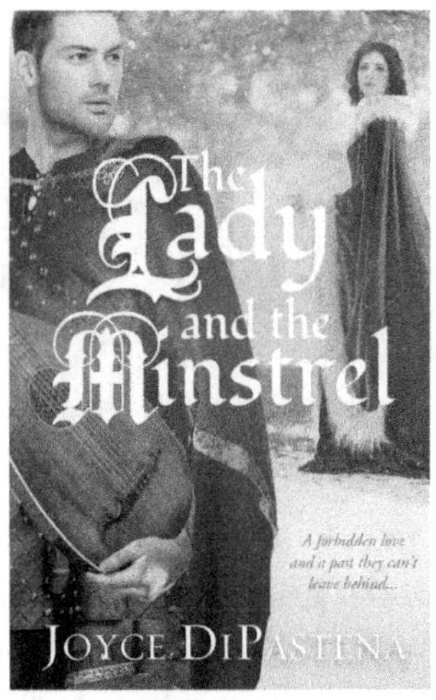

I hope you enjoyed reading *The Lady and the Minstrel*. If you did, would you please consider ~

Recommending this book to a friend.

Leaving a review on the website where you downloaded this book. Just a few words about what you liked about the story will help other readers find and enjoy this book too.

Subscribing to my newsletter at joycedipastena.com so we can keep in touch about future releases and follow along with new books I'm writing. Turn the page to learn more!

Thank you so much for reading *The Lady and the Minstrel*!

Join Joyce's Medieval World

Visit joycedipastena.com to sign up for Joyce's newsletter and receive a free copy of her medieval romance, *Loyalty's Web*. Her newsletter is sent out three times a month and includes announcements on new releases, special promotions and offers, periodic giveaways, historical trivia, and more! You are free to unsubscribe at any time.

Notes for the reader

Fact and Fiction

The *Lady and the Minstrel* is a work of fiction that incorporates both historical events and historical events with a literary spin. Which are which in the story, a reader might legitimately wonder?

Most readers will recognize King John as an actual king of England who ruled in the 13th century. He is the King John of the fictional world of Robin Hood and the King John of the real world of Magna Carta. Though he possessed many qualities that might have made him a very good king, he chose, more often than not, to nurture those qualities that have made him go down in history as a very bad king.

The two rival counselors I ascribe to King John, the Earl of Saxton and the Earl of Gunthar, are both characters of fiction, but King John was certainly fickle enough to have played the two men against each other if they had actually existed. You can separate the other fictional characters from non-fictional ones by reviewing the Cast of Characters included at the beginning of this book.

What else is fact and what is fiction in this story?

The palace of Westminster was, in fact, the principle residence of the kings of England during this era of the Middle Ages. Although the city of London lay a mere 2 miles away, Westminster was not then considered part of the city. The origins of the palace extend back as far as when Cnut the Dane ruled over England. Edward the Confessor rebuilt the palace after a fire, and King William II (William Rufus, son of William the Conqueror) added to this palace the Great Hall, the largest hall of its kind in Europe. This hall still stands today, but nothing else of the original palace does. The palace suffered multiple fires through the years, including an extensive one in 1512 and such a devastating one in 1834 that only the Great Hall remains of the palace as it stood in 1214, the year of *The Lady and the Minstrel*. No floor plan exists for the original palace or the palace of 1214. Therefore, aside from a description of the Great Hall that was given to me by Evelyn Tidman, I have allowed my imagination to "build" the remainder of the structures and rooms described in my story, including the dungeon. I could find no record that Westminster Palace in 1214 actually held a dungeon, but as mentioned above, there is no existing floor plan to definitively say that *no* dungeon existed, either. (A reader might ask, "What about the Tower of London? Isn't that where royal prisoners were housed?" The Tower of London was also a royal residence in these days. Although occasionally used as a prison, that was not its original purpose and it had not yet evolved to the prison status it would later achieve under the Tudor kings.)

It is fact that King John stole the beautiful and very young Isabella of Angoulême from his own vassal, Hugh de Lusignan, the Count of La Marche, while she was betrothed to the count. La Marche was one of the most powerful men in the county of Poitou and not a man to take such an insult to the feudal contract between him and the king lightly. That this hasty, passionate, and arrogant act by the king, combined with other provocations, led to the rebellions referred to in my story by the Count of La Marche and his relatives is fact. However, that supporters of La Marche attempted to ambush King John and steal back the queen shortly after their marriage, along with the parts played by my fictional characters Garoux Beckford and Arthur Marcel, are literary inventions for the story.

Also fact was John's attempt to settle the differences between himself and La Marche by betrothing his daughter to La Marche's son and heir. The Lusignans did, in fact, rebel again and held the castles of Mervant and Voucant against the angry king. John successfully assaulted both castles, and after humbling the Lusignans, completed the betrothal between their families. (The marriage never took place. Instead, after King John died, his queen, the notorious Isabella of Angoulême, returned to Poitou and married La Marche's son herself.) However, as much as the Lusignans had reason to hate King John, the plot between them and the French that Kit Beckford mediated is another of my literary inventions.

After humbling the Lusignans in June 1214, John did in fact turn his attentions to finally attempting to confront the French. The fever that befell his camp on his march towards the border of Maine is my invention. The events that followed this fictional pause are, however, fact. The Poitevin baronage had always been reluctant to throw their support to King John, regardless of their feudal contracts with him, and when push came to shove, they did indeed refuse to fight against the French. John wrote an urgent letter to England attempting to summon more soldiers from those shores, but it was too late. His allies were defeated at the Battle of Bouvines, John had not enough support to carry on alone, and thus he returned in defeat to England.

One area that may be fact *or* fiction is the language spoken in England by 1214. From the days of William the Conqueror in 1066, French had been the language of the ruling classes of England. Scholars are not agreed as to when English came into use by the upper classes of England. Some believe it was as early as the late 12th century, others claim it was spoken by the early 13th century. Still others insist English as the common tongue came later. Literature written in English began appearing in the early 13th century, but the first English government document to be published in English (the Provisions of Oxford) was released in 1258 in the reign of King John's grandson, Edward I. My own theory is that people did not speak French for centuries, then simply wake up one day suddenly speaking English. There must have been an evolution from one language to the other, and it likely happened over decades, and surely over the century and a half between the Norman Conquest and the reign of King John. We cannot judge by the written language alone. The written word always lags behind the spoken vernacular, especially among populations that were largely illiterate, as was the case in the Middle Ages, and thus provides few records that reflect what may have been the common speech versus records of "official" correspondence of various sorts.

Mostly likely, many of the upper class had become bilingual by the year of *The Lady and the Minstrel*. When I write in my story of my characters speaking English versus the French they hear in Poitou, I do not imagine them speaking the language we speak today, but a blending of the two languages, Norman-French and Anglo-Saxon, that was evolving into something unique and distinct. Of course, I could be wrong. Sadly, we possess no recordings of how people actually spoke in those days. But this is the theory I use for all my novels set in the late 12th-early 13th centuries. Readers may, of course, do their own research on the subject and come to other conclusions.

Finally, there is the question of what happened to John's nephew, Arthur of Brittany. The account of Arthur as told in this story is historical. Some of King John's enemies, including the French, attempted to put the boy forward as the legitimate heir to the throne after the death of Richard I. Arthur was captured in the course of a rebellion against John, imprisoned, and ultimately simply disappeared. Some accused John of ordering his murder or even murdering the boy himself (Arthur was only 15 when he was captured), but no body was ever found. The fate of Arthur of Brittany is one of the great mysteries of history.

Suggested Reading List

(for readers interested in a further study of subjects
addressed in The Lady and the Minstrel)

All about Castles

Bottomley, Frank. *The Castle Explorer's Guide*. New York: Avenel Books,
1979.

Clothing of the Middle Ages

Bradfield, Nancy. *900 Years of English Costume*. New York: Crescent Books,
1938.

Brooke, Iris. *English Costume from the Early Middle Ages Through the Sixteenth
Century*. Mineola, NY: Dover Publications, Inc., 1936.

Fabrics of the Middle Ages

Labarge, Margaret Wade. *A Baronial Household of the Thirteenth Century*. New
York: Barnes & Noble, 1965.

Rosalie's Medieval Woman: Medieval Fabric, Fur and Leather Names.
   http://rosaliegilbert.com/fabricnames.html

Timekeeping in the Middle Ages

Farrell, April. "Court Will Begin at Half-Way Terce: Keeping Time in High
Medieval Europe." (Essay) September 2004.
   http://www.troynovant.com/Farrell-A/Essays/Medieval-Timekeep
ing.html

Medieval Heraldry

Bestiary: Heraldic Monsters & Medieval Critters.
    http://www.modaruniversity.org/Monsters.htm

Fox-Davies, Arthur Charles. A Complete Guide to Heraldry.
    http://www7b.biglobe.ne.jp/~bprince/hr/foxdavies/fdguide11.htm

"Heraldry (Charge): Animals." *Wikipedia: The Free Encyclopedia.* Wikimedia Foundation, Inc.
    http://en.wikipedia.org/wiki/Charge_(heraldry)#Animals

Coins: King John vs. King Philip

Coin of King John: The Fitzwilliam Museum.
    http://www.fitzmuseum.cam.ac.uk/dept/coins/exhibitions/CoinOfThe Moment/John/

Coin of King Philip: Wikimedia Commons.
    http://commons.wikimedia.org/wiki/File:Capetingi,_filippo_II_augus-to,_denaro,_1180-1223.JPG

The English Channel as the British Sea

The Old Map & Clock Company (map).
    http://www.oldmap.co.uk/England-and-Wales.php

Medieval Villeins

Bennett, H.S. *Life on the English Manor*. Cambridge, England: Cambridge University Press, 1937.

Duby, Georges. *Rural Economy and Country Life in the Medieval West*. Philadelphia, PA: University of Pennsylvania Press, 1968.

Gies, Frances and Joseph. *Life in a Medieval Village*. New York: Harper & Row, 1990.

Christmas Song the Robert Sings

Although the song quoted in Chapter 10 of *The Lady and the Minstrel* does not appear in written form until the 1500s, it possibly traces its roots back to the 12th century. See "Personent hodie", *Wikipedia: The Free Encyclopedia.* Wikimedia Foundation, Inc.
http://en.wikipedia.org/wiki/Personent_hodie

England Under the Interdict

Cheney, C.R. *King John and the Papal Interdict.* [PDF]
https://www.escholar.manchester.ac.uk/api/datastream?publication Pid=uk-ac-man-scw:1m3082&datastreamId=POST-PEER-REVIEW-PUBLISHERS-DOCUMENT.PDF

Krehbiel, Edward Benjamin. *The Interdict.* Washington, D.C.: The American Historical Association, 1909. Google Books.
http://books.google.com

McLynn, Frank. *Richard & John: Kings at War.* Cambridge, MA: Da Capo Press, 2007.

Spence-Jones, Henry Donald Maurice. *The Church of England: The Medieval Church.* London: Cassell and Company, Limited, 1897. Google Books.
http://books.google.com

Warren, W.L. *King John.* Berkeley: University of California Press, 1961.

John's Campaign in Poitou in 1214

McLynn, Frank. *Richard & John: Kings at War.* Cambridge, MA: Da Capo Press, 2007.

Warren, W.L. *King John.* Berkeley: University of California Press, 1961.

"War of Bouvines (1202-1214)," "Campaign of Bouvines (1214), "Battle of Bouvines (29 July 1214." Xenophon Group: Military History Database.

http://xenophongroup.com/montjoie/bouvines.htm

Herbs and Uses Mentioned in *The Lady and the Minstrel*

Culpeper's Complete Herbal. Hertfordshire, England: Wordsworth Editions Ltd, 1995.

McLean, Teresa. *Medieval English Gardens*. New York: The Viking Press, 1980.

"Tanacetum parthenium (Feverfew): Uses." *Wikipedia: The Free Encyclopedia.* Wikimedia Foundation, Inc.
    http://en.wikipedia.org/wiki/Tanacetum_parthenium#Uses

University of Maryland Medical Center: "Feverfew."
    http://umm.edu/health/medical/altmed/herb/feverfew

LearningHerbs: "Yarrow."
    http://learningherbs.com/remedies-recipes/herbs-for-fever/

Morgan Botanicals: Herbal Blog. "Yarrow . . . A Local Favorite."
    http://www.morganbotanicals.com/herbal-blog/entry/yarrowa-local-favorite-.html

Whispering Earth: "The Multiple Benfits and Uses of Yarrow."
    http://whisperingearth.co.uk/2011/09/28/the-multiple-benefits-and-uses-of-yarrow/

Medieval Wedding Ceremony

Emilie Amt, editor. *Women's Lives in Medieval Europe: A Sourcebook*. New York: Routledge, 1993.

The English Language in Medieval England

Heys, Jacquie. *French as a Mother-Tongue in Medieval England*, 2001.
    http://homes.chass.utoronto.ca/~cpercy/courses/6361Heys.htm

"History of the English Language: Middle English." *Wikipedia: The Free Encyclopedia.* Wikimedia Foundation, Inc.
http://en.wikipedia.org/wiki/History_of_the_English_language#Middle_English_.E2.80.93_from_the_late_11th_to_the_late_15th_century

Story of William de Briouze

Warren, W.L. *King John.* Berkeley and Los Angeles: University of California Press, 1961.

Story of Arthur of Brittany

McLynn, Frank. *Richard & John: Kings at War.* Cambridge, MA: 2007

Warren, W.L. *King John.* Berkeley and Los Angeles: University of California Press, 1961.

Acknowledgments

I never thought LinkedIn would be of much use to me as an author, but through a LinkedIn group called Historical Novels, I received help and suggestions with *The Lady and the Minstrel* literally from around the world. When I became stumped with such research questions as: "What was the English Channel called before it was called the English Channel?" and "How much literary license can I take in describing Westminster Palace of 1214 since descriptions for that year are scanty at best, and the medieval palace burned down in the 1800s," I received a plethora of helpful answers from this wonderful group! I wish to express my thanks to everyone in the LinkedIn Historical Novels group who took the time to offer comments and guidance, literally too many people to cite by name here, except for two:

Evelyn Tidman found a photo of the windows in the great hall of Westminster Palace, the only portion of the medieval palace to survive the 19th century fire. Evelyn kindly scanned the picture from a book called *London, the Biography of a City*, by Christopher Hibbert, and emailed it to me. This page and the description that accompanied it became the foundation of my heroine Marguerite's initial impressions of Westminster Palace. Chrissie Parker, who, like, Evelyn, lives in England and (an extra bonus for me) has worked in modern-day Westminster, proved a treasure trove of information on historical Westminster, London, and the weather in England, as well as referring me to numerous links to websites that my own research efforts had failed to turn up. Both women reached out to me purely from the generosity of their hearts, and I will forever be grateful to them both.

I also wish to thank my numerous beta readers who helped me polish-polish-polish this story for you. My deepest appreciation goes to:

(First round betas): Sara Acevedo, Donna Hatch, Jeannette Johannsen, Tina Scott, Margaret Turley, and Kathy Heare Watts; and (second round betas): Celeste Hansen, Wanda Luce, Melanie Mason, and Alison Miller Woods.

About the Author

Joyce DiPastena illuminates the Middle Ages for modern readers through heartfelt historical romance. However many changes a few centuries may bring, she believes that stories of love can unite people across time.

Joyce grew up in southern Arizona and can easily withstand summer temperatures of 115 degrees, as long as she's sitting in a restaurant, movie theater, or under a ceiling fan—inside an air-conditioned building. She can be bribed with chocolate chip cookies and enjoys attending the Arizona Renaissance Festival every year. She holds a degree in history, specializing in the Middle Ages, from the University of Arizona. Joyce currently resides in Mesa, Arizona with her black cats, Nyxie and Calypso, who bring her good luck every day.

Joyce loves to hear from her readers. Email her at joyce@joycedipastena.com, visit her website at joycedipastena.com. join her newsletter, or connect with her on Facebook, Twitter/X, Amazon and BookBub. (Just search for "Joyce DiPastena." She's the only one there is!)

www.ingramcontent.com/pod-product-compliance
Lightning Source LLC
Chambersburg PA
CBHW060808120726
47909CB00006B/1831